BROKEN BY DAYLIGHT

BEASTS OF THE BRIAR
BOOK FOUR

ELIZABETH HELEN

LUNA FOX
PRESS

Published by Luna Fox Press

First Edition published September 2024

Interior Design © 2024 by Elizabeth Helen

Cover Design and Illustration © 2024 by saintjupit3rgr4phic

Ch. 34 and 105 illustrations © e_haez

Ch. 90 and 122 illustrations © Salome Totladze

Identifiers

ISBN: 978-1-998945-04-7 (eBook)

ISBN: 978-1-998945-07-8 (paperback)

ISBN: 978-1-998945-06-1 (audio)

To Susan, Stevie, and Aje for believing in Rosie.

CONTENT WARNINGS

Broken by Daylight is the fourth book in the multi-book Beasts of the Briar series. It is a why-choose romance that ends on a cliffhanger. It contains explicit sexual content (M/F, M/M, and MMF), mature themes, and is intended for audiences 18+.

Trigger Warnings: Fantasy violence and gore; torture; imprisonment; on-page flashback of death of parents and siblings; physical and emotional abuse from a parent against their adult children.

CHRONOLOGY

Age of the Cosmos
Years unknown

A glorious time that is shrouded in mystery. Very few fae who lived in this age still remain today. It is said the Above hung from a canopy in the cosmos. All the light, magic, and goodness of the world emanated from the Gardens of Ithilias, a celestial rosebush.

A young fae woman named Sira desired to create her own realm and stole one of the heavenly flowers. She fled the cosmos and, using the might of her stolen rose, forged a new realm known as the Below. In the dark, Sira was able to use the rose to breed creations of her own, monsters crafted of darkness and rot.

For the treacherous act of stealing the rose, Sira was forever banished from the Realm Above. Enraged that she and her creations were not accepted by the Above, Sira waged a great war. Sira's creations mercilessly attacked the fae of the Above. Though the fae were courageous, they knew not the ways of war. Sira destroyed the Gardens of Ithilias and all that was good and beautiful in the world fell to darkness and despair.

Age of the Vale
0–1025

A young fae woman named Aurelia, filled with courage, was able to save four roses from the Gardens of Ithilias. Infused with the roses' magic, she forged a new world consisting of five realms. The first four realms—known as Winter, Spring, Summer, and Autumn—became safe havens for the survivors of the Above. In the fifth realm, Aurelia grew a magnificent tree that housed the four roses. The tree, known as Castletree, channeled the last light of the Gardens of Ithilias and provided strength and stability to all. So grateful to Aurelia were the survivors of the Above that they named her Queen, and the land of Castletree became known as the Queen's Realm. She appointed a High Ruler to each of the seasonal realms and blessed them with celestial magic from the sacred roses.

Queen Aurelia was a dauntless and spirited ruler who was determined to see her people thrive. More powerful than any other fae, she was able to change the world around her, including the shape of plants, animals, and even other fae. Under her rule, the world she created, known as the Enchanted Vale, prospered and great civilizations flourished.

However, peace was not to be, for down in the darkness, an enemy schemed. While Aurelia ruled five lands of light and prosperity, Sira's realm was one of darkness and rot and her only subjects were her monstrous creations. Sira began to manipulate fae from the surface realms into joining her, promising them power and ancient magic. Using the first rose stolen from the Gardens of Ithilias, Sira threw herself into creating armies of darkness.

Attacks from the Below against the Enchanted Vale became more frequent until finally war broke out. The Gloaming War waged for hundreds of years. Desperate to end the suffering of her people, Aurelia and the High Rulers devised a plan. The first High Ruler of Spring, High Prince Rafael, was a masterful blacksmith and believed he could craft weapons of immense power, if only he could access ore from the Above. Though the fae had lost their way to the ruins of the Above, Aurelia and the High Rulers traveled across the Enchanted Vale in search of fallen shards from their first home. After a great journey, they recovered five shards, and from this, High Prince Rafael extracted ore enough to craft five mystical weapons: the Sword of the Protector, the Hammer of Hope, the Trident of Honor, the Lance of Valor, and, most powerful of all, the Bow of Radiance. Aurelia put an enchantment on all five weapons so that they could only be used by someone who possessed one of the Queen's tokens, necklaces blessed by her magic. Without a token, anyone attempting to wield the weapons would find their blood turning to rot. Aurelia gifted the weapons to her loyal High Rulers, keeping the bow for herself. With the aid of these divine weapons, as well as the Queen's Army, a dedicated force of soldiers, Aurelia was able to keep her realms protected.

Sira's forces were defeated but her spirit was more enraged than ever. Sira turned to a new source to try and regain power. With dark and perverse magic, Sira was able to open windows between the worlds. She used these to seek a greater power than any in the Enchanted Vale. In her search, she found Malekai Furiondemius, Baron of the Green Flame, a godlike entity who traversed the paths between universes, conquering whatever lands he desired. Though Sira's window was not powerful enough for the Baron to step within this world, he began to fill her mind with ambitions. Together, they designed plans to claim the Enchanted Vale for their own.

As the Gloaming War finally came to an end, Aurelia bade the Queen's Army return to the monastery they called home and recalled the divine weapons, for they were only to be used in times of war. The only exception was the Sword of the Protector, which she allowed High Princess Elowyn of Winter to keep. She named the High Princess of Winter, Protector of the Realms, with the instructions that if she were ever unable to rule as Queen, the Protector of the Realms would serve the Vale in her place.

Aurelia's closest confidants reported that Aurelia had lamented that the centuries ruling the Vale and the memories of battle weighed heavily on her . . .

Age of the Missing Queen
1025–1450

Queen Aurelia disappears. Although grief blanketed the lands with the loss of the beloved Queen, four new High Rulers inherited the realms: High Prince Erivor of Winter, High Princess Isidora of Spring, High Princess Sabine of Summer, and High Princess Niamh of Autumn. The realms maintained stability and peace. Four princes were also born during this age: Keldarion of Winter, Ezryn of Spring, Daytonales of Summer, and Farron of Autumn.

In the Below, Sira was lost to her envy of Aurelia's beautiful realms and creations. She desired above all else to create the perfect entity: a child of her very own, one who would put the rest of the world to shame. After beseeching the Baron, he granted her greatest wish, impregnating her with a child: a fae of the Below and of the Green Flame.

Growing up in the Below, Sira's young son, Caspian, was raised to inherit his father's magic, the power of the Green Flame. With Aurelia gone, Sira turned her attention to her new goal: finding a power that would allow her to open a gateway between this world and the Baron's, so Caspian's father could step through and join them. Sira envisioned a future where she, Malekai, and Caspian ruled not only the Below, but the surface realms, as well. She even dreamed of rebuilding the Above and ruling the land that once shunned her.

Though full-out war was avoided, tensions remained high between the Below and the surface realms. High Prince Erivor of Winter and his wife, Princess Runa, devised a plan to incapacitate the Below's forces. They intended to take back the rose that Sira once stole from the Gardens of Ithilias. Without such power, the Queen of the Below would no longer be able to create her monsters.

Erivor and Runa's valiant attempt ultimately failed. Although they were successful at gaining the rose, they were ambushed before they were able to escape the Below. Erivor and Runa survived the attack; however, the rose was lost. Without the rose in her control, Sira's power was significantly weakened and many of her creations became feral, no longer answering to any master.

Meanwhile, Sira's young son lived within the boundaries of his birthright: as half his blood was tied to a demi-god from another world, Caspian was not able to stray far from the Below. He tested these limits as much as possible, including visiting the human world, where he was befriended by a young couple with secrets of their own. Caspian developed the mysterious ability that would one day become his namesake: control over thorns.

In Summer, High Princess Sabine passed Summer's Blessing and the title of High Ruler to her eldest son, Damocles.

Age of the War of Thorns
1450–1501

High Princess Isidora has died while passing Spring's Blessing to her eldest son Ezryn. Prince Ezryn inherited the throne of Spring.

Sira, enraged by the loss of the rose and her lack of power, devised a plan to not only find the rose, but weaken the surface realms forever. She sent her now grown son Caspian undercover to gain the trust of the four realms while secretly doing her bidding.

During a fateful Rainbow Festival held at Castletree, Caspian appeared at the door, distraught and hurt. He implored the High Rulers to take pity on him, despite the fact he was well known as the son of the Queen of the Below. Claiming to have escaped his mother's clutches, he promised intelligence and aid to the surface realms in their plight against the Below. As Protector of the Realms, High Prince Erivor chose to imprison Caspian.

However, Erivor's son, Keldarion, desired to trust the Prince of the Below, and convinced his father to set Caspian free—under his watch, of course. Keldarion, eager to prove his worth, believed Caspian could have the answers to many of the problems they faced. The young Winter Prince desperately wanted to succeed at the mission his parents had failed at: retrieving the stolen rose that was lost somewhere in the Below.

Caspian began to immerse himself into Keldarion's life, attending functions with him, training alongside him, and even befriending Keldarion's companions, the princes from the other realms. Keldarion's most trusted ally, the High Prince of Spring, however, never warmed to Caspian. The Prince of the Below played his role dutifully, both assisting Keldarion, but also secretly using his thorns to return to the Below, reporting to Sira. Though Keldarion attempted to maintain a strictly neutral relationship with Caspian, the tenacious spirit of the mysterious Prince of the Below captivated him. Little by little, harsh words gave way to lingering glances and talks of strategy became long conversations late into the night.

However, Keldarion was betrothed to Lady Tilla of Spring. On the day of their wedding, he fled the altar. He was intercepted by Caspian, where the two admitted their feelings for one another and were intimate for the first time. While this occurred, the Below launched an attack on the capital of the Winter Realm, Frostfang. Caspian was blamed for the attack and banished from the surface realms.

Against the wishes and advice of all those around him, Keldarion refused to believe Caspian would betray him. He followed Caspian down to the Below, where they decided to continue working together to find the lost rose. Keldarion took up residence in Cryptgarden. The persistent feelings and newfound intimacy between Caspian and Keldarion continued to grow. Within each other, they found solace and a connection like neither had experienced before. As their search for the rose persisted, passion and partnership evolved into a loving relationship.

In Autumn, High Princess Niamh passed Autumn's Blessing to her eldest son, Farron.

Down Below, Keldarion and Caspian made a fae bargain of everlasting love, with the fateful words: "Let me take no other but you. If one day, my vow shall prove false and I lie with another, let them serve you in repentance until you tire of them as I did your heart. And if ever there is no love between us, let this bargain melt away like snow under rain." This particular bargain was specific in its terms that it could not be rescinded; it would only break if no love remained between the two. Under the terms, should either of the fae princes lie with another, that person would magically be sent to the other and fall into a thralldom, intent only to serve the one who had been betrayed until they said otherwise.

Desperate not to lose her son's allegiance, Sira took Caspian to visit the Fates, so that he could see the pain Keldarion would cause him in the future.

Despite the vision, the Prince of the Below and the Prince of Winter continued their mission and were ultimately successful: they found the lost rose. Keldarion organized an elaborate celebration in Frostfang.

Worried that she was losing control over Caspian, Sira decided to organize a betrayal against her own son but wanted to frame the surface realms. She planted a member of her inner circle into the Winter army and had them pose as a loyal soldier. Then, she had her servant reveal condemning information to Keldarion's closest confidant, High Prince Ezryn, outlining Caspian's true allegiance to the Below. Ezryn took Keldarion's army and attacked Cryptgarden, destroying much of the city. Keldarion led the army away and told Caspian there was a mistake and the soldiers arrived at his command, unwilling to reveal that Ezryn ordered the attack. Distraught, Caspian still agreed to attend the celebration.

At the great celebration when Caspian was supposed to be recognized for his loyalty to the surface realms and for retrieving the lost rose, the Prince of the Below ordered a vicious attack against the capital. Princess Runa of Winter was murdered during the siege, Frostfang was occupied, and Prince Keldarion was kidnapped. Thus began the War of Thorns.

Battles scoured the land. Autumn faced a deadly fight against a goblin force that ended with a mudslide destroying both armies. The Great Scriptorium of Alder was destroyed during an attack on Coppershire. Spring was able to hold its borders but nearly the entire royal family of Summer, save Prince Daytonales and Princess Delphia, were killed during a siege of Hadria, the capital of Summer. Prince Daytonales inherited the Blessing of Summer. High Prince Ezryn of Spring rescued Keldarion from his imprisonment in the Below.

High Prince Erivor led a valiant assault on Frostfang with intentions to liberate his people. He successfully recaptured the city but was felled in the process. Keldarion inherited the Blessing of Winter and the title of Protector of the Realms.

With newfound power, Keldarion sought revenge against his old ally, the newly dubbed Prince of Thorns, Caspian. With incredible power, the two fought across the Anelkrol Badlands. The battle caused massive damage to the area, including the creation of the Great Chasm, a deep and vast canyon that revealed tunnels straight to the Below. The rose was caught in the turmoil and destroyed.

Ultimately, the surface realms were victorious. Caspian and Sira survived the war and returned defeated to Cryptgarden.

A year passed with Castletree being overseen by the four young High Rulers: Keldarion of Winter, Ezryn of Spring, Daytonales of Summer, and Farron of Autumn. Recovering from the war, the realms lacked true leadership as all four of the High Rulers struggled to rise to their positions.

Age of the Curse
1501–1526

An Enchantress appeared at Castletree and cursed the four High Princes for their negligence. The curse forced the princes to spend each night in the form of hideous beasts, as well as tying their life forces to four enchanted roses. The more time passed, the more the roses wilted. If the roses were to die completely, the curse upon the princes would be complete, trapping them as beasts forever. Ashamed and hopeless, the four princes hid away, waiting for the day they could break their curse: when they found their fated mate and that person accepted the bond. Stewards were appointed to rule the four realms in the princes' absence.

Down Below, Sira adopted a child and raised her as her own. Ever ambitious, Sira discovered the curse and once again saw an opportunity to claim the Enchanted Vale for herself. Slowly, she began to put plans in place for her complete and utter takeover. Caspian grew a great briar bush around Castletree, causing the Queen's Realm to become known as the Briar. His thorns wrapped around the once-powerful tree and were believed to suck the vitality from its roots.

Age of the Rose
1526—

A young woman from the human realm discovered the Enchanted Vale and found herself at Castletree . . .

DRAMATIS PERSONAE

Rosalina O'Connell, daughter of George and Anya, and fated mate of Keldarion, Ezryn, and Farron

Curious and wistful, Rosalina O'Connell spent her first twenty-six years living in Orca Cove, a small town in the human world. When her father went missing, Rosalina accidentally wandered into the Enchanted Vale while searching for him. After finding herself imprisoned by a fae prince, High Prince Keldarion of Winter, Rosalina bargained, wiled, and worked her way to freedom, finding peace and acceptance in the fae realm. She later discovered she was half-fae and daughter to the missing Queen of the Enchanted Vale. Rosalina is fated mates with three High Princes: Keldarion, Ezryn, and Farron. She also has a mysterious connection to the Prince of Thorns, as he is able to speak in her mind, and a strong bond with High Prince Daytonales.

George O'Connell, husband to Anya and father of Rosalina

An accomplished archaeologist, George O'Connell lost his wife Anya twenty-six years ago and has spent most of Rosalina's life searching for her. This obsession caused him to be an absent father. When George found his way to the Enchanted Vale, it set him on course to make amends with his daughter while finding clues to his wife's whereabouts. George has been struck with illness and is being tended to in the Autumn Realm.

Anya O'Connell/Queen Aurelia, wife to George and mother of Rosalina

Anya went missing twenty-six years ago. She is said to have been an outspoken and free-spirited woman, who loved her work as an anthropologist and was known to collect trinkets from around the world. Rosalina has recently discovered that Anya is also Queen Aurelia, the Queen of the Enchanted Vale. Aurelia is known for creating the Enchanted Vale, her immense bravery, and her love of language. She suddenly disappeared five hundred years ago.

Sira, Queen of the Below, mother of Caspian and the Nightingale

One of the first fae who hailed from the Above, Sira coveted the ability to create. She is responsible for stealing a rose from the Gardens of Ithilias, creating monstrous creatures such as goblins, and waging war on the Above. She rules from her tower in the Below, forging dark pacts with a god from a different world, and raising her two children: her eldest son and her adopted daughter.

Caspian, the Prince of Thorns, son of Sira and Malekai Furiondemius, and brother to the Nightingale

Child of the Queen of the Below and an evil god from another world, Caspian has never felt a sense of belonging. He strives to manipulate others to maintain a sense of control in a life where he has almost none. Caspian has the ability to control thorns, a power only wielded by three others in history: Queen Aurelia, Rosalina O'Connell, and his adopted sister, the Nightingale. Hated by many fae of the surface realms, Caspian has caused his share of chaos, including several supposed betrayals against Keldarion and the creation of the Great Chasm. Now, he does his mother's bidding while also secretly aiding Rosalina.

The Nightingale, daughter of Sira and sister to Caspian

The Nightingale was adopted as a baby twenty-five years ago by Sira. She loves her brother Caspian above all else, though both will betray the other if necessary. She works hard for her mother's approval. The Nightingale has a particularly close relationship with Prince Kairyn of Spring. She also seeks vengeance for an unknown affront against her by Rosalina.

Keldarion, High Prince of Winter, Sworn Protector of the Realms, son of Erivor and Runa, and fated mate of Rosalina

Keldarion first received Winter's Blessing during the War of Thorns. The majority of his reign has occurred while residing at Castletree, as he was cursed only a year after his coronation. Though known for his temper and standoffish nature, Keldarion has proven he will do anything to protect those he loves, even if he has to destroy himself in the process. He is fated mates with Rosalina O'Connell but refuses to break his curse due to a bargain he holds with the Prince of Thorns.

Erivor, late High Prince of Winter, husband of Runa and father of Keldarion

Erivor was a renowned leader to not only the citizens of Winter but to all the realms. He was felled during the War of Thorns while leading the force that would eventually recapture Frostfang.

Runa, late Princess of Winter, wife of Erivor, and mother to Keldarion

Runa was lauded for her wisdom and beauty. Stories say icy rain fell across all the lands of Winter when she was killed during the siege of Frostfang.

Irahn, Warden of Voidseal Bridge, brother of Runa, and uncle to Keldarion

Irahn lives in the wilds of Winter as the Warden of Voidseal Bridge. A stern and pragmatic man, he has no lofty ambitions nor craves power, but rather has dedicated his life to protecting Winter from whatever ills may crawl out of the Great Chasm.

Ezryn, former High Prince of Spring, son of Isidora and Thalionor, brother to Kairyn, and fated mate of Rosalina

Ezryn was once a famed warrior across the Vale. He was praised for his martial prowess, as well as his talent for command in battle. Ezryn dutifully served under both his parents. Isidora willingly passed Spring's Blessing to her son. Unfortunately, overcome with the new power within him, Ezryn accidentally killed his mother in the process. While living at Castletree, Ezryn was cursed by the Enchantress for the malice he bore in his heart. Years later, Ezryn fell in love with Rosalina and discovered she was his fated mate. When the curse began to break, he was once again overcome with power; his fear of losing Rosalina as he did his mother only caused the magic to grow more out of control. After destroying Spring's sacred grove and nearly killing Rosalina, Ezryn was arrested by his own soldiers. His throne was usurped by his brother, and he was banished from Spring. He earned the moniker "the Prince of Blood" for his brutal retaliation against the force that held Rosalina hostage.

Isidora, late High Princess of Spring, wife and fated mate of Thalionor, and mother to Ezryn and Kairyn

Isidora was the beloved High Princess of Spring. She wore a helm of starlight silver and wielded a broadsword of the same metal. Though she had a stern and imposing disposition, it is said she was the only one to show true empathy and understanding to her youngest son, Kairyn. It was with great pride and resolve that she passed her Blessing to Ezryn, believing he would be the greatest leader Spring had ever seen, though she was never able to see that wish come to fruition.

Thalionor, late Prince of Spring, husband and fated mate to Isidora, and father to Ezryn and Kairyn

Thalionor was known as a powerful soldier and inspiring commander. However, after the death of his fated mate, Thalionor succumbed to his grief, unable to serve as steward of Spring without the assistance of the majordomo Eldor. Eventually, Thalionor's state worsened, and he developed strange physical symptoms. He was killed by Caspian; an act Ezryn has sworn revenge against the Prince of Thorns for.

Kairyn, High Prince of Spring, Emperor of the Green Rule, son of Isidora and Thalionor, and brother to Ezryn

Kairyn always followed in his brother's shadow. Quiet and introspective as a boy, Kairyn was never the dutiful soldier Ezryn was, nor did he possess his brother's innate ability for leadership. When he witnessed his mother's death at the hands of his brother, Kairyn was overcome with grief and challenged his brother to the Rite: a dangerous duel that could result in one of the brothers dying or being unhelmed. Kairyn lost the duel and was instead banished to serve at Queen's Reach Monastery, a punishment he saw as dishonorable and pitying. While serving at the monastery, Kairyn witnessed the corruption of the High Clerics, as well as his brother failing to uphold the realm. He also became acquainted with the Nightingale, a beautiful woman from the

Below who promised him everything Kairyn believed Ezryn had stolen from him: glory, honor, and love. With the Nightingale's assistance, Kairyn organized a coup against the High Clerics, claiming their title. With his newfound position, he was able to help the villages that had been denied aid. He then set his sights on Spring. While secretly working with the Below, Kairyn preyed on his brother's loyalty and sense of honor, ultimately usurping the throne and banishing Ezryn from Spring. Now, Kairyn has taken the position of Emperor of the Below's Green Rule and has begun working toward the complete takeover of Summer.

Daytonales, High Prince of Summer, son of Sabine, Ovidius, and Cenarius, brother to Damocles, Decimus, and Delphia, and fated mate to Wrenley

Daytonales, referred to as Dayton by his friends, never thought he would be the High Prince of Summer. As a third-born son, he spent his days enjoying fights in the arena, drink, and the companionship of beautiful people. However, after most of his family was killed in the War of Thorns, Dayton was forced to assume the title. Deemed a drunk and a dullard, Dayton hid away in Castletree, allowing his young sister to serve as steward. Dayton was cursed by the Enchantress for his avoidance. However, Dayton's relationship with Farron and Rosalina has reminded him there are things worth fighting for—especially now that Dayton has found his fated mate in Wrenley, the beautiful young acolyte. Unfortunately for Dayton, he's not in love with her and has yet to break his curse.

Sabine, late Princess of Summer, wife of Ovidius and Cenarius, and mother to Damocles, Decimus, Daytonales and Delphia

Sabine was a descendant of the Huntresses of Aura and the former High Princess of Summer before she passed the Blessing to her eldest son, Damocles. Sabine was known for her fierce love for her husbands and children, as well as her fearless nature. She was killed amid the siege of Hadria during the War of Thorns. Many say her spirit still shines in her daughter, Delphia.

Ovidius, late Prince of Summer, husband of Sabine, partner to Cenarius, and father to Damocles, Decimus, Daytonales, and Delphia

Ovidius was a great warrior, a stern man who loved his family fiercely. He was killed amid the siege of Hadria during the War of Thorns.

Cenarius, late Prince of Summer, husband of Sabine, partner to Ovidius, and father to Damocles, Decimus, Daytonales, and Delphia

Cenarius was beloved across the realm for his ability to light up a battlefield, a tavern, or a strategy meeting with a joke or song. He was killed amid the siege of Hadria during the War of Thorns.

Damocles, late High Prince of Summer, son of Sabine, Ovidius, and Cenarius, and brother to Decimus, Daytonales, and Delphia

Damocles was a legendary hero of the Enchanted Vale. Some said he was the most powerful warrior to walk the realms. A serious and determined leader, he loved his family and wished to see them achieve the glory he knew they were capable of. He took particular interest in Dayton, wishing him to reach his full potential. Damocles never shied away from a fight and always resolved to face battles head-on. He was killed amid the siege of Hadria during the War of Thorns.

Decimus, late Prince of Summer, son of Sabine, Ovidius, and Cenarius, and brother to Damocles, Daytonales, and Delphia

Like his older brother, Decimus was a great warrior and skilled gladiator in the arena. He often had a playful rivalry with his younger brother, Dayton. He was killed amid the siege of Hadria during the War of Thorns.

Delphia, Princess and steward of Summer, daughter of Sabine, Ovidius, and Cenarius, and sister to Damocles, Decimus, and Daytonales

The youngest-born of the four royal families across the seasonal realms, Delphia was only a small child when most of her family perished in the War of Thorns. With her brother residing in Castletree, she was forced to serve as a child steward of Summer. Such responsibility has made Delphia wise beyond her years, though she still possesses the boldness of her parents and brothers. She became close friends with Eleanor when the young Autumn Princess served as a ward of Summer.

Farron, High Prince of Autumn, son of Niamh and Padraig, brother to Dominic, Billagin, and Eleanor, and fated mate of Rosalina

Farron was a reluctant leader when his mother first passed the Blessing of Autumn to him. He carries the weight of many failures in leadership during the War of Thorns and was cursed by the Enchantress for his cowardice. However, Farron learned the strength of his heart through his love for Daytonales and his fated mate, Rosalina. With Rosalina's love, Farron was able to break his curse and help his people. After his mother perished in a battle outside of Coppershire, Farron has become anxious about losing more of his loved ones and has shown curiosity toward the magic of the Green Flame that may prevent a permanent death.

Niamh, late Princess and steward of Autumn, wife of Padraig, and mother to Farron, Dominic, Billagin, and Eleanor

The former High Princess of Autumn, Niamh believed her son Farron would be a great ruler and willingly passed the Blessing on to him. She served as steward during his reign but was still treated as the true ruler and held the loyalty of the people. She died in battle but was able to see her son become the leader she knew he could be.

Padraig, Prince and steward of Autumn, husband of Niamh, and father to Farron, Dominic, Billagin, and Eleanor

Jovial and lighthearted, Padraig is both a talented war commander and a loving family man. After the death of his beloved wife, Padraig assumed the role of steward to assist his son in ruling Autumn and does everything he can to protect his people.

Dominic, Prince of Autumn, son of Niamh and Padraig, and brother to Farron, Billagin, and Eleanor

A young prince, Dominic is the twin brother of Billagin. The brothers have had to learn to defend themselves in times of strife. They have trained to be spies and now pride themselves on their skills at navigating deadly terrains, even the Briar.

Billagin, Prince of Autumn, son of Niamh and Padraig, and brother to Farron, Dominic, and Eleanor

Dominic's twin brother, Billagin tries to maintain an optimistic attitude, even in times of peril. Recently, the twins were entrusted with leading George O'Connell across the realms in search of his missing wife. When George fell ill, they dutifully saw him back to Coppershire and now watch over him.

Eleanor, Princess of Autumn, daughter of Niamh and Padraig, and sister to Farron, Dominic, and Billagin

The youngest member of the Autumn royal family, Eleanor, or "Nori," serves as a ward in Summer. Fascinated with the macabre, Nori often gets herself in trouble when she conducts arcane experiments. Close friends with Delphia, the two princesses rely on one another when the rest of the world seems against them.

Wrenley, acolyte of Queen's Reach Monastery and fated mate of Daytonales

A demure and sweet acolyte who served at Queen's Reach Monastery, Wrenley has found herself in dedicated service to the new High Cleric, Kairyn. After being rescued by Dayton, Wrenley wishes to help and protect him however she can, especially after she discovers he is her fated mate.

Marigold of Spring

A proud and boisterous woman, Marigold once directly served High Princess Isidora and helped raise Ezryn and Kairyn. Now, she serves at Castletree. Caught in the curse, Marigold spends her nights as a racoon. She loves Rosalina fiercely and will do anything she can to help her. Marigold has recently reconnected with her old flame, Eldor.

Astrid of Winter

Despite being cursed to turn into a hare at night, nothing can dim Astrid's upbeat attitude. She is proud of her position at Castletree and loyally serves Keldarion and the other princes. Astrid was Rosalina's first friend at Castletree and continues to be her close confidante.

Eldor of Spring

The majordomo of Keep Hammergarden in Spring, Eldor, or "Eldy," dutifully serves the royal family of Spring. During Thalionor's steward-ship, Eldy completed the majority of tasks as Thalionor was suffering with the grief of his wife's death. With Rosalina's help, Eldy was able to escape the occupation of Florendel by the Green Rule, and now lives at Castletree with his beloved, Marigold.

PART ONE
PRISONER OF THE DEEP

PROLOGUE

West bank of the Nile, outside of Luxor
1904

The young man wiped the beads of sweat off his brow and blinked up at the wavering horizon. The unforgiving sun had been blazing down on him all day, but he'd been unable to tear himself from his work. Dust covered every inch of his skin, his neck was burned from the sun, and his khakis were stained from the ochre sand. But as he stared down at the uncovered ruin before him, every physical ailment melted away.

A lost world right beneath his fingertips. History, long covered by the earth, now seeing the sunlight for the first time in thousands of years. His heart near beat out of his chest for the wonder of it all.

He stood and arched his back, pulling off the wide-brimmed hat that was meant to protect him from the relentless sun. A canvas of stone and sand stretched before him. He would be returning to Luxor in a few days to meet with the leader of his expedition. Every morning, he thanked whatever it was—God, the stars, fate, or simply Lady Luck—that he'd found his way into the employ of an eccentric Italian who had taken him here. Egypt was like no place he'd ever been before. Not the wilds of his homeland, a world away across the sea, nor the busy streets of London that he'd traveled to in search of employment.

Egypt could throw everything she had at him: blistering sunburns, sand in every crevice of his body, agonizing days with no discovery to be found. But when he looked down at the broken slab he'd just carefully unearthed with a brush and scalpel, it was all worth it.

It may just be a piece of rock with a carved hieroglyph to someone else, but to him, it felt like his own version of magic.

The rest of the archaeological team, dressed in matching sun-faded khaki, busied about him. The rhythmical clink of pickaxes striking the hard earth filled the air, sometimes cut with the call of a desert bird. Camels milled around the dig, carrying canteens of water and fresh fruit brought in from Luxor.

"Nice-looking find." Someone clapped a firm hand on his shoulder, and the young man turned to see his colleague, Samuel Rowell, smiling at him. Samuel's large, round head matched his large, round body. He was experienced on digs and had taken the young man under his wing.

"Finally got this part clear of the sand." The man bent down and pointed to the hieroglyph on the slab.

"What does it say?" Samuel asked.

"I don't know. Beautiful, isn't it?" The man trailed a hand along the image. It seemed to whisper to him in a voice he couldn't understand.

"Boss says there's likely a tomb nearby. Keep your head down and eyes peeled." Samuel's gaze drifted to the side, and he crossed his arms. "Jesus Christ."

"What?" the man asked, still unable to take his eyes off the hieroglyph.

"*She's* back again," Samuel muttered. "That nosey broad from last week."

"Who?"

"Ah, you lucky bastard, you were in Luxor with the boss and didn't have to deal with her. She came to the site and started digging right where we were working! I told her to scram, and she laughed in my face. It's no place for a woman here, that's for certain, and definitely not a smart-mouthed one like her."

The man raised an eyebrow, imagining Samuel's usual red face becoming even more beet-like while in confrontation with this woman.

"I had to deal with her last week," Samuel groaned. "Your turn. Tell her to get out of here."

"I'm busy!" the man exclaimed, gesturing back to the ruin.

Samuel gave him another clap on the shoulder. "You'll be busier if she steals one of our discoveries and the boss finds out that you let her on site. Off you go."

The young man sighed, staring longingly at his work, desperate to give a shot at trying to interpret the hieroglyph. "I'll be back for you," he muttered and headed off in the direction of the woman.

Her back was to him, and she was bent over in the sand on the edge of the dig, an open case of tools at her side. A camel stood quietly nearby, loaded with canteens, a bag overfilled with textbooks, and even more tools. She was certainly prepared.

The young man's feet sank into the soft sand as he approached. She didn't turn around as he stood behind her. She wore tight-fitting khaki pants and a white blouse, with tall leather boots covered in dust. Her curly brown hair was pulled into a ribbon at the nape of her neck. He cleared his throat. She didn't turn.

"Excuse me, ma'am."

Again, ignored.

"Ma'am?"

She didn't budge, instead busying herself with a scalpel now, clearing away some of the debris from whatever she was working on. Fed up and eager to get back to his own project, the man looked at the sun behind him and adjusted his position, causing his shadow to stream over her work.

"Do. You. *Mind?!*" the woman snarled and turned.

Their eyes met and the man blinked. Her expression was filled with anger but to him it was the most beautiful sight he had ever seen. He had gazed upon the tomb of Tutankhamen, flown in a hot air balloon above the Serengeti, traveled by sea across the Atlantic, and yet no wonder could compare. Her nose twitched with her scowl, brown eyes flashing golden in the sun.

Had he seen her before? No, and yet, it was as if she'd lived within his mind for all his life. Like every piece of him was crying out, *I've been waiting for you!*

He was in love. That had to be it. What else could it be? Love at first sight. He'd thought such a thing only a silly idea from children's fairy-tales. But this felt as it had when he uncovered his first ruin. Like sunlight hitting a place that had been hidden in the dark for a thousand years.

Magic.

Her nose stopped twitching. The dark brows, jutting down, softened and her lips parted into an O.

The man would not be surprised if a hundred years passed and they became covered in sand again, for time stilled between them.

Then she whispered, "You're in my light."

With a certainty he had never felt in his twenty-five years, the man replied, "You *are* my light."

Yes, this was true love, and she felt it, too—

The woman burst out laughing. "Excuse me?"

The man stopped. Caught himself. *You* are *my light? What does that even mean? Heavens to Betsy, I've been in the sun too long.*

He shook his head and tore his gaze from hers, afraid he'd get lost again in whatever *that* was. *That was heatstroke, that's what* that *was.*

"This is a closed dig, ma'am. You're not allowed to be here. This site belongs to Mr. Schiaparelli." There. That's what he was supposed to say, and he'd said it. Good. He turned to leave—

She laughed again. It was brash, a donkey's bray. It was the damned most beautiful thing he'd ever heard.

"This site doesn't *belong* to anyone. How can you *own* history? How can you own the languages and the religions and the past that is carved into this stone?" She turned around. "If you'll excuse me, I'm quite busy actually discovering something useful, instead of just carving up rock to shove in a glass box."

The man sighed and looked back at Samuel, who was busying himself plucking dates out of a jar. He had tried to send her packing. What else could he do? His own work awaited—

He bent down beside her. "What are you working on?"

She gave him a sidelong look. He offered a genuine smile, as a peace gesture, and she returned it with a relenting sigh. Before her was a sun-washed slab of broken stone. She'd assembled the pieces like a puzzle. "I've been looking for these segments for days. See how they fit together? Once I have the last section, I'll be able to read it."

"You can interpret the hieroglyphs?"

A smile broke across her lips. "Yes. I have a special interest in languages."

He stared down at the pieces, the middle missing. One empty spot. But he recognized the shape, the jutting bit here, the indent there. "I'll be right back."

Carefully, ever so carefully, the young man returned a few minutes later, carrying the slab he'd uncovered. Her eyes widened as she saw it. With deft fingers, he slotted it right between the other pieces.

"It fits," she whispered.

"Well?" he urged. "What does it say?"

She traced the symbols. "Roughly, it says . . . Here lies the Queen."

They met each other's gaze. "It's true," he whispered. "This is the Valley of the Queens."

Her eyes glittered. "That's why I'm here."

Then she quickly packed her tool kit, stood, and walked to her camel. "A brilliant discovery always makes me hungry. I must go back to the city now." In a fluid movement, she mounted the beast and her shadow fell over the man, her eyes sparkling like chips of gold.

"Wait!" the man cried. "Will I see you again?"

Her voice was light, as if she knew something wonderful that he didn't. "Oh, you won't be able to keep me away."

As she drew the reins, her white blouse shifted, and the sunlight caught a necklace she wore. It shimmered every color of the rainbow, a luminescent flash of light. The man squinted against the gleam. A rose.

"What's your name?" he asked.

"Anya. Yours?"

"George," the man replied. "George O'Connell."

Anya smiled that knowing smile once again before turning her beast and striding off across the horizon. George could not look away, not even after she became nothing more than a tiny dot amid the dunes.

He had the very distinct feeling his life would never be the same.

I

DAYTON

Damocles would never have let this happen.

When my brother was High Prince of Summer, the streets of Hadria were filled with laughter. Stalls were packed with fresh fruit, clothes, and pottery, and sand would settle between the cracks of the cobblestone streets from fae returning after a day of swimming in the turquoise ocean.

Dried blood is the only thing that stains the stone now. Probably from someone who was beaten last night for disobeying the *Emperor's* mandatory curfew.

Throwing up my hood, I dart out of the alley and onto the main strip. There's a flow of fae heading toward the Sun Colosseum. Those without necessary jobs are required to attend the games.

Kairyn's games.

The thought makes me sick.

The air feels thick as soup and sweat drips down my brow. Between the cramped rows of people, it's nearly suffocating.

"Keep moving," calls one of the armed guards lining the streets.

Kairyn doesn't have his toxic plants here to control the people of Summer. He's probably too far away from his realm for that magic to work. But a few thousand Spring soldiers, former Queen's Army, a fleet of airships, and an entire horde of fucking *goblins* will do the job just the same.

"Clear the streets," one of the goblins calls. "Emperor Kairyn is coming. Clear the streets!"

Fae scurry away from them in fear. Goblins, creatures of the Below, now dictate orders to *my* people.

Gritting my teeth, I follow the crowd and make my way to the Sun Colosseum. Its tall columns rise before me like a mountain. I duck behind one of the huge marble pillars. I know I should get back to my lodgings, but it's so different now without Farron. With just *her*—

"Prince Daytonales," a voice hisses. I turn to another cloaked figure and pull them deeper into the shadows.

"Not so loud, Claudius."

"Apologies, m'lord," Claudius says. He's a young fae with dark hair and a cunning smile. He runs one of the fish stalls on the wharf, which are still allowed to operate, though it's a cover for his other activities. One of my few contacts in the city, Claudius is a dealer of secrets and he has become invaluable to me these last few months. "Another update on your sister. A sailor reports that he saw her ship around Veritas Bay, not two days past."

My relief at Delphia being sighted alive mixes with the worry of her being so close to the capital. *Don't come back, Delphie. There's nothing you can do.* Stars, there's nothing I can do.

We learned that Delphia had escaped with Farron's sister, Eleanor, when Kairyn first attacked the city. Reports said they initially tried to fight back, but between his fleet of airships and three armies, Summer hadn't stood a chance.

Not to mention, Summer doesn't have a High Prince on the throne.

My throat tightens as I ask the next question. "Any news on the Golden Rose?"

Claudius tilts his head, giving me a sad smile. "Nothing besides the whispers of hope. There have been no sightings and the guards won't talk. If she's in Summer, it's a place even I don't know about."

My heart constricts. When we first left Spring months ago, Farron had been able to follow the tug of his mate bond in the direction of Summer, but then the pull had suddenly vanished.

He doesn't think she's dead. We know Kairyn and his crony, the Nightingale, have used suppressant magic like this before but the scary thing is, he hasn't felt a flicker, not for the three months we've been here.

My hands curl into fists. *I'll find you, Rosie. I promise.*

"If I may, m'lord," Claudius steps closer, lowering his voice, "there are people in the city who will fight. Who *want* to fight against the Green Rule. A resistance is brewing."

The Green Rule—that's what Kairyn's calling his occupation of Summer, sanctioned by the Below. I look around. Most of the soldiers are occupied with ushering people into the arena. Inside, Kairyn has imprisoned half the legionnaires of Summer, forcing them to fight in his twisted games. The rest of our army is imprisoned in Soltide Keep, the prominent fortress in Hadria and my childhood home. Whatever resistance Claudius is speaking of would be comprised only of the common folk of Summer. I can't risk my people like that. "No one hates this more than me, but it's not the right time. It would only get more people killed."

Claudius nods but can't hide the disappointment on his face as he slinks back into the crowd. He doesn't understand. I can't lead anyone. I don't even have my magic.

There's a faint crackle, like an echo beneath my skin, but I can't summon anything. It's been too long since I've returned to Castletree. The damned Prince of Thorns stole my token and even being in my own realm isn't enough to restore the Blessing.

Another roar echoes from the crowd, and I peer through the pillars, catching a glimpse of the sacred sands of the arena. The stands rise around them in an oval shape. The Emperor's Box sits at the very top, an elevated seating area with the best view of the fights. Within the box floats a glowing, brilliant object. The Bow of Radiance. Kairyn has it.

The way he's treating this sacred space, this sacred object . . . It's perverse. My people, my legionnaires, are forced to fight in his games and if one gladiator or a team wins three matches, they are allowed the privilege to try and wield the Queen's own bow.

Everyone's burned up on contact with it.

The only way to wield the bow is to wear the Queen's token, and that was lost five hundred years ago when she left the Enchanted Vale.

Leaving the arena, I turn a corner and come face to face with someone who *could* save the city.

A mural of my family painted onto the wall of the Sun Colosseum. Or my family how it once was before the War of Thorns. There were seven of us, and we were so close. My mother married twice, a custom common among fae in Summer. They weren't mates, but there was so much love between all three of them. My two fathers treated each other like brothers, and both adored my mother, Sabine. In the mural, Delphie is a newborn, and Mother cradles her tightly. My mother has her blond hair curled in loose knots around her face. Even in the painting, her gaze is still intense, eyes like chips of turquoise. Gauzy pink fabric twists down her tan arms.

Delphie's birth father, Ovidius, stands over them. He may not have been my blood, but he was still my father. The mural depicts him just as I remember, tall and broad-shouldered, with dark brown skin and full lips in a stern line. His long, black hair is pulled into tight braids that fall over his chest. Ovidius taught me to fight and to know when patience is warranted.

On his other side is Decimus, his other biological child. A smile brightens on my face looking at him. I can hear his voice offering advice, teasing me, or giving commentary on fights in the arena. The dimple in Decimus's cheek is straight from our mother Sabine's face, while his brown skin, black hair, and shining eyes all came from Ovidius. I see so much of him in Delphie now.

My fingers trail over the mural, to the other side of my mother, to Cenarius, my birth father. His long blond hair is depicted in thick curls. He was always in the ocean, always finding some way to make us laugh. I learned all of my best jokes from him.

My hand drops before I let it touch Damocles. It would feel like a betrayal to even do so after what I let happen to his city.

What I let happen to *him*.

Damocles, the eldest-born son of Cenarius and Sabine. Damocles the hero. Damocles the wise. Damocles the perfect.

He stands there with the seashell token of the Queen around his neck and a stern line to his mouth. I don't think I ever heard him laugh. There isn't time for jokes when you've got a realm to run.

"It's the royal family!" a light voice says, and a young girl runs up to the mural. Quickly, I back away behind an archway, but for some reason I can't help but watch.

The girl places her hand over the image and whispers, "When is Damocles coming back to save us?"

A woman walks up and places a hand on the girl's shoulder. "Damocles is dead, you know this. Daytonales is the High Prince now."

The young girl tilts her head at the mural. "I don't know who that is."

"Summer has not seen him in a long time."

"Maybe Princess Delphia will come back and save us."

My heart near shatters in my chest.

A shadow falls over the girl and her mother, and it's suddenly so quiet. The kind of quiet that only fear brings.

The crowd parts as Kairyn struts forward, tall and broad, adorned by his metal helm and a swishing black cape. Fuck, the bastard must be sweating buckets—just more proof of his insufferable pride. Maybe if I'm lucky he'll boil away in that walking chamber pot.

Dozens of Spring soldiers flank him. Even if they didn't, there isn't a single person in this city that could fight him and win.

Not while he wields Spring's Blessing.

I pull my hood lower over my brow, resisting every urge to rush into the street and confront him. To demand to know where Rosalina is. Order him to let her go.

But I'll be no use to Rosie dead.

"There is already a savior here, child. I will keep you safe the way your loathsome Prince of Summer never could. I have restored Spring to its former glory, and Summer is next." Kairyn tilts his owl helm at the child. "All you need to do is kneel."

He says the words as if he knows I'm here. I stagger farther back into the crowd.

Magic crackles through the air. The kind of magic only a High Ruler can wield. It's the Blessing of Spring. Kairyn only has access to such power because he manipulated Ezryn into passing the Blessing to him.

Dark vines writhe from beneath his hand, breaking into the wall, tearing apart the mural. Broken pieces of my family turn to dust upon the street.

One by one, the crowd drops to their knees, heads bent in submission. I should kneel, I should submit. But I can't.

I can't fight either, not yet. So, I slink into the shadows.

But Kairyn isn't the only High Prince not hindered by a curse.

Farron.

Farron will find a way to save us. He always does.

2

FARRON

My paws pound against the wet earth, each step sending me bounding through the briars. How long have I been running? Days? Weeks? I don't remember. But I know I haven't stopped. Freed from the Enchantress's curse, the wolf barely needs to sleep. I've survived with only the adrenaline rushing through my body and the odd goblin that dares to show its face to the Autumn wolf.

I've never spent this long out in the Briar, but without my token to magically transport me to Castletree, traveling by cover of bush and darkness is safest. I'd rather face the goblins here than Kairyn's soldiers, who now block the pass from Summer to Autumn.

Briars tear at my fur, but I ignore them and sunlight sneaks through gaps in the huge, twisted thorns all around me. Through the breaks, I spot the glimmer of a rolling hill dotted with heather. *I'm almost home.*

But I don't know if I'll ever be able to call a place home if she's not there.

It's been three months since I last set eyes on my mate. My last image of her—screaming and crying in pain as Ezryn was marched through the streets of Florendel—is etched into my mind. After that, I'd lost my wits to one of Kairyn's corrupted plants. Dayton had found me. Saved me, as he's always done. But he'd had the help of . . .

My fangs gnash together, and a growl rumbles through my chest unconsciously. I don't want to think about Wrenley right now. Every fraction of energy I have has to be focused on the power of my legs, the strength of my paws. The will of my heart.

I burst out of the Briar, suddenly bathed in orange light. The smell of an apple grove wafts in the breeze, and I inhale deeply. For the first time in days, I pause and take in the Autumn realmlands. With the purple briars at my back and my realm before me, I allow myself a sense of hope.

Rosalina is alive. I know this in my heart. Even though I can't feel our bond the way I should, it hasn't slackened, only numbed. Wherever she is, the Nightingale must be keeping her magic at bay. But we'll find her. I know we will.

I take off running again. The wolf's instincts are sharp. Even so deep in the wilds, I know exactly the direction of my home city.

The last few months have been nothing short of torture. Dayton and I traveled to Summer hoping to find Rosalina and warn the steward, Dayton's younger sister, Delphia, of the oncoming invasion. We were too late. By the time we arrived in Hadria, Delphia had fled to the sea and Kairyn sat upon her throne. My own sister, Eleanor, is a ward of Summer. A pain shoots up my chest. I can only hope she's still with Delphia, safely in hiding.

Dayton, Wrenley, and I found a small apartment in the slums to shelter in while we tried to find any information. Where are the Princesses of Summer and Autumn? What is Kairyn's next move?

Where is Rosalina?

I'll find you, I say through my numb bond. *I won't ever stop. Your love is my guiding light through the darkness. No force in the Vale can keep us apart.*

She can't hear me, but I hope my love is strong enough to make it to her somehow. There can be no magic in all the world stronger than that of a mate bond.

I stumble, paws sliding against the slick grass as I run downhill.

I'm not the only one with a mate bond.

The image flashes through my mind: Wrenley, holding the will-o'-wisp to her chest. The beam of light shooting straight at Dayton.

Logically, I knew this was bound to happen. I always knew I couldn't keep him. That he didn't belong to me.

So why does it feel like my heart will rip out of my chest every time I think of the acolyte's hand on his? Of how she always flutters right in his shadow, watching him with that focused gaze of hers?

Staying with Dayton and Wrenley in our Summer slum had to be a unique brand of torture, devised just for me. Sometimes I wish he'd just do it—just accept his bond and mate with her already. At least then he'd break his curse. But as always with Dayton, no force in all the realms can compel him to do something he doesn't want to do.

Or maybe he wants to be with her. Maybe I was just in the way. Stars, they could be mated already, for all I know. He might have decided it was time the minute I left.

I hadn't wanted to leave, but we'd exhausted every option in Hadria and were no closer to finding Rosalina. Even Wrenley, who had secured her position once again as one of Kairyn's acolytes, heard no useful information. I couldn't take another moment in that little apartment, wondering when Dayton would finally say yes to Wrenley and accept his bond with her.

The two of us certainly hadn't been intimate since Rosalina's disappearance. Though, there were many dark days I craved his comfort, when the loneliness and fear for my mate seemed too strong. I imagined going to Dayton and falling into his arms as I've done so many times before.

But how could I when his true mate was right there?

Faster, I need to run faster before my thoughts eat me alive. The hill gives way to a familiar forest. The Emberwood, the place where I broke my curse and made love to my mate for the first time. *We'll come back here again, you and me. I will take you in my arms and kiss you a hundred times, no, a thousand times, because I will never have my fill of you. Then we'll fall among the leaves and make love like it's the first time again. The first time of infinity.*

Coppershire isn't far now. That's why I left Dayton. I told him there was nothing I could do here and, with no word from Keldarion or Ezryn, we had to seek help elsewhere. The people of Autumn will come to Summer's aid.

Silence fills my mind as I run the rest of the way. Every patch of heather, every stone and tree, seems familiar now. My powerful legs send me bounding up the final hill that overlooks the city.

I stop. Down below, Coppershire glimmers bronze in the dying light. Outside the city walls, fighting on the same field that I fought upon nearly half a year ago, are Autumn soldiers barely holding their own against a goblin horde.

My heart thunders in my chest. What is this? I search the battlefield, but I see no commander, no denizen of the Below shouting orders. These are goblins straight from the Briar.

My father leads the soldiers, cutting down three goblins with a single giant swing of his sword. His familiar voice booms over the chaos, shouting orders and motivating his troops. Anger swells in me. I lost my mother on this field. I won't lose anyone else.

Fire licks at my paws as I sprint down the hill. The flames spread, engulfing my entire body until I'm more fire than wolf. Every day that passes since I broke my curse, I become more and more reacquainted with the full breadth of my power. But what good does it do me if I can't get Rosalina back?

A soldier spots me, eyes wide with awe. He raises his spear and lets loose a triumphant cry.

A few goblins turn to stare at me, terrified looks flashing across their faces. But it's too late for them to escape. I swing my flaming paw, knocking them aside. My maw is a torrent of heat, snapping necks and tearing heads from spines.

My father's face lights up as he sees me making my way to him. "Hail the High Prince of Autumn!" he cries. "Hail!"

The rest of the soldiers take up the cheer, lauding as I cut through the enemy ranks. One by one, the goblins fall to flame and teeth. A few try to retreat, stumbling back up the hill, but my father's soldiers cut them down. Within the hour, what once was a great horde is now ash beneath my paws.

I walk through the smoking field, suddenly abashed at the look of adoration from the soldiers. There's only one person I want to speak to right now.

"My boy!" His booming voice carries over the din. I peer through the smoke to see my father's giant body hurtling toward me. He wraps his arms around my snout, and I nuzzle against him.

"You came in the nick of time, didn't you?" He pulls back and puts a spark out on his bushy, red beard. I shift, body shimmering back into that of a fae. My father shrugs out of his hooded cape and hands it to me.

I hug the cape around my shoulders. "What was that, Father? I've never seen a force of goblins so brazen on their own."

Father leads me toward the city gates. "That's the third attack this month, boy."

Third attack this month? How can that be? "I don't understand. Who's commanding them?"

"I don't know." He shakes his head. "Maybe no one. They're pouring out of the Briar faster than ever. Don't you worry, boy, we've kept our gates standing." He stops before the wall surrounding the city and looks at me with a sad smile. "I'm just so happy to see you, son. Been a quarter since anyone's heard word of you. I feared the worst."

"My Queen's token was stolen by the enemy. I've had no way to travel to Castletree."

"Where's Rosalina?"

"Gone," I whisper. "The enemy has her. I've been in Summer trying to—"

"They say Hadria's fallen and the Golden Rose has been kidnapped. Is it true, then?" my father interrupts. His eyes shine, and I realize he's holding back tears. "What's happened to our Nori?"

I take a deep breath. "There are still fae resisting Kairyn's rule. Word is Delphia escaped on a ship. No doubt she'll have taken Eleanor with her, too."

Father squeezes his eyes shut. "Your mother's essence is with her, watching over her. I know it."

"I do, too," I whisper.

I follow my father inside the city walls, every step heavy. He tells me of the past goblin attacks, of how they're running out of good steel without trade with Spring, of how the farms closest to the Briar are too dangerous to harvest now and must be abandoned. I see the look of hope in the people's gazes as I pass, as if I've come to fix everything.

How can I ask my own people to come to Summer's aid when they're barely surviving as they are?

As we approach Keep Oakheart, my heart sinks further. Is there truly no way to fight this? Are the realms doomed?

My gaze drifts across the way, to the Alder Tree. Inside lies a hidden treasure, one only I know about. A crown of Green Flame plucked from my mother's murderer. Perth Quellos had wielded the Green Flame with evil purpose, but what if someone could control it for good? Could such magic be used to protect those I love so I wouldn't have to lose anyone again the way I lost my mother? What if I could—

I force my thoughts away. There's no time for experiments. Not when my mate is missing, and my realm is falling. More than ever, I wish there was someone I could turn to for advice.

"Have you heard from Keldarion or Ezryn?" I ask Father.

"Ezryn, no. I heard he was banished from Spring for killing a bunch of holy acolytes in Queen's Reach Monastery."

"No, that's not true."

"What is true is there hasn't been sight of hide nor hair of him. Keldarion was here about three months ago. He's since returned to Frostfang."

"What? Kel went back to Winter?"

"Aye," my father says, and a mischievous twinkle appears in his eye. "Word is, the High Prince of Winter is *pissed*."

3

KELDARION

I slam the door to my chambers in Keep Wolfhelm, the Winter Realm's stronghold. Ice cracks the wooden floor as I try to control my ragged breathing.

"Careful," a voice purrs, "or it will start to look like the Winter Wing in here."

Caspian lounges on a plush chair by the fire. Sprawled sideways, his long legs hang over the arm, his dark hair falling in waves around his face. It looks as if he's been walking through the snow and it only just dried.

A deep rumble sounds through my chest, and I turn away from him. "You're back."

"Don't jump with joy now," he replies.

I throw off my heavy, embroidered jacket. Pale pink light flickers through the window, the first sign of sunset amidst a light dusting of snow. Soon the sun will set, and I will be confined to my chambers as the beastly wolf.

I look around my room, though it hardly feels like mine. This place still carries the essence of my parents. Such grandeur, with rich woven tapestries depicting scenes of battle, hanging on dark wood walls. My canopy bed, draped in velvet curtains of midnight blue, stands at the center. The scent of burning wood fills the air, mingling with the faint aroma of pine from the nearby forest. I look to the stone hearth and fire-light dances across the chamber, dispelling the chill of the Winter night.

But it's none so bespelling as the man watching me.

I cross to him. "You're alone."

Caspian's lavender eyes dart away, and if I didn't know better, I'd swear there was a flash of sadness there. "My latest plan didn't work."

I see it then, the weariness on his face. I cross to the hearth and place a hand on the mantle. "The council advised against my request to march our army to Summer. As High Ruler, I don't need their support, but I'd lose what little control I have here. My people don't trust me."

"Kel." Caspian stands. "If you march your army out of Winter, Sira will invade. She's watching Winter closely."

"Then my people will think I'm allied with the Below—again."

Caspian steps in front of me. "Now, what would cause people to tell such nasty rumors about you?"

I grab him by the collar and slam him against the wall. "You promised you'd help me find her."

Anger flashes in his gaze and he breaks away from my hold. "You think I destroyed Kairyn's airship for fun? They'd already moved her by the time I got to it. Do you know what my mother did to me when she found out? Thankfully, she thought I destroyed it out of jealousy. Otherwise, I would be dead."

I sigh, unsure what to say. I know Caspian's been lying to Sira about helping me find Rosalina. She's a dangerous woman, and not even her own son is safe from her wrath. "Your people have her, Caspian. How can you not find her?"

"Look," he says, running a hand through his hair, "I'm not exactly on great terms with the new High Prince of Spring right now. If my mother even suspects I'm interested in finding Rosalina, she might just kill her to spite me. You don't understand how careful I have to be."

Anger rises in my chest, but I know it's not directed toward Caspian. Not all of it, at least. He's been trying to help, in his own way. Though I still don't understand why he's so fascinated with Rosalina. Is it just because she's my mate, or is there something more?

I stayed only briefly in Castletree before returning to Winter, trying to see if there was any way to make Kairyn answer for his crimes. With more and more monsters pouring out of the chasm, and my already tenuous hold on my realm, there had been no other solution but to come to Winter.

Caspian was able to assure me there were rumors of Dayton and

Farron in the Summer Realm, and I have no doubt they are looking for Rosalina as well, as neither has returned to Castletree.

"I can't even *feel* her, Cas." I shake my head. "Do you have any idea what that's like, to know she's out there, but not be able to reach her?"

"I can imagine."

"I don't know if she's scared or hurt or—"

"She's alive," he says. "I know. You'd feel it otherwise. No magic suppressant could block out that pain."

A deep growl rumbles in my chest. I tried to count on others, but again I am left on my own. I cross the room to the window.

"Kel, I know that look," Caspian says. "What are you thinking?"

"That I need to do what I should have done a long time ago. I'll go to Summer and find her myself."

Caspian is in front of me in an instant, his brow furrowed. "You can't. You don't even know she's there."

"Then I'll tear Kairyn apart piece by piece until he tells me where she is."

"Oh yes," Caspian snarls, "I'm sure it'll go exactly like that. Do you remember what he was like in the throne room? His power has only grown since then."

"I tried to wait for you. I tried to rally my realm. No more waiting. I'll have to run as the beast." The enchanted doorway between Castletree and Keep Soltide is closed, and since Kairyn stole my token, I have no way to use the mirror in Castletree.

Caspian stops me with a palm on my chest. "I can take you to the briars bordering the Summer Realm."

Thorns break through the wood, tangling around us. Drawing me closer to him, his fingers clutch in my shirt. "Say you could beat Kairyn with his unconstrained Blessing of Spring. How do you intend to escape the three armies he has in Hadria?"

My chest presses against his as the thorns and shadows draw us under. My lips end up by his ear, then I lower them to his neck. "Then you better be close by."

"I can't," he says, voice as silky as the shadows caressing us.

"Can't?" Without meaning to, my teeth nip at his neck, hard enough to bruise. "Or won't?"

"Kel," he whispers, and the sound is so desperate, so full of want, it almost consumes me. His voice is dangerous, and it's dangerous to trust him. But for Rosalina, I will do anything.

I let his shadows and thorns pull us through the Vale. We'll find her. If *he* doesn't find her first.

Even though he hates me, even though he lost his power, I know there is no length Ezryn will not go to in order to rescue our mate.

4

EZRYN

rack.

The man's screams drown out the sound of his next two fingers breaking. I drop his limp hand and stand above him patiently. I'll wait for him to stop screaming.

It doesn't take long. He's already learned that I'm not a patient man.

The filth raises his watery gaze to me. He's collapsed on the ground, his other hand tied tight to his torso with rope, his ankles bound. He doesn't look like a member of the former Queen's Army. Now, he looks exactly like what he is. A raider. A rat. A traitor.

"Let's try this again," I say calmly. "Where. Is. She."

Anger flashes across his blood-streaked face. "I don't fucking know. I don't! I swear, I don't!"

I sigh. I know he's lying. It's in the shift of his eyes, the tremor of his lip. If he doesn't want to talk, that's fine. There are two of them, after all.

It would be heresy to still refer to these men as Queen's Army. They deserted their post and their morals when they chose to follow my brother. Kairyn, High Cleric of Queen's Reach Monastery and the new High Prince of Spring, has allied with the Below and decided to name himself Emperor of the Realms. So far, he has claimed the seats in Florendel and now Hadria. Where he goes, his minions follow, waging their destruction upon the land.

Pulling a knife from my back pocket, I place it at the base of the man's ear. "You're having trouble listening," I growl.

The smell of urine assaults my nose.

"Where is she?" I ask again, slowly, calmly. The man shakes but says nothing. My voice grows to a booming roar: "Where is she?!"

"Emperor Kairyn has her somewhere no one will find her!" the second man calls. He's slumped in a pile beside the cave wall. Despite his own torso and ankles being bound with rope, this one's still got some fight.

I stride over to him. The cave is dark, dusky light filtering in. Beyond, the desert sand wavers with heat. Soon, it will be near freezing but the cold and dark never bother me. I imagine it will bother these two though.

The fire that raged upon the nearby village is now extinguished; flames dwindled to mere embers. I was staying in the small settlement for the day, refreshing my supplies of water and food, when Kairyn's soldiers descended. Patrollers, they said they were. Summer belongs to them now, after all. They demanded everything they could of the people: their food, their water, their supplies. When the village refused, they set fire to it.

It wasn't hard for the villagers to stop the fire once the soldiers were dealt with.

There had been ten. Now, there are two.

A breeze drifts through the mouth of the cave, wafting my dark hair before my eyes. It's been three months, and I don't know if I'll ever get used to it. I wear only cloth. The only Spring steel left to me is my mother's sword, which I keep sheathed and undrawn. I will not taint it with the blood of traitors.

I yank the man up by his hair until we're eye to eye. "Where is the Golden Rose?"

The man, eyes swollen from my fists, has a delirious grin on his pockmarked face. "Who? You mean the Dandelion? That's what Emperor Kairyn calls 'er. Nothing but a little yellow weed, ready to be torn out."

I slam the man against the rock wall of the cave and plunge my knife into his thigh. He cries out, only making me twist the blade more. "Do you feel that?" I growl. "My knife's right in the perfect spot to bleed you straight out. Tell me what you know, or I'll tear it out right now and let you drown in your own blood."

The man licks his red teeth. "Look at him, Aldridge. Those torn-up ears. Don't even look like real fae, does he?"

"Just tell him, Laughy," the first man—Aldridge—says.

"You know where she is." I slam Laughy hard against the rock wall again. His head cracks against the stone and blood drips down over his neck. "Tell me!"

Laughy begins to chuckle. "So, this is how I go! By the Prince of Blood, himself. I've heard the rumors. An airship downed in the Suadela Sands. A troop of soldiers left mangled on the border. They whisper of you among the ranks. 'The Prince of Blood,' they say! 'He's coming for us!'"

"Now he's found you," I growl.

Laughy shakes his head and smiles. "You'll never get to her. Kairyn's got her locked up so tight, not even the Prince of Blood could get through."

I snap, drawing the knife out in one swift movement, then drive it back into his other thigh. Blood gushes onto me and the man screams.

"You're out of time. In one minute, you'll have passed out. In two, you'll be dead."

Something shifts in Laughy's eyes as he gazes down at the blood surging from his thigh. "D-doesn't matter if I tell you. You won't be able to get to her—"

His words are cut off in a scream as I drive the knife point through his bicep.

"She's on the prison barge!" he cries. "It's floating thirty klicks off the coast of Hadria. West of the Byzantar Isles! Kairyn's watching over her himself. You'll never—"

I drop the man face down. A gurgle erupts as he tries to lift himself out of the pool of his own blood. I turn away.

The remaining filth trembles as my shadow overtakes him. "He told you what you want to know! Haven't you had enough, Prince of Blood?"

"I have," I say, my voice a low gravel. "But he hasn't."

The sun dips below the horizon. The cave goes dark as the wolf rips out of my skin, a massive beast of tangled bone and black fur.

The man's scream is cut off as his neck snaps in my jaws.

I take off across the sands, cutting south for the capital of Summer. I don't care what they call me. I don't care if they're right. I *am* the Prince of Blood. Every waking minute since I left Florendel has been spent searching this godforsaken realm for my mate. Now, I finally know where to find her.

If I have to tear the mountains from the earth, the clouds from the sky, the water from the sea, I will do it. Nothing will stop me from finding Rosalina.

5

ROSALINA

T. *Tom Sawyer from* The Adventures of Tom Sawyer. *U. Ursula Brangwen from* Women in Love. *V. Vin from* Mistborn. *W. Wendy Darling from* Peter Pan. *X . . .*

Fucking X! I always get stuck at X. There's got to be some literary character I've read who starts with X. Surely, one of Tolkien's orcs. Or wasn't there a prince in *Game of Thrones*—

"Look at me when I'm talking to you," the helmed man growls and grabs my shoulders, giving me a small shake. "Are you even listening?"

I sigh and drag my gaze up to Kairyn's black helm. There's a shining silver streak down the front, repaired by Spring steel from when it had cracked in the storm by Sylvanita Lake. It doesn't keep the helm from looking any less cruel though. It's like peering into a void, all light disappearing beneath the carved feathered brow.

"You messed me up," I say dully. "Now, I have to start over."

A. Aragorn from The Lord of the Rings. *B. Bridget Jones from*—

Kairyn grabs my chin, the leather of his gloves warm against my cool skin.

It's hard to feel warm six hundred feet under the sea.

"How many times must we do this, Rosalina?" Kairyn sighs. The usual timbre of his voice takes on an exhausted tone. "Tell me what I want to know, and we can stop these little visits."

"Why would I want to stop them?" I ask, unable to bring any emotion to my voice. "After all, you're such good company compared to the fish."

I tilt my head toward the walls of my prison. Three of them are made of glass. No Spring steel bars needed here. Even if the air wasn't infused with the Nightingale's magic-sapping concoction, there's nowhere to escape to. Just miles of ocean on every side.

It's been three months since I was captured and brought aboard Kairyn's airship. I'd recognized the turquoise ocean from my brief visit to Summer a year ago and had known we were somewhere off the coast of Hadria. They transferred me from the airship to a massive, floating barge. The contrast between its harsh, dark metal and the brilliant sky and ocean had been stark.

That was the last time I felt the sun. They'd taken me down, down, down into the depths of the prison barge. I've lived every day since then in this cell with one metal door and three glass walls, wearing the same pair of tattered white trousers and shirt they gave me when I arrived. There's a thin mattress and a contraption to use as a toilet, and the fish outside and that's it.

I turn away from Kairyn and stand by one of the glass walls, staring out at the blue sea. I was lying, of course. The fish are far better company than him. We're so far down that only the faintest glimmer of daylight can penetrate, but it's enough that I've been able to track my days here by scratching a little line on the floor with my nail. If I wasn't a prisoner, I might even find the view spectacular.

The deep blue sea spans out all around. Fish of every hue swim back and forth in front of my three walls. I'm never alone; they seem to swarm here, as if wanting to keep me company. I don't even mind the strange ones: the ones with scales black as oil and eyes that glow like gemstones. I wonder if the Below has an ocean, too.

Kairyn comes up beside me. He visits me nearly every day. I call them visits because the word "interrogation" sets my heart racing.

"It doesn't have to be this way, Rosalina," he says softly. My name in his mouth makes me want to gag. I can still feel his vines wrapping around my body, squeezing the breath out of me. "I know how lonely it must be here. No freedom. No magic." He gives a long exhale. "No mate bonds."

A shudder trembles through me. Every day, I fight so hard to keep his poisonous words from affecting me. Whether it's with stupid word games or imagining I'm somewhere—anywhere—other than here, I can do it. I can keep his darkness from seeping into me.

But every day, it gets harder and harder. As if the sea is swallowing me whole.

I sink to my knees.

Kairyn drops down beside me. "It's all right, Rosalina. I'm here. You're not alone." Carefully, he moves a strand of matted dark hair away from my eyes. "This can all be over, little Dandelion. Just tell me what I need to know—"

It gets harder. But I won't stop fighting for them. For myself.

With a roar, I throw my body against Kairyn's, sending him backward. "Go to hell, you monster!"

I clamber over him. He's so much bigger than me and stronger, and he could call an entire unit of guards in at any second. I won't win my freedom by doing this, but that doesn't matter. I just want him to feel the pain he's caused me, caused my mates, just for a second. Just to remind him he's not dealing with a dandelion.

He's dealing with a fucking Queen.

Pinning his shoulders down with my knees, I wedge my hands under his dark mask. There is no greater shame for a royal of the Spring Realm than to reveal their face to anyone other than their fated mate. A shame he forced upon my own mate. A shame I will *make* him endure.

I push as hard as I can, but three months of consuming only rationed bread and water has made me weak. The helm inches up with agonizing slowness. Kairyn bucks beneath me. "Get off, you bitch!"

A strong chin emerges, and a desperate excitement rises. I want him to suffer as I've suffered.

"Get off!" Kairyn jerks his torso, throwing me to the ground. He staggers to his feet. His whole body shakes as he places his hands on his helm to wedge it back over his chin.

I draw my head back and spit. A glob of spittle lands right on his bare skin before he can slam his helm back over it.

We stay there like that for a minute: his armored body shadowing me upon the floor. In the three months I've been imprisoned, he's never hurt me physically. Never used torture to get the information he wants. I wonder if this is the moment he breaks.

"Emperor, are you all right?" a guard shouts from outside the metal door. "We heard a scuffle."

"Stay out," Kairyn growls back. "Stay out!"

He takes a heavy footstep toward me. Then another. I shuffle backward until my spine is pressed against the cold glass, trapped between the sea and a madman.

"I was tasked with keeping you safe," Kairyn says. "Tasked with finding the answers to my questions. If I can't accomplish this, then you will be sent to someone who can." He takes another step closer until I'm completely engulfed in his shadow. "Trust me, Sira does not keep her guests in such fine conditions as I."

Sira, Queen of the Below. The arch-nemesis of my fae mother.

"So, I ask you again," Kairyn breathes, "my three questions."

I close my eyes. *B. Bridget Jones from* Bridget Jones's Diary. *C. Chani from* Dune.

"Where is the moonstone necklace?"

D. Mr. Darcy from Pride and Prejudice.

"Where is Summer's token?"

E. Effie Trinket from The Hunger Games.

His voice rises in pitch, growing raspy, near hysteric. "Where is my brother?"

I flick my eyes open and stare at him, bent down only an inch in front of my face. "Rot in hell, asshole."

He pounds his fist against the glass, right beside my pointed ear. I flinch. "Where is the moonstone necklace?"

"I don't know." I give him the same answer I always do. In the first few months, I realized they were infusing my food with some sort of truth serum to stop me from lying. Well, the joke was on them. Just because I had to tell the truth didn't mean I was going to tell the truth they were looking for. They've stopped bothering with the serum now, having realized I wouldn't fall so easily into that trap.

And this is the truth—I don't know where the moonstone necklace is. Caspian took it from me, and I have no idea where the Prince of the Below is. But I do know I have to do everything I can to avoid it falling into Kairyn's hands. Whoever wears the moonstone necklace can wield the Bow of Radiance, the most powerful of all the divine weapons.

Kairyn slams his other fist on the opposite side. "Where is Summer's token?"

"Not on me," I growl, another truth. After Ezryn killed the Turquoise Knight up at Queen's Reach Monastery, I took Dayton's necklace back. How was I to know I wasn't going to see him again? Now, I keep my gaze focused straight on Kairyn so as not to shift it to the flimsy mattress they call a bed. They didn't know I had his necklace when they imprisoned me here. I've hid it in a slit within the mattress for safekeeping.

"Where is my brother?"

This question, I know, is not for Sira. This is all Kairyn. He must assume I know where Ezryn would have gone after we were separated in the throne room. Joke's on him, again. I can't predict Ezryn's movements any more than I can predict the trajectory of a shooting star. So, this answer I give from my heart. "I wish I knew."

Kairyn's asked me these three questions nearly every day, and I've given him the same three answers.

What else can I do? My heart, which should be erupting with the mate bonds tying me to Kel and Farron and Ez, is silent. I have no idea where any of them are. Where Dayton is. Where Caspian is.

It's just me and the fish.

Kairyn pulls back, but his helm is still focused on me. He's deciding something. He's lost his patience with me. Will this be the day I'm sent down to the Queen of the Below?

I drift my gaze past him to the schools of fish outside my window. I suppose I'll come to miss even this tiny bit of light when I'm rotting beneath the surface. The brilliant colors swarm past the glass in frantic motions.

I blink. There's something else out there, in the deep water. Not a fish. A girl.

6

DAYTON

No light streams out of the tiny apartment window, but that doesn't mean she's not home. We keep the curtains drawn to attract less notice. Slowly, I enter.

She is here. My mate.

Wrenley's smile broadens as I arrive, and she crosses to me, resting a hand on my arm. "Dayton, you're back. I was worried about you. Well, I always worry about you, talking to all those people out there."

"I'm all right," I say, dropping my bag near the door and throwing off my cloak in such a way it causes her to move her hand from my arm.

The air hangs heavy with the scent of sea salt and mildew. The walls, once adorned with vibrant frescoes, are now cracked and peeling. Flickering oil lamps provide the only source of light, casting eerie shadows that dance across the floor.

The furnishings are sparse and worn. In one corner, a rudimentary hearth serves as the kitchen, backed by smoke-stained walls. Pots and pans hang haphazardly from hooks above. A rickety wooden table sits in the center of the room. Wrenley has piled it with items she's pilfered from the Summer Palace. She returned to her job as an acolyte by claiming she was lost after the attack on Queen's Reach Monastery. She's been learning what she can from Kairyn, but it's dangerous work.

"Good haul," I say, raising a brow as I look upon the table, laden with bread, fruit, and a jug that might be wine.

Gods, I hope it's wine.

She skips to it. "The fig bread is great with a little olive oil, and the grapes make the most satisfying crunch!" She picks up a grape and slowly brings it to her mouth before sinking a sharp canine into it. The juice spills over her full lips.

Despite being an acolyte, she knows how pretty she is, with her sapphire eyes and wavy brown hair. I often notice people's lingering glances on her the few times we venture out together. It would be so much easier if I was the one who couldn't look away.

"Makes me sick to think of Kairyn and his goons eating food grown by the very people he invaded." I reach for the wine and pour a full glass into a wooden cup.

"Did you learn anything that could help today?" Wrenley asks.

I take my cup and saunter into the next room. This one has nothing but threadbare cushions scattered on the mosaic floor. That's where the wolf sleeps. There are two narrow alcoves in the back of the apartment, containing nothing but drab sleeping quarters, simple cots with moth-eaten blankets. One is where Fare stayed all those months, and even though she could sleep in the palace, Wrenley sneaks out and spends most nights here with me.

"There's been another sighting of Delphia," I say.

I collapse down onto one of the cushions, and Wrenley sits down on the floor across from me, concern flicking over her features. "I hope she doesn't try anything brash."

I can't help the smile that twinges at the corner of my lips. "Are you kidding me? Being brash is in my sister's blood."

"But if a High Prince doesn't stand a chance against Kairyn, what chance does a little girl have?"

"Delphie's stronger than she looks."

"Aren't you worried?"

"Of course I'm worried. There's still no news on Rosie. Farron's been gone for weeks. I thought for sure Kel or Ez would have sent word by now, but we haven't seen or heard anything from them. Fuck, I'd even welcome a visit from Cas if he'd tell us something useful."

"And I'm working at Soltide Keep. If Kairyn discovers—"

Shit, I probably should have mentioned her too. "Of course, and you. I don't know how you do it, serving that monster every day."

"I have a lot of experience serving monsters."

Right. Before Kairyn dispatched the High Clerics, Wrenley served them in Queen's Reach Monastery. That was before the Nightingale kidnapped Rosalina, and Ezryn painted the monastery red getting her back.

Or so Wrenley says.

I wish I could speak to Ezryn about it. I don't want to believe such things about him. But then again, I wouldn't doubt the lengths he'd go to for his mate.

Tilting my head, I study the woman across from me. Would I go to the same lengths for her?

"What I mean," Wrenley says, when I don't reply, "is aren't you worried about your sister? You keep putting yourself in these dangerous situations, and if something happens to you . . ."

I pause, catching onto her meaning. "My Blessing would pass to her."

"Kairyn would stop at nothing to hunt her down. Her Blessing wouldn't be cursed like yours is. Even with such a power, Delphia would never be able to stand against Kairyn and his forces."

Explaining the curse and showing my wolf to Wrenley hadn't been my favorite thing ever, but Fare had been there, and he made everything easier. Surprisingly, Wrenley had taken it all in her stride.

Though, I know she wonders why I'm not motivated to break my curse. Why I haven't even kissed her. How can I get to know her, really? How can I even think about her when my realm is occupied? My sister is a runaway, Rosalina is missing, and I bloody miss Farron so much it hurts.

With my free hand, I touch the metal cuff around my forearm, the one forged from our bargain. We struck it on the battlefield of Autumn, so that my strength might belong to him as long as he never forgets that moment. The moment where we both finally claimed our love out loud. *What would you do if you were here, Fare?*

It comes to me in an instant. Wine sloshes over the lip of my cup as I stand. "We'll go to her."

"What?" Wrenley rises quickly.

"We'll go to Delphie. Claudius said she was spotted along Veritas Bay," I say. Farron would never abandon his family. He would do anything for them. "We can rent a sailboat and find her. I know where she would conceal a ship around there."

"Where?"

But I'm already packing my bag, throwing in clothes and waterskins. "We'll find her and make sure she's not doing anything rash. Maybe she has information on what's going on with the other realms."

"I'm not going to sea—I can't."

"Then stay," I say, making my way to the kitchen.

Only silence echoes behind me, and I turn to see tears pooling in her eyes.

"Shit, Wren, I'm sorry. I didn't mean it that way." Then I shrug. "I thought you'd like going out to sea. Wasn't your dad a fisherman?"

Wrenley shakes her head and steps closer to me. "I'll go. One of the other acolytes owes me a favor. She could say I'm sick for a few days. I'll just have to put a few things in place tonight."

"I only meant this could be dangerous."

She gently touches my chest, fingers resting over my seashell necklace. Farron strung it for me, and for many years it held the token of Summer. Wrenley's staring at the necklace's newest addition, a nautilus shell, gleaming gold. The one she gave me from her own necklace, the day I saved her from drowning.

"Where you go, I go," she says softly.

I force a tight smile. "Once we figure this out, we'll figure *us* out. I promise."

"I've waited years for this, Daytonales. I can wait until you're ready."

"Thank you." I look out the small window to the peek of blue beyond. "At dawn, we head to sea."

As I stare at the horizon, I feel like it's calling me in a way it never has before. A tether drawing me deep beneath the blue waves.

7

ROSALINA

A girl . . . swimming through the water.

I blink my eyes again. She can't be more than sixteen, if that. The dappled light casts ripples over her dark brown skin, and her eyes meet mine. I *know* her. I've seen her before.

She wears a tight-fitting suit of turquoise blue, her black, curly hair splayed out in the water. Around her face is a translucent bubble. I watch carefully as her chest heaves in and out. An air bubble for breathing . . . Ingenious.

"Ignoring me again, Rosalina?" Kairyn breathes, and I quickly tear my gaze back to him. If he turns around, he'll see her.

"No," I say. "I mean, I've told you everything I know."

"We both know that's not true. You are my brother's mate. Surely, you know of his intentions. Where he could be hiding out. Unless he abandoned you? I wouldn't doubt it. He abandoned me, after all."

"Why don't you get rid of this anti-magic air, and I'll ask him through our mate bond for you?" I force a smirk and chance a look past his helm again.

The girl has reached the glass and holds up a pointed silver tool. A flash of red explodes where the tool meets the glass. My heart hammers against my chest. She's *melting* the glass. What kind of fire burns underwater, let alone hot enough to melt glass this thick?

Kairyn stills, then begins to turn.

"Wait!" I cry and grab his arm. We both look at my hand on his armor. Quickly, I retract it. "I do know where he is. I'll tell you. Just don't send me to Sira, and I'll tell you everything. What Ezryn's doing, where Dayton's token is. All of it."

In this one way, Kairyn is similar to his older brother. His body becomes perfectly still, a near statue as he contemplates my words.

Then he looks behind him.

The girl has burned a half-circle into the glass, about two feet long. Her eyes widen as Kairyn looks at her, the expression of surprise strangely familiar.

Kairyn lets loose a bellow. "Guards! Deploy the outer defenses!" He rounds on me. "Treachery! I knew you were lying. You would not so easily give up your mates."

Of course I wouldn't. I would die before I let this monster touch one of my men again. Though, his choice of wording is wrong. Dayton isn't my mate, as much as my heart wishes him to be.

The whir of the tool becomes audible as the girl quickens her pace. She waves frantically at me, and her meaning is clear.

I'm getting out of here.

I spring past Kairyn, placing my hand close to the glass. It shimmers with heat. Within her little bubble, the girl smiles as I approach, then refocuses on her work. I see now she's making a circle in the glass. Once it connects all the way around . . .

"A rescue attempt? How valiant," Kairyn says. His heavy footsteps reverberate behind me. "Good timing. My defenses are starving."

A chill runs up my spine as two dark shapes appear in the water behind the girl. She doesn't notice, too intent on the melting circle. The shapes grow larger and larger until I make them out—

I slam a fist on the glass near her face. "You need to get away now! Go!"

Her light brown eyes widen, and she turns. Two massive sharks torpedo toward her, jaws opening. These are no ordinary sharks, appearing as if they swam straight from the abyssal depths. Sleek and sinewy, their skin is a sickly shade of indigo, almost opaque, as if absorbing every iota of light that attempts to cut through the water. Long, needle-like teeth jut out from their gaping maws.

She kicks off from the glass and darts upward. The sharks surge after her.

Kairyn places his gloved hand in the middle of the melted circle. The smell of burning leather hits my nose. "How irritating," he murmurs. "Regardless, her blood shall soon paint the glass."

No, no, no, this was my chance to escape. That girl is risking her life for me. She was so close—the burning circle is almost completed. If only she had a chance to finish.

Adrenaline surges through my veins. I have to get out of here. I don't know what's happening to Castletree or my friends or the rest of the realms. My father is sick. My mates are lost, two of them still cursed.

I will *not* stay caged.

The heat from the burning glass wavers across my cheeks. Just outside of that is freedom—even if it's freedom in death. I need to break the glass. But I don't have a tool like she did. I would need something strong to crack it open.

Something like Spring steel.

"Hey, Kairyn," I whisper. "That armor looks heavy. Ever tried swimming in it?"

He tilts his helm at me, and I strike. I grab him around the shoulders and *push*. He's huge, but I use the force of his body against him, sticking out my leg so he trips over me. With a roar, I shove his stupid owl helm straight against the heated glass. The sound is a sickening crunch as the helm smashes into the weakened barrier. Shockwaves ripple through my hands. I stumble back and so does Kairyn.

We both take a breath.

Spiderwebs trickle across the surface of the heated section, and then, with a resounding crash, the glass gives way. Water bursts into the cell. I slam against the metal door. Kairyn lands next to me, pinned by the force of the water.

I turn to look at him with what must be a delirious smile on my face. My bare feet find purchase, and I push myself to standing, leaning against the wall for balance. The water is frigid cold, but I don't care. Something else is happening.

I suck in a deep breath. The air pressure has changed, the force of the seawater displacing whatever was floating around in here.

All at once it hits me: a white wolf howling up at a blue moon. The lick of fire against my skin as I run and run and run. The crunch of bone and taste of blood in my mouth. My mates are out there, somewhere. Looking for me.

I intend to find them.

Kairyn flounders in his heavy metal, pinned against the corner of the wall as more and more seawater plunges into the cell. He makes a garbled sound, calling for help likely. With my own beastly roar, I feel the force of my magic flood my body, a dam breaking inside of me just as it has in my cell. Water lifts at my command, and I plunge it over the top of the new High Prince of Spring, cutting off his cries for help.

Fighting against the flood, I make my way over to my bed. With a deep breath, I duck down, grasping for the slit in the mattress. My fingers clutch around the chain with a single seashell token. I put it around my neck and tuck it into my shirt.

Outside, I see three silhouettes darting through the water. The girl swims at an impossible speed, just out of reach of the two sharks. I need to get to her now.

But how? I can't make it six hundred feet up to the surface, let alone help her. She has made a bubble around her head; some form of water magic I've never tried before.

"Come on, Rosie," I say. "Now or never."

The water's up to my waist now, and if I don't do something soon, I'll drown here with Kairyn. "Bubble, bubble, bubble." Little baby bubbles emerge on my fingers, but nothing controllable, nothing I could trap air in.

"Come on!" I can do it. I've done harder things before, things everyone else thought impossible. I turned an arrow to water, summoned golden roses, transformed my friends into birds—

And if I transformed them, I could transform myself.

I place my hands on my neck and close my eyes, picturing the fish that surrounded my prison for these three long months. The gills that sucked the oxygen straight from the water.

A surge of magic courses through me, eager to be let loose. Delicate slits rise up beneath my fingers along both sides of my neck.

"Holy shit. I did it."

I look around as if there's someone to congratulate me, but there's only Kairyn, floundering against the waves, completely pinned by his armor and cloak. His helm pops out of the crashing, white water. "Stop!"

The water is past my collarbone now, so I take a deep breath and plunge under. Water drifts past my gills, relieving the ache in my lungs as if I've just taken a huge gulp of air. Ahead, the gap where I smashed the melted glass still shimmers with heat. I take one last look at Kairyn, unable to get to the surface of the cell, then swim out of the hole.

The open sea surrounds me. Blue everywhere: above, below, around. Fear creeps in at the openness of it all, the endless abyss.

But I've just spent three months in a box. I could use a little openness.

I kick my legs out, trying to fight my blurry vision to catch sight of the girl and the sharks. When I turn, the immensity of the prison barge swarms over me. It appears almost as an underwater mountain, a hulking structure with a steel hull encrusted with barnacles and seaweed. How long has this thing been here and what was it used for before?

Something rushes past me, and my vision becomes nothing but white bubbles. I shake my head to see the young girl beside me, eyes wide with panic.

"Move!" she mouths. She grabs my arm and urges me forward.

I feel the sharks before I see them, the force of their movements sending water spiraling around me. Their eyes are hauntingly large and vacant, driven solely by hunger.

Water rushes into my mouth as I attempt to scream. I fling out my hand, feeling for the one thing that has always protected me.

My golden thorns find root in a patch of seaweed on the hull of the barge. It's like coming back to myself. The girl tugs me again, but I stop swimming and face the sharks. Just as their jaws open to wrap around us, I *pull* on my thorns. They erupt from the barge and entangle the sharks' tails, yanking them back against the steel.

The girl blinks at me, and her lip quivers. She tangles her fingers in mine and points up.

Our legs kick in synchronization. Her free hand swirls before her and the water pushes us faster toward the surface. *She's very talented in water magic.*

Within minutes, we breach the water's edge. For the first time in months, I see the sun. I cry out as it burns my eyes, but hardly have time to think before someone's grabbing me around both shoulders.

I'm pulled up by two women, before I'm tossed down onto the wooden ground. Eyes still burning, I try to take in my surroundings: a wooden ship with huge white sails drawn. I stagger to my feet and look around for the girl who rescued me.

But I see another girl first. She looks about the same age as the first, not more than sixteen. She has long, straight auburn hair, pale skin, and golden eyes I would know anywhere.

In a deadpan voice, she says, "Hi. Glad you're alive."

"Th-thanks?" I stammer.

The girl turns to my rescuer, who's wringing out her black curls, the bubble around her face now gone. "So, how'd the Autumnfire drill work?"

"Perfectly," my rescuer responds. "First time I've ever said that about one of your experiments."

Autumnfire. Those golden eyes. I hold the gaze of the second girl and know we've met once before. Eleanor, Farron's little sister.

One of the women who dragged me onto the boat turns to the young girl who saved me. "What are your orders, captain?"

The young girl walks to the wheel and grabs the spokes. "We secured the cargo. Set sail for the open ocean. Let's see these bastards try to outrun *The Deathly Sky Dancer!*"

Now, I know. We have met before. With all the adrenaline coursing through me earlier, I hadn't been able to place her. But the confidence I saw in her just now has assured me of it.

I was rescued by Dayton's little sister, Delphia. The steward of Summer.

8

DAYTON

Our skiff cuts through the turquoise water, white sails filled with wind. I shift the rudder at the stern and peer into the horizon. There's something ahead, too far to make out.

"Grab the tiller," I tell Wrenley. She takes my place without complaint.

I stand and walk carefully to the bow. The fishing skiff Claudius lent us is small, barely big enough for two, but it's quick and can handle the open sea without too much fuss.

I hold on to a rope and lean forward. The salty air whips my hair back. It's been decades since I've been upon the ocean like this. No land in sight, only the sky and sea before me. Though my magic has long been empty, my heart stirs. Just as Kel is most at home in a frosty wasteland, *this* is where I belong. Salt on my tongue and a whole horizon to tame.

"What do you see?" Wrenley calls from behind me.

"Nothing yet."

"There's a spyglass down by the lamp."

I rifle through the junk Claudius left in the skiff: three fishing harpoons, a net, a jug of oil, a lamp for late-night expeditions, and a packet of matches. Finally, I grab the spyglass and hold it up to my eye.

"Stars be damned," I whisper.

"What is it?"

"I think . . . I think it's the First Sands."

"The *what*?"

"The First Sands," I say louder, so my voice carries over the wind and she can hear me properly. Every Summer child knows about the Arena of the First Sands. It was Summer's first colosseum, not a structure of rock and dirt like the one in Hadria, but a giant floating barge. It was built so both the land people of Hadria and the sea people of Aerantheis could celebrate together.

That was centuries upon centuries ago, a relic long thought shipwrecked or lost. Mentions of it disappeared from recent history, the same time as the people of Aerantheis did.

Wrenley releases the tiller, walks up beside me, and gestures for the spyglass. I take another long look before I give it up. The barge is circular in shape, with massive arches and columns complete with Summer's intricate carvings. Everything has been reinforced with metal: steel plates cover the hull and bars crisscross between the pillars. This kind of metalwork has only been seen in . . .

"Spring's taken it over," I snarl, handing the spyglass to Wrenley. "It looks like a damned prison."

"If that's true, we have to be careful," she says. "Kairyn's forces could be all around us right now." The boom of a cannon echoes across the waves, and I snatch the spyglass straight from Wrenley's hands. Then I see it, east of the barge. A wooden schooner, white sails filled with wind, streaking away. A black flag snaps back and forth painted with a horse's skull over crossed bones. Though I've never seen the flag before, the ship I recognize instantly. How could I not?

"That's *The Trident's Glory*," I say. "The fastest ship in Summer's navy." Though, the name has been scrawled out. I close my left eye to get better focus with my right while looking in the spyglass. Yes, there's paint smeared over the name. I can barely make out the new letters: *THE DEATHLY SKY DANCER.*

"Who the fuck renamed it?" I growl.

But my heart is beating too fast to concentrate on the desecration of such a fine ship. I adjust the spyglass, focusing on the helm. A smile breaks across my face. There she is, shouting orders and holding tight to the wheel as if she were some grizzled old sailor. My baby sister, Delphia.

"Oh no!" Wrenley cries, grabbing my arm. "Look there!"

A second schooner emerges from behind the barge, twice the size of my sister's ship. A large cannon at the forecastle oozes with smoke. Thankfully, they weren't close enough to hit *The Trident's Glory*. But they're gaining fast. I set my gaze upon the helm of the enemy schooner. I've spent these last three months trying to be as numb as I possibly could, not wanting to feel the loss of Rosie, the hopelessness for my brothers, or the guilt of not being what Wrenley needs. But all of that numbness fades away as I set my sights on Kairyn.

He's bent over the railing leading up to the helm, shoulders shaking. His cape looks soaking wet, and water drips from under his helmet over his black chest plate. A soldier walks up to him with a blanket, and he shoves the man away.

That bastard *took* Rosalina. He mutilated Ezryn. He betrayed us all. Now, he's coming after my sister.

Not if I get to her first.

My teeth grind together so hard, I'm surprised they don't crack. I throw the spyglass to the ground and look at Wrenley. "We have to get those bastards away from my sister's ship! Let's get this boat moving. Hard to lee! Full to the wind!"

Wrenley blinks her giant blue eyes at me. "What?"

"Hard to lee—don't you know? Your father was a fisherman, for stars' sake!" Anger cuts through my words as I rush to the stern to do it myself.

"Doesn't mean he paid any attention to me," she snaps.

"Just make sure the ropes don't get caught. We need to catch *The Trident's Glory*."

"I thought you said it was the fastest ship in Summer?"

I flash her a grin. "The fastest ship is whichever one I'm sailing."

With the wind at our back, our skiff takes off across the sea heading straight between Kairyn's platoon and my sister's ship.

"What's the plan here, Day?" Wrenley screams, bracing herself against the edge as our skiff crashes over the waves. "That's a big ship and we're just . . . we're just us."

I rush forward to adjust the ropes and hover right over her. I hold her gaze and smile. "Exactly. We're us. That's all we need."

A blush rises on her cheeks, and she looks away.

As we get closer, voices ring out over the waves. "Secure the hatches! Enemy fire incoming!" my sister cries. Her voice is so young, still in adolescence. Leave it to Delphia to have a whole ship at her command while also still sleeping with a stuffed doll.

Another voice rings out louder. Kairyn has stalked to the bow of the ship and points a leather finger toward my sister. "Send that piece of junk to the bottom of the sea!"

"You've got the boat, Wren!" I snatch the fishing harpoon and tie its line to the sturdy cleat on the front of the ship. Then I hold the wooden shaft of the harpoon in my right hand and brace a leg on the railing. "Get us right in front of that ugly ship."

"Right in front of the cannon?" Wrenley screams. Quickly, she puts her hood over her face, covering herself from view.

"Exactly."

Our skiff shoots before the giant boat. I stare up at the forward cannon, arching my arm backward.

"Go left, left, left," I direct. "There!"

I throw the harpoon and it sails through the air, the barbed tip catching the rim of the cannon's carriage. I grab its line and take a deep breath. There's no magic left in my body, but I've never preferred spells when brute strength would do. I bounce the line in my hand, feeling the weight and tension. Then, with all the strength left within me, I pull.

"Keep it moving!" I roar to Wrenley.

The cannon creaks: the harpoon's barbs are unmovable, latched tightly onto the ridges. I brace my feet against the gunwale of the skiff and throw everything I have, everything I am, into towing the line. It cuts into my palms and red blood oozes out, but I don't give a damn.

Kairyn's finally going to learn that no one fucks with my family.

The armored bastard himself runs over, watching as his cannon screeches across the wooden deck, pulled by the force of our skiff. "Someone get this harpoon *off!*"

One of Kairyn's men runs up to him. "Shall I give the order to attack that skiff?"

Kairyn stares down at me. I hold his dark, void gaze, muscles trembling. We look at each other for a heartbeat, then two, and then I hear him repeat: "Get this harpoon off!"

The Trident's Glory is still ahead, but I need to make sure there's enough of a gap for her to escape. My arms struggle against the rope. "Take the skiff round her port side!"

Wrenley does what I say, clumsily adjusting the tiller. The wind tugs our sails, and our skiff banks to the left, tracing a dangerous arc around the imposing hull of the ship.

The harpoon line snaps taut, and I let out a bellow to hold it as it drags the cannon across the schooner's deck. Shouts ring out as Kairyn's men attempt to hold down the cannon, but our skiff is too fast, the cannon has gained too much momentum. As we swing the line full-way around, the cannon turns completely, barrel now facing the helm.

"The cannon's incapacitated! What's next, Day?" Wrenley yells.

I let the line go and stare down at my shredded hands. "I'm going to kill the High Prince of Spring."

She reaches for me, but I shirk away. "It's too dangerous!"

I grab the second harpoon. "For him."

"Forget the cannon!" Kairyn's screaming at his men. He storms back and forth across the deck. "Catch the princess and bring back my prisoner!"

"The idiot!" Wrenley cries. "The damned fool!"

"I couldn't agree more. Now, get to the tiller."

I stand with my second harpoon perched over my shoulder, and line up my target. Kairyn doesn't even notice me; he's too busy screaming at his men. He's covered completely in Spring steel, armor so hard that the barbed tip of this harpoon would be like hitting it with a toothpick. But I've spent decades passing time sparring with the previous High Prince of Spring. I know exactly where every slat in the armor is, how there's a gap right between the helm and the collarbone.

I hold up my left hand to help me aim. The harpoon's tip shimmers in the light. My mind reels with the strength of the throw, the angle with the wind.

Then I have it. The tip lines up right where I need it to. "This is for Ez," I whisper. I draw my hand back and release—

"Ahh!" Wrenley cries, falling against me. The harpoon goes wide, snagging into the wooden deck right at Kairyn's feet. He looks down at it and then up at me, fists clenching.

"Stars damn it, Wrenley!" I roar. "I fucking had him!"

"I'm sorry, I'm sorry." She shrinks under my gaze. "My foot got caught in the rope. I was just trying to follow your orders."

There's no time to waste dwelling on it. All I have is one harpoon left and an entire ship to take down. But I've never been one to be discouraged. One harpoon took out their cannon—

Their cannon with the breech wide open, the barrel packed with gunpowder.

I look down at the rest of the supplies Claudius left in here.

"When I say so, Wren, we need to get out of here. Not a minute after I say so, not a second after. Right away. You hear me?"

"What are you planning?"

"We need to be quick. Quicker than our skiff can go." I grab her face with my hands, smearing bloody marks on her cheeks. She stares up at me as if the world is in my eyes. "Remember the fountain in Florendel? How you controlled the water?"

"Yes." She places her hands over mine.

"I need you to do it again. We need a current under this skiff. Get us straight in the wind then you concentrate on the water below us. Can you do it?"

"For you, anything," she whispers.

"Great." I drop my hands. I need to be quick. It's a wonder Kairyn hasn't asked his troops to kill us already. With all the Queen's Army deserters he has, we'd be like fish to their trained spears.

I tear my shirt off and wrap it around the tip of the harpoon, before dousing it in oil from the canteen. Then I grab a match. "Ready, Wren?"

"I think so."

"You can feel the water?"

"I don't know."

I stare down at her, holding her ocean-blue gaze. "I can't do it with you this time, but you know me now. You know what it feels like. I believe in you."

She takes a deep breath and nods. There's such a determination in her expression, a fierceness I can't help but admire.

"All right, then—" I light the match, igniting the harpoon. "Now!"

Wrenley pulls the ropes, filling our sails with wind. At the same time, the water rushes up beneath our boat, speeding us away.

I stare at the barrel of the cannon on the enemy ship. Take a breath. Throw.

The fiery harpoon arcs through the air before cresting straight into the barrel.

A thunderous explosion erupts, echoing across the seas. Flames engulf the schooner, dancing wildly along the timber. The heat of the blast throws me back, and I slam hard against the deck of our skiff.

Wrenley cries out, clambering over me to the bow. "What did you do?"

My ears ring but I'm able to sit up and crawl over to her side. The hull of Kairyn's ship is torn wide open, now a mess of smoke and sea spray. The stern of the ship still bobs in the air.

My fists clench together. Kairyn's being helped to his feet upon the helm by two soldiers. The monster lives.

Wrenley breathes a sigh. "You're okay."

I look down at my torn-up hands. "Nothing I can't handle." Shakily, I stand then help her up. "That'll slow them down. Come on, let's get to my sister."

I take the tiller, and with Wrenley assisting the current, we slide up alongside *The Trident's Glory* . . . or rather, *The Deathly Sky Dancer*, as it is now named.

"I'll be damned," someone calls from over the deck, a voice too high-pitched for such crass language.

And there she is, scowling down at me in the way only a sister can.

"What can I say, Delphie Girl? I like to make an entrance." I beam up at her.

Delphia rolls her eyes but she's smiling, too. She looks behind her at her crew. "Lower the ropes!"

I abandon our skiff—with a promise to make it up to Claudius—and begin climbing the rope. I'm going to squeeze my sister so tight, then yell at her until my lungs give out. What in the seven realms could be so damned important on that barge that Delphia would risk her own life and that of her crew?

I leap over the side of the boat and scan the deck for Delphie.

But I see someone else first.

She glides toward me with such grace, it has to be a figment of my imagination. But this must be real—no other sight could cause my heart to beat so wildly.

I see Rosalina.

9

FARRON

Even in sleep, George O'Connell seems restless.

Rosalina's father lies nestled within soft white blankets in a private room in Keep Oakheart. After he got ill on the road with my brothers, Billagin and Dominic, they brought him back here. We made plans to transfer George to Spring, where the most talented magical healers live, but that was impossible after Kairyn took over.

Glowing orbs that appear like little harvest moons bounce around the room, bathing it in golden light. Incense burns on the end table, a mix of juniper, cedarwood, and myrrh. Outside, a soft wind blows red and orange leaves against the window.

Though his eyes are closed as if in sleep, his mouth moves constantly in an unintelligible mumble.

I stand at the end of the bed, unable to sit but unable to leave. Dom and Billy are crammed together in an armchair, whispering among themselves.

"No change at all?" I ask again.

They peer up at me, two pairs of matching golden eyes. "Not in months. Father's organized care for him day and night. Tried everything. A soother, a healer, a bloodletter. He sleeps and he talks to himself. That's it."

"When was the last time you saw him act like himself?"

Billy chews on his bottom lip. "Well, when we were traveling through the realmlands, he had bad days and good days. Sometimes, he'd seem just like himself, then the next morning, he could barely stand. When we got him back here, he was pretty much delirious."

"But then Kel came to visit him!" Dom says, shooting forward and knocking Billy to the floor. "Remember? Kel came about, what, three months ago?"

"That's right!" Billy says, picking himself up. "About a day before Kel's visit, ol' George was nearly acting like himself again. Walking around, talking, eating, all of that. Kel came the next day and they sat and chatted for ages. But after he left . . ."

"Things went bad again. Not right away. He was normal for a few weeks. But then he declined." Dom's face falls, and I realize just how much Rosalina's father means to my brothers. "Now, he hasn't woken up at all."

I walk around the edge of the bed and touch George's face. His brown hair, flecked with gray, has grown longer. Wrinkles line the corners of his eyes and around his lips. His mutters are quick, urgent.

"Has anyone been able to understand what he's saying?" I ask the boys.

Billy shrugs. "We get bits and pieces. Like 'Rosalina,' he says that a lot. And he talks about Anya, too."

"Anya . . ."

"His wife," Billy clarifies.

"I know." I shoot my little brother a glare.

"The rest of it is nonsense," Dom says.

I lean down to George's chest, my ear twitching. If there's one thing I've learned from searching through texts and papers for decades, it's that often nonsense can be the most truthful of all.

George's voice trickles out between quick breaths: "Mask on, Annie! Mask on. To Vimy now. Ridge painted red. Planes overhead. Sound like angry wasps, don't they, Annie? Stay close to me. Told you I'd come back. Promised I would. Watch out! Take cover!"

I suck in a breath. Annie must be his wife, Anya, but what of the rest? There's some truth in here, something I don't yet understand.

I pull away. None of it makes any sense. Bone-deep exhaustion fills every part of my body and mind.

My brothers look at each other, then come up on either side of me. Normally, I'd be expecting some sort of prank or trick, but this time, I wrap my arms around each of them, and they wrap theirs around me.

"We'll watch over him, Fare," Billy whispers.

"Promise," Dom says.

I squeeze them tighter. "I know you will."

I step away and make to leave the room when it hits me.

My heart erupting. A star shooting across the realms. I feel a matching pulse over the hills and desert. A matching pulse in Summer.

My mate bond . . . I can feel it again. That means Rosalina . . .

"I need to get back to Castletree. Now."

10

CASPIAN

rip, drip, drip.

D   A circle of emerald crystals lines a pool, bleeding phantasmal green energy into the water. The pool sits in the middle of a cavern. What isn't covered by crystals is jagged black stone.

Sira, the Queen of the Below, beckons me to follow her. There's a slight change to her regular attire. Today, a sparkling green cape flows off her shoulders.

The color of the magic that fills the pool.

My father's magic.

And my own.

"Come along, Caspian."

I follow my mother, taking in the immense cavern. Green crystals scatter the rocky earth and crawl up the walls. Each one grows toward the giant crystal ring surrounding the pool.

The crystals have been growing for over twenty-five years. Each time I step foot in this place, they're bigger than before, pulsing with arcane energy.

"It's coming along wonderfully, isn't it?" Sira says, following my gaze. "If only Aurelia could see the fruits of her sacrifice."

These crystals grow through the Below all the way to Aurelia's green crystal cage, which, drop by drop, sucks her power.

"We've been patient, my love," my mother continues, "but it is almost time."

Patience wasn't what my mother had in mind when she first captured the Queen. She'd tried to take *all* of Aurelia's magic at once, but the Queen almost died before the power could be taken. My mother has since perfected her method.

I make my way to my mother through a small gap between the crystals and look down into the depths. The water bubbles and pops on the surface, and not for the first time, I wonder just how deep it goes.

"Shame, I forgot my bath salts." I grin.

My mother ignores me, instead transfixed on her own beautiful reflection wavering in the water. Honestly, it's no surprise she was able to seduce the Baron of the Green Flame into—whatever this is. With their mutual love of world-ending destruction, it's no wonder they found such camaraderie.

"Soon, we will have drained enough of her essence for the gateway to open," she continues.

I keep silent. Mother has been raving about this for years, but she's never been able to fully open the passage between worlds. By what means she reached the Baron of the Green Flame at my conception—or however *he* reached *her*—remains a mystery to me. All I know is he can't materialize here until Mother gathers enough arcane energy to power this gateway. I pray this feat is beyond even her.

"When it does, your father will step through and finally teach you how to take full control of your magic."

Yes, my magic. The Green Flame that writhes within me. I've only used the magic a handful of times, and mostly by accident, such as when Keldarion betrayed me, and I created a giant chasm in the Winter Realm. Though, there were other times on purpose, like when my sister threatened Rosalina, so I obliterated her Dread Knights with the flick of my wrist.

My mother believes that I don't know how to awaken it. She doesn't understand that every moment of my life, I'm trying to repress it.

"The Green Flame has conquered many worlds before," Mother continues, "and soon he will aid us in ruling this one."

"You know," I say, staring into the pool, "I don't know a lot of conquerors, but my understanding is they don't love to share power. How do you know he won't destroy us too?"

"You are his blood. He made you to rule." She strokes my arm. "If he tries, you will destroy him. You are more powerful than anyone in this world or the world beyond. You have his magic and mine."

And hers. I absently stroke the thin rose-gold bracelet on my wrist. "No pressure then."

Sira's heels click as she circles the pool. "We must take risks to achieve our vision. You know I was once of the Above. They were content with mediocrity. I had the gall to dream, to create, and I was heralded as a demon for doing so. Aurelia wanted me down in the dark. Well, now she's learned things can still grow in the darkness."

Standing above the pool, bathed in green light, she looks akin to a god herself, and I can't help but tremble.

"Once all the divine weapons are secured, we will open the way to the Above and I will build my own empire from its ashes." Sira's voice darkens, terrible and deep, full of malice. "Your sister will rule the Enchanted Vale, and you, my darling boy, who cannot survive in the light, will claim the Below as your kingdom."

Or I could throw my body over hot spikes, which sounds just as fun as *that* future. Truly, the greatest disappointment of being sired by a primordial being is that his blood just doesn't seem to like the Enchanted Vale— at least not in my pathetic half-fae body. Maybe I've got some tether to this damned pool, or maybe the godblood running through my veins rejects the surface world, but while Sira and all of her pure faeness can go where she pleases, I keep throwing up black gunk whenever I stray too far. "Ah, Birdy and Kairyn; who wouldn't want those two as their new rulers? So sane of mind, the pair of them."

Sira crosses to me. "I know you are jealous of your sister taking both Spring and Summer, but did you really have to destroy one of Kairyn's airships?"

She says the words so calmly, as if she hasn't had me whipped and beaten so terribly that it took my body weeks to recover. But I stay silent. It's one of few mercies that she believes jealousy was the reason I brought the airship down. If she knew what Rosalina *is* to me . . .

There would be no force in the Below that could save her from my mother. Death would be a mercy. I can't even begin to imagine the torture my mother would put Rosalina through to control me.

"There is still Winter and Autumn for you to claim." My mother purses her lips. "Perhaps start with Autumn. Even with his full power, that prince is nothing but a boy playing with fire."

"Farron's not as weak as you think," I say, then realize it might sound too close to a compliment, so I quickly add, "The Autumn Prince's spell was one of the only things that thwarted the Green Flame."

"Perth's first failed experiment." Sira shifts her eyes to the green pool. "Nothing but feeble echoes of the true power."

Ah, dear Perth Quellos. He's not a quitter, I'll give him that. Last I heard, he'd left the comfort of his laboratory on a mission I wasn't privy to.

Ice roils through my veins. The pool begins bubbling before twisting into a whirl. The Green Flame inside of me sparks to life, growing hotter with the intensity of the magic within this space. "What's happening?"

Sira kneels before the pool and dips her slender fingers into the water. "The magic is not yet strong enough to send your father through. But Caspian, he is sending us a gift."

I rush to my mother and yank her up. "You shouldn't touch that."

Her smile is wild with frenzy. It's a smile I've glimpsed on my own face more than once . . . usually when I'm about to do something crazy.

"This is for you, my son." She clutches my face, the green liquid cold as ice as it drips down my cheek. "We will use this gift to capture the Winter Realm. The Enchanted Vale will bow to us."

Hazy fog writhes from the liquid. Noxious fumes rise in eerie tendrils. Shadows dance across the surface, then one breaks free. A figure shrouded in darkness, its skeletal form glinting in the dim light. Bone by bone, it climbs from the pool, movements stiff, as though puppeteered by unseen hands.

Or hands from another world.

Armor hangs off its pale bones. Maybe once it was resplendent, but now it only bears the scars of battles long forgotten. In its bony grasp, the skeleton wields a pair of swords unlike any I have ever seen. The blades gleam. Sigils I don't recognize adorn the hilt; the faded image of a large winged lizard curled around a tree.

Emerald flames swirl beneath its rib bones and light the caverns of its eyes. It snaps its head to me with an unnatural click. Then it's not the skeleton's face I'm staring at, but *his*.

Pain radiates through me, and I crash to my knees, green flames coursing through my vision. There's ringing in my ears, and I have the odd sensation of being pulled somewhere far away, though I'm not moving.

When I open my eyes, a wave of nausea rolls through me. There are tall marble pillars and high windows that show a barren landscape of snow and ice, though by looking at the shape of the jagged mountains and falling snow, I know it isn't the Winter Realm or anywhere else in the Enchanted Vale.

Before me are towering stairs that lead to a massive throne. An even more enormous figure sits upon it. The power radiating off him hits me like a wave, and I can't look away from his eyes. They're green—unsurprisingly—along with the flames licking off his glittering black armor, and the huge broadsword he grips pointed into the ground beside the throne.

"Greetings, Caspian. Stand." His voice is deep and commanding. Each word is not just spoken, but rather, a decree that must be obeyed.

His face is foreign to me, yet familiar; something I've felt all my life but never seen. There's an unsettling beauty to his features, sharp and dangerous, like a concealed dagger. The longer I stare, the more they seem unnaturally perfect, as if each detail of his face was crafted by an artist. Even his grin seems made with exact precision.

Long, ashen-white hair drapes over his shoulders. His skin, the color of bone, diffuses the glowing green light, highlighting his sharp jaw. My gaze catches on the tips of his ears, which veer out from the curtain of his hair. They're pointed, like a fae's, but longer than I've ever seen the likes of in our realm. Pieces of shadowy-black armor elegantly fit together on his body, forming a suit worthy of the divine—or the infernal.

"Who are you?" I gasp, my words hoarse, each one an effort to get across to this place—this world.

"I've had many names over the ages." His voice is a deep rumble. "Some have called me Malekai, the Green Flame, or the Baron, but you, Prince, know me by a name none other do."

I swallow, fingers curled at my sides. I force myself to stand.

"I've forged worlds and created armies, but I have never created life such as you. I have never had a son. An heir."

Panicked heartbeats careen in my chest, and I desperately try to keep my face blank. The dark marble floor goes translucent below me, and I'm looking down on myself, kneeling before the pool, my eyes flooded with green.

But it's what's pouring out of the pool that has my heart ablaze. Row after row of Green Flame skeletal soldiers. They file from the pool, moving with purpose, a legion of the damned marching forth from their watery grave.

I watch, transfixed, as they assemble at the base of the pool, a relentless tide of bone and sinew. They seem to pulse with dark energy. An army of the undead: not one created by Perth, but soldiers of my father's own creation.

The sight fades as he pulls me back into his throne room.

"I grant this army to your mother," the Baron says. "Prove your obedience and worthiness, and I shall grant you this and more."

Something snaps within me, my vision fracturing as I picture Sira—picture myself—leading this army around the Enchanted Vale, watching realm after realm fall to it.

"What if I choose not to slaughter thousands of innocent fae?" I snarl, my hair falling across my face. "What if I'm *not* worthy?"

I'm not sure what I expected from my omnipotent, godly father, but laughter wasn't it. He laughs deeply, then sets down the sword, writhed in green flame, and leans his forearms over his knees.

"Caspian," he smiles, "I made you. I can unmake you just as easily."

II

EZRYN

I thought I'd miss it more. The helm.

Throughout the centuries of my life, it was a constant reminder of who I was, what I valued. My realm. My honor. No matter where I went, people knew who I was. First, son of Isidora and Thalionor, heir to the Spring throne. Then, the High Prince of Spring himself.

Now, I'm grateful for my anonymity. No one knows my face. With my hair grown long enough to cover my one identifiable feature—the ragged ears, points cut off by my brother's blade—I could be anyone. A pauper, a merchant.

A member of Kairyn's army.

I shift in my stolen armor. My brother's forces consist of goblins gifted from the Below, the deserters from the Queen's Army, and the Spring soldiers he's rallied to his side. I'm in a platoon of ex-Queen's Army soldiers aboard a ship bound for the prison barge. A nameless face, unknown to everyone.

Except her.

I know you.

Even before I removed my helm, it was as if she could see right through me, to the blood and bone and soul beneath. It had felt like we'd known each other our whole lives and were just waiting for the chance to meet. She had loved me in the darkness—and I returned her love with more darkness.

If I am not worthy of basking in her radiance, then I will walk behind her as a shadow. As her shadow, I will engulf any who would dim her light. If darkness is all I have, then I will use it to serve her.

I'd executed my plan over the course of a few days. First, I'd stolen the armor and identification from a soldier undeserving of title or breath. Getting into Hadria was easier than I thought; my brother and I had both served my father in times of battle. Every procedure, security measure, and tactic Kairyn has implemented could have been taken straight from my father's own war strategies. For anyone else, these would have proved formidable, but I knew each step, each phrase, to get within the city and secure myself a place on a relief ship sailing out to the prison barge. My father would be proud.

Father. I keep my face expressionless, although the thought of who my father once was compared to who he'd been at the end of his life causes my ribs to ache. *I could have saved him. I could have made him better—*

But the *traitor* had taken that away from me. That spawn of the Below robbed me of my father and helped destroy my rule. I always knew Caspian was incapable of honor.

I thought Kel had finally learned it, too.

Turquoise water splashes up against the porthole. My fellow soldiers and I stand quietly below decks. Long hours have passed. Based on the increased sound of footsteps and shouting above, I surmise we must be getting close to our destination.

I touch the roughly drawn map tucked into the vambrace on my wrist. Yesterday, after I'd found out which ship would be sent to the barge, I snuck into the captain's quarters and found a map of the prison, the manifest, and a list of ships due in and out. Though there was no mention of Rosalina by name, I'll be able to find my way to the cell blocks.

If she's still here, the dark part of my mind whispers.

An hour ago, I'd felt the light in my breast *erupt*, springing back to life like a desert suddenly awash in a rainstorm. *My mate bond.*

Whatever they'd been doing to Rosalina, it had stopped. I can *feel* her again, distantly, but she's there beside my heart. Where she belongs.

Are you out there, Rose? I'm coming for you.

Can she hear me? Probably not. Too far away.

Or perhaps my mate bond is damaged. I would not be surprised if I ruined it as I ruined everything else. My mind drifts back to the time at Sylvanita Lake when it had felt like every broken and jagged piece of me was softening. Because of her.

Because she loved me.

The curse laid upon me by the Enchantress had begun to break. With the breaking came a rush of magic I hadn't felt since my mother passed the Blessing of Spring to me. Magic I have always been too weak to wield. For decades, I dismissed my brother as nothing more than a wild, frenzied child. But I am no better.

Shame rushes over me as I remember what I did to Rosalina. What I did to Spring's sacred place. I can only imagine what other destruction I would have caused if I had allowed my curse to break.

The wolf controls me. I need him.

"All hands on deck!" a voice calls from above.

We've arrived.

Briny wind and bright sunlight bombard my face as I walk up to the top deck. A circular structure bobs in the waves, a hulking, hideous thing that is part ship, part Summer arena, and part fortress.

I try listening to the bond within my chest, but it feels distant, echoey. Is she here but still under some magic-inhibitor or did that scum in the desert lead me astray? Regardless, this place will have the answers I seek.

Our ship is tied up in an external docking port on the edge of the floating fortress, and the soldiers line up for security checks before entering. Several smaller skiffs are tied up beside it, and I note their location for mine and Rosalina's escape.

I slip to the back of the ship, rid myself of the clunky stolen armor, keeping only the scabbard that houses my mother's sword, then leap across the gap between the ship and the barge, quiet as a cat.

Staying on the outside, I use the broken pillars reinforced with Spring steel to climb away from the soldiers and up the side of the barge. When I find an opening, I check for guards, then duck inside, feet whispering over the metal floor.

Stooping down in a shadow, I consult my map, counting the floors I climbed up. The highest-security cells are below the surface of the water. So back down I go.

I weave through the labyrinthine passages of the barge, trying my best to stay in the outside ring. Guards patrol in pairs, but I avoid each one, hiding among the shadows or holding on to the outside of the ship. Finally, I weave my way down to the main floor, where I see part of the structure is cut open to allow an internal dock.

A mauled schooner is moored, the front half nothing but tattered timber and streaks of gunpowder. I creep closer, hiding behind barrels and other cargo strewn around the dock.

The hairs on the back of my neck stand on end. The ghost of a feeling washes over me. It has no scent, yet I know it's rotten. It has no sound, but my ears ring with screams. It does not touch me, yet I feel it in every fiber of my body.

He's here. The thing he stole is calling out for me.

"We'll send all the fleet after them, sire, promise! They won't get far!" a voice urges.

Another sniveling voice says, "It was the runaway princess, sire, and the High Prince of Summer. But we'll hunt them down—"

There's a clatter, then gagging. "There is *no* High Prince of Summer. I have taken his realm. He is a threat to the peace and sanctity of the Vale. I will end him as I did the last High Prince of Spring."

Breath comes ragged from my throat. I'd know that voice anywhere. It haunted my mind for years. I peek out from the barrels and see my younger brother, Kairyn, holding up one of his minions by the throat. His armor is both soaking wet and charred.

I fling myself back behind the barrels. *Dayton was here. Does that mean—*

"Now, I want every bloody ship we have scouring the Byzantar Isles for those rebels. Bring me back the Golden Rose or this whole prison will be torn down to the depths of the Below," Kairyn roars.

She's escaped. I can't catch my breath. *Rosalina has escaped and she's with Dayton.* My brother, not of blood but of fellowship.

Kairyn had set a trap for me in the Spring Realm, and I walked straight into it, giving him my magic, my realm, and my honor. Now, I am void of all three. My mother's sword sits heavy on my back. Slowly, I reach behind to grab the hilt.

My fingers tremble on the metal. His face looms in my mind's eye. Not the feathered owl brow of his helm, but my brother's true face, the one I'd gazed upon as he squeezed the last ounces of breath from my lungs.

Every life I've claimed in the last three months has led me here. I thought I was coming for Rosalina, but it was my brother I found. Our fates tied together, always to lead back to one another until one of us strikes the final blow. I tighten my fingers on the hilt of the sword.

Ezryn! Stop! The memory of Rosalina's scream roars in my head. She hadn't wanted me to fight Kairyn in the Hall of Vernalion. But didn't she understand? There was no other way. He had *wronged* me, wronged our people. There were so many reasons I had to fight, that I have to fight now—

But I cannot draw it. My chest heaves too quickly. I cannot draw my mother's sword.

My next thought strikes me like an arrow: *I have to get out of here.*

The last time I took up arms against my brother, I only hurt Rosalina. I had the chance to save her, and I chose vengeance instead. I won't lose her again for the benefit of my long-forsaken honor. Finding her is all that matters.

Cursing, I look back around the barrel. My brother and his two accomplices are gone. So is my chance to kill him.

I look down at my shaking hands. If Kairyn has disappeared and Rosalina has escaped, there's nothing for me here. I need to get out before I'm discovered.

Quickly as I can, I make my way back from the internal dock to the edge of the barge. I'll commandeer one of the skiffs and slip out to the Byzantar Isles. Perhaps there, I can get word of Rosie and the runaway princess's ship she has escaped upon.

I round the last corner to the external dock and count the rotation of the guards. When there's a gap, I dart forward and leap upon the nearest skiff. I'm no sailor like Dayton, but I can catch the wind. I bend down to unravel the rope when a shadow casts over me.

"Did you really think I would let you escape, brother?"

Ice runs up and down my spine. Slowly, I drop the rope and stand, meeting the metallic gaze of Kairyn.

"I knew you were here," he says softly and touches his chest. "It feels you, you know. Sometimes, at night, the magic seems to cry out. It still grieves for my disappointing predecessor."

I can't speak. A suffocating storm of fury and fear rages within my chest. He nearly killed me. He has an entire army at his disposal. He's got the damned Blessing of Spring.

He took my mate.

"What did you do to her?" I growl. "What did you do to my mate?"

Kairyn laughs, the sound reverberating between us. "My men talk about you. The Prince of Blood, that's your new name. Too stately for the ragged vagabond you've become. You've left a wake of corpses across the realm."

A low growl ebbs from my throat. "Where is my mate?"

"When will you realize that you're not the hero?" Sunlight glints off his mask. "Rosalina didn't need you. The lives you took were for nothing. How does it feel, brother?" His voice grows breathier, more frantic. "How does it feel to be the villain?"

"No!" I draw my sword, but I'm too late.

Kairyn heaves his arms up. Great strings of seaweed erupt from the deck, wrapping around my arms, my legs, my torso.

"Fool!" Kairyn cries. "When will you learn? You *cannot* overpower me. I am stronger than you ever were. You have *nothing!*"

Nothing but thousands of reasons to kill him. I tear against the binds, but as soon as one breaks, another takes its place. It can't all have been useless. All the deaths, the blood I spilled, the men I broke.

"Stop fighting," Kairyn growls.

"Never."

The seaweed tightens around my wrists and ankles and pulls, tearing me in four different directions. I wince against the pain. "Then I will end this for both of us," Kairyn says.

Heat explodes in my joints. I lash against the bindings, but nothing breaks.

A cold breeze caresses my skin. A breeze far too cold for the Summer Realm.

Kairyn and I both turn to the open sea.

Waves freeze into floats of ice before cracking again. But there's someone leaping from ice floe to ice floe. Even from this distance, I can see the wrath held in his body, the piercing blue gaze.

"I would run if I were you," I say to Kairyn.

The High Prince of Winter is here.

12

KELDARION

Saltwater transforms to ice beneath my feet as I surge toward the floating prison. My mate bond riots in my chest, the reawakened tether like a lifeline. She's no longer here, but I feel her across the horizon. Another tie calls me to this place.

Mate of my mate.

Kairyn stands on a skiff bobbing in the water, tied to the dock of the prison barge. Wrapped in sea plants is Ezryn, that unfamiliar face trapped in a pained grimace.

I haven't seen him in three months, since he stormed out of Castle-tree. No one has had word of him. For all I knew, he could have been dead.

Despite the animosity between us—and the fact he's tied up by Kairyn's magic—I feel relieved to see him. *He's alive.*

And I'll be damned sure to keep it that way.

I raise my arms, turning the spray of water around me into icy javelins. I'm level with the dock, and they shoot directly toward Kairyn. He cowers, but one strikes his armor and breaks. Bloody Spring steel.

"Where is she?" I roar. Another spray of ice daggers shoots toward him.

Kairyn staggers off the skiff and back onto the dock. The seaweed around Ezryn slackens. The tendrils whip out to grab my arms, but I reach out with my magic, turning the water on the weeds to ice. They crack and fall uselessly to the ground.

Kairyn takes a step back, and I slow to a stop, balancing on an icy floe beside the skiff. Though being in Summer may seem like it would hinder my Winter magic, both realms' strength lies in the water and the wind. The ocean is like endless ammunition around me.

"Not so tough when you're not surrounded by your corrupted plants, are you?" I snarl to the usurper.

Kairyn's breathing is audible even across the crashing waves. "I should have expected my brother wouldn't dare show his face alone. Oh, great and powerful Keldarion, always too little. Too late."

Ice crackles as I craft a huge, jutting spike that rears toward Kairyn. "This realm does not belong to you. Nothing belongs to you, monastery boy."

Kairyn touches the small, brown token around his neck. A light emerges, growing until it forms the shape of a giant war hammer. He swings it over his head, smashing it down upon my ice spike. "The Vale will belong to me. It has been promised. You barely hold Winter. My Sapphire Knight sits as steward upon the Spring Throne, enacting my rule with the Sword of the Protector. Runa and Erivor would be ashamed of you."

The use of my parents' names sends a storm of rage through my chest. Still balancing upon the ice floe, shining daggers dart up from the sea at my command, hailing down upon Kairyn. He flinches, unable to bat them all away with his hammer. Blood runs out from between the gaps of his armor.

Ez staggers to his feet, throwing off the last of the seaweed and rolling his shoulders. He draws the sword at his back.

Kairyn collapses to the deck, then peers up through the void of his mask. "Are you going to kill me, Keldarion? Where would the Blessing of Spring go? I have no heir and it won't go back to my big brother. It's never happened, not in all the ages. Perhaps it shall be lost forever."

"I don't fucking care," Ezryn growls.

"Of course you don't," Kairyn says. "You only care about the realm when it suits you."

I step off my ice floe onto the dock. "Where is Rosalina?"

"He couldn't keep her," Ezryn answers. "She's gone. Escaped upon the sea with Dayton."

Ah, my Rose. Look at us here to rescue you. Of course you could do it yourself. In my heart, I never doubted. I knew I would see you again.

Ice crystallizes in my hand, forming a long spear. I hold it up above Kairyn. He grabs the hilt of his war hammer.

I'm quicker. My spear shoots down, pinning his cape. Then I turn, transforming as I leap over the dock and onto the sea. My body shifts to that of the white wolf. My paws land upon ice. "Get on," I say to Ezryn.

"What?" His brown eyes flash, darting between me and Kairyn. "We have to fight him!"

"Now is not the time." As much as I would like to think I could end Kairyn in a single blow, I know with the full might of Spring's Blessing and the Hammer of Hope, this is no guaranteed battle. Getting to Rosalina is more important.

Besides, Kairyn's words sit heavy in my mind. What would happen to the Blessing of Spring upon his death, with no heir?

"Get on, Ezryn," I growl.

I see the war in his eyes as he looks from me to Kairyn. Soldiers flood down onto the dock, carrying spears, bows, and swords. Kairyn yanks my ice spear free and cracks it in half.

"Get on!"

Ezryn leaps onto my back and seizes two fistfuls of fur. I run.

With each step, I summon ice to form below my paws. The waves crack the floes quickly, the water too salty and warm.

Arrows fly past us; I hear them whizzing by my ears and feel their rush close to my paws. Ezryn smacks one away with his blade.

"Your realm will belong to me!" Kairyn cries, but his voice is far away.

Step after step, wave after wave, we break across the ocean until the arrows stop coming. Until Kairyn's voice is a distant memory.

I dare not speak to Ezryn first. I can only imagine the hatred he's held for me these last three months.

My pace slows. I haven't used that much magic since my last battle with Kairyn. My body feels drained, each ice floe an effort.

The small island I left from shimmers on the horizon. *Almost there.*

"Are we going to find Rosalina's ship?" Ezryn asks. I nearly start at the sound of his voice. It's dull, emotionless. No thank you for the rescue, but I didn't expect that from him. Rescuing each other is what we've always done.

"No. I won't be able to make it that far out to the open sea. But Rosalina's regained access to her magic; I can feel our mate bond again.

Knowing her, she'll want to return to Castletree, and she'll be able to do so with her thorns as soon as she hits dry land. We'll meet her there."

Ezryn's grip tightens in my fur. "I can't go to Castletree. Kairyn is High Prince of Spring, not me. That's his domain now."

"Your brother won't dare show his face while Farron and I still hold our realms."

My body gives out as soon as we reach the shallows. Ezryn topples off into the sea, and I shift back into the form of a fae.

We trudge through the waist-deep water until we reach the beach. I practically collapse onto the soft white sand.

Ezryn stands over me. This new him—this one with the scowl I can now see instead of just feel—stares down at me with a look of confusion.

"Even if I wanted to return to Castletree, neither of us have our tokens. How do you intend to get there?"

I crawl up the beach. My pack sits beside a palm tree. I rifle through it without meeting his gaze, pulling out and donning a pair of trousers and a shirt.

"Kel," Ez says warningly, "how do you intend to get to Castletree?"

"Now, now. Let's be reasonable," a smooth voice says. Caspian steps out from behind another palm tree, dressed in a long black coat and tight pants, far too fine for a deserted island. "We're all friends here. Did you locate our little Flower?"

I turn to Cas. "She's escaped on a ship bound for the Byzantar Isles. I can only imagine her first intention will be to return to Castletree."

Ezryn staggers backward. It isn't rage on his face but hurt. He looks at me. "You . . . you tricked me."

"Ez, listen—"

"Murderer!" Ezryn draws his sword with both hands, eyes blazing. "I'll kill you!"

Then he charges at Caspian.

"Ez, no!" I reach for him, but thorns tangle up my arm.

"I don't have time for this. If that's how you're going to be, not-so-metal-man, then fine. Stay on this island. See if I care," Caspian snarls. Thorns erupt around him and more of them tangle around my body.

Then we're swept below the earth together, leaving Ezryn alone.

13

ROSALINA

I t's him.

Dayton stumbles across the ship as if he's drunk, but I don't think he is. His eyes—blue as the water surrounding us—are too bright.

His lips form my name, though I can barely hear his voice over my bounding heart.

"Day," I say.

He pulls me against him.

The embrace is crushing in the best way, forcing all the air from my lungs. I wrap my arms around his neck, and he lifts me up, my face burrowing into his bare chest. After months and months of fear, in this moment, everything is okay.

I'm safe here in his arms.

"Rosie, Rosie, Rosie." His large hand fists in my hair, and he murmurs frantic words. "Stars, I was so worried about you. Are you all right?"

"I'm with you. I could fly." I look up at him. The glittering sun makes his hair shine like gold.

Dayton's breath is still ragged as he looks down at me, and I know it's not just my imagination. Every part of him missed me the way I missed him. He thought of me just as much as I thought of him.

"Kiss me already," I whisper.

His turquoise eyes narrow, full lips parting, but then he pulls away.

Something is different. The last time I saw Dayton, he and Kel were being imprisoned and the Nightingale was stealing me away to the monastery. Before that, he'd used his bargain with Farron to give his strength to save me. *What's changed?*

"Rosalina?" A chirpy voice breaks between us.

I step away from Dayton to see Wrenley walking over with cat-like grace. She wears a pair of cropped breeches, a fluffy white blouse, and a green cloak. Her curly brown hair has grown just below her jaw.

"We were all so worried about you."

"What are you doing here?" I know the words are rude, but she worked for Kairyn, the man who imprisoned me for three months. Kel said she rescued them from Keep Hammergarden, but I didn't think she'd *stay.*

Dayton looks between us. "Wren's been a big help. She's working for Kairyn undercover to get us information."

A bout of nausea courses through me at the use of the nickname. *Wren.* Why is he calling her that? For a moment, I think I'm going to be sick over the edge of the boat. "Yet your sister was still the one to rescue me," I say, regretting it immediately.

Why do I feel so upset all of a sudden? He's been out here *looking* for me and so has this girl. *Wren.*

"I'm sorry," I say before anyone can reply. "It's been a long few months."

"You don't have to apologize for anything," Dayton says. "I'm just glad you're okay."

"Where's Farron? He feels far away."

"He went back to Autumn for help, but if you can feel him, he can feel you. I haven't seen Kel or Ez since Spring, but I'm sure it'll be the same for them. They'll try to find you, I'm sure of it."

"Ezryn is coming?" Wrenley asks, eyes flashing. "He's a monster—"

I shoot her a look. "It's Kairyn and his soldiers who are monsters."

"Hey, let's all calm down." Dayton steps between us.

Tears pool in Wrenley's blue eyes. "Excuse me if I'm not as used to death and violence as all of you. I joined the monastery to serve the light of the Queen and he ravaged it—"

"Look, a lot happened in Spring," Dayton says, raising his hand as if to touch her, but then lowers it. "When Ezryn finds us, he'll explain everything."

"Ezryn would *never* hurt the innocent," I snarl. "Why would you even question that, Dayton?"

"I'm not. I'm just trying to have a little compassion, okay?"

I curl my hands into fists. "He'll come to me soon enough and you'll see."

"Look, as much as I love this little conversation, we've really got to get going." Delphia stomps over and eyes us with raised brows, as if seeing her brother surrounded by arguing women is not an unfamiliar sight.

"Hey, Del." He smirks at her then pulls her into a hug.

It's there only for a flash: the fierce captain who rescued me turns into a little girl in her brother's arms. But then she pushes him away, still smiling. "We can talk later. For now, we have to get out of here."

"Aye, aye, captain," Dayton says.

"All hands on deck! Prepare to weigh anchor," she says, a new pride to her words. "Hoist the sails and trim them tight!"

Within a few moments, the crew has us sailing again, heading away from Dayton's small ship. Dayton joins in the work naturally, and everyone around him brightens. Whispers of the High Prince of Summer filter through the crew.

Soon, Dayton, Wrenley, Nori, and I find ourselves in the captain's quarters, a map spread out on the desk before Delphia.

"We have to keep moving," Nori says, index finger trailing across the map's blue ocean. "Kairyn's airships travel quickly and can see for great distances."

"There's a rumor the Huntresses of Aura took one down," Delphia says.

"The Huntresses are a myth," Nori responds in her dry monotone.

"No, they're not! My grandmother was a Huntress." Delphia glares. "Tell her, Day!"

"Indeed, she was. Right now, my priority must be returning to Castletree. I can't summon any magic if I don't," Dayton says.

"I'd like to return to Castletree, as well," I say. "It's the first place my mates will look for me. We could use the other High Princes' help."

"But how will we get there? Going back to Hadria is out of the question," Delphia says. "It's Kairyn's primary base in Summer and swarming with soldiers. Plus, the way from Keep Soltide is closed. It can only be opened by the High Prince, but there's no way we could make it past all those guards."

The token of Summer sits heavy in my pocket. I need to give it back to

Dayton. But even now, it's useless without his magic. "I can summon thorns to bring us back to Castletree, but I can't do it in the ocean. I have to draw them from the earth."

Delphie's smile widens, and she gives a sidelong glance at Nori. "Then we make land."

"Somewhere beyond the laws of Hadria," Nori agrees.

A laugh bubbles from Dayton's chest. "Never did I think I'd be going there with my little sister."

"Where are we going?" I ask.

"To the Byzantar Isles." Delphie moves the token of the ship across the map. "A hive of scoundrels, pirates, and outlaws. We're heading to Corsa Tuga."

14

ROSALINA

"Corsa Tuga!" Dayton exclaims as we step off *The Deathly Sky Dancer* and onto the dock. "I'd tell you some stories of when I came here when I was younger, but I really don't want you looking at me differently."

I smack him in the chest. "I'm not sure there's much that could surprise me now."

He turns around, walking backward. "It's only because I haven't told you my best stories of the Byzantar Isles."

A gust of salty breeze courses over us. It weaves through his hair, and, with the broad smile on his face, he's never looked so beautiful. I stumble, and he quickly helps me regain my balance, throwing an arm around my shoulder and leaning down to whisper in my ear, "This story involves a mischievous parrot, a treasure map drawn on a napkin, and a daring escape aboard a makeshift raft made of rum barrels. One of which Farron was stuck inside."

A laugh bubbles out of me, and I find myself leaning closer into his embrace. "I can't believe you brought Farron here."

"I brought Farron everywhere with me when he visited Summer. Though he complained, he always followed."

"I think that smile of yours can compel people to do just about anything."

Suddenly, that smile falters. He steps away from me before pulling his hood up. "Cover your face. We don't want to draw too much attention here."

I nod, following his instructions. We fitted ourselves with cloaks before disembarking the ship. It makes the heat even more relentless and beads of sweat cling to my brow.

"We've got some rooms at the Salty Kraken Tavern," Delphia says, coming up behind us. "There's an alley beside it. Might be a good place to grow your thorns."

I nod and follow the group into the city. Beyond the docks, the town is alive with bustling markets. The breeze is thick with the scent of spices mingling with the briny sea air.

"It's crowded here," I whisper.

"Kairyn hasn't expanded his reach to the Isles yet," Wrenley says, coming up beside me, silent as a cat. "They're small and difficult to navigate to as they're left off of most standard maps."

Delphia falls into step with us. "Many fae escaped here when Kairyn attacked. Some of the pirates are smuggling weapons and supplies to the underground resistance in Hadria."

"Hadria and Corsa Tuga are usually at odds, but the two cities have formed an uneasy alliance in the last few months. Nothing like having a common enemy to bring people together, right? The pirates don't want Kairyn in charge any more than the citizens of Hadria do," Dayton explains.

There is a certain way of life here, one that feels vibrant and alive. As we meander deeper into town, my gaze is drawn to the colorful array of shops lining the cobblestone pathway. THE MYSTIC EMPORIUM is written on a flapping wooden sign, but I can't see anything beyond the dust-covered windows. Another sign reads THE BUCCANEER'S BLACK-SMITH, where an artisan hammers away at molten steel, forging weapons.

Farther down the street, SIREN'S TREASURES catches my eye with its sparkling window display. Pearls glisten like moonlight on the waves, while intricately carved coral pieces seem to whisper secrets of the sea. I linger for a moment, enchanted by the otherworldliness of it all.

Dayton comes up behind me, resting a hand on the small of my back. "It's said that a long time ago, the sirens used to come to Corsa Tuga all the time. They'd walk among the fae and swim in the canals." He gestures to the waterways that run up and down the city streets.

"Wait, they can walk?"

"Sure. Sirens lose their tails if they step on land, but you can always recognize one by the dusting of scales on their cheeks in the sun." His thumb brushes my face, and the only thing I feel there is a blush.

I saw a siren once, down in the Below. She had sung at Caspian's birthday party, and Ezryn said she was likely there due to a bargain. It makes me sad, perhaps because once I had been trapped myself due to my fae bargain with Kel. But I found my way to something better. Maybe she can, too.

Suddenly, I remember I still have Dayton's token tucked in my pocket. Up ahead, it appears Nori, Delphia, and Wrenley are engaged in a conversation with a vendor, and Nori is trying to purchase some sort of cursed-looking charm.

"This is yours." I take out the token. He still wears his other necklace, the one strung with seashells. My gaze catches on one shell in particular. A nautilus shell, gifted to him by the acolyte for saving her in the river.

I quickly press the token necklace into Dayton's palm and look away.

"How did you get this?" Dayton asks.

"Long story. The Turquoise Knight tried to touch the Bow of Radiance, and it turned him into dust. But it left your token . . . and the Trident of Honor. Day, it's *inside* the necklace."

"So, it's true. I was never sure. As Protector of the Realms, Kel was the only one with a sacred weapon, and he preferred to keep it as far away from him as possible." Dayton moves to unstring his necklace.

"Wait." I grab his wrist. "Kairyn doesn't know I have this, and he asked me about it every day while I was captured. They want all the weapons, and now, this is the only one they don't have."

"This is why you're the smart one." He smirks. "Though, how did you get the trident inside of the necklace?"

"It's because—"

"Hey, you two, hurry up!" Delphia calls from up ahead.

"I'll tell you later," I say. I still haven't told Dayton what I've learned about myself, that I'm daughter to Queen Aurelia . . . and I can wield her bow.

"Thank you, Rosie. I mean it." He leans toward me before straightening and tucking the token into his pocket. "I can't believe you got this back."

We quickly catch up with Delphia, Nori, and Wrenley.

The five of us finally make it to what must be the tavern district. The air takes on the distinct tinge of alcohol. Even though it's still morning, laughter echoes out of the buildings, followed by slurred shanties.

"We'll be stationed here while we wait, resupplying the ship," Delphia says, stopping in front of the Salty Kraken.

"Three days," Dayton says. "Then I'll be back."

"Better be," Delphia replies as she lets herself be pulled into a tight hug.

"Give these to my brother. I'm sure he'll find you at Castletree." With an eerily straight arm, Nori holds out a heavy black bag to me.

Gingerly, I take it. The contents seem to be an odd mixture of firm and squishy. "Uh, thanks."

"Just some things I found on my travels. They may be useful to him."

I smile. Though I haven't been able to spend much time with Nori, I know from Farron's stories that she's not exactly what one would call expressive. This gift to Farron must be her way of saying, "I miss you and I love you."

Before she can walk away, I snatch Nori in my arms, squeezing her as tight as I can. "Now I can give Farron a hug from you."

Nori's body stiffens, then relaxes. "Yeah. Whatever," she says softly.

I pull away from her, and she scuttles over to Delphia's side.

"Are we ready to go?" Wrenley stands by the entrance to the alley.

"You're coming?" I ask.

"Of course I am," she says.

We head down the alley, slinking into the shadows, and I take a deep, steadying breath. Out of the edge of my sight, I catch Delphie and Nori peering around the corner of the alley, watching intently.

"Hold on to me. I haven't done this that many times before," I say to them.

"Are you sure this isn't dangerous?" Wrenley asks, a knot creasing between her brows.

Very dangerous. You should probably stay here so you're not accidentally impaled by a thorn, I think before I shake my head and reach out to grab her hand. "It'll be okay."

She snatches her hand away the instant I touch her, lips curling back, panic flaring in her blue eyes.

"Rosie will take care of us, Wren. She's very powerful." Dayton grips me around the waist and reaches across to grab Wrenley's shoulder.

She takes a deep breath, then twists her hand in my cloak.

"All right," I say, golden briars rising around us. "Let's go home."

15

ROSALINA

We crash through the briars and land in a heap at Castletree's entrance hall. My golden briars fall among Caspian's purple ones. I lie there for a moment breathless, limbs tangled with Dayton and Wrenley. But there's never been a bigger smile on my face.

I'm home.

Through my blurred vision, I see the familiar door, the mirror, and the fireplace. The Prince of Thorns' briars tangle all the way to the top of the ceiling.

He's still holding the castle together.

"You're not the most graceful, with that form of travel, are you?" Wrenley grumbles.

I don't care about her whining because my chest is filling with an unmatched warmth, an igniting fire.

"Farron," I breathe, and push myself up, dropping Nori's bag.

He's standing at the top of the stairs, tears already streaming down his freckled cheeks.

I run toward him. I don't care that I probably smell like seaweed, or my clothes are tattered. Farron, my *mate*, is here.

"Rosalina!" He leaps to the bottom of the staircase and grips me tight around the waist.

We fall in a tumble, and it's like the briars reach up to catch us. His lips are on my cheeks, wet with salty tears. "I felt you. I wanted to run to Summer, but then I knew you'd come here if you could and told myself to wait just a few more hours and . . . here you are."

He breaks off in a choking sob, and I don't think my heart could love him any more. Gently, I take his auburn waves between my fingers. How often did I picture that color during the endless days and nights beneath the sea? Wishing I could see the gold of his eyes again, his smile?

"Farron, you're here," I whisper, and bring my lips to his. "You're here. You're here."

"Let them try to take you from me again," he says, a growl to his words. His kiss is just as powerful, devouring me.

Dayton coughs.

Farron pulls away, and we both look up to see Dayton smirking down at us. I slide myself off Farron, knowing he probably wants to see Dayton too.

But all Farron does is tilt his head. "Hi, Day."

"Hey, Fare," Dayton replies.

"Wrenley," Farron says.

"Farron," Wrenley says.

I look between them, the tension taut, but a high-pitched scream breaks the silence. "ROSALINA!!"

Astrid bounds down the steps, quickly followed by Marigold and Eldy. My own incoherent babbles spill out, and I stumble over the thorn-covered steps to fall into a giant group hug.

"You made it back okay!" I sob. "I'm so glad!"

The last time I'd seen them, I'd changed the three of them into birds so they could escape the Spring Realm.

"Are you kidding? That was fun." Astrid winks. "Though, I still prefer hopping!"

"I'm grateful for our little winged adventure," Eldy says, throwing an arm over Marigold. "I've still been able to change into a bird, so I've been turning every night at the same time Marigold does. It helps me to understand my beloved's affliction a little more."

I wipe my tears with the heel of my palm. "How have you all been?"

"Without any of the princes at Castletree, we've been keeping ourselves busy," Marigold says.

"Lots of places have crumbled and need repairing," Astrid says.

"Lots?"

"It's not so bad, dearie." Marigold pats my head.

But from the worried look that passes between them, I can tell it's not good. Moreso, now that I've gotten a moment to breathe, I can feel Castletree's wounds as if they were my own. It's worse than when I returned from Orca Cove and found all of Castletree covered in ice. There's an almost sweet smell tinging the air, like rot.

"The important thing is that you're home," Marigold says. "And now, so are two of the High Princes."

My chest tightens. Keldarion and Ezryn aren't here. I make my way down the stairs to stand in a semi-circle where Dayton is filling Farron in about my escape with Delphia and Nori.

Farron pulls me against him, kissing my ear and whispering, "Marigold's right. Nothing else matters. We're together now even if it's not the way you envisioned. I'm sorry about Day, Rosie."

Ice floods my veins and I step away from him, every nerve suddenly on edge. "What about Dayton?"

Farron's eyes flash with something feral, and he whirls to Dayton. "You didn't tell her?"

Dayton opens his mouth then closes it.

"Tell me what?" I snarl.

There's a fracturing in Dayton's face as he looks at me. "Rosalina . . ."

Rosalina. Rosalina? He *never* calls me Rosalina.

"Tell me what?" I choke out.

It's Wrenley who crosses to Dayton and puts her hand on his chest. "That Dayton and I are mates."

PART TWO
FATED IN THE STARS

16

FARRON

"Oh, you're mates," Rosalina says. Her eyes are wide, her voice shaky. She holds her hands up, stepping away from Wrenley and Dayton.

I could *kill* Dayton. A growl rises in the back of my throat. "I can't believe you didn't tell her."

"I was going to," Dayton says, storming up to me. "But between battling Kairyn and assisting in Rosalina's rescue *alone*, there really wasn't time."

"Are you saying I should have been there?" I shove him in the chest hard enough for him to stagger back. *"You're* the one who told me to leave."

Dayton shakes his head, fury lighting his eyes. His lips curl over his teeth as he snarls, "And you were so happy to run away."

The ground shakes, and I grasp his arm instinctively to steady myself. The briars writhe beneath us and, above, some of the high glass windows crack.

"Hey, listen!" Astrid yells. "Something's wrong with Rosalina!"

We whirl. Tears cut rivers down Rosalina's dirt-stained cheeks. "I'm fine, r-really," she says, staggering away from Astrid and the other servants with unsteady feet. "I suddenly feel s-so—"

Rosalina falls hard to her knees. Dayton and I lunge toward her, but a force sends me flying back, a swirl of wind surrounding Rosalina's body.

"Rosalina!" I yell, staggering to my feet.

Her eyes are wide, and they've turned completely gold. Though her lips are parted, there's no sound, only the wind breezing around her. With eerie apprehension, I realize it reminds me of Ezryn when he lost control of his magic.

There's another rumble, but this one comes from a different part of the castle. Flavia, the castle's seamstress, runs from the Summer Wing, a few other staff trailing behind her. "It's collapsing! The Summer Wing is collapsing!"

"It's my rose . . ." Dayton breathes, voice ragged. "I don't have any magic."

"Go to the High Tower," I say, then turn to Marigold. "Do you have a list of everyone who was stationed in the Summer Wing today?"

"Already on it, boy!" she says, pulling out a slim pocketbook from her apron.

The room shakes again and screams sound from deep within the halls of Summer. Eldy holds on to Marigold's arm, and Astrid clutches desperately to the banister.

"Dayton, go!" I round on him. "You need to protect your rose in the High Tower!"

He looks desperately from Rosalina to a few more staff running out of the Summer Wing. "No," he growls. "I need to save my people."

In a fluid motion, he leaps into the form of the golden wolf and bounds into the Summer Wing.

What do I do? What do I do? Panic rises within me. Flavia and other staff surround Marigold as they try to take count of everyone. Wrenley is still on her feet, watching Rosalina with an expression of fear and fascination.

Rosalina. There's not just wind around her now, but water. Salty, briny water. Her hair tumbles around her face, wild and unkempt. A steady stream of tears cascades down her cheeks and flows into the tempest.

Her pain hits me like a wave. Pure sorrow. A deep despair echoing in her heart where a raging storm thunders. I know this pain.

I've felt it myself.

Heartbreak.

"Rosalina!" I cry. "I'm here. I'm here."

But my words don't reach her through the storm. She's completely still. I *need* to get to her. I throw myself into the bubble of water and wind surrounding her. The elements rip my clothes and tear at my skin. I fall back, breathless and bloody.

Another huge quake shakes Castletree. Wrenley screams, falling to her knees, gripping the thorns in a desperate attempt to steady herself. The golden wolf rushes out of the Summer Wing with several staff members on his back and one in his mouth. He drops them in a heap before he looks down at us, forlorn. "The wing is flooding," he gasps. "One of the staff is hurt."

He turns just as a wave of water crashes into the main hall, pouring down the stairs in a thin layer. I look from Rosie to the staff members. I can't leave her.

"It's Zearia!" Astrid calls. "Her leg is bleeding really bad!"

"Put pressure on it!" Where is Ezryn? I need to protect Rosie, I need to help Dayton, and I need to shelter my staff.

I knew Castletree was weak, but how can we be losing an entire wing? Could it have been the Prince of Thorns? Did he sense Dayton's magic was diminished and launch an attack?

Then, as if he can read my mind, a tangle of thorns sprouts in the entrance hall. The Prince of Thorns appears. But he's not alone. His slender fingers grip tight to the arm of . . .

Keldarion.

"What is going on?" the High Prince of Winter growls.

There is only one way to fix this.

Fire licks up my arms as I stalk forward. "The Summer Wing is collapsing, and it's his fault!"

I lunge at Caspian, but Keldarion steps between us. "No, it's not." He grips Caspian roughly by the back of the neck, pulling him close. "I know you've been using your thorns to keep Castletree standing. Now, save it."

Caspian's expression goes from startled to wistful as he stares across at Kel, then drops his eyes to the storm that is Rosie. "I can try. But it's not going to be easy."

"When is anything involving you easy?" Keldarion says almost softly.

Softly, in a tone I haven't heard directed at Caspian in over twenty-five years.

"This is such a fucking mess." Caspian stalks forward and rolls up his sleeves. I don't know if I've ever seen him look so angry, his face contorted in a sharp scowl before shifting into a wide-eyed stare. His gaze is trained on Wrenley. "Housing Kairyn's acolytes now, are we? I thought I was the only monster allowed in Castletree."

Wrenley says nothing as she watches the Prince of Thorns with an almost bemused expression on her face.

Caspian makes it to the top of the stairs in two bounds, and his eyes widen as he stares down the corridor of Summer. He stretches out his hand, perspiration dotting his brow. "I can't keep it standing. It's too far gone. All I can do is buy you a little time."

Castletree shakes, and another torrent of water rushes from the Summer Wing.

"Dayton!" I yell.

Caspian grits his teeth, thorns coming up to twine around his legs and keep him steady. He curls his fingers, lavender eyes closing.

Is what Kel said true? Have Caspian's thorns been helping us all this time? The thought is so wild I can barely process it.

There's a growl, and the Summer Wolf rushes out, laden with more staff. His legs shake and he collapses.

"Is that everyone?" I yell.

"I think so," Eldy calls back, looking over Marigold's shoulder as she makes furious checkmarks on her notepad.

"Farron, help!" Astrid is in front of me, holding Zearia. A nasty gash runs down her leg, bleeding fast.

"Lay her down." I kneel on the ground, trying to steady my breath and concentrate on the healing magic Ezryn taught me.

Keldarion runs over to me, gaze fixed on Rosalina. "Tell me what happened."

"Rosalina and Dayton just arrived. And . . . we were talking—" My words jumble as soon as they leave my mouth. "Rosalina just fell to her knees like this. I don't understand what's happening to her. The Summer Wing started to collapse. Dayton's magic is so weak, perhaps that's why."

"This isn't just the Summer Prince's weakness," Caspian snarls from the top of the stairs. "The Queen created Castletree. Rosalina's magic is affecting it."

"How is that possible?"

Keldarion steps toward her. "Because Rosalina is the Queen's daughter."

17

ROSALINA

I'm back in my prison, being swept out into the open sea. I've never been lost in a storm this wild.

I gasp and flounder. Waves crash into me with a sudden force, driving me deeper, deeper, shattering me into fragments, like stars in the night sky.

Drowning again.

Something is wrong. Something is very wrong.

All I know is I *hate* these waves, the taste of salt, the burning, burning sun that blazes each time I make it to the surface.

No, that's not true.

I guess I just believed I belonged in these waves with him, too.

But I can't calm this storm.

Each flicker of my heart casts me amid this tempest. I am uncontrollable and wild.

I think I'm going to drown here.

I break through the ocean, and instead of heat hitting me, I'm struck with a chilled breeze. A huge wave crests above, threatening to drive me back under. The base of it freezes, getting colder and colder, until all the sea around me is entirely frozen.

A voice plays on the wind: "Rosalina. Rose."

I know that voice.

Mate.

The storm fades into a mist, and ice binds my legs to the briars. Large hands grip my face.

Keldarion sits across from me. His clothes are torn, chest crisscrossed with small cuts, but he's smiling as he looks at me. His white hair falls over his shoulders in a tangle, strands shining silver in the light.

"Kel," I say, voice hoarse. I feel so weak, even forming his name is a challenge.

"My Rose," he says.

"I hurt you . . ."

"Never." He tugs me free from the thin layer of ice encasing us to the floor and pulls me into his arms, kissing my cheek tenderly.

Everything about me feels wrong and hollow, like I've lost a piece of my heart. But Keldarion is holding together what's left.

"What happened?" I collapse against his chest. A thin layer of water leaks down the stairs. Staff rush through the foyer. Farron's leaning over someone, blood on his hands, and Caspian is *here*. He's taking off his cloak and handing it to Dayton, who's naked.

At the sight of the Prince of Summer, a fresh wave of grief cascades through me and I struggle to breathe.

Something feels different about Castletree. Worse. Rubble and bark crowd the hall to the Summer Wing. Water seeps out beneath the debris.

"Can we fix it?" I croak.

Kel looks over at Dayton who slowly shakes his head. Confirmation of what I already feel inside. The Summer Wing is destroyed.

A heart's cry escapes me, and tears stream down my face.

"It's all right." Keldarion smooths down my hair, carrying me to sit beside Astrid and Marigold. Then he storms over to Farron. "How did this happen?"

Farron steps away from his patient and shakes his head. "Like I said, we were just talking—"

"What did you say to her exactly?" Caspian asks smoothly, gliding down the steps. Dayton follows him, Caspian's cloak wrapped around his waist.

"We told Rosalina that Dayton found his mate." Farron gestures to Wrenley, who sits only ten feet away from me.

Keldarion gives a low growl, then walks over to Dayton and punches him on the nose.

18

EZRYN

Everything makes me angry.

The sun, too bright for my naked eyes. The turquoise sea in the horizon that seems too peaceful for this debauched place. The constant jabber of vendors hawking their wares and the boisterous laugh of drunks despite it being early in the morning. Three times already I've nearly snapped the wrist of a would-be pickpocket, making me miss my armor; no one would ever have attempted such a thing if I was dressed in Spring steel.

What else can I expect from the immoral hive that is the pirate town of Corsa Tuga?

I should count myself lucky. The deserted island Keldarion abandoned me on was one of many used by the smugglers that inhabit these isles. I spent the night alone on that island, my wolf's body curled around a palm tree, thinking of all the ways I could have killed Caspian. He'd ended my father so swiftly; perhaps I could learn something from the murderous wretch. Don't think. Don't hesitate.

I won't be taken aback by Keldarion's betrayal again. Three times now, he's chosen the Below spawn over me. I only have myself to blame for thinking he'll ever choose otherwise.

This morning, I'd been awoken by a group of smugglers and bartered my way aboard their vessel to Corsa Tuga, home to the most lawless and dishonorable fae in all the four seasonal realms.

I suppose I'll fit right in.

If there's any word on Dayton and Rosalina's vessel, someone here will have it. I only hope I have the right price.

The dock square is nestled on the bustling waterfront. The smell of fish guts, spices, and unwashed feet mixes with the briny sea air. Weathered wooden planks echo underfoot as I observe each vendor, looking for one that may sell information.

Patched sails are repurposed as makeshift awnings, and stalls are crafted of stacked crates or barrels of rum. One merchant sells colorful cloth said to be cut from the Queen's own gowns, and another peddles tiny daggers, claiming they're genuine Spring steel. I catch myself mid-eye roll, remembering everyone can now see when I do that.

But nowhere do I see the most beautiful woman to ever walk the Vale, nor the muscle-bound, most likely shirtless, warrior that I pray is watching over her.

An angry voice cuts over the din, one that sounds too innocent to be in this place of scum and villainy.

"Look, I've offered you ten denarii already. That's double what it's worth." The girl's voice grows louder. "Will you make the deal or not?"

My gaze drifts over to a vendor sitting on a stool behind a slanting wooden stall. The man's frame—more barrel than man—is covered in both tattoos and what appear to be barnacles. Squinting eyes peer out from beneath a weather-beaten tricorn hat that sits atop a clump of greasy, matted hair as he sizes up the two young women before him.

Stars be damned.

The girl scowls up at the vendor, appearing very much like a mouse glaring up at a vulture, but seemingly unbothered by it. Because of course she wouldn't be. It's in her blood not to fear, her mother being one of the most intrepid women to ever walk the Enchanted Vale and her fathers being two of the most accomplished warriors. Not to mention the legacy of her three older brothers.

Delphia, steward of Summer and sister of the High Prince, is dressed like a common urchin. Her black hair is swept back in a tangle, and a streak of oil shines across her dark brown cheeks. Her clothes would better befit a rubbish pile than a lady of the royal family, though I can tell the fineness of the dual blades holstered at her hips. I last saw her at Princess Niamh's funeral in Autumn, and Dayton had doted on her as he always did.

Despite her scrappy appearance, she carries such maturity in those eyes. She's been a child ruling an entire realm with no guidance, no support, no family. Now, she's lost the only home she's ever known and she's here, in Corsa Tuga. This is no place for a young person, let alone Dayton's sister.

"I ain't trading this valuable product for ten measly denarii," the barnacle-covered vendor snaps. "Why should I trust the coin of a streetling, anyway?"

"Fine. We'll keep our coin," says the girl standing beside Delphia, her voice deadpan. "If you won't make the trade, we will find other ways to procure the item we seek. Perhaps I shall pluck a hair from your chin and make a spell of my own, one that turns your will to mine. Or I could turn your eyes inside out with a simple incantation, and we can sift through your wares as we see fit. Would that be preferable to our streetling coin?"

"Nori, *please*," Delphia snarls.

Stars be double-damned. Not only is Dayton's little sister here in this wretched town, but so is Farron's. Eleanor stands with her arms crossed, her outfit equally as decrepit as Delphia's, though she wears a skirt while Delphia wears trousers. A harsh sunburn has formed across her nose over her otherwise nearly translucent pale skin. Her long auburn hair has the bangs cut blunt over her eyes and hangs straight down to her waist.

What in the seven realms are they doing here?

"Is that a threat, streetling?" The vendor stands up, towering over the two girls. They stare up at him with matching wide-eyed gazes.

"You two dirty dock urchins get the fuck out of my sight and your hands off my wares before I *take* your hands *for* my wares." He snags a cleaver off his belt and holds it up above them.

It's instinct. Before I even contemplate what I'm doing, I'm in front of the girls, holding the vendor's wrist with the perfect amount of pressure to be just on the edge of breaking.

"I would be careful with such words, merchant," I say calmly. The cleaver falls from his hand and embeds in the stall. He stares at me with a look both fearful and angry. "You never know who will visit your fine establishment. You may find yourself speaking with Her Royal Highness, Princess Delphia of Summer, and Her Royal Highness, Princess Eleanor of Autumn. When they wish to trade you their hard-earned coin for one of your fine wares," I give a disdainful look down at the assortment of crap he has laid out on the stall, "then you should, in fact, respond with grati-tude. And dignity. And thanks."

I drop his wrist and place his hand on the stall. Then, I pick up the cleaver, toss it into the air, watch it twirl three times, before catching the hilt and slamming it down right between his splayed fingers. "In fact, you may find yourself so honored to be visited by such gracious company that you gift them whatever such item has won their affections."

I allow myself to do something I've never bothered with before. I smirk. "What say you, fine merchant?"

The merchant looks down at the cleaver, perfectly placed between his fingers. His barrel-like chest heaves in and out. "Fine! Fine. Take the damned feather. Probably not even real anyway."

Nori's hand jerks out, snagging a large, ratty black feather from the stall and stuffing it in her pack.

I nod down at the girls. "You two. With me." No way I'm letting Dayton and Farron's sisters walk around this wretched place alone. If I hadn't stepped in, they could have lost their hands. Besides, if they're here, they must know something about Dayton's whereabouts.

The girls exchange a look with each other then follow behind me.

As soon as we're out of the dock square, I tug the backs of their shirts and direct them into an alleyway. "All right, ladies, would you like to explain—"

Delphia shoves me into the wall of the dark alley, then swings up her dual blades, placing one at my neck and one at my ribs. At the same time, a bright light shines from between Eleanor's hands; she's holding a small pumpkin with a carved face, the eyes and jagged mouth glowing. Red mist wafts out of the orifices of the pumpkin, smelling of . . .

Apple cinnamon?

Delphia snarls up at me, then turns to Eleanor, face changing as she gives an exasperated sigh. "Nori, I thought you said it was poisonous gas!"

Eleanor smacks the pumpkin. "I think I left my gas one on the boat. This is the aromatherapy spell."

I raise an eyebrow, and Delphia just sighs again, then turns back to me with a vicious expression. "Who the fuck are you, stranger? How do you know who we are? Speak, or I'll gut you here in the alley!"

This would be slightly more intimidating if I hadn't presented her with a dollhouse for her last birthday—a gift picked out by Marigold.

But, of course, the girls don't recognize me. They've never seen the Prince of Blood before.

"Whoever he is, he's no friend of ours," Eleanor says in that detached voice of hers. "Only an enemy or an idiot would trumpet that the

Princesses of Summer and Autumn are here on Corsa Tuga. Some of the pirates here would sell us out to the Green Rule for a single coin."

The Green Rule . . . So that's what Kairyn's calling his new empire. I suck my throat back a smidgen away from Delphia's shaky blade. "Well, I'm no enemy, so I'm afraid that makes me the other one."

"Give me one reason I shouldn't bleed you out," Delphia snarls.

I take a breath, then move. First, I knock her blade away from my throat with a strike to her forearm. Then I spin away from the blade at my ribs. A quick nudge to the pressure points on her inside wrists, and she drops her blades. I grab them out of the air, give them a spin for good measure, then hold up the tips to her and Eleanor's throats.

The girls stare at me, wide-eyed and gasping.

I retract the blades and spin them again, presenting the hilts to Delphia. "These are good swords. Your brother has ones just like them. I'll tell you the same thing I'm always telling him. Mind your spacing. Too close and you'll entangle yourself; too far and your strikes will lack power."

Delphia grabs her swords and takes a step back. "Are you a sorcerer?"

"No," Eleanor says. Her golden eyes flash and she steps toward me. For a child, she also has so much wisdom gained too young. "It is Ezryn."

"High Prince of Spring?" Delphia whispers.

"Not High Prince anymore," Eleanor says. "The Prince of Blood."

"How do you know that name?" I ask lowly.

Eleanor waves a dismissive hand. "The dead whisper it all around you."

I pull away from her and eye the empty space around me warily.

"You look different without your armor," Delphia says, stepping closer to me.

"Obviously. He's got a face now." Eleanor rolls her eyes, and Delphia sneers at her.

I back up against the wall, suddenly feeling like I'm under the spyglass of these two young fae. "All right, all right. Yes, it's me, Ezryn. I've come to find your brother and the Golden Rose. Are they here?"

Delphia crosses her arms. "*We* rescued the Golden Rose. The royal family still has friends. One of my sailors has a friend who was commissioned as a shipwright to work on Kairyn's prison barge. Through him, we were able to get it all: prisoner list, schematics of the underwater cells, and even a security detail."

I raise my brow, impressed. "You risked your lives and the lives of your crew for a woman you barely know. Why?"

Delphia's gaze is fiery. "The Golden Rose gave Autumn the miracle they needed. Maybe she can be the miracle Summer needs, too." Then, as if embarrassed, she waves her hand. "Of course, my dumb brother shows up at the last minute and takes all the credit."

"Where are they?" I ask.

"They went back to Castletree," Delphia says.

"Using the golden briars," Eleanor adds, and I see the look of reverence on both their faces and why not? To see Rosalina's magic for the first time is a sight never to be forgotten.

Delphia turns and starts to walk out of the alley. "We're meeting them back at my ship in three days' time. You can meet us there if you want. I'll tell you where it's docked."

I stalk behind her. "I'm not letting you wander around this town unchaperoned."

Delphia gives me a glare that could wither even Rosalina's roses. "I'm the steward of Summer. I don't need anyone to look after me."

"I'm acting on behalf of your brother. That trumps even stewards."

"Great," Eleanor growls, grabbing Delphia's elbow. "Now we've got a *babysitter*."

High Prince to babysitter. "It's only three days. Then you'll be rid of me, and I'll be pleased to be rid of you."

Three days. I've survived goblins, monstrous plants, and my brother. Two teenage girls can't be that much harder.

19

KELDARION

The Summer Wing is gone. There are not even any ruins to inspect. The hall that once led to it is nothing but a pile of roots, rocks, sand, and mucky saltwater. The enchanted hot springs, Dayton's quarters, and the training grounds are no more.

Dayton, Farron, Caspian, and I stand among the ruins. Astrid took Rosalina to her room, while Eldor and Marigold are taking care of the displaced Summer staff and finding a room for Dayton's new mate, Wrenley.

"I don't suppose if I break my curse, the Summer Wing will just grow back?" Dayton asks, leaning an arm on one of the boulders. His nose is still red from where I hit him. Well deserved.

Farron picks up a piece of limp seaweed. "I don't think so, Day. The castle, like the realms, was created by the Queen."

"Oh, you mean Rosie's mother?" Dayton shakes his head. "Damn, I feel like I should be surprised, but I'm not."

"It's not Rosalina's fault the Summer Wing collapsed," I say. "She was imprisoned for three months, and this is the first time she's returned to Castletree since she discovered the truth of herself."

Sadness flickers on Farron's face. "The influx of magic she must have felt, then Dayton's news, combined with the weakened state of the Summer Wing . . ."

Dayton steps forward, throwing his arms out to the sides. "What I'm hearing is this is all my fault!"

A growl rises in my throat. "How did you expect her to react? You *made her* fall in love with you."

"Shut up, Kel," Dayton snarls back, anger flashing in his eyes. "Neither Rosie nor I ever said anything about *love*. You love her, Kel, and I fucked her and Farron does both. Seems like the little princess has got it pretty good."

"Stop it, Dayton," Farron says, gaze cutting. "I know you're hurting, but that's just cruel."

A strange laugh bubbles up from the Prince of Summer. "Hurting? Me? No, I'm the luckiest motherfucker in all the realms. The answer to the curse has waltzed right into my life. I can break my curse whenever I want and stop being this mangy mutt."

"Then why don't you?" Caspian's voice is sharp as a knife's edge. He's been so quiet, I could almost have forgotten he was here, if not for the shadowy presence always at my back.

Dayton growls. "Oh yeah, and what's this about shadow boy's thorns actually helping?"

"All this time, you haven't been sucking the magic from Castletree?" Farron narrows his eyes.

Caspian turns to me. "Did she tell you?"

"Oddly enough, it was her faith in you that made me believe it."

A strange expression passes across Caspian's face, and he turns away, kicking the shallow water. "Let's just say what happened here would have happened a long time ago without my help."

Farron grabs Caspian's arm. "Why help Castletree, and then betray me? Why attack my realm? Whose side are you on?"

"My own side," Caspian snarls. "For the moment, I don't want your stupid tree to fall. Is that not good enough for you?"

"It's good enough for now," I say.

Dayton lets out a bitter laugh. "Maybe it's good enough for you, Kel. I didn't realize we were trying to relive the War of Thorns. Don't you remember what happened last time you two allied?"

Caspian slides behind me as I advance on Dayton. "Weren't you listening, Daytonales? Our home would be destroyed, our curses forever bound to us, the roses wilted, if it weren't for Caspian. So be very careful with your next words."

A storm flares in his eyes, but then a smile curves up his face. "Answer me this, Kel. Where's Ezryn? I bet he doesn't agree with your little arrangement, either."

"Ezryn has made his choice, as must you all," I growl. "Tomorrow, once everyone has rested, we will restore our roses. Then, we need to forge a plan. Meet at the High Tower tomorrow morning."

"Yes, master," Dayton sneers and stalks away.

Farron gives a wary look between me and Caspian, then follows Dayton.

A moment after they leave, Caspian snakes around me. He puts his thumbs into my belt and looks up at me through dark lashes, his lavender eyes sparkling. "Thank you, Kel."

Dying briars lie among the stone, but living purple ones still writhe and twist around the entrance hall, all throughout Castletree. All throughout my room. I cup his cheek with my palm, seeing it redden beneath my touch.

"No, Cas," I say. "Thank you."

20

ROSALINA

I take a deep breath, soaking in the familiar scents of old books, candles long burned down to the wick, and mahogany furniture. Astrid had left me to settle in my room, but after I'd bathed and changed, it felt too empty, so I'd followed the pull to Farron's room instead. I needed something to ground me, to tether me back to the earth. My bond led me here.

I sink to my knees at the foot of his bed and rest my forehead against the wooden frame. A position of surrender, but surrendering to what? My breath comes ragged from my throat, and I can't seem to get a proper lungful. It's all too much. I've been pulled from the watery monotony of my cell into the light, and my eyes can't adjust.

Dayton has a mate. Someone who's not *me*. Everything that's been thrown at us, I've faced head on. I always believed we could do this together. But this . . . This isn't something I can fight and I don't know if I have the strength to face it.

Silent tears run down my cheeks. How could I lose control of myself? The Summer Wing, the home of the Summer staff who can't return to Hadria, is gone. Because of my selfish heart. Every step I've taken has been wrong. My love has only ever been a burden to Dayton.

How can I even begin to imagine rising from the floor? Where do I go from here? Keldarion is still bound by his bargain with Caspian, and both refuse to bend. My father is sick, and I haven't seen him in so long. He *needs* me, and I can't even rise from the floor. I scratch at the skin of my chest. My other mate bond is so quiet, so distant. *Where are you, Ezryn? I lost him, I lost my mate. He could be hurt or scared or dying and he left me . . .*

A choked sob escapes me, and I hug my arms across my body to try to keep myself together. I should be grateful. I was rescued from prison. Dayton can break his curse. I'm back home . . .

So why are the pieces of me so jagged?

"Rosie."

A voice echoes in the room, and I turn.

Farron stands in the doorway. I catch his gaze, and in that single, lingering look, hope flashes back in my heart.

"Fare."

I remember what I used to think of him, back when I'd first come to Castletree. Like he had waltzed straight out of a book of fairytales. He looks like that now, wearing a vest woven with threads of russet and burgundy. Elaborate patterns of acorns and oak are stitched into the fabric. His cravat is perfectly tied and tucked into the vest, a brilliant amber. The fitted chestnut brown trousers are tucked into tall leather boots, embellished with golden filigree. One of his pointed ears is adorned with a golden ear cuff, intricately designed to resemble tiny leaves and vines. His tousled auburn hair falls around it.

Yes, he still looks like that fairytale prince. But now, I know that when he laughs, he tilts his head back so far, his reading glasses can slip right off his face. Or he has the habit of falling asleep in the library, and I'll find him with ink smeared on his cheek. Or how when he's worried, a wrinkle forms on the inside edge of his right eyebrow, but not his left one.

That wrinkle is there now as he stares at me.

I hold on to this moment. It's something I would picture in my mind's eye over and over again while I was locked below the surface. Reuniting with my mate.

I stand for him.

"Rosie," he repeats and staggers toward me.

"Farron." His name is my lifeline.

I run to him, and he envelops me in his embrace. My whole body gives out, falling against him, but he holds me up, holds me strong. This is home. This is peace. This is safety.

"My mate," I breathe.

My hands run over his back, in his hair, his face, under his shirt so I can touch his sacred skin. He pulls me tighter against him, breathing in the dip between my neck and my shoulder, his lips all over me, first my collarbone, then my ears, then my cheeks, then my eyelids, then my mouth.

I let it all drift away, the sorrow, the exhaustion, as I fall completely into his embrace. I am a battery, drained, and he is an entire lightning storm, bringing me back to life. His lips are soft at first, barely more than a whisper over mine. I tug his hair then draw his face closer, and he changes, now hungry, seizing my breath. I don't ever want him to stop.

His lips don't leave mine, our kiss long, desperate. When he does pull away, he blinks down with his golden eyes, and my heart skips a beat. My *mate*. He's so beautiful.

"I thought I lost you," he whispers.

"Never," I swear to him. "I never gave up hope. All those days in that cell, I knew it wasn't the end. I knew I would be back here with you, in this moment, in your arms. I wouldn't have it any other way."

A shaky smile breaks across his face. "You see the world so beautifully."

"*You* are my world."

He pulls me close again, and I nestle my head in the crook of his neck. His strong hands run down my hair. "I love you, Rosalina. I love you so much. All of this—we can do it. I promise you. You and I, as long as we're together, we can . . . We can do this, okay?"

I know what he means. He's not talking about the realms being overthrown or breaking curses or saving the world.

He's talking about losing Dayton.

Tears spring to my eyes, and I bury my face deeper into his chest. This heavy grief wraps us together. "How, Fare? How do we do this?"

He pulls back, thumbs wiping away my tears. His own face is wet. "One heartbeat at a time."

I squeeze my eyes shut. One heartbeat at a time.

Lub-dub.

My love for Kel, held forever at a distance.

Lub-dub.

My love for Ezryn, echoing off his impenetrable shell.

Lub-dub.

My love for Dayton, now an evil thing, something to be spurned and buried and forgotten.

Lub-dub.

My whatever this painful and consuming feeling for Caspian is.

Lub-dub.

I open my eyes and stare at Farron. My best friend, my first true love. The first man to make me feel like I was someone worth loving.

This heartbeat is for him.

I trace the lines of his face, treasuring each one.

"I won't lose you ever again," he breathes. "I'll make sure of it."

"You are mine, High Prince of Autumn," I say, reveling in the truth of it.

"And you are mine, Queen of the Vale." He sinks to one knee and bows his head. Keldarion must have told him the discovery of my lineage.

I lift his chin with a finger. "So, you know."

"I'm both shocked and not surprised. Though, knowing the truth, I want to go back and reread everything we've ever found about the Queen. It will all have such a new light. In fact, there was one text I—" He looks toward the door, but I pull him up to his feet and back into my arms.

"You're not going anywhere," I laugh.

He laughs too, throwing his head back. Thankfully, he's not wearing his glasses, or they would have been tossed straight across the bedroom.

Laughing together—it feels so good. For a moment, I forget about all the empty spaces in my chest.

"Rosie." The way he says my name, like all his dreams are wrapped up in it.

I'll keep them safe, Farron, I think. *I'll keep you safe.*

We kiss again, soft and slow. A kiss filled with those dreams. His skin grows warm beneath my touch, and a white light shines through my closed eyelids. I blink open.

"Farron," I whisper, "you're . . . glowing."

"Huh?" He looks down at his hands. A soft white light radiates from his skin, warm like the coals of a fireplace. "Oh, what do you know."

Another laugh bubbles up my throat. *"Why* are you glowing?"

"I think it's my magic telling you how happy you make me."

It's amazing that despite feeling like I know Farron with my whole heart, there's still new depths to the love and magic we share. This is the first time our magic has ever manifested in this ethereal glow. What else is our love capable of?

He gives me that smile, the one that I can never resist mirroring on my own face. I step back from him, then reach behind my back and loosen the ribbon of the corset around my dress.

Then I let the dress fall.

Farron's eyes roam over me, and his smile fades, turning into a hungry grimace. I swear his golden eyes flash black.

I think of his love, of the pure happiness I feel in his embrace, of my mate bond so strong and alive in my breast, beaming out for him. I think of an Autumn sunrise, warm light chasing the chill off the heather. I think of the fire that burns between us.

A soft glow radiates beneath my skin, shimmering out toward his.

"I can do it, too," I say.

"I see that," he says, voice now low and raspy.

"Now, High Prince of Autumn," I say, "I've been waiting three months for you. Remind me who I belong to."

21

ROSALINA

F arron doesn't say anything. He moves with an otherworldly speed and I'm caught up in his arms, thoroughly kissed, and spun onto his bed. His weight falls over me, the soft fabric of his clothes rubbing against my bare skin.

I kiss him feverishly and blindly tear at his clothes, yanking off the cravat and ripping open the buttons of his vest. He struggles out of his shirt and trousers, and I have to push him away from me so I can drink him in. Seven *realms*. How did I survive under the water without being able to look at him?

He's so gorgeous, his body lean, skin shimmering with light. The taut muscles of his chest move up and down with his rapid breath. I want to worship every inch of him.

His naked body against mine is pure euphoria. I realize now how touch-starved I've been these last three months, my only company the fish and Kairyn's visits. Every place Farron's skin touches mine feels alight.

He runs his hand down my neck before hovering it over my breast. A pained expression crosses his face.

"Something wrong?" I ask.

"No, I'm just preparing myself." He sucks in a breath. "You have *no* idea how badly I've missed these."

A full-body laugh hits me, and he grins in response. "You're so damn cute," I tell him.

"We'll see about that." With that unearthly grace and speed, he palms my breast with one hand and cups my pussy with the other. I gasp and tense against the contact, then melt into his touch.

"Fuck, Rosie," he moans, slipping two fingers inside of me. "I've missed this pussy."

"How much?"

"*This* much." Another two fingers press within me and Farron increases his pace.

There's no time for softness, for slowness, now. My hunger for him is explosive, ready to burst out of my chest. I reach down and seize his cock. That melting sensation surges through my body again, a sense of relief just to hold it in my hand.

I stroke it from base to tip, whispering with each caress, "I love you. I love you. I love you."

The hand on my breast is replaced with his mouth. He sucks hard, gently nipping at my skin. His thumb drifts over my clit, and a shiver runs up my spine.

I feel my orgasm building quickly within me, my body so eager to respond to his touch. But this isn't enough for me. I want all of him.

"Inside of me," I gasp. "I need you inside of me. *Now.*"

Farron looks up from between my breasts. "I could never say no to you."

He sits back on his heels, and I spread my legs around his waist. I'm torn between the delirious ecstasy of watching him like this, his gorgeous body hovering over me, and the feeling of emptiness without his skin directly against mine.

"Come back to me, darling," I whisper.

His smile is so soft, his eyes filled with love. Then he drives his cock into me, and I nearly explode into stars right then and there.

His weight falls over me again. I wrap my legs tight around his hips and my arms around his neck, as if I could hold him this close to me forever. I don't ever want to let him go.

We move together, our mate bond cocooning us until I feel like we're one body, one soul.

He murmurs in my ear, near whimpers: "You feel so good, Sweetheart. So good. I love this pussy so much."

His cock sends tingles up my body. With each thrust, the sensation intensifies, the tingles growing into a crescendo. My body feels like embers caught in the rushes, swirling into a raging wildfire.

I suck in a deep breath. "Fare, Fare—"

He captures his name as it leaves my lips. One hand pinches the nipple of my right breast, and the other tangles in my hair. "Give yourself to me, Rosie. Give it to me." He thrusts again, the feeling of his cock radiating throughout my whole body.

My chest heaves, my breaths quicken, and I feel as if I'm about to break. As Farron's thrusting grows more erratic, the pleasure starts to meld into a burning desire that swells within me.

"Farron, I . . . I can't hold back much longer."

His response is a low growl, punctuated by his hips pounding into me. It's as though we've entered another realm, one where the only thing that matters is the love we share. I can feel my orgasm building, an unstoppable fire that's about to consume me.

His movements send jolts of pleasure and pain up and down my spine. My nails dig into his back, pulling him deeper. I can't help but moan, the sound echoing through the room, filling the air with our ragged breaths and cries.

His thrusts become more urgent, more feral, as if he too is trying to hold on for just a few more moments. He grips my thigh and hikes it over his shoulder, the movement allowing his cock to penetrate my deepest core.

"Tell me you'll never let me go," I beg.

He releases my leg and clutches my sweat-slicked face. "Never, Rosalina."

The primal fury in his words is almost enough to push me over the edge.

Farron's eyes are locked on mine, the intensity of his gaze matching the passion surging through me. He knows I'm close, and he thrusts deeper, harder, as though trying to pull every last ounce of pleasure from me.

I can feel the wildfire inside me spreading, about to consume me whole. My nerves are taut, the anticipation nearly unbearable. "Farron," I cry. "Farron!"

My glow intensifies, melding with his, and I surrender. My orgasm bursts forth like a wildfire caught to the wind, my every nerve like dry leaves eaten by my flames. A sound leaves my lips, not a sob, but a wild war cry. My body, once imprisoned, now reclaimed.

Farron wraps me in his arms as I come down, but he doesn't stop thrusting. I squeeze around his hardness, grounding myself with his body.

"Good job, Sweetheart," he whispers. "So good for me."

His movements grow desperate, so quick his body is a near blur. He growls low in his throat, eyes flashing, and slams into me once more, burying himself to the hilt. It's like a floodgate has been opened, his cock pulsing inside of me, spilling his seed deep within.

"You're mine," Farron growls, his voice hoarse with desire. "Always and forever. You're everything to me."

With that, he collapses on top of me, his weight pinning me to the bed, our bodies slick with sweat. We lie there, panting heavily, our hearts pounding. His cock stays nestled within me, connecting us fully.

"I love you," I whisper, my voice breaking with emotion. "More than words can say."

He raises his head, his eyes filled with love and adoration. "In the starlight way." I knot my fingers in the waves of his auburn hair. *My mate. My best friend. The love of my life.* I want to give Farron everything I am. All of my glowing moments, and my faded ones, too. I know he'll keep them both safe. I want to bathe him in my sunshine, and dance with him in my rain. I want to know that when I feel like I'm losing myself, I'll never truly be able to, because every bit of me belongs to him.

Farron gazes down at me quizzically. "Everything all right, Sweetheart?"

"I'm not ready to sleep yet." I lick my lips, suddenly vulnerable but not afraid. Farron is my sanctuary. "I love you so much, Farron. So much, I can barely contain myself."

He smiles. "I love you, too."

I sit up, pushing him back against his heels. "I want you to know every part of me. To claim every part of me." I narrow my eyes and look up at him through my lashes. "A piece of me no one has ever had before."

Farron blinks then looks down. "Oh . . . I understand." He tucks a dark curl behind my ear. "Let me take care of you, darling."

An excited energy sings between us. Giggling, I lie back down. "How do you want me?"

"Just like that." He clambers over me to the bedside drawer and pulls out a pretty turquoise vial. Oil shimmers as he coats his fingers. "We'll go slow. You just say the word, and I stop. You're in control. Got it?"

"Got it."

Gently, he lifts one of my legs over his shoulder and kisses my calf. A shiver of anticipation runs up my spine. He strokes his hand over the soft skin of my thigh, then traces the seam of my pussy, then further down.

His slick fingers whisper over my rim, and a tremble courses through my body.

"Okay?" he asks softly.

"Okay," I breathe back.

"Do you remember what it was like our first time?" His voice has a slight hitch to it, and I wonder if he's nervous. He presses a little harder against me, and another delicious shiver runs up my body.

"Of course. How could I ever forget? It was one of the best moments of my life."

A ripple of pleasure builds as he slowly presses a finger inside. "Mine too. Our first time together, and it was in a rainstorm in a pile of leaves. That's really no way to bed a Queen."

I laugh lightly, breathing as he pushes deeper. "Well, I didn't know I was a Queen then and besides, no four-poster bed could compare to those leaves in that moment."

"I suppose you're not exactly opposed to activities outside of the bedroom." He flashes me a cheeky grin, and I realize what he's doing. Distracting me and relaxing my body. I sigh against him, loosening my muscles.

"Let's see," I murmur. "There's been the forest, the library, the kitchen—"

"You told Marigold you'd tripped and fallen into the flour. I don't think she believed you."

I laugh again. All these memories, and we've only just started our lives together. "I need a hundred more years with you, Fare. A thousand more years. A million!"

"Eternity would not be long enough," he says, and his finger slips deeper inside of me.

I let out a moan and press myself harder against him. *Yes*, this is what I needed. All of him, all of me. Forever and ever and ever.

The pressure inside of me releases, and Farron sits back. "I'm going to fuck your ass now, Sweetheart," he says, his voice ever the gentleman.

I sit up on my elbows and hold his eyes with a stare. "Take me, Farron. Take all of me."

He drips oil over his cock, which is already hard again. The liquid shimmers over his length. My heart beats rapidly against my chest. His cock, both glowing with his inner radiance and now shiny with oil, seems worthy of a painting.

Farron positions himself at my entrance, his face right over mine. With his hot breath on my lips and the head of his cock pressing against my rim, my excitement feels ready to explode within me.

Then he captures my mouth with his and pushes into me at the same time. Pain and pleasure burst through me. His cock fills me up completely, my tight canal gripping him with each movement. He bites my lower lip as he thrusts. Every fiber of me blooms with sensation, a feeling of fullness like nothing I've ever experienced.

"Okay?" Farron breathes.

"Okay," I breathe back.

His hands tremble as they run over my breasts, and I notice his eyes nearly rolling back in his head. *My body* does that to him. *My body!*

Because he is my mate, and we are made for one another. This piece of myself I thought too intimate to ever offer was so easy to give to him. He is my refuge and always has been. Since the moment I came to Castletree and saw him there in the prison, I knew he was my haven. I tried to rescue him then and have never stopped trying. Now, with each pump inside of me, I feel like he's rescuing me from the darkness that was threatening to overtake me earlier.

"Your ass feels so fucking good, Sweetheart," he moans. "This is *mine*. You are mine."

Hunger rages in my chest, and I run scratches down his back. "*Harder*, Fare. Harder!"

He growls and increases his pace. I cry out. My skin grows brighter, reflecting in his golden eyes. His light shines brighter, too, warmth radiating over me. I am on fire, a meteor hurtling toward his earth.

Farron and I have been together so many times now, in so many places. We've made love, fucked like animals, and worshiped one another as if we were gods. But this is different—this is a complete surrender of my body to him and I don't ever want it back.

Farron holds himself up on one arm, then reaches down and strokes my clit. The single electrifying touch combined with the relentless pressure within me sends my body over the edge. I unshackle from reality, my nerves exploding from top to bottom.

"F-Fare!" I manage. "I'm coming."

His light grows so bright, his features are nothing but wavering mist. "Me too. Where—?"

"Inside me, Fare. I need you inside me!"

My light bursts forth with his, and together, we erupt. Farron cries out. His cock pulses within me, filling me even fuller than I thought possible. His light radiates out in great beams, and my own joins his. I am a bucket of stars, spilling out across the sky.

The world seems suspended in a breath. Farron's full weight falls over me, his breathing heavy. I wrap my arms around him and take in the scent of his skin.

We stay like that for a few minutes, hazy with ecstasy. Farron starts to untether from me with a few sloppy kisses that send me into a fit of laughter again. I miss his touch instantly as he gets up, but he's back soon enough with a warm, wet towel.

After cleaning up, Farron dresses me in a pair of his pajamas. Something about his soft striped trousers and shirt is so much comfier than my own. He pulls me back into bed with him, and I lie on his chest.

My light has puttered out, my control of magic nowhere near as nuanced as his, but his skin still has a subtle glow.

I trace my fingers over his bare chest. My own living starlight.

He kisses my brow. "So," he whispers, "what do we do next, Rosie?"

"We keep going," I say back.

One heartbeat at a time.

22

ROSALINA

Very carefully, I place the last sugared doughnut onto the top of my tower.

"Going to fix the castle with sweets?" A voice carries from the entrance of the kitchen.

I jump and my hand bumps the pile, toppling my tower. I blow the hair away from my eyes with a long sigh. "Great, Cas, now I'm going to have to start again."

The Prince of Thorns saunters in past the huge stone oven, gliding his hand along the wooden table in the center of the room.

I haven't spent too much time in Castletree's kitchen, but it's quite the cozy space. Set below the main level, it's made entirely of stone. Dried herbs hang by the arched windows, streams of red midday light flickering through them. Two pantries stand side by side: one overflowing with vegetables and grains, the other chilled by Winter's magic, stocked with an array of colorful berries, tubs of creamy desserts, and jugs of fruit juice and iced tea.

Since being back at Castletree, I've made sure to drink my contraceptive tea. It's got a bitter taste, but thankfully one cup will last me a whole month.

"You've been busy," Caspian says, eyeing the table laden with food: jewel-toned berries, a platter of ambrosia grapes, tiny tarts with flaky crusts and fillings of sweet cream, and a platter of pastel-hued cakes with edible flowers. There's also a pot of honeysuckle tea brewing and a few jugs of fae wine. I know I'll have to be careful with that, figuring the last time I indulged, I ended up showing my ass to Keldarion. But that was only because Day—

A sudden pang of grief ripples through me at the memory of that night. When Dayton had first taken me to the Summer Realm. First kissed me.

You were the first of the princes to kiss me.

I grip the edge of the table and breathe in through my nose. "It wasn't hard," I say, my words too high-pitched. "The chef Oliviana helped me for a bit. I'm just finishing up."

Caspian eyes me carefully, like he can feel all the pain inside of me with just a look. He seems content to play along for now, and pops a berry into his mouth, the juices painting his lips red. "What is all this for?"

"I'm having a sleepover with Astrid and Marigold."

He raises a dark brow. "Just how much do you expect a little rabbit and raccoon to eat?"

"And with Wrenley," I say.

Caspian stiffens but doesn't respond.

"She's going to be part of our lives now," I continue, not sure why I feel the need to justify myself to the Prince of Thorns of all people. Maybe I need to hear myself say it. "It's only polite to try to get to know her."

"Princess," Caspian says, anger lacing his words. "What happened to the Summer Wing wasn't your fault. You don't need to do something you'll hate just to ease some feeling of guilt that shouldn't even be there."

"I lost control of my magic."

"Lucky just some parts of the tree fell apart. When Ezryn lost control of his magic, he almost *killed* you."

The thought of Ezryn in such pain sends another stab of longing through my mate bond. *I'll find you soon*, I think. "Speaking of Ezryn," I say, "I know why you killed his father."

"To continue overthrowing Spring and assist in building my mother's dynasty."

"No," I say, crossing my arms. "It was one of the things I spent a lot of time thinking about during my imprisonment. Thalionor was sick. He was going to turn into a monster like that plant rat, wasn't he? The pus that dripped from under his helm was the exact same as what that monster had around its maw. Perth Quellos must have been poisoning him."

Caspian avoids my gaze. "Are these cream-filled tarts? Very delicious."

"Caspian," I say, "why didn't you tell Ezryn what was wrong with his father?"

"It wouldn't have mattered. Ezryn would have wanted to try to save him. But Thalionor was moments from turning and he might have killed you—" He stiffens, then says quickly, "Might have killed us all. I couldn't take that chance."

"Tell him when you next see him, then."

"He won't believe me."

"Caspian," I snarl, smacking his hand away from the tarts, "won't you even try?"

"Like you're trying, with all these?" He gestures to the table of sweets. "You're going to make yourself miserable for what? Do you even know if you can trust Wrenley? She's still Kairyn's acolyte."

"And you're the son of the Queen of the Below."

He grits his teeth but says nothing more.

"Besides," I say, "I have to make this right."

"Getting to know the little bird chirping in Dayton's ear isn't going to put Castletree back together."

I dig my fingernails into my palms. "I'm supposed to protect Castletree, not destroy it."

Caspian crosses to me and places a finger under my chin, forcing me to look up at him. "What are you *supposed* to do? Being her daughter doesn't burden you with some responsibility. You didn't sign up for this. Just because you have magic doesn't mean you have to use it. You could leave."

I shake my head and turn away from him. "Like you did?"

"You're upset with me."

"Why didn't you come for me?" I whirl to him, and fresh tears spill over my cheeks. "I was Kairyn's prisoner for months and you didn't come for me."

Pain flickers across his features, and he grits his teeth. Then he grabs me around the waist. "I *tried. Believe* me when I tell you I tried."

Breath surges out of my throat as he moves us across the room, pressing me against the stone wall. He dips his head, soft hair brushing against my cheek. "I tore myself apart trying to get you back. I wish I had done more. I wish mine and Kel's plans had worked faster."

Slowly, I thread my fingers through his hair, and the small sound he makes has my stomach flipping. "Every sunrise, I would whisper the names of everyone I wished to see again, Kel, Farron, Ezryn." My voice hitches. "Dayton, my friends here, my father, and . . . and you, Caspian."

He looks up at me, eyes like a star-swept sky. "You shouldn't be saying my name like that, Flower."

"Were you and Keldarion looking for me *together*?" I ask.

"Give us the right motivation and anything is possible." He leans closer to me, lips an inch from mine.

I suck in a tight breath as I feel his hand curve up the side of my waist. "Are you intending to stay at Castletree?"

"I'll have to return to the Below shortly, but with Kel, Dayton, and Farron giving their magic to the tree, I can lessen my hold on the thorns a tad. It makes it easier to stay on the surface. Perhaps I'll even have a few days here to keep an eye on things," he purrs.

"Where will you be sleeping?" I ask as his teeth lightly graze my collarbone before resting on my neck. "Keldarion's room?"

Then his lips are brushing mine as he speaks. A not-quite kiss. "What use does a wolf have for a big bed?"

That not-quite kiss isn't enough for me. Not now. Not after everything we've lost these last few months. I put my hand on the back of his neck and pull him toward me.

Our lips meet, and my body seems to sing at the connection. At first, he stiffens at my touch, then melts into me, a low growl resonating through his chest. His kiss is everything I remember: glittering starlight and the dark spaces between. My fingers tangle in his soft hair, and he tugs me closer in response.

Is this how Kel felt when Caspian kissed him all those years ago? Lost in starlight and shadow? But that's not quite right. Because despite the rush of blood in my head, the dizzy sensation that threatens to overtake me as his kiss deepens, I don't feel lost.

In his arms, I am found.

I pull my mouth away just enough for a breath. I know what the others would say. I shouldn't play these dangerous games with Caspian. Neither should Kel. "Tomorrow, my touch could keep him fae all night," I manage. "So, I'm sure it'll be you on the floor."

Caspian licks from the corner of my lips to my ear. "Why don't I join you both and find out how big the bed really is?"

23

ROSALINA

Everything is finally ready. Everything is ready and normal. Because it's totally normal to have a sleepover with your two best friends, and the girl who is now mated to a man you're trying hard to forget you're in love with, all while on a three-day break from trying to save a realm from the tyrannical younger brother of your mate.

I look around my bedroom in the Spring Wing. The only thing left to do is enjoy the present. Or at least try to. After working all afternoon to make everything perfect, it's almost time for the festivities to begin. I am *so* not doing this just because I feel guilty, like the arrogant, stupid, perfect-haired Prince of Thorns suggested.

"I think these are going to be absolutely perfect." Flavia, the castle's seamstress, holds up four custom-made nightgowns.

"These are amazing!" I rush over and run the fabric between my fingers. The dresses look spun from threads of moonlight, shining like light skipping over a pond. The bodices are adorned with tiny pearls, with delicate frills of lace sewn around the hem.

"So cute!" Astrid says, hopping up and down.

Flavia has made two human-sized dresses, and two small enough to fit a racoon and a rabbit. The sun hasn't set yet, but for most of the night, they'll be in their animal forms.

"I think Wrenley will really like this," I say, quickly changing into my own nightgown, then holding hers up to the light.

Flavia clears her throat. She's always so elegant. Her blue and green hair is swirled in a dramatic updo, and she wears a simple black dress.

"Aren't you happy Dayton found his mate?" I ask. "You won't have to become a peacock at night anymore."

Flavia exchanges a sidelong look with Astrid and Marigold before stepping forward to cup my face. "I suppose we just all thought it would be you."

My heart sinks, and I wring my hands in the silken fabric. "Thank you for this. It was really kind of you to make them. Are you sure you don't want to stay?"

Flavia had overheard my idea of a sleepover from some of the other staff and jumped at the chance to create some new nightdresses.

"Nonsense, lovely. It was a welcome distraction from everything." She gives me a smile and makes to leave. "I'm going to have a restful sleep tonight."

Flavia opens the door and gives a little chirp. "Oh, hello, Wrenley."

"She's here!" I shoot a panicked look at Marigold and Astrid. A part of me wasn't sure she was going to show up. She hadn't seemed overly enthused when I'd invited her earlier.

"Well, let her in, girlie," Marigold says, placing a hand on her hip.

"Come on in, Wrenley," I say, leading her inside.

Wrenley's eyes dart to every corner of my room before landing on me. "*What* are you wearing?"

"A nightgown!" I say, plastering the biggest smile on my face. "There's one for you as well!"

Wrenley awkwardly takes it, and I grab her arm. Immediately, she jerks out of my grip. "Come see the rest of the room," I say quietly.

When I first arrived in Castletree, my cherry blossom tree had been in full bloom, sprouting pink blossoms. But now, it's a little wilted. Actually, it's *a lot* wilted, with bare branches and a mulchy floor.

"Farron taught me a fairy light spell." I point to the top of the tree where tiny little lights bob around the branches. "He helped me drag in all these pillows and blankets." I gesture to the mounds of cushions all throughout the room. "Oh and see here!"

"There's more?"

In the far corner is the spread of all the food I made. Beside that is a big pile of snow that I'm using to store bowls of ice cream and cold drinks. "Kel made that. I've never used ice magic before. Though, there's always time to practice. Not in the training arena though, because that's, uh, collapsed . . ."

I trail off awkwardly as Wrenley gives me a flat stare.

"Why don't you head into the privy, dearie, and put that gown on?" Marigold places a hand on Wrenley's back and directs her to the attached washroom.

"Ugh . . ." I rub my hands over my eyes once she leaves. "Why am I such a mess?"

"You're doing great, Rosalina!" Astrid smiles.

There's a light knock on the door. "Come in," I sigh, flopping down on the cushions.

"Thought I'd see how it's going," Caspian says, sliding inside and raising a dark brow. "Oh, very cozy."

The privy door opens, and Wrenley walks out wearing the frilly night-dress. With her short brown curls and heart-shaped face, she looks younger than when dressed in her acolyte robes.

Caspian snorts when he sees her. "Nice pajamas."

"Shut up," Wrenley sneers, throwing her own simple dress to the end of my bed. I've got to give it to her. Not many people would talk so carelessly to the Prince of Thorns. Though, I suppose one must be fearless to work with Kairyn. I wonder how long Wrenley's served as a Golden Acolyte. Did she work with Kairyn before he took over the monastery? Was she there when he was first banished to Queen's Reach Monastery?

"No, I mean it," Caspian says, stepping farther into the room. "Pink is really your color."

"Leave her alone, Cas," I say. "You haven't complimented me at all."

"Flower, you know I'd prefer you with nothing on at all."

I launch a pillow at him, which he dodges easily, smirking.

"Now, there's a man who isn't afraid to speak his mind." Marigold sighs.

"What are you doing here?" I growl. "*You* weren't invited."

"Thought I'd bring my favorite girls a little gift." He holds up an elegant purple bottle.

"That's my idea of a gift." Marigold saunters over.

"Careful, darling," Caspian says so slyly, a blush crawls up Marigold's cheeks. "There's something special about this wine."

"What is it?" I ask, an edge to my voice.

Cas tosses the wine from hand to hand. "My sister, the Nightingale, dabbles with potions. This wine is infused with her truth serum. One sip, and you won't be able to lie. Thought it might be fun for some of your games." He sets the bottle down and strides from the room. "Not that any of you have anything to hide."

THE NEARLY FULL moon has risen in the sky, casting its luminous gaze through my window. So far, I've eaten my weight in tarts, participated in an embarrassing round of charades, and we've attempted to do each other's hair. This was hindered by the fact Marigold and Astrid turned into animals, and Wrenley wouldn't let me touch her.

The acolyte sits on the floor, picking at the lace of her nightdress, as we prepare to play another game.

"All right," I explain. "This one is from the human world; it's called Never Have I Ever. Everyone holds up five fingers, and we take turns saying things we've never done. If you have done it, then you have to put down a finger and have a drink. The first one to lose all five has to . . ." I bite my lip, thinking. "Has to take a shot of that disgusting whisky from the Autumn Realm."

"Marigold, you'll have to hold up your fingers for me," Astrid giggles.

"Never have I ever gotten drunk with woodland creatures," Wrenley says, a curved smile crawling up her face.

"A first time for everything," I say.

"Sounds fun, girlie," Marigold says. "But let's make it interesting. Break out the prince's wine and make sure no one lies."

"Are we sure that's a good idea?" Wrenley says. "Do you really trust what's inside?"

"No," I say, but I pop the cork and pour the liquid into three cups and one little saucer for Astrid. It's smooth and looks to be flecked with stardust. "But I trust Caspian."

Wrenley snorts, and it almost reminds me of the way Caspian laughed when he first saw her. "Wait, you're not kidding. You really do trust him?"

"For better or worse, and I've got nothing to hide," I say, taking a sip of the wine. It's sweet and smooth with undertones of blackberry and a lemony tang.

Marigold takes a cup in her little racoon paws, and Astrid laps up a sip, the wine coloring her white muzzle purple. I hand the last cup to Wrenley. "You don't have to drink if you don't want to."

Wrenley takes it and sips. "What would an acolyte have to hide?"

I place the truth wine down in front of me. As long as no one says, *Never have I ever been in love with the Summer Prince despite him having a mate*, then this shouldn't be awkward at all.

"All right," I say, trying to think of questions that will apply to the fae realm. "Never have I ever gone skinny dipping."

Wrenley rolls her eyes but doesn't lower her finger. Astrid gives a little giggle. But it's Marigold who lowers her little racoon finger.

"What?" She smirks. "I had quite the nightlife before this curse."

Wrenley bursts out with a laugh. I'm so surprised to see her laugh, my own bubbles up. "Something funny?" I ask.

She shakes her head, voice lowering. "I was just imagining her doing that as a raccoon."

"Hey." Marigold fluffs her full cheeks. "This form is quite good in the water, I'll have you know."

The four of us chuckle a bit more. "You go, Wrenley," I say.

She chews on her lip. "Never have I ever made a fae bargain."

Both Astrid and Marigold shake their heads. I sigh, lowering one of my own fingers, thinking of the two bargains I've made: the one with Caspian on the battlefield and the one with Kel to find his mate. *That icy bastard. He knew the whole time it was me.* "Got me, Wrenley."

She combs a hand through her hair, looking away. "Bargains are binding. I can't think of a worse fate than being bound to someone."

Astrid's ears go straight up. "I've got one that's going to get Rosalina."

"You guys can't gang up on me!" I laugh.

"Never have I ever," Astrid says, "been in love."

"Ahh, my dear Eldor." Marigold sighs dreamily, lowering a finger. "It's the facial hair, I tell you."

"You got me, Astrid." I smile, thinking of my mates. But . . . it isn't only my mates that my heart calls out for.

"Well, I've never—" Wrenley starts confidently, but then it's like the rest of her words won't come out. The truth wine. I'd almost forgotten we'd taken it. She shakes her head, her expression going from confused to angry. "No. I'm not in . . ."

Astrid and Marigold exchange a wary look before Astrid ventures, "Maybe your mate bond makes you fall in love."

"It doesn't do that," she snaps.

"Well, I fell in love with his abs at first sight," Marigold hiccups, then laughs. "And that's the darn truth."

"Lucky Dayton," I breathe out, then stand quickly, heading for the privy. "Excuse me for a second."

The moment the washroom door closes, my tears fall. Wrenley really does love Dayton. She loves him. She couldn't fake that, not with the truth wine. Was that Caspian's purpose, to show me how much Wrenley loves Day? Is he trying to help me get over this in his own twisted way?

I slide down the bathroom door, putting my head on my knees, painting my nightdress with my tears. "But I love you, Dayton," I whisper out loud. "I love your smile, how you make me laugh. I love the feeling when you kiss me. I love how you light me up in the darkest moments. I don't want Wrenley to be your mate. I wish it were me, Day. I wish it were me."

I shake my head, hugging my legs. I hate myself for thinking such an ugly thought, for being able to say it out loud with the truth wine. If I really loved him, I'd want him to be happy with her. To break his curse, to regain his magic and save his realm.

"I'll try to make it easy for you, Day," I whisper to myself. "I'll try to love her because I can't love you anymore."

WHEN I FINALLY DRY MY tears and leave the bathroom, I see Astrid and Marigold are in a fit of giggles, still engrossed in the game. Wrenley is surprisingly still here, swirling her finger in the top of her wine like she's brewing a potion.

She looks so uncomfortable, it reminds me of myself, sitting in the cafeteria at high school, surrounded by everyone who had their own inside jokes.

I sigh, walk over to the spread of food, and start dishing up bowls. "Hey, Wrenley, will you come here for a second?"

She stiffly stands then walks over to me.

"Try this," I say and hand her a bowl.

"What is it?" she asks.

"Elderberry swirl ice cream. Trust me, it's delicious."

Wrenley raises a curious brow and takes a bite. "Interesting."

I place a hand on my hip. "What's your favorite flavor?"

She tilts her head. "I guess it would have to be elderberry swirl."

"Wait, are you telling me you've *never* had ice cream before?"

She shakes her head slowly.

I look over to Astrid and Marigold. "We'll be right back!"

Marigold hiccups, which sends Astrid into another burst of laughter. I turn back to Wrenley and hold out my hand. "Come with me."

Wrenley doesn't take my hand, but she nods. I lead her down into the kitchen, then into the cold room.

We stand in front of rows and rows of glass containers full of ice cream. Moonlit mint chip, elderberry swirl, pixie peach melba, starlight sorbet, unicorn dreamsicle. I remember a day during my first month in the castle when Astrid and I made labels and chose the names for all the flavors the chef had created. "The flavors are a little different from the ones I grew up with in the human world," I tell her as I scoop a little of each into a bowl, "but these are all very good. Trust me."

Wrenley watches me with a curious expression. Then, after a long pause, she asks, "What's your favorite flavor?"

"Oh, that's easy." I carry the two bowls and spoons back into the main kitchen. "Cookie dough. But when I'm sick, vanilla. Peanut butter when I need to celebrate. Of these fae flavours, probably . . . unicorn dreamsicle."

I jump to sit up on the counter. After a moment, Wrenley mirrors my movement, taking a spoon and trying a few of the flavors. "The starlight one is good," she says softly.

"You know those hot summer nights when you're a kid and the sun seems like it's never going to set?" I ask. "On those nights, my father and I would walk down to the wharf and get ice cream, then we'd sit and look at the water. Sometimes we'd get lucky and see a seal or an eagle. The best was when we'd spot an orca. Orca Cove is where I'm from."

"In the human world," Wrenley says.

"Yeah." I touch the tips of my pointed ears. "I thought I was human for a long time."

Wrenley takes another bite. "Your father . . . what's his favorite flavor?"

"Moose tracks. It's filled with peanut butter cups, and he'd pretend they were moose poo when I tried to take a bite." I laugh. "Then, he'd act like he was doing magic and turned them to peanut butter and chocolate. He'd let me have as much as I wanted."

She stills, spoon halfway to her mouth.

"What about you and your father?" I ask. "Did you do anything special together?"

"I've never met my father," she says, then her eyes widen.

"You told me he was a merchant and a cartographer."

She drops her spoon into the empty bowl and jumps off the counter. "I lied. When you were telling me about your father, it made me jealous. Listen, I've got to go."

My heart clenches at her admission and the fact she had to say something so personal just because of Caspian's drink. "I'm sorry."

She pauses by the door, a flicker of sadness crossing her face. "No, Rosalina, I'm sorry."

24

FARRON

It's so bright in the High Tower, it's almost offensive. Buttery morning light seeps into the room, casting a kaleidoscope of colors across the ground from the stained-glass windows.

Dayton kneels before his turquoise rose, head bent low, golden hair falling over his shoulders. His full lips are slightly parted, cheekbones sharp, square jaw clenched. *Stars, he's beautiful.* He looks like a marble statue, and I don't think even the greatest sculptures of Summer could capture his magnificence.

A dramatic rainbow plays over the hard planes of his chest. I want to place my hand there and see the colors swirl over us both. I want to run my tongue from his jaw to his ear, where I'd whisper how much I love him.

How much I still love him; despite the fact he's found his mate. I think I love him even more. Because all my love for him is trapped, burning a hole beside my heart. A fire like this could turn me to ash from the inside out. The only thing tethering me to life is Rosalina.

But instead, I walk toward him and say, "Your rose looks terrible."

A muscle feathers in Dayton's jaw. "I thought being here would help, but even the soil around it looks rotten."

I step over the briars. *The briars.* It's so strange to look at them now as help rather than the enemy. So many crisscross and tangle around the High Tower. I always believed they were stealing Castletree's magic. If

Keldarion's words are true, if the briars are keeping Castletree standing, then they're protecting the roses. *Protecting Keldarion.*

Did the Prince of Thorns never fall out of love with Keldarion? Even so, it doesn't justify what he's done over the years. The lives the War of Thorns took. Keldarion's parents, Dayton's family . . . all collateral.

"Let's see," I say, kneeling beside him, keeping far enough away so that our bodies won't brush.

Dayton's turquoise rose sags, the blossom almost touching the ground. At its base is a pile of discarded petals. The surrounding soil reeks with the sickly sweet scent of rot. This isn't good. If Dayton's rose wilts, he could be stuck as a beast forever, and no mate bond could save him. No wonder he's had such a hard time accessing his magic.

"Uh," I mutter, struggling for words. "I'm sure it'll perk up once we all pool our magic."

Dayton straightens. "You'd think it would be like Ez and Kel's. They're like me. They found their mates but their curses aren't broken, either."

Keldarion and Ezryn's roses are both wilted, but nowhere near as bad as Day's. They look like they're slowly dying . . . but not *rotting.*

"Fuck," Dayton swears and stands, storming into the one dark corner of the room. He covers his eyes, but not before I catch a tear falling down his cheek.

My self-restraint breaks and I stand, crossing to him. All it takes is the brush of my fingers against his arm for him to pull me into an embrace. His grip is crushing. His head dips to my shoulder, tears soaking my vest. I feel so guilty because being pulled close to his sun-kissed body is what I've wanted for so long. I feel like I'm on some sort of high, inhaling the salt and sand scent of his skin.

"I don't want to be a beast forever," he says in a broken rasp. "But I don't want . . ."

His voice trails off, but the unsaid word hangs heavy between us.
Her.

Because there's only one way he can save his rose. His mate's love.
Wrenley's love.

How many times have I seen him like this? How many times have I seen the great Daytonales cry? A handful of times at most. But he's never looked as broken as this.

I feel my own tears pool in my eyes, and I shake my head, feeling foolish. "Sorry, I'm supposed to be making you feel better."

Then his large hand is on my face, calloused fingers wiping away my tears. "I thought it would be better once I got Rosie back," he says hoarsely. "She was *all* I could think about, from the moment I woke until sleep claimed me. I just needed to know she was safe. But it's consuming me even more."

We're so close now, hip to hip. I can feel his every breath as his chest moves against mine. I know I shouldn't, but I ask, "What's consuming you?"

"Rosalina," he says. "You."

"Day . . ." I move to step away, but he grips me tighter.

"I slept in the library last night, and when I woke naked among the shelves, all I could think about was you two. It felt like my body was going to tear itself apart unless I could be inside of you both."

I flutter my eyes closed. "You shouldn't be saying these things. You have a mate."

His thumb brushes over my mouth, and my whole body quivers. He doesn't move away, the tip of his thumb pressing between my lips, slowly pulling them apart.

"Just one kiss, Fare," he whispers.

I blink at him. He looks almost delirious. For so many months, he's tried to be so good to Wrenley. So why now? Why is he breaking apart now?

Make him remember our love. A wicked thought crosses my mind. It sounds like Caspian. But I can't. His rose . . . Day's rose is so weak.

There's only one person who can save Dayton now. And it's not me.

"Come on, Fare," Dayton whispers. "One last kiss."

I thought every part inside of me was broken, but this shatters me even more. "We've already had our last kiss."

I turn away, my mind grasping for the memory of that moment as if it would help me hold on to him. When he found me wandering the streets of Florendel—did we kiss then? Why didn't I hold on tighter, savor the taste of his lips? Just kiss him for one moment longer.

Steps sound on the stairs. I quickly wipe away my tears, watching Dayton do the same. The door opens, and Keldarion and Rosalina walk in. Rosalina's gaze flicks between us as Keldarion holds the door for her. Her eyes are too keen to hide anything, and a wave of sadness and understanding passes through our bond.

"We'll have to stay here for a while," Keldarion says. "Without the High Prince of Spring, it will be harder to restore life to Castletree."

Rosalina usually stands to the side of us, but today, she goes to kneel before the Spring rose. "I'll see if I can do anything."

"Aren't you a little bitter, Rosie?" Dayton mumbles. "He couldn't break his curse and ran away. Left this place."

Rosalina shakes her head. "I'll find him again. My heart is resilient. I'll love Ezryn forever."

Even though she said Ezryn's name out loud, a part of me wonders if she also meant Dayton.

The Summer Prince digs his fingers into the rotten soil beneath his turquoise rose. Kel takes a place before the sapphire rose, and I take my position in front of my own. It is a bright orange, blooming amid my mate's golden briars.

"Together," Rosalina says.

The four of us bow our heads. A dam breaks within me. Magic flows into Castletree through my rose. But Castletree doesn't only take; magic flows up through me from Castletree itself, from her roots that weave deep into the earth of the Enchanted Vale.

My mind hums as we stay bent together. Magic courses around us for an hour, for two, until I forget my hands, arms, my legs. My body feels misty, and my entire self is filled bit by bit with this enchanted energy. Finally, a voice breaks through the haze in my mind.

"That's enough," Rosalina says. "That's as much as we can give."

We all fall back with a strange sort of weariness. Exhausted, but in a good way. My magic feels stronger, and as I look at Keldarion's rose, I see it has risen slightly. Surprisingly, the Spring rose has perked up too. Lastly, I look to Dayton's. The soil no longer appears rotten, the color of the petals brighter.

He sees me watching him, then smirks, waving his hand as a thin stream of water comes out and splashes me in the face. I can't help but give a small chuckle, especially when I hear Dayton's own booming laughter. With a mischievous grin, he shoots another spray of water toward me.

"Seems like the Summer Prince has found his magic," Keldarion says, freezing the stream. Dayton flashes a grin at him.

The earlier weight feels lifted, even though all we've bought for Dayton is time. Renewing his magic hasn't changed anything.

Frantic footsteps sound on the stairs, and we lurch to our feet. Keldarion crosses in two steps to Rosie and clutches her against him.

Rintoulo, the butler, bursts open the door with an anxious expression.

"What is it?" Keldarion growls.

"Master," Rintoulo gasps, "a visitor just came through the Autumn door. It's Rosalina's father."

25

KELDARION

We rush down the stairs, Rosie at the forefront. Her every movement is frantic, nearly tripping over the briars that lace the stairway, pricking herself on a thorn as she pulls open the door. But as we run out to the mezzanine above the entrance hall, she slows. Tears shimmer in her eyes as she covers her mouth. "Papa!"

George stands in the hall below, looking around with his usual expression of wonder. It's the same countenance he wore the first night I ever set eyes on an O'Connell. If only I knew how much throwing that old man in prison would change my life. Regardless of what Marigold thought of me in that moment, I can never regret it.

He wears a white nightrobe, and his feet are bare, but his face is shaved, evidence of the fine care he's received in Autumn. His blue eyes are full of such life that one would never know he was previously bedridden.

A smile breaks across his face as he sets his sights on Rose, and his shoulders relax. "My girl."

"Papa!" She takes the stairs two at a time, dashing across the hall and into his arms. Love and happiness wash over me through our bond, and I can't help my own smile. Farron and I exchange contented looks, then head down the stairs toward them, Dayton trailing at our heels.

A strange shiver runs down my spine, and I look up to see a large cluster of briars by the bottom of the stairs. Caspian sits atop them, dangling one leg down, eating a plum. He watches Rosie's reunion with a bemused expression.

"You're all right?" Rosie asks, putting her palm to George's forehead.

"I feel just fine," he chuffs. "A bit groggy, I suppose. I opened my eyes, feeling like I'd been away for a hundred years."

"You mean, been asleep," Rosie says.

George shakes his head. "No, it didn't feel like sleeping at all."

Before he can say more, a few members of the staff rush over to greet him. Many of them have gathered in the doorways, delighted smiles on their faces. Though George only stayed at Castletree for a short time, he had the same effect as Rosalina on everyone who lives here, their open hearts making people instantly feel welcome in their presence.

Farron, Dayton, and I hang back, waiting for our own turns to say hello to the old man. I find myself straightening, checking my shirt for wrinkles—of which there are plenty—and attempting to smooth back my hair. Farron, always presentable, chuckles at me.

Something catches the corner of my eye. A sudden movement in the doorway leading to the dining room. The acolyte from Queen's Reach Monastery pokes her head out from behind the corner. What was her name? Winnie? Wirley? No, Wrenley. That's right. I suppose I should know it now that she's Dayton's mate.

I start to look away from her, but something in her gaze makes me pause. Her short brown hair falls over her blue eyes, but her stare remains transfixed on Rosalina and her father. There's a sense of bewilderment to her, as if laying eyes on a gryphon or a winged horse or some other make-believe story from a children's tale.

With hesitant steps, she creeps out from the doorway and enters the hall, staying behind all the staff waiting to greet George. Her movements are stiff, as if she's in pain as she takes each step. But her eyes—those huge blue eyes—remain entirely focused, unblinking.

I nudge Dayton in the ribs. "Is your mate all right? She looks upset."

Dayton glances her way for half a second, then shrugs. "She's fine."

Wrenley's eyes grow bigger, now shining. Her hands form into fists. She starts to shoulder her way through the crowding staff.

Caspian jumps down from the briars above us, lithe as a cat. He says nothing to me but pushes past the staff and snags the acolyte's wrist.

"What the fuck are you doing?" Dayton lunges forward. He grabs Caspian by the back of his tunic and pulls him away from Wrenley. "Don't touch my mate."

Caspian yanks himself loose of Dayton's grip and smooths the lining of his coat. Then he looks up at Dayton through his lashes with the smarmiest grin I've ever seen him muster. "Oh, Sunshine, I *live* to touch your mate."

Dayton pulls back his fist.

"Wait!"

The cry halts Dayton an inch away from Caspian's nose. It's George, pushing through the crowd to get to the two of them. Out of the corner of my eye, I notice Wrenley retreating and quickly dipping back into the dining room.

"What's happening, Papa?" Rosalina asks.

George stands between Dayton and Caspian, then places a hand on Caspian's face. Caspian sucks in a deep breath, body going rigid, expression . . . nervous? Is that possible for Caspian?

"These past few months, I've lived inside of dreams," George says. "Watching moments play out that are so familiar, it's as if I've lived them, yet when I search my memory, they're like stories from a book I read about myself. Sometimes, I saw things that felt outside of my own being. Towering green crystals."

"Go on," Rosalina urges.

"I saw Anya's reflection in those crystals." George places his other hand on Caspian's face. His brows lower. "And this boy was looking back at her."

26

ROSALINA

"I saw her. Anya. Trapped between the crystals, speaking with this raven-haired lad." Papa's hands tighten on Caspian's face. "What do you know of her? Tell me!"

My chest heaves rapidly. I place a hand on my father's arm to lower his grip away from Caspian. Is what Papa saying the truth? Is my mother alive and has Caspian spoken to her? Or are these the ravings of a sick man?

I hold Caspian's gaze. His own chest moves quickly, in time with mine. He doesn't speak, doesn't even blink.

"It's true," I breathe. "You knew where my mother was and you never told me."

A symphony of low growls erupts behind me, and I turn to see three wolves stalking toward us. Rage exudes from each of them, from the pulled-back maw of the Winter wolf, revealing his icicle fangs, to the trembling fire ruff of the Autumn wolf, flames licking each step. The Summer wolf makes my heart seize; Dayton's wolf looks like a ship-wrecked beast, the golden fur dripping briny water, tangles of seaweed and shells encrusting his body.

"You knew where the Queen of the Vale was this whole time?" Keldarion growls. The staff scatter before this monstrous pack, and even Papa staggers away. "All these years, you've let her rot?"

My father said he saw green crystals; I've seen them, too. They belong to Sira. Which means my mother is in the Below.

I hold out my hand to stop the three wolves from getting any closer to Caspian. He's backed up against the wall, not even daring to wield his sharp tongue.

The wolves stop at my command. I stride toward the Prince of the Below and unleash my rage upon him.

Golden briars surge out of the ground, sending pieces of the stone floor flying. I fashion my thorns sharp as daggers and explode them all around Caspian. A prickly cage spikes into the wall, imprisoning him, the thorns all inches from his skin. He flinches back, throat bobbing. His fear only fuels my anger.

"All this time, you've known who I am. What I am," I breathe, words choked with sorrow and rage. "You *know* what my family means to me. What my mother means to me. How could you keep this a secret?"

"Because he's never been on our side," Dayton growls. "Ezryn's right. We should gut him while we have the chance."

"Silence!" I yell, and my voice booms through the entrance hall. I point at Caspian. "Be honest, Caspian. Because right now, the only reason I can think why you wouldn't tell me is because everything has been a lie. Whatever goodness you have shown me was all fake. Whatever feelings you made me believe you had—"

"It's not fake, Rosalina," he breathes. Caspian closes his eyes and sighs. "Yes, I've known the whole time. I've spoken to your mother in the morning, then come and listened to you cry from missing her in the evening and I never told you." He shoots a glare toward Papa. "If it were in the Fates' designs, I never would."

A scream erupts from my throat, and I shoot my hand forward. One of my thorns grows longer, jerking right against his Adam's apple. "You lied to me!"

"I never lied to you," he whispers. "I just never shared."

"A lie by omission." My emotions roil in my chest: hurt and betrayal and anger and, somewhere deep underneath them, relief because *she's alive, she's alive, she's alive!*

The wolves flank me, and I lace my fingers through Kel's fur on one side and Farron's fur on the other, the juxtaposition of cold and heat shocking.

Caspian breathes shakily through his nose. "Listen, Rosalina. It does you no good to know this truth. It will only torture you. Your mother is imprisoned. She has been for decades. There is *no* way to break her out. It would be suicide to even consider it." His eyes flash. "I will not tell you how to find her, not even if my life depends on it. For what awaits down in the depths where she is kept is a fate worse than death."

I snarl and throw my hand forward again, inching that thorn harder and harder against his neck. A drop of blood blooms on his skin, and he sucks in a breath.

One more push and . . .

Someone puts a hand on my shoulder. I turn to see Papa. His face is so pale, eyes sunken. I drop my hand. My golden briars wither, and Caspian falls to the ground, clutching at his neck.

Papa needs me right now. Caspian is . . .

Caspian is no different from what he's always been. A spider, spinning truths, waiting for any stupid fly to stick to his words.

I meet Caspian's shining gaze. "You have until tonight to tell us everything you know or else I will let my mates decide what to do with you. A Princess does not treat with traitors."

Arm around my father, I stride from the entrance hall, leaving Caspian to the wolves.

27

FARRON

I feel oddly light as I walk through the halls, hands in my pockets. Of course, my heart aches for Rosie, for the betrayal she was so certain would never be done to her. But my mind, on the other hand, feels alight.

The Queen is alive, and Caspian knows where she is.

It's like finding a textbook that's fallen through the cracks, the one that has exactly the chapter you need. Or finally translating the last cipher and the whole puzzle becoming clear. The information is *here*. There are answers to be had.

It's just a matter of clicking the pieces into place.

After Rosalina gave her ultimatum, the Prince of the Below had skulked off, and the rest of us had separated.

No one will go looking for him, I know that. Dayton hates him, Rosie's furious, and Kel's loyalty has been proven misplaced once again.

So, if anyone's going to turn the Prince of Thorns to our side, it's going to have to be me.

I remember when he cornered me at his birthday party down in Cryptgarden. *You and I are alike, Farron,* he had told me. I hadn't wanted to believe it. Wouldn't accept that I could be anything like that traitor. But now I understand that it goes beyond who lives above or below the surface.

Maybe Caspian wasn't wrong.

I'm not sure why I decide to try the library first, but that's where I find him. He's lying on a table, staring up at the mural on the ceiling, and tossing an apple up and down in the air.

He doesn't fit here, his sharp edges too shadowy for the bright oranges and yellows of the library. I quiet my steps so as not to alert him to my presence and lean an elbow against a bookshelf.

Caspian has dropped his black cloak, which lies like pooled oil on the floor. In contrast to his usual attire, his shirt seems too casual, just a loose black shift, the laces undone to his breastbone. Dark hair spills over the edges of the table. His mouth, usually twisted in a smirk of some kind, is set in a firm line.

He looks . . . sad.

I can understand what drew Kel and Rosie to him in the first place. Even for the fae, he is an otherworldly beauty.

One of the books I'm leaning against slides out from under my elbow and clatters to the floor. I lose my balance, barely catching myself on the shelf.

Caspian sits up, startled. When he sees me, he rolls his eyes then lies back down, continuing his game of catch with the apple. "Has the great High Prince of Autumn come to chastise me?"

"No," I say, attempting to regain my composure. "I happen to like libraries."

"Sure, sure, that's why you're here." His sigh seems to reverberate throughout the entire library. "It's a hopeless cause."

"What?" I walk over and lean against the table he's on.

"Saving the Queen." Caspian doesn't look at me, still focused on his apple. Up, down. Up, down. "I know it's so much more entertaining to imagine me as your perfect villain, entrapping the bloody Queen of the Vale in my dungeons Below and manipulating all of your gnat-like minds. But that's not why I kept the truth from Rosalina. From any of you." He catches the apple, and his fingers turn white around it. "Saving her is a hopeless cause. I should know. I've tried."

I stare at him. All these long decades, I've hated this man. Hated him for how he lied to Kel, for the war he brought upon the Vale, for the lives of so many of our loved ones who paid the price for his deception.

At the same time, he's kept Castletree standing where we could not. He's saved Rosalina's life and he's here, pouting on a table in a castle of monsters that want to kill him, instead of running back to Below and telling his mother everything he knows.

He reminds me of someone. A boy who hid in an alder tree. But his hideaway is not a place, but a mask he wears around everyone to keep them from understanding who he truly is.

"Nothing to say?" Caspian throws the apple up in the air again.

I catch it, bring it to my lips, and take a bite. "I understand now."

"Understand what?" he spits.

"You, Caspian, are afraid."

He sits up, scoffing. "If you're not, then you're more foolish than I thought, little pup. You have no idea what my mother is planning."

I duck in front of him. "Then enlighten me."

"What good would it do? Even with your curse broken, you're no match for her. There's no winning this fight. Best we can do is stay alive. I'm trying to keep you fools that way, and stars know it's no easy task."

"So, let me get this straight." I take another bite of apple right in Caspian's face. "The Prince of Thorns, renowned for his love of games and wagers, is too afraid to even check the stakes?"

Caspian pushes on my chest and shoves away from me, stalking toward the book stacks. "Listen to me. This is where you all have it wrong. You think Sira is the one who needs defeating. But it's not her you should be afraid of."

"Then who?"

He looks back and smiles. "It's me."

"Why, Caspian? If you wanted to kill us, you could do it right now. Use your thorns to crush Kel, Dayton, and Ezryn's roses. Without them, you could take me out easily. You won't do it, whether because you're insane and just like to torment us or because of some sort of strange sense of loyalty you have. So why should we be afraid?"

Caspian grabs a book, flips it open, tosses it over his shoulder. "I told you to make me human. How's that going, professor? Any spells in any of these? A curse, even? Fuck, I'll take a bargain if it would work." Book after book he opens, slams shut, throws behind him. I cringe each time the spines hit the hard floor.

Finally, I can't take it anymore. I drop the apple and rush over to him. I snatch the next book he picks up out of his hands and place it back on the shelf. He goes to grab another one, but I snag his wrists and hold them still. "You don't have to be afraid of this," I say quietly.

He sneers down at where our skin touches. "Of what? *Holding hands?*"

"Of telling me one true thing about you." I offer him a crooked grin.

"Come on. You already think we're incompetent idiots. What am I going to do with one little secret about you?"

The moment stills between us. Neither of us moves. He's considering it.

Then, he looks up at me and his eyes are pure green. Emerald flames flicker over where our hands touch. Instead of radiating heat, it's like they burn with *power*, their fuel the very energy between us.

"There are things beyond your comprehension, Farron, son of Autumn. Entities that make queens seem like commoners. My entire existence is to be a conduit for this kind of force. I was made to bring about the end of the Vale as we know it." His voice becomes a whispered breath, and then he blinks, eyes returning to lavender. The flames around our hands flicker out. "I cannot let this happen."

I take a shaky inhale. "If you're human, Sira won't be able to use you."

"Can you do it?"

"No." I turn the corner and walk to a different bookshelf.

"Farron!"

Caspian runs after me, nearly bumping into my back. I pluck a book off a shelf, a very special book. The one Caspian stole from the alder tree. "There's only one person who can."

"I have asked her and asked her and asked her," Caspian says. "Aurelia cannot turn me."

"Then she's a better liar than you." I flip open the book, filled with lost tales of the Queen. "First evidence: the people of Aerantheis. She changed them from fae to sirens. Second evidence: the people of Calandorin. She turned them from fae to birds. Third evidence: the princes of Castletree. She changed us into something beyond fae, beyond animal." I slam the book into his chest. "The Queen can turn you. But you're going to have to break her out of prison first."

I hold my breath as I walk back to the table he'd first been lying on. For a long minute, he does not follow. Then, like a skulking cat, he appears from behind me, eyes wide and questioning. "It can't be done."

"What? Rescuing her?"

"Yes," he says. "It's impossible."

I lean back on the table in the position he previously was in. "Oh yeah? Like how making golden briars is impossible? Or thorns holding up all of Castletree? Or Kel actually admitting to someone he was wrong? I don't know about you, but we seem to like to do the impossible."

"It's suicide."

"Sounds like waiting for your mother to turn you into some evil god bomb is suicide, too."

Caspian kneads the bridge of his nose. "You're not listening to me. My mother is vicious. If she finds out I'm plotting against her, her vengeance could—"

I sit up, grab his wrist, and glare at him. "I don't care what your excuse is, Cas. My mother was the bravest and most generous woman to ever live. She's dead. Dead because of your mother and whatever magic she's letting into the Vale. You and I may both be absent a mother's love now. But not Rosalina. If you're too afraid to try for yourself, then do it for her. Give her the family you and I will never have again."

We stare at each other, matching scowls and heavy breathing. Caspian tears out of my grip and stalks to the window, looking over the Briar. I walk toward the exit. "Think about it, Cas. Work with us, break Aurelia out of prison, and take your humanhood as a reward. Then you can run away from the Vale and never think of us again. You don't have to be a great hero. But for once in your damned life, you don't have to be the villain."

28

CASPIAN

It's been weeks since I've spoken with the Nightingale alone. Not many things surprise me, but finding my adopted sister here, lurking about Castletree, is one of them. I can only imagine she's shocked to see me too.

She shouldn't be here, doing whatever she's doing. Spying, sneaking, plotting. For all her skills as an assassin, this is bold. Too bold.

My briars lift me up to the side of the castle to one of the great branches that flows out through the turrets. Like the rest of it, Castletree's roof is a mixture of the canopy of a tree and the stonework of a building. There are still leaves this high up, though dark lines of rot shoot through the wood. I felt someone using my briar pathways and came up to investigate.

Birdy sits on the edge of the branch, which is thick as a rampart, and swings her legs in the air. Dusk is setting, and the Briar is painted in strokes of brilliant pink and purple.

Fear and protectiveness war within me at the sight of her at Castletree, clad in her iridescent armor. Where did she come from? Cryptgarden? Hadria?

"What are you doing here?" I ask. "Did Mother send you to spy? Castletree isn't safe for the likes of us. You're in danger."

She doesn't say anything. I sit beside her. Her eyes shimmer, the dusky rays playing across her face. She's not wearing her usual mask, the absence of it making her look younger. Innocent, even.

I tuck a short strand of hair behind her softly pointed ear. "You look beautiful like this," I murmur.

"Shut up," she says.

"I mean it." My voice is soft. "What are you really doing here, Birdy? Spying on them? Spying on me?"

"I've been watching you," she spits. "Would you like to explain what you're doing playing nice with the enemy?"

I sigh. Farron's words from earlier sit heavy in my chest. "I know you won't believe this, but it's true. I'm trying to keep you safe."

She quickly wipes the edges of her eyes. *Has she been . . . crying?* "You're right. I don't believe you. I know how things work for people like us, Cas. We look out for ourselves. We have to."

I smooth a wrinkle in my pant leg. "I'm going to look out for you. We're family."

She scoffs and shakes her head. "We're *family*? What, you want us to act like the little, perfect, happy family they're pretending to be in there?" She gestures down, toward the castle. "They make me *sick*. Imagine giving someone that much control over your life!"

"I don't think it's so much giving control to one another but trusting in someone else. Having faith that someone will do right by you—"

"Listen to yourself!" Birdy stands and glares down at me. "What, next you'll be telling me you want to join their delusional little cult."

I jump to my feet. With Castletree's branches and the Briars in the distance, Birdy is bordered by dark beauty. Her short hair whips in the breeze, and that mouth I rarely get to see is set in a frown. I wish more than ever I could see it in a genuine smile. "Birdy."

She takes in a breath. "No, Cas. Don't say it."

"Birdy."

Tears fill her eyes. "Don't tell me you're joining them."

"I've only ever stayed for you, Birdy. You know that. I would have run away twenty-five years ago if it weren't for you."

She grabs my shirt jacket and wrings her hands around it, voice a broken rasp. "Fine! Then run! Just don't join them, Cas, don't do it." She buries her head in my chest. "Don't make me kill you."

I wrap my arms around my sister's back and hold her tight to me. "I have to do this. You know what will happen to me if I don't. Sira will bring about the destruction of everything we know, and I'll be the blade she uses to do it."

"Better to go down in flames than to submit," Birdy growls to my chest.

I close my eyes, pain striking my heart. Still, after everything Sira's done to her, she won't accept that she's always been a tool.

"Come with me," I whisper.

Birdy pulls back. "What?"

"Leave Sira. Put away the Nightingale and forget about your plots. I'll keep you safe. You don't need Mother or your metal dog. I'll look out for you, I promise—"

"Ugh!" She shoves away from me and stalks to the very edge of the branch, right where it starts to thin. "Stop it. Just shut up, okay? It's so great for you that this little crew of rabid idiots accepts you. Where would I go? Do you think they'd just open up a room for me in this creepy zoo? 'Oh, great, let's let the Nightingale stay!' No! I'd be thrown out again."

"I would never leave you—" I reach for her, but she tears out of my grip.

Pink light shines across her nose, and as she stares up at me, she looks so much like she did as a little girl, forced to grow up in the dark. "You're leaving me right now."

A sharp pang pierces through my chest. Everything I've done, all the secrets I've kept, has been to protect her. My sister, who didn't deserve to be beaten and screamed at and abused in the depths throughout her life. My sister, who loves glittery things and accidentally snorts when she laughs but can also slit a man's throat without a single thought. My sister, who's never understood just how loved she is.

"Come with me," I say again. "Help me rescue Queen Aurelia."

Birdy practically hisses, then curls away, hugging herself and shaking. "How could you do that? You're abandoning me. It's all happening again."

"Birdy," I whisper, my own voice broken with a sob. Anguish wells up inside of me, mingling with a profound sense of betrayal. But I know I have to do this. Farron is right.

Either choice is suicide. At least this option gives Rosalina a chance. Gives Birdy a chance.

Light-footed, I walk out on the edge of the branch and wrap my arms around her. She sobs loudly, desperately. There's nothing I can do but hold her.

"We don't know the truth about the Queen," I whisper.

Birdy takes a steadying breath. "I don't care, Cas. Even if I wanted to join you, I couldn't."

"That's your fear talking." I narrow my eyes. What ties her to the Below? She doesn't have the sickness like me. Loyalty to my mother, of course, but it's something else. Something deeper.

Kairyn?

The scent of salt and nectarines lingers on Birdy's hair. She must have just come from Hadria. Reporting to the so-called Emperor? *Or visiting him?*

She sinks her nails into my forearm, holding on as if for dear life. "You don't know everything, as much as you'd like to think so."

"I know this is what I have to do."

Birdy turns in my arms so she's facing me. A few leaves tremble from the tree and adorn her dark hair.

"So, are you going to tell your new friends my plan, then?"

I raise an eyebrow. "Are you going to tell Mother mine?"

We stare at each other for a long moment. Then she sighs. "Let the best child win, I suppose. I'll keep your secret, and you keep mine."

"Deal. You're playing a dangerous game. You can't pull this off forever."

"I don't need to do it forever. Just until the Summer Realm is mine."

An uneasy alliance with my sister. Another secret to keep from Rosalina. Oh well. She'll figure it out soon enough. "We'll both be traitors to Mother in our own way."

Birdy looks out over the Briar. "She wouldn't expect anything less."

I drink her in for a moment. No army, no armor, no swords. Just a girl in the sunlight.

"You should go," she says. "You don't want your little friends to see you with me."

I turn, unable to say the words I wish I could. *Goodbye, little sister. I'm sorry I wasn't able to do right by you.*

"Caspian?"

I look back. "Hmm?"

Birdy doesn't meet my gaze. Instead, she wrings her hands in her skirt. "Are you still in love with the Winter Prince?"

"Unfortunately."

She looks down. "What does it feel like?"

A breeze rustles through my hair. I cast a gaze to the side of Castletree that houses the Winter Wing, the wood blue with frost. "It's like being stuck in the eye of a storm you can't escape. It's suffocating, consuming. It's waking up every day with a weight on your chest, wondering if today will be the day it crushes you entirely. Love is continuing to drink poison because it's also the only antidote. For me, it is a battle that if he wins, I lose, and if I win, somehow, I still lose. Love is the only reason I still choose to draw breath."

Birdy is silent and still. "Oh," she finally says. "I was afraid you'd say something like that."

I stay there watching her in the dying light for a moment more, hating the world for turning my sister into a monster. Hating the world for making her fall in love with one.

29

ROSALINA

"You should really eat something, Rose," Keldarion says.

"I'm not hungry." I burrow my face into the crook of his neck.

I'm sitting on his lap in the dining room, a table of food spread before us: steaming potato leek soup, crusty rolls, a crisp salad with tomatoes, olives, cucumber, and passionfruit tarts for dessert. As delicious as it all looks, my stomach is still in knots. *This whole time you knew. You knew who I was, knew where my mother was being held.*

There's no response in my mind. Good. I don't want to talk to Caspian anyway.

"Just a few bites," Keldarion urges.

Reluctantly, I reach for one of the passionfruit tarts and nibble on the crust.

"I always get chastised when I have dessert before dinner," Dayton drawls. His words are slurred. With an important meeting on the horizon, the Prince of Summer is drunk. His plate is also empty, though he's helped himself to more than a few glasses of wine.

"Perhaps when you are as perfect as my daughter, you can get away with it," my father says. Farron chuckles at that, and even Dayton cracks a half-smile.

Keldarion leans down to my ear. "He's right. You are perfect."

I certainly don't feel perfect, but his words make me blush regardless.

My father sits at the end of the table with Farron. Surrounding their plates are rotten mushrooms, dead animal skulls, strange trinkets, feathers, and scraps of paper, all dug out of the bag Nori instructed me to give her brother. The two of them have been having great fun going through the pieces, muttering about leaching mushrooms and ancient spells.

The table feels empty, and it's not Caspian I'm missing (good riddance to the liar) or Wrenley (thankfully, Kel agreed that, despite being mates with Dayton, it isn't necessary for her to be in on all Castletree business). It's Ezryn.

I can tell through our mate bond that he's very far away. My heart cries out for his. I need to find him soon.

May I come in? Caspian's smooth voice caresses my mind. I jolt, and Kel rubs a soothing hand up and down my back.

No, I shoot back to Caspian with as much venom as I can muster.

Well, too bad. Your princes and father are idiots, and if you ever want to play happy family, you need me.

Why bother asking if you're just going to waltz in anyway, you pig? I think vehemently. "Kel, hand me a bread roll."

"Would you like it buttered?" Kel asks.

"Give me the oldest, hardest one you can find."

He shakes his head, reaching around me, and then deposits one in my hand, just as the grand doors of the dining hall open. I chuck the bread roll as hard as I can where it bounces off Caspian's thick skull.

"Nice shot," Kel says.

But I still glower. *You let me hit you.*

What can I say? His star-flecked gaze shifts to me. *I'm a masochist when it comes to you.*

Heat crawls up my neck, and I turn away.

"Close the doors, Caspian," Keldarion orders. "Sit down and prepare to tell us everything you know."

"Everything?" Caspian steps closer, his black cloak fluttering behind him like a shadow. "We'll be here a long time."

"Everything about my wife, you vile miscreant!" Papa says, voice gruff as he slams his palms down on the table.

Caspian raises a brow, a serpentine smile on his face. "Ah yes, the long-lost Queen of the Enchanted Vale. Aurelia."

Caspian eyes the chair next to Kel, so I slide off my mate's lap and onto it, so he doesn't get any ideas about taking my seat. The Prince of Thorns gives a long sigh and sinks into a chair beside me.

"Her name is Anya," my father says, but something glazes over his sapphire-blue eyes. "It was, wasn't it?"

"That's the name you always told me," I say.

"So, you're actually going to help us?" Farron asks.

"For now," Caspian says, rocking back in his chair.

Papa's eyes are wide as saucers. He's been searching my whole life for my mother, and now to speak with someone who's seen her . . . I can't imagine what he must be thinking.

"Here are the facts. Yes, I've spoken with Aurelia, but not much. It's a dangerous trek to her cell, and if I dwell too long, my mother could get suspicious," Caspian says. "Aurelia doesn't believe I'd ever act against Sira. Which is fair, figuring it's my mother who trapped her in the Below."

A collective ripple of energy pulses through the princes at the confirmation, a deep instinctual fury to protect their Queen. It surges in me too. Sira . . . I mark the name in my heart.

"Twenty-five years ago, the Queen returned to the Vale and placed her curse upon the princes," Caspian continues.

A weighty silence settles over the room. "So, it's true," Farron whispers. "The Enchantress was the Queen. We theorized this must be the case, but a part of me never truly believed the Queen would curse us."

"Why not?" Keldarion says. "We inherited her realms, her magic, her people, and returned such grace with negligence. It's no wonder she would enact retribution against us."

I look down at my hands. The same magic I used to transform my friends into birds for their rescue had been used to curse them. What else was my mother capable of?

What else am I capable of?

Caspian drums his fingers on the table. "Shortly after cursing you, Sira captured Aurelia and imprisoned her in the Below."

"How could Sira manage such a thing?" Keldarion growls.

Caspian holds up his wrist, showing the frosted thorn bracelet. "With one of the strongest forms of magic in the Enchanted Vale. That of a bargain."

"That's preposterous. Our Queen would know better than to bargain with Sira," Farron says.

"She never told me the details, though I know it was for love." His eyes flick to my father.

"She would never," Farron continues.

It's my father who says gruffly, "No . . . she would."

"What are you saying, Papa?" I ask.

My father's eyes are a deep well of memory. "I do not know this Sira, but I know my Anya. She was rash and bold, and there was never anyone quite as clever as her. It was that cleverness that often got her in the most trouble. Her confidence would get the best of her, but I was always there to bail her out."

"Look, it doesn't matter how she got there, the problem is that's where she is. Sira's got her in the deepest part of the Below, caged in a labyrinth filled with traps, in an impenetrable prison," Caspian says, and then he turns to me, nothing but blazing stars in his lavender gaze. "This is why I never told you, Princess. There's no way to get her out."

I stare him down. "Well, Caspian, I've read thousands of stories, and in none of them is the damsel ever left in the dungeon. We *will* rescue my mother."

A FEW HOURS LATER, the dining room table has transformed into a diorama of the Below, represented by various soups, bread rolls, fruit, and vegetables. Currently, we're bent over a bowl of potato soup, which represents the Green Flame pool Cas filled us in about. Apparently, now we've got undead skeletons milling about the Below, and their creator chomping at the bit to join them.

Across the table, my mother is represented by a passionfruit tart trapped in a prison of celery sticks. The celery sticks are, of course, the green glowing crystals Sira is using to siphon her magic. A line of them crosses the table back to the deadly Green Flame pool.

"I'm telling you," Caspian says again, "not even a divine weapon could break these crystals. They grow from the ground like trees, yet they're indestructible."

"What about the pool? Can we break apart its structure?" Keldarion asks.

"Maybe," Caspian says. "That's just rock, but it would take a great deal of magic, and you wouldn't want to be anywhere around that liquid when it's spilling out. Even if we destroy the pool, Sira could just drain more and more life from Aurelia and start again."

"So, we need to get Anya out," my father says, staring intently at the tart as if it's really his wife.

"We will, Papa."

"Well, isn't this jolly fun?" Dayton says, voice near incomprehensible from wine. "After this, let's make the Sun Colosseum out of bread rolls and drown a carrot Kairyn in soup. That'll certainly get him out of my realm."

"At least we're trying to figure this out, Dayton," Farron snaps.

"And how far we've come." Dayton leans across the table to reach for the wine.

His movements are clumsy, and he knocks an empty carafe over. It rolls, toppling the potato soup and celery crystals. They spill across the table, right into Nori's treasures.

Farron yells, desperately trying to salvage the supplies, as the celery sticks hit the dark mushrooms. They turn black, shriveling up. "Dayton, you've made such a mess!" Farron shouts.

I watch the wilted piece of black celery that touched the mushroom. Its darkness spreads from one celery stick to another.

"Wait," I say. "I think Dayton might be on to something."

"I am?" Dayton says, blinking doe-eyed at me.

"Yes." Quickly, I reassemble the celery crystals, making sure the path is connected all the way to my mother's prison, then, using a napkin, I pick up a mushroom. "Tell me about this, Fare."

"They're called the leach mushroom," he says. "They only grow on a few select islands in the Byzantar Isles. This species thrives by draining energy from nearby plants or animal carcasses."

"All right." I place the leach mushroom on one piece of celery. Instantly, it turns black, before sprouting to the next one, then the next, until the rot shoots across the table and devours the sticks surrounding the tart.

"She's free!" my father gasps.

"Congratulations, you destroyed some vegetables." Caspian rolls his eyes. "These crystals are formed from the Green Flame's power and infused with Aurelia's magic. It'll take more than a little mushroom to destroy them."

"Maybe there's a way we can find out if it will work," Farron says softly. "Wait here."

Dayton stills, probably sensing the same seriousness in Farron's tone as I do. Farron returns shortly and sets a bundle of cloth on the table. Slowly, he pulls back the edges to reveal Perth Quellos's shattered crown. The one he used to harness the Green Flame's magic and raise an undead army.

"Why do you have that?" Caspian snarls, voice full of venom.

"I thought it might be useful to understand the enemy's power," Farron says.

"You don't want to know that power," Caspian says. "Trust me."

"It's broken anyways." Farron lines up the shattered pieces of crystal. "But is this the same kind of stone? Will it work for our experiment?"

Caspian chews his lip, still looking displeased. "Similar enough."

"Let's try. Now, this experiment might not show exact results. For example, I could plant the mushrooms and help them respawn with my magic. The crystals would also be buried in the earth. This, at least, will tell us if they'll have any effect."

"All right, enough science talk," Dayton urges. "Try it."

Farron places one of the mushrooms beside the crystal. We all peer over, and I let out a small gasp, seeing a bit of the crystal turn black, but it doesn't spread to the others.

"See, it's not strong enough," Caspian bites.

"But the mushrooms aren't planted in the ground," Papa urges. "A living shroom would be stronger than this dead one, don't you think? I say we give it a try."

"Technically, mushrooms aren't *planted*. They're attached to the mycelium—"

"We don't just *try* to destroy a gateway to another realm," Caspian interrupts. "We do or we die. There's no third option. The Below isn't a forgiving place for testing experiments."

Farron knocks the shards away. "Caspian's right. We can't expect something of the natural world to triumph over such ancient magic."

"Fare," Dayton says intently, and everyone stills. "You know that spell you performed in Autumn to put the dead to rest. What if you did that?"

"Intensify the mushroom's leaching ability with your own magic," I add on.

Farron shakes his head. "That spell was for souls."

"So, rewrite it." I grab his hands. "Change the story. Change how the magic works."

His auburn hair falls in his eyes as he shakes his head. "Reworking a spell that powerful . . . I'm not talented enough for that."

"Now who's afraid?" Caspian drawls, grabbing more celery to place around Aurelia.

Farron's gaze lingers on him, before he whispers, "Fine. I'll try."

"It's settled!" My father beams. "We need two teams. Farron, obviously, will go to the pool."

"I'll have to go with you," Caspian says. "You'll never get into that chamber without my help."

Farron sneers but stays quiet.

"The second team," my father continues, "will be waiting to get Anya when the chain reaction breaks her cage."

"Oh yes, traversing the deadly labyrinth in the pits of the Below," Caspian says. "I'm sure you'll have lots of volunteers for that."

"I'll go," Keldarion says. "The Queen cursed me because I dishonored my role as the Protector of the Realms. I will defend her husband at all costs."

Warmth swirls within me at the protectiveness in Kel's voice.

"I'll go with them," I say.

Caspian levels me a glare, then slowly uncrosses his boots and stands, looking down on me. "Too bad for you, Princess. You haven't heard my one condition for offering my help."

"What is that?"

"If there is to be a foolhardy rescue, you are not going."

"That's bullshit." I wave my arms in the air, looking at the rest of the princes for support. "If my mother is in the Below, I have to go find her."

Caspian just sits back down, crossing his legs and looking bored. "Then find someone else to help."

Anger bubbles within me.

"Rose," Keldarion says, "it will be dangerous. I know you could handle it, but the Queen's magic lives in you. You're the Vale's final hope."

"I have barely a fraction of the Queen's magic," I say, even though I understand his reasoning. "My bow was the most powerful thing I had, and Kairyn stole that."

Dayton perks up for the first time all evening. "Then take it back."

"How would I do that?"

His smile is dazzling. "By winning Kairyn's games. Enter with me in disguise, and we'll win your bow. Once it's in your hands, you can use it to take down Kairyn and the Nightingale."

"Ezryn is in Summer," Keldarion says. "He's searching for you. Return to Summer with Dayton and find Ez. The three of you can work on liberating Summer while we rescue the Queen."

Despite the sense of this plan, I can't help casting a glare at Caspian simply because I don't like being told what to do.

Keldarion looks down at Dayton, tone serious. "Take Wrenley with you as well. You know what you need to do to reclaim your realm."

Dayton's only answer is a tight nod.

"Good," Caspian says. "Glad we've got that all figured out."

"If Ezryn were here, he'd tell me this was all a ploy to lure the High Princes to the Below," Keldarion says softly.

Caspian's smile darkens. "If Ezryn were here, he'd try and remove my head from my shoulders."

The thought of Ezryn hating Caspian so much makes my stomach twist into knots. Though to be fair, I'd felt my own fair share of rage against Caspian earlier.

"I can take Farron down with me by thorns," Caspian says, "but the only way through the labyrinth is to walk. You'll find your magic will dwindle the closer you get to her enclosure. You can find your way there from a path at the very bottom of the Great Chasm."

"Good thing I've never needed magic on my adventures," my father says with a twinkle in his eye.

"Let us say the plan works. How do you suggest we escape once we've freed the Queen?" Keldarion asks.

"With this." Caspian pulls a small seed from his breast pocket. "Plant this and it'll return you to Castletree."

Keldarion takes the seed carefully, tucking it away. "We're counting on you."

"Don't think this is more than it is. I just don't want some green tyrant destroying the Vale," Caspian sneers. "My mother cannot find out I'm helping you."

"It's finally happening." My father dabs his eyes. "Anya, I'm coming."

Slowly, I reach out and clasp Dayton's hand. "And we will free Summer."

30

CASPIAN

I sit on the edge of the pond in Castletree's gardens, staring into the clear water. She approaches like a sunrise, a subtle warmth slowly crawling up my skin until my whole body glows like a damn star. *Mate.* My mate.

Not that she has any idea, or if she does, she keeps that part of herself hidden.

I can't blame her. I wouldn't want to be my mate either.

"Caspian." Rosalina waves her hand, and my briars uncoil, making a path for her. The twilight paints her in a hazy orange, pink, and gold that filters through her gossamer skirt.

The stars must have been feeling particularly cruel when deciding to pair me with someone like her. How can we be mates? My blood is devouring flames and wicked shadows. Rosalina is light and love and beauty.

It's better if she doesn't know. Besides, if Farron is right and Aurelia can turn me human, what will happen to our mate bond? Perhaps fate will bestow upon me a small mercy and break the bond, so neither of us will have to be burdened with it. Though, I assume I won't be so lucky. It was all too easy to speak in her mind and feel the pulse of our connection, even when her faedom was trapped within her. Not to mention, I suspect certain humans may hold more magic within them than they think. Rosalina's lineage, especially.

"Quite the retreat," Rosalina says, sitting on the opposite side of the pond from me.

After everything that's transpired today, I'd needed to be alone. The last place I wanted to go was back to the Below. So, Castletree's gardens seemed as good a spot as any. Not that there's much garden besides my thorns now.

"I didn't even know there was a pond here," Rosalina continues.

The water is nearly hidden beneath curled briars. It would be impossible to get to without asking the briars to move. But I left a gap in this particular thorn bush, letting rainwater feed it, and surprisingly, after all these years, the water is still clear.

"What can I say?" A smile crosses my face. "I like to protect beautiful things."

Rosalina lets her hand rest on one of the briars, nose crinkling in concentration. She's thinking of my secret that's not quite a secret anymore. I can only hope the princes keep it to themselves. If my mother ever found out . . . it would be the end of everything.

"The briars at Castletree help hold the structure up," I explain. "I had to cast them wider, using the surrounding land to help feed life back into the castle. I'm powerful, but not powerful enough to keep Castletree standing on my own."

"It hurts you," Rosalina says. "The rot . . ."

"You mean my delightful black goo?" I say, rubbing my nose absently. "Yes, well, that has happened since I was a child. I can't survive above ground forever. Using so much energy on Castletree speeds up the process."

The warm summer air breezing through the briars tugs at the curls in her hair. "Are you okay right now?"

"As okay as I can be. I don't have to channel as much energy into the briars when the princes are here, sustaining Castletree with their magic. I might even get a couple days on the surface, if I'm lucky. But who knows? Every dawn is different." I shrug. There's a flash of concern on her face, so I quickly add, "How did you find me, Princess?"

"Marigold told me you went outside and then I . . ." She trails off because the answer isn't in words. It's a feeling. Of course she knew where I was.

"Well, I know you haven't forgiven me," I say, tossing a pebble into the water. "So, why are you here?"

"I'm here—"

"To make sure I'm not leading your mates into a trap?" I finish for her.

"Once you all go down Below, you have the power, Caspian," Rosalina says. "It's up to you to protect them."

"As soon as Kel and George enter the labyrinth, they'll be beyond my help. Farron, however . . . I'll do my best."

She chews her lip, gazing at me.

"If you don't trust me, trust in our common enemy. I don't want the Green Flame coming to the Enchanted Vale any more than you. Freeing the Queen will ensure Sira can't siphon her magic again."

"If my mother is free," she says, "she'll surely take back Summer and Spring and the Below will lose control over those realms."

"Kairyn and the Nightingale will lose control," I clarify. "What do I care about the surface world? I can't even survive here."

Rosalina shakes her head; we both know there's nothing I can truly say to get her to trust me. "You should have told me, Cas. About who I was, where I came from. You should have told me about my mother."

"You know why I didn't," I say.

Her face scrunches in anger and she tosses a large rock into the water. "Yes. No. It's impossible to know what's going through your mind. God, even now you can't admit this is *where* you want to be. You can't even fully take our side."

I crawl closer to her and grip her trembling hands. "I'll do everything in my power to bring your mother back and protect your mates, Rosalina. How about that? I promise you."

"It's a start." A few drops of her crystal tears fall onto our intertwined hands. "You're still keeping secrets from me, aren't you?"

"Many, but only two you'll truly hate me for," I answer truthfully.

"Does my mother know I'm here?"

"I've told her what I can, but it's dangerous to exchange too much information."

Rosalina nods. I crawl even closer to her until her breath caresses my face. "Do you forgive me?"

Something devious flashes in her smile, teardrops still dotting her full lips. "On one condition. You allow me to do something to you."

"Anything," I say instinctually. My body, my heart, my soul . . . it all belongs to her. She can do anything she wishes.

"Wonderful," she whispers.

Her lips are only a breath away from my skin as she moves closer, and it takes every ounce of self-control not to grab her and devour her here.

"Caspian," she whispers, fingers digging tight into my jacket. "I hope you know how to swim."

Then my mate grabs me and pushes me into the pond, where cold water embraces me and the only thing I hear is her laugh.

31

ROSALINA

"Can you shut up and get me something dry to wear?" Caspian snarls over Keldarion's boisterous laugh. We stand in the doorway to the Winter Prince's room.

"What can I say?" I explain. "The path to my forgiveness was pushing him into the pond."

Caspian just grumbles, shuffling inside, dripping water onto the ice-covered floor.

"You know where to look," Keldarion says, ignoring Caspian and crossing to me. He scoops me up and dips his lips to my neck. "I've been looking forward to tonight."

"Me too," I whisper back. Since I spent my first night at Castletree with Farron, and my second at my sleepover, we agreed tonight, before we depart tomorrow, I'll spend with Keldarion. He won't turn into a wolf as long as we're touching.

I've been wondering all day if we'll have a repeat of the night he gave in and touched me with his magic. It's too much to hope that he'll finally decide to complete our mate bond.

But with Caspian here, on our side . . .

"I'll send him away," Keldarion whispers.

"He can stay," I reply, "if you want."

"If I want?" There's a hint of mischief in Kel's voice. "What do you want, Rose?"

As if we sense the other's intent, we both turn to Caspian, a large towel wrapped around his shoulders as he stands before Kel's armoire. He turns to us, a surprised, almost shy look on his face as he sees our gazes on him. Lavender eyes, full lips parted, wet tendrils of hair falling in waves across his eyes—he is beautiful.

The expression doesn't last more than a heartbeat, turning instantly to the cocky, arrogant grin I know so well.

"Oh, I see now, Flower," Caspian says with a serpentine smile. "You know, there are easier ways to get me out of my clothes."

The Prince of Thorns drops the towel and saunters to the bed. He changed while Kel and I were talking, and Keldarion's pants, too large, hang dangerously low beneath his razor-sharp hip bones. A thin line of hair snakes up to his belly button. His chest is cut with lean muscles that rise to his elegant neck.

He must know I'm checking him out, but I realize this is the first time I've seen the Prince of Thorns completely shirtless. He runs a hand over the velvety sheets. "I've been particularly fond of this bed lately. It's much comfier than the one in Frostfang."

"Did you two spend a lot of time together while I was gone?" I raise a brow.

Still holding my hand, Kel leads me to the armoire where he pulls out a silken nightdress. "I was willing to make any alliance in order to find you."

"He kicked me out of his bed on full moons, though." Caspian pouts. "And he only let me kiss him once."

Keldarion grabs my wrist. "I'm sorry, Rose. He surprised me and—"

"It's okay, Kel, really," I say, meaning it. As much as my trust in Caspian comes with strings, there's no jealousy or possessiveness when it comes to the three of us. Kel turns around, blocking my body with his as I change into the nightdress. It's the color of silvery moonlight, the fabric clinging to my body like a second skin. Delicate snowflake-patterned lace adorns the bust and hem of the dress. I step out from behind Keldarion and enjoy the way Caspian's eyes widen, the slight tremor of his lips as he takes me in.

"You kissed me and then Kel?" I say, placing a hand on my hip and staring pointedly at Caspian. "Seems like you're obsessed with us."

"Undyingly." Something in the dark tone of his words makes my heart skip.

"Though, I'm curious." Caspian puts his hands behind his head.

"Whose kiss did you prefer, Rosalina? I think you should give my lips another try, just to make sure you have it memorized."

"Trust me, I do," I say, meaning the words to come out in a snarl, but instead they're hardly anything but air.

Keldarion's predatory gaze shifts between us, and my possessive, jealous mate doesn't seem possessive or jealous at all. Instead, he links his large hand with mine and leads me toward the bed. He's changed as well, now wearing a low-cut shirt and pants.

I crawl into the bed, tucking myself beneath the covers. I'm careful not to touch Caspian as Kel shifts in on the other side, making the whole bed sink with his weight.

"What are you still doing here?" he growls to Caspian without any real venom behind the words.

Caspian tilts his head, then crawls over the top of me to get closer to Keldarion. "First, say whose kiss you liked better. Mine or Rosalina's."

"Rosalina's."

Caspian's smile deepens as if that was the answer he was expecting. He turns to me, driving his knee between my legs over the blanket. "In that case, Rosalina should give me lessons."

Lightning-fast, Keldarion grabs Caspian's jaw and drags him away from me. "You're being annoying. Purposely." He flicks Caspian away, and the Prince of Thorns lands in a heap on the other end of the bed.

My own sneaky smile spreads across my face, and I turn from Caspian, crawling into my mate's lap. "He's obsessed with kissing. How about we show him how it's done?"

Blue fire simmers in Keldarion's gaze as he grips the back of my neck and pulls me against him. He moves agonizingly slow, lips velvety. He doesn't even open his mouth, keeping the kiss chaste. A wave of anticipation lingers in my belly, yearning for more. I know Caspian is watching, if only by the deep male groan he emits.

With gentle pressure, Keldarion parts my lips, his tongue slipping into my mouth, filling me with the cool taste of frosted berries and pine. His large hand grips my neck, thumb a gentle pressure at the column of my throat, my mouth and body becoming pliant as he deepens the kiss further, taking me, sucking, biting my lip. A shiver runs through my whole body when he finally pulls away, his half-lidded gaze enraptured, though I'm sure I look stunned stupid by all of it.

When I come back to myself, I turn to stare at our audience. Caspian lies leaning on one arm, but his other hand rests above the top of his pants, fingers dipping beneath the band. The thin fabric does nothing to hide his arousal.

A part of me wants to tease him, but at the sight of him watching us, all I feel is a curling desire deep within my body. Keldarion must feel it through our bond because he slides his hand down my back before cupping my bottom, fingers twisting in the fabric.

"Don't stop on my account," Caspian says.

I drag my hand down Keldarion's chest. "You could see a lot more if you'd rescind your bargain, Caspian."

"Is that what you think?" He smirks, crawling to us, then grabs Keldarion's wrist. His fingers trace the frosted thorn bargain bracelet. A replica cuffs Caspian's wrist. "Fine then. Keldarion, I rescind the bargain."

32

KELDARION

Caspian's starlight eyes are wide, smile venomous. *I rescind the bargain.* Did he just say those words? Words I've dreamed of, hoped for . . .

No. It will not work.

"Say it back," Rosalina urges, breath heavy in her throat.

I grip Caspian's slender wrist. "I rescind the bargain."

Caspian's smile deepens. Nothing happens. If anything, I only feel the thorns dig deeper into my skin.

"Wait." Rosalina looks between us, "Why didn't it work?"

"Not all bargains can be revoked by mutual agreement," Caspian says, finally dropping my hand. "We worded our bargain so cleverly. If ever there is no love between us, let this bargain melt away like snow under rain. Unfortunately for the Winter Prince, he still loves me. It's certainly not anything on my end."

"I do not," I snap at him. "You must hold some obsession with me yet."

It's a lie, of course. There's a piece of him in my heart I cannot get rid of.

"You begged me to rescind it before," Caspian says harshly, "but you must have always known it would never work. There's only two ways for you to break your curse now, Winter Prince. You kill me or you trust me."

My brash and beautiful mate wiggles on my lap, lips dipping to my neck. "He's right. We can break the curse tonight. Take me. I won't go far. I want you so badly."

Her hips press down, tempting my already erect cock. Stars, if there isn't anything I want more in this world than to slip inside of her, to let our love come together, release my magic . . .

But there are some things I want more than even that. To keep her safe.

"No," I growl and lift her off of me. "The moment our lovemaking ended, you would become his thrall, and I wouldn't be able to stop him from taking you Below. You'd be powerless to resist him, not in control of your mind or magic. Your only thought would belong to him until he releases you from the spell."

Rosalina grimaces and smacks Caspian on his bare chest. "He wouldn't do that. Tell Keldarion you won't do that."

Caspian looks to Rosalina, then me. "No, Keldarion," he says deadpan. "I'll happily sit here and watch you come into your full magic, then release your beautiful mate the moment she comes under my power."

Rosalina huffs and falls to the bed in a heap. "You could at least try to sound convincing."

Caspian just shakes his head. "He won't believe me."

That's true at least. I can have him here. I can be in an uneasy alliance. But I will not trust him with what I treasure most in this world.

"Not yet at least," I say, my own words surprising me. "Perhaps if you are true to your word and help us rescue the Queen, then we can arrange something."

Caspian looks startled, then rises on his forearms to stare at me. "Are you sure, Keldarion? Being present for your first time having sex in twenty-five years, that's quite the occasion."

I grab his jaw, thumb caressing his full lips. "Thought you'd want to be there, figuring you were there the last time."

He flushes, breaking away from me and running a hand through his hair.

Rosalina lets out a long sigh. "So, what I'm hearing is I'm not sleeping with anyone." She pulls the blankets up around herself in a dramatic display.

I exchange a glance with Caspian, and something electric passes between us, something even I don't have the power to resist. We both turn toward Rosalina.

"Here's how it's going to work," I say, and she pokes her head out from under the covers. "We can touch you, but you must be a good girl and not touch us, all right?"

Her small intake of air is the only answer.

Caspian crawls toward her, but I grip his arm, hard. "If I get any sense you're trying to manipulate our bargain for your own agenda, you will not be welcome back."

"I promise. Use me however you want," he pleads. "Just please, don't ask me to leave."

33

ROSALINA

Keldarion, Caspian and me . . . Is this really happening? All I know is my heart is thrumming in my chest, and I want this. I want *this*. If the expressions on their faces are any sign—animal-bright eyes, hungry smiles—they want me just as badly.

Kel rolls next to me, and Caspian kneels on my other side. "Ready to come out of the blankets, darling?" Kel asks.

I nod, and Keldarion slides the blanket down, revealing the silken fabric of my nightdress. Caspian lets out a small breath and reaches for me, but instead of touching my body, his long fingers caress my jaw. His features are soft, almost reverent, as he gazes down at me.

Kel might not trust Caspian yet, but I'm willing to wait as long as it takes for that trust to grow between them.

"You look nervous, Cas," Keldarion says, shooting him a pointed gaze. "She's not that terrifying."

"I'm not nervous—" Caspian snaps.

Keldarion reaches across me and grips the back of his neck, then pulls him into a rough kiss. Caspian makes a surprised sound in the back of his throat, mouth opening to Keldarion, his lavender eyes wide before they close as he sinks into the kiss.

Warmth spreads deep within me as I see them together, watching Caspian tangle his hands in Kel's wild white hair. When they break apart, they're both gasping. Kel brings his mouth to Cas's pointed ear. "Watch her face as she comes. It's the most beautiful sight."

"As I what?" I stammer.

Keldarion straightens, poking Caspian in the chest so he falls in a heap beside me. Kel's smile oozes male confidence as he crawls beneath the covers and spreads my legs. There's nothing but a lump beneath the blanket now as the Winter Prince disappears under them.

The Prince of Thorns' naked shoulder brushes mine. I inhale a sharp gasp.

Caspian turns to me, tugging on the strap of my nightdress. "I bet she doesn't have any panties on. You have such an aversion to them, don't you, Rose?"

I flush, then feel the scrape of Kel's stubble as his cheek brushes my inner thigh. I groan at the first soft flick of his tongue across my center. My back sinks into the pillows as I squirm.

Caspian lets out a gasp as well, as if he's anticipating this just as much as I am. "What's he doing?"

"He's teasing me," I moan.

Kel knows exactly what he's doing, only lightly licking me while kissing the surrounding skin, causing me to heat. My inner walls tighten and every nerve in my body craves him. Finally, he brings his whole mouth to my center and sucks. I throw my head back, grasping the sheets with one hand. With the other, I mean to do the same, but instead I grab the solid muscle of Caspian's thigh.

He murmurs something unintelligible before pulling me against his chest. Cas's lips dip to the crook of my neck, just as Kel drives his tongue deep inside me, lapping at my wet heat. An almost inhuman moan escapes me.

"How does it feel, Flower?" Caspian murmurs.

Working through the fog in my mind, I search for words. "Amazing. God, I could feel this for a thousand years."

Keldarion shifts, coarse stubble rubbing my leg, his voice muffled from beneath the blankets. "I would be here forever if I could."

Then he forcefully pushes my legs apart, diving deep inside me with his tongue. My breath matches the cadence of his mouth.

"Your heart is racing," Caspian says, drawing his hand along the top of my chest, fingers dipping beneath the snowflake lace.

I lean into the solid press of his chest against me, grasping his wrist. "Just touch me already." I guide his hand beneath my dress.

Caspian lets out a deep groan as he palms my breast. "It's like touching the clouds."

Keldarion places one of his huge hands on my thigh, gripping me tight, keeping my legs spread wide. His other hand massages the top of my clit in soft circles. "Kel," I cry out, core heating, stomach tightening. "The blankets, remove them. I need to see—"

Caspian does so with his free hand. I nearly pass out at the sight of Kel between my legs. My beautiful silken nightdress is bunched up to my stomach. The powerful muscles in my mate's back strain against his tight shirt as he sucks, sucks, sucks me harder and harder. My mind turns hazy, and I tangle my hands in his white hair.

"Fuck," Caspian swears, turning to look at me. "I have to watch you come, Princess."

My breath comes ragged. Caspian massages my breast, rubbing his thumb against my sensitive nipple. He grabs it and pulls hard.

"Cas." I swear, fingernails digging into his shoulder. He doesn't stop, palming me, pulling and tugging hard.

"Look at me as your mate makes you come," he commands, lavender eyes wild.

Kel's pace increases. I dig my heels into the mattress and grip his hair so hard, I'm surprised I don't pull it out. *God*, he feels so good. My breath is thick in my chest, my muscles tightening. Then, in a sudden rush, everything releases. A gentle shiver trembles through my body and then unfurls into a crescendo of pleasure.

Kel doesn't stop devouring me as I come apart. Caspian's hand stills on my chest, and through the white flashes of my vision, I see his expression, the wide-eyed gaze and parted lips.

My body surrenders to the moment, every muscle tensing and then relaxing in a blissful rhythm.

Keldarion crawls up from between my legs, laying his heavy weight on top of me, and I feel the evidence of his arousal pulsing hot between my legs.

"You are sensational," I breathe, kissing him, tasting my own heat on his lips.

"Trust me, Rose," he says. "It is you who is sensational. You are made of sun and honey."

Caspian's hand is still trapped between us, and I feel his heavy breath as he looks down at us. "So beautiful," is all he mutters.

"And delicious," Keldarion says before pulling Caspian into another kiss. This one seems to send the Prince of Thorns into a frenzy. His tongue drives into Kel's mouth, tasting every part of him, every part of *me*.

When he pulls away, his eyes are so dark, they almost look entirely black. They flash down between my legs, still wide open. My pussy is very much on display.

Kel tracks the movement and grips the ends of my dress, pulling it up. "As beautiful as this is, I am ready to gaze upon you in all your magnificence."

He throws the nightdress to the ground. I lie back on the plush bed, completely bare, arms above my head, hair spread out like a curtain around my face. Kel gazes down with a worshipful stare. But Caspian . . . A flush starts at his neck and works all the way up until his face is entirely red.

Kel gives him a sidelong glance. "Embarrassed, Cas?"

He throws a hand over his eyes, looking so adorable I think I might melt. "No, I—"

"Blushing for me?" I purr, raising myself up on the backs of my arms. "Do you get this red with all those fae in the Below?"

"No," he says. "They mean nothing to me."

"But I do," I whisper.

"Yes." His voice is a broken rasp.

"Why?"

He says no more, but I feel it, the unanswered question floating between all three of us. Something enchanted, something dangerous, something I'm too frightened to grasp. My heart careens in my chest so loudly—

I sit up and press my naked body against Caspian's. My breasts melt against his bare chest, my thighs straddle his hips. Then I grip his face and kiss him. Wildly, mouth open, wet and messy. I devour him the way Kel devoured me, in an I-need-you-desperately kind of way.

Caspian responds with an animalistic hunger, hands threading in my hair. He pushes me back to the bed until he's crushing me, his cock pressing through his pants to grind against my aching core. I scratch my fingernails down his back and pulse my hips up against his, desperate for the friction. He pulls away long enough to groan my name before diving back into the kiss. His hands glide up my body to caress my breasts, kneading them as we rock together.

"Fuck," Keldarion says, a broken moan.

I turn my head as Caspian licks his way to my ear. Kel's sitting on his knees watching us, his hardness evident through his loose pants. I smile at him, loopy and desperate.

"I could come just watching you two," he says.

Something wild flits through me, and I loosely thread my fingers in Caspian's hair. "I can't make you come, Kel. But he can."

34

CASPIAN

Ice-frosted kisses, powerful hands, taut muscles, and deep groans of pleasure. It all flashes before me at Rosalina's words. *But he can.* Would Keldarion truly allow me to touch him again? Cautiously, I raise my head from the crook of her neck and gaze at the Prince of Winter.

There's an almost bewildered expression on his handsome face.

"My body is irrelevant," Keldarion says. "We would both be more than happy to pleasure you until dawn."

"He's not wrong," I agree, licking from the corner of her lip to her ear. I'm rewarded with the softest mewl that has my cock hardening. Stars, I want to sink inside her. I want to be inside of her so much, I think I'll be sick with it.

But the bonds I've rebuilt with Kel these last few months have been tenuous at best. Fucking his mate before he does would certainly strain them.

Besides, if I join with Rosalina in such a way, there will be no hiding what blooms between us.

She'll know I am her mate.

Though, the way she's looking up at me now, running her long fingers along my jaw, it has me stupidly thinking . . . perhaps that wouldn't be such a bad thing.

Her swollen lips curve into a wicked smile. "What if that pleases me?"

The desire in her words ignites a lust that pulses through our shared bond. Stars, it's a wonder they don't feel me there.

"Well, if it's for you, the icy brute can't resist, can he?" I say and kiss her again because I'm not quite ready to leave this moment yet.

This wild, unexpected moment.

"What will you do, darling, while I see to your mate?" I murmur against her lips.

"Kel can give me something to keep me occupied," Rosalina says huskily.

As she speaks, I feel soft snowflakes flutter over my back and hair, and then Kel is pressing something cold and long into her palm. I sit up to examine it, then roll my eyes.

"An icicle in the shape of your dick," I say, crawling off her. "That is so very . . . you."

"Come here, Cas," Keldarion growls and grabs me around the waist.

Then his mouth is over mine, and I am lost in his wild storm. The initial contact is an intoxicating memory. No wonder I thought this kiss could save me.

Thought this prince could save me.

And as he pushes me down to the mattress, a part of me still does.

He kisses my neck before biting hard enough to bruise.

"Fucking mark me," I groan, digging my hands into his hair. "Do it again. Fuck, Kel."

His laugh is a low rumble through his chest. Lightly, he laps the sensitive skin before biting down again. My body trembles at the sensation, basking in it. So many people have tried to brand me over the years with the lash of their whips or the commands I never wanted to obey. But his scars are the only ones I want to bear.

And hers.

I turn my head to Rosalina. She's sitting up, knees spread as she gently moves the ice in circles around her pussy. She's so gorgeous.

"It's supposed to go inside you, Flower," I say.

Her lip trembles. "Just working up the courage."

I glide my hand down Kel's chest until I palm him through his pants. "Did you have to make it as massive as your cock?"

"She likes it," he smirks, "like you did."

To that, I have no response, my breath heavy in my throat at the new flood of memories. The bastard has the gall to push his hips down, pressing his length harder into my hand.

Biting my lip, I flash a look at him. "Lie on your back. Your mate wanted to see you come, and I'm of a mind to obey her."

"Good boys," Rosalina purrs.

"Be grateful of this bargain, Rose," Keldarion growls, lying on his back, his gaze never leaving hers. "Or you don't want to know what would be happening to you right now."

She presses the tip of the icicle against her entrance, body shuddering. "Maybe I do."

"Ahhh," I groan, my own cock becoming uncomfortably hard. "You're distracting me, and I've got a job to do, one I'm particularly good at. Though it's been a long while since I've sucked cock."

The tremble through Keldarion's body and Rosalina's cute gasp are more than satisfying. But it's Kel's vulnerable gaze meeting mine as I start to work the laces of his shirt that truly undoes me.

"How long?" he asks.

My fingers are still on the laces of his shirt. "You know I've fucked other fae. What do you want me to say?"

He brushes the stray hairs from my face with his knuckles.

"Fine," I continue. "I haven't sucked anyone's cock, and no one's fucked me since you. Every time I did sleep with someone, it just felt . . . empty. Like eating food but not being able to taste it. Is that what you two want to hear? Besides, I haven't been with anyone since she asked me to stop."

"You did that for me?" Rosalina brushes a tear from my cheek.

I hadn't realized she'd moved so close.

Hadn't realized I'd started crying.

Fuck, I'm so gone.

"That *is* what I wanted to hear," Keldarion says, primal command lacing his words.

Rosalina kisses my shoulder before backing away from us. "I wish I could stay between you."

"Maybe one day you can," Keldarion says. "Consider that your motivation, Cas."

"Trust me." I grab the edge of Keldarion's shirt and pull it over his head. "I'm motivated."

His chest heaves, covered with thick dark hair, scars and muscles visible beneath. His masculinity is the perfect contrast to Rose's soft figure.

I'll prove it to you, I think. We may never be able to break our bargain, but I'll prove to him he can trust me.

I just have to prove it to myself first.

Playfully biting his nipple, I work my way down his chest until I get to his pants, then quickly work them off to reveal his cock. My heart stutters in my chest as I gaze down at him. So perfect, no one in the Below has ever compared.

Of course, I was never in love with any of them.

A smile quirks on Kel's lips. "Are you going to stare at it or suck it?"

Rosalina giggles, leaning back on the pillows, returning to teasing herself with the ice. There's enough pleasure radiating from her to not feel guilty about not touching her right now.

"I was just thinking about how beautiful you are," I say. "Both of you."

Now it's their turn to blush, and I take the opportunity to take Keldarion's cock in my mouth. No teasing licks. I don't have the patience for any of that. I wrap my lips around the tip and sink deep.

Keldarion gives a deep sigh, as if he's been waiting for this for a long time, and I suppose he has. I don't think anyone's touched his cock since . . . since me.

It gives me an idea. I break off, saliva dripping down my lips. "Flower, come here."

"I said no tricks," Keldarion growls.

"No tricks," I say. "Just don't come yet."

Rosalina crawls on all fours toward us. Her heavy breasts swing in such a tempting way, I can't help but reach out and grasp one, pulling down on the nipple.

"I want to give her one taste of the most delicious Winter treat." I lick his length, prominent veins rubbing against the flat of my tongue. "Think you can hold off coming to give her one taste, Prince?"

"Y-yes," he groans, teeth clenched.

I grip Rosalina by the back of her neck and guide her down. "Open wide, Princess."

She sighs deeply as her pink lips wrap around his massive cock. Her mouth looks so small and delicate around it. She slides lower and lower, a deep moan echoing from both of them. I grab the base of Kel's cock, helping him hold back his pleasure, and fuck, she's not even close to my hand yet.

"Deeper," I command. She obeys, and I can almost make out the shape of him in her throat.

She slides back up quickly, gasping for breath, eyes wild with pleasure and more than eager to continue.

"Get her away," Keldarion groans. "Gods, Rosie, you feel too good."

"Kel," she whimpers, sliding back to the plush bed. "I want you so badly."

"I know, love. I want you too."

Guilt simmers through me. "Let's make you come, Kel."

With each deliberate stroke of my tongue, I trace the contours of his cock, feeling its velvet surface stiffen further beneath the gentle pressure. Salty precum drips into my mouth, making my lips sticky. I take him fully to the back of my throat, using my hands to play with his balls, gently squeezing the soft surface.

Keldarion's moans deepen to a rasp, and I know he's getting close when his large hand tightens in my hair. I could tease him more, but I'm as eager to taste him as he is to release. He doesn't need to ask me where to come.

He knows.

I increase my pace, slamming his cock against the back of my throat, my saliva and his precum coating the surface. My mind blurs as his pleasure nears climax.

His cock stiffens.

"Fuck, Cas," Keldarion says, broken beautiful words.

I fucking love when he calls me Cas. His cock twitches and spasms beneath my palm. In a sudden rush of sensation, his pleasure floods my mouth, salty and sweet. I pump my hand, trying to milk every last drop.

But I don't swallow like I usually would.

Keldarion's chest heaves as I rise. He looks at me, a soft expression that makes my heart stutter. But it's Rosalina I turn to next. She's watching with a similar expression, legs spread, the icicle a quarter of the way into her pussy.

I place my hands on either side of her head. *Open up*, I say in her mind, because, well, I can't use my voice right now.

She parts her lips. I lean closer, then kiss her, spilling Kel's pleasure into her mouth. She moans as she accepts it, grasping my hair.

"Oh, Cas, yes." She licks my lips for any last drop. "Kel, you taste so good."

A quick glance over at the Winter Prince shows he's just as aroused by this as we are. But I'm not done with our little Rose yet. I reach between her legs and grasp the end of Kel's icicle.

ELIZABETH HELEN

"How did you like having that enormous cock in your mouth, pretty?" I begin to push it deeper, and she squirms. "Now imagine that big cock fucking you raw, filling you so full of cum, you can't be filled any more."

Her only answer is a broken cry as I start to move the icicle in and out of her with a new rhythm, fast, then slow, then fast. "How deep can we get this, Flower? How deep do you want it?"

"Deeper," she gasps. "More, Cas."

I grin, looking down at the beautiful sight of her pink pussy being filled. Her wetness and the melting ice coat my palm, and I inch the massive shape deeper and deeper inside, feeling the resistance of her inner muscles.

"Let me soothe your heat," Keldarion says, closing the distance between us. He runs a hand along her stomach to cup her breasts. His hand sinks deep into her soft flesh, molding and unmolding the shape beneath his powerful grip.

He kisses her, no doubt still tasting his own cum on her lips. I take the opportunity to shove the icicle all the way into her. Her moan is muffled against her mate's lips. I press my palm flat against her mound, feeling her slick pleasure merge with the icy water.

"I don't know about you," I smirk, "but after all this excitement, I'm parched."

I kiss them first, their lips still locked together, before making my way down her body until I get to her center. My lips are still caked with Kel's cum, but I don't care as I press them to her entrance, cold and warm all at once. He was right. She tastes like honey and sunshine. I lick her folds, dancing my fingers around her clit.

"Oh, Cas," she whimpers. "Damn, I love this."

With each leisurely lick, I explore the contours of her pussy, tracing intricate patterns against her smooth surface. Kel was right. It would be easy to live between her legs for a thousand years. I'll never be done with the feel of her, the euphoric taste of her pleasure dripping onto my tongue. Knowing how full she is with the ice cock only spurs my excitement.

"Come on my lips, Flower." Each lick across her center is bliss, bringing me deeper into a haze of pleasure.

Keldarion grips me on the shoulders and moves me so I'm lying on the bed next to her. "Did I do something wrong?" I gasp, light spinning in my vision.

"Absolutely not." Rosalina smiles. "But there's been a change of plans."

Keldarion brings his face close to mine, wild hair tickling my shoulder. "We decided she's going to make herself come at the same time as I make you come."

Now my heart truly stops. I hadn't even heard them whispering. Or perhaps they used their mate bond to speak in each other's minds. "I always knew you two would conspire against me."

Keldarion has already gripped the too-big pants I'm wearing and easily slides them off my hips. I can't remember the last time I was this bare before someone. In the Below, I always left something on. Never showed anyone my full self.

All three of us here, naked, open, vulnerable. A part of me wants to shut my eyes, overwhelmed by it all. But then Kel is running his palm down my chest, a million memories swirling in his eyes as he looks down at me.

"His cock's as pretty as he is," Rosalina purrs. She's got the end of the ice again, working it in and out of her pussy. It's smaller than it was before, melted by her heat.

"One day maybe you'll feel how pretty this cock would be inside you," I say back.

"Keep dreaming, Cas," Keldarion says.

"Rosie's played with your toy," I say. "Now she can have mine."

Without a thought, I summon briars stripped of their thorns. Two crawl up to wrap around her ankles, spreading her legs wider, and a third probes her entrance.

"What do you say, Flower?" I smirk. "Let me in?"

Gingerly, she places the ice to the side, and I guide the briar up, letting it slide inside her and explore.

Rosalina lets out a whimpering sound, gripping the bedpost and biting her lip.

"If it's too much, you take control and stop them," I say.

"Oh god!" she says in response, writhing as the briar begins to work in and out of her already tender pussy, plunging deeper and deeper with each stroke.

"As for you," Keldarion says, "how do you want to come, Cas? My mouth or my hand?"

Butterflies flutter in my stomach, and I can hardly believe he's above me. This is terrible. I'm so far gone. "Your hand on my cock," I whisper, then point to my lips. "And your mouth here."

"Predictable," he says, lowering his weight to one arm beside my head, while his other gently caresses the contours of my length. He wraps his entire hand around it, squeezing hard as he rubs up and down. With each stroke, I feel the knots of tension unravel, melting away beneath his skilled hands.

"Kel," I whimper and reach between us to grasp his cock. "Hard again?"

"How can I not be with what you're doing to her?"

Two briars are still tight around her ankles. I seek for control of the one inside of her. Through my connection, I'm able to feel her muscles contract and tighten around it as it fucks her fast, matching the pace of Kel's hand.

"How fucking beautiful you look beneath me," Keldarion growls, kissing me with a furious passion. He rubs my cock against his own and the sensation is pure bliss.

"I can't last," I gasp. "Fuck, Kel."

"Come for me, love."

"It's been a long time since I've come," I pant, "and not been completely alone after."

Kel strokes faster now. "Oh, how I've enjoyed your little presents."

Stars, this feels so good. My head rolls back, fingers clasping the sheets. "I only did it to make you jealous." I shouldn't admit to that. No one I've been with has made me feel like this, and being in *her* presence is even more electrifying. "Did it work?"

He leans over me, chest pressing against mine, hand still furiously working my cock. "You know it did." He kisses me, teeth biting my lip hard enough to draw blood as he pulls away.

But that look in his eyes, that possessive tone that claims me—it's near enough to send me over the edge. I tilt my head to the side, seeing Rosalina strung up in my thorns, eyes rolled back to white as my magic works her. "Ready to come, Flower?"

She responds in little gasps and sobs, the only intelligible words our names. "Cas, Kel, I-I—"

I feel her body explode, my own pent-up release not able to withstand the pleasure surging through our bond. Frantically, I grasp for Kel's hard cock, needing to feel his release. It's as if something has awakened between the three of us, transcending words and language.

"Kel, Rose—"

My pleasure surges forth, a torrent of warmth spilling into Kel's palm, and I surrender to him and his touch, feeling his own release coat my body. Beside us, Rose collapses, gasping and smiling.

Keldarion kisses me, and all I feel is warmth. I wish I could grab Rosalina but it's still too soon. Is it too soon?

The reckless Winter Prince doesn't seem to care. He grabs her around the waist, lips still locked to mine, and pulls her between us. She's still gasping for air. Our hands and mouths and legs intertwine. I don't ever want to be untangled.

WE LIE breathless for what seems like an eternity. Keldarion stirs just as the dusky pink light of the impending sunset drifts over us. Kel helps us both up and into the attached privy to wash. Kel is quickest, of course, leaving Rosalina and me alone. We don't speak. I can't stop looking at her, the perfect curves of her body, the long fall of her dark hair. She's taking me in too, a flush across her cheeks.

You were made for me, I think.

I must be getting sloppy because her flush deepens.

By the time we come out, Keldarion has fresh linens on the bed and two soft long tunics laid out.

"Kel's clothes are quite comfy," she explains, sliding one on.

I do the same, seeing the tunic fall to my mid-thigh. The two of them crawl into the bed, and Rosalina looks back at me. "Aren't you coming?"

Kel growls. "I'm not going to kick you out now."

But I just shrug and point to my nose, where a small line of black rot drips. "I can't." I wish I didn't sound so pathetic. Despite only exerting the smallest fraction of my magic, this rot will always win. At least I was able to spend a while on the surface this time. It was a treasure.

"No, no, no," Rosalina says, crawling to the edge of the bed. She loops her arms around my shoulders. "You don't feel that sick, right? Cuddling is the best part, I promise."

"I don't think it works like that, Princess," I say, stroking her hair.

"Stay, Cas." Rosalina presses her lips to mine, fingers tangling in my hair, and starlight blooms bright inside my chest so hot, I wonder how she doesn't feel it. Maybe she does. Maybe she always has. Maybe she just doesn't know what to call it.

I deepen the kiss, pushing her backward on the bed. I don't know if it's my imagination, or just the fact that dying in their arms is preferable to the Below, but I sense some relief from the sickness in my blood. I crawl into the bed beside Kel and Rosalina. "Just for a little while."

Rosalina lies down curled in Kel's arms, her head on his chest, and I lie on her other side, wrapping my arms around her waist, pressing my chest tight to her back.

"Are you comfy, Cas?" Kel asks, his arm outstretched long enough to play with the ends of my hair.

"Very," I say, dipping my head into Rosalina's hair. Feeling safer than I have in twenty-five years, I drift to sleep.

PART THREE
MAROONED

35

ROSALINA

"Be careful," I say to Papa. He wraps his arms around my waist and squeezes me tight.

"You too, Rose. But not too careful. Take risks when you're ready and rest when you need to. But most of all," he pulls away to hold my gaze, "don't be afraid of the fire within. It's never led you astray before."

My chest tightens, and I sniff back tears. I have to be strong for him, for all of them.

I stand in the entrance hall with Papa, Kel, Farron, Caspian, and Dayton. I've already had my weepy goodbye with Astrid and Marigold this morning—I don't think I could stand another one.

We'll all be going our separate ways after this. Caspian will use his thorns to transport Papa and Kel to Voidseal Bridge. From there, they'll follow the Great Chasm deep beneath the earth to find the labyrinth my mother is imprisoned in. Meanwhile, Cas and Farron will continue to Cryptgarden, where the green crystals await. They've arranged to destroy the crystals in nine days; Caspian thinks it will be enough time for Kel and Papa to make their way through the labyrinth. My stomach twists, thinking of how everything will have to fall into place perfectly for them to pull this off.

But if anyone can, it's Caspian, Farron, Kel, and Papa.

Dayton, Wrenley, and I will use my thorns to head back to Summer.

Hopefully, Delphia's waiting for us without incident. We'll head to the capital, Hadria, and fight in the games to reclaim my bow. I close my eyes, feeling an ache in my chest. We'll find Ezryn in Summer, too. I need to tell him . . .

Tell him what? I forgive him? I don't know if I do. In Spring, it was as if he couldn't see past his vengeance against Kairyn. But I know I have to find him. My heart depends on it.

I give my father one last hug. "Say hi to Mom for me."

Papa turns away, but I catch him wiping the corners of his eyes.

Keldarion waits patiently. Dressed in a blue traveling cloak, leather pants, and a white shirt with loose laces, he looks even more handsome than when he's in his finest garments.

He sweeps me in his arms, dipping me low for a kiss that takes my breath away. I tangle my hands in his long white hair. "We'll be back here before we know it, won't we?" I ask. "You and I, together?"

"Nothing in this world or the next could keep us apart," he vows.

"I'm trusting you with my father's life," I whisper. "Keep him safe, Kel. Please."

"Your father will see no harm as long as I'm with him. This is my duty. It is time for me to do what I've needed to do all these years and be the Protector of the Realms."

"You've always been my protector, Kel."

He kisses the top of my head and tightens his embrace. "When I see your mother, I'm going to tell her how strong her daughter is. How brave. How she's saved the princes of Castletree." A low chuckle rumbles through his chest. "And I'm going to ask her why she cursed us so badly, too."

I allow myself a laugh and kiss Keldarion one last time. For now. We have overcome so much: frozen waters, banishment, loss, bargains. He's right—nothing can keep us apart now.

I drift out of his embrace and over to Farron. He shifts uneasily from foot to foot. Anxiety roils through our bond. I know working with Caspian must be so hard for him, especially after what the Prince of Thorns did to Autumn's sacred alder tree. "Fare, look at me."

He grabs me, holding as tight as he possibly can. His chest heaves with breath. "I said I wouldn't lose you again, Rosie."

"You're not going to."

"I know. I won't let it happen."

I offer him a smile and tilt his jaw down toward me so I can capture his mouth in a kiss. "Don't worry. Dayton's going to look after me and Caspian's going to look after you, too." I shoot a look at the Prince of Thorns who's fussing over the wrinkles in Dayton's shirt. Dayton swats him away.

"Yeah, look after me. More like murder me in my sleep," Farron says under his breath.

"I trust him. He'll stick to his word. So, watch out for him, too, okay? For me?"

Farron sighs deeply and squeezes me. "Fine."

"Did you say goodbye to Dayton already?" I ask.

Farron's gaze drifts over my head. "Yeah, we said a few words."

Now's not the time for me to pry. I know Farron's dealing with Dayton's new circumstances in his own way, as am I.

My mate runs a languishing look up and down my body. "How am I going to be without you for stars know how long?"

I give his nose a gentle tap. "If you get lonely, just kiss Caspian."

Farron's face erupts into a red flush, and I laugh, giving him one last kiss before forcing myself away.

Lastly, I turn to Caspian. Despite saying he was leaving, he spent all night wrapped up with Keldarion and me. Thankfully, he was free of black goo this morning.

It was a night I'll remember forever.

The Prince of Thorns bows low and takes my hand, kissing it whisper-soft. Looking up through his lashes, he offers a curved grin. "Wish me luck, Princess. I'm off to save the world."

Before I can respond, he moves to stands in front of Kel, Farron, and my father.

Their impending absence is a tangible ache in my chest. I want to sink to my knees and sob, but I force myself to be strong.

"Good luck," I whisper, voice breaking. "I love you so much."

My father smiles, Kel nods, Farron squeezes his eyes shut, and Caspian winks. Dark purple briars erupt from the ground, wrap around their bodies, and then they're gone. Disappeared beneath the earth.

I nearly collapse to my knees, their absence like a gravity pulling me down. But instead, I squeeze my eyes tight, take a shaky breath, and stand straighter. They're being strong for me, for my mother, for the sake of the realms. I have to be strong, too.

Dayton places a hand on my shoulder. "Ready, Rosalina?"

Wrenley has crept around the corner. I guess she didn't care to be here for any of the goodbyes. Why would she? If anything, she's been more distant and quieter than I've ever seen her since arriving at Castletree. Even now, there's a shadow of grief in her eyes.

But she has her mate here with her. Dayton will look after her, as he'll look after me in the arena. I stare up at his ocean eyes, the too-serious expression on his face. We'll work together to get my bow back and save Hadria from Kairyn's occupation. We'll be like . . . business partners.

That's better than losing him entirely, so I'll take it.

"I'm ready. Get in close," I say.

Wrenley stands on one side of me, and Dayton goes on the other. I take a deep breath and look around the hall. Castletree, my home. *I won't let you down*, I promise. One day, all of us will be back here within these halls as we should be.

"Let's find Delphia and get out to sea as soon as possible," I say. Golden briars swirl up around us. I close my eyes and concentrate on Corsa Tuga: the salty scent of the sea, the colorful buildings, the many ships in the harbor—

We surge under the earth, my briars transporting us in a golden cocoon. I keep my focus on Corsa Tuga. The busy marketplace, the sunwashed dock—

"Cannon fire!" Dayton cries.

We emerge in an alley just off the main market strip. Dayton bowls into me and Wrenley, pushing us to the ground. I try to catch my breath, but shrapnel whooshes over us. My ears ring with the explosion.

A shadow crosses over me, and I blink up at the sky. It's one of Kairyn's airships.

The Byzantar Isles have been found.

36

ROSALINA

My heart explodes against my chest as we run. Dayton has one arm around me and the other around Wrenley, shouting orders. We duck under an awning as the rooftop above it bursts into rubble. Merchants and pirates alike rush past us, screaming.

"That ship's going to take down the whole city," Dayton yells.

I chance a look up. This airship is different to the one Kairyn transported me in, but clearly part of Spring's fleet. Fashioned from obsidian wood, the hull glistens with a dark emerald polish. Strange sigils are etched along the planks, symbols I've never seen in the Vale or human world.

Rising high above the deck, the mast stands tall, the rigging appearing more like beams of emerald-green energy than rope. The black sails unfurl like the wings of a great bat, casting an eerie glow in the air. Soldiers and goblins patrol the deck, setting off cannons upon the city and firing green-fire arrows upon the buildings.

"We need to get to the harbor and find Delphia's ship," Dayton says. "Come on." We dart down the main street, leaping over rubble and cracks in the cobblestone. My legs burn, and my lungs feel like they may give out, but I can't stop.

A *boom* erupts around us as a cannon demolishes the building across the street. Wrenley cries out, falling from the force of the explosion. I turn around and grab her arm, hoisting her up. "We can do this."

She yanks her arm out of mine. "I know."

"Don't stop!" Dayton circles back, pushing us forward. "The harbor's just ahead!"

The turquoise sea glitters as we crest the hill. The dock has been mostly decimated, wood splintered like shards of bone. Many ships flee across the horizon. Small green figures dart over the ruined dock and leap aboard vessels attempting to depart. Goblins, I realize.

"There!" Dayton points. Still attached to a piece of dock is a ship bearing a black flag with a horse's skull. Delphia stands at the helm, shouting orders to her crew.

I still as Dayton and Wrenley rush forward. Dayton looks over his shoulder. "Come on, Rosie! Let's go."

"What about Corsa Tuga? The people?" Another cannon shoots from the airship, sending a row of market stalls flying. "We can't leave them to be destroyed!"

Dayton makes a pained, exasperated expression. "What do you want to do, Rosie? Bring the damn airship down?"

"Yes. That's exactly what I want to do."

"There's no time!" Wrenley shouts, pulling on Dayton's arm. "We have to go."

Dayton looks between me and Wrenley, then his eyes dart to his sister's ship. The goblins swarming the dock have surrounded it, and some attempt to board. Delphia draws two blades, rushes to the side of the ship, and kicks a goblin into the water.

I touch the side of Dayton's face. "Once they're done with Corsa Tuga, they'll set their sights on the ships escaping. I have to do something."

"I know," he says.

"And you have to help your sister. Get her ship moving. I'll meet you there, I promise."

Indecision flickers in his eyes, but I don't let him waver. "Go!" I push him toward the harbor, and then turn and run in the opposite direction before he can stop me.

Gulping, I stare up at the dark shadow ahead. Taking down an entire airship—how hard can it be?

A pile of barrels have been blown against the side of a flat-topped building. That will do. I dash toward them, quickly hoisting myself up on the first barrel before ungracefully clambering onto the one stacked atop it. Thankfully, I'm dressed in breeches and an off-the-shoulder cream top cinched with a corset instead of one of my usual dresses. I can only imagine how much more inelegant this would look otherwise.

Breathing heavily, I haul myself up from the barrels onto the roof. Shingles slide beneath my feet, the structure worn from nearby explosions. I find my balance and focus on the sails of the airship. It's flying low, and with this amount of height, I should be able to tear right through the black canvas.

Magic resonates through my body as I channel my inner strength. A golden briar snakes up from the cracked cobblestone at the foot of the building and weaves toward me. I think of the bow Caspian crafted for me months and months ago, how the thorns would do my bidding. My golden briars weave into a crescent moon shape, strong yet elegant, the bowstring crafted of the thinnest golden vine. An arrow forms in my hand of the same strong briarwood.

I can't let this ship stay in the air—it will hunt Delphia's ship until we're nothing but carnage across the sea and I can't let it continue to tear apart Corsa Tuga.

I close my eyes and take in a slow breath, letting all my muscles relax. Dayton's lessons come back to me; my body remembers the feel of a bow, the strength still in my muscles. I open my eyes, pull back and fire.

The golden arrow shoots across the sky and rips through the black canvas sail.

Nothing happens. It continues to move, no stutter, no slowing.

This is fine, I tell myself. *I'll just have to think bigger.* I nock three arrows onto my string.

My arrows careen through the air and slash three more holes through the sails. This time, the ship jerks, dipping forward. Then, the hull hums with emerald light, and the ship straightens again, carrying on.

I blink. What just happened? I ripped its sails and—

My eyes catch on a soldier standing at the railing of the airship. He snarls up at the ripped sails, then stares at me. He draws his own bow.

Oh, fuck.

I look around, but there's no cover on the rooftop. I have to move fast or—

The arrow whizzes through the air, its aim true. I don't even have time to react before I'm knocked over and flattened against the rooftop. The arrow hisses right over me.

Right over *us*.

I blink up at the man who knocked me over, who's now hovering above me, staring with eyes of darkest brown.

Ezryn, my mate, has found me.

37

ROSALINA

I'm on my back, breathless and overwhelmed, as my mate lies over me. His expression is as shocked as mine must be.

Ezryn. He threw me to the ground right before the arrow could strike.

He found me. Again.

His face, framed by tousled dark brown locks—so much longer than the last time I saw him—is still so new to me. Yet as my gaze drifts over each rugged feature, I can't help but think: *Mine. Mine, now, forever. Mine.*

Our eyes meet in a silent exchange—a thousand words passing between us without ever being spoken. With trembling fingers, I reach out to trace the contours of his face, memorizing every angle and line as if to commit them to memory for eternity.

"Rosalina," he whispers.

"Ezryn."

Our gazes linger, charged with unspoken intensity. Ezryn leans down, his lips drawing closer to mine. Time seems to slow to a crawl as our breath mingles.

I sat in prison for three months thinking of all the things I would say to Ezryn when I saw him again. How I would scream and yell and spit. *How could you jump across that chasm? How could you leave me?*

All that anger seeps out of me as his hand caresses the side of my face. Yes, I've waited three months. I can't wait a moment longer.

I grab the back of his head and pull him to me. Our lips meet, and his touch is like lightning splitting the sky. Every piece of me is alight, electrified. Longing and belonging swirl through our bond, a contrast both painful and beautiful. I melt into him, my body molding against his as if trying to bridge the distance that had lain between us.

Cannon fire rackets in the distance, and I feel the heat of a nearby explosion. My hair whips up with the velocity of another arrow, but I don't care about any of it, not in this moment. It's only us, lost in this sweet surrender.

Ezryn pulls away and stares down at me, a look of reverence across his face.

"Hi," I whisper.

"Hello, my lo—Watch out!" He grabs me around the shoulders and rolls. We tumble over one another to the very edge of the roof, barely missing a volley of arrows.

Quickly, Ezryn jumps to his feet and hauls me up. I pull on his loose shirt. "I need to get on that ship and bring it down."

"That one?" he says glumly, looking up at the airship.

"Yes!"

"All right." He removes the bag he was wearing on his back and starts rummaging through it. "You want on that ship? I'll get you on that ship." He pulls out a coiled rope attached to a grappling hook.

"Where the hell did you get that?" I ask.

He shrugs. "Turns out I'm a pretty good haggler."

The metal gleams in the bright sunlight as he swings the hook around and around, gaining momentum. "See the descended ladder on the starboard side? We'll use that to get on the deck. The ship is just about in position. Hold on to me and whatever you do . . . don't let go."

I sling the bow over my body, with the string across my chest and the wooden bow itself at my back. Then I wrap my arms around Ezryn's neck. "Why do I have the feeling I'm going to regret initiating this?"

A dark shadow blocks out the light as the airship gets closer. With a practiced flick of his wrist, Ezryn launches the hook toward the ladder hanging off the side of the airship. The rope trails behind it like a lifeline.

The hook finds its mark and secures onto the rungs.

"Ready?" Ezryn asks.

"I don't think SO!" My voice arcs into a scream as Ezryn grabs the rope with both hands and leaps off the building. The wind whips past us as we fall through the air. For a heartbeat, it feels as if we're freefalling, the ground soaring up to greet us.

Then, with a sudden jolt, we're pulled upward, the rope of the grappling hook taut. I scream, scrambling tighter onto Ezryn's back. Wind lashes my hair and makes my eyes water. Corsa Tuga is a blur beneath us.

Hand over hand, Ezryn climbs up the rope until we reach the ladder. I release my vise grip on him and grab the rungs, trying to steady my rapid heart. The hum of the ship's engine whirs loudly. Before we climb over the railing, Ezryn stops me. We face each other, each holding on to one side of the ladder.

"All right," he says. "I've got you on the ship. What's the plan?"

I make a face at him. "What plan? I have no plan! I just want to stop this thing from shooting everybody!"

His head tilts in such a way that reminds me of how he used to look in his silver helm. "Okay then. We have to clear the deck, bring the ship out to sea, and then get to the engine. Follow my lead when we're up there. This isn't the first time I've taken down one of these things."

I raise a brow. *What have you been doing these past few months?*

"Ready?" he asks.

"Ready," I say.

With one final leap, we clamber onto the deck, face to face with a crew of soldiers and goblins.

"Take the wheel!" Ezryn cries and draws a massive blade from the scabbard on his back. "I'll deal with this lot."

"Take the wheel?" I repeat incredulously. "I don't know how to sail or *fly* a ship!"

Ezryn's blade moves with deadly precision, striking down two goblins with a single swing. "It's easy!"

The wheel is a massive thing, forged from obsidian, the spokes sharp like fangs. A goblin stands on a box, arms stretched as far as they can go to hold on to each side of it. A sword dangles off its hip.

I draw my bow and nock an arrow. "Care to move or will I have to shoot you?"

The goblin drops the wheel and faces me, maw open in a horrible snarl. This isn't one of our local moss-covered Briar goblins, but one of the Green Flame, its eyes glowing with infernal hatred.

"Too slow," I growl and release the arrow with a sharp twang. It finds its mark in the chest. The goblin staggers back. I rush forward and snatch its blade right from the scabbard, draw back my arm, and sever its head from its body.

"Good luck coming back after *that*," I growl. Quickly, I run over to the wheel and grab the spokes. "Okay, I've got the wheel. What now?"

"Get us out over the open water!" Ezryn cries, parrying the blow of a spear-wielding soldier. He swings his blade back, swift and sure. Already, bodies litter the deck.

"Get us out to open water," I murmur. "Sure, can't be that hard."

There's nothing left to do but try. I tighten my grip on the spokes and spin the wheel as hard as I can to the left. The ship careens to the side, deck angling upward in a sharp diagonal. A goblin screams and falls over the side of the deck to the ground below.

Ezryn steadies himself on the mast, while kicking one of the soldiers backward. He follows the goblin, tumbling overboard. "Hold her steady, Rose!"

"I'm trying!" I cry, correcting the other way. The ship balances out with a thud.

Okay, nice and easy. I can do this. I relax my fingers on the wheel and concentrate on the sea below. The ship is heading over Corsa Tuga, but I've got to get it out past the harbor. Slowly, I spin the wheel. The ship follows my command.

"That's it!" Ezryn says. He ducks under the legs of one soldier, his blade up to cut them down the middle, before leaping to his feet and spinning in an arc that downs three goblins.

My chest heaves as the airship surges over the destroyed dock and out over the ocean. There's only one other ship going in this direction. I recognize its crew.

Dayton runs back and forth across the deck, pointing up at us. His voice carries over the wind and hum of the engine: "Keep up with the airship! Don't lose it!"

Delphia at the helm snarls back, *"I'm* the captain! I make the orders!" She spins her own wheel, following right after us. "Keep up with the airship! Don't lose it!"

With a grunt, Ezryn takes the head off the last soldier. The deck is quiet as he stands amid the pools of blood, his white shirt stained red, face speckled.

"What's next?" I ask.

He gives a half smile. "Now, let's crash this ugly thing. Come on."

Warily, I leave the wheel and follow behind Ezryn. He leads me over to a metal hatch and flips it open. "My brother may have been the engineer behind these airships, but he didn't have a way to power them. That was until he joined with the Below."

He jumps into the hatch, not even bothering to use the ladder. I scoot down the rungs into the dim underbelly.

"The engine room is this way."

"How many of these things have you been in?"

"I took one down on the outskirts of Hadria and another just over the border. Once you clear the crew, it's not hard." He opens a door, and the humming grows louder. A brilliant emerald light shines into my eyes. "You just have to take out the energy source."

I step into the engine room. A huge green crystal sits atop a dais. My face reflects in the fractals.

"How do we destroy it?" I ask.

"Smash it." His voice is a low growl. He draws his blood-soaked blade and presents me the hilt. "Would you like to do the honors?"

"Better back up," I mutter. Ezryn complies, and I hoist the blade up, gritting my teeth. With a roar, I swing the blade and crash it into the crystal.

"Good work." Ezryn takes back his sword and slides it into the sheath. "Now that the engine is broken, we've got to get off this ship."

I let him pull me back up through the hatch and onto the deck. With a cry, I see the ship is nosediving through the air, heading straight toward the water. We have maybe ten seconds before we'll be thrashed among the waves.

"Jump!" a voice screams from below. Dayton's standing on the railing of *The Deathly Sky Dancer*, gesturing to us. "I'll catch you."

Ezryn and I exchange incredulous looks. "I'm out of ideas," he says.

"Then let's trust him." We leap up onto the railing. Ezryn grabs my hand in his. I squeeze.

"One," I count.

"Two," he says.

"THREE!" We jump together, careening through the air. A salty spray and the bracing gust of ocean wind billows toward us, and my heart surges into my throat.

Dayton roars from down below and a giant wave comes up to meet us. Ezryn and I are swept up in the water. Salt stings my eyes and my lungs fight for breath.

Then we crash onto the deck of Delphia's ship. The water splashes away. I push up onto all fours, coughing. A giant crash sounds, and I look over the railing to see the airship hurtled into the waves, the mast splitting in two.

I look at Ezryn, also on all fours, dripping water. He meets my gaze and smiles.

"Welcome back," I say. "Missed us?"

For the first time since we consummated our mate bond, there's a lightness in his eyes. "You have no idea."

38

ROSALINA

I'm still catching my breath, soaking wet on the deck of the ship, when a force nearly knocks me over to get to Ezryn.

"Ez!" Dayton cries, wrapping his arms around my mate, who hasn't even stood up yet.

Ezryn allows himself a laugh and leans into Dayton's embrace. "Good to see you, Daytonales."

Dayton pulls back a little and cups Ezryn's face. He stares at him intently. "I forgot how damned handsome you are. Who needs armor when you have such rugged charm?"

Ezryn rolls his eyes and pushes him off, but I can feel the familial love pulsing through our bond. My own heart blooms to see them together, these two men I love—

A gasp sounds. Wrenley runs over and grabs Dayton's arm, pulling him up and away from Ez. "Don't get close to him, Dayton! Get away!"

"What are you doing?" Dayton gets his footing and roughly removes Wrenley's hand from his arm. "Stop."

"That monster," she snarls and points a condemning finger down at Ez, "is the Prince of Blood."

Ezryn stays perfectly still, just kneeling in the puddle of saltwater that's accumulated underneath him. Something hard flickers in his gaze.

"He's a murderer," Wrenley continues. "He killed everyone in Queen's

Reach. Not just the soldiers, but the acolytes. Women. *Children.* He's a demon, Dayton! Cast him overboard and avenge my people!"

"I never—" Ezryn begins to growl, but I stand up and step between them.

"You don't know what you're talking about, Wrenley," I say calmly, but the accusation sends heat flickering beneath my skin.

Her lip trembles, and she takes a step backward. "You don't see it. He will *hurt* you. He has struck down his own people—"

"*Enough,*" Dayton growls. "Watch your words. You don't know what you're saying."

Slowly, I reach for Ezryn, but he steps away from me, shadows falling over his gaze.

"I do know," Wrenley urges. "I was there! I saw him!"

"She would accuse me of such acts," Ezryn says, shooting a glare toward her. "She served my brother directly."

"I told you," Wrenley whispers to Dayton. "He will come for me next."

I look between Ezryn and the acolyte. Ezryn has lived in fear of what he's capable of for so long. To be accused directly of such atrocities, claims I *know* are false, seems a cruel injustice.

But there is genuine fear on Wrenley's face. Perhaps, in the chaos, she was confused about what happened. "Wrenley, I was there that day. I was captured by the Nightingale, one of Kairyn's puppets. Ezryn rescued me, but he never—"

"The Nightingale," Wrenley says lowly, "is *not* one of Kairyn's puppets."

"But you are, aren't you?" Ezryn says. "You served him faithfully. Why should we trust you?"

"Ez, she saved mine and Kel's life from Kairyn. She's not a puppet." Dayton sighs deeply and takes her hand. "She's my mate."

Ezryn's muscles stiffen the exact same way mine do at those words. *My mate. My fucking mate.*

"Enough yakking." Delphia steps between us. Though she's so much shorter and younger, she carries the presence of a queen. "This is *my* ship, and I won't have any squabbling aboard. Is that clear?" She stares each of us in the eyes.

I look down at my feet and mumble, "Yes, ma'am."

Adjusting her tricorn hat, she turns to Wrenley. "Ezryn is a member of my crew. I say if he stays or goes, and I say he stays. If that's a problem, I can show you to the door. Though, around here, it's called the plank."

Pure rage crosses Wrenley's features. Her hands tighten to fists and her lips become one thin line. Beside her, I watch Dayton barely holding back his laughter.

"Fine. If you'll excuse me." Wrenley turns on her heel and storms below deck.

A weight lifts from my chest, and I take in a deep breath. Ezryn runs a hand through his dark, wavy hair.

"So, when did Ez become a member of your crew?" Dayton asks Delphia.

"Met him in the market." She shrugs. "He helped us get this."

At that moment, Nori walks over with her usual awkward shuffle and holds up a large black feather tinged with red.

"A ratty feather?" Dayton raises a brow. "Wow, great find, Del."

"This is not just any feather." Delphia fixes her brother with an adorably frustrated glare. "It's from a Pegasus and you know what that means."

"That Hercules was actually a fae?" I chime in, resulting in receiving my own adorably frustrated glare.

Delphia grabs the feather from Nori and holds it up to the sun. "No, it means the Huntresses of Aura do exist and they're in the Ribs."

Ezryn and I exchange confused stares. For once, during my time in the Vale, I'm not the only one out of the loop. "I'm not sure what to ask first. Pegasus as in the winged horse? What are the Ribs? Who are the Huntresses of Aura?"

Delphia runs a hand along the feather, an almost dreamlike expression crossing her face. "Pegasus are the greatest steeds to ever traverse the Vale. Their legs are more powerful than any horse, and they can fly higher than a gryphon. They have a fierce sense of justice and loyalty. Hurt one, and the herd will seek vengeance for their fallen."

Nori says in her deadpan voice, "The myth says they've only ever been tamed by a nomadic group of Summer fae known as the Huntresses of Aura."

"They're not a myth!" Delphia says. "My mother's mother was a Huntress. Wasn't she, Day?"

"So Mom said."

Delphia grabs my arm and yanks excitedly. "The Huntresses of Aura are fierce warriors, blessed by the Queen with boundless courage. They ride their winged horses across the realm, maintaining tranquility and balance in nature. They nurture all the flora and fauna. Legends say, hundreds of years ago, Summer fae began digging too deep into the Suadela Sands to try and compete with Spring's mining. It hurt the animals living there, so the Huntresses destroyed the operation and, another time, a dam was built into the River Gami, and none of the fish could make it to the sea. The Huntresses destroyed the dam and flooded the surrounding area, creating huge oases. And—"

"*And* they haven't been seen in hundreds of years," Nori says blankly.

Dayton takes the feather from Delphia and sniffs it. He rubs off some of the red coloring, painting his own fingers. "Red clay. This came from the Ribs all right. Whether or not the Huntresses are a myth, the dangers of the Ribs are not."

"What are the Ribs?" I ask, unable to stop my smile at Delphia's excitement.

Ezryn takes a turn examining the feather. "The most northern part of Summer. It is a desert wasteland of red sand, huge gorges, and craggy cliffs. I've never been there myself. Not many fae have and lived to tell the tale."

"Many years ago, explorers from Summer tried to build outposts up there to allow better access to Autumn," Dayton explains. "But it's inhospitable. The sands will steal your breath, the wind will slice you open, and if somehow you survive all that, the creatures living there will pick your bones clean." He shakes his head. "Your feather is a nice keepsake, Del, but why are we talking about this?"

The wind seems to shift around Delphia, blowing her dark hair up in a halo around her face. "If anyone can help us take Hadria back, it's them."

Dayton sighs. "Come on. Say you found them, what then? They're said to have never treated with the royal house, besides the Queen herself. They have always followed their own agenda."

"This isn't just noble houses bickering!" Delphia cries and shoots an arm out to the sea. The crashed airship bobs as an eerie skeleton in the distance. "Look at that! These things are unnatural. They're hurting the ocean and all the people of Summer. I have the blood of the Huntresses, and I know they do what's right." She slaps her chest. "This is *right*."

I can't help but feel in awe of this little girl, barely a teenager, knowing her convictions so strongly. I was never sure of myself, never trusted what I believed in. Not until I came to Castletree, at least. But Delphia is like a tidal wave.

Dayton rubs his eyes. "What are you saying, Delphie?"

She sets her jaw. "I have to go find them."

Nori steps up beside her. "Then I will accompany you. If these Huntresses are real, I shall be the first person in recent history to record it."

Dayton lets out an exasperated groan and paces away. "Rosie and I can't go with you. We must get to Hadria and beat Kairyn at his own game. It's the only way to get back the Bow of Radiance." He flashes a look at me. "Rosie's our only shot of defeating him."

"Is that a good idea?" Ezryn grabs my wrist. "If Kairyn's running the games, then you know they're rigged."

"Well, we'll just have to spring the trap," I say.

"Even if that means running straight into it." Dayton grins.

Delphia pulls out a rolled-up scroll from her back pocket and unfurls it to reveal a map. "We're here in the Byzantar Isles. We'll sail northeast. You can drop Nori and me off here, at the Caelum Outpost. It's the last spot of civilization before the Ribs. We can make our way on foot from there." She stares up at her brother determinedly. "Then you can captain my ship and take it to Hadria."

"Del," Dayton whispers. "I can't let you do this. It's too dangerous."

She stares up at him, expression hard. "I've been leading Summer alone for twenty-five years. I am well-acquainted with danger."

Even though I know fae age differently than humans, it's still a wonder to me that Delphia is actually far *older* than me, even though she looks and seems like a teenager. It's hard to wrap my head around how slowly the fae mature and how long this child has been left to rule . . .

Dayton paces away. "You can't go alone. No way. What if you take this crew with you—"

"They're sailors, not soldiers. Besides, you'll need them to man the ship if you want to make it back to Hadria," Delphia says.

"Then there's no other choice. I'll have to go with you," he says.

Delphia places a hand on her brother's face. It's a surprisingly tender action. "You're the only undefeated gladiator to ever fight within those sands. If the Golden Rose is going to have any chance of winning that helmed rat's games, you're the one who's going to give it to her. Be strong, big brother. We must each travel our own paths to save our home."

He puts his hand over hers, and tears shimmer in his eyes. His voice cracks as he says, "No, Del, I can't let you do this by yourself. I can't lose you, too."

A beat of silence passes over the deck before Dayton turns and stares at . . .

Ezryn.

My heart sinks. I know what Dayton is about to ask.

Ezryn is looking out at the horizon. He closes his eyes as he feels Dayton's heavy gaze on him. "Don't ask me, Day."

"Ez—"

Ezryn storms toward Dayton, grabs his arm, and pulls him away from the others but I can still hear his harsh whisper, "Do not ask me to do this thing, brother. You do not know what I have done to be here. To return to her."

"I know, I know." Dayton grabs Ezryn's shoulders, then puts his hands on his face, his hair. "I have no right to ask this of you. How can I? But I will. I'll ask it."

Ezryn's eyes squeeze shut. "Please, don't—"

"Accompany my sister and see her safely across the desert. Protect her with your life."

Pain sparks across my mate bond, both mine and Ezryn's. My knees buckle, but I turn away so Ezryn cannot see the anguish on my face. Because through that pain, we both know there's only one choice Ezryn can make.

"I have just returned to my mate." There's a hitch in Ezryn's voice. "I swore I would protect her—"

"Give me that vow," Dayton says. "I will take it, and I will see no harm comes to her. As you will see no harm comes to my sister."

"It is my blood who you will face," Ezryn says. "Kairyn awaits in Hadria—"

"Let me take vengeance for you, brother," Dayton says. "Let no more kin's blood stain your hands."

Ezryn paces away and lets out a growl of frustration. He shoots a hand toward Delphie and Nori. "How am I supposed to protect them? They're half-feral! They spent the three days in Corsa Tuga causing more havoc than a crew of pirates."

"She will listen." Dayton gives a pointed look at his sister, and she rolls her eyes.

"How can you trust me with this task?" Ez's voice lowers so much, I can barely hear it. "Your mate would tell you I'm a childslayer."

"My m-m—Wrenley has been through a lot. Don't mind her. It doesn't matter if she trusts you," Dayton says. His eyes search Ezryn's face, pleading. "I trust you with what is most precious to me. Say you will do this thing."

Ezryn closes his eyes and takes in a deep breath. Then he looks to me. *Tell me what to do,* he whispers in my mind.

But more words crash through, words I don't think he intends for me to hear: *I can't do this. I failed to protect you against Kairyn. How can I protect them?*

I look over at Dayton, the pain etched on his face. Their brotherhood is so strong; I can't imagine him trusting anyone else besides the princes of Castletree with such a task. Then I look to Delphia and Nori. Two brave young women who are risking their lives for the people of Summer.

Finally, I look to Ezryn, the mate I thought may be lost to me forever.

How can I bear to have him leave my side again? We only just found each other. It's not *fair.*

Nothing about these last few months has been. Yet, we face it all the same.

Ezryn will protect Delphia and Eleanor. His heart is strong enough. Dayton knows it. I know it. Ezryn needs to know it, too.

Which means I have to let him go.

Even though every part of me is screaming, I hold my mate's gaze. I swallow back my tears and lift my chin. Through our bond, I say, *The people of Summer need you. You must accept this duty.*

A look of sorrowful resignation crosses Ezryn's face. "Fine," he rasps. "I'll do it."

Kel and Papa in the labyrinth. Farron and Caspian in Cryptgarden. Ezryn, Delphie, and Nori out in the Ribs. Dayton and I in the arena.

Do I have enough hope for all of us?

39

EZRYN

The whetstone slides effortlessly across my mother's sword. Tenderly, I work the edge, making sure the blade is never dull, never dirty. I care for and protect this sword as I should have cared for and protected my mother.

Light flickers off the steel, but besides the lantern, my cabin is dark. After the decisions were made about our next plans, Dayton and Delphia had sequestered themselves in the captain's quarters to look over sea charts, and Rosalina had stalked off below deck.

Huxton, a scrappy red-haired member of the crew, had offered me this small cabin. It's nothing more than a wooden room with a desk, a chair, a lantern, and a rickety bed, but I'll treasure even a few nights of sleep with a warm roof before facing the Ribs.

What am I doing? Agreeing to Dayton's plea to watch over Princess Delphia and Princess Eleanor is madness. The last three days chaperoning them around Corsa Tuga have been torturous enough. Delphia has all of her brother's bravado and only a quarter of his skill to back it up and, three times already, I've caught Eleanor attempting to prick my finger and get a few drops of blood for 'research.'

What could have possessed me when I agreed to take them deep into the wilderness of Summer?

I close my eyes. I know the answer.

Whatever my Queen's commandment, I will obey.

How can Rosalina still trust me after everything I've done? How can Dayton, especially when his sister's life is at stake? I saw the pain etched across his face. Dayton has experienced so much loss in his life. His fathers, his mother, and his brothers fell in the War of Thorns. What man could endure more?

I still hear it ringing in my ears in the dead of night: Farron's scream as he held his mother's body on the battlefield. I was too late to save her. I can't hear that sorrow again, not if I have a way to keep his sister safe.

He killed everyone in Queen's Reach. Not just the soldiers, but the acolytes. Women. Children. The acolyte's voice drifts through my mind. I didn't. I *know* I didn't. Even in the blood frenzy that'd overtaken me as I stormed Queen's Reach Monastery, I never laid steel to one of the acolytes.

But can I keep Delphia and Eleanor safe?

There is no other choice. I *will* keep them safe.

I slam the sword back into its scabbard and place it on the floor. What does it matter what good I do now? None of it will erase the evils of my past. My hands are stained—does it matter with how much blood?

Closing my eyes, I think of Rosalina's face. It is the only thing that calms my racing heart. I had been on the dock in Corsa Tuga with Delphia and Eleanor when the attack started. I ran up into the city proper to scout the situation, only to see Rosalina standing on a rooftop. It was as if my life had been given back to me. The months without her, it was as if I were walking through an endless mist of blood, my only mission to return to her.

I've just gotten her back and now I have to leave. Even though it kills me to do so, even when every fiber of my heart screams to stay.

But she didn't need me to break her out of prison. She won't need me in the arena; there is no fiercer spirit than she and Dayton has never lost a fight within the Sun Colosseum. She could have no better companion.

If Kairyn is there . . .

A pit opens in my stomach, a gnawing sensation that snaps at my ribs. Thoughts scatter like startled birds, and all I can feel is his hammer on my chest, the breath seized from my lungs.

I am not as powerful as him. Not only that, but I have no control. The vengeance that possessed me was like a demon, and I do not trust myself that it will not rear up again.

I cannot protect anyone against Kairyn, so I must trust Dayton to do so in my place. I will go where I belong—into the wilds with the monsters.

A loud, angry knock sounds at my door. I rise and open it.

Rosalina stands there, a scowl across her perfect face. Seven realms, she is a true beauty. Her long brown hair is especially wavy from the saltwater, and a small sunburn has formed right across the bridge of her nose, only making her frown look all the more innocent. She wears clothes that must have been lent to her by one of Delphia's crew. A linen dress of turquoise showcases her long neck and collarbone, and a black corset is tightly tied and pressing up her luscious breasts.

"Why didn't you come find me?" she asks, crossing her arms.

"You left. I thought you wanted to be alone."

She pushes past me and storms into my room. Gently, I close the door.

"No, I didn't want to be alone. It's you who always wants to be alone, Ezryn."

Oh. She's angry.

With me.

"I'm . . . sorry," I offer.

"Oh, great, you're *sorry*. Well, that makes me feel better!" Her light brown eyes shimmer. "I shouldn't be surprised at this point, should I?"

"I've upset you."

"Oh, you think?" She throws her hands into the air. "For whatever reason could I be upset?"

"Because . . . I didn't come and find you?" I guess.

"Because you *left me*, Ezryn," she snarls. Angry tears flash in her eyes. "You left me and Kel there in the throne room. We had a chance to escape, and you chose your revenge over us and now you're leaving me again."

My body stills. The flicker of the lantern across the walls seems too bright, the crash of the waves outside too loud. I can barely remember that moment; there was only my hatred and my shame, emotions that felt as much living, breathing entities as Kairyn did.

"You agreed that I must go—"

"So what?" Rosalina storms right before me and shoves me in my chest. It's not hard enough to make me move, so she does it again. Tears stream down her cheeks. "I spent three months in Kairyn's prison, *hating* you. Hating the fact that you chose Kairyn over us. Hating the fact that you would have killed yourself and robbed me of my mate if it meant bringing Kairyn down with you. Hating that your honor meant more to you than our love." Each point is marked with a firm shove against me.

I snag her wrists to stop her from attacking me. "One day, I will get vengeance for what he did to you. I vow it."

"Don't you understand?" she yells. "That's the problem! If you're constantly meeting his storm with your own, you'll only bring the whole world down with you."

"He *hurt* you."

"You hurt me," she breathes. "You hurt me every time you doubt the strength of your heart. Every time you believe your worth only comes from how much blood you can spill. Every time you hold on to the curse because you think that's what you deserve."

Silence hangs between us. "Rosalina, I never wished to bring you such sorrow."

"I will take the sorrow because it comes with the joy." Her eyes sparkle with a fierce intensity. "But I will not let you destroy yourself because you think there's no other way. You're too smart and good and funny and *kind* for that, Ezryn. Until you see that, the beast will never leave you."

My breath catches in my throat, and I stare down at the floor, unable to meet her gaze. I know what she wants from me. To let go of the wolf and all the shame and malice he holds within him.

But without the wolf, what will be left of me?

"Without killing Kairyn, how else can I protect you, Rose?" I breathe.

"I don't want vengeance." Her voice cracks. "I only want you."

Her rage—I can take it. I can take all of it, the words, the shoving, the vitriol. But the pain—knowing I am the cause—breaks me. Emotion floods my heart: anger and longing and love. Our bond is alive with all the emotions. Her anger is her love, as her grief is her love.

"You have me, Rosalina," I breathe. "Wherever I go, you have me. Whatever desert I leave my footprints in, whatever wilderness I inhabit or mountain I scale. It was set by the Fates and bound in the stars. You have me."

Tears run silently down her cheeks, and in my mind, I hear her voice: *Promise me you'll come back, Ezryn. Vow it. On your knees.*

I do.

I sink to the floor and stare up at her. "Whatever it takes, I will return to you, my Queen. If I have to crawl, I'll crawl. If I have to swim through rivers of fire, I'll swim. If I have to defy the Fates themselves and rearrange the stars, I will do it."

She looks down at me, a goddess looking at peasants from her throne in the clouds. "Stand."

I do.

She cups the side of my face, and I lean into her touch. Her other hand caresses the line of my lips, my nose, my jaw. "I'm still angry with you," she whispers.

"As long as you feel something for me." Unable to hold back a moment longer, I grab her around the waist and kiss her.

She kisses me back, a woman starved. I cannot get enough of her taste; I wish I could devour her whole, right here, right now. Finally, when breath can wait no more, I pull away and bury my nose in the crook of her neck. I inhale deeply.

Her sweet scent mixed with salty water and . . .

Lavender.

A growl roils up my chest. "Rosalina, why do I smell *him* on you?"

"Who?"

"The murderer. *Caspian.*"

She pulls away and blinks up at me. "Ez, he's—"

Primal jealousy surges through my veins, a wild dog unleashed. His scent is on her, on what is *mine* by bond. "He killed my father!"

She grabs the side of my face, eyes searching for some sanity in my own. "Ezryn, listen to me. Your father was dying. He was poisoned by Perth Quellos. If Caspian hadn't ended his life, he'd have turned into something like that plant monster that nearly killed us by the lake. He spared your father a horrible fate."

"The lies of a snake!" I roar, tearing away from her. "He's a murderer."

"That's what Wrenley called you," Rosalina snaps. "I know better."

I pace back and forth across the room. "This is Kel's fault. He's trapped you with his own lust for Caspian."

"My feelings are my own," she asserts.

The words make a growl surge up in my throat. Desperately, I fight against the urge to claim her right now. To mark her so completely that Caspian would never dare to touch what is mine again.

"He's risking his life to save us," Rosalina continues. "We're all trusting him. Not just Kel and I, but Farron and Dayton, too. I would never do anything to hurt you, Ez. I truly believe Caspian wants to do right by us. By you."

Her words are meaningless to me compared to the anguish on Kel's face when he found out Caspian was storming Frostfang. Compared to the green scar that cut across the Anelkrol Badlands, creating a rift in the world where all manner of Below scum can freely ascend. Compared to the sound of my father choking on his own blood as Caspian's thorns cut through his chest. "He's a traitor, Rose."

She approaches me and grabs my hands, kissing the knuckles. I almost pull away, but she holds me still with her gaze. "I know you, Ez. Know the deepest parts. There is darkness in you, but there is also light. I will have you as you are, and I will have Caspian as he is." Her voice lowers to a husky plea. "Will you have me?"

I breathe in a ragged breath. Within the depths of my soul, I know there are no lengths I would not go to in order to keep her safe. Caspian has her in his clutches, as he has Kel.

I will have to kill him. There is no other way.

For now, my mate stands before me, claimed by another man's scent. Primal need sends the blood raging through my veins. I will have to rectify this immediately. She has become the very definition of my existence, her mere presence turning me into both predator and protector.

"I will have you," I say lowly.

She steps back from me and undoes the laces of her corset. She slips out of the sleeves of her dress and lets it whisper to the ground. "Then prove it."

40

ROSALINA

Ezryn stares at me like a man undone.

That's how I feel. Unravelled, the edges of me frayed and spooled on the floor.

There's so much pain within me, I don't know what to do with it. I can't take another goodbye when we've only just said hello. Yet, I know he has to do this. There's still something jagged in his gaze, something I only ever felt but never understood before his helm came off.

If he faces Kairyn as he is, Ezryn will fall.

So, it has to be this way. We'll fight for Summer from across the realm, with our mate bond to lead us back together.

The pain threatens to consume me, so I turn my attention elsewhere. There are so many other emotions fighting within me. Anger is much easier to deal with.

I *am* angry at Ezryn. Angry that he let his vengeance rule him; angry that he can't open his mind to Caspian. Angry that he's leaving me again, even though I know that's what he needs to do.

As I stand naked before him, with his gaze darkening with primal hunger, I let myself feel another emotion, too.

Lust.

"I don't want to think about tomorrow or the next day," I breathe. "I don't want to remember anything that's happened to us. I only want to exist within these four walls." I take a step toward him and look up through my lashes. "Can you make the rest of the world disappear for me, Ezryn?"

He drifts a hand up to my face and runs a thumb down my lips. "I can do anything you ask, Baby Girl."

"Then take it all away," I whisper. "Make me yours."

He reaches behind my head and grabs my hair. Slowly, so slowly, he winds it around his hand until he can move my head with a tug. "Submit to me."

"I am a princess." My voice is ragged, and my breasts heave, the points of my nipples brushing against his chest. Ezryn steps closer, and I take a step back until he has me pinned against the wooden wall. His grip on my hair slackens. "I don't submit."

He wedges his knee between my legs. I gasp. Unable to stop myself, I grind down upon him, my pussy already wet and aching.

"You *will* submit to me," he growls.

Yes, I fucking will, I think. But I'm not going to give him the satisfaction of saying it out loud. Not yet, at least. He's going to have to work for it.

I lean forward, as if to kiss his neck, and whisper, tenderly, sweetly, "Make me."

Then I push him away and run.

He spins, eyes wide, as I dart to the other side of the room. It's so small, there's nowhere really to go, so I jump up on the bed. I give him a taunting smile. His pupils are so blown, his eyes are more black than brown.

"You want me to hunt you down, Petal?" he asks and stalks toward me. He flashes a wolf's grin.

I run a hand across my breasts, over the expanse of my stomach, before trailing one finger through my slit. I pull it out and hold it up, slick and gleaming, before popping it into my mouth. Never breaking eye contact with him, I swirl my tongue around my fingers, lapping up every last drop.

"That's *mine*," he growls then lunges.

I give a half-laugh, half-cry as I dodge out of his way. He falls onto the bed, and I scramble over the top of him, rushing to the other side of the room.

He props himself up on both hands and turns to look at me. There's a primal fire in his expression. A fire I want to stoke. "Where are you going to run, Petal? The longer you keep me from what is mine, the longer I'm going to punish you for it. Do you understand?"

"Why do you make it sound so tempting?" I raise a brow.

He gets up and stalks toward me. "Be a good girl. Get on your knees. Tell me you submit, and I'll forgive you for making me chase you. This is your last chance, Petal."

I offer him a sweet smile and walk up to him. He looks down at me with a self-satisfied smirk.

"On your knees," he says.

I move as if to kneel, then shove him hard in the chest. He falls back onto the bed, and I take the opportunity to run behind the desk, laughing.

"That's it." Ezryn stands. The outline of his cock strains against his trousers, so hard it looks painful. "I've given you chance after chance." His voice lowers a notch. "Now, you're mine."

I make to run to the other corner of the room, but he's quicker. He moves with an impossible speed, suddenly appearing in front of me.

"Mine," he repeats.

Then he grabs me around the legs and heaves me over his shoulder.

"Ezryn!" I laugh, but my laughter is immediately cut off by a sharp *crack* against my ass. "Hey!"

"I warned you, Petal. I'm going to use you until I see fit to stop." He slaps my ass again *hard*. "But you're a good girl, aren't you? You can take it."

Heat rushes over my bottom, sending tantalizing need through me. I squirm in his embrace. This position of surrender only makes me crave to give more to him.

"Tell me you can take it," he growls.

Not only can I take it, but I want it all and more.

So, I slap his ass back.

He stills, and I bite my lip, waiting with breathless anticipation.

"Oh, Petal," he purrs, "you're going to regret that."

I'm flung off his shoulder onto the bed. I scramble backward, but he pounces over me, grabbing both of my wrists in one of his huge hands and pulling them over my head. He drives his knee against my pussy again.

His free hand trails over my jaw. "You say stop, I stop."

I lean forward and kiss him, capturing his bottom lip between my teeth and biting down. "Don't stop."

His eyes flash like those of a predator set loose in a field of prey. He tightens his grip on my wrists and places his mouth over my breast. His tongue flicks over my nipple, making me buck my hips, seeking more of the contact with his knee. He responds by thrusting it harder against me. The promise of bliss simmers in my core.

He sucks deeper, teeth raking over my nipple, before he bites down. I cry out, the pain transforming into pleasure.

Looking up from between my breasts, his expression is near possessed with lust. "Tell me, Rosalina, are you a good girl?"

"Yes," I whimper. "I'm your good girl."

"So, are you ready to submit to me?"

I lean forward and lightly bite his neck. "No."

"I was hoping you'd say that."

Ezryn jumps up and sits on the edge of the bed. Then he flips me over so I'm on my stomach and pulls me onto his lap. I let out a moan, the feel of his hard cock pressing against my side like an irresistible lure. I don't know if I've ever been so vulnerable, totally naked against his fully clothed body, my ass in the air and my sopping pussy against his thighs. Desperate need surges through my body. I want him to use me this way, to be his completely in this moment.

"Look at you." Ezryn runs a hand over my back before patting my ass. "Mine to play with as I wish."

He strokes my hair and caresses the point of my ear. Shivers run up and down my spine. "My pretty girl. Too bad you were trying to keep your pretty pussy from me earlier."

Crack!

He spanks my ass with a firm hand. I cry out and push my center harder against him.

"You wouldn't do that again, would you?"

I'm breathless, my words stolen by cries of desire.

Crack!

"Would you?"

Heat blooms on my ass.

"No," I whimper.

Crack!

Another punishing blow that makes the press of his cock even more torturous. "Why not?"

"Because I'm a good girl."

Ezryn leans down and kisses the hot skin. "Yes, you are."

He pushes my legs apart and cups my pussy. A purely male growl rumbles through his chest. "I've missed this."

"It's yours," I whisper.

He presses harder against it. "I *know*."

Two fingers slip into me, and immediately I tighten around the feeling of fullness within. I've craved his touch for so long, I can barely contain myself.

"Do you like that, Baby Girl? Do you want more?"

"Yes, oh god, yes, Ezryn."

Another finger plunges within me. There's no gentleness, no teasing. I can feel his desperation for my body as fervently as I feel my own. His cock is steel against my side, and I reach back to stroke it—

"No," he growls, tossing my wrist away. "You are *mine* to play with. I'm going to fuck you until you can't remember any name but mine. Until you only smell of me and my cum."

I can't respond, my entire body rocking on his lap with the force of his fingers inside of me. A relentless pressure builds in my core, sending my body tingling.

Ezryn uses his other hand to cup my hanging breast, tugging and pinching the nipple. The added sensation makes me cry out. I can practically taste my impending release. I'm right there on the edge, about to explode into oblivion—

Ezryn pulls his fingers out.

I crane my neck to look up at him, a horrified expression on my face. My body still tingling with anticipation.

He holds eye contact as he licks his fingers clean, an evil mockery of what I did earlier.

Oh, my mate thinks he's so *clever*.

I move.

The primal energy he'd embodied earlier sinks into me, and a growl resounds through my own chest. I push him to the bed and straddle his hips. With desperate urgency, I yank off his shirt revealing the muscled torso, dark hair, and tawny skin. I know if I sit back and stare at him as I so want to, he'll take control again. I'm too hungry for him to wait.

I duck my head into the expanse of his chest and inhale. He smells of mahogany wood, musk, and rain-kissed foliage. The heady scent sends my head spinning.

I look up at him. "I need to come all over your cock. Right now."

He looks down at me with an expression more wolf than man, and I know he's not done with me yet. Slowly, his large hand gently caresses my chin before his fingers wrap around my throat. "How much do you want my cock?"

I exhale. "So much."

His grip tightens. "Take off my pants then."

MY FINGERS SHAKE as I pull apart the lacing of his trousers. This moment is one I cannot rush. I grab the waistband and slowly, ever so slowly, pull down.

When his cock is freed, it springs outward, bobbing against my face. My heart throbs against my chest, and I lick my lips as my eyes run up its base. I can't help myself. I lick the tiny pearl on his tip, before sucking the head into my mouth—

Ezryn tightens his grip on my neck and pulls me upward. "You have a job to do, Petal," he growls. "Come on my cock. Now."

Well, I can't say no to that.

I position myself over him and take a deep breath. Already, the girth of his head pressing against me has my body trembling.

"Take me, Baby Girl," Ezryn says. "I am yours."

I plunge myself down upon him.

My mate's cock fills me so completely, I cry out. Each thrust on top of his cock sinks me deeper into a state of blissful surrender.

His hands glide down my body, and then without breaking his rhythm, he flips us. I'm on my back as he continues his relentless assault of my pussy, reminding me just how at mercy I am to this fae's strength.

Wildness flickers in his gaze. Deep within those brown eyes is a primal sort of emotion. One, I imagine, that strikes fear into the hearts of our enemies. To me, it ignites.

I loop my arms around his broad shoulders and lift my mouth to his, kissing him deeply before dragging my lips along his sweat-soaked skin.

"Rose," he growls deeply. He slows his pace to deliberate thrusts, hitting so deep I think I may split in two.

There's a twinge of pain as he ravages me, but it makes the pleasure so much sweeter. With each thrust, I claw at his chest, a wild animal. The sound alights something in his wolf-bright eyes.

He grabs my shoulders and moves me. My world spins, and I realize my head is hanging off the edge of the bed, neck exposed. He clasps a hand around my throat, leaning over me with pure domination in his expression. His cock remains deep within me. "Do you remember the day we first met? I had your beautiful neck in my hand just like this."

"Imagine if you'd taken me like this out on the bridge instead of dragging me inside." Each word makes my throat bob against his skin.

"I could have had you screaming my name so many months earlier." He lays a kiss on the corner of my mouth.

"I scared you back then, didn't I?" I ask with a hint of a smile.

For one moment, his gaze softens. "Petal, you scare me now."

I know he's only teasing me, but my stomach tumbles regardless. All my life, I've been so powerless. Always at the whims of others. Yet, even though Ezryn's on top of me with his hand over my neck, I've never felt so in control.

Ezryn squeezes, briefly cutting off my breath. The sensation shudders through me, causing my inner walls to clench around his cock. I know he can feel it because he gives a satisfied grin.

"Tell me what you want, Petal, while you still have use of your words."

"I only want to feel your cock inside of me. Take everything else away," I gasp. "Even my breath."

His fingers flex, a small movement that betrays so much more: his lust, his barely held restraint. "If it's too much, tap my arm," he says.

I nod, but I trust him completely. Through our bond, he can feel my emotions, my thoughts.

Ezryn kisses me, and when he pulls back, his grip tightens. Instinctually, I try to gasp—and realize I can't. Heady excitement rushes through me. He continues moving, his cock penetrating deeper and deeper. My head bounces on the edge of the bed.

As my vision darkens around the edges, every sensation heightens. A rush of euphoria courses through my body.

"So good," Ezryn growls. "You like being choked when you're fucked. You like it rough, don't you, Rose?"

His grips lightens and I gasp in. One breath is all I get, and a flash of his face: feral and possessive, dark waves falling over his brow. My pulse beats wildly against his calloused hand.

"You." He thrusts hard. "Are." He pulls out all the way. "*Mine*." He shoves back into me.

Unfettered bliss floods through my body, this rush of being at his mercy, of being his to play with. He releases my neck and I inhale, tears springing to my eyes.

Ezryn runs his hand down my chest and palms my breast before wrapping his strong arms around my shoulders. We fall back onto the bed, me on top of him, our bodies still entwined. Neither of us slow our movements.

He pushes my sweat-slick hair away from my face. "You did so good, Baby Girl."

"You did pretty good yourself," I say, voice hoarse.

We move in a rhythmic pulse, his hips undulating against mine with such precision, I can't believe this is only the third time we've done this. It's not enough. It will *never* be enough.

But he's leaving. He's leaving again, and I don't know how many more hours we have together. The thought brings the anger back. I slide my fingers through his chest hair, scratching at the skin beneath. My movements become faster, pounding, unrelenting. Tears fill my eyes, and I don't hold them back.

He grabs my hips and slams me down upon his cock. His eyes shine, and he breathes rapidly through his nose. His own emotions flood through the bond: jealousy, protectiveness, grief. Love.

I toss my head back and close my eyes, losing myself to the cadence of our bodies. I am consumed and consuming. I hate him and I love him. I forgive him and I don't.

More than anything, I miss him so damned much and he's right here with me.

"Petal," he breathes. "Kiss me."

We don't stop rocking against each other, but I shift and lean down. His lips whisper over mine.

"I submit to you," he murmurs. "Fully. Completely. Forever."

I cross the threshold into euphoria. Warmth radiates through my body, not from within, but from him. My eyes start to close, but I fight it, not wanting to look away from him. He breaks underneath me, my name coming out as a roar. His cock pulses, sending my own pleasure spiraling further.

As he promised me, there is no past. No future. Only the exquisite bliss of being wholly and unequivocally satisfied. I tumble into his arms. He pulls me close and kisses my eyelids, the corners of my mouth. I scratch at the skin over his heart.

His curse remains unbroken. Through the bond, I feel the beast curled so tightly around his heart, protecting it, growling when I get too close.

He's not ready yet.

Maybe he never will be.

But I'll take him as he is.

I snuggle deeper into his embrace, willing myself to stay in this oblivion for a little while longer.

"I don't ever want to let you go," I whisper.

"Tell me to stay by your side. I will do whatever you ask."

I suck in a ragged breath. "We can't be selfish."

"I know." He peers down at me, dark curls falling over his eyes. "But I think we could be a little selfish tonight."

He rolls on top of me, and I shower him with kisses between my laughter, falling back into oblivion.

41

DAYTON

The breeze dances through my hair, carrying the scent of salt and wet wood. I press my hands onto the ship's rail, looking out at the vast horizon. The bruised purple clouds of dawn are being swept away by white wisps over an azure sky. Waves lap against the hull, nothing but untamed waters and blue skies ahead.

"It's going to be a clear day, I think." Delphia comes up behind me. Her tricorn feathered hat shields her face from the sun.

"You can tell these sorts of things?"

"Of course." She leaps up on the railing of the ship, holding on to the ropes with reckless abandon. There's no point in telling her to be careful. She's too much like me.

So, I hop up beside her, holding myself steady with the rigging. A blast of salty water splashes up to pelt my skin. My ears twitch as I hear the crew murmuring our names, no doubt watching every move of the royal family.

"You're really sure about going off on your own?" I ask.

"I'll be fine," Delphie says. "Besides, I won't be alone. I'll have Nori and your grumpy old man friend."

"Don't let him hear you say that. Ez is hardly an old man." I grin. "But he *is* grumpy."

"This is important. I can feel it in my bones. The Huntresses of Aura are out there. They'll help Summer."

I take her in, hair blowing, eyes flashing. "You're brave, Del. Braver than all of us. I should pass my Blessing on to you, and you could save Summer."

"W-what?" Her amber eyes widen. "No."

"You would be a High Princess, Del. You're already powerful with magic. Imagine if you had the Blessing."

"Stop it, Daytonales," she says, taking off her hat and smacking me in the chest.

"It was a compliment!"

"You have to always stop thinking that you aren't good enough, that you aren't worthy."

"I'm not, Del." I look away from her out to sea. "It was never supposed to be me. You know I'm cursed. I can't even unlock half my magic."

She tips her head. "Isn't that why you brought that girl with you? Isn't she your mate, the key to breaking the curse?"

"It's not that simple."

"I get it," Delphie says, and she walks along the edge of the railing, her balance impeccable. "The curse mentioned love, and love is always complicated. But it doesn't mean you should pass your Blessing along. I don't want it."

I follow her, using the ropes to hold myself steady. "You can't mean that. The people adore you. You've been an incredible steward to Summer."

"Exactly, I've done it. I've done it for twenty-five years." Her face tilts to the sun. "This is what I want, Day. The open sea. Adventure. Searching for the lost legends of Summer. I don't want to live in a stuffy castle with old men and big decisions."

I can feel it in the tone of her voice, the wondering gaze. This is her truth. Her desire. But she's put it aside all these years while I've hidden in the dark.

Delphia turns to me. "Besides, you say you were never meant to be High Prince, but I think you're the best suited of us all."

Truth rings in her words, but I can't help but wave my hand to silence her. "No, Del. Damocles was a great leader. He was wise and powerful. Decimus never got the chance, but there was no one stronger than he was."

She turns and puts a hand on my arm. "That's true. Damocles was great, and Decimus was strong, and they burned so bright, it's hard to see beyond it. Their light was the cold sun of morning and the chill of sunset. Dayton, you've always been the midday sun to me, warmth and power and everything they both were combined."

I shake my head. "Maybe, but neither of them were idiots like me."

"You can't keep dwindling your own flame just because you're afraid of what it might mean if you burn brighter than both of them."

WITH DELPHIE'S words still heavy in my heart, I make my way below deck and tap on the door to Wrenley's room.

"Come in."

She's lying on the simple wooden bed, face pale and a little green.

"Seasick?" I ask and move to sit on the end of her bed.

"Just a little queasy." She runs a hand through her curls, trying to smooth them down.

"It can happen if you haven't been on the water in a while."

Her eyes close, and she says nothing.

"You're upset with me." I let out a breath.

"I don't understand why you don't believe me. How can we let him on our ship?"

"Listen, I know Ezryn frightened you in the monastery, and fear makes us see strange things. But I believe him. He's my brother."

"And I'm your *mate!*" Tears prick the edges of her eyes.

"I know," I say. "I know. What he did was to protect *his*—"

"Rosalina," Wrenley says, then gestures to her bedside table. "She brought me green apples."

"Supposed to help with seasickness."

Rosalina. She's with her mate now. Maybe it would have been better if she had gone to the Below. But I can't help the satisfying feeling of her still being with me. Of her mates leaving her with me to protect. It warms something inside of me. *Mine* to protect. Even if she had come down the stairs yesterday morning, smelling like Keldarion *and* the Prince of Thorns, the scent of desire sitting on her skin like a brand. I can't believe Kel had allowed that, but I shouldn't be surprised, figuring the same sickly smell was wrapped around him.

Rosalina and Caspian.

How deep does he have his thorns in her? A memory flashes. "Wrenley, why did the Prince of the Thorns grab you at Castletree? He said he *lived* to touch you."

"I-I'm not sure," Wrenley says. "I've never seen him before, but I've heard stories. He probably figured out you were my mate and wanted to unnerve you."

I run a hand through my hair. "You're right. He acts that way with Rosalina, too."

"Because she's Keldarion's mate, and he loves him."

"Everyone knows that tale, I guess," I say. "That's why I assumed Caspian hung around Rosalina at first, just to bother Kel. But he's been pretty persistent at saving her life. I'm worried it's something more."

Wrenley's breath hitches. "Is Caspian in *love* with her?"

I know Rosalina spent some time with Wrenley at Castletree, but the level of worry for her from my mate surprises me. But that's how Rosie is, enchanting anyone who spends time with her.

"Don't worry, her mates won't let anything happen to her, no matter how obsessed Caspian is."

"Yes, all her lovely mates and you?" Wrenley stands and smacks the green apple off the bedside table. "She's still here for you to protect. Everyone will always choose her."

A million emotions war in her voice, and I don't know what to say to quell a single one. "Rosalina is part of the plan to take back Summer." I stand and open the door. "Maybe I should go."

"What about me, Dayton?" She storms over and places a hand over my seashell necklace. "What about *my* part of the plan? I can help you break your curse."

"I know, Wren, I just—"

"Just what? I'm tired of waiting." She clutches her fingers in my shirt, pushes herself up on her toes, and covers my mouth with hers.

Bile rises in the back of my throat, but I force myself not to pull away. Mate. She's my mate. She is kind and beautiful and can break my curse.

So, I kiss her back, putting a hand on her waist, the other cupping the back of her neck. I open my mouth slightly to inhale her scent, black cherries and bitter apple. Her fingernails claw into my chest, and I don't know how much longer I have to keep my lips to hers before I *feel* something. I've kissed thousands of fae. Why can't I force myself through this one?

Distant footsteps sound, then a voice. A voice I know. I move to pull away, but Wrenley clutches me even tighter.

"Wrenley, I found these ginger sweets. Thought they might help—"

I break away, gasping. Rosalina stands in the open doorway, hair loose, a pile of candies in her palm.

Wrenley drops back down to the flats of her feet, cheeks flushed, hair mussed.

Plop, plop, plop. The sweets fall from Rosalina's fingers one by one.

"S-sorry," Rosalina stammers. "I, uh, I didn't mean to interrupt—"

"It's all right." Wrenley reaches forward and grabs the last ginger candy from Rosalina's palm. "I'm sure this will help."

Rosalina glances to me, depths of emotions swirling in her gaze. Hurt, betrayal, sadness.

But what right does she have to feel any of that? She's been with her mate all night and all morning. Her mate who loves her. Not to mention what she let Cas do to her yesterday. She gets to keep Farron for the rest of her life, and he gets to keep her. They get to go live their perfect little lives together, being Princess and Prince of the fucking Vale.

What right does she have to any sort of sadness?

So, I answer the look with a grin and throw an arm around my mate. "Thanks, Rosalina, she's feeling better already."

Then I kick the door shut in her face.

42

FARRON

Everything about the Below makes my hair stand on end, and Caspian's creepy sister's room is no different. Though, there is something fascinating about breaking into the Nightingale's private chambers. Besides the table filled with potions and half-finished concoctions, every other nook and cranny is filled with trinkets. Most are from the surface realms, though there are some oddities from the human world too.

She displays even the simplest objects as if they're priceless treasures. I pick up a fork engraved with a human sigil, which she had placed on a mirrored tray.

"She's particularly fond of that one." Caspian looks over at me. "Brought that to her for her tenth birthday. She used to brush her doll's hair with it."

"Curious," I say, placing it back down and looking at a music box over-flowing with jewels. I can tell by just a glance that most of them are costume baubles made for children. "You actually care about her, don't you?"

Caspian is bent over the Nightingale's potion table, picking up bottles and examining the labels. After a beat, he says, "She's my sister."

She's also a crazy psychopath who's loyal to the fae who took over Dayton's realm. But I bite my tongue and cross the room to Caspian. He still doesn't look up, but says, "She has nobody else."

As much as I love arguing with Caspian, I stay silent. My thoughts drift to my own sister and the turmoil in the Summer Realm. *Dayton will make sure she's safe.*

"So, should we be worried about the Nightingale wielding the Green Flame, too?" I ask.

"No, she's not my biological sister." He straightens, holding a bottle with a vibrant orange liquid inside. "This will be perfect."

"What will this do again?"

Caspian pops the cork. "Smell it."

I inhale a blend of citrusy tanginess and sweet floral undertones, reminiscent of freshly picked oranges kissed by the sun. "This will really help us?"

"Yes." Caspian shoves the lid back in the bottle and tucks it in his bag. "We'll mix this into the drinks, and everyone will be temporarily adrift in beautiful ecstasy. Trust me, a party is the perfect distraction. Everyone will just assume I've gone off to fuck someone."

"You'll be with me."

Caspian tugs on my belt, drawing me close to him, and says with a sly laugh, "Now, be practical, Farron. We'll have an important job to do. There won't be any time for such *base* activities."

I push away from him, turning before he can see the flush rising to my cheeks. "I know what we have to do."

We've planned it down to the day, to the hour. In nine days, we'll sneak into the chamber with the pool and spread the fungal spores that will hopefully destroy the crystals and cause a chain reaction to break Aurelia free. We'll have to hope Kel and George arrive in time and haven't become lost in the labyrinth.

"How's your little spell going?" Caspian asks.

I think of the crumpled paper still shoved in my bag, words scratched out and rewritten. "I've still got time to work on it."

Caspian leans on the desk, regarding me with a half-lidded gaze, his dark hair loose. "I could help you, if you'd like."

Another bitter retort knots in my chest. "I suppose you know a lot about death."

"Unfortunately. It's my birthright."

The light catches in just the right way to see the glimmer of green in his eyes. "How were you born, Cas? Do you know?"

He pushes away from the table and paces the room. "Not all the details, only that my mother has always been obsessed with power, with retaking the Above and returning to it. But one of her spells went wrong, and it didn't connect her with the Above. It connected her with *him*."

"The Green Flame."

"The Green Flame. The Baron. Malekai Furiondemius. A thousand names for a thousand conquered worlds," Caspian says, voice biting. "Sira was always jealous of the beautiful things Aurelia created, when her own turned twisted and corrupt. So, she asked the Baron for a child, one as powerful as it was beautiful."

"You," I breathe.

"Me," Caspian says. "The Baron promised her I would be the answer, that with his flame and her shadows, there would be no one that could stand against me."

It's the truth, I think, though I don't admit it to Caspian. I'm sure even Keldarion knows there is no power in the Vale that can rival the man before me.

Or there wasn't. Not until Rosie arrived.

Another thought strikes me. I've hardly ever seen Caspian use the magic of his birthright. It's the thorns he's drawn to.

"Sira became pregnant with me," Caspian continues, "and she continued to commune with the Green Flame. His attention becomes more and more fixated on this world and the magic of the land. It's why we must ensure the gateway never opens. If he makes it to the Vale, Farron, there will be nothing left."

He does want to protect it; protect a world he can't even survive in himself. "We will," I say, meaning it. "We're going to stop it and yes, I would like your help with the spell."

"Good." Caspian gleams. "And you're going to need my help getting ready for the party because there's no way I can bring you looking like *that*."

I can't help but laugh, running a hand through my hair. "We'll see about that."

"Come on," Caspian says, turning. "We've got what we need. We should leave before Birdy returns."

"Right." I follow him, but something on the table catches my attention.

The Nightingale has an assortment of strange ingredients strewn across the table of potions: powders, gels, herbs, dewdrops in a jar. There's one flower that draws my attention. It shines with a light blue glow. I know this plant, one that goes by many names. Friar's Lantern.

The Deceiver's Bloom. The Lonely Lover's Flower. Rosie found one in the Emberwood, which confused the will-o'-wisp she held.

"Coming, Farron?" Caspian calls from the entrance of the chamber.

"Right behind you," I reply and quickly pocket the flower before heading after the Prince of Thorns.

43

ROSALINA

So much has changed these last few months. At times, Ezryn feels like a new person after all the layers I've uncovered. But in many ways, he's still the same knight-in-shining-armor who gave me a room filled with cherry blossoms.

Through my sleepy eyes, I see him kneeling on the floor, methodically sorting the contents of his pack and laying out his sword and gear. His armor is made of leather and cotton now, swapped for bright silver metal, but his careful movements are all the same.

I pull the rough blanket up over my shoulder, unable to leave the warmth of the covers yet.

"Did you sleep well, Petal?" Ezryn asks, standing.

"Yes," I murmur. Even though his curse hadn't broken, our mate bond was strong enough to stop his shift, so long as he was wrapped in my arms. *The same as Keldarion.* For the first time, Ezryn and I spent the night entwined.

It was so peaceful, rocked by the gentle ocean waves, our naked bodies entangled, and my lips pressed to his chest, inhaling the intoxicating scent of his skin.

He's wearing only loose dark pants now, and the lantern light paints patterns on his muscular chest. *So handsome.*

Yawning, I stretch. There are no windows in our little room, but I can hear the call of seabirds. We must be near land. Soon, Ezryn will leave.

Throwing my feet over the side of the bed, I get up, the blanket falling to my feet in a dark pool. I cross to my mate and wrap my arms around his shoulders, pressing my naked body against his back. He's so warm.

A low growl rumbles in his throat, and he reaches up to hold on to my forearms.

"You're still wearing your armor," I murmur against his skin.

"It's different now," Ezryn says, gesturing to the clothes before him.

"No, the armor within you. Ez, talk to me."

He gives a long sigh, then spins, sitting on a small stool and pulling me onto his lap. My legs fall to either side of his waist. Ezryn tilts his head, gaze roaming over my body, as his knuckles lightly brush my back. "I don't think I'll ever stop being spellbound by your beauty."

I weave my fingers through the waves of his dark hair, the tips of my breasts brushing his bare chest. "That's not what I meant."

He draws me into an embrace, his facial hair rough on my shoulder. "My mother used to be a brilliant tracker. She could find a man lost in the mountains using week-old footprints or lead herself out of the depths of a wood by navigating the moss on the trees. She never lost her way. Not in the wilds, not in her convictions." His throat bobs. "Rose, I don't know my way."

I know he's not just talking about navigating the Ribs and locating the Huntresses. His dark eyes shine with a vulnerability I rarely see in him. The expression makes my heart catch. Yesterday, we sweated out so much of the anger I carried. What was left slips out of me now. For all the mistakes Ezryn's made, I've known they were never truly out of malice, but from hurt. From shame. Feelings I too carried for so long.

"You'll figure it out, Ez. I know you will." I take his face in my hands, forcing him to look at me. "You found your way back to me, after all."

He places a hand above my heart then peers up at me through his lashes. His voice is barely a whisper. "Have I?"

"Of course." The bond within my chest sings, but I know what's between us is so much more than just the twining of fate. Our love has grown quietly, steadily, since I first saw him on the bridge at Castletree. From quick glances across the dining table to sharing our deepest pain, Ezryn and I have always been on this path. The one that leads us straight to the other.

"I thought I may have lost you forever," he says. "How can you find forgiveness for me?"

"No matter what comes at us, you always find your way back to me," I breathe. Seeing him like this, I know he's still the man I fell in love with. Despite all the pain he endured—and inflicted—over the last few months, I still have hope in him.

Ezryn blinks up at the ceiling, eyes shining. "Then I shall do it again. I will come back to you, Rosalina. I swear."

"I know." I smooth down his hair, feeling my own throat tighten. "You'll protect those girls, and you'll find the Huntresses and bring aid to Hadria."

"What if I cannot do it?" His voice darkens. "What if only the Prince of Blood can?"

I grab Ezryn's chin and hold it tight. "You are a good man, Ezryn. A strong man. You, not the Prince of Blood, will find a way to do this. If you don't trust yourself, then trust me when I say I believe in you. Can you do that, Ez? Can you trust me?"

He collapses his head into the crook of my neck. His voice almost sounds boyish. "I suppose."

"Do you remember what I said to you when I first saw you without your helm?"

He pulls back to stare at me, words near reverent. "I know you."

"I know you," I repeat. "I *know* you, Ez."

I hope he understands exactly what I mean within those three words. That I know his wounded soul, the one desperate to be the perfect leader, son, brother. The perfect mate. The soul that feels like it's never good enough. Yet, I also know the man who would do anything for his realm, including giving up his magic because he thought it was right. I know the man who would do anything for his mate, even fighting to the top of the tallest tower in the Vale. The man who would turn into a monster for love.

"I know you, Rosalina," he responds.

"You don't need the Prince of Blood or your beast. You don't even need your helm. Trust this." I place my hand over his heart. "I do."

"Rosalina." His rough hand caresses the side of my face. "There are no words in any of the languages I know that could convey the depths of my love for you."

"Your heart knows the words. I feel them through the bond." I trail kisses up the side of his jaw before landing on his scarred ear. I wonder if, one day, he'll let me heal his scars, as he once healed mine. I don't think he's ready for me to ask him that yet, so I settle for a feather-light kiss on the jagged tip instead.

He wraps his arms around my waist and tugs me even tighter to him. "It's going to be a long road, Rosalina."

"I know. But I'll be here at the end of it. I promise."

I stay chest to chest with him for as long as possible, treasuring each heartbeat, not knowing when I'll once again be held in the sanctuary of his arms.

44

ROSALINA

Ezryn's kiss still bruises my lips, even as he fades into a speck in the distance, heading into the wilds of Summer with Delphia and Nori. Our bond feels like a string pulled too taut—we're not meant to be this far apart. I'm not meant to be this far apart from any of them.

Only when I can no longer see the shape of him do I let go of the ship's railing.

Wrenley looks like a cat who got all the cream, sitting cross-legged behind the wheel, pointing her pretty face up to the sun. Guess she's over her seasickness. The late afternoon sun glistens off her dark hair. She opens her eyes and meets my gaze, her own blue as the ocean. I swear I've seen that color blue somewhere before.

"We're starting course to Hadria," Dayton says, interrupting my thoughts. "We'll dock at one of the bays outside the city and sneak in. This ship would be too noticeable in port."

He's talking to me without looking at me. It's the first thing he's said since I accidentally walked in on him and Wrenley kissing.

The thought sends a wave of nausea through me, and I quickly push it away. Of course Dayton would kiss his mate. Of course he should.

"I don't love the look of the sky," he murmurs, teal eyes narrowing. Wispy gray clouds cut across the horizon.

Dayton leaves to speak with the crew, to get us on course, and do whatever it takes to sail a ship. I need to find some space to think. I head to the bow and sit on a crate beside the railing. Misty water sprays up to coat my heated face.

I feel so far away from so many people I care about. Farron, Caspian, Kel, and Papa are in the Below. Ezryn, Delphie, and Nori are in the desert. I can't do anything to protect them.

Heavy footsteps sound, and I look up to see Dayton walking toward me. He's lost his shirt, skin glowing bronze in the orange light. A striped bandana is wrapped around his head, holding back the tangles of his golden hair.

"Trying to look like a proper pirate?" I can't help but smirk.

He grabs one of the ropes and smiles back. "Just trying to fit the mood. I'll be a gladiator soon enough. The arena I know even better than the sea."

"You seem to know the sea like the back of your hand."

"I do, but the arena . . . The arena I know down to the very marrow of my bones." His voice is a deep fever, and a wildness sparks in his eyes.

"Do you really think I can do it?" I ask. "Fight with you in these games?"

"You took down an airship. A few monsters from the Below won't be a problem."

"I won't be able to use my thorns, though," I remind him.

"Right." Dayton sits on a crate beside me. "There will be bows though, and we'll go over your sword work. I'll be there the whole time."

This is okay, talking to Dayton about our mission. This I can handle. "Aren't you nervous? You'll be competing in front of your people, most of whom haven't seen you in a long time."

His smile only broadens. "Kairyn is an idiot. He's trying to twist the Sun Colosseum into his own dark playground. But he can't hold domain over a place he hasn't shed blood. I fought in the games my whole life. Most royals do one or two big fights to show their worth, but my family couldn't get me out of there."

"Why's that?"

"In the arena, I felt alive. There wasn't any worrying about the future. You make a decision, or you die. The crowd may be screaming, but for me, it's the one place where everything is quiet. Kairyn can hold his games, but he can't control what happens on the sand. And he doesn't know something very important about me."

Dayton's hair is a wild storm as he speaks, blue eyes flashing with memory and mirth. "What doesn't he know?" I ask.

"I've never lost a game in that arena. I'm the only one in the entire Vale who can claim that." He reaches across and grabs my hand. "I don't plan to start losing now. We'll win the three matches and get your bow. Then you'll blow apart the sky."

His words set my heart to a gallop, but instead of getting caught up in it, I pull away. "Wouldn't you be more powerful in the arena with your curse broken?"

Dayton stiffens. Then he smiles, but it's not his usual one. It's slower, more lopsided, cruel. "Maybe I would have already broken it if you hadn't interrupted us earlier."

"Oh, you're just—" I interrupt myself and stand, fists clenched.

"I'm just what, Rosalina?"

"I'm leaving."

Dayton leaps up, grabbing my arm. "No, say what you want to say."

"Fine. I think we should be careful with what we tell Wrenley about our plans. Especially if she's still working under Kairyn at the palace when we return."

His grip tightens. "I knew you didn't like her."

I shove him in his perfectly muscular chest. "I never said that. I'm *trying*, Dayton."

"So am I. You're the one making it hard for me."

I reel and dig my hands into my hair. "*I'm* making it hard? I spent the night with her. I've tried to be her friend. God, Dayton, how am *I* making this hard for you?"

He doesn't answer. His chest heaves, half his face cast in shadows from the clouds.

"Dayton?"

He moves toward me.

Some instinctual part of me takes a step back, unnerved by the wildness in his gaze. "I could have broken my curse with her before we went to Castletree, you know," he growls. "I could have done it a thousand times over by now."

My back presses against the mast, but Dayton doesn't stop advancing. "A year ago, can you imagine how lucky I would have felt to find a beautiful mate who wants nothing more than to adore me?"

"I'm sure you think you're very lucky," I spit. The wind is violent now, tossing my hair every which way.

"I don't, and I blame you." Dayton places a firm hand on either side of my head. "This is all your fault. I was fine before. You made me stop pushing Farron away. You made me believe in some sort of destiny. You made me believe love was real. You have ruined everything, and I will never stop loathing you for it, Rosalina."

My heart near beats out of my chest, and electricity tangles in the air as Dayton grabs my chin and pulls me toward him—and I can do nothing to stop him.

Bright blue light covers my entire vision. I scream, and Dayton tugs me back against his chest as a bolt of lightning strikes the mast with a deafening crack.

"Storm incoming!" one of the crew calls.

"That came on too fast!" another shouts from the crow's nest.

The boat rocks as waves crash against the hull, sending a spray of water on deck, but Dayton keeps an iron-clad grip on me. A torrent of rain erupts from the clouds, soaking us. Another strike of lightning sparks across the sky, illuminating the dark clouds. In a flash of light, I see the crew's panicked faces, and Wrenley, staring down at us from the upper deck. Her face is wild and furious, eyes like electricity itself.

"We need to secure the ship, then get everyone below deck," Dayton says.

I nod, and he steps away from me, in one moment transforming from the carefree Summer Prince to a commander of the sea.

"Batten down the hatches," Dayton calls. "Secure the cannons and get below deck!"

Pitch-black clouds turn the sea into a churning darkness. Huge waves pelt the ship on all sides. I scramble, terror seizing my body. Dayton keeps shouting orders while the crew work furiously to take down the sails. The lightning that struck the mast has left the sails hanging awkwardly.

Furious wind whips through them, tearing the canvas. Other crew members attempt to tie down the cannons and barrels. Farther up, Dayton ushers some crew below deck.

"Come on, Rosie!" he shouts.

I run toward him on the slick ground, struggling to maintain my footing as the ship pitches and rolls with the swell. The ship dives forward as we slide down a huge wave. I fall to my knees, suddenly nearly horizontal on the slick surface. I need to stop myself.

My first thought is to summon my thorns, but the ocean floor is too far away. Scrambling, I reach out and grasp the side railing, stopping me from slipping farther.

Dayton's shouting, running toward me, but he's barely audible over the cacophony of the storm. With a groan, the ship levels, and a huge wave pours over the deck, soaking me, but I keep my grip tight on the rail until I'm sure we're no longer pitching down.

"I'm okay," I gasp, standing, wiping the water from my eyes.

Dayton stops, a stupid, relieved look on his face. "Come on, Rosie," he calls, before throwing his arm around an injured crew member. Quickly, I rush after them.

A crack sounds through the air. The top half of the mast snaps. I retreat and it barely misses me as it strikes the side of the ship, breaking apart the railing and tumbling into the churning ocean. My breath is ragged. If that hit me—

A rope swings in my vision, trailing after the mast. I don't have time to move. It strikes me in the stomach, and I slam against the deck. Another icy wave pours over the side of the ship, engulfing me and dragging me closer and closer to the edge. *No, no, no, no.*

My fingernails cling uselessly to the slick surface, and I scream as I careen closer and closer to the broken railing. Magic. I have to use magic. The water turns to ice beneath my fingers, causing me to slide faster. "No!"

The ship tilts and I spin, missing the opening but slamming my head hard against the railing. Pain radiates through my skull. The world spins and dips, and it's so cold. My body becomes limp as a ragdoll before all goes black.

45
DAYTON

"Everyone's here?" I gasp, peering down the hall below deck. Wrenley is huddled with the rest of the crew. *Good, good.* "Rosie, get down." No answer. I turn. Only pelting rain and wind. She was right behind me. "Rosie?"

I rush back up on deck. "Dayton, it's not safe up there!" Wrenley yells after me. I ignore her.

There's only one crew member left above deck, the first mate, Huxton. He's tied himself to the wheel and has a wicked, crazy grin on his face.

"Huxton!" I yell, each step an effort. "Anyone else on deck?"

"Nay, captain!" he calls. "Just me and the storm!"

"Rosalina!" I scream, throwing myself into the wind and rain. These waves are like nothing I've ever seen: fifty feet high at least, pitching the ship up and down, crashing over the deck and rolling off the bridge. I don't see any end to them. "I'd like to know what fucking sea deity I pissed off today."

I jump down to the lower deck. The mast is gone, causing a huge gap in the railing. Then I see her, white shirt, brown hair. Rosalina lies limp, her body against the remaining intact railing. *She's so close to the opening.*

"Rosie!" I rush toward her.

"Dayton!" Someone grabs the back of my shirt. I spin. Wrenley.

"What are you doing here?" I scream, grabbing her by the shoulders. Tears or rain melt down her face. "I couldn't leave you."

I shove her toward the stair railing. "Hold this and don't let go. I'll come back for you."

She nods, terror clear in her eyes. She followed me . . . Was it the pull of her bond? I can't wonder about it. Right now, I have a princess to save. I run across the deck, sliding and lurching forward.

"Big one incoming, captain!" Huxton shouts.

I look ahead. Rising a hundred feet above the ship is the biggest wave I've ever seen, black with a foaming white maw.

"BRACE YOURSELF!" Huxton yells.

I grab what's left of the mast and hold on. Icy water pours over me as the ship dives deep into the waves. The rope on the mast scrapes my palm bloody, and just when I think the damn ship will never rise, the water falls away and we bounce back into the storm.

My heart sinks. Rosalina is gone, fallen overboard. I run toward where she was, knowing I have only a few precious moments.

"She went over!" Huxton yells.

"I know!"

"The other one too!"

I stop and look back to where I'd left Wrenley, clutching the railing. *No . . .*

Two opposite sides of the ship. I won't be able to save them both. Might not even be able to save either.

One of them is my only chance at ever breaking my curse, at not becoming a beast forever and the other . . .

The other is Rosie.

"See if you can spot the girl and throw a barrel and rope over the port side! Keep the crew safe," I yell to Huxton, and then leap onto the railing. Below the sea is a roiling eddy of black water. It'll be near impossible to stay afloat. Ridiculous to think I can find her. The roar of the storm fills my ears, drowning out all other sound as I leap off the edge.

The icy water swallows me whole as I sink deeper and deeper into the darkness. Its grip is suffocating. I'll never be able to keep an oxygen bubble steady in this water. I'll just have to hold my breath.

I open my eyes. It's so dark. Lightning flashes, illuminating sinking wood and spiraling ropes. *Where are you? Where are you?*

Something ignites in me. Deeper. She's deeper. I descend, propelling myself down into the endless ocean. In another flash of lightning, I see her, brown hair floating around her face as her limp body sinks deeper and deeper and deeper.

I force myself downward, willing the ocean to carry me faster. My magic hasn't felt this strong in a year. The lightning fades, and it's almost entirely black, but I know where she is. She's right in front of me.

Fingers straining, I connect with cloth, then hook my arms around her waist and kick to the surface.

Breaking through the storm-swept waves, I hold her tight in my arms. There's nothing around us but thundering water, no sign of the ship, only the broken pieces it left behind. *They'll get through it and so must we.*

Holding Rosie against my chest, I swim to a large plank of wood and haul her body onto it, before crawling up after her. She's not breathing.

Panic swells in my chest. I lean down and part her lips, breathing oxygen into her lungs.

It does nothing.

I pull her lifeless form tight to my body. "Rosalina, I swear to all the stars, if you wake up, I'll never have another drink in my life." I press my mouth to hers again, breathing into her lungs. "Baby, please wake up."

She sputters, then coughs. Then I see the most peculiar little slits on her neck. *Gills.* "When'd you learn to breathe underwater?"

Her smile is weak, but beautiful. "Just something I picked up." She grips my shoulders tight as our little raft sways in the turbulent sea. No sign of ship or land. "You jumped in after me?"

I search for any regret within me but find only relief that Rosalina is all right. We fall back to the plank together, exhaustion taking over.

"How are we going to find our way home from this?" Rosie rasps.

I hold her tight, dangling one of my arms into the open sea.

The current is alive. Alive in the way Ezryn can control the earth, and Kel the ice, and Fare fire. This current is mine to command. *Safety,* I think, my magic rippling into the surrounding ocean. *Carry us somewhere safe.*

Arms banded around Rosalina, all goes hazy. The last thing I see is the flicker of something shiny beneath the water.

46

EZRYN

"**M**y brother told me all about the curse. So, you really turn into a big wolf at night?"

"Yes."

"Whoa, that's awesome. Can you do it whenever you want?"

"Yes."

"You could do it right now?"

"Yes."

"Will you?"

"No."

"Oh. But if you did . . . could I ride on your back?"

"No."

"Ugh, you're so annoying. So, when all four of you wolves are together, and one of you starts howling, does it compel everyone to start joining in?"

"No, well, yes, I guess so." I stop, my feet sinking into the sand, and blink the sweat out of my eyes. I can't take any more of these insufferable questions. Eleanor has been walking right beside me since we left Caelum Outpost. Not a few steps away. Not a few paces in front or behind, but *right* beside me. Every passing moment has been spent answering some question about Castletree or the Blessings, and now she's moved on to the curse.

I peer out at the wavering horizon. We've been trekking for several hours now, and the sun sits at its highest point in the sky, beaming down relentlessly. The memory of cool sea air and salty breezes is far away. There's no road beyond the final outpost, only golden sand and sun-baked earth.

All we have to go on is a ratty feather caked in red clay. I know the Ribs are the most northern point of the realm, and so I navigate using the sun, as seems fitting in Summer. Once the sand shifts to red, we'll know we're close.

My gaze is drawn to the towering red rock formations up ahead, punctuating the landscape like broken bones. They rise abruptly from the desert floor, narrow and tall, with flat tops. Their long shadows drape over the earth.

I take in a deep breath, the dry air scratching my nose, and adjust the three packs on my back. Somehow after the first hour of walking, I'd ended up with both Eleanor and Delphia's bags.

"Why'd we stop?" Eleanor says, blinking up at me with an owlish expression that reminds me of her eldest brother.

"I don't like the look of those rocks," I say. "Hey, Delphia, get back here."

Delphia is up ahead. Unlike Eleanor, she's wanted to be ahead of me the entire time. I didn't mind when I had sightlines in every direction, but anything could be behind these rocks.

Myths and legends are abundant in the Vale. I've learned that even the most far-fetched tale usually has some inkling of truth to it. So, though there may not be drakes camouflaged as mirages, or elementals in the shape of whirlwinds, the Ribs have stories told about them for a reason.

"Delphia, get back here!" I shout when she doesn't respond. She doesn't even have her twin blades; they're strapped to her pack which is currently hanging off my left shoulder.

"I just want to check these out!" she calls back, running toward the towering rocks.

"Delphia, steward and Princess of Summer, daughter of Sabine, Ovidius, and Cenarius, sister to Damocles, Decimus, and Daytonales, get your behind *back* here this instant or I'll—"

"You'll what?" she calls. "Send me to my room?" She cackles before turning and running toward the rocks.

A growl rumbles in my throat, and I shoot a glance down at the smirking Eleanor. "Don't laugh at that."

I take off, doubling my pace to try and catch her, while Eleanor sighs and keeps stride beside me, moaning, "I *hate* running."

Well, I hate sweating my skin off in this barren wasteland while being pack mule to two defiant, ungrateful little girls, I think, but save my breath for running. For the thousandth time today, I wonder why I agreed to do this.

For Dayton. For Farron. For the Summer Realm.

For fuck's sake!

Delphia has reached the rocks and started climbing up one of them. I heave in a breath and move faster.

Shadows drench Eleanor and me as we reach the towering formations.

"Get down," I growl to Delphia, who's hanging a few feet above my head.

She glares at me. "Shush."

"I swear on the seven realms, if you don't get down—"

"Fine!" She jumps down, landing gracefully, only the smallest cloud of dust whiffing up around her boots. "Just be quiet."

I cross my arms. "I *want* to be quiet, but you're the one gallivanting across the desert, without a single thought—"

"No!" She puts a finger to her lips and whispers, "Be quiet and listen."

Immediately, the hairs on the back of my neck rise. There shouldn't be anything to hear except the wind and the shift of sand.

"I hear it," Eleanor murmurs. "It sounds like . . . a lullaby. One my mother used to sing."

Delphia drifts away, pointed ear twitching. "It's not a lullaby. Listen closely. It's an old tavern song. My brothers would sing it together all the time."

I still my breathing and let all the other sounds drift away. Yes, I hear it now. An otherworldly voice from a memory. Each note is filled with a sense of longing and sorrow, yet the melody makes me smile. It's the song the captured siren sang the night we all descended Below. Last time I heard this song, Rosalina sat upon my lap, her body soft and radiating warmth in such a cold place. If only I could hold her like that again.

If I close my eyes and drift into the song, I can—

I snap back into myself. How are we all hearing music this far out into the desert? It's not possible.

Unless . . .

A myth about monsters in the Ribs comes rushing back to me. Suddenly, the song doesn't sound like the siren's voice anymore. It's a hideous, mocking jeer, devoid of tune or melody.

Eleanor's leaning against the rocks, eyes closed, tears dripping down her face. I snatch her collar and pin her tight against my side, before spinning. "Delphia!"

Delphia's wandered out into the open sand; a huge smile spread on her face. Like Eleanor, her eyes are closed, and tears paint her cheeks. "Sing it again, Dammy," she calls. "Once more!"

"Delphia!" I roar and lunge for her.

But the harpy is faster.

Great black wings streak out of the sky. Hooked talons sink into Delphia's shoulders.

The song disappears, replaced by Delphia's scream.

47

KELDARION

The only light in the Great Chasm comes from the lantern Uncle Irahn carries. It burns valiantly in the pitch-darkness, causing shadows to flicker along his and George's faces. Our elevator continues its creaking descent down, down, down into the deep. We're long past the torches held by the other Voidseal workers. No one's mad enough to go this far down.

But no one's ever tried to rescue someone from Sira's prison before, either.

George and I spent yesterday traveling from Frostfang, with George riding atop my wolf's back. The old man proved himself a keen rider. "No harder than riding the ostriches down in Jacksonville! Mr. Fraser opened up a farm. I was quite taken with it."

In the time we've been traveling together, I've learned, much like his daughter, George has a story for everything. Though, where Rosalina's stories come from her books, George's all come from his own history. Crossing the Anelkrol Badlands reminded him of a failed expedition he and Anya were a part of on the HMCS *Karluk*. The massive bridge across Voidseal prompted a memory of fastening a lock to the Ponte Milvio with his and Anya's names on it to symbolize everlasting love. Though I've poked my head into the human realm from time to time, these places and names mean nothing to me. Yet, it's as if I can see everything play out in my head; George speaks with such vivid imagery, his mind as sharp as ever.

The one common theme in all of his tales is Anya. She's always with him, the focus of his attention. It's as if just by saying her name, something within him alights.

Now, George leans over the edge of the elevator, trying to peer into the murk. Uncle Irahn grabs him by his coat and yanks him back. "You'll lose your nose that way, boy," Irahn says gruffly.

George gives a sheepish grin and taps his foot impatiently. Despite being a human and traveling with a giant wolf for days in the most unforgiving place in the Vale, he's shown no fear. No nervousness.

I, on the other hand, am filled with dread. There's nothing to distract me here with the dark so consuming. Only the irritating rattle of the elevator and the cold. The dread sinks deeper into my bones.

I'm not afraid of the Below or whatever Sira throws at me in her labyrinth. But I'm responsible for Rosalina's father, the most important person in her life, and possibly—if things go according to plan—I'll be responsible for her mother, as well. I have to bring them home safely. Have to give Rosalina a chance to see both her parents again.

The elevator creaks to a halt. We've been descending for what feels like hours; the stillness unsettles me.

"This is as far down as it will go," Uncle Irahn says. "You're on your own now, boys."

He opens the door, and we step out into an icy tunnel. Uncle Irahn hands both me and George a lantern, though they do little to help. It's as if their light is swallowed immediately.

"Thank you, Uncle," I say.

To my surprise, my uncle hugs me. "I don't know what's so damned important down here, boy, but I better not randomly wake up one morning with a Blessing in my chest."

"I'm not going to die," I say. For the first time in so long, I'm confident in that. There is too much future for me. Too much for Rosalina.

Uncle Irahn nods. That's as much emotion as I'll get from him.

George and I walk into the tunnel. The elevator creaks as it ascends back toward the light.

"Only one way out now," I mutter.

With each step, I sense we're leaving Winter behind and entering the Below. The air is warmer, and I shed my large coat. Eventually, we don't even need our lanterns. Glowing green scars cut across the walls: remnants from when Caspian created the Great Chasm in the first place.

"What is this place?" George asks, running a hand along the stone.

"The result of a temper tantrum," I mutter. "Now, it's an entryway. Sira could send an army through this gap if she wanted to. The only thing standing between her and Winter is the Voidseal Guard."

"A temper tantrum. I do believe you'll have to explain further," George says.

My voice is raspy. I don't want to tell this tale. But all my stories seem to be filled with tragedy, and George has given me so many, I suppose I owe him one. "Before the realms existed, there was only the Above, home of the first fae. Many legends have been passed down about what it was like, but all agree it was a place of light, of hope. It was lit by a magical rosebush known as the Gardens of Ithilias."

"So, heaven exists," George mumbles. "At least, a version of it."

"Whatever it was, it doesn't exist anymore. Sira stole a rose and created the Below. She waged war on the Above and eventually destroyed the rosebush. Everything would have been lost if it wasn't for Aurelia's courage. She saved four roses from the bush before Sira destroyed it and used those to make Castletree and the realms."

"Aurelia," George whispers. "Aurelia. Anya. My Anya."

Green light glows off my skin as I talk. "Years and years after Aurelia left the Vale, the Below was still waging war on the realms. Everyone knew Sira was using the rose to create her monsters, so a plan was put in place by my parents to retrieve the rose. Unfortunately, they were ambushed while escaping the Below. My parents eluded capture, but the rose was lost in the attack. Neither the surface realms nor the Below had control over it."

One step in front of the other. One word after another. I can't let myself get tangled in the memories of my parents.

Of him.

"Despite the best judgment of many, I made an alliance with the Prince of the Below, who swore he had abandoned his mother and all allegiance to this dark realm."

"The dark-haired boy. The one I saw in my mind's eye speaking with Anya. There was something familiar about him . . ."

"Yes. Caspian. We decided to work together to find the rose. I even lived in the Below for a time while we searched. Eventually, we succeeded."

246

"A valiant mission indeed," George says. He watches me out of his peripheral vision, and it's as if he's reading me like a map. There are so many unsaid parts of this story. The love. The desperation. The bargain. But I don't need to tell George for him to understand.

"Ultimately, our alliance was not to last. An ally of mine attacked Caspian's home, and in return Caspian stole back the rose and led an army against Keep Wolfhelm. My mother perished in the battle, and I was captured by the Below. Thus began the War of Thorns, a terrible campaign that would claim the life of many fae."

George sighs deeply. "There is no greater tragedy than friendships torn asunder by war. Pain knows no allegiance."

"Just like Caspian," I mutter. "The War of Thorns raged across all four realms. Frostfang was occupied, and the Below led a force against Autumn."

"Ah, Dom and Billy spoke of this when we passed by the chrysanthemum field outside of Coppershire. They said a huge mudslide destroyed both the fae and goblin armies."

I nod. "Those armies recently fought again, raised by Perth Quellos's evil magic. Thankfully, Farron has now given them eternal rest."

"You were captured during all of this?" George asks.

"Caspian chained me to a mountain within the Below." I shrug as if this fact is no more jarring than saying I was out of town. "Ezryn, the same ally who first attacked Caspian's home, climbed the mountain and rescued me. Although Ezryn was High Prince at the time, his father was able to hold back the Below's forces against Spring, so Ezryn stayed to assist Winter. I gave him command of my army. He and my father worked together to take back Frostfang."

"You went after Caspian yourself," George says. It's not a question. Insightful, just like his daughter.

"I needed to reclaim the rose. At least that's what I told myself. Truly, I wanted Caspian to hurt the way he had hurt me. I challenged him, and we battled across the Badlands. I knew he was powerful, but during our fight he . . . erupted. This chasm, the tunnels, the green light—that was all a result of his betrayal."

"Or his love." George shrugs.

"Caspian's love has always been a tempest." My boots are too loud on the stone, the green scars too bright. "The rose was destroyed during our fight out on the Anelkrol Badlands. Sira could not use it to create any more of her armies, but nor could we use it to take control of them. The monsters, such as the goblins in the Briar, became wild, untamed. All suffered."

"You're sure the rose is gone forever?"

I take a rumbling breath. "Yes."

"How do you know?"

"Because I did it myself." Images flash into my mind. Lavender eyes flooded with green. Ice battling with shadows, with thorns, with emerald fire. "My father died in the process of retaking Frostfang, and I received Winter's Blessing. Between my newfound strength and Caspian's Green Flame, our magic was untethered. The rose was the cost."

"What came of this war?"

A joyless laugh escapes me. "Nothing. Hadria and Florendel were able to hold their borders, and after the mudslide destroyed the armies in Autumn and Frostfang was retaken, the Below had no choice but to retreat. As far as Caspian and I were concerned, when the rose was destroyed there was nothing left to fight for but the death of the other. I suppose there was a limit even to our anger."

George is silent for a few moments; a strange occurrence for him. Then he says, "I've spent my life finding remnants of things people thought destroyed, and I've come to learn nothing is ever truly lost. Perhaps, Keldarion, a little piece of heaven may still be here in the realms."

"Your delusion is charming."

"So I have been told." George smiles, then flicks his gaze past me. "Ah! Looks like we're about here."

The dim purple light of the Below's horizon filters in through the tunnel. We quicken our pace until we step out from the cloistering walls into a massive chamber.

A colossal structure looms before us. The walls of the labyrinth rise into the murky sky. The stones seem ancient, yet unmarred by time. Intricate carvings adorn each one, depicting grisly scenes of torture and violence. I can only imagine how much time it would have taken to carve them. Grotesque creatures of stone stand on either side of the open entrance, their forms distorted beyond any recognizable beast in the Vale.

The maze is so large, there's no way to tell how far back it goes or how long it stretches. But somewhere beyond it is the rightful Queen of the Enchanted Vale.

"Last chance to turn back, George," I say. "I can do this without you."

"No, you can't, boy," George says. He closes his eyes and touches his heart. Then, he snaps his eyes open and takes three steps into the labyrinth. "Left, I should think."

"How do you know?" I ask.

He smiles back at me and taps his heart. "She's my little piece of heaven."

I stay frozen to the spot. Within these walls are dangers like I've never experienced—the darkest and most vile creations of the Below—and I'm going to be led by an old human man trusting his heart.

Well, I've done stupider things.

I enter the labyrinth and follow behind George as we walk straight into the heart of evil.

48

ROSALINA

Waves crash against my mind in a gentle rhythm. Grainy sand coats my lips and cheeks. I flutter my eyes open, and it's bright, so bright. Not just the sky, but white sand and brilliant green foliage. Disoriented, I slowly push myself up, sand clinging to my damp clothes. The scent of salt fills the air.

I take in my surroundings. The flotsam and jetsam from the ship lie scattered across the beach, wood and barrels and rope. I rub my eyes, trying to make sense of what happened. Memories flood back in fragments: the fierce winds, the roaring waves, and the desperate struggle to stay afloat. Dayton pulling me from the water.

Dayton.

"Day—" I gasp, voice hoarse. There's a shape farther down the beach. I stagger to my feet. "Day!"

I run over, sink to my knees before him, and heave him onto his back. Damn, he's heavy. Dayton starts to cough and sputter seawater on his bare chest. Relief washes over me.

"Hey, Blossom," he croaks, dragging his knuckles across my cheek.

I can only imagine what I look like right now: waterlogged with wild sea-crusted hair, and ripped clothes.

"Any sign of the ship?" Dayton sits up.

We must have been out for hours. The sea is smooth as glass, azure water spreading as far as I can see, but no sign of any ship.

"Do you think they're all right?" I ask.

A pained expression crosses Dayton's face. "Most of them."

It's still hard to fathom. He jumped into the water, abandoned his crew, his mate, to save my life.

Dayton staggers to his feet and pulls me up as well. "We must be on one of the smaller Byzantar Isles. Most of them are uninhabited."

Towering palm trees sway gently in the breeze. The beach gives way to foliage that leads up to a high point on the island.

"I could use my thorns to take us back to Castletree or Corsa Tuga," I explain. "But I've never been to Hadria. There are no thorns there to travel to." I'm sure Caspian has some about, but it would be too risky. That could take us right into the heart of Kairyn's stronghold.

Dayton shakes his head. "If we go back to Castletree, the only way to get to Hadria would be on foot, and that could take weeks. Corsa Tuga will be in shambles after Kairyn's attack. We'll find no help there."

"So, what do we do?"

Dayton turns his gaze from the sea to the middle of the island. "We'll find high ground. Perhaps from up there, we can see *The Deathly Sky Dancer* and make a signal. We'll also need to find food and water."

From the position of the sun, it's late afternoon, but the heat has almost already dried my soaking clothes and hair. My stomach twists. We're truly on our own out here.

Dayton does a quick scan of the beach, looking for anything useful, but there's nothing but driftwood and rope.

He leads us into the jungle. The beach disappears behind us almost instantly, and we're engulfed in dense bush. Vines drape from towering trees, creating a verdant labyrinth. Yet Dayton seems to know where to go in an almost instinctual way.

About an hour into traveling, he motions for me to stop and then clambers up one of the trees, swatting down two coconuts with a stick.

"There's an easier way to do that." I smirk up at him. A golden briar shoots up from the earth, knocking the remaining coconuts free.

"Think you could make me a little knife with that?" he says, jumping back down to the ground.

I'm not as practiced with it as my bow, but after a few moments, I manage to craft something with a sharp edge. Dayton takes it from me and cuts open the tops of the coconuts. "Drink."

I hadn't realized how parched I was until the liquid slid down my throat. It's slightly sweet, with a nutty undertone. As soon as I finish one, Dayton hands me a second, which I take eagerly.

"We should keep going," he says, then continues into the jungle.

I keep following him. It's uncomfortable, the humidity coating my skin with sticky sweat, and although my clothes have dried, they're salt-crusted and stiff. I just know my inner thighs are going to be raw and red tomorrow.

But it's also beautiful. The jungle is alive with bright blooming flowers and the symphony of chirping birds . . . which I can hear clearly because Dayton has barely spoken two words since we've left the beach. I walk up beside him.

"Is everything all right?"

"Yes."

"Day?" I grip his arm and he whirls around to face me.

"Why didn't you go below deck when I asked?"

"I was *trying*, but I got knocked over!" It suddenly comes back to me: the words he spoke right as the storm hit. How he *loathes* me. "Do you regret jumping in after me?"

"No, of course not." He runs a hand through his hair. Something's clearly still bothering him. "Just drop it, okay?"

"Look, I know this isn't ideal, but we'll find the ship again. We'll get back to the crew and . . . and your mate."

"I might not even have a mate anymore," Dayton snaps, then continues into the jungle.

My stomach sinks. What does he mean? What happened after I passed out? "Dayton, wait."

I rush after him, and we break out of the treeline onto a rocky outcrop overlooking the island. The vista stretches before us. Below, the lush greenery meets the glittering ocean. There's not a single ship on the horizon.

"What do you mean, you might not have a mate anymore?" I ask.

He shakes his head, avoiding my gaze. "I mean, we have no idea what happened to the ship. No idea where they are."

A warm breeze tousles my hair, and I step closer to him. "Can you *feel* her?"

"What do you mean?"

I place my hand on my chest. "I can feel my mates in my heart. Even Kel, despite not completing our mate bond. I would know if they were dead."

252

Dayton shakes his head. "I don't think it works like that for me."

It makes me sick to help Dayton strengthen his bond with Wrenley, but he's clearly worried about her and it's my fault they're separated now. I step closer and guide his hand over his heart, but when I move to pull away, he keeps my hand cupped in his. My fingertips graze his sculpted chest.

"Tell me what to do, Blossom," he rasps.

"Close your eyes," I whisper. "Mine is like a warmth beside my heart. My mates flicker in the flames."

He tilts his head, and his lips brush my hairline. "I don't feel anything—"

"Just think about her," I say. "The feel of her. Make a shape in your mind."

"Mmm-hmm." He presses his hand on the small of my back, drawing me closer against him.

My eyes close. "Imagine your heart is an arrow. Where does it lead you? Where is it guiding you?"

His other hand tightens around mine, and I feel the vibrant beat of his heart. I breathe in, getting lost in the intoxicating scent of his salt and sunshine skin. I squeeze his hand and he instinctively draws me closer, my heart beating in a wild tandem with his own.

"I feel something," he says, and even without opening my eyes, I hear the smile in his words. "Like . . . like something beside my heart that isn't my own."

"That's her," I whisper, a silent tear running down my cheek.

I feel a flame in my own heart spark, one that doesn't feel like Kel, or Ez, or Farron. But I'd believed so vividly that Dayton was my mate before, I won't be fooled by this phantom flame again.

"Thank you, Rosalina," he mumbles, words slurred as if drunk. It's like he's in some sort of daze. He leans down, his mouth gliding across my temple, salt-crusted lips caressing my cheek.

"Dayton," I say, my heart beating like a war drum in my chest. My whole body is a moth drawn to the flame of his lips.

"Just a thank you," he rasps, the edge of his mouth touching mine.

"Dayton, we can't." I shove him in the chest and stagger back into the jungle.

I hear him swearing behind me. I don't slow, needing to get some space between me and the Summer Prince. Stupid. I was so stupid to let him touch me. Stupid to let him get so close.

"Rosalina, I'm sorry. I got carried away." Dayton catches up and grabs my arm. "Will you just listen to me?"

There's a snap of rope. Dayton looks down, then up at me. "Oh fuck."

The grass and dirt beneath our feet shifts, revealing a rope net. It draws upward, whipping us up into the air and then dangling us from a tree high above the ground. My arms and legs tangle with Dayton's. Before I can summon my thorns, before I can even scream, a silhouette emerges from the edge of the treeline. A fae, holding a huge trident in one hand.

We're not alone on this island.

49

EZRYN

"Delphia!" My voice cracks as I watch in horror as the harpy tightens its talons into her shoulders and whips back up into the sky. Delphia screams, the sound not of a steward or a princess, but a terrified little girl.

I push Eleanor back against one of the pillars and run out into the sand, tracking the winged monster's movements. The creature laughs, its hypnotic song replaced by a half-human, half-animal cackle. The harpy is a twisted amalgamation of woman and bird. She cuts through the air with an eerie grace before landing atop one of the rock formations.

I know these creatures. I've seen them only once before, but not here. It was down in the Below during one of my visits to Keldarion when he lived there. I remember the traitor Caspian speaking to me of them, how they were a creation of Sira's. His words from decades ago filter through my mind: *The Queen of the Below has always been jealous of the Queen of the Vale. Aurelia made fae into birds, so Mother wanted to make fae into birds. You can see, Mother wasn't quite so talented.*

Have these monsters escaped from the depths and found salvation here?

Whatever the reason, they need to die. Now.

My heart rails against my ribs. I can get up there. I just have to figure out—

"Ezryn?" Eleanor says quietly.

I ignore her; I need to concentrate. The formations are about one hundred feet high. I could scale them, but it would take too long—

"Ezryn?" Eleanor says again, louder.

I don't have time for her questions. "Not now, Eleanor."

"EZRYN!" her voice ascends into a shriek.

I spin just in time to watch a second harpy fold in its wings and dive toward her. It spreads its gray-black wings at the last second and seizes Eleanor's arms in its talons.

"Eleanor!" I lunge for the monster, but it's too late. It jerks her up into the air, shrieking in delight, an old crone's voice mixed with a bird's screech.

No, no, no, no. They're gone. They're both gone. I *promised* Dayton, and through Dayton I promised Farron, I would keep their family safe. I can't lose them, not like this.

I grit my teeth. I *won't* lose them. These abominations will die before they steal another drop of fae blood.

I move without thinking now. Grabbing the grappling hook off my pack, I swing the rope in huge circles for momentum. I fling the hook forward. It lodges into one of the rock formations, but nowhere near high enough. It will still take me too long to get up there. The monsters' cackles are louder now, and one of the girls is screaming.

A shadow passes over me as two more harpies cut across the sky. They're heading for the rocks, too. They're hideous things, with faces that vaguely resemble those of fae women, but the proportions aren't right. Their eyes are too big, the color black within black. Their jowls are sunken, cheeks caved in. One opens its mouth to screech, revealing a maw of needle-sharp teeth.

I stare at the scaly legs descending into talons. They're not quite bird feet, but a twisted semblance of faedom. The long, sinewy toes taper into sharp points, with sickle-shaped claws perfect for gripping. I turn my attention to its breast, covered in mottled, tattered feathers. Unprotected.

With a mighty heave, I swing the grappling hook back into the air. This time, it hits its target. The steel prongs make a squelch as they drive into the harpy's chest. I grab the rope and pull.

The harpy gives a piercing cry but keeps flapping. Its companion looks down and cackles before descending to one of the rock formations. With a roar, I pull harder, dragging the harpy down toward the earth. A putrid odor washes over me as I yank the monster closer. It's so strong, I can almost taste it, the smell of rot thick and cloying. Every desperate flap of her wings is redolent with the stink of carrion. Bile rises in my throat, but I fight it down.

With one last pull, the harpy is right above me. She grimaces, revealing sharp yellow teeth, chunks of rotten flesh poking out from between them. Patches of wiry hair sprout from her scalp in clumps matted with filth.

I lunge, grabbing hold of her ankles. She cries out and takes off into the air. My stomach loops as the ground drops away beneath us. Wind whips my face, stinging my eyes and stealing my breath, but I refuse to let go. Black blood drips over my face from the puncture wound in the harpy's breast.

With each beat of her powerful wings, the harpy carries us higher and higher until we hover over the rock formations. Nausea roils through me. The rocks are each topped by a nest. They're little more than crude piles of sticks and dried vegetation, but all heaped with festering carcasses and gnawed bones.

The harpy shrieks and starts thrashing above one of the nests. I let go, and don't think. Not about the disgusting gushing sound my boots make as they land in the nest, not about the height. Not even about where Delphia and Eleanor are.

I act on instinct and by now, my instincts for killing are perfect.

There's not enough room up here to get a hard enough swing with my sword, so I unsheathe one of Delphia's instead. Her twin blades are small; this one is like a long knife in my hand. But it's just what I need to slit the throat of the harpy, retrieve the grappling hook, and kick the creature over the edge.

My shoulders heave with my ragged breath as I scan the horizon. Three harpies leap up and down on the edge of a nest on one of the flat-topped rock spires in the distance.

I measure the length between the nest I'm on and the next closest one to the harpies: about ten feet. I clench my fists and roll my neck. Not much room in this nest for a running start, but it will have to do.

Rotten sinew and brittle bones crack beneath my feet as I run then leap. I land in the next nest with a thud, rolling over a half-eaten carcass of what might once have been a horse. Then I'm up and leaping to the next one before I give myself a chance to think.

With jump after jump, I cross the rock spires. As I approach, I see the girls huddled together, backs pressed to the edge of the nest as the three harpies surround them. The monstrosities screech and cackle, poking at the girls with their wingtips. Delphia grabs a bone from the nest and swings it wildly. One of the harpies shoots out a foot, grabbing the bone in its talons and cracking it. Delphia screams.

Eleanor buries her face into Delphia's shoulder and raises her hands. A shower of sparks flies from her fingertips. An ember catches on one of the harpy's feathers, and it begins leaping up and down, desperately trying to snuff it out with its fae-like maw. The other two harpies laugh hysterically.

Rage boils through me. I take each jump faster, more recklessly. With every beat of those monsters' wings, my fury intensifies. Blood courses through my veins. Already, I can feel their wings snapping under my hands, feel the splatter of their blood as I make them pay.

With a primal roar, I charge forward, taking the very last jump and landing in their nest. The world around me blurs into a whirlwind of motion as I launch myself at the first harpy. Delphia's blade cracks through the breastbone and I push harder until I feel the spurt of heart's blood.

The second harpy screeches and bats its wings to get away, but I'm faster. I cut this one horizontally. A gush of foul innards spill from its belly before I kick it over the side.

The last harpy hovers protectively over her prey, attempting to shield the girls from my sight. One of her talons grips Delphia's tunic and slices through the skin. A line of blood courses across Delphia's collarbone.

Red floods my vision. I snag the harpy around the neck and pull her away from the girls. She beats at me with those dirty wings, but I wrestle the monster to the ground, pinning her beneath me. Her leathery skin cracks as she bites at my neck.

With a sound as animalistic as the harpy's, I drive the blade down into her chest. Her neck. Her eyes. Her wings.

Black blood splatters over my face, but I don't stop. I stab and stab and stab. This monster must *pay*. The muscles of my arm scream, and I can barely get a breath in. My vision is red and black spots, but I don't stop stabbing.

Finally, my blade hits rock. I take in a shaky breath. The creature below me is so mutilated, I've cut all the way to the bottom of the nest. My hand stills.

My hand and Delphia's beautiful blade, modeled like her brother's, are both pitch-black with monster blood. Sitting back on my heels, I try to regulate my breathing.

I blink the blood out of my eyes and turn to the side. The girls have their arms wrapped around each other. They're shaking, their eyes wide and haunted.

They're afraid.

Not of the harpies.

Of me.

I try to wipe the blood off my face, but there's no part of me that's unmarred. I can't even clean Delphia's blade. "Girls . . ."

A soft whinny sounds from the other side of the nest. It's coming from beneath the body of the first harpy I killed in this nest. Grateful for any distraction from staring at the horrified looks the girls are giving me, I get up and walk over to the body. With a shove, I roll it off the edge.

Beneath it quivers a white foal. At least, I think it's white, though its coat is covered in harpy blood and tucked tight to its body are . . .

"Seven realms," I mutter. "Delphia, you were right."

"What is it?" she asks, her voice shakier than I've ever heard.

"Come and see."

The girls don't move. I turn to them and try to smile. They both stare at me with the same etched look of fear.

I return to them and hold out my hands. "Come on. You'll want to see this. I promise it's okay." I look from Eleanor to Delphia. "You can trust me. It's not going to hurt you."

The princesses look at each other, silent words passing between them. Then they each take one of my hands. I walk them over to the other side of the nest.

The young Pegasus blinks up at them and gives a little whinny.

"You were right, Delphia," I whisper. "The Pegasuses are here. We're going to find them, okay?"

Delphia sinks to her knees. Her body shakes and tears rush down her face. She holds her hands out, and the foal sniffs her fingers before leaning into her touch.

"They're real," she cries. "I knew they were real!"

Eleanor falls to her knees beside her and runs her hands over the foal's body. Then she blinks up at me. "We'll save her, won't we, Ezryn?"

"Of course we will."

Two hours and a complicated pulley system using my grappling hook and rope later, we're back on the ground. All four of us.

The girls chatter excitedly about names for the foal before deciding on Drusilla, the name of Delphia's grandmother. The little beast trots happily beside them. Besides a few talon marks, the foal is unharmed.

It is completely unafraid of them, I think. This is no wild animal. It has been raised with the fae. *We're going to find the Huntresses. I'll bring them back to Summer with Delphia and Eleanor. We're going to survive this.*

Though the foal has eased some of the pain and fear, I can still sense it from the girls. A wariness they'd never had before.

Good. It's what's needed to survive. If I have to be a killer to keep them safe, I will be. Even if they hate me for it.

50

DAYTON

Instinct takes over and I grab Rosie's golden thorn knife from my back pocket and slice open the rope trap. I land on both feet, and easily catch Rosie, who falls into my arms.

"Stay down, love," I say and hurl us both to the ground just as the trident careens over our heads and embeds into the tree.

I grab Rosie beneath her arms and haul her to her feet. Branches break behind us. I chance a glance back at our hunter, a tall figure with a dark hood shadowing his face. Male, broad-shouldered, and radiating power.

"I can use my thorns," Rosalina hisses.

"No," I say. "Don't reveal who you are yet. I can handle one man."

The shadowy figure rips the trident from the tree with a *crack*. The weapon has a long reach, but once I get past his defenses, a quick strike to his chest should take him down. I zig-zag toward him, feinting left as he drives the trident in my direction, then duck, planning to come up right in front of him.

The handle of the weapon smacks me in the side of the face, and I go down hard in the foliage.

Never stay down. Stay down and your enemies will seize the advantage, turning the tide against you in an instant. Old lessons play in my mind. The figure pulls the trident back, poised to strike. I roll to the side, trident spraying up dirt and leaves beside my head.

I somersault, leaping up at his back. Dagger in hand, I move to strike.

The bastard has already turned, trident's prongs slicing three red lines across my chest. While I'm still reeling in shock, he gives a dissatisfied grunt and kicks me in the stomach.

"That's the last time you touch him," Rosalina growls.

"Now you're done for," I croak.

Light glistens across the jungle and, with a scream, golden briars erupt from the ground, snaking toward us in great arcs. The shadowed figure turns from me then leaps *onto* the briars, bounding over them toward Rosie. He raises the trident above his head.

I see the shock on Rosalina's face. She tries to change the briars' path, bringing them up to strike the man, but he cuts them in half with a wave of the trident.

"No!" I scream, and a torrent of water shoots from my palms.

The man doesn't even turn, just thrusts a hand behind him, a gale of wind blasting the water away.

The man jumps, poised to attack Rosie.

I'm across the jungle in a single instant, blocking her body with my own, feeling the sharp slice of the trident against my back. I push her to the ground, grunting as we roll away.

"Dayton!" she gasps, gripping me tight around the neck.

The shadowy figure paces, watching us, no doubt anticipating our next action. This man responds like he knows my every move.

And hers. Like he knows exactly how to counteract her thorns.

"I can take us back to Castletree," Rosalina whispers.

"I'm not done yet," I growl. "Damn, I wish I had my swords."

"You do have something," Rosalina says, touching my pocket.

And the token within it, which holds the Trident of Honor. I don't have time to think through the gravity of what it means to wield a weapon of such caliber. I've always been one to react to the situation as needed, and right now, I need a damn weapon.

The foliage breaks behind me as the man approaches. I reach into my pocket and pull out the token, throwing it over my neck. I think of the trident. With a flash of brightness, it appears solid in my hands. A glow emits from it, illuminating Rosie in teal light.

"I promised Ez I'd protect you," I say and I almost do something stupid, like finish that kiss I tried to give her earlier. At the thought, warmth spreads across my chest. I've never been so sure this bastard threatening her needs to fucking die.

I leap up, meeting his trident with my own in a metal clang. I press forward, but he steps easily over every root and rock. His movements are fluid, almost mesmerizing, as he mirrors my stance with uncanny precision.

We dance between the shadows of the trees, the heat of the jungle sweltering. Sweat beads on my brow as I struggle to keep up with the relentless assault. With each move, he anticipates my next step.

I need to outsmart him and end this quickly. I feign a stumble, expecting to catch him off-guard and strike at his opening. He meets my thrust, and the prongs of our tridents interlock. I drive my heels into the ground, putting all my weight behind the attack. Fuck, this bastard is strong.

Then, to my astonishment, he takes one hand off his trident. From his free hand, a blast of water erupts, striking me in the chest, shooting me backward. The man rushes forward and strikes his trident into the ground, pinning mine to the earth.

"Now, there's a weapon I haven't seen for ages," the shadowed figure speaks, staring down at our interlocking tridents.

That voice . . .

He fought like he knew my every move because he *does*.

The shadowed man throws back his hood, and my old master stares down at me.

"Justus," I breathe, staggering up on my forearms. "What are you doing here?"

"Still teaching you, apparently." He flicks my trident into the air with his own, where I reach out a palm to catch it. "Follow me."

DUSK FALLS OVER THE ISLAND, casting everything in a hazy pink glow. Justus's cabin lies perched at the highest point. The ocean stretches all around us, sapphire waters blending with the fiery hues of the setting sun.

The hut is simple, weathered wood and a palm-frond roof, built only from what the island has to offer. I rest outside of it before a roaring fire, flickering light dancing across the violet earth.

Justus sits across from me, stirring a bubbling pot of stew that is cooking on the fire. He's one of the oldest fae I know. Long gray hair is tied at the nape of his neck with a leather cord, and he's grown a scratchy beard. Nicks and scars line his weather-worn face, and his voice has the gravel of a stone bed. I think Rosalina had been quite surprised when I'd gone from a death match in one moment to bounding over and hugging the man the next.

But it had suddenly all made sense. I wasn't in any danger. Neither was Rosalina. Sure, I'd been nicked a few times, but that's just how Justus works. *You don't learn if you don't get hurt, especially someone as thick-skulled as you, Daytonales.*

Rosie had come around, especially when he mentioned something about stew and a warm place to sleep. The door to the cabin opens and she steps out. Her hair falls in salt-thick waves around her face, and the top of her nose is slightly burned. The sun has brought out a small splattering of freckles on her cheeks. It's cute and reminds me of Farron.

"I feel like every inch of me is covered in sand and salt and more sand," Rosalina grumbles.

"After you eat, there's a stream nearby, and you may make use of my extra clothes," Justus says, then turns to me. "She's one of the reasons you lost the fight."

"Huh?"

Rosie walks closer. The firelight sparkles in her hair and eyes like it wants to join with her. She sits down, giving me a quick smile, before turning to Justus.

"Is it so wrong to protect your allies?" she asks.

"It is if it puts you in jeopardy. You can't protect anyone if you're dead." He ladles a cup of stew into a coconut bowl. "You two will have to overcome that if you're to fight in the arena together."

"Dayton told you about that?" Rosalina gives a quick nod of thanks as she accepts the stew.

"No time to waste," I say.

Justus hands me my own steaming bowl, and I eagerly bring it to my lips, taking a sip and swallowing sweet potato, pineapple, and gummy roots.

"So, you trained Dayton?" Rosalina asks.

"He unfortunately forced that task upon me," Justus says.

I can only laugh at the memory. "Damocles and Decimus were both trained in the palace, but I used to get bored with my lessons and sneak out. I was only a child at this point and preferred to play with the other kids in the foothills around Hadria. They told me stories of an ancient fae warrior masquerading as a goat herder outside the city. I thought if anyone could teach me to beat my brothers in combat, it was him."

"I believe the words you first said to me were, 'Teach me to be a hero,'" Justus says, sipping his own bowl.

"Well, I figured only a hero could beat them," I reply.

"So, you agreed to take Dayton on as your student?" Rosalina's eyes light up. There's nothing that girl loves more than a story, and I intend to give her a good one.

"Oh, it wasn't that easy. I went up there every day for a month, and every day he sent me packing, saying he was just a goat herder and he had nothing to teach me. But on the thirty-first day, he said I obviously had energy to burn, and I might as well be useful while I was up there. He had me shovel the goat pen. *But* he corrected my hold on the shovel and when I sparred with Decimus later that day, I didn't drop my swords."

Rosalina looks between us eagerly, urging us to continue with her eyes.

"It went like that for a while. Work, work, work, with the occasional hint. It wasn't until I told him I had signed up for the Luminae Games that he finally relented, and our training began."

"Because you were a *child* entering into one of the most dangerous arena fights in all of Summer."

"That child became the youngest to ever win those games," I say, downing my stew and holding out my bowl for more. "Thanks to your training."

"What are the Luminae Games?" Rosalina asks.

"A specific type of tournament that makes use of an ancient artefact recovered from the Above," Justus explains. "The artefact, known as the Orb of Ancestors, allows the royal family of Summer to commune with the memory of past leaders and great gladiators who gave their lives upon the sands."

"But during the Luminae Games, we use it for something else," I say.

"The orb is used to bring ancient warriors back to the arena," Justus says. "Their memory, etched in light, comes to life to fight again, testing the new gladiators of Summer."

"Trust me, a blade of light can kill you just as easily as a real one," I say. "After that, our training truly began."

"I thought I could make you a hero," he says.

A pit forms in my stomach at the sadness in his words. I know I have to ask, but the words are heavy on my tongue. "What are you doing out here? After the War of Thorns, I looked for you, but you disappeared—"

Justus shakes his head. "I failed Summer. Failed your mother. Failed all of you."

"You didn't fail them," I say, staring straight into the flames. "I did."

"No one failed anything," Rosalina says. "Will you help us prepare for the arena?"

"I could not help him before," Justus says. "I could not stop this war. What can I offer now?"

Rosalina looks over at him, a fire in her eyes. "Dayton *is* a hero. He may not see it, but he has saved me again and again. He's back now, despite everything, despite his curse, to reclaim Summer."

"So, the curse is real?" Justus asks. "I have heard whispers."

"Yes. You'll see soon enough." I flick my gaze to the approaching sunset.

"You have a way to break it," Rosalina says. "Your mate is alive and awaits you."

The thought makes me feel even heavier. I rest my head in my hands and look up at Justus. "I understand how you combated my moves in the fight. But you did the same with Rosalina and her thorns. It was like you knew exactly how she worked. You never fought Caspian in the war, so how could you know her magic?"

"You're right. I never fought Caspian." Justus stands and looks down at us. "But I know how to combat the thorns because I was trained by the one who first wielded them."

Rosalina and I exchange a stunned glance.

"Take my cabin and rest. Tomorrow, I will teach Aurelia's daughter some tricks," Justus says. "For you, Daytonales, you are already a master at your dual swords. Now, it's time to learn how to wield my old trident."

With that, he walks into the woods.

"He really is an ancient warrior." Rosalina gasps. "He *knew* my mother."

His old trident. "He knew your mother," I say, as it finally dawns on me. "Because he was never a goat herder, just as he was never actually Justus. He's Aeneas, the first High Prince of Summer."

51

ROSALINA

H ands full of clean tunics, I follow Dayton through the jungle
until I hear the soft bubbling of water. He pushes back a leaf as
tall as me, revealing a silvery stream cutting through the
foliage.

"Wow," I gasp. "It's beautiful."

Dayton stares at me for a moment, then walks downstream. "I'll go
behind this bend to give you some privacy."

"Right," I say, trying to ignore the disappointment that swirls inside of
me as I watch him disappear around the corner.

Leaving the dry clothes on the bank, I strip down to my bra and
panties, not willing to go completely naked in the jungle in case Justus
wanders over. The stream is cold yet refreshing. Dirt and sand float off me
as I wade deeper. *Gross.*

I take a plunge and work furiously at the mats in my hair, desperately
wishing for some conditioner. Then I scrub my skin, before returning to
the stream's edge and grabbing my clothes to give them a wash in the
deep water as well.

As I work, the sounds of the jungle come alive: a chorus of birds
bidding farewell to the day, the chirping of crickets, the rustle of leaves,
the murmur of the stream, all blending in a harmonious lullaby. I close my
eyes, surrendering to the serenade of the jungle.

Something slimy prickles on my arm. Opening my eyes, I see a giant black bug attached to my forearm. A bloodcurdling scream erupts from me.

Water splashes and suddenly Dayton is in front of me, the trident gleaming in his hands. It's like he moves faster in the water than out of it. He grabs my shoulders and whips his head back and forth, searching for injury. "What is it, Rosie?"

"My arm," I squeak.

He looks down, notices the bug, then bursts out laughing. The trident disappears into light and flows back into his necklace. He's been wearing it on a separate string since he first faced Justus. "That's a nightfire caterpillar, Blossom."

"A what?"

He tilts his gaze to the sky. I notice he hasn't completely stripped either, wearing only tight black shorts. "Should be about time," he murmurs.

"Yeah, about time to take this *off* me!"

"During the day, they look like this, but when night approaches . . ." His movements are slow, careful, as he gently taps the black bug three times. "They change."

The caterpillar shudders, sending a strange tingling sensation up and down my arm. There's a small crack and then two translucent wings appear from it, a soft orange glow emanating from its shell. The wings flutter once, twice, then it lifts into the air.

"Wow," I gasp.

"Just wait," Dayton says, grabbing my arm and spinning me toward the trees. "It just takes one."

Suddenly, the whole emerald forest is filled with fluttering orange lights, like dancing flames rising into the sky. The Summer Realm's version of fireflies.

"It's so pretty," I whisper, running a hand over the water that ripples with their reflections, like a hundred sparkling suns.

"Quite the scream, for such a little thing," Dayton says, squeezing my arm.

"I'm usually not scared of bugs," I say, trying to regain some dignity. "It just startled me."

"Sure, Blossom." Dayton smirks.

"Hey, I didn't grow up in a place where there are bugs as big as my hand."

Dayton laughs and snatches my wrist. "Nah, it was bigger. Your hand is tiny." He lines his up with mine, and I feel his calloused fingertips against my palm.

"Only compared to yours," I breathe, not taking my hand away.

He tilts his head. His hair looks longer wet. Burnished golden ends curl over his damp collarbone. "Your shoulders are burned," he says.

In a swift movement, he disappears beneath the water, and all I see are bubbles popping on the surface. I shift from foot to foot as I wait, feet sliding over the smooth rocks and silty sand.

Dayton emerges a moment later and takes a deep breath, a strange root in his hands.

"What is that?" I ask, raising a brow.

"Lotusweed." Dayton tears the bulb open, and a gooey pink liquid oozes out, which he coats his palm in.

A cooling sensation spreads over my skin as he rubs a hand along my shoulders and collarbone.

"You'll have to let this dry above water before rinsing it off," Dayton explains. "It'll help soothe the burn."

His large hands move softly over my skin. He caresses my chest, fingers nearly brushing the tops of my breasts. My body shivers, and a sinful heat clenches in my core.

I can't banish the memories of how he's touched me there, grasping my breast with his whole hand, the melody of kisses he left over my body with his lips. I flick my gaze away, desperately trying to think of something else. I know I should step away, but it's as if I'm addicted to his touch.

He moves to my back, sending shivers down my spine. I can't help but let out a soft moan as I practically feel the heat evaporating from my body.

Dayton's breath hitches as he lifts his hands. Disappointment flutters inside me. *Why can't I ever keep my mouth shut?*

"Turn," Dayton says.

I do, every instinct in me obeying him.

He smears a line of pink goo over my nose. "Can't have your nose this red. Though it is cute."

My cheeks heat at his compliment, and he quickly paints them with the lotusweed as well. Though, I think we both know my cheeks aren't burned.

Dayton steps away from me and rubs his hands together beneath the water. "Guess I'll stay close by, so you don't get scared again."

"Good call. You never know, I may spot a particularly frightful monkey."

"Monkeys are no joke." His grin widens. "Got in quite the battle with one as a kid. It kept stealing my coconuts."

I smile as Dayton continues on with another story of chasing a monkey through the city when it stole Farron's glasses. I know I should look away, but I can't. Can't help but notice the hard lines of his muscles as he stretches and washes the sand from his hair. How his stomach ripples, the tempting line of hair that dips below his waistband. How I'm envious of the droplets of water that caress his body.

"Time for this to come off," he says suddenly. Then Dayton lunges at me, tackling me beneath the water.

We plunge into the cold depths. Here, where no one can see us, his hands are all over me, rubbing away the lotusweed goo. I open my eyes underwater and see his are wide, taking in my barely covered body. His hair flows in golden waves around him.

Dayton smiles when our eyes meet. He leans in close.

Does it make me a horrible person if one of these times I don't push him away?

But it's not a kiss. He brushes away the rest of the goo from my face, then drags me to the surface.

"Thank you," I say.

His gaze is already on the sky. "Think we lingered too long. Looks like I'll be making my way back as a wolf."

"I like your wolf," I say.

Something flashes in Dayton's gaze, an emotion I can't quite place. He's unusually quiet as we step on shore. I take Justus's clean clothes and go behind some trees to change. The tunic is long enough to be a dress, and I secure it around my waist with a rope belt before gathering the rest of our clothes in a bag.

When I walk out from behind the trees, the wolf is sitting as patiently as a golden retriever.

My nose crinkles as I look at him. His fur has always been covered in seaweed and shells, but it looks worse than ever. Barnacles are crusted along the sides of his face and sickly pale coral is tangled among his golden fur. *His curse is intensifying . . .*

A deep pain cuts through me. We won't be on this island forever. Soon, we'll return to Hadria, and Dayton will need to complete his mate bond. That's the only way to break his curse.

I can't help him with that.

But there are still some things I can do.

"You look like you've been rolling in the surf." I run my fingers through his fur, pulling out the seaweed and shells. He stays quiet as I do, but every so often, he knocks me with his massive snout or nearly trips me with his tail. Finally, I've freed all of the debris and tossed it to the jungle floor.

"Rosie," he says, "do you think it was fate that brought us to this island?"

I've finished my job, but I can't remove my hands from the wolf's soft fur. I turn to look into his seafoam eyes. "You're part of this realm, Day. Not just one of the people, but part of the land, as well. Perhaps the tides knew this was where you needed to be."

He gives a long sigh, then trots back in the direction of Justus's cabin. "So, it is fate."

I hike my bag over my shoulder and struggle after him through the thick foliage. "Why do you sound so upset about that?"

Dayton shakes his head, golden fur blowing in the warm night wind. "The thing is, I've been trying to convince myself this whole fate thing is a hoax. Because I haven't liked a single twist fate's woven for me."

I stay rooted to the spot as he breaks through a thick line of trees. Dayton's words slowly make their way through my mind. Fate. Fated mates. *Is he talking about Wrenley?*

52

CASPIAN

Waking up with the Autumn Prince in my bedroom wasn't something I ever imagined happening. Farron is curled on the floor beside my bed in a bundle of blankets. He didn't want to share with me.

Misty light shines in from the floor-to-ceiling balcony, illuminating my room. My bedroom is one of the few places in the Below I can stand. A beautiful vanity sits against one wall, next to a large wardrobe overflowing with garments of deep purples, rich maroons, and black. I cross to it and throw on a sheer robe, knotting it at my waist.

The crystal-lit fireplace crackles with sparks of bright pink, blue, and yellow.

Opening my door, I find breakfast already delivered. Carrying the silver tray, I cross to my bed and remove the lid to uncover a platter of freshly baked pastries and a bowl of pomegranate seeds. A pot of hot coffee steams beside it with small cups of cream and sugar.

"What's that delicious smell?" Farron mumbles sleepily. He sits up, yawning and stretching. His shirt rides up to reveal his stomach.

"Sorry." I take a bite out of one of the pastries. "Only enough for one. I don't usually have overnight guests."

"No, you prefer to send all your friends to us," Farron sneers. He reaches up and snags the bowl of pomegranate. "Yet somehow, you weaseled your way into becoming the overnight guest," he adds.

My hands are still on the coffee pot as I flash back to that night. Not just the physical sensations—which had been exquisite—but sleeping beside them. Rosalina in my arms, Kel's hands in my hair.

"Are you jealous? Rosalina is quite the work of art."

"She tells me everything, you know," Farron says, finishing the bowl and reaching for my half-eaten pastry. "No. I'm not jealous. Unlike you, I prefer to trust people. If it's Rosalina's heart's wish, I will not stand in the way."

It's more complicated than that. I know why it doesn't tear Farron apart. *Because we're all her mates.* But I lied to Farron about that, or at least let him believe I wasn't. It won't matter. If the Queen makes me human, it might very well destroy my mate bond. Then neither Farron, Kel, nor Rosie will be burdened with me.

Ezryn will probably throw a fucking party.

"Right," I say and stride to my closet, grabbing a few pieces and tossing them to the floor in front of Farron. "Our special event occurs in four nights, but it's never too early to prepare to look your best. It will be a masquerade, so no one will see your face. Though, you can't very well go in a cute little leaf-lined vest."

Farron rolls his eyes but gathers the clothes and pads into the attached bathroom. Meanwhile, I take a seat at the vanity, arranging the small pots of gels and powders.

"I'm not coming out in this!" Farron calls from the other room.

"If you don't like it, it means you'll fit right in at a Cryptgarden party."

There's a long sigh, and Farron shuffles out. A smirk tugs at the corners of my lips. He looks positively delicious. My leather pants cling to the lean muscles of his legs. The silk shirt is cut deep enough to show the contours of his chest. A black velvet cloak drapes over his shoulders. As he stands before me, dressed in my clothes and bathed in darkness and desire, I can't help but feel a surge of possessiveness wash over me. *He's going to be such a spectacle at this party.*

"Sit down across from me," I say, patting the second stool.

Farron groans, plucking at the pants, and sits down.

"There's still a few days to the party," I say, picking up a pot of black smoky powder. "But we should prepare your look." As much as I'd love to get this whole thing over with tonight, we have to give Kel time to get through the labyrinth.

"I thought my face would be covered."

"Most of it. Close your eyes."

Farron does, and it seems a shame to cover his face with anything. He is so effortlessly beautiful—the splash of freckles across his nose, his thick lashes and brows, the parted lips, and his wild auburn hair that he hasn't even bothered to smooth since waking up.

"Is this some sort of trick?" Farron asks. "Or are you using magic to make me look as enchanting as you?" His golden eyes flash open. "Not that I—"

"You think I'm enchanting?"

"No," he says quickly.

"I don't even have to add blush, Autumn Prince. You're already red."

He gives a low growl in the back of his throat and closes his eyes. "Can we just get this over with?"

I begin by adding some smoky black around his eyes, then bronze under his cheekbones.

"I didn't take you for it," he says.

"Take me for what?"

"A reader."

I glance away from him to my overcrowded bookshelf in the corner. "Kel said the same thing when he first came here. When you grow up in the Below, there's not much that can help you escape."

A muscle feathers in Farron's jaw. Maybe he's thinking of escaping from his own world, but I can't fathom what Farron would need to escape from. He grew up with two doting parents, loving siblings, and a realm that adores him.

Maybe he's thinking the same thing because his next question surprises me. "What's your favorite type of book to read?"

"Why are you even bothering asking? I already saw you checking out the books last night." I sigh, rubbing gel through his hair, changing the auburn to a deep brown. I take to styling it as well because he's practically hopeless. "When I was young, I liked to read stories of the four seasonal realms. They seemed so different from down here."

Farron is silent for a moment, and I realize his hands are near on my waist, unconsciously playing with the tassels of my robe. "There're some books in Castletree's library I think you might like. I could find them for you after all of this is done."

"Okay."

"Okay."

His fingers still as if he's finally realized how close his hands were to me. But he doesn't move away.

"But you'll have to check them out properly," he says, smiling. "Or else Rosalina will kill me."

"We wouldn't want that. Open your eyes. I'm done."

He does, turning to the mirror. He was always beautiful, but now he looks devastating. Dark-lined eyes, rouge-stained lips. His hair brushed to one side, looking just the right amount of disheveled.

"Imagine if Rosalina could see you now," I say.

The wave of desire that pulses off him is maddening. My breath slows to deep intentional rasps. His golden eyes look like gemstones in a black wall.

"I guess you're good at some things," Farron says, hand patting my thigh through the sheer robe.

Stars, I haven't even gotten dressed. What do I look like? My reflection shows my hair is a mess, and my own cheeks are flushed.

"What do we do now?" Farron breathes.

There are a million answers I want to give him, but right now, there's only one that matters. I lean forward and reach past him, grabbing the crumbled piece of paper on the vanity. "Now that you look like a dark prince, we write a spell befitting one."

53

ROSALINA

My legs feel like rubber as I sit at the edge of the stream. The cold water is a huge relief to my aching muscles. The late afternoon sun burns hot in the sky.

Justus hands me a flask of cold water and goes to perch nearby on a high rock. Behind him, the stream stretches like a glimmering ribbon, a tapestry of colors scattering the bank—emerald ferns and bright yellow flowers as big as my head, their sweet fragrance carrying on the breeze. It looks so different in the daylight.

"You did well today," he says.

"Dayton taught me everything I know," I say. The Summer Prince has run up to the cabin to fetch a late lunch for us.

"He's a good teacher, and you're a fast learner," Justus continues. "You have a strong handle on the basics. Give it a few years and you could be a real competitor in the arena."

Justus spent the day teaching me the basics of how the games work, as well as the skills that would be most useful in the arena. That meant learning proper footwork, so I don't get knocked over easily, and if I do, how to get up quickly. We went over a few moves with the dual swords, but mostly defensive techniques. Dayton will be handling most of the combat, while I'll focus on getting a bow and providing ranged support.

"Thanks," I say, flushing a little. "I'm really just going to try to stay alive in there."

"In Kairyn's games," Justus says, "there is no other goal. You win or you die."

While I was working with Justus, Dayton stayed nearby, practicing some techniques with the trident. But when Justus sparred with him, Dayton fumbled every round. He's been unusually quiet.

"Dayton will be there," I say. "So, we'll win."

A grave look passes over Justus's face. "At this rate, he doesn't have what it takes to win in the arena."

"How can you say that?" I ask. "He's *never* lost before."

"He's never fought in the arena with you before," Justus counters. "When I came upon you in the jungle, his every stance, every action, was a direct reflection of your position."

I drag my wet hand over a rock, leaving a dark sapphire trail. "He made a vow to my mate to protect me."

Justus waves his hand. "Dayton is protective, I'll give you that. But there's something different about him when you're around and that might just help you win Kairyn's twisted games."

"I thought you said I was his weakness."

Justus smiles broadly. There's a gap between his two front teeth that gives him an almost youthful charm. "Only because you two haven't figured out how to turn that into a strength yet."

Before I can question him more, Dayton breaks through the foliage, a basket of fresh fruit in his arms. He sets it down beside the riverbank, then takes an apple, bouncing it off his elbow before angling it toward me with a grin.

I reach for it, but it fumbles out of my grip. Instinctively, I shoot a golden thorn from the ground, and it spears the apple right beside me.

"Good catch, Rosie," Dayton says, peeling a banana, then flopping down into the water on top of a giant lily pad. "If only you could use that in the arena, then you'd have no problem."

"We're betting on Kairyn letting you participate for the sport of it," I remind him, "but they can't know it's me. They'd never let me participate in the games or get close to the bow."

Dayton turns to his trainer. "Since you're more ancient than I ever realized, did you ever live in the fabled Above? Do you think Kairyn will truly be able to open a way there if he gets all five of the divine weapons?"

Justus stills. "He may be able to open a way yet. But for what reason he would want to is beyond me. Sira left nothing of our home realm but ash, dust, and ruin."

Memories upon memories play on his face. This fae knew my mother and once lived in the same realm as her. I know very well how painful some memories are, and don't want to pry. Dayton must sense it too because he stays quiet.

Perhaps he'll share more when he's ready. We'll be here with Justus another day at least. This morning, we asked him if he knew of a way for us to return to Hadria. The old master was insistent he had one but refused to elaborate.

"Can you tell me what my mother was like?" I ask. Papa has told me stories of her, but they were about Anya, the human. It may have been a part of who she was, but it wasn't all of her. I long to know this other side. The one of the Queen.

Justus's face softens. "She was a vicious fighter when she needed to be, with a cunning mind. Though, it was her kindness that truly set her apart as a leader. There wasn't a soul too small in the Enchanted Vale for her to help, from the lowest forest thrush with a broken leg to the greatest noble. Aurelia aided them all."

Even after all these years, there is a reverence in his words when he speaks of her. A part of me wants to tell him that she's alive, that right now, the High Prince of Winter and my father are rescuing her. But Caspian was adamant that no one else can know. It would be too dangerous if his mother got wind of what we're planning. I silently vow that once we save her, there will be a chance for her to reunite with her first High Prince of Summer.

"She looked a lot like you," Justus continues. "I'd have known who you were even if I hadn't heard the rumors of the Golden Rose or seen you use the briars."

"She used briars like me, didn't she?"

"Down to the same color," Justus says. "She always did have a fondness for roses. The Queen's greatest strength was change. She transformed a tree into a castle and barren empty land into enchanted realms. Because she created it, she was connected to all of it. Not just the briars and the earth, but all who are born from it. People of land, sky, and sea."

People of the sea. "The sirens," I whisper. "I remember reading about the ancient city of Aerantheis. She saved the people by transforming them into sirens. Is that really true?"

"Indeed," Justus says. "They are a powerful people, able to summon legs upon land and a tail in the sea."

Dayton dips his head back into the water, dappled sunlight playing over his chest. "I might have seen a siren after the shipwreck. A glimmer of silver in the water."

"Maybe they helped us to shore," I suggest.

"It's not a far-off idea, young Rose," Justus says. "The High Prince of Summer and the Queen's daughter in the ocean together would have felt like a great well of power. One you'll have to draw upon to return to Hadria."

"What do you mean?" Dayton asks, sitting up.

"If you want to get home, the sirens are your only hope," Justus says. "But Daytonales, if you leave before mastering the Trident of Honor, you'll never reclaim Summer."

54

ROSALINA

The sky is a canvas painted in hues of coral and lavender, streaked with wisps of cotton candy clouds that catch the dying light of the setting sun. I walk along the powdery sand, my bare feet leaving imprints behind me.

Dayton walks closer to the water, sinking up to his ankles in the wet shoreline. Waves lap up his legs before curling back out to the sea. Seagulls wheel overhead, their cries almost joyful. The salty breeze carries with it the scent of brine and seaweed, mingling with the sweet fragrance of tropical blooms that dot the shoreline.

It's so peaceful here, so tranquil. For a moment, it almost makes me forget about everything waiting for us in Hadria. We spent the rest of the afternoon training with Justus, but Dayton got no closer to mastering the trident. So, we'll be here for another night.

There's nothing to do but wait. Dayton shifts closer to me, his fingertips grazing mine. I wish I could grab his hand, but I smile up at him instead. "It's beautiful here."

His teal gaze doesn't leave mine. "I agree. The Summer Realm suits you."

There are far worse places to wait. In this moment, we're free to wander these sandy shores, to lose ourselves in the beauty of the fading day. Soon, the wolf will take him again. I turn my head to the sinking sun, letting its warmth seep into my soul like I'm one of the trees in the lush forest.

"Want to watch the sunset from here before we go back?" Dayton asks.

"Sure." I take a seat on the silken sand, knees drawn to my chest, toes just touching the ebb and flow of the waves.

Dayton collapses beside me. He isn't wearing a shirt, as usual, just loose cropped pants. He stretches his hands over his knees, dangling the token of Summer from his fingertips. I notice he hasn't strung it back with the rest of his shells, instead just corded it on its own with a thin piece of twine.

"Damocles wouldn't have had any trouble wielding this trident," he says softly.

"Your brother had the Blessing of Summer before you, didn't he?"

Dayton nods. "Yes, my mother passed it to him before she became pregnant with Delphia."

"Dayton," I say cautiously, "you've never told me what happened to your family."

A muscle feathers in his jaw. "I don't talk about it, not with anyone. People know what happened, but it's not a pleasant story, Rosalina."

It's almost like I can feel it within him, festering and coiling. Something eating him away from the inside out. Slowly, I reach out and place a hand on his arm. "Your family seems to be on your mind a lot since returning to Summer. If you'd like to talk about it, I'm here to listen."

Dayton shakes his head, hand clenching around the token. "I know what everyone thinks of me, the drunken Prince of Summer. A coward who let his brothers die. But the truth is, it's so much worse than all of that. I feel like I've lost you once already. I can't lose you again to this truth."

It takes me a moment to register his words. Lost me once . . . lost my love. Lost the chance to love me. Waves of grief flow through me.

I crawl in front of Dayton, wet knees sinking in the ground. I grab his face and force him to look at me. His teal gaze blinks open, tears clinging to his lashes like dewdrops on morning petals. "I'll always stay with you, Day, I promise. You're not going to lose me." His tears fall over my fingers, but I hold on, making him believe it. "We're a team. Help me understand what you're going through."

He places his large hand over mine. "That better be a promise, Blossom."

"Promise."

Dayton stares at me for a moment longer before flashing a lopsided grin. "You know, water nymphs are feisty creatures, but in my youth, I happened to have a special friend and—"

"Oh, come on." I roll my eyes. "What does this have to do with—"

"I'm getting to the point. She happened to teach me a unique trick with my magic, one of memory and water. Come here."

He widens his knees and I position myself between his legs, facing the water. Dayton reaches around me, and with a flick of his wrist, a wave rises before us in the shape of a shimmering fan.

"After Caspian created the Great Chasm and attacked the Winter Realm, the War of Thorns began," Dayton says. "All the seasonal realms against the forces of the Below. Hadria, the capital of Summer, has always been nearly impregnable, with its high walls and back to the sea."

Colors and images flicker across the fan of water, showing a large wall. A fae that looks almost like Dayton, but with short cropped golden hair, stands atop it.

"What's this?" I whisper.

Dayton's breath brushes my ear. "It's my memory."

"That's Damocles," I say.

In Dayton's memory, the former High Prince of Summer gleams golden as a god, tanned skin, with hair the color of honey. A helmet with a red plume is tucked beneath his arm. His breastplate is beaten gold, and he wears a skirt crafted of red leather strips. His eyes are blue, so similar to Dayton's. But where Dayton's gaze is all the depths of the ocean, Damocles' gaze is still as a pond with no wind.

"We'd received a report that forces of the Below were planning to march on Hadria through the Suadela Sands," Dayton explains.

"Was it Caspian?"

"No," Dayton says. "He was preoccupied with Winter. This was Sira's own force. Damocles wanted to march our army out of Hadria and meet them in the open before they got a chance to lay siege. Decimus claimed we'd have power over them in our own land, that we knew the sands better than they ever could."

Another figure appears in Dayton's memory. A shorter man, but broad of shoulders, with dark brown skin and short black hair.

"Decimus," I say. "He has the same smile as Delphie."

"I know," Dayton says. "It was Ovidius's smile. He didn't grace you with it often, but when he did, it was something special."

"What did you think of meeting Sira in the open?"

A slight hitch trembles in Dayton's voice as he continues, and I place my hand on his leg to steady him. "I advised against it. I told him we should keep our legionnaires inside and pick off the enemy as they approached the wall. My brothers would hear none of it. Decimus told me I was a coward. Damocles told me I was afraid. He ordered me to march with them at dawn. Our parents and Delphia would stay safe in the castle, and us three brothers would ride out together. It was the last thing I ever heard him say."

The water shifts again, revealing the shouting face of his brother.

"Did you follow his orders?"

Dayton's chin dips to my shoulder, voice a low mumble. "No. I did what everyone would expect. I got drunk. I slept through dawn and their departure, passed out in some barn where no one could find me. I woke up choking on smoke."

In the memory, I see rampant flames as Dayton rushes from a barn and into a city of chaos. People run wild, buildings burn, and goblins brandish weapons.

"It was all the Below's trick," Dayton says, anger tinging his words. "Sira had lured all the vile nightmares of the desert to do her bidding. She ordered them to dig tunnels beneath our city and ambush the people within. No army was left to defend them. What Damocles and Decimus found when they rode out was not a force of the Below struggling through the desert, but one adept at it."

In the watery vision, flames lick the walls of Soltide Keep as Dayton enters. The next memory strikes me in my heart. A bloody massacre of soldiers and goblins litters the floor. I watch as Dayton falls to his knees in front of his two fathers. Jagged spears run through their lifeless bodies.

"I was too late to save them," he says.

"You could have been killed too," I say.

"I took a sword from each of them," Dayton continues. "They are the swords I still wield today. At that moment, I knew I had to find my mother and Delphia. The palace was swarming with goblins, so I leaped out a window and climbed the vines along the outside walls. I nearly fell off multiple times, I was still so sick with drink. But from that height, I could see the sands beyond the wall. How little Damocles' army had traveled. How surrounded they were.

"I got to Del's bedroom and found her and my mother. They had furniture barred against the door as a horde tried to break it down."

Dayton's mother sparkles with a fierce glint, her hair the same color as her son's. Delphia, looking much younger than she does now, clings to her mother's legs. Through the waves, I watch the reunion. Sabine shoves Delphia into Dayton's arms, ushering them to a corner of the room and pressing a stone to reveal a secret passage small enough to crawl through.

Dayton and Delphia crouch before it, their mother kissing them both.

"What did she say to you?" I ask.

Dayton's voice is hoarse. "That I had to take Delphia to safety while she held back the force. That the goblins would surely find this passage if they came upon an empty room. I tried to tell her to let me stay instead. She refused, saying she only wished to give her children a chance. But I know the real reason."

"Day—"

"I was in no state to even hold a sword."

"You don't know that," I say. "She trusted you with Delphia. She would not have wanted you to sacrifice yourself for her. No mother would."

Dayton tugs me against his chest, head dipping to the crook of my neck, speaking the story only to my skin. "We fled through the tunnel and into the streets of Hadria, but nowhere was safe."

I watch as Dayton carries Delphia through the streets, each turn, each corner drawing more and more goblins and other wicked creatures after them. He turns back once, looking to the palace, only to see a figure in purple satin fall from the tower and into the ocean.

His mother.

Delphia screams, and he covers her eyes. They round a corner only to be caged between a burning building and a troll crushing columns with his massive hammer. They run back into the streets, goblins gathering on all sides. Then Dayton pitches forward, going to all fours, Delphia tumbling from his arms. Dayton's mouth widens in a scream.

"What happened?" I whisper.

"It came to me . . . the Blessing of Summer," Dayton says. "It tore through me like all the fire of the sun. All I could think was . . . they're dead. My brothers are dead."

The memory of Dayton withers on the ground, his skin becoming luminescent. Beyond this memory, the sun sinks lower on the horizon, casting sapphire-rich shadows across the beach. The sky is a riot of color: fiery oranges, rosy pinks, and dusky purples, all swirling together.

The memory of Dayton rises, glowing from our own sun, and draws his swords.

"What did you do?" I whisper.

"I suppose," Dayton says, "I got angry."

The vision plays out in a blur: his swords flashing and magic dancing from his fingertips. He sees Delphia to safety atop the gate and rallies the surviving soldiers in Hadria to drive the invading forces out. Finally, Dayton rides out himself to the remnants of the battle.

That's when I witness magic as I've never seen before, the magic of a High Prince not bound by a curse or weakened by a sick Castletree. Dayton is a god unleashed, swords sweeping, great torrents of water flooding the sands and sinking whole legions of Sira's army. The Queen of the Below herself is there, riding atop a giant scorpion before fleeing in the face of such power. The memory is so quick, as if it's unimportant to Dayton.

It's the next image we linger on. Dayton finds Damocles after the battle is won; body blood-soaked. Dayton cradles him in his arms, rocking the limp body over and over and over, repeating the same phrase. The vision has no sound, but I don't need to hear it to read his lips. *Take it back*, he shouts to his brother, to the sky. *Take it back, take it back, take it back*.

Dayton waves his hand, and the memory falls away, ebbing back to the sea. "I never wanted to be the High Prince of Summer. It was never supposed to be me."

I turn around to face him, my own tears streaming down my face. "Dayton, I don't think you've seen what I have. You were a hero. You saved Hadria."

"No, Rosie, you *don't* see," he says, pushing away from me and standing. "If I hadn't run away from my duty and had ridden out with them, maybe I could have saved them somehow."

I push myself up. "Then you wouldn't have been there to save Delphia."

"Or maybe my mother would have escaped with her," Dayton counters. "Trust me, I've gone over it a thousand times. All I know is I let my brothers go off to battle without me, and they died. They died and I, the one who stayed behind, got the great Blessing of Summer. How is that fair or just or right?"

"Maybe staying behind was the best thing to do," I snarl back at him.

"You sensed the city was in danger. Dayton, you can't change the past, but you can look at the good you did. You saved Hadria all on your own."

He shakes his head, golden strands blowing in the wind. "We won the battle but lost so much more. It was my fault. The Enchantress was right to curse me for what I did."

The sun dips below the horizon, and the Summer Prince shifts before me to the cursed wolf.

55

CASPIAN

There's always been a beauty to the Summer Realm that captivates me. Especially in the Serenus Dusk Chambers attached to the Sun Colosseum. The gauzy drapes surrounding the bed flutter in a sea breeze that cools the sandstone room. Glittering shells and jewels are encrusted on everything from the bedposts to the vanity. If I got up from the bed and wandered to the window, I'd have a stunning view of the arena, and then beyond it, the turquoise sea stretching out until it melded with the sky. Where I've always felt cloistered in the other realms, there's a sense of freedom in Summer that I can't deny.

I stretch out over the bed and undo a few more laces on my shirt. The sweltering heat, however, I could do without.

It won't be a long visit here; not only can I feel my lungs filling with sludge, but I don't know what kind of trouble Farron is capable of getting into while left alone in Cryptgarden. Dangerous games are my favorite, but I'm used to playing them alone. One wrong move and the Autumn Prince could be discovered. A chill runs up my spine despite the heat. Not that I *care* what happens to Farron, per se, but I am giving this hero-thing a try. It wouldn't do to lose my partner so quickly.

I know the reason for my visit is approaching because the walls seem to shake with each reverberation of his step. Not that I am here to visit Kairyn, but where that walking pile of scrap metal goes, so does my sister.

Birdy swings open the door and storms in. She's not in her armor or mask. I like her like this, with her hair down, and the curve of her mouth visible. It's etched in a frown right now, but there's always a chance I can see it in a smile.

"You lost her? You *lost* her?" the raspy voice of Kairyn says as he follows behind her.

"Yeah, well, you lost her first!" Birdy snarls, rounding on him and slamming the door.

"Well, well, well, if it isn't the happy couple."

They both jerk their gazes to me. I can only imagine Birdy's glare is echoed on Kairyn's face.

"Do you always have to show up unannounced?" Birdy asks. "Get off my bed. Why are you even here?"

"Just checking up on you. Very nice accommodations here above the arena. Your cages are always gilded, aren't they, Birdy?"

She ignores me and strides to the vanity. She sits down and runs a brush aggressively through her short hair. It's curlier than usual, smelling of saltwater.

Kairyn leans against the door, head tilted back in exasperation. It's a strangely casual posture for him, one I'm not so familiar with.

"Don't mind me," I urge. "Carry on with your argument. Something something lost her?"

"The Golden Rose," Birdy snaps. "I lost her location once she went out to sea. It's not my fault. You *know* I have no mobility on the ocean."

"Yes, tricky thing about the thorns is you can grow them in the ocean soil, but the swim is the killer." I flash a grin at Kairyn.

"Maybe fate is on our side for once and she drowned," Kairyn mutters.

"We aren't so lucky," Birdy growls.

So, Rosalina's gone missing. That's better than her being in Birdy's clutches. I can only assume Rosalina and Dayton have a plan.

Whatever it is, I won't say it's going to be brilliant, but it's probably going to be spectacular.

Kairyn walks over to the vanity and stands above my sister. Slowly, almost delicately, he lifts a strand of dark hair and tucks it behind her ear. "We'll find her."

Birdy leans her head against his hand. I sit up and blink. Birdy does *not* like to be touched.

"And the High Prince of Summer, too," she whispers. "It's coming together, Kai. His Blessing will be mine."

Kairyn stiffens. "Let me kill him for you. I could do it. With Ezryn's Blessing—"

She stands suddenly and faces him. "It's not Ezryn's Blessing—it's yours. We've talked about this. If you kill Dayton, it will go to his damned sister, and you lost her, too."

"Dayton." Kairyn says his name like a curse. "Now you're calling him by that ridiculous nickname."

"It's really not that ridiculous," I chime in, examining a thread on my cuff. "Sea Puppy would be a ridiculous nickname. Or Fred, because what does that have to do with it all? But Dayton is actually quite a normal—"

"Why are you even here?" Kairyn growls, stomping toward me. "You're a layabout. A distraction. A good-for-nothing—"

"Careful." I smile. "You're starting to sound like my mother."

"No, Caspian, you be careful," Kairyn says darkly. "If you don't remember whose side you're on, you're going to get your sister killed."

My movements are quick, graceful. Deadly. Before Kairyn even has a chance to step away, I'm holding a sharp dagger made of pure shadow to the sliver of neck that shows between his helm and his chest plate. I smile up at him, though I know my eyes are radiating darkness. "I don't care what they call you. High Prince. Emperor. God. I will keep my sister safe above all else. Suggest otherwise again, and I'll protect her against the man capable of mutilating his own brother."

Silence echoes in the room. Kairyn's chest heaves up and down. "I did what I must."

"Is that what you tell yourself in the dead of night when you remember what you did to him?" I breathe.

Then there's a hand on my wrist, yanking it away. "Caspian, *stop it.*" Birdy gives me a glare that could dim a will-o'-wisp. "I don't need you showing up and keeping an eye on me. I've got everything under control. Soon, I will sit on the throne of Keep Soltide with Summer's Blessing. I'll oversee all the realm—"

"Ah, so your metal dog will run Spring and rule over a bunch of thralls, and you'll sit in your seaside palace, leader to a group of subjected fae who hate you."

"Hate me. Fear me. Love me. I care little for it," she spits. "But I'll be out of that wretched squalor in the ground, and you'll rule the dirt and darkness, Cas. Like it or not, Mother will see we are ascended. Better I have some say over my fate, lest she chooses for me as she chose for you."

I take a shaky breath in through my nose. "All the pieces must be in place. Sira's not ready for such moves yet."

"The time will come soon enough." Kairyn walks over to the window and looks out. "The celestial lands await. Sira will see herself once again in the Above."

"Right, right, Mother does love to look down on us all." I choose my words carefully. "Little problem with the weapons though, isn't there? You've got four under your control, even if you can't wield the bow yet, but that sneaky little Summer trident's gone missing, hasn't it?"

"*She* knows where it is," Birdy rasps. "I should have interrogated her myself." She looks up at Kairyn. "You're too soft."

"What would you have me do? Torture her? She's my brother's mate," he says.

"My brother! My brother! My brother!" Birdy spins in a circle. "Will I never cease hearing of Ezryn? He's as good as dead. You have his Blessing! Forget him!"

Kairyn leans over the windowsill, the breeze blowing back his black cape. "He's alive. He hunted my soldiers through the sands. He came to me in the prison. I hear his voice sometimes, screaming out my name—"

"Green Flame, rid me of this incessant chatter of fucking Ezryn," Birdy cries, covering her ears with her hands.

My teeth grind together. These two are nearly as dysfunctional at making a plan as those four princes. "Back to the Above . . . Any luck with finding someone to wield the Bow of Radiance? Word is it's the grand prize in your twisted little games."

Birdy paces across the room. "It's ridiculous. This idiot's willing to let every peasant and pauper good enough with a sword put their hands on it. They've all burned up, of course. But I could do it. I can wield it—"

"No!" Kairyn yells. He turns away from the window and storms over to her. His hulking body basically enshrouds her. "It is too much to risk. We'll find someone strong enough to withstand it."

"*I'm* strong enough, Kai," she says softly.

He takes her hand, so small in his giant gloved ones, and lightly runs a finger over her palm. A wave of nausea comes over me that has nothing to do with the sludge.

"I know you are," he murmurs. "But as I trust you with your plan, trust me with mine. If there is someone else capable of wielding the bow, I will find them. There is no reason for you to risk your life."

She rolls her eyes but doesn't pull away as quickly as I expected. When she does, her eyes linger on the shadow of his dark helm. "There is no time to waste. I'm going to the docks to get word on the storm." She flicks her gaze to me. "Lovely visit as always, Cas. Next time you see me, you may be addressing me as High Princess of Summer."

"You've always been a princess to me, Birdy," I say softly.

A smile seems to fight to grace her lips. She quickly turns and strides out the door. Kairyn goes to follow, but I grab his arm.

"You can't let her try to wield the Bow of Radiance," I say. "Whatever you do, don't let her touch it."

"I know," he says back. "You're not the only one who would do anything to protect her." Then he whips his arm away from me, turns, and storms out the door.

I stand alone in the room, the only sound the crash of waves outside. Kairyn doesn't want her to touch the bow because he's afraid she'll turn to ash.

But I know if she touches that bow, it's the realms that will burn.

56

DAYTON

The clash of tridents echoes through the jungle as I face my master. His movements are fluid and precise. Meanwhile, I feel the weight of my own failure with every strike, dragging me down like anchors into a tempestuous sea.

Maybe I could blame it on this new weapon—I always favored the dual swords—but Justus made sure I was well-versed in all weaponry. *You never know what you'll be forced to wield in the arena,* Justus had said over and over. *Never know when your sword may shatter, and you must pick up your comrade's spear on the battlefield.*

It's not a lack of skill that has been fumbling my grip, that has him pinning my trident again and again and again.

I let out a frustrated breath as I dig it out of the soft earth. It had glowed when I first wielded it, but now it looks ordinary and dull. "Isn't this thing supposed to be legendary?"

"A divine weapon is only as legendary as the person who wields it," Justus says. "Again."

Another sigh, and I gesture to Rosie sitting in the shade of a tree. "Shouldn't she have another turn?"

"Rosalina has finished her lesson for this morning," Justus says. "She did a damn fine job of it."

"Ahh." I toss a wink her way. "Guess we can't all be as perfect as you."

She smiles reassuringly. "You can do this, Dayton. Win the next one for me."

I haven't won a single spar against Justus since we arrived on this damn island, so I'm not sure where her confidence comes from. I can't help but stare a moment longer, her big brown eyes shining amber in the sunshine.

How can she still look at me like that after what I'd told her yesterday? *Hero.* She'd called me a hero. If it were anyone else, I would dismiss them entirely, but Rosalina is always truthful. She's so good and kind and brave. How can she see those things in me?

I still can't believe I was able to talk about it. I hadn't realized how trapped inside of me those memories were until they played out before us. Being with Rosie made it easier.

"I'll try, Blossom," I say and turn back to Justus. He stands waiting, wearing only light-leather armor and worn sandals.

The rumors have never done the first High Prince of Summer justice. He may use a different name now, but he can't hide that sense of power.

"Come on, boy," he says. "Let's get to it."

Heaving in a deep breath, I tighten my grip on the Trident of Honor and charge. With each thrust and parry, I struggle to keep pace, my movements hesitant and faltering against his relentless onslaught.

Sweat drips down my brow. We need to return to Summer and enter the games, which means winning a spar against him. But there's no opening, no move I can take to gain advantage. This stupid trident seems no more powerful than any other hunk of metal.

"Would you like to know why I decided to train you, boy?" Justus growls.

"Because I wouldn't leave you alone?" I say, driving the prongs of the spear toward him, which he easily dodges.

"No." He sweeps his own trident beneath my legs, and I fall hard to the ground. "Untapped potential. The same as I see in you now. Wells of it."

I push to my feet, barely blocking a blow aimed at my face.

"I watched your brothers fight in the arena," Justus continues. "They were as powerful as they would ever be."

"So, you took pity on me, the youngest brother."

"No, I saw in you the only one worthy of Summer's Blessing."

"That's not true," I growl, anger rising in me. "My brothers were near gods."

Justus gives a humorless laugh, slashing across my shoulder. "Damocles was so obsessed with glory, it made him brash. He made decisions to elevate his status as a revered victor. Decimus was strong, but it made him reckless, made him think he was invincible. They were unworthy of Summer's Blessing."

"Be quiet, old man."

"Why? It's what you've always known deep in your bones, Daytonales. That's why they're dead." Justus lunges, his trident slicing through the air. I narrowly avoid his attack before countering with a swift thrust of my own. Our tridents clash with a metallic clang, the force of the impact reverberating through my arms.

"That's not true," I growl.

"You've been holding yourself back your whole life. Admit *why*."

I shake my head, hair falling in my face. "I haven't. I'm the only undefeated gladiator to fight in the Sun Colosseum. I couldn't have done that if I was holding back!"

"Another lie. Even holding back, you're twice as good as anyone there."

I press forward, seeking an opening in Justus's defenses, but he moves with fluid grace, deflecting each of my strikes effortlessly. His experience is evident, his movements calculated and precise. I grit my teeth.

"I watched you spar against Damocles your whole life," Justus says. "Watched you fumble and lose every time. Maybe not consciously, but still, purposefully."

"He had Summer's Blessing!" I shout.

"Even with it, you could have beaten him. Couldn't you?"

Memories of sparring with my brothers come back to me in flashes. Could I have defeated Damocles? An uncomfortable sensation pricks in my belly as I realize I already know the answer.

"You've always been able to see every tell of your opponents. You saw theirs too. Tell me the truth."

My heart careens in my chest. Feinting to the left, I quickly pivot and lunge toward Justus's right side, aiming for an exposed flank. But he anticipates my move, smoothly sidestepping my attack and countering with a rapid series of strikes. I barely manage to parry each blow, feeling the strain in my muscles with each block.

"Damocles," I grit out, "was always observing the crowd in the arena. Even when we practiced, he was always looking around to see if our parents were watching. It made him distracted."

"And Decimus?"

"He was overconfident," I say. "He'd come out swinging, but in a prolonged battle, he'd tire easily. Put him against a quick opponent and he couldn't keep up."

"Yes. Magic never called to them the way it did to you, isn't that right?" Justus continues. "They made you feel lesser for your call to the sea, for the wind at your command, but it was only because they knew they could only reply with their blades."

As the intensity of our fight escalates, I struggle to keep pace with Justus's relentless assault.

"Your brothers were right about one thing," Justus says. "You are afraid."

Sweat beads on my brow as I focus on maintaining my footing, searching for an opportunity. *This needs to end.* I turn to Rosalina. One hand is clutched to her heart.

"You are as afraid now as you were then," Justus continues. "Afraid of what it would mean if you challenged your elder brother and won. Admit to me what you've always known!"

"I don't know what that is!"

"You don't hate yourself because you let your brothers leave without you. You hate yourself for hiding your strength your whole life. For muting your potential with drink and gallivanting."

My vision grows hot, and I press back the attacks. "Sounds like a fucking great time to me."

Justus laughs bitterly. "Say it, Daytonales. What would have happened if you'd shown your true potential? The potential I saw in the mountains while training you? The one you only reveal like glimpses of the sun through clouds?"

"I don't know what you're going on about, old man!"

"The Blessing doesn't always go to the eldest when passed willingly. Your mother could have chosen any one of you. Damocles had the Blessing when Hadria fell. It passed to Decimus before it came to you. Neither of them could save the city, yet you did. *You*, Daytonales."

With a sudden burst of adrenaline, I seize the moment, unleashing a flurry of strikes in rapid succession. Justus defends himself skillfully, but I manage to find a gap in his armor, grazing his side with a well-placed thrust. "Damocles was the greatest. He always wanted to be High Prince. He said he was born for it."

"What if he was wrong?" Justus yells. "Tell me what you know!"

Justus's trident slices forward with precision. I meet his strikes head-on, parrying each blow. The clang of tridents shatters the air, yet all I hear are the words of the Enchantress: *Here stands the fool, who escapes within the flesh for fear of his fate. Who languishes his time and talent. Here stands a beast who will let his realm go to rot as long as his mind is muddled enough not to comprehend.*

I wasn't cursed because they died. I was cursed because I abandoned my realm, because I refused to wield the gift as a High Ruler should.

"Tell me what you know!" Justus screams again.

"She should have chosen me!" I shout back. "If my mother had passed the Blessing to me, they all might still be alive."

With a swift feint to the left, I catch Justus off-guard, closing the distance between us in a flurry of motion.

"What does that mean, Day?" Rosalina calls. She's moved closer to us, eyes shining.

What does that mean? What does it mean? *Hero*, that's what she called me. If I let go of the fear, of the guilt, what does it mean? My skin seems to hum, a torrent of fire inside my chest. Tears and sweat drip down my cheeks.

"It means," I growl, "I was meant to be the fucking High Prince of Summer."

With a surge of determination, I channel this newfound energy. The Trident of Honor glows bright beneath my palm, light dancing along its length.

Justus's eyes widen in astonishment. For a moment, time seems to stand still as the world holds its breath, captivated by the raw power coursing through me.

With a resounding cry, I clash my trident against his. A great burst of light shines between us, and Justus falls to the ground, his trident snapped in two before him.

He stands, smiling. "Well, High Prince of Summer, it seems you're ready to reclaim your realm."

57

ROSALINA

Nerves roil in my gut as we approach the ocean. I step inside Dayton's large footprints.

Today, we return to Hadria . . . *if* I can get the attention of the sirens. Justus was adamant they are the key to us returning to the capital, though I'm still not entirely sure what that means.

After finally winning the match against Justus, Dayton tucked the trident back into the protection of Summer's token. There's a confidence radiating off him like rays of the sun.

The water is warm as we step into its depths, waves swirling around our knees. Looking over my shoulder, I see palm trees swaying in the gentle breeze, their fronds casting dappled shadows upon the sugar-white sands. Justus sits beneath one, watching us.

"Any idea what we're supposed to do?" I whisper to Dayton.

"Hey, I did my thing. This is all you." He nudges my shoulder with his own. "Though, when we were drowning, I think a part of me called for help without realizing it. Maybe that's how the sirens found us."

"Somehow I don't think they're going to hear me from here."

"Remember what Justus said? The Queen was connected to everything in the Vale because she created it. I have her Blessing. Perhaps that's what the sirens felt."

I turn to look up at him. "That sounded surprisingly wise."

"Don't get used to it, Blossom." He smiles, and it's so dazzling, my heart clenches painfully in my chest.

"Maybe it's like how, through my mate bond, I can sense Kel, Ez, and Farron, even if they're far away. What if in a different way, I have a connection to the Vale?"

"Look there, a school of angelfish." Dayton grabs my hand and points it in their direction. "See if you can *feel* them."

"Okay." I lower my hand, but he doesn't let go of it. I don't want him to. The ocean, the Blessing of Summer, and even me, the daughter of the Queen, are all connected.

The colorful fish dart among the coral reef, then disappear from sight, but I close my eyes, willing a part of me to follow. A jolt of electricity travels through my body as I realize I'm still with them. Appearing as bright stars in my vision, they swim deeper and deeper into the depths of the ocean. A sea turtle glides past them, and carries me with him, flowing into the melody of the sea.

"Farther out," Dayton says. "We need to go deeper."

He's with me. I feel the flame of Summer's Blessing burning beside my heart.

In my mind's eye, I push us farther into the ocean's depths. Specks of light like stars blur past us. Each one is alive, each one a part of the Vale. "It's all connected," I whisper. I can feel them, from the smallest plankton to the mighty whales, to creatures I've never seen with my own eyes before. Their energy intertwines. I feel the pulsing rhythm of the currents, the veins of life feeding the ocean.

A shock of light and pain suddenly pulses through me, and we pause our search. Dayton squeezes my hand tight, feeling it too. I refuse to open my eyes and lose this tether. A new creature swims across my mind's eye, one I feel no connection to. A creature of shadow.

"Corruption from the Below," Dayton says lowly.

"It feels so different," I say.

"It's not part of the Queen's magic."

Steadying my breath, I push past it, continuing our search, and release a call into the void of the sea. *Help. Please, I need your help.*

The waves stir around my legs. A deep rippling of magic courses back to me. With a melodious hum, their presence surrounds me. *Golden Rose, we are coming,* says a chorus of voices, sounding like the song of the sea itself.

Gasping, I open my eyes, the bright sun blurring my vision. "They heard me!"

"Rosie, that was amazing!" Dayton gathers me in his arms, lifting me out of the water. "I've never felt anything like that before. It was incredible."

I bury my head into his shoulder, wrapping my legs around his waist. "I couldn't have done it without you. I felt you guiding me in the ocean."

He pulls back but doesn't put me down. "I felt you as well." There's a splash, and Dayton drops me to the water. "They're here."

From the depths of the sea emerge two sirens, their graceful forms gliding effortlessly through the shimmering waves. Their hair, a cascade of iridescent strands, catches the light, casting ethereal reflections upon the water. They sit before us, tails curling below them.

I clutch Dayton's arm, unable to let go. They're as beautiful as they are terrifying, with eyes like gemstones and delicately ridged ears like the fins of a fish. One's hair is a light green, while the other's is pale pink.

"Greetings, Golden Rose," the siren with the green hair says. "I am Nereida. I have heard your call."

Beside her, the siren with the pale pink hair giggles, looking between Dayton and me. She looks younger, almost embarrassed. "Wow, a princess and a High Prince. They're both so beautiful."

"Quiet, Callistia. We are here to aid, not gawk," Nereida says. "My sister insisted on coming when we heard your call."

I see now that they share the same blue tails and brown skin. Taking a deep breath, I kneel in the water.

"Thank you for coming. We need help. We fell overboard and got separated from our ship," I say. "Would you be able to bring us back to it?"

"Oh, we know you fell from a ship." Callistia claps her hands together. "It was Tethys who saved you. He was bragging about it to everyone in Aerantheis."

"I knew I was saved by a siren!" Dayton says, dropping into the water beside me.

Callistia's blush deepens. Like the siren I saw in the Below, Callistia wears nothing over her chest. Flat jewels cover her torso and parts of her arm. Though, Dayton hasn't even glanced at her breasts. Perhaps finding his mate has made him turn over a new leaf.

"Aerantheis," I say, turning back to more important matters. "That's where you live?"

"Yes," Nereida says. "Aerantheis was saved by your mother many centuries ago. In return, we will do all we can to aid you, Golden Rose."

"Do you know what happened to our ship?" I ask. "Were there any other castaways?"

"Your ship survived the storm. Last I heard, it was spotted harbored safely in Hadria."

"That's amazing news!" I exclaim. "Can you help us return to Hadria?"

"We will lead you there," Callistia says, clapping again and smiling.

Dayton turns back to his mentor. "Will you return with us?"

Justus walks over. "Aye, I will return to Hadria in time. But I will make my own way there."

"How?" Dayton raises a brow.

"You have your beast. Perhaps it is not all a curse from the Queen, but partly a gift. Such as the one she granted me." In a flash of brilliant light, Justus changes into a golden eagle and lifts off into the sky.

"Would you look at that," Dayton says. "Secrets upon secrets."

"Maybe he's right," I say. "Farron has found strength in his wolf since breaking the curse."

Dayton doesn't respond, but his expression sobers.

"You must change as well," Nereida says.

"What do you mean?" I say, turning to them.

Callistia splashes her tail out of the water, a mesmerizing shade of blue reminiscent of the ocean's waves. "Well, you can't expect to swim all the way there with *legs*."

Her meaning becomes abundantly clear.

I'm going to need to turn Dayton and myself into sirens.

58

DAYTON

As someone who has turned into a wolf almost every night for the last twenty-five years, you'd think a little change wouldn't be that big of a deal. But there is just something incredibly wondrous about being transformed into a siren.

It didn't even take that long to get the feel for swimming like this. Rosalina took a little longer to adjust to her tail than I did, but I didn't mind being close to her and helping her out one bit. As amazing as she made *me* look with a twinkling teal tail, I haven't been able to take my eyes off of her since we dove beneath the sea.

Rosalina gleams like a jewel. Her tail is golden, each scale casting a shimmer upon the ocean floor, and her chestnut hair flows around her face like a crown of Autumn leaves. Across her torso is a top of iridescent pearls and seashells, gifted by one of the sirens that have joined us on our journey.

More and more sirens have felt our presence in the ocean as we travel to Hadria. They've flocked to see the High Prince of Summer and the Golden Rose.

"We'll be passing Aerantheis soon," Nereida says, her voice clear despite being underwater. "The other sirens will return home, and we will continue on to Hadria."

"Amazing." I smile, still in awe of being able to breathe and communicate below the surface.

Rosalina is up ahead, surrounded by Callistia and a dozen other sirens. Not only was she gifted the top, but also a crown of shells and pearls, and a bracelet of shark teeth. I can tell by her smile and the cadence of her voice that what Rosalina treasures most is not the gifts but getting to know these people. She's soaking up their stories, their friendship, the way plants soak up the sun. As always, her smile is infectious to those around her.

"There it is." Nereida points. "Aerantheis."

Far below us, the city of the sirens rises from the ocean floor. The spires and domes are adorned with coral and sea flowers that sway gently in the currents. The buildings seem to dance in the dappled light from the surface.

"Dayton, look!" Rosalina barrels into me, and we spin, twirling together, bubbles billowing around us.

She clings to my neck as I try to steady us by flapping my tail, but I only brush against her. We end up horizontal, her below me.

"Sorry," she says, flushing. "I'm not quite used to this tail yet. I wanted to make sure you saw the city."

"I see it," I say, guiding the hair from her face as the current gently pushes us upright.

"It's so beautiful," Rosalina says wistfully. "I wish we had time to visit."

The lost city is a kaleidoscope of color and movement. Schools of vibrant fish dart between the coral buildings, their scales catching the light. Illumination shines from the depths. Magic? Deep sea plants? I'm not sure, but an ache of longing pangs in my chest. I wish to see it up close, to explore and learn the stories.

I pull Rosie tight to me, our tails entwining. "We'll come back. We'll explore all the sunken ships and the city and attend a siren ball."

"You promise?"

"I promise," I say. "If for no other reason than to figure out how to access my siren cock. Surely, it must be here somewhere."

"Dayton!" she chides, laughing.

"I'm serious, Rosie." I gesture to the smooth surface of my tail. "What did you do with it?"

"Ask a siren—"

I tug her close, bodies pressed together. "Maybe this will help."

She doesn't push me away, instead letting her hands hang loose over my shoulders, her lips pressed close to my skin. I can feel the smoothness of her pearl top against my bare chest, her delicate curves, the silky feel of her tail against mine.

That's new, and not entirely unwelcome.

"There's so many dangers on the surface," she whispers. "It feels safe down here."

"I know, love. I will never let anything happen to you."

She pulls away slightly, brown eyes reflecting all the ripples of the ocean. "Because of the vow you made to Ezryn?"

That should be the reason, shouldn't it?

But the truth is, I wasn't even thinking of the vow I made to Ezryn when I jumped in after her instead of my mate. Wasn't even thinking of her being the Queen's daughter and what that meant for the Vale. I was thinking of the woman I first saw in the hot springs, who blushed when I introduced myself. The woman who looked so at home in the Summer Realm and conned me into buying her anything she wanted at an over-priced market. The woman who saved the man I love from his own darkness. The woman who took the haunted stories of my heart and held them like a treasure. The woman I know I can't exist in this world without, even if it means living a separate life.

All those things flash through my mind, but I pull away from her and smile.

"It's only fair, after all. Ez is looking after my sister." Then, because I can't bear to see her reaction, I turn and follow one of our siren guides. "Come on, we aren't far from Hadria, and the games await."

59

KELDARION

There's no way to tell time in the labyrinth. The purple haze that permeates the Below never changes, and the temperature is always cool but never cold. The only two signs that the hours have passed are the comings and goings of my wolf's form and George's insistence that Anya feels closer to him.

I walk a few steps ahead of him, following a long, straight stretch of the maze. The walls tower around us so high, they'd be impossible to climb. I only let George walk in front of me when we come to a junction and he must tell me which direction to go. At all other times, I keep pace protectively in front of him; I don't want him walking into a trap. My shoulder still stings from a grazing spear that shot past us a few hours ago.

So far, we've survived every obstacle lurking in this horrible place. We outran the statues that came alive, their axes held aloft, ready to swing. We avoided the floor that opened up to a pit of snakes. George had been caught in the stare of a mask with sapphires for eyes, but I'd been able to rip him away. Every step, every turn, every wall we pass, could hold the next danger.

I pause and wait for George to catch up. He hurries to my side with a smile. No amount of danger seems to dismay him. Farron had warned me to watch him carefully; George had been so sick only last week, deep in a slumber he couldn't awaken from. He seems strong now, never asking for a rest, and quite capable of maneuvering the trials we've faced so far.

And yet . . .

"Did I tell you about the time Anya scaled Mythispire and walked the whole mountain range? She told me the story when we were climbing Mount Kilimanjaro. Said the trek was similar in elevation. Now, she never needed to take a breather—"

I peer down at him as he talks, giving only minimal grunts to show I'm listening. His stories . . . They're all mixed up. He combines fae lore in with places from the human realm. He retells stories of Anya's life in the Vale. But he never knew Anya was actually Aurelia.

Though his body seems strong, it's as if what he's learned about the Enchanted Vale during his adventures across the Autumn Realm with Farron's little brothers is getting confused with his memories.

"Quiet," I say suddenly, placing a hand on his chest. In the distance, I see a silhouette up ahead.

Our next trial?

"We could go back," I say. "Find a different path and avoid whatever this is."

George's brows lower. "No. Anya is this way. I can feel it."

I let a flicker of magic ignite on my fingertips. "All right. Let's meet our new friend."

Trepidation fills my steps as we walk closer. This is no trial, at least not one like any of the others we've experienced so far.

The figure moves in a way that is both fluid and disjointed. Her head twitches on her neck, and her legs bow as she walks toward us. Each movement is spasmodic, as if her limbs are being jerked by an invisible string.

As we get closer, I notice the color of her skin—a muted blue—and the huge, weathered tome she balances on her forearm.

I've met her before. She looked different then, but the feeling is the same.

"It's a Fate," I whisper to George.

He narrows his eyes. "Friend or foe?"

"Neither."

"Should I be on guard?"

"Won't matter if you are," I say. "She knows everything you've ever thought. Every action you've ever taken. It's all there in her book."

For walking toward us is Clio, the Chronicler of Lives. She stops as we get closer, cradling her book and smiling with her gently pointed teeth visible. Like her sisters, the Fate is blind, her eyes covered with black bandages that give way to a flowing veil.

"Who is she?" George asks quietly.

"One of the three Fates. No one knows where they come from. Some say they were fae of the Above, transformed when the Gardens of Ithilias fell. Others think they've come from outside the Vale, from a world far different than ours. They see things that once were and things that have yet to come."

George runs a hand through his wayward hair. "Well, that's quite the company!"

I nudge George. "Take note of her book. She can see the entirety of time itself. Every piece of history is etched into those pages."

"They work for the Queen of the Below?"

"They don't work for anyone, but they've decided to reside in the dark," I say. "Usually if one wants to consult with them, it's a matter of hunting them throughout the Below. If you come across one, it's for a reason. They come bearing *gifts*, so they say."

"And what a gift I bring for you today. Something very special. Very important. I have sought you out for this purpose." Clio's voice crosses the distance between us, a voice so soft and sweet, and all the more unnerving for coming as it does from behind her sharpened teeth.

"Why is that, Clio?" I call.

She moves quickly, all four limbs jerking as if pulled by strings held from above.

"My sisters and I have been watching you, Keldarion, High Prince of Winter, and George of the O'Connells." A smile twitches across her mouth. "We are most impressed by your journey."

"Thank you kindly—" George begins before shrinking back. Clio reaches for him with her pale blue hand, her long nails sharpened to points. Stitches run up the length of her skin, as if she's barely held together.

She caresses his cheek and shivers. "A human. What a desperately delightful experience. You die so quickly; I am honored to touch your flesh."

"The, uh, honor is all mine," George says.

I grab her wrist and remove it from George's face. She jerks her head toward me and hisses.

"We don't want any gifts," I growl. "Let us pass."

"Terribly rude this one," she says in her slow, sweet voice. Pulling back, she flips through the pages of her tome. "Ah, yes. It started here. The two hundred and third Hearthlight Festival. Your father had recently passed, and Sveran Ironhall asked if he could have his dagger. You told him to take a long walk off a short pier into the Great Iskvalldan Lake, for it might be the only thing vast enough to contain his ego. Or perhaps it was the time—"

"Enough," I snarl. "We'll take your gifts and be on our way."

She slams her book shut, and although I doubt there's anything beyond those bandages, it's as if I can feel her gaze. The tome disappears and is replaced by two smaller books. She hands one to each of us, then gives a breathy laugh and switches them. "Always good to read something new, isn't it?"

George immediately begins examining the book, a violet, velvet-covered thing. Mine is weather-worn leather.

"Farewell, travelers," Clio says. "I shall enjoy chronicling the rest of your journey."

With a final crack of her neck, the Fate disappears, leaving us alone in the passageway.

George looks up at me. "I should know better than to open books from strangers we meet in a labyrinth, but color me intrigued."

"This is . . . unprecedented, to be certain," I say. "We should—"

Before I can get the words out, George opens the cover of his book. His eyes turn white.

I roll my own to the sky. "Fuck it," I say and open the cover.

There are no words, no ink, no pages even. Instead, there's a bright flash of light then complete darkness. My stomach roils, as if I'm falling out of the lift in the Great Chasm, down, down, down. I land on all fours and squint up into the sun.

This place . . . I've never seen it before. I'm surrounded by dense forest. The scent of pine and damp earth fills my nostrils. Sunlight filters through the canopy, casting dappled shadows on the forest floor.

Laughter sounds, and a small boy runs by. He's crafted a makeshift bow and arrow from a few bendy branches. A knit wool cap sits atop his dark hair, and he sports a red and black checkered shirt. No clothing the youth of the Vale would wear.

This is the human realm.

Creamy light floods my vision, and the images change. Water sprays upon my face. I steady myself on the steel railing of a ship. A young man, head low as he scans a notebook, walks toward me.

"Pardon me," I begin, but he doesn't look up. He walks straight *through* me. A chill runs up my spine.

"Trowels, brushes, shovels, pickaxes, sifters, tape measurers, rulers, notebooks, pencils, compass, map of the Nile . . . I'm forgetting something," he murmurs to himself.

That distracted mumbling—it's familiar. Before I can think further, the light floods my vision once again. Now, I'm blinking up into the blinding sun. The heat is nearly all-consuming, but I push myself up. Giant, triangular structures of stone surround me. I gasp, staggering backward, trying to take in their size.

"Boggles the mind how the blocks were moved up the superstructure! How do you think it was done? Ramps, leverages, counterweights?" A man's voice tears me from my thoughts.

I turn to see a man's back. A woman, hidden by his silhouette, laughs and says, "Oh, darling, when the human spirit sets its sights on something, nothing is impossible."

She steps out from behind him to touch his shoulder. My heart thunders in my chest. Rosalina. It's—

It's not Rosalina. It must have been the heat clouding my vision, but the way her dark eyes squinted up at him, the curl of her hair *just so* over her brow, the smile . . .

It's not Rosalina. It's her mother.

I stagger forward. The man she's touching smiles down with eyes of crystal blue.

This is George's life.

Suddenly, the images rush faster through my vision. Anya lounging on the bow of a wooden ship as it traverses a river past banks of sand, while George fumbles with a clunky black box that suddenly emits a blinding light. George chasing Anya through the dense woods of his childhood, raindrops falling across her face as she laughs and smiles. Them sitting across from each other at a wooden table, her cheeks streaked with tears. George wears a tan tunic with matching pants and a broad-brimmed hat of the same color. He holds a letter in his shaking hands.

"I have to go," he says.

She stands and screams, "I left to escape war! I will not go back!"

Mounds of mud dripping with blood. Bangs ricocheting in my ears so loudly, I fall to my knees. Dancing and laughing through a crowd of people. The heat of a jungle, then the bitter winds across a field of ice. A long, narrow metal structure, like the hull of a great ship, surging across the horizon, emitting great plumes of steam. Music like I've never heard before, a gorgeous low tone, as a man blows into a brass tube while Anya and George stare at each other in a smoky, dark room. She brushes a hand across his cheek and murmurs, "I will love you across the ages."

More and more images flash before my eyes; I see them for only a second, and yet it's as if I'm there with them. I feel the weight of the years pass over me.

This isn't a lifetime. This is more than that, more years than any human has ever lived.

The last image scars itself into my mind: Anya, gaze intense, clutching a baby to her breast. She grabs George's hand; he looks younger than he does now, dark hair without the speckles of gray.

George takes the baby from her arms and gently rocks it back and forth. "Our sweet Rose."

"I'll protect you both," Anya whispers.

The light flashes again, and then darkness grips me. The purple fog wafts back into my vision, and I blink to settle myself.

I'm still standing in the labyrinth. The leather book crumbles to flecks of ash in my hand, and I swear I hear a soft, sweet sigh as it disappears.

George blinks over at me, his book vanishing as well.

"How old are you?" I rasp.

"Fifty."

I shake my head. "No, you're a lot fucking older than that."

George grimaces. "That's impossible. Tell me what you saw."

I close my eyes and try to describe the memories in as much detail as possible. George's breathing quickens. "I don't understand," he mumbles. "Those events you're talking about—they happened decades before Rosalina was born. How could I have been there?"

"Do you remember them?" I ask.

He kneads his nose. "Yes. No. Bits and pieces. They happened, I *know* they did. But how is that possible?"

The intensity in Anya's gaze in the last memory plays in my mind. *What did you do?*

George slumps against the wall and rubs his eyes. "I saw him. The dark-haired boy who spoke to Anya."

"Caspian," I whisper.

"You made a bargain with him. One of eternal love."

Of course, Clio would share such a personal memory. "A bargain of eternal love on my end, but not on his. It was one of his many tricks. He had sought out the Fates beforehand and seen I was to have a mate. The bargain with me was a trap all along."

George shakes his head. "No, that's not right. I saw it. He made the bargain with you, and then went to the Fates with his mother. There, he saw a vision of you and Rosalina. I felt it, Keldarion. There was . . . sorrow. I don't know how else to express it. Sorrow of the soul."

My legs slacken, and I stumble back against the wall. "Caspian . . . Caspian made the bargain before he saw the vision?"

"So the Fate would claim. You did say she was the Chronicler of Lives, so I'm inclined to believe her."

If Caspian made the bargain without seeing the vision of Rosalina and me then . . .

Then it was the truth. He *did* love me. He had wanted everything that I had wanted in that moment.

I look down at the intertwining snowflake and thorn bracelet. All these years, I had thought only I was keeping the bargain alive with my stubborn, ridiculous love.

But he loved me once.

Does he love me still?

"Come on. Let's keep moving," I growl.

Caspian is counting on us.

60

ROSALINA

Nereida and Callistia lead us to a sandy bank beneath the docks of Summer. Here, out of sight, I press a hand to Dayton's beautiful tail. It was surprisingly easy to make this change, almost easier than transforming Marigold, Astrid, and Eldy into birds.

Maybe it's because of the way I connected with the sirens. Or maybe because it's been my dream to be a mermaid since, like, *forever*.

Dayton's tail shimmers away, and he stretches out his long, muscular legs. Heat rises to my cheeks as he turns away and starts to dig in the bag we brought, packed with our clothes. Nereida had given it to us, claiming the fabric was completely waterproof.

"Ah, good on you, Rosie." Dayton laughs. "My cock has returned to me, just as it was."

"Have you thought about how you're going to disguise yourself here, Golden Rose?" Callistia asks, ignoring Dayton. "There are a lot of people in this place who wish you harm."

"She's right," Dayton says. "I'm going to enter as myself. If my legionnaires are in that arena, then I need to show them their High Prince stands with them. No doubt Kairyn will be arrogant enough to let me try."

"But they'll never let me enter, knowing I can wield the bow against them," I agree. "They're betting on someone they can manipulate into doing their bidding. We won't let that happen."

"Can you do it, Rosie?" Dayton asks. I turn to him just as he's lacing his pants. He throws on his tunic and long cloak. "Can you kill Kairyn when it comes down to it?"

"Yes. For what he did to Ezryn. For taking your realm, I could." Though, my voice wavers. Kairyn is still Ezryn's brother. And I've never killed anything, except for Perth's monsters . . . and Lucas, though he was a monster in his own right.

Dayton's seashell necklace gleams in the sunlight, and I notice he's restrung the token of Summer on it. It won't be obvious from afar that he has it, but I know what it symbolizes. The High Prince of Summer isn't hiding anymore.

"All right," Dayton says, then raises a brow. "As pretty as they are, it's time to lose the scales."

I flop my golden tail in the shallow water, sad to see it go.

"What if you don't lose *all* your scales?" Callistia says. She hikes herself up high enough on the sand to be completely out of the water. Her tail shimmers into two legs, but it doesn't make her fully fae.

Callistia's pink hair still shines with an otherworldly gleam, and her ears remain webbed. Scales dust her thighs, across her arms and chest, and even along her neck and cheekbones.

"That's brilliant," Dayton says. "I've seen a few land-dwelling sirens in Hadria over the years. They're rare, but still around."

"Life on land." Nereida sighs. "I can't imagine who would choose that over the sea."

"Dayton, you could say I rescued you when you fell overboard," I say. "Callistia, can you help me?"

When I changed Dayton and myself earlier, I'd gone about it practically, only giving us tails and gills. But if I were to adopt the other siren features—the webbed ears and scaled upper body—no one would recognize me.

Callistia kneels beside me, and I place my hands on the sides of her face, studying the shape of her ears and the scales still glimmering on her skin. It's different than using my thorns to recreate objects like bows and arrows. This power originates deep within my chest, a guiding bolt seeking for something deep within Callistia.

I dive inward, feeling how her essence sparkles, then lead those changes to me. Magic flutters over my skin, soft as a butterfly's wings. I feel my legs again and kick them in the surf.

"Amazing!" Callistia smiles.

I open my eyes, and Callistia helps me to my feet. I catch my reflection in the water. I look different than I did when I had the siren's tail earlier. My hair is completely golden. My eyes have changed color too, shining bright as coins. Scales of the same color shimmer along my legs and stomach.

"You look amazing, Rosalina," Nereida says. "Though I was partial to the tail."

"She looks beautiful!" Callistia chimes. "Doesn't she look beautiful, Prince Dayton?"

It's only then I realize he hasn't said anything. Maybe it's because I'm naked, or almost naked. I still have on the pearl top, but it hardly provides coverage, and my stomach, legs, and everything in between are bare.

Dayton's face is flushed, and the muscles in his throat bob as he swallows. "Hmm?"

He didn't react at all when Callistia changed, and she was even more naked than me.

"Hand me the bag," I say.

He tosses it to me with a fumbling throw, and I quickly dress in my ratty, shipwrecked clothes.

"I don't know how we'll ever thank you." I throw my arms around Nereida and then Callistia.

"No thanks needed," Nereida says. "We're pleased to aid you in any way we can. If there is anything the city of Aerantheis can do for you in the future, please let us know."

"Thank you. I won't forget this," Dayton says, smiling.

"I will see you again, High Prince, Golden Rose." Callistia turns to me. "One last thing. Have you decided on a name? You can't go by Rosalina anymore."

I place my hands on my hips. A name for a siren. I smile, thinking of one of my favorite movies from my old life. "Call me Madison."

WE SPEND the rest of the afternoon in Hadria. Dayton found his confidant, Claudius, who reported that a ship with a black flag did dock outside of Hadria with a crew loyal to Summer who snuck in after dark. He didn't know if there was a girl named Wrenley among them, but he did have a small bag, given to him by the crew. Thankfully, it included

Dayton's dual swords. He'll need to use them in the arena, as it'll be too dangerous to let Kairyn know he has the trident.

When we returned to the apartment Dayton rented, there was no sign of Wrenley. He collected some coin, and we used it to buy some new leather armor in the market.

It was an entirely different experience than the first time I was here. Goblins and soldiers lined the streets, and the vendors looked terrified of every transaction. This was not the vibrant city I fell in love with.

Pain is still etched on Dayton's face as we leave the bazaar.

"We'll bring it back to how it was," I assure him.

"I suppose you'll be wanting another stuffed nonsense as your reward." He manages a smirk.

I smile back. "Two, in fact."

Ahead of us, the Sun Colosseum emerges majestically, its pillars glowing in the warm afternoon light and casting violet shadows over the streets below. As we draw nearer, the roar of the crowd sounds in the air. The games are on.

"Are you sure we shouldn't look for Wrenley some more?" I ask. "Perhaps we could find one of the crew and—"

"There's no time," Dayton says, tilting his face toward the sun. "We need to get into the barracks before sunset."

Though there are rumors of the High Princes and their curses, and the people of Autumn have accepted Farron's wolf as a protector, it may be an entirely other thing to see one wander the streets of Hadria.

"Besides," Dayton continues, "Wrenley knew I was planning to join the games; she'll find me. Maybe she went back to her work in the palace to spy on Kairyn."

"I don't think we should tell her about your token or who I am. Not that I don't trust her," I quickly add. "It's only . . . I was Kairyn's captive for months. If he suspects something, he could use her to get information."

A muscle feathers in Dayton's jaw, and he nods his head. "We're almost at the arena."

As we draw closer, Dayton throws back his hood and the reaction is immediate. The crowd lining up for the games begins to murmur, and I hear his name on the wind. The name Damocles is whispered too, like a ghostly echo.

Dayton acts like he doesn't notice, though I'm sure he does. He doesn't even turn his head as he walks straight up to a small booth, where a soldier of Spring sits with a long piece of parchment in front of him.

Dayton slams his swords down on the marble counter. "I'm here to enter the games."

The reaction from the crowd is palpable, and when the soldier looks up, his eyes widen in recognition. "What are you doing here?"

"I told you. I'm entering the games."

"Y-you can't," the guard stammers. He quickly says something to another soldier in the booth, who runs off. "Don't move."

"Are the games not open to any citizen of Summer? I am a citizen of Summer."

"N-no, you're the High Prince," the soldier says.

"Oh, am I now?" Dayton's voice oozes confidence. "Then as High Prince, I command all of you Springlings and gobbos to pack up your ugly asses and get the fuck out of my realm."

The crowd laughs, and a few fae begin to cheer. He's already having an effect on the people, and he hasn't even entered the arena yet.

Red blooms across the soldier's poxy face. "Summer is under the Green Rule now. I'll let you in the barracks, but Emperor Kairyn will hear of this!"

Dayton picks up his swords, swirling them before sheathing the blades. His smile is vicious as he says, "I'm counting on it."

PART FOUR
PRINCE OF THE ARENA

61

FARRON

"Be honest. Purple or navy cloak?" Caspian holds them both up to his body.

I look up from my book. I'm reclining on his bed, trying to ignore the Prince of Thorns while he tries on different outfits for the upcoming masquerade party. "They both look nice."

"But which one is more striking? Which one will draw the most eyes?" Caspian purrs.

"You could show up naked and still somehow be the best dressed."

He tosses the cloaks to the side. "Thinking of me naked, are you, Farron?"

I slam my book down, but he's already crawling on the bed toward me. "No, I wasn't, I—"

"Don't be embarrassed. I look amazing naked." He laughs. I've heard him laugh before, a smoky, ethereal sound, but I'm not sure he's ever laughed because of me. A man could get drunk on that laugh.

It draws one out of me too. Caspian must have gotten bored with picking apart his wardrobe because he practically plops down on top of me and reaches for my book. "What are you reading?"

I honestly don't remember, not with him on top of me. His nose wrinkles as he flips through the book, black hair tossed across his brow.

Then Caspian's ears twitch, and he's throwing back the velvety blanket to get beneath them. "Get under the covers, Farron."

"What?"

"Get under the fucking covers now," he rasps, a deadly serious expression on his face.

I'm so taken aback that I do what he says, allowing him to grab my hair and put me between his legs. "Oh," he whispers, just as I hear the door click open. "It would be helpful if you pretended to suck my cock."

Then he lets out a truly haunting sound, part moan, part growl, as he caresses my hair beneath the sheets. It's followed by a female's scoff and a metallic huff.

Immediately, I know who's in the room with us. The Nightingale and Kairyn.

"Excuse me," Caspian drawls, the pinnacle of indifference. "I have company."

"Of course, he languishes while we work to secure the realms for the Green Rule," Kairyn says.

"This is important, Caspian," the Nightingale says, voice muffled. She's probably wearing her signature mask. "Kairyn and I don't have time to be hunting you down here in Cryptgarden when we're needed in Hadria. Speak quickly so I don't have to stay a second longer than I need to. Do you know the location of the Golden Rose?"

"Yes, she's under these covers, sucking my—"

"This is serious," the Nightingale snarls.

They still haven't found Rosie. Caspian told me they'd lost track of her. I'm so far Below, I can barely feel her through our mate bond, but I'm confident I would feel *something* if she were in danger.

"She's trapped in an impenetrable underwater prison," Caspian drawls. "Oh wait, that's right. A child broke her out."

"ENOUGH!" Kairyn roars, and something smashes. "Daytonales has abandoned her and enrolled in my games with some sea siren. What's his plan?"

The mention of Dayton's name sends a pulse of longing through me. Kairyn's wrong. Dayton would never abandon Rosalina. It was always the plan for them to enter the games together, with Rosalina in disguise. Could she have adopted the form of a siren?

"Perhaps he's just an arrogant bastard who can't resist a challenge." Caspian gives a long sigh and slaps my cheek. I guess that's a cue for me to move. My cheek brushes his thigh. His pants are softest silk, and slowly I mimic the movement he's looking for. "Isn't that something you should have figured out, Birdy?"

The Nightingale inhales a shuddering breath. "We can salvage this, Kairyn. Everyone in Summer knows he's enrolled in the games. If you imprison him, it'll only enrage the people more. Why make him a martyr when you can humiliate him in his own arena?"

Humiliate the only person who's never lost in the Sun Colosseum, I think. *Unlikely.*

Caspian threads his hands into my hair, dragging me dangerously close to his cock, which I can now see the distinct shape of through his loose pants. Holy fuck, is he hard?

"Humiliate the only person who's never lost in the Sun Colosseum?" Caspian says. "Unlikely."

"He hasn't played in my games," Kairyn snarls.

My breath is ragged. It's getting warm beneath the covers. Caspian's leg twitches, and he makes a deep sound in the back of his throat, which I'm not entirely convinced is faked.

As he moves his knee, I can just see out of the bottom of the covers. The Nightingale is in her prismatic armor standing next to Kairyn's massive frame. My body quivers in anger at the sight of them. One of my fists tightens, entwining in the sheets, the other on Caspian's thigh.

"We must devise something truly horrible for him to face in the arena," the Nightingale gleams. "Thank you for nothing, brother."

There's the slam of the door, and Caspian immediately grabs me by the shoulders and drags me out from beneath the covers. We're nose to nose, breath mingling.

"Rosalina—" I start.

"Nearly positive she must be the siren," Caspian says. "I'll go to the surface and check."

"Thank you."

He swallows, and I watch the muscles in his throat bob. "Sorry about that."

"Did you just apologize to me, Cas?"

His smile turns devious. He grabs my hand and drags it lower and lower until I can feel the hard shape of his cock. "Can't say I didn't enjoy it though." He moves his leg, rubbing against my hips. "And you did too."

"Cas."

He tilts his head. "What? Your Summer boy is confused, and you miss getting fucked."

Ahh. I know what he's doing. I understand because Dayton did this to me for years. He felt something inside him, something he didn't understand, so he needs to dismiss it with a crude remark. But two can play at that game.

I squeeze his hard shape. "I was actually thinking about how it would be to fuck you."

"Do you want to end up in the fucking labyrinth?" Caspian's face turns red, and he pushes off me, standing. "I'm going to Summer."

Then thorns erupt around him, and he disappears.

IT'S LATE when he returns. The light never changes down here, but the fire has dwindled to crystal cinders. I realize I've fallen asleep in his bed, wrapped in the soft blankets, and for some reason I don't make a motion to leave.

Caspian stands before the wardrobe, methodically removing all his layers until he changes into soft, loose pants. They look much too large for him, and I wonder if they once belonged to another High Prince that frequented these rooms. He goes to the door and tests the lock twice, then raises a barrier of thorns. Then he checks the lock of his balcony three times before crossing to the privy. It's so quiet, I can hear his rapid breath. He's paranoid. Does he do this routine every night?

The bed sinks with his weight. "Tired of the floor?"

"Just don't touch me," I say, then, "Was it her?"

"Yes," he says. "She was sleeping. I just watched her for a little while. Rosalina makes a very beautiful siren."

"Good." I roll over, holding my pillow. Dayton will take care of her. Stars, she can take care of herself. But it doesn't stop the ache of missing her. "Thank you for helping us, Cas."

"I know it's not enough," he says, so softly. "You know, I only ever wanted you princes to see the real me, to feel something when you saw me. I think, for a long time, to be hated was enough because it was *something*. It was better than nothing."

Is this his way of saying sorry? Of offering an explanation? I don't know. I'm not sure about anything anymore since coming down here. "Was it really all an act, Cas?" I whisper. "All those years ago? Working with Kel, befriending us, saying you had abandoned the Below and wanted to help the realms? Was it all a set-up to steal the rose from the Gardens of Ithilias and begin your War of Thorns?"

Caspian grumbles something, then mutters, "Yes. It was all an act. My mother sent me as a spy. I was destined to betray Keldarion. To betray you all."

I shift, searching the darkness to find any hint of truth in his eyes. For so long, I've berated myself and Kel—and even Rosie, at times—for being so foolish as to fall for the Prince of Thorns' manipulation. But lying here with him now, I'm reminded of how he was in the past. "I don't believe you. Maybe the plan was to deceive us, but at some point, you wavered, didn't you? You were our friend, and you did love Kel."

"Kel sent an army to destroy Cryptgarden," Caspian snarls. "At least one of us succeeded at deceiving the other. It was my fault for ever believing I would be accepted outside of the Below. I stuck to my mother's plan, and I stole the rose back. So what? Kel would have done the same in my position. They call it the War of Thorns, but it was my mother's campaign. Once the rose was destroyed, I had no interest in any of it. I'd already done enough damage at that point."

"The Great Chasm."

"It was an accident," he murmured. "If that's what I can do with what magic flows through my veins now, then I can't imagine what I'll be capable of if my mother gets her wish, and I am forced to accept the full might of my legacy."

"We won't let that happen," I say. Keldarion and Caspian's battle across the Badlands outside of Frostfang is practically a legend among the fae now. I'd always assumed the creation of the Great Chasm was Caspian's last effort to destroy Winter.

Was it really just an accident? A loss of control while fighting the man he loved?

I narrow my eyes. "Your allegiance never fully returned to the Below. You bolstered Castletree as soon as it started to get sick. What changed your mind?"

Caspian runs a hand along his wrist. In the dim light, I see his fingers caressing a gold bracelet. "Aurelia showed me kindness once. Castletree is important to her. It was the least I could do in return. Besides, even after everything, there are things inside that castle I can't bear to lose."

Secrets within secrets. I think I understand Keldarion and Rosalina a little more. I know I've already pushed him enough, so I don't press further. Instead, I say, "I'm going to sleep now. If you accidentally kick me in the middle of the night, it wouldn't be that big of a deal."

The Prince of Thorns laughs—the kind of laugh I could get drunk on—and then he's beside me, his leg over mine, head on my pillow close enough that his long hair brushes my cheek. "Like this? Would this be a big deal, Autumn Prince?"

I groan and attempt to push him away without any real effort behind it. But somehow it only brings him closer, his head falling to my shoulder.

"Or this?" His hand snakes beneath my shirt, and even though everything with Caspian naturally feels sensual, this gesture feels more comfort-seeking than anything else. So, I let my arm fall around him and I wonder to all the stars why falling asleep next to the Prince of Thorns doesn't feel like the most terrible thing in the world.

"Goodnight, Cas."

But he doesn't answer. He's already asleep.

62

DAYTON

Through the grates in the barracks, I watch the fight outside. Kairyn's got three Summer legionnaires pitted against some creature he's dragged from the Below. A chimera, by the looks of it.

Fighting monsters from the Below is not uncommon in the Sun Colosseum, but it was always by choice. Now, my people are forced to risk their lives.

Torches mounted around the arena paint the sands with long black shadows. I have an hour at most before the wolf takes over.

Despite it being mandatory attendance, the crowd buzzes with anticipation. They don't want to see legionnaires of Summer die any more than I do.

The chimera's lion-like body tenses, its goat's head casting a sinister gaze. The Summer legionnaires are armed with swords and shields, at least. The chimera lunges with a deafening roar, claws slashing through the air. My comrades evade the creature's deadly strikes. One lands a slice across the chimera's flank, but the beast barely flinches, its hide resilient.

"That thing ate three men yesterday. We can only hope its full belly makes it slow," a familiar voice says from behind me.

I turn. "Tilla!" I rush forward and clutch her in an embrace. "What are you doing here?"

Her body stiffens, and she backs away from me. The last time I saw the blacksmith, she was leading a group of Spring refugees to the Winter Realm.

"Kairyn's forces ambushed us on the pass," Tilla says. "It was like he knew exactly where we were going to be. His cursed army transported most of the citizens to prisons in Florendel, while our fighters were taken here to the arena."

"I'm sorry, Tilla. It lifts my spirits to see you alive, though." Somehow, Kairyn finds out everything: the mountain pass, the location of Corsa Tuga. There's a new scar across Tilla's cheek. Raven-haired with tawny skin and eyes that shine like chips of onyx, Tilla's always had a fierce sort of beauty, but I don't think I truly appreciated her until we reconnected a few months ago in Spring. I know for certain I didn't give her the respect she deserved when she was engaged to Keldarion.

Another roar sounds from outside. The chimera is dripping blood, but pursues the soldiers relentlessly, driving them against a wall. *Your back to the wall means your enemy knows you have nowhere to go.* I think of one of Justus's lessons, gritting my teeth.

"You volunteered for this madness?" Tilla raises a brow. "Please tell me you have a plan, and this isn't all some plea for a glorious death upon the sands, Daytonales."

"I have a plan."

"That sea creature you dragged in . . . is she part of it?"

"Madison's my partner." I turn to see Rosalina surrounded by legionnaires on the eating bench, no doubt enchanting them with tales of the sea. So far, we've been treated like any other captives here. I've been in the barracks a million times, and it's all pretty much the same. The mess hall, the viewing area to watch the fights, a training pit stocked with wooden weapons and a sample of armor to choose from. They confiscated my swords, though I did demand to have them back for our first fight tomorrow. We'll see if they comply.

The only difference is now the exits are blocked. You fight or you die.

There's a shift in the crowd outside, a stillness. The kind of silence that only happens when the battle is near over. The legionnaires maneuver around the monstrous beast, their swords flashing in the sunlight. Then, seizing a fleeting opportunity, one of them delivers a decisive blow, plunging her sword deep into the chimera's side. As the creature stumbles and falls, defeated, a wave of jubilation washes over the arena. Sitting in the Emperor's Box, I see a looming dark shadow stand and leave. *Even you can't control the arena, Kairyn.*

He hasn't come down to force me into prison yet, which means the plan is working. He's going to allow me to fight.

My gaze stays locked on the Emperor's Box where a glowing object hovers above a pedestal. Rosalina's Bow of Radiance. *It'll be ours again soon.*

"You've already stirred the hearts of your soldiers with merely your presence," Tilla says. "I cannot wait to see what flames you ignite upon the sands."

"Down here, Tilla, we're not soldiers," I say, slapping her on the shoulder. "We're gladiators."

I'm NOT sure my wolf is going to fit. I stand in my box of a room. Each gladiator is given one, consisting of nothing more than a single bed and a basket for our things. I'd wanted to stay in Rosie's room, but there would really be no space for that. At least she's in the chamber right beside mine, so I'll be able to hear if anything goes amiss. I'd sleep outside her door if a giant wolf wouldn't draw too much attention.

Rosalina had been delighted that Tilla was alive, and only a little disappointed she couldn't have a formal reunion. As much as I trust Tilla, it's safer if no one knows who Madison truly is.

I tug off my shirt and throw it in my little basket and start on the clasps of my pants just as my door opens. Maybe Rosie decided she wanted to stay in my room after all. "Ro—Wrenley!"

My mate stands in full acolyte robes, white hood drawn over her hair. In her hand is a tray of star-shaped biscuits.

"You're okay!" I tug her inside, closing the door. "You survived the storm. I thought the waves might have taken you."

Something akin to sadness flickers in her eyes. "They did almost. Huxton was able to throw a rope over for me."

I clutch my chest, breathing a deep sigh of relief. Thank the stars my decision to rescue Rosalina hadn't condemned Wrenley.

"You're okay, too." She sets the tray on the bed and then wraps her arms around my neck. "I was so worried about you. We searched all over when you fell off the ship."

"I got lucky. A siren rescued me."

"The one you brought with you to the arena? Dayton, they're all talking about it. Kairyn is furious. But he thinks he can humiliate you out

327

there. I don't know what, but there's something horrible planned for your match tomorrow."

"Whatever it is, I can handle it."

Wrenley's eyes shimmer as she looks up at me. "Even with your power as it is now?" Then her hand is on my arm. "You wouldn't have to worry about sunset or lacking magic if—"

I step away from her and look at the tray on the bed. "You're right. It's almost sunset. You shouldn't be here."

"I don't care, I had to see you. I even volunteered to hand out blessings of the Queen to the fighters as a way to get down here."

"Blessings of the Queen," I say, taking a bite of the star cookie. It's dry. "Can't hurt."

"Dayton, where is Rosalina? She fell from the ship in the storm. Did the sirens rescue her as well?"

"I don't know. I couldn't find her."

She gives me a speculative gaze. "Yet, you returned to Hadria without her?"

"I'm sure she made it to shore. Rosie's a great swimmer. Besides," I walk over to her and tuck a loose strand of curly brown hair behind her ear, "if she were in danger, one of her mates would have felt it and come running. I had to return to the capital."

"Yes, they would," she says, then, "So, you really don't think she's dead?"

"No, it'll take more than a little wave to get Rosie."

"Trust me," Wrenley says, picking up the tray of star-shaped cookies. "I know."

I nod my head toward the door. "You should probably get going. You know, with sunset approaching and all that."

Tears shimmer in her eyes. "You would send me away so soon? We only just reunited." Her hand trails down my chest. "Didn't you miss me, Dayton?"

Actually, I barely thought of you at all, I think, but I can't say that out loud. "Of course I did."

"I've missed you so much," she says softly. "I didn't realize it until we were separated, how much these last few months being with you have meant to me. Ever since my parents died and I came to live in the monastery, I've only ever had myself. But you look after me now, don't you?"

My throat tightens, and I have an urgent desire to step away from her, but she looks so distraught. "You know I won't let anything happen to you, Wren."

Her lip begins to tremble. "You say that, but do you mean it? I saw how you treated Farron and Rosalina. So much gentleness and care. To me, you're always so distant. They aren't your mates. I *am*."

The words hit me like arrows. I want to stumble away from her, but I force myself to stay still, to not let the anguish show on my face. I've put Wrenley through enough.

"I can make you happy, Dayton, if only you'd let me try," she says and stands on her tiptoes, lips turned toward mine.

Magic shimmers through my body as the last rays of sun dip below the horizon. My body shifts, transforming into the golden wolf. Wrenley gasps and lurches back, pressing against the door.

Water drips from my paws. Rotten seaweed tangles through my fur. Barnacle-covered shells are embedded in my skin, and the smell of rancid fish hangs heavy in the air.

"I will try harder, Wrenley," I say, the wolf's voice more guttural than I've ever heard it before.

She looks me up and down, fear flashing in her eyes. "How can you stand to be like this?"

I turn away from her and slump onto the floor. "Trust me. There are harder things to bear."

63

EZRYN

A spark ignites within the kindling as I strike the flint against my dagger. Carefully blowing on the embers, I stoke the fire to life, feeding it dry grass until it stands on its own. I sit back on my heels and blow into my hands. Though the days in the desert burn so hot the sand is scorching to the touch, the nights carry a chill.

The sun hasn't fully set yet; dusky light paints the horizon in brilliant orange. Luckily, the night after the harpy attack passed without incident. . The princesses, despite their occasional whining, have kept a good pace. Though, I noticed Eleanor ceased her endless questions, and Delphia no longer ran ahead of us. *We grow up in the wilds*, I think. It's the necessity of nature.

The thought sounds exactly like something my father would say. The hardened—at times brutal—belief that any hardship is an honor as long as we have the strength to survive it. It's how Kairyn and I were raised.

Until we return to Hadria, the girls are my responsibility. Is this how I want to treat them? Like soldiers?

Tonight, we were lucky to have come across a small oasis tucked into the dunes. I've made our fire among the palm trees, using their fronds and bark as tinder. Bushes and patches of greenery remind me there is still some life in this barren place. A pool of water provided much needed relief from our filthy clothes. I'd scrubbed my hands until they were raw, finally ridding myself of the harpy blood which had dried and soured on my skin. Unfortunately, even after scrubbing it in the pool, Delphia's blade seems permanently stained with harpy blood.

The girls are on the other side of the pool, taking turns holding a large palm frond up to the foal we found in the harpy nest. The little beast chomps greedily and flaps its wings in delight. Another mouth to feed with four wobbly legs was exactly the last thing we needed, but I couldn't leave the Pegasus up there. Not with the small shimmer of hope it had ignited in the girls' eyes. Besides, it reminded me of a lesson my mother once told me long ago.

We don't know best when it comes to nature's will, Ezryn. Would you tell the grass how to grow or a bird how to fly? Would you try to show a deer how to run or the sun how to shine? Nature knows best. But if you're a patient enough listener, she might teach you.

I had wanted to keep heading north, but the foal—Drusilla, they'd dubbed her—had whinnied and pulled until we followed her westward. Sure enough, the sand turned to red clay beneath our feet. Peering past the descending sun, I can see steep rock canyons in the distance. *Is that where you're hiding, Huntresses?*

The girls start to make their way back from the pool, leading Drusilla with another palm frond. I need to get them settled in their bedrolls before the sun dips. Last night, we'd been fortunate enough to find an abandoned cave in an outcrop of rock. With only one entrance, it was simple enough to guard. I'd tucked the girls at the very back of the cave with a fire, then followed the short path to the front where I'd stayed awake, watching all night. Every muscle in my body was tense with apprehension—I kept expecting something to creep out of the shadows and barge past me, heading straight for the girls. At the same time, I was afraid one of them would wake up and come and check on me. Instead of the man, they'd find my wolf.

I know they're both aware of the Enchantress's curse; their brothers have informed them. But I don't want them to see the monster I become each sundown.

I've already scared them enough.

A knot tightens in my chest, and the twig I'm holding snaps. I can't rid the image from my mind: their faces, splattered with blood as I drew my blade down on the harpy again and again and again. I told Dayton I would protect them, and I did. But at what cost?

I take a shaky breath. Ezryn hasn't been able to keep anyone safe; only the Prince of Blood can.

"You don't know what you're talking about," Delphia snarls, slumping down by the fire, her back leaning against the felled trunk of a palm tree.

"I'm not stating opinion. These are facts and as much as you love to pretend your opinions are facts, they're scientifically inaccurate," Eleanor says in her usual dry tone, sitting against the other side of the trunk. Drusilla gives a concerned whinny and lies down across the fire from them.

"Well, your facts are stupid," Delphia says.

"Good one," Eleanor snorts.

I dust off the charcoal from my hands and sit between them, leaning back against the tree. "What are we fighting about this time?"

Delphia looks away from me, crossing her arms. I notice there's a shimmer in her brown eyes.

"Delphia?" I ask softly.

"Nori says Hadria is lost," Delphia says. "Doesn't matter if we find the Huntresses or not, we won't be able to stop the Green Rule and they're going to come for Coppershire next. She says none of us are ever going to go home again."

"It's a conclusion based on a series of facts. I believe in being prepared," Eleanor mumbles. She digs in her pack and pulls out a string and an assortment of tiny animal skulls. I've noticed her scooping them up anytime we passed skeletons picked clean. She starts to thread the skulls onto the string.

I look between them, at the defeat on Eleanor's face, the dying hope in Delphia's eyes. *Do I treat them as soldiers and prepare them for the realities of war?*

My thoughts shift to Rosalina. The Prince of Blood couldn't save her. What kept her going, what's always kept her going, is her invincible tenacity. Her ability to seek out the single flash of light in a pitch-black sky. What would she say to these two?

I nudge Delphia then Eleanor. "Listen, I know how it feels when you're faced with an enemy that seems so much stronger than you. Every step feels insurmountable. But the fight doesn't stop as long as you keep rising. Let them knock you down again and again. You just make sure you get up." I look between them. "Defeat is the hearth that forges resilience. You'll see your homes again, and you'll be all the stronger for it."

The girls look past me at each other, speaking in that silent language I don't understand. Then Delphia blinks up at me. "Do you really believe that?"

I believe in Rosalina, and she believes that. "Of course."

"But you were banished from your home. Do you think you'll see it again?"

I suck in a breath. Long have I mourned the verdant smell of Florendel, the roar of the waterfall down the mountain, the clatter of steel in the air. No, I don't think I'll ever return to Florendel.

More than that, my other home was taken. Never again can I set foot in Castletree, not while Kairyn remains High Prince.

I have no home. A prince, now an orphan. A vagabond. Homeless and unmoored, a seed adrift with no place to plant myself—

Plant yourself in me. I will keep you safe.

I close my eyes, Rosalina's voice drifting through my mind. When I'd held her in my arms, it didn't matter that we were aboard a ship, sailing across unknown seas. Her heart is my home.

I look up at the sky, bejeweled with stars. "Home is more than the roads you've walked before or the walls that once sheltered you. You will find it within the bonds you've forged and the love you've shared. That is something that can *never* be taken from you." I hold each of their gazes in turn. "You two are a home for each other. You will protect and shelter each other. Do you hear me?"

"Yes," Delphia whispers and looks over at Eleanor. The Autumn princess nods.

"I'm here to protect you too," I tell them. "I'm not going to let anything happen to you, all right?"

Again, they look at each other in silent conversation. My stomach turns as I see the flash of trepidation in their eyes.

They're so innocent, these two, and yet both have faced so much. So much loss, so much war. They don't deserve to live in such fear. Rosalina ordered me to accompany them because she thought I could protect them. But have I not only added to their ordeals? I was no hero rescuing them yesterday, but a monster in my own right. I can still feel the power coursing through my veins with each killing blow.

Is there another path for me? One not drenched in blood?

"I-I'm sorry if I frightened you yesterday," I manage. "Your brothers are two of the most important people in my life. I have to do right by them, and when that creature—" I cut off, and realize my hands are shaking. I did what I had to do to protect them. Why do I feel such shame?

There's a light touch on my arm, and I look down to see Delphia's hand. "It's okay. I'm not afraid of you," she says.

"Me neither," Eleanor says. She grabs my hand and pulls it into her lap, then ties a string around my wrist. I realize it's a bracelet she's made, decorated with little animal skulls. I hold it up to the firelight.

"My brother's mate says you've done a lot of bad stuff," Delphia continues. "I don't believe her, but even if you have, it's okay. My brother's done a lot of bad stuff too."

"Mine too. A lot of people blamed him when the Scriptorium burned down," Eleanor says. "Sometimes, I blame him for making Mom so sad those last few years. She tried to hide it, but I wonder if he came home more, if she would have been happier, you know?"

Delphia looks into the fire. "Yeah, I know what you mean. I feel angry at Dayton sometimes. He lives in Castletree, and I live in Soltide. He's got all of his friends there, and I've got no one. Not a mom or a dad or any siblings. I mean, there's my teachers and the council, but once all the decisions are made, there's no one to sit with me in my room." She looks up, and I notice her fighting back her tears with a smile. "At least, until Nori came."

Words feel stuck in my throat. We princes have done so wrong by those who love us most. When our families needed us, we hid away. By every right, Delphia and Eleanor should hate their brothers. "How did you find forgiveness for them?" I ask quietly.

Firelight reflects in Delphia's eyes. "Nobody taught me how to be steward. I felt scared so much of the time. Scared I was going to make a wrong decision. Scared I was going to hurt the people counting on me. Sometimes, it made me feel so overwhelmed, I couldn't do anything. I would think and think and think, and I'd get all these ideas and intentions. It was just too much. So, a while ago, I decided that all I needed was one good reason. Every time I had to make a decision, I just needed to find one good reason to do something," she says. "I used to go around and around in my head. Should I stay mad at Dayton forever? But I had one good reason not to." A small smile tugs at her lips. "I love him."

I stare down at her. Silence passes through the oasis, the only sound the crackling fire.

Was there ever any love between Kairyn and me?

"Maybe if you're feeling scared like you were with the harpies," Delphia says, "you could find it helpful just to find one good reason. You know, like you don't have to fight them because you're scared, and you hate them, and you're angry all at the same time. Just pick one reason to stand up to someone and go with that."

"That's good advice," I concede. A sense of peace whispers through the oasis. We sit in easy silence, watching the fire, as I contemplate Delphia's words. *One good reason.*

Rosalina should have been the only reason I needed not to chase after my brother during our fight in the Hall of Vernalion. The frenzied rage that had overtaken me had been like a living entity in my chest. I'd felt it again in the harpy nest.

There must be another way to protect those I love. A way that doesn't result in me losing myself in the manner I've done before.

I wish I could stay here for longer, but the line of the horizon is bright orange, and any minute the sun will slip away. "All right, girls, time for bed. Get out your bedrolls."

"Aren't you going to sleep by the fire?" Eleanor asks as I stand up and walk away.

"No, I'm going to be on watch at the edge of the oasis. Don't worry. I'll look out for you."

The girls exchange a look again, but I turn away. On the other side of the oasis, behind a bush, I shed my clothing, carefully tuck my new bracelet away, and wait for the last rays of sun to fade.

The beast seizes my body, erupting out of me with thick black fur and sharp claws. I shake, the bones matted in my fur rattling together.

I pad out from behind the bush, readying to patrol the edges of the oasis.

"Whoa!"

"He's HUGE."

Jumping back, I'm faced with the two gaping faces of Delphia and Eleanor.

"What are you doing here?" I growl. "I told you to stay by the fire!"

I step back, trying to shrink into the darkness. I don't want them to see the glint of my fangs or the moss that grows through my fur. I don't want them to look upon this monster that's supposed to protect them.

"This is so fascinating," Eleanor says, stepping closer and touching one of the bird skulls tangled in my fur.

"Sharp!" Delphia squeals, grabbing my lip and examining my teeth.

"Hey." I growl again, backing up, but the girls keep approaching.

"Look how pretty his tail is!"

"You really are big enough, we could both ride you. Then we wouldn't have to walk."

"All right, all right." I nudge their backs with my snout. "To the fire."

335

The girls trudge dutifully back toward their bedrolls. Drusilla is fast asleep, legs in the air and wings splayed.

"Now stay," I tell them and start to turn away.

I feel a small hand on my back, fingers running through my fur. "You're so warm," Delphia says. "I thought you'd be cold, but you're warm."

Eleanor places her hand beside Delphia's. "And soft, too."

They're not afraid, I think. *Even when faced with the most horrifying parts of me.* A strange sensation thrums in my chest. *Or am I not as frightening as I've always thought?*

With a sigh, I turn back to the fire and thud down, sending up a cloud of dust. "I can keep watch from here, if you prefer."

They nod and walk back to their bedrolls.

I curl in on myself and close my eyes, just for a moment. Just for a moment to feel the warmth of the fire.

Two shapes lean against me. I crack an eye open to see Delphie and Nori snuggled together, pressed against my side, no mind to my fangs or claws or matted fur. I still, not even daring to take a breath.

There were a thousand reasons I shouldn't have agreed to this mission.

But there are two damned good reasons to stay.

64

ROSALINA

I'm not sure what's more terrifying: Kairyn's cross-armed stance as the crowd in the Sun Colosseum chants Dayton's name, or the gorgon slithering toward us.

My feet slide over the gritty sand as I retreat further. The gorgon is massive, twelve feet tall and twice as long. With a male humanoid body, it sprouts a coiling serpentine tail with shimmering green and brown scales. Its fae-like face is marred by two protruding fangs.

"Don't stare too long, Mads," Dayton says, darting in front of me.

"I thought you said it had to be staring at me *and* touching me in order to turn me to stone," I snarl.

"Better not to take any chances." Dayton turns to the audience and flashes a dazzling grin that is met with thunderous applause. "Cover me. I'm going back in."

"Okay." My webbed fingers clutch tight to the wooden bow.

I'm okay with hitting targets, even moving ones, but I can't seem to land a shot here. Not under the eyes of thousands of people, beneath the oppressive heat of the Summer Realm. Not with the traitorous High Prince of Spring watching with his calculating gaze and my bow glowing on a pedestal beside him.

This is what we're fighting for: the way to defeat him.

"Ready to dance, snaky?" Dayton says. An echosphere, a small glowing ball, swerves before him, booming his voice to the entire arena. Dayton rushes forward, and the gorgon raises its curved sword.

I take aim at the creature's unblinking gaze and release an arrow. It goes wide. *Dammit*. I need to get closer.

Dayton's running around the gorgon now, making the shot even more difficult. A clang rings out as their swords meet. I've seen Dayton fight before, but never like this. His intent is razor-sharp on the sands. He's a blur of elegance and lethal precision.

But the gorgon is no easy foe. It's a creature of the Below, created by Sira herself, a horrific blend of fae and snake. They live in deep caves in the Suadela Sands, Dayton had quickly explained when we first saw our opponent. They're vicious, often known for sneaking into Summer villages and taking prisoners. No doubt they volunteered to be here to try their might against the gladiators.

With a deft flick of its wrist, the gorgon slashes at Dayton, aiming for his exposed side, but Dayton is too fast. He deflects the blow with one of his swords and strikes with the other.

I can't let him do this alone.

"I will take pleasssure in gutting you, Ssssummer Prince," the gorgon hisses.

Dayton dodges another blow, leaping over its tail. "Someone's hiss-terical today, but your insults are as sharp as your tail."

Fury flashes across the gorgon's face, and it lashes out its tail care-lessly. Dayton easily jumps backward and slashes a line across the gorgon's back, dripping inky-green blood. *He's riling it up to make it careless.*

The Summer Prince leaps back again, and the gorgon is wide open. This is my chance. I nock an arrow to my bow and run closer. Dayton told me to stay back, but I can't hit it from that far away. I plant my feet firmly and fire.

The arrow strikes the gorgon in the arm. His curved sword drops. The monster reels, flashing its fangs. "Where are your sssscales, little sssiren? Should have ssstuck to the sssea, instead of drying up on the sssand." It lunges at me, coiled tail unfurling, venomous fangs bared.

Dayton jumps between us. He strikes it across the chest, but it whirls, wrapping its massive tail around Dayton's body, pinning the Summer Prince's arms to his sides.

"No!" I cry out, my voice mingling with the collective gasp of the crowd.

Barbs in the gorgon's tail dig into Dayton's skin, and his blood drips out of the coil onto the sand. Every instinct in me wants to call my thorns and rip this creature in two. I can't reveal myself, but I won't let Dayton fail.

Dayton's got his eyes closed, and the creature bends in closer. If he locks gazes while it's touching him, he'll turn to stone.

"You'll make sssuch a pretty ssstatue," it hisses, drawing a clawed hand along Dayton's face. "Asss will your sssiren."

"Don't you fucking touch her," he snarls, then, "And you spit on my cheek." He struggles but can't get his arms free of its tail.

"Trust me, Day!" I call. Then I draw my bow, my hands steady despite the chaos and roar of the crowd. I take aim, my focus narrowing to a single, critical point.

With a twang, the arrow flies true, slicing through the air and making a satisfying thud as it pierces the gorgon's tail. Dayton breaks free from its grasp, his swords flashing in the bright light of the arena. He launches himself forward, blades singing. With a swift, decisive strike, he plunges both swords deep into the heart of the monster. A final, fatal blow that sends the creature and Dayton crashing to the ground in a tangle of scales and blood.

For a moment there's only silence. Then like a storm rolling over the sea, the crowd begins to roar. Dayton rises from the corpse of the gorgon, shaking green blood off his blades. He walks over to me, flashing a dazzling smile. "There it is. Have you ever heard such a beautiful sound?"

"They're cheering for you."

"They're cheering for *us*." He sheaths his sword and grabs my arm, raising it up.

We did it, our first victory. Only two more until we win our chance to claim the bow. The crowd is on their feet, Dayton's name ringing through the air. My breath is ragged, heart pounding. But as I look at Dayton, he's not staring at the crowd. His gaze is straight on Kairyn, watching from the precipice.

A challenge. A warning.

The High Prince of Summer has returned.

65

ROSALINA

It's too hot. I love Summer, with the sun, the beaches, the golden sand. But it's too bloody hot. Sweat drips down my brow and I clutch my pillow tighter as my stomach cramps. How much longer can this last?

After Dayton and I returned victorious from our battle, we were greeted with cheers and applause from the other gladiators. Tilla pulled us aside and told us how seeing Dayton in the arena had spread a wave of hope through the captured warriors. She knows we have intentions to defeat the Green Rule, and she assured us that when we move against Kairyn, there are those who will fight with us.

Then, during training, in the combat pit, *this* happened to me, and I returned to my small room to lie down. I'm not sure how long ago it was now, only that if it doesn't stop soon, I might die.

A knock sounds on my door. "Who's there?"

"Day."

"Come in," I groan, not bothering to change into my siren form. Keeping the form up isn't exactly hard—more of an unconscious action, like breathing—but right now all I can concentrate on is this agony.

Dayton closes the door behind him. He's holding a tray of food and places it on the floor beside my bed. His hair is damp from washing off the blood, and his bare chest glimmers with a light sheen of sweat. Around his waist, he wears a simple white wrap, showing off the muscles of his long legs. Watching how that powerful body moved in the arena this morning, and now seeing him clean and nearly bare . . .

It's torture.

"I'm not hungry."

He kneels beside the bed. "Come on, a little posca never did any harm." He holds up a brothy soup with herbs floating on the surface. "Besides, a gladiator has to eat."

"I'm hardly a gladiator." I force myself to sit up and gingerly take the bowl of soup.

"You won a match in the Sun Colosseum. Even Keldarion can't say that. Imagine the look on his face when we tell him."

At the thought of my mate, a wave of agonizing heat ripples through me. The spoon drops into the soup, splashing liquid over us.

"Rosalina!" Dayton cries, taking the soup away. "What's wrong with you? I thought you were just tired, but what is this? Venom? Did the gorgon bite you? Tell me."

His teal eyes blaze with worry. But how can I tell him this? It's *embarrassing*. I clutch my blanket around my shoulders and squish myself into the corner of the bed. "Don't worry about me. This will pass. I'll be okay for tomorrow's match."

"Dammit, Blossom, you're burning up." He touches my forehead, and then he's sitting on my bed, pulling me into his arms. "I can go look for some medicine."

"It won't help." I know I should pull away, but instead I find myself leaning my head on his chest. His heartbeat is so fast. "Not with this."

"What is *this*?"

I squirm against him, feeling a sudden wave of relief. "I think my *wilde courtship* is affecting me. Did you ever hear Farron talk about it?"

"A little maybe," Dayton says. "I don't remember what he said."

I let out a sigh, my hand curling into a fist over his hard stomach. "It's a physiological response from being away from my mates. Specifically, Kel because we've never completed our bond. Basically . . . my body craves him. Last time this happened, my mind even brought me to Kel in my dreams, but I think he's too far down in the Below now. There's no relief unless—"

"Unless you get some icy dick?" Dayton laughs.

"Hey! You have no idea how uncomfortable this is." I smack his chest and raise myself up to look up at him.

Bad idea.

In the candlelight, he doesn't even look fae; he looks like something more, a sculpted god made of shadow and light. Burnished golden hair, piercing eyes, full parted lips.

"Think of a time when you desperately craved something, craved it so badly your whole body ached," I say. "But you knew you could never have it. You'd just have to live with this feeling until it consumed you. Can you imagine that?"

"Yes, Rosalina, I can." His grip tightens on my arm. "I can very much imagine that."

I shut my eyes and it floods into my mind: a vision so vibrant and real it doesn't even feel like my own. Dayton closing the distance between us, devouring me with an open-mouthed kiss. Our flimsy clothes are ripped off when we break away for air. There's no foreplay, no touching, no time for any of it. He takes me, fast and urgent, in a desperate, animal way. His hard cock stretches my inner walls, pounding faster and harder with every stroke. Our hands claw at each other, hair pulled, lips bitten. Until . . . until I explode around him, and he fills me deep with what I so desperately crave.

"Day." A whimper slides out of me before I can stop it. Wetness pools between my legs, my whole body rippling from my imagination.

Except it's not just my imagination. We've been together twice. I almost wish we never had, that I never knew what it felt like. Wish I didn't know his kisses taste like sunlight and his body inside mine feels like being tossed in a glorious storm.

One of his hands cups my face, and the other lightly grazes my back. I open my eyes, his face right before mine. Has he bent closer?

"You should go," I whisper.

"I'm not leaving you like this."

"There's nothing you can do to help."

A strange mix of sadness and anger crosses his features. "Look, I might not be able to help you the way one of your mates could, but I can't leave you. Don't ask me to."

What about Wrenley? I want to ask the question. But at the thought of her, anger surges through me, and I snag his arm, holding it hard enough to bruise. "Then don't."

"I'll stay."

"I guess your presence is sort of distracting." I need him to stay, but it can't be in the way that I want. Not when he has a mate. "Will you tell me a story?"

"If you eat your dinner." He hands me the tray.

Grumpily, I take it and dip a slice of bread spiced with dill into the soup. The broth has a vinegary taste to it, but it's refreshing. While I eat, Dayton recalls a story of the time his family took a ship to the Moon Coral Isles. Memories come alive from his words: diving to watch the fish with his brothers, creating animals out of sand with Delphie, and bonfires on the beach roasting beets and pineapple.

His deep voice is so soothing, and it's not often that I get to hear him speak this freely about his family with such a happy cadence. He takes my bowl when I'm finished. I can't help but lay my head on his chest as he starts a new story of the time his fathers and brothers pranked him by placing him in a small schooner when he was asleep and letting it drift out with the tide.

"Joke's on them." He smirks. "Woke up in the middle of the sea, but it was the first time I met a siren. We had a lot of fun before she brought me home. Which also reminds me of the time Fare and I first met a selkie."

"I want to hear that," I murmur, lips moving against the salt-kissed taste of his skin. "Just remember to leave before sunset." There are no windows in the room to tell the time, but it can't be past late afternoon yet.

"Of course," Dayton says and continues with the story.

His presence has eased my discomfort for now, and I find myself drifting off to the soothing sound of his voice.

"IT'S OKAY, Baby. Tell me what's wrong."

Another moan ripples through me, pain clenching in my stomach, body burning. My eyes flutter open. My head is on Dayton's chest, his arms draped around me.

"I must have fallen asleep," I croak.

"So did I," Dayton says, handing me a glass of water from the tray. "Woke up to you, uh, writhing."

I take a sip, heat flushing my cheeks. My *wilde courtship* is back with a vengeance.

"Look, you really should go. I can manage."

"We've been through this. I'll stay as long as I can." He leans closer. "Now, tell me where it hurts the most, Baby."

I gesture to my stomach. He pulls me so I'm sitting between his legs, then lifts up the simple white shift I have on.

"Wait, I'm not wearing, uh, I'm not wearing anything underneath and —" I cut off, and I can practically hear Caspian's laugh in my head, *An aversion to underpants, Princess?* But it just so happens, there is limited clothing given to the gladiator contestants of the arena, and I have to ration what's clean.

"Don't worry," he says. "I'll be the perfect gentleman, and not touch you anywhere else, all right?"

"Okay," I say. But it's hard to believe when I feel the hard shape of him against my back.

"Just relax," he tells me.

I lean against him as one of his large hands comes to cover my stomach, and he begins to rub soft circles. I remember Kel did the same thing when my mate bond brought me to him in the north through my dreams. But that had a different ending, one where we got carried away. I can't let that happen here . . . I can't . . .

But *oh*, his hand feels so good, soothing the ache inside of me. His other hand wraps around me, rubbing my shoulders. His lips are by my ear.

"How's that feel?" he asks, continuing his caresses. "Does it help? I can't stand seeing you in pain. I want to help you, Baby. I want to help you so damn much."

"I feel so good." My whole body relaxes against his chest, and my bare legs fall open, brushing against his.

He inhales sharply, a deep rumble sounding in his chest. Is my *wilde courtship* making him able to smell my arousal? He shouldn't be here . . .

"This is a bad idea, Day."

"You know me, I've never been one for a good idea." His circles around my stomach get larger, fingertips brushing the top of my center.

A wave of unabashed pleasure courses through me, and I dig my heels into the mattress and buck against him, feeling him. Feeling his need.

His other hand caresses my face, pushing the hair back, before grabbing my jaw. The move screams possession as he pulls me back against his muscular chest. His wet lips brush my ear. "Tell me to stop, Rosie. Fucking tell me to stop."

I bite my lip, my mind muddled with an insane amount of pleasure. Every sweep of his hand is like fractured stardust across my skin. Every sweep is more and more dangerous as his circles get larger and larger. He slows each time at the base of my belly button, rough fingertips brushing my midriff. Each small movement has my body convulsing with ecstasy.

He spins me, and I steady myself on his forearms, eyes whirling with stars. His golden hair falls in thick waves over the pillow. His chest heaves, dotted with sweat. My fingertips dig into his skin, nails scratching pink lines. I'd crawl inside him if I could. My hair falls loose, a dark curtain over my face.

God, I hope it's concealing my face. I know my expression is nothing except pure desire and want and . . . love.

"Rosie, don't you feel this?"

And I do. His desire through the thin wrap. The desperation in his voice. It echoes in every part of me.

"Dayton, we can't."

"You think you'll die without Kel tonight?" he growls, golden hair wild, eyes a storm. "That's how I feel about you. It's how I've felt about you every damned day since you were taken. It's tearing me apart."

I need to stop him, stop this. But I'm barely tethered to the earth. I'm swept away by every piece of him. "Day . . ."

"I've never felt more at my beast's mercy than when I'm around you." He tosses me onto my back, fingertips digging into my shoulders, pressing me deep into the bed. "The wolf inside of me is desperate to claim you."

My shift rises up, revealing every part of my body. My legs brush his. I need to push him away.

He grabs my calf and runs a hand up my leg to my inner thigh where he drums his fingers. His other hand brushes my stomach, up to my ribs and below my breast, which heaves up and down in a desperate cadence. His large hand caresses my face, parting my lips, cupping my jaw, as if he's trying to memorize every part of me.

Then he leans closer, and the feeling of his chest pressing against mine is the most intense sensation of my life. I feel his heartbeat reverberate in my own chest.

"Even if it's not right," I whisper, "Day, there's a part of my heart that will always belong to you."

Tears pool in his eyes, and he smiles. It's so beautiful, like the sun breaking through the clouds.

"Stars, I know, Rosie. I fucking know. I want this. I want you. I choose you." His eyes shine. "It's why I saved you instead. Why I saved you in the storm."

Something shatters the fogginess in my mind. "What?"

He dips his head to my neck. "It's why I saved you in the storm."

I push against his chest until we're sitting up. My shift falls back over me. "You said instead. Instead of *who*?"

His face blanches, but then turns into a challenging smirk. The same one he gave to Kairyn earlier in the arena. "Wrenley fell in, as well. I knew I could only save one of you."

He states it like a fact, no remorse or regret.

"You saved me instead of your mate?"

"And I'd do it again." He clutches my hand, holding it tight to his chest.

My heart rages, mind spinning. He saved me. He chose me.

"Dayton, what if she had drowned? You'd be your wolf forever. What about Summer? What about your curse?"

"I—" His breath is heavy, chest heaving. "She's fine."

"You didn't know she would be, though!" I cry. It now makes sense how upset he was on the beach. "Day, tell me, please. Tell me you saved me because of who my mother is. Tell me you saved me because I'm the only one who has wielded the Bow of Radiance and survived. Or for stars' sake, tell me you saved me because of your vow to Ezryn."

He's silent for a long while, calloused hand still gripping mine. All I can hear is the *thump, thump, thump* of his heart. "I can't."

Tears run across my cheeks. "Leave my room."

He stares me down, a storm swirling in his eyes. For one wild moment, I think he's going to reject everything I said. He's going to kiss me despite it all. I don't know how much longer I can stay afloat before it pulls me under.

"As you wish," he snarls and finally lets go of my hand.

He takes a few steps and then clutches the wall. A rippling courses through his body and he transforms into his wolf. It's so big, it crashes against the basket of my things, snapping it.

"The sun must have just set," I gasp. He can't go outside now.

A growl emits from the wolf. He circles once before throwing himself down on the floor. "I'll sleep here."

Agony pulses in my throat. His golden fur is tangled with shells and seaweed. Slowly, I reach a hand down to him, but when I get close, he growls again.

"Get some sleep, partner," he snarls. "We've got a big match tomorrow."

66

ROSALINA

The metal gates rise, and Spring soldiers shove us between our shoulders to guide us into the arena. Kairyn has transformed it overnight. Huge plants snake through the sand, flowers stand as tall as me, and vines drape over crumbled pillars and broken statues.

"Kairyn has certainly set the stage," I whisper. In the bright light, the scales dusting my arms gleam gold. Today, I wear a simple leather chest plate over a white shift and sandals on my feet to maximize quick movement.

"Looks like he's found a use for all the things he broke raiding Hadria," Dayton growls.

We step into a patch of sunlight, and as the crowd catches sight of their prince, a thunderous roar erupts that shakes the sands.

Dayton raises a sword to the crowd, a dazzling grin spreading across his face, as we approach the center of this twisted arena. I still haven't caught sight of our opponent yet.

"Look up there." Dayton nudges my shoulder.

I follow his gaze to see a spinning orb of light in the center of the arena. A golden circle twirls around it like the rings of a planet. It's much larger than the tiny echosphere that hovers around to boost our voices.

"That is the Orb of Ancestors," Dayton says. "Remember when Justus told you about how I won the Luminae Games? This is what we use. Inside, it holds the memory of all the fighters of this arena. It can create an illusion of them to fight upon the sands. Kairyn thinks he can best me with an ancient warrior? He will be sorely surprised."

"Don't be so cocky," I hiss back. "We don't know who he's going to summon."

Dayton sends another grin up at the crowd and is met with a welcoming roar. "Don't worry. I've fought dozens of these matches, and not one has proven to be a challenge I cannot face."

Still, something twists in my gut. The crowd goes quiet as the so-proclaimed Emperor steps forward in his box. Kairyn's black cape hangs pin straight in the humid air, and my only consolation is that he must be boiling beneath all that heavy armor.

"People of the Summer Realm, you have joined us for a most spectacular match," Kairyn's voice, amplified by an echosphere, booms across the crowd.

I feel more than hear the wave of displeasure as Kairyn addresses the crowd. Booing him would only harm the people, with all the soldiers he has stationed among the audience. In the pulvinar beside Kairyn are numerous Spring soldiers, former members of the Queen's Army, and several white-robed acolytes. I don't spot Wrenley among them. I do, however, see the Nightingale gleaming in her prismatic armor. I haven't seen her since she fled the monastery. I could have killed her with the Bow of Radiance, but I let her go instead.

I'm still not sure if that was the right call.

"My subjects!" Kairyn raises his gloved hands in the air. "I have seen how you enjoy watching your former Prince of Summer fight in the arena."

Despite the use of the word "former," the crowd still roars a cheer, Dayton's name growing into a chant. Dayton soaks it in, raising both swords as a boisterous laugh bursts from his chest.

Kairyn doesn't seem bothered by this new display of affection for Dayton. If anything, he stands straighter. Anticipation coils in my gut. *What do you have planned, snake?*

"I wish to please you, citizens of Summer," Kairyn says. The owl helm tilts, the single silver streak glistening. "You have enjoyed watching one Prince of Summer fight in the arena, so why not three?"

The orb above the arena spins faster and faster until beams of light shoot from it and begin to take shape upon the sand in the form of two large fae males. One holds dual blades like Dayton, the other a shield and sword. Even if I didn't recognize them from the mural, even if the crowd didn't begin to chant their names, I would know who they are simply from the empty expression on Dayton's face, the sound of his swords falling to the sand.

Kairyn has returned Damocles and Decimus to the arena.

"Pick up your swords, Dayton," I breathe.

The two warriors prowl forward. They look fae and yet, they don't. At times, their bodies are a solid illusion, but when they step into a beam of sun, they gleam entirely of light.

"Of course, we would find our little brother in the arena," Damocles' voice roars, an echosphere carrying it to the crowd. "It's where he always escaped his royal duties."

"I will give him the royal reckoning he deserves." Decimus bangs his sword against his shield. As he does, a wave of black shadows passes through the light.

My heart sinks further. This isn't like the Luminae Games Dayton mentioned. I would bet Kairyn has somehow corrupted the memories of his brothers into these twisted spirits.

They're almost at us. Dayton hasn't moved, hasn't picked up his swords.

"Day!" I scream, pulling him to the side just as Damocles makes a running leap.

Heart in my throat, I pull us behind a huge fern, abandoning the swords for now. I keep running until we're covered by the plants. The crowds cheer louder, Damocles' name a chant. He must have stopped to rile the audience up.

Dayton mentioned that while he was training with Justus. *Damocles was so obsessed with glory, it made him brash. He made decisions to elevate his status as a revered victor.*

"Look at me, Day." I grab his face.

He shakes his head. "Kairyn's fucking sick for doing this."

"It's not them. You know it's not. It's just a twisted memory."

He grits his teeth. "Everything is ruined. Even if I kill the illusions on the sand, it'll look like I'm murdering my brothers."

Dayton's right. This is twisted. Far too twisted and clever for Kairyn. I wonder who came up with it . . . the Nightingale? It must have been. Why else would she be here if not to watch?

The plant splits and Decimus is before us with a crazed look in his eyes. He grabs me around the waist and hurls me twenty feet through the air. I scream, feet kicking, arms flailing. I land hard with a crack. Quickly, I sit up and pull my broken bow out from under me. *Better my bow than my bones.*

Across the sands, I see Decimus fly across the arena in a huge gale of wind. He crashes against a pillar, the stone crumbling. Dayton's hand is outstretched, a shimmer of magic dancing from his palm.

The sand shifts, and Damocles runs toward me. His golden hair is cropped short, face menacing. He leaps and plunges the swords down, striking the sand just as I roll out of the way. I reach into my belt and pull out my short sword. I'm not as comfortable with this as my bow, but it's all I've got.

With a cry, I slice it across Damocles' calf. He hisses, red blood spurting from the wound before it turns into fractured light on the ground. I scramble up. I haven't deterred this warrior. He lunges, striking a blow that almost cuts through my leather chest plate.

Justus's lessons crash through my mind at lightning speed. *Block, get away.* All I know is I'm outmatched here. I swing my short sword and Damocles blocks it with no real effort.

"What's a pretty little siren doing so far from the sea?" he says, approaching me with deadly intent. "Was my brother's call enough to pull you from the ocean? It's unfortunate he will be the death of you, as he has been for so many."

Damocles knocks the short sword from my grasp, and it skitters over the sand. I back up as quick as I can but hit a stone wall. If I don't use my thorns now, I'll die. Damocles raises his sword—

It's met with a clang that sounds through the arena as Dayton steps between us, blocking the attack.

"Get away from her," he snarls, voice tinged with fury.

"He finally joins the fight," Damocles says. "I thought you would sleep through it."

Dayton snarls, matching Damocles blow for blow. Quickly, I search the arena for Decimus. He's recovered from the collision with the pillar and races toward his brothers.

"Dayton! Look out!" I cry.

He catches my meaning, bringing up his sword just in time to block Decimus's attack. I have to help him. He's outnumbered and they're all content to ignore me now.

Running back to the remnants of my bow, I pick up the pieces. It's snapped in two. Quickly, I tear off a chunk of one of Kairyn's creepy vines and wrap it around my snapped bow. It's not much of a repair, but it'll have to do.

Running back to the fight, I glance up at Kairyn and the Nightingale. I see they're both on the edge of the pulvinar staring with rapt attention.

Well, watch this.

I draw back the bow, take aim, and shoot. It goes wide, the bow twanging awkwardly in my hand. Dammit. Hopefully, they didn't watch that one.

Drawing a second shot from the quiver on my back, I aim it at Decimus's broad shoulders. The arrow hits, and he roars, rearing back. Dayton takes the opportunity and strikes him across the chest. The light flickers. He almost has him.

The crowd gives a collective gasp of anticipation. Dayton hears it. I see it in the way his precise movements slow.

"Strike down your brother now," Damocles snarls. "Give him another death as you did when you left him on the battlefield."

"No, I—" Dayton stammers, turning just in time to block Damocles' attack.

"Show everyone the death you caused," Damocles says, driving forward, pushing Dayton back into Decimus.

"Our little brother always falters when there's a decision to be made." Decimus pummels into him with the bulk of his shield, pushing Dayton straight into Damocles' swords.

I scream. Blood spurts from Dayton's wounds as the swords draw out of his body. He gags, blood dripping from his lips.

"No!" I yell. Magic crackles within me as I run forward. But I don't reach for my thorns. Instead, I connect with the plants of the arena, plants Kairyn created. Those of Spring, those of my mate's magic. A towering coil of vines beside the brothers collapses. Both Damocles and Decimus back up, and I pull Dayton to the other side.

The vines create a divide between us. I grab Dayton around the shoulders and drag him deeper into the plants' embrace, silently asking them to rise up around us. Hopefully, it's not noticeable to Kairyn from this far away.

As soon as we're shielded from the view of the crowd, I press my hands to Dayton's bloody stomach, searching for my healing magic. I know that power must be inside me, but I've never accessed it before. I should have had Ezryn teach me the way he taught Farron.

Snarling, I remove my blood-soaked hands, rip the hem of my dress, and wrap it around the wound. At least no one can hear us in here.

Dayton grips my shoulders tight. "Get us out of here, Rose. I can't do this. I can't win."

Every instinct in me wants to summon my thorns and spirit us away from here. But that would mean abandoning Summer, the chance at my bow. Abandoning all the people here, counting on us.

"That's not true," I say. "Justus said you could win against your brothers. You know their weaknesses. You *told* him."

"It's one thing to know it and another to do it." Dayton shakes his head, blond hair wild. "They're my *brothers*."

"No, they're not. It's not them. Kairyn is doing this to frighten you. He's doing this because *he's* frightened."

"Oh, I'm sure he's quaking in his metal boots."

Outside, a call begins: Dayton's name on his brothers' lips as they search for him.

"Kairyn is afraid," I say, gripping the back of Dayton's neck. "He saw how you ignite the crowd. He's not strong enough to corrupt their minds here. Not in this realm, not in *your* realm. He can only rule with fear, and you take that away. You give the people hope."

His lips tremble, still red with blood. "Killing my own brothers in front of my people? How can I . . ."

"They're nothing but corrupted memories. Remind the people of Summer what a true hero is. Remind them that it's not Kairyn, or Damocles, or Decimus who is the High Prince of Summer." I lean my forehead against his. "It's you. Now go out there, face them, and burn so bright you blind the sun."

67

DAYTON

Gods, I want to kiss her. She's beautiful of course, even if she doesn't look like the Rosie I'm entirely used to, with her golden hair and scale-brushed cheeks. But there's a light in her that always shines through. "Did I ever tell you how cute these are?" I say, flicking her webbed ears.

"Day!"

"Listen to me, Blossom." I grab her hand. "This is something I have to do on my own. Can you keep yourself safe?"

"I understand. Don't worry about me," she says.

"All right then. I've got a crowd to entertain." I wink and leap up from behind the vines and into the bright light. Pure adrenaline is keeping me going at this point, and I refuse to acknowledge the pain that stems from my wounds. They're bad, but if I don't push through it, we'll be dead, and that's worse.

The sun burns my eyes, and I blink to adjust my vision. Damocles and Decimus stand near the center of the arena.

"Was that my name I heard?" I say, the echosphere amplifying my voice to the arena. "Sorry, just needed a quick nap."

Laughter roils through the crowd. Good. The only thing Damocles hated more than me being a shit was a good time and a smile.

Sure enough, my older brother's light-stricken glare reflects in the glint of his steel. Beside him, Decimus looks nothing if not sturdy and determined with his red shield and sword.

Both my brothers are formidable opponents on their own, and here I am, trying to take them both on. But I always was one for bad ideas.

I tighten my grip on my twin blades, feeling their familiar weight. I know I can't match their strength head-on, but I have other advantages— agility, cunning, and the fact that I'm not made of fucking light. I dart forward, using the dense foliage to conceal my movements.

Damocles charges, blades flashing in the sunlight, his confidence palpable. I evade his blows, dancing between the pillars like a shadow, waiting for the opportune moment to strike. Decimus moves to flank me, his shield raised defensively, but I refuse to be cornered. Instead, I lead them on a merry chase, darting in and out of cover, wearing down their stamina.

"Are we fighting or dancing?" Decimus roars. He swings his sword at me *hard*. I spring out of the way, and it strikes a pillar, causing the whole thing to crumble.

"Nice one, Dec." I smirk, flitting backward. "You always were the strongest of us brothers."

Damocles huffs. "He wishes." My eldest brother, never one to be outdone, slices his twin blades through a huge vine blocking our path.

Very good, I think. *Keep tiring yourself out.*

"The real Damocles could have done that to stone," I call.

"What riddles do you speak, little brother?" Damocles spits.

The warriors of light never realize what they are, but the crowd does. I have to remind them these are just illusions.

"I'm only saying it's a good thing you're here, brothers." I narrowly duck below a combined strike from both of them. "I always wondered if I kept my record of wins in the arena because I never faced either of you. Now, we'll see who the true champion is."

"Not one so cocky and foolhardy as you," Damocles spits.

Damocles' blades slash through the air with deadly precision. I spring into action. With a swift motion, I dart to the side, ducking behind one of the pillars. Damocles follows, his arrogance driving him without hesitation. But as he moves to strike, I vanish into the shadows.

Meanwhile, Decimus presses the attack, his shield raised in a defensive stance. I can see the strain in his movements, the weariness creeping into his limbs. I unleash a flurry of strikes, my twin swords a blur of steel as I barrage him from all sides. His shield wavers, his defenses faltering.

The crowd roars its approval. But I can't just play with them. I must have the strength to end this. To claim what's mine in front of the people of Summer. The Blessing is mine. I need to show them why.

Something glimmers golden in my peripheral vision. Rosalina.

I'll win this for her. For the man she believes I am. A man who can save his people. A man worthy of his Blessing.

"Hey, brothers, did you ever think you'd fight a High Prince upon the sands?" I leap into the open.

"An unworthy title for a coward," Decimus roars, closing in. His shield pushes me back, his sword a relentless barrage of strikes. I parry and dodge, my muscles screaming with exertion, the heat unrelenting, but I refuse to yield. I press forward, exploiting the chinks in Decimus' defense, until finally, his strength wanes, and his attacks falter.

"No," I growl back. "To fight in the arena is an honor. It is our way. What's dishonorable is chopping your brother's ears off and begging for the Blessing through twisted words. You are unworthy of being a High Prince." I point my sword skyward to Kairyn. "What's twisted is making the people of Summer watch the princes who died defending them in battle fight in your games, while you dine with the servants of those who gave them the true death."

"Shut it off—" Broken words, Kairyn's words, the echosphere cutting in and out. "Stop him—"

The crowd roars in response, anger and repulsion evident.

"I will end this for them. I will end this for Summer," I snarl. It doesn't matter now if the people hear me. They'll see what I plan to do.

There's no hesitation in me now. My brothers appear as nothing more than flickers of light. It's not Damocles, not Decimus.

I land between them, feet shifting in the sand as they move to attack me on all sides. In the arena's pulsing heart, amid the ancient pillars and verdant greens, I stand, twin blades glinting with resolve. This was always my world more than theirs. They fought in it; they did their duty. But never did they win the crowd like I did. Never did they find the pure flash of life between strikes of the sword.

As the crowd's fervor crescendos, I seize the moment. With a deft twist, I disarm my brothers, their swords clattering like forgotten echoes. With each strike, my heart races with the rhythm of their fading breaths.

My swords find their marks with haunting precision. Damocles and Decimus's eyes widen, hearts pierced by their brother. As I hold their gazes one final time, I wonder if this is how they looked at the end, on that battlefield, as their life ebbed, as they felt the Blessing of Summer float away . . . Did they think of me?

Think of the brother that abandoned them?

"I'm sorry," I say, tears flowing down my face. The magic flickers out, their bodies drifting away into motes of dusty light. "I'm sorry I couldn't save you. But I promise, I will do whatever it takes to save our people."

Their forms drift away entirely, and my swords are as clean as when I stepped into the arena. The only blood left on my chest is mine.

The ringing in my ears fades, and the roar of the crowd breaks through. Cheers for me, mixed with something else. Voices rise in protest, cries of anguish mingling with shouts of condemnation as the crowd rails against the cruelty displayed by Emperor Kairyn.

A presence stands before me.

"Whatever it takes," Rosalina says.

So, she heard me. That explains the tinge of sadness in her voice, the same one writhing through me now.

I will see the Summer Realm freed from this tyranny. Whatever it takes. But we both know what it'll take for me to reclaim Summer.

My full unbridled magic.

There's only one woman who can give me that.

And it's not the one beside me.

68

KELDARION

"Come on, George. Not much farther."

I'm not sure if my words are true. The prison at the inner sanctum of the labyrinth could be right around the next corner or on the other side of this damned maze. As certain as George has been at each fork in the road, we could be getting farther and farther away with every step.

And I'm not sure how many more steps George has in him. He still manages that assured grin, but his face is pale, his movements slow. I wrap an arm around his shoulders to keep him steady. Rosalina would beg for us to take a break, but we rested not long ago. We can't keep stopping.

There isn't much time left—only three more days before Farron and Caspian break the crystals. If it happens before we're at the prison, it will all be for nothing. We're running out of time.

"You're a good sport, you know that?" George pats my chest.

"I would do anything for your family," I say. "If I have to carry you through this maze, I will."

"Let's hope it doesn't come to that." George tilts his head to the right as we approach a T-shape in the maze.

I turn us right, only to be faced with a huge archway carved with cherubs. Beyond, it widens to a walled grove. The ground is purple grass, dotted with rocks that shine like amethysts. Trees glowing with iridescent leaves tower nearly as high as the walls. Bright pink butterflies flitter to and fro.

"Well, if this isn't a nice change of pace!" George exclaims. It seems to have given him a second wind. He pushes off of me and heads with urgency into the grove.

"Careful. Nothing is placed in the labyrinth without reason."

At the far end of the grove lies another archway: the continuation of the maze. There must be some sort of trap or trial here. Each step is dangerous.

"Keep an eye out for anything out of place," I warn George.

"Like that pile moving over there?"

"What?"

George points to a cluster of trees across the grove. At their base lies a large lump covered in brilliant pink butterflies. It shifts and moves, as if awakening from a great slumber. I stand protectively in front of George.

The pile heaves upward, a mass of butterflies flapping. Standing, it's nearly ten feet tall. A woman's shape begins to form amid the crowding butterflies. Long white hair falls out from beneath the shroud of living creatures. A large butterfly covers her face, the spots upon its wings appearing like ghastly eyes peering through me.

"I saw that you would pass this way, Keldarion, High Prince of Winter," the giantess says, her lips covered by butterflies. She begins to walk toward us. Her arms swing like pendulums, much too long for her body. Her legs, too, seem unnaturally thin and elongated.

"I hope we didn't keep you waiting, Philiris," I say. I knew we'd come across her eventually. The Fates are never far from each other.

"Of course not. I knew when you'd be here." Her butterfly eyes loom over George, and her whole head twists nearly upside down upon its long neck as if getting a better look at him. "Though some of you are harder to see than others."

"This is Philiris, the Visionary," I say to George. "Another of the Fates."

"Many have come to me before." Philiris's voice is deeper than her sister Clio's, a strange, echoey sound that seems to originate from within all the wings covering her body. "I have shown a great many futures that have come to pass. The last to see me was the youngest son ofSpring. The flutter of the wings depicted a great and terrible future. So, it has come to be."

"Knowing the future has never helped me before," I growl and grab George's arms. "Whatever you're going to offer us, we don't want it."

We start to walk past her when a massive expanse juts out before us: a culmination of all the small butterflies flying together to form Philiris's giant wing. "I wasn't going to offer to show you your future, Keldarion, High Prince of Winter. Or even yours, George of the O'Connells." Her head twists all the way around so she can look at us. "But the future of the Prince of Thorns and his Golden Rose . . . That is what the wings have shown me."

I should go. Keep walking. Spring every trap in this grove if I have to. But I can't move my feet. "You . . . you know Rosalina's future?"

Philiris sighs, her butterflies rippling with sound. "The wings of the future flutter endlessly. I catch sight, here and there."

"Show me." George pulls out of my grip and walks up to her. "I would see my daughter's fate."

Philiris places her unnaturally long fingers over George's face. A butterfly springs into existence, forming a mask across George's brow, with spots for unseeing eyes.

"No," I say, reaching out and grabbing her spindly wrist. "I'll do it."

"High Prince?" Philiris asks, pulling the butterfly from George's face.

I look at Rosalina's father. "Seeing the future can set even the most determined man to hopelessness. I have lived with such despair for decades. Let me bear this burden."

George holds my gaze for a long time, before finally, he nods.

The butterfly flits up from Philiris's palm then lands on the bridge of my nose. All goes dark.

I see her. Rosalina. She sits on a throne at the top of a huge staircase crafted of intertwining purple and golden thorns. Her long legs are crossed, the milky skin I long to touch visible from the high slit in her dark gown. A crown of thorns adorns her hair.

I stagger up the stairs toward her. Heat radiates on all sides of me, but not the normal warmth of fire. This heat seems to chill and burn all at once, raking my skin with clawed fingers. Emerald fire licks the edge of the stairs. Faces form in the blaze, screaming mouths and eyes agape, before vanishing in the next flicker.

Rosalina taps her fingers on the armrest, mouth curved in a frown. Her eyes, usually so kind and warm, are vacant and dull.

A flash of emerald fire blazes beside her, and then another figure appears. He stands above her, dressed in blackened steel, armor too formidable for his frame. Spikes jut out from the pauldrons. His black hair falls below his jaw, and a wicked smile curves his lips.

A smile I've spent forever trying to burn out of my mind.

When Rosalina sees Caspian, her face alights. But not in the way I know, such as the girlish smile when she tells a joke and is the only one who laughs, or the sultry smirk when she knows she has me right where she wants me. This is something else, something feverish.

The smile of a thrall.

Caspian grabs her by her neck to guide her up. His own expression is one of feral hunger. He nips at her bottom lip, tugging it away and biting down so hard, blood dribbles down her chin. The act only seems to make her more desperate for him. She scratches at his chest plate, trying to push every inch of her body against his.

My heart is a thundering drumbeat in my ears. This isn't jealousy—I shared Rosalina with Caspian only days ago. I know she has other mates who worship her body in the way she deserves. But this sight before me . . .

This is not Rosalina. If I were to break my curse by making love to her, it would send her straight into Caspian's arms. And this is what will happen.

It doesn't matter if Caspian loves me. He loves her, too, and if the only way he can have her is by making her his thrall, he will do it.

Caspian grips her around the neck again and forces her down to her knees. She stares up at him reverently. As if he is the love of her life. As if he is a god.

And as I look around at the green fire burning everything in the horizon, I realize that's exactly what he is.

A dark god with his dark queen.

"No!" I scream. The fire has created huge welts over my skin, but I don't care. I surge up the staircase, hands lunging for Caspian.

Caspian turns and a crooked smile forms on his lips. "Hello, lover," he says.

Then I've fallen to the ground, my fists ripping out the purple grass. The staircase and the flames are gone, revealing only the grove. I look down at my skin. No burns, yet the chilling heat lingers in my bones.

"What did you see?" George asks, running over to me.

I ignore him and stare up at Philiris. "Will it come to pass? Is there no other future for her?"

She drifts over to me, moving a piece of hair out of my eyes with her stretched finger. "I only see the future, High Prince. It is you who makes it."

"I will not let that happen," I vow. My voice is ragged, desperate.

"Some things are set. For example," her butterfly eyes look from me to George, "you are both destined to find your rose shattered. Go back to the place where all was lost."

My Rose . . . shattered? No, no, I won't let that happen. It can't be our destiny! "What do you mean? What do you mean?"

But the Fate says nothing. She starts to shrink in size, her butterflies careening away from her in a blur. Before me stands a small, naked woman, her skin completely rotten. It hangs off her bones in folds of mottled gray and green, emitting a sickly sweet scent. Only one butterfly remains, the one covering her face. "Goodbye. I will see you again, Keldarion, High Prince of Winter. But not you, George of the O'Connells. Farewell."

Then as if her bones were ripped out of her, the rotten skin tumbles to the ground in a heap. The butterfly covering her face flits off into the sky.

"Philiris!" I scream. "Wait!"

"What did you see, boy?" George yells, shaking me. "What did you see?"

But I cannot tell him. For if that future comes to pass, it is because of me. Because I fail to protect Rosalina.

No. It will never be like that.

I let my heart guide me with Caspian before, let his words sink beneath my bones until I gave him everything. I felt it happening again the night I shared with him and Rosalina, desperate to trust him again.

I was fooled last time, and it shattered me. But now I don't only have myself to protect. There is Rosalina.

No matter what my heart wants, it must become stone. This vision is the truth. I have to protect Rosalina from Caspian.

Winter will fall to the Green Flame before Caspian puts his hands on my mate again.

69

ROSALINA

"Kairyn is summoning us both to the Serenus Dusk Chambers." The door to my room flies open as Dayton rushes in.

I sit up on my bed where I've been resting after today's match. "What are those?"

"They're suites and halls attached to the Sun Colosseum," Dayton answers, words clipped and angry. "During long games, my family and other nobles would reside there rather than return to Soltide Keep."

"Why does he want us there?"

"I don't know. One of the guards explained we must be *prepared*. I said I would get you, but I don't like this."

My heart lurches in my throat. "Kairyn must be furious after your performance in the games today. The people were enthralled by you."

"It's a full moon tonight. He knows that as well, I'm sure," Dayton says.

"We can't let him get to us," I say, pacing my room. "He's going to try to rile you up. Whatever his bait, we can't rise to it. Our only goal is to be allowed to continue and enter the final match."

The muscle in Dayton's jaw twitches.

"Dayton, are you listening?"

"Yes." He touches the Summer token on his necklace. "Or I could get close to him tonight and gut him with the trident."

"Kairyn's magic isn't cursed. He's too strong. We need the support of your people and the bow."

There's a banging on my door and a booming voice carries inside: "All right, time to go."

Quickly, I unfasten Dayton's seashell necklace. "If they look too closely at you, they might discover the token. Best to take this off."

"Do you really think it's safe here?"

I kneel in a corner of my room beside my bed. From the dirt, I summon a tiny bramble of thorns that wraps around the necklace to protect it. "Safer than with Kairyn."

Dayton gives a long sigh and extends a hand to help me up. "Well then, little siren, let me escort you into the belly of the beast."

I'VE NEVER FELT SO EXPOSED and so revered. Like a walking jewel.

Shortly after we were brought to the Dusk Chambers, I was taken into a separate room and attended to by two fae females.

They stripped me down, washed my body and hair, all while remarking on how they'd never seen a siren up close before. Then they *painted* me. Unlike the paint Astrid used before I went to Caspian's birthday party in the Below, this paint did not form cloth. It stuck to my skin like a second layer until every inch of me was covered in gold.

"To match your hair," one of them explained.

Very little covers the rest of my body, only a draping of gold-painted shells woven on a thin string that dangles across my chest and hangs off my waist. My feet are left bare. My already golden hair is curled into loose waves.

Now, I walk through the halls, keeping my head high. I will not be embarrassed or ashamed by this. This is just another layer to my disguise. Siren, gladiator . . . and if Kairyn wants to dress me up as a jewel, then I'll be that, as well.

"Just through here," one of the attendants says as we pause before a gauzy curtain. Behind it, I hear the faint murmur of voices and the melodic hum of music.

Footsteps sound behind us, and I turn to see Dayton being led by two attendants of his own.

Breath catches in my throat. If I'm a jewel, he's a golden sword. Every hard edge of him glitters. His body is painted as well, and only a delicate curtain of shells dangles from his jutting hip bones, showing off the powerful muscles of his legs. They've left his hair down as well, brushed with gold powder. The ends graze his broad shoulders, and the shimmer on his face accentuates the square cut of his jaw.

That glimmering face curves into a snarl when he sees me. He breaks away from the attendants and roughly grabs my arm. "You can't go in there looking like *that*."

"Oh, you think I'm pleased about your get-up?" I shoot back. "That little skirt is hardly enough to cover your, uh . . ."

He flashes a white grin. "I know. It's breezy."

"Be careful!" One of the attendants bursts between us. "You'll smudge the paint."

Dayton is forced to step back, and a new layer of gold is applied to my arm and his hand. Before we can say another word, we're ushered inside.

Immediately, I'm overwhelmed by the scent of mingling perfumes, wafting delicately amid the lively chatter and soft rustle of silken garments. My heart quickens at the spectacle before me. This isn't just any Summer Realm party—it's reminiscent of something out of the Below, an extravaganza that blurs the lines between proper and sensational.

Music drifts through the air. A harpist plucks delicately at the strings, while flutes trill with an otherworldly lilt. All eyes turn to us as we walk into the celebration, the chatter of the crowd fading to a hushed whisper.

Marble columns rise majestically around the room, adorned with intricate carvings. The walls are draped in sumptuous fabrics, rich hues of crimson cascading like blood. Marble statues stand sentinel in alcoves, their serene faces illuminated by flickering torchlight.

But those aren't the only beacons in this place. Blue lights dance merrily in the air, casting a soft glow. "Will-o'-wisps," I whisper, leaning closer to Dayton.

"They sometimes float into the Serenus Dusk Chambers and around the arena during games. I didn't know what they were until you and Farron taught me about the wisps in Autumn. My mother said they were spirits drawn to the great gatherings of life here." Anger flashes in his gaze. "Not that this is a gathering of life. Look at these people. I recognize half of these Summer and Spring nobles. Spineless sycophants. The rest must be from the Below."

"They might be just as trapped as we are," I whisper back.

"Or maybe Kairyn's giving them an excuse to let out their dark side."

My gaze is drawn to the figure seated upon a throne at the head of the room, clad in full black armor that gleams ominously in the flickering candlelight. When the owl helm's gaze meets mine, a shiver runs down my spine. *He doesn't know it's me,* I remind myself. *Not with the makeup, not as a siren.*

We stop before the throne, and Kairyn stands. "Ah, Daytonales. So pleased you could make it."

"Yeah, well, I heard the food was better than in the barracks." Dayton smiles.

There's a small ripple of laughter through the audience, and I see the annoyance in the shift of Kairyn's stance.

Beside Kairyn are a handful of his loyal acolytes, clad in robes of white and gold. I spy Wrenley holding a tray of bubbling drinks. Her big blue eyes are wide as she gazes at Dayton.

As she gazes at her mate.

"We were all delighted to see your little performance in the arena today, Daytonales," Kairyn says. "Would you like to know who you and your little fishy friend will be fighting next?"

"Unless it's you in full gladiatorial garb showing your ass to the sun, then I don't really give a shit."

A low metallic growl sounds through Kairyn's helm and he gives an agitated gesture with his hand. Hard metal steps sound in the hall, and a looming figure approaches. The newcomer is nearly as tall as Kairyn and plated in coppery armor with a golden spear in his hands. The Bronze Knight, wielding what should be Farron's Lance of Valor. Farron's beautiful golden leaf token hangs from the knight's neck.

"Do you think," Kairyn's voice lowers, "the little Autumn Prince will feel his lost relic taking your life? Perhaps he will seek revenge, only to meet the same fate."

A low growl sounds in Dayton's chest, and he surges forward, but I grab his arm. "Save it for the arena."

Dayton stills, muscles tense.

"Just as one day, I will finally put an end to the plague that is my brother with the Hammer of Hope." Kairyn touches the wooden square, the token of Spring, at his neck.

Now it's my turn to bite my tongue. After everything Kairyn has done to Ezryn, it's still not enough.

"You'll never be the ruler Ezryn was," Dayton growls, voice low and dangerous.

"Are you implying you know so much about leadership, Daytonales?"

Kairyn chuckles. "It's almost embarrassing how easy it was to take your realm. Damocles would be ashamed."

"Do not say his name," Dayton roars. I squeeze his arm.

"You're nothing more than a shadow of him. A failed remnant of a greater man," Kairyn says.

I narrow my gaze. If that isn't the pot calling the kettle black. Thankfully, Dayton's pulse has steadied under my touch, and he's reassumed that blasé look from earlier. Letting Kairyn rile us up will only hurt our cause.

"Look at you, practically a prisoner while I sit upon the throne that was once yours. Do you even know why I've brought you here?" Kairyn asks.

"Well, I'm assuming by the way you've dressed me, it can only be to appreciate my male physique?" Dayton chides. "How long has it been since you've removed that armor and gazed at your own cock?"

"Dayton," I hiss.

Kairyn's body tenses with anger, fists curling at his sides. "No." He takes a step down the stairs that lead up to the throne. "As a participant in my games, you belong to me. But I don't want to keep you all to myself. You proclaimed yourself High Prince in the arena, yet I see no token, and I certainly don't feel the magic of a High Ruler."

The muscles in Dayton's throat work as he swallows.

"Tonight, you can be prince of the people." Kairyn spreads an arm out to our audience, all watching with rapt attention. "Wars are expensive, you see. Tonight, these lovely fae will bid on the pleasure of you and your partner's company."

"I'm not fucking anyone," Dayton growls. "And neither is she."

Kairyn shakes his head. "Is that all that's ever on your mind, Summer Prince? Fucking and drinking? I am not offering anything so base. The people here are curious about your ways. They pay for the company of gladiators and of the wonders of the sea. Eat, drink, and share stories, all while knowing every moment you spend with them is fueling the Green Rule."

Kairyn sweeps past us to address the crowd. "Do we have an opening bid to spend the night with the gladiator Daytonales?"

The nobles begin to throw numbers into the air like rain. "Two thousand denarii," I whisper. "Is that a lot?"

Dayton grunts. "A skilled blacksmith might earn a thousand denarii in a year. These people are fools to throw that amount of coin at Kairyn."

"That amount for *you*."

He leans in and whispers, "If anyone touches you tonight, I'll do worse than relieve them of their hands."

"Then I'll do my best to keep my distance, partner."

"Three thousand denarii!" A Spring servant calls out the bids. "Going once, going twice, sold!"

A woman in draping spiderweb silk jumps up and claps her hands together, eyeing Dayton with a hungry gaze. He sighs.

"If it's any consolation, I don't think your fishy sidekick will go for such a price," I say.

"I don't like this."

"Telling stories, being charming for a few hours . . . we can handle that." I lower my voice. "We'll steal it back and buy a thousand stuffed animals."

"It's a promise, Blossom. Though, I don't know if you and the princes will fit in a bed with all of those." His face softens, and he turns away.

My stomach twists in sadness as I watch him go. The woman and her friends greet him with cheers of glee, handing the prince a goblet of wine.

They are citizens of the Below. Perhaps there's something we can learn from them.

"All right." Kairyn waves a dismissive hand, already looking bored. "The siren."

My bids start low.

"Twenty denarii!"

"Thirty-five!"

"Forty."

A male with a protruding nose and a pointy, rat-like chin prowls forward. Stringy brown hair falls in greasy strands to his shoulders. "I've always been curious about the elusive sirens." He reaches a crooked hand to one of the shells at my waist.

"If you want to touch, Duke Vermil, you must pay." The auctioneer steps over, and the male retracts his gnarled fingers. "We have forty. Do I hear fifty?"

"One thousand," a sweet voice says. A young woman stands next to a cubiculum covered by gauzy curtains. "My master would like to bid one thousand denarii."

I wrack my mind. Has she bid before? One thousand denarii—that's almost as much as Dayton went for.

Duke Vermil licks his lips. "It seems I'm not the only one with such desires. I bid one thousand and fifty denarii."

My stomach sinks. If anything, the price increase made this male want me more. I know Kairyn said we only had to talk with these people, but I don't think that's what this duke has in mind.

"Five thousand denarii," the girl says. I try to get a look at her through the crowd. She has straight black hair and smoke-lined eyes.

The duke's face blanches. "It seems someone knows more than me."

"Six thousand," another bidder says, a burly man near the back of the hall.

Kairyn gives a huff of approval, watching this play out. I meet Dayton's wide eyes, concern on his features. He doesn't like this any more than I do. What are these people going to expect of me with this much money on the line?

"My master will bid twenty thousand," the slight girl says.

"Thirty thousand," the duke hisses, spittle foaming from beneath his teeth.

"Forty thousand," says the fae in the back.

My heart rate increases and sweat beads on my brow, threatening to ruin my paint. *No, no, no.* I don't want to be here anymore. I told Dayton I could do this, but I'm not sure I can. If I use my thorns to protect myself, our ruse will be up and—

"One hundred thousand denarii," the girl says. "My master would like to bid one hundred thousand."

The room goes silent. Even the musicians pause.

"One hundred thousand denarii," the auctioneer stutters and looks at Kairyn.

"Sold," Kairyn says. "If your master can pay."

"I assure you he can," the girl says confidently.

"Very well," Kairyn says and looks at me. "The deal is done."

The duke scrunches his face up in anger, then stalks away.

"Come with me, miss," the slight girl says as she walks over. Her red eyes glint with mirth.

Wait. Red eyes . . .

"Astrid?"

She gives a little giggle and takes my hand. "Shush. I'm in disguise."

My nerves calm, and I follow her through the crowd. She's heading for a private room, hidden by black curtains. None of this makes any sense. What is she doing here, away from Castletree? Who is her master? The only person she's ever called master is Keldarion. He can't be here, can he? He's supposed to be in the Below.

Then I feel it, something burning deep into my chest. For a wild moment, I know if I grabbed one of these wild will-o'-wisps, it would lead a light straight beyond those veiled black curtains.

"Just through here," Astrid says as she pulls back the veil and ushers me through.

But it's not Keldarion lounging on the chaise inside.

It's the Prince of Thorns.

His lips curve into a tantalizing smile. "Why, hello there, little siren."

70

DAYTON

A trail of drool leaks from the woman's mouth onto the floor. The others in this alcove aren't faring much better. Ladies of the Below are sprawled out around me, snoring. I suppose they're not used to our Summer wine.

My eyes keep drifting to the gauzy curtains where Rosie disappeared over an hour ago.

I know Rosie can take care of herself, and going over there might alert Kairyn to just how much I care about my partner, but it doesn't make the waiting any easier. One hundred thousand denarii for the company of a siren. Just who is behind that curtain?

I grab another goblet off the table and down it. An array of fruit, dates, and crusty bread with oil for dipping is laid before me. I already stuffed myself as soon as my companions passed out. It's much better than the food in the barracks. I even wrapped some extra in cloth, hoping to bring it for Rosie and Tilla later, but I'm not sure how I'll smuggle it out.

Not like they gave me pockets in this ridiculous get-up.

It didn't look ridiculous on Rosie, though. She was like a golden goddess. When I think of the curves of her body, her gold-dusted lips, it's no wonder some minion paid one hundred thousand denarii just to bask in her presence.

Fuck, I'd give every star in the sky.

I adjust my position and try to shift my thoughts away from Rosalina. This outfit does little to hide my growing desire.

"Fancy a drink?" A servant comes around with a tray of wine goblets.

"No, thank you," I say.

"Dayton." The voice lowers. "It's *me.*"

Wrenley stands above me, holding tight to the tray. "Come on, follow me. I don't think your buyers will notice your absence for a long while."

She weaves through the crowd, white robes trailing on the marble flooring, and takes me to a secluded cubiculum covered by a white curtain. Inside, there is only a chaise, a low table, and a platter of olives.

Wrenley sits down and pats the seat beside her. "I noticed this one wasn't being used. It's been so hard to sneak away and see you."

Guilt tightens in my gut as I look down at my mate. Sure, nothing really happened with Rosalina the other night. But I'd held her in my arms, touched her body, and stars know, if she had let me, I'd have done more.

Rosalina said she was taken over by her mating frenzy, but damn, there was a fire burning through me as well. One like I've never known. My cock was steel hard. Even after she fell asleep, the instinct never left me. All I wanted to do was rouse her from her slumber and kiss her and claim her and empty my seed deep inside.

Why did I agree to do this mission with her? I'm not only in agony because of her beauty but because of who Rosalina is. In the arena, she's fierce and valiant.

I would never have won the fight against Damocles or Decimus without her.

My brave, kind, beautiful girl.

Who isn't mine at all.

"Dayton?" Wrenley says. In the dim candlelight, with the way her curls fall across her brow and the furrow of her nose, she looks a little like Rosie. A lot like Rosie, actually. "Is everything all right?"

"Yes, I'm listening." I sit down next to her. "I'm sorry I've been distant lately. I'm going to try to do better by you, Wren."

Because to break my curse, I don't just have to find my mate. She has to *love* me. Could Wrenley do that?

"Do you really think we can make this work?" I say softly to her.

"I do." She reaches out to grab my hand. "The stars would not have aligned our fates, if not."

"I guess you're right," I say and then add, "How are you doing?"

"I'm all right. Kairyn is furious at you for your remarks this evening. Why do you chide him with such untruths?"

"Untruths." I smirk. "I meant what I said. I'd face him if he showed up on the sands of the arena, dressed in nothing but gladiator gear! I'd like to see that, wouldn't you?"

Wrenley looks me up and down, then her face turns entirely red. "Why would I—"

"I'm just teasing you," I say, tucking a strand of hair behind her ear. "It's what I do when I'm nervous or scared or just feel like being a shit. Which is a lot of the time."

"I've noticed."

Her face shines in the dim blue light. A small will-o'-wisp bounces into our alcove. All night I've watched drunk partygoers try to catch them and place them on their chests to see if any light bursts forth. So far, I've seen none.

"A will-o'-wisp." Gently, I extend a palm to it.

Wrenley smacks my hand away, and the little creature flutters out of the alcove. "Are you crazy?" she snarls. "You can't let that nasty little creature land on you. What if someone sees our mate bond? What do you think Kairyn would do to me?"

I give a long sigh. I've upset her. "Thought I would be romantic. I guess I wasn't thinking."

She shakes her head, tears brimming at the edges of her eyes. "I'm just worried about you. You have to face the Bronze Knight next."

Her worries are justified. Rosalina told me that even Keldarion couldn't defeat one of Kairyn's knights when they wielded a divine weapon. "I've never lost in the Sun Colosseum."

"You can't afford to be so arrogant," she says. "What will happen to the Blessing of Summer if you fail?"

"It will pass to Delphia," I say slowly.

She shakes her head. "Such a burden to place on a child already laden with so much responsibility. You know the moment she inherits the Blessing, Kairyn will stop at nothing to imprison her."

My heart thrums in my chest. Wrenley's right. I've already inflicted such pain on Delphie. If I broke my curse, she wouldn't have to be the steward anymore. She could just be a kid, like she deserves. "I want to do right by my family."

Wrenley's long lashes lower as she places a hand on my shoulder and guides my other hand to her waist. "I want to help you, Dayton."

"Then cheer loudly." I smile. But she's drawing closer, and even though every instinct in me is screaming to push her away, I know I shouldn't.

"That's not what I mean." Her chest presses against mine, and she threads a delicate hand through my hair.

"Do you really want this, Wrenley?"

"Yes," she breathes. "Do you know how many times I've repeated that night on the ship in my mind? Your lips on mine."

It takes me a moment to search my memory for it. I'd completely forgotten I'd kissed her on the ship right as Rosie walked into the room. *Fuck it.* Why does Rosie need to be in my head all the godsdamned time?

Tightening my grip on her waist, I pull the acolyte onto my lap and snatch her jaw. "Then let me give you another memory to think of while you spend long days looking into that ugly black void."

I kiss her. I can tell she's surprised because her mouth is open, and she makes a small gasp. But then she's kissing me back, hands gliding over my ears, down my neck. How many seconds is good for a kiss? I force myself to stay another two, but she's the one who breaks away first.

Her face is flushed, brow furrowed—

"Oh shit," I sigh, looking at the gold paint now covering her white robes.

"I should change before Kairyn sees and you should get back before one of your patrons wakes up."

"You're right."

I stand, towering over her. Before I leave, she touches my arm. "Tomorrow, I'll come to your room. I want to help you, Dayton. I want to be your mate."

Something like a knife twists in my chest. "Okay."

"See you then."

Wrenley scuttles off into the crowd, and I make my way back to my lovely ladies. But I can't help but take the long route past Rosie's cubiculum, just to eavesdrop a little.

But I don't hear voices.

I hear the sweetest, most perfect, moan.

Fire bursts through me, red blinding my vision, and before I can stop myself, I throw back the curtain.

71

CASPIAN

"Well, don't just stand there. Come in," I say.

Rosalina's shocked face turns into a snarl, and she stalks forward and smacks me across the face. I could have stopped her, but I probably deserve it.

"What was that for?" I ask, massaging my cheek. "Did you want to get bought by one of those whelps?"

She places a hand on her hip. "One hundred thousand denarii to Kairyn and his tyranny, Caspian? You should have let me sell for less."

"I couldn't," I say. "Besides, you're worth far more. But if it means that much to you, I'll steal it back."

"Where's Farron? Aren't you supposed to be looking after him?"

"The little pup is safe and sound in my room, probably reading the most boring book off my shelf."

"How could you bring Astrid here?"

"Prince Caspian came to Castletree looking for an assistant. Don't worry, Rosalina, I volunteered." Astrid gives a huge smile. "Marigold and Flavia had a lot of fun dressing me up like someone from the Below."

"She's done very well in this little game," I say. "But I suppose it's time to hop this little bunny back to her burrow."

Rosalina's face softens, and she pulls Astrid into a firm hug. "How is everyone at Castletree?"

"We're all right, but we all miss you and the princes," Astrid says.

"I miss you all too." Rosalina pulls away and lets out a laugh. "I've got gold paint all over you."

"Don't worry about it," Astrid says. "Marigold asked for a detailed account of what you were wearing. This will help me describe it. I love the siren look, by the way."

"Ready, my dear?" I ask, sitting up.

Astrid hops up and down. "Ready! It was *so* fun traveling here through the thorns!"

"Yes, your screams of joy were delightfully loud." I wave my hand, tangling the girl up in a bushel of thorns. She had been handy. I couldn't trust anyone from the Below for this little act. While Kairyn knows I'm keeping an eye on Summer, it would have been too suspicious for me to bid on Dayton's mysterious siren. Plus, I thought Rosie might like to see a friendly face.

"Goodbye, Astrid," Rosalina says as the thorns weave into the ground.

I lean back on the chaise and eye her. "I'm ready to accept your thanks now."

"What are you wearing?" Rosalina walks to the low table and picks a grape off the platter. "You look ridiculous."

It's bloody humid in Summer, so I opted to blend in with the locals and wear a one-shouldered black toga, bound at the waist by a coil of thorns. "You're one to talk, Goldie."

She turns, the paint smeared across her curves from the hug with Astrid. Stars, I wish I was the one to have smeared it. "I like it," she says.

"So do I." My voice pitches lower. "The rabbit was right; you do look alluring with those ears."

Rosalina saunters toward me, the seashells chiming together, giving an oh-so-brief glimpse of what lies beneath. She leans down, golden hair spilling over one shoulder. She flicks me on the nose. "Astrid's a hare."

Rosalina moves to straighten up, but I grip her arm and hold her stare with my own. It's so easy to lose myself in the depths of her golden eyes. Besides the color of her eyes and hair, and the fishy ears, all her features are the same. "Kairyn's a fool. I would recognize you anywhere."

"Sure, Cas," she whispers.

"No, Rosalina, I would. I would know you in any form anywhere in all the Vale. By the gentle curve of your smile and the way the air sparkles when you're around." I draw myself closer. "In the night's tapestry, I would know you as a star or as a bloom in a field of flowers. Did you know there is a particular cadence to your heartbeat? Especially when you're around me. I could pick it out in a symphony."

"Don't be dramatic, Cas." Her breath brushes over my lips.

"Dramatic?" My smile curves. "Dramatic would be saying that even if there was nothing left of me but shadows, I would know you." But it's not dramatic, because when my mother brought me to my lowest, when she sank me deep in pain and draped me in the dark, I thought of Rosalina. *I thought of you and found my way out of the shadows and wished I could make my way to your light again.*

I'm here now. Her words caress my mind like the loveliest melody.

Gripping the back of her neck, I pull her against me. Her lips part as I slip my tongue between her teeth. She makes a soft sound of surrender. I turn us until she falls beneath me, hair spread out over the red fabric like a crown. "I missed you," I say.

The words hang heavy in the air. *I missed you.* Why did I tell her that? Why did I say that out loud? Of course, she won't say it back. She'll have missed Kel and Farron and even that grumpy Spring bastard, but not—

"I missed you too," she says, hand smearing gold across my cheek.

Something melts in my chest. It's all worth it. Dealing with Farron, sending Kel to his likely doom, this fire in my chest . . . it's all worth it if it's for her.

I kiss her again.

Her touch is soft and delicate, yet filled with an intensity that leaves me breathless. I savor the taste of her, a mixture of roses and honey. Her fingers weave through my hair, her body arching to mine, and I can feel every inch of her painted curves.

"Caspian," she says against my ear.

I can barely get her name out, driving my hips down into hers. "Rose."

"Stop." She pushes against my chest, face hurt and *angry.* "You're glowing."

Through the gauzy curtains shines a line of gold light, slamming straight into my chest.

A moment later, a busty woman with a red face—obviously drunk out of her mind—bursts inside. She holds a will-o'-wisp to her chest. "My mate is in here!" she giggles and then hiccups. "He's gorgeous."

Rosalina jumps up and stands in front of me. "He's *not* your mate," she hisses, so full of venom that the woman takes a step back.

"Fucking Farron," I murmur and adjust the letter in my breast pocket.

As soon as I do, the glow disappears. I look up at the woman. "What light?"

She blinks, looking down at the will-o'-wisp on her chest, then over at me. "You should go," I say. Thankfully, she obliges. Rosalina turns to me, and I hand her the envelope. "From your mate."

Carefully, she peeks inside. "A letter and . . . a flower. A Friar's Lantern. Why would he send me this?"

I shrug. "I'd keep the envelope closed unless you want more suitors to interrupt us."

Carefully, she places it on the side table. "You two have been getting along?"

"As much as necessary."

"You smell like him a little. Along your neck mostly."

I rub the spot subconsciously. "Is that why you were all over me? If I'd known that, I would have snuggled up with the little pup a long time ago."

She laughs. It's a beautiful sound.

And I'm an idiot.

"Tell me, Flower, why were you so sure I wasn't her mate?"

Rosalina tucks her hair behind her webbed ear. "I was just trying to save her the agony of being mated to you."

"Agony. Are you so sure that's what it would be like?"

She turns to me, eyes wide and lips parted. The disguise of the siren fades away, and now she's just a gold-painted Rose. "Yes. I'm sure."

Before she can say more, I cross the room and lift her in my arms, gripping tight to her hair. Brown waves shimmer where the gold dust has fallen off. Her legs wrap around my hips, and I drop her to the chaise.

"I want to take this off," I say, touching her shell top.

She nods, and I untie it, letting it clatter to the floor. Soft paint slides beneath my fingers as I begin to rub her, circling her nipples, tugging on them until they're taut. My fingerprints mark her. Her hands glide over my body in such a desperate way, I wonder if she's been thinking about that night we spent together as much as I have.

My attention drifts lower, over the softness of her stomach, to touch the shell skirt just barely concealing her. "And this?"

"Destroy it," she gasps, then, "But not really, because I don't want to walk out of here naked."

Carefully, I untie and place the shell skirt on the ground. "As if I would let that happen. There's only one other fae here I'd be at peace seeing you like . . . *this*."

For a moment, her face pinches in confusion, but then I slide my hand between her legs, and she gasps. Her eyes roll back in her head, lost in pleasure. My budded flower ready to unfurl. I grip her thighs and pull them apart.

"You know there are people just outside," I say.

She threads her fingers in my hair and guides me lower. "Don't tell me you're getting nervous."

A desperate kernel of sound breaks out of my mouth, and I dive between her legs, nuzzling, before running my tongue along her center. There's at least one place that's not painted. *This is mine.*

It's as delicious as her lips, the sweetest nectar. Amid this frenzy of pleasure, my mind slips into hers. She's completely and utterly consumed by me. Predatory need surges through me at the thought. Every fiber in me wants to enter her, and when I rise to capture her lips again, she begins to paw at my clothes.

Grabbing her wrists in one hand, I bring them above her head. "No, Flower. Why is everyone so eager to see Keldarion in the labyrinth?"

She laughs, and I wish I was as funny as the hulking gladiator, so I could make her do it again.

"Come on, Cas," she purrs. "I know you want me to touch you."

Of course I fucking do. The only question is . . . can I control myself around her?

I've never been good at resisting temptation. "Fine, a little taste. For my princess."

"Tell me if you need me to stop," she breathes, and there's nothing but trust in her bright eyes.

Rosalina slips off my clothes, and the light breeze tugs through my hair. I suddenly wish we weren't so exposed here, weren't concealed by only sheets of fabric.

I want her all to myself.

"You're so beautiful," she whispers. Her lips softly brush over my newly exposed skin, tongue dipping into the hollow below my neck, sending the most delicious shiver through my body. She pushes me down, my back hitting the chaise. Her teeth nip at my skin as she makes her way lower and lower.

My cock aches, standing sword straight. Her long lashes lower as she inspects me, and a strange heat crawls up my neck. She slides her hair over her shoulder and her warm breath sweeps over me, causing my cock to quiver and bob.

Her pink tongue inches out of her lips, and I bunch the fabric in my hands, nearly dying from the anticipation.

Slowly, she licks from my balls to my tip, wet and silky.

"That's a cute sound, Cas." She smirks.

"What sound was that?"

"A whimper."

My face heats. I wasn't even aware I had made a sound. However, I cease to care as she swirls her tongue around my tip before closing her lips and slowly taking me into her throat. My hips buck, and I fist my hands in her hair as if that will keep her here forever.

Who am I kidding? I'll barely last ten minutes at this pace.

She continues moving up and down my cock, her hollowed cheeks tight. Her rhythm is near perfect, and I tangle my fingers in her hair as she moves.

"You feel so good, Flower," I rasp. "You're doing so well."

My praise urges her on, and she goes so deep, I hit the back of her throat, causing her to gag a little. "Keep making sounds like that and I'll accidentally fill those pretty lips with my cum."

She pops off, saliva dripping from her lips. "I'd swallow every drop of you."

My whole body clenches, cock becoming painfully stiff, and I push her away, staggering to the other side of the room.

"You're too good, beautiful," I gasp, taking myself in my palm.

Rosalina looks enviously at my hand. "Better safe than sorry, I guess. I don't want to get sent to Keldarion because of your bargain."

"You don't make it easy on me," I grunt. "Not when you look like that."

"Should I get dressed?"

I squeeze myself at the base, holding back a powerful releasee. "Don't you dare, Princess."

Rosalina sits up, the soft curves of her stomach bending in the most delicious way. I keep my gaze on her as I pump my cock. *This doesn't count for the bargain; we're not even touching.* The gods know I've come to her image almost every night these last few months.

"Kel would never be this careless with you," I say.

Her gaze sharpens. "You're not Kel."

"Glad you've noticed." I rub my thumb over the tip of my cock. It twitches in my hand, desperate for release. "Flower, I want to come inside you so badly."

She gives a sly smile and lies back, fingers grazing her entrance. "Now you're starting to sound like Kel."

I laugh, breath growing heavy. "Is that what you want? To be filled completely? By me? By Kel? By all your mates at once?"

Her eyes flutter and her fingers work faster. "Yes."

My grip grows near painful, I'm clutching myself so hard. "I imagine it dripping down your thighs. Fucking delicious."

She gives a moan, her back arching up.

"Don't you come, Rosalina," I say, dark command echoing in my voice. "I'm going to make you come."

She gives me a pointed glare but runs her hands up to her stomach. The movement—and her submission to my command—is enough to send me over the edge. I give a ragged moan as my cock hardens and cum spills out onto my palm. Fucking loads of it.

I sigh, body shaking. She's watching with a hawk's bright gaze, something animalistic on her features. *My darling's just as desperate for me as I am for her.*

I move to wipe my hand on a cloth napkin.

"Wait." Rosalina jumps up and crosses to me, her full breasts swaying.

She grips my hand then brings a finger to her lips, licking the moisture off.

The sensation ignites something in me, something primal and deep and dangerous. The feel of her mouth is fucking incredible, but not near enough.

"You like that?" I growl. "How about this?"

Roughly tugging her closer, I rub my cum-splattered palm against her pussy.

"Caspian!" she cries so loud, I'm surprised the whole damn party doesn't hear it.

"You're so wet already. From my mouth, from your desire. Now from my cum." My fingers slide easily inside her. Her body melds against mine, and she desperately grips my shoulders to steady herself.

"Cas, Cas," she gasps. Her mouth is wide open against mine, and I inhale her air. Sinking two fingers inside her, I begin to pump in and out.

"Do you like that, Rose? Tell me you like that."

She's beyond words, desperate moans escaping her lips.

I pull my hand out and grab her leg, lifting it up to my hip. I squeeze her soft ass with my other hand. She's trembling so much, I think I'm the only thing keeping her standing. Sinking my hand deep within her again, I curl my fingers to stroke her sensitive core. She bites down on my shoulder, stifling a whimper of her own.

A growl escapes me and I increase my pace, the wet sound of her pussy intoxicating.

"Yes, Caspian, yes. I'm going to—"

I dig my fingers into her soft thigh, then kiss her with a wild desperation, just as I remove my hand.

She breaks away, trembling. "Cas? No, I—"

I scoop her in my arms and carry her back to the chaise. "You're on the most intoxicating edge of pleasure, Rose. I intend to let you hover in this bliss."

As I lay her on the chaise, I can tell even the change of fabric is stimulating to her in this heightened state. Everything from the lightest brush of my lips to the flick of my fingers is going to feel like fucking starlight.

I'd keep her this way forever if I could.

I throw myself on top of her, capturing her lips in a kiss. I'm careful not to touch her pussy yet. She threads her fingers through my hair, her tongue exploring my mouth. It lasts longer than I intend, and I pull away, running a hand through her silky hair.

"Cas," she whines, her voice breathless and heady with need. "Tell me something."

"Anything," I lie as my fingers circle her entrance, wet from my mouth and cum, and her own desperate desire.

"Why didn't you try harder to convince Kel?" she asks. "To convince Kel you'd let me go if he and I made love? I know you wouldn't keep me as a thrall, or whatever he's afraid of."

"Because, Princess," I shove two fingers into her, and she gasps, "I can't even convince myself."

The start of my name turns into a moan. Her hands claw at my back as I ravage her already swollen heat. From this angle, I can truly admire her, that pretty pink pussy, glistening with our mutual desire. I don't dare take her. There's no way I would be able to control myself once inside her.

"You belonging completely to me, every part of you at my mercy? I would be good to you, good to you like this, but not so good as to give you up. Keldarion won't give in because he knows how much I *want* you."

Her eyes squeeze shut, body bucking against my hand, and I curl my fingers inside her. It's time to let her come. She can't hold back her climax any longer. She shudders around my hand. Her face breaks into a gorgeous eruption of pleasure, a long moan escaping her lips. Lips I capture and whisper against, "Because I want you all to myself."

Rosalina falls back to the chaise, and I don't let her go. I can't even remove my fingers from her warmth. She blinks up at me with a look so adoring, it's almost like she's my thrall already.

But I know she's too much of a romantic to believe a word I just said.

Maybe she's making a romantic of me too, because despite what I said out loud, I wouldn't change a single thing about her.

Besides, it's too damn satisfying getting her to submit by her own volition.

Rosalina tilts her head to the side. "Dayton?"

I turn, seeing the Summer Prince standing with the curtain drawn. I let out a huff. "You just missed the grand climax, Sunshine. Either come in or show that aroused cock to the whole party."

72

ROSALINA

Dayton's gaze doesn't leave mine. He stares as my body trembles and twitches from *that* feeling. The feeling Cas had given me. I understand now why Kel is so wary of his shadows. Once you fall beneath them, can you ever get out?

Caspian and I are both completely naked. Caspian's fingers are still inside my pussy, soaking up the last shocks of my orgasm. I feel like a melted candle, nothing but bliss wavering through me. I can't tear my eyes away from Dayton. His glorious body moves closer and closer, his long, hard cock barely concealed by the shells wrapping his waist.

Did he see Cas and me? Is that why . . . Then, I notice the smeared fingerprints across his torso and shoulders.

"Who *touched* you?" I snarl, raising myself up on my forearms.

"You're actually concerned about that? Look at you."

Caspian straightens and tilts his head toward Dayton, dark waves cascading over his shoulder. "Come here, you hulking pile of muscle."

Dayton gives him a wary gaze but then steps closer. Caspian removes his hand from me, then wipes it on Dayton's muscular thigh. "There."

A deep growl emits from Dayton's throat, and he grabs Caspian by the shoulders, seeming to not even care the Prince of Thorns is naked. "What were you doing to her?"

"Everything you *wished* you could the other night," Caspian purrs.

How does Caspian even know about that? Quickly, I get up and gather my clothes, no matter how flimsy, and begin to tie them on.

Dayton tugs Cas closer. "I have a mate."

Caspian draws his hand down Dayton's rippling chest toward his very evident arousal. "I know you do. One you're too scared to truly satisfy."

Dayton moves as if to toss the Prince of Thorns away, then pauses, "Why the fuck do you smell so much like Fare? Is he here?"

My heart breaks at the desperation in Dayton's voice. I can only imagine how much he misses Farron.

"We've been cuddled close every night," Caspian rasps. "Don't you think it's cute how his little nose twitches when he sleeps? Or do you never get to see that because of the whole wolfy thing?"

Dayton snarls and roughly throws Caspian to the chaise.

"Stop it. Caspian is just trying to rile you because he actually cares about Farron," I say, walking between them, and turning to Cas. "You're being a dick. Tell Dayton you'll protect Farron down there."

Caspian gives a long sigh and pulls on his toga. "I actually came here to find a safe place to plant thorns. We'll need to make a quick getaway once we grow his little mushrooms. And alas, I should be doing just that."

"Caspian." I reach out and grab his arm. "Thank you."

"Anytime you want to come, darling, just think of me." The Prince of Thorns winks.

"No, that's not what I meant." My face burns. "Thank you for everything else."

"Right." Caspian turns to Dayton. "Good luck in your next match, gladiator. You'll need it."

With that, the Prince of Thorns disappears in a flurry of briars.

I let out a breath, wondering if Dayton is mad about what he walked in on. But he knows I've been with Caspian before, and he hasn't told me who touched him. Was it the woman who bought him or . . .

Dayton brushes the hair off my shoulder. "You should change back before we go out."

Nodding, I shift into my siren form. For some reason, in that moment, I'd wanted Caspian to see *me*.

Why didn't you think I was her mate? The answers twist like a firestorm beside my heart.

AS WE'RE ESCORTED BACK to the barracks, the pink blush of morning is just cresting through the white stone of the colosseum. I'm glad we have a day off today after being up all night. The party ended shortly after Dayton and I left the private room. I didn't see Kairyn or Wrenley again. The third fight is tomorrow, so we'll need to use today to rest and train.

We enter separate bathing chambers to wash off the paint, and I change into a simple white shift. Dayton is waiting for me outside the baths, damp hair looking a shade darker.

We walk back to our rooms together, and he pauses outside my door. "You should try to get some sleep."

"You too, Day," I say.

"We should practice with a spear in the morning. Meet at the training pits?" His words are clipped, and he keeps avoiding my gaze.

"All right."

"Rosie, uh, Rosalina . . . we're going to have to do whatever it takes to win this," he says. "I can't lose my realm to Kairyn. I can't let my people suffer because of him."

I swallow, my stomach churning. "I know."

He shifts awkwardly from foot to foot. "I took some food from the party. Here." He places a package wrapped in cloth in my hand and walks away.

I stand there for a moment, watching his silhouette disappear. *Whatever it takes.* Fingerprints smeared across his golden chest . . .

Inside, I sit on my bed and open the wrapped package Dayton gave me, snacking on the treats. Then, I pull out the letter Caspian delivered.

I drop the pale blue flower onto the sheets, then unfurl the parchment. In true Farron fashion, it's long, every inch of the page covered in his messy scrawl. He talks of his adventures with Caspian, and the ridiculous outfit Caspian dressed him in, and how irritating the Prince of Thorns is. Tears fall from my eyes and smear the ink as he writes how he misses me and Dayton. Of how brave I am, and how I can do anything I set my mind to. It gives me the courage I didn't know I was so desperately craving.

Only at the end of the letter does he write of the flower.

I found this on the Nightingale's potion desk, of all places. Can't get it out of my mind. What reason could she have for experimenting with such a thing? Rosie, this is important.

But I'm out of paper, and Cas says he has to leave now. I miss you so much, my brave, wonderful mate.

I love you in the starlight way.

Farron

I wipe my tears and bring the letter to my lips, kissing it. Falling back to my bed, exhaustion threatens to pull me under. Slowly, I trace the edges of the flower.

The Deceiver's Bloom.

Rosie, this is important.

73

EZRYN

Towering cliffs loom on either side of us as we make our way through a gorge. My footprints trail behind me in the red clay.

It's eerily quiet here, besides the occasional screech of a vulture. I catch them circling above, waiting for heat or dehydration to take us.

I have no idea how long this canyon stretches. Our goal had been to make it to the red clay sands, and we're here, as deep into the Ribs as one can get. The only sign we're going in the right direction are the giddy steps of the Pegasus foal leading our party.

Drusilla beats her white wings, flapping a few feet into the sky before descending again. She turns around as if to urge us forward, an impatient whinny echoing in the canyon.

"Be careful," I murmur to Delphie and Nori, who flank me. "We don't have good sightlines. There could be anything in these crevasses—"

My words are cut off by a sharp *thunk* to my neck. I stumble backward, grasping at my throat. I yank out a small dart and hold it up. My vision wavers, the black-feathered dart becoming two.

"Run," I whisper as the world goes dark.

MY EYELIDS FLUTTER, reluctant to part, as consciousness stirs within me. My limbs feel heavy, and my mind is covered in a thick fog. With a groan, I push myself upright.

The world swims into focus, hazy and disjointed. I can't even take in my surroundings.

"Delphie? Nori?" I try to say, but my throat is dry. Where are the girls?

The scent the desert blooms wafts into my nose, punctuated by something stronger—horse musk. I claw back what consciousness I can and will my eyes to clear.

I'm in a room cut into red rock, its walls adorned with carvings my eyes are too blurry to make out. The ceiling opens up to the sky; the sun sits just past midday, which means I haven't been unconscious long.

"Ez? Are you okay?" Nori's voice. A wavy image beside me clears, and I see her staring at me, an uncharacteristically worried expression on her face. She's on her hands and knees but unbound like me.

"I'm fine," I say. "You?"

"Yeah, I'm okay."

I breathe a sigh of relief. "Del?"

Nori nods forward. "She's, uh, she's talking. With *them.*"

I focus my eyes toward the direction Nori nodded. In the center of the room sits a throne, hewn from rugged stone but adorned with feathers. A woman sits straight-backed, a fierce expression on her face. Atop her head is a magnificent headdress; like the throne, huge feathers jut out, arranged in a way reminiscent of—

Reminiscent of a Pegasus.

"We found them. We found the Huntresses," I gasp.

As my mind further clears of its fog, I now see the room we're in is a hive of activity. Women clad in rugged leathers stand in groups on either side, talking to each other. Each is unmistakably a warrior, their muscles honed. For every Huntress stands a Pegasus. Some are huge, towering over their companions, while others are the size of horses. They come in every shade from black to grey to white, to lightest blue and palest pink.

Most magnificent of all is the young girl standing before the Huntress on the throne, facing her down with equal ferocity.

"My name is Delphia, daughter of Sabine, granddaughter of Drusilla. I am the steward of Summer, and I have come to ask for your aid in this trying time." Her voice carries through the chamber. Gone is the young girl I walked with, who cooed over the foal or squabbled with Nori; instead stands a leader. I'm reminded of Sabine's presence.

"Welcome Delphia, daughter of Sabine, granddaughter of Drusilla," the woman says. Even seated, I can tell she's tall. Her skin is bronzed by the desert sun, face weathered. She wears a white tunic belted at the waist with rope, with light leather armor that has seen its time in battle. "I am Matron Valeria. Welcome to the home of the Huntresses of Aura."

I see Delphia fight her smile. "We have crossed the realm to find you, by sea and by sand."

"You are quite determined," Valeria muses. "Now, would you like to explain why you have stolen one of our flock?"

She looks to the corner of the room, where the foal, Drusilla, nuzzles against a large Pegasus the same shade of white.

"We didn't steal her!" Delphia insists. "We saved her from a harpy's nest. As I was saying, we have come a long way to find you."

Valeria waves dismissively. "Tell me, what business does a child of the capital have with us?"

Delphia falls to her knees. "We beg for your assistance. Hadria has been overtaken by dark evil. My brother, the High Prince, has been deposed of his throne. I was tasked with the protection of the city. My mother's mother was a Huntress. Your blood runs in my veins. I call upon our order to assist in retaking the city of Hadria for the good of all Summer—"

"Our order!" Valeria scoffs and looks to a group of Huntresses at her side. "This capital spawn calls herself one of our order! Yes, yes, I remember your mother's mother. Drusilla was valiant. Brave. Then she left to be at the side of a High Prince and concerned herself with politics. She forgot the skies."

Delphia staggers up. "She did not forget. Her memory has passed to me. My blood remembers the skies. Please, Hadria needs—"

"We do not involve ourselves in the politics of the realms," Valeria snaps. "Century after century, we did our part to protect what we could. More often than not, it was the High Rulers causing such ills against the balance of nature. Our hearts can take no more. We remain here, where our steeds and spirits can be free."

I lick my lips, wanting to stand, wanting to run to Delphie's side. But she sets her jaw. "This isn't about politics. This is about the people! This is for the good of every living creature in Summer, the good of the realm!"

"Who knows what is for the good of the realm?" Valeria says. "Only the Queen. If she has abandoned you, then there is no reason for us to risk our sanctuary."

I close my eyes and grit my teeth. Then I stand. "If it is the Queen's word you need, then let me give it to you. I am fated mate to Rosalina O'Connell, the Golden Rose, daughter of Queen Aurelia. She seeks your swords and wings in this battle for Summer."

Silence echoes in the chamber. Valeria stands and strides over to me. She grabs my chin and tilts my head each way, examining me closely.

"Let me see your blade," she says finally.

I draw my sword and present it to her. She takes it and holds it up to the light. "I fought beside the wielder of this blade once. She was a mighty warrior. Together, we cleared a grove of blighted dryads that stretched along the border of Summer and Spring." Her gaze pierces into me. "That makes you Isidora's son. Ezryn."

"Yes."

She hands me back my blade and returns to her throne. "Here in our midst, we have a child steward begging a throne back for her brother and the supposed fated mate of the Golden Rose. He is a Prince of Spring, yet he bears no Blessing nor helm. What am I to do? Am I to trust the word of these strangers?" She looks to the Huntresses at her side.

"The Queen's daughter needs our aid," Delphia urges. "Together, we can retake Hadria."

"Retake Hadria for whom? One noble or another on the throne makes no difference to us."

"You don't understand," I say. "The man claiming himself to be Emperor is a servant of the Below. He must be brought to justice."

"And you are the one to do so?" Valeria raises an eyebrow. "I have seen your justice, son of Isidora. Yes, we've watched you across the desert these last few days. You are not a hunter. You are a slayer. There is no balance in your justice."

"I kill only those who deserve it," I growl.

Her voice booms between the walls. "Who are you to pass judgment? I have heard of this Golden Rose, but I see not the mate of a Princess. I see a storm ready to rip root from earth. We cannot fly in a storm, slayer son of Isidora."

Panic breaks across Delphia's face. "Please, you have to help. I've come so far to find you. My brother is counting on me!"

Nori runs up and grabs her arm.

My thoughts begin to frenzy. "I'm not leaving until you understand why you *must* help us," I say.

Matron Valeria turns to Delphia. "Your companion says he is a voice for the Queen. Aurelia would never suffer such discord. Unless there is a sign from our Queen, we will not help you."

Delphia looks down, defeat evident in her gaze.

"How can you do this?" I roar. "People are dying! All of the Vale is in danger! You must help—"

A small hand grabs my arm. Delphia looks up at me, gaze empty. "It's over, Ezryn. Let's go."

She and Nori walk toward the exit of the chamber.

No, this can't be it. We can't have come all this way.

I can't have failed again.

74

ROSALINA

"Remember to block." Dayton's wooden sword slams against my shoulder.

Hissing, I bring my two swords up to guard my face, and he taps them with a satisfied smile. "I prefer the bow," I say.

"Then maybe don't snap it in half so I'm forced to watch your pitiful excuse for swordplay. Again."

The midday sun beats heavily down into the open-air training pit. Grainy sand shifts beneath our feet. Knocking wood sounds in the air as other gladiators train around us. Though, I notice their gazes constantly drift to Dayton.

Tilla's right: his presence *is* igniting. There's been a change since the last match where Dayton defeated his brothers. It's reminded his legionnaires and the other gladiators that he's not just the third-born son. He *is* a High Prince.

Dayton puts me through a few more rounds, mostly practicing footwork and building on the defensive techniques Justus taught me. He starts wielding a spear, showing me how to block and how far away I have get in order to be out of its range. We'll be fighting the Bronze Knight and his Lance of Valor in the next battle.

A few more hours slip by, and I take a break to eat dried fruit and bread and sip some lukewarm water. But Dayton doesn't stop, instead choosing to spar with a spear wielder.

Dayton disarms him in a moment. The man begins to apologize, but Dayton just wipes his forehead and shouts. "Can anyone here offer me a challenge?"

A few more legionnaires face him, and he downs them in moments. Pairs, then triples, attempt to face the High Prince. Dayton sweeps them away, each landing flat on their back, clouds of dust rising up around them.

His chest heaves, a red sunburn scalds his shoulders, and sweat coats his skin. His eyes almost glow, and for a moment he looks more beast than fae. No one moves to challenge him, and he stalks off to the wooden pell, hacking at it with his swords.

A match begins in the arena, and most of the gladiators leave the training pit to watch, while the rest are chased away by the afternoon sun. Dayton and I are suddenly alone.

Still, Dayton makes no move to stop training. I ladle a fresh cup of water and bring it over to him. "You should drink."

"Not thirsty." He doesn't turn to me. Doesn't even look at me.

I stalk away, put the cup of water down, and pick up my sword instead, stomping back over to Dayton.

Intercepting his sword with my own, I glare up at him. "Are you going to tell me what's wrong or are you just going to take it out on this wood?"

His eyes are cloudy. He backs up from the pell. "Nothing's wrong."

"The way you treated the other gladiators isn't like you."

We shift over the open sand. He's barely listening, his concentration fully on sparring with me. I can barely keep up.

"Are you upset with me?" I ask, just barely blocking a hard blow. "Because of Cas?"

A low growl sounds in his throat, and he sweeps my feet out from under me. My swords go flying and I tumble back. Dayton catches me and lowers me to the sand, pinning me there.

His golden hair is a halo, face soft for the first time all day. "I told you to watch your footwork."

"I know."

He shakes his head, and that near-void look returns. "No, Rosie. I don't care. You're free to fuck who you want and so am I."

He straightens and turns, not offering to help me up. Nausea roils in my stomach, and I scramble after him. "What do you mean?"

He chucks his swords across the sand. "We've trained enough for today."

I reach out for his arm but hesitate before grabbing it. "Dayton."

"I need to talk to you, but not here."

"Okay."

In silence, we walk to my room. The moment my door closes, he says, "Wrenley's coming down later. We're going to break my curse."

The room spins. My vision fades in and out. Steadying myself on the wall, I open my mouth, but find it empty of words. There's no sentence in all the world that could describe how I feel.

"We both know I can't face the Bronze Knight as I am now. Everything is ruined if the match is lost. I can't overthrow Kairyn, free my people, or protect . . . protect you."

I always knew this was coming, that this was where his path would lead. But now that the moment is here, I'm not ready for it. Not ready at all.

"Rosalina," Dayton says.

Power ripples out of my body, and my siren disguise fades. I squeeze my eyes shut, forcing it all down. I can't let what happened to me last time happen again. That power destroyed an entire wing in Castletree.

Surprisingly, I find my eyes are dry. "I understand. But I can't stay here."

"You're leaving? Our fight is tomorrow."

"Do you expect me to just sit here while you're fucking her next door?" I gesture to the wall, hating the jealousy tinging my words.

The anger seems to ignite something in the Summer Prince. The void expression on his face fades to a smug smile. "Well, you said you under-stood. So why not?"

"I'll lock my door and make a small thorn portal to Castletree. I'll be back by the morning."

"That's it then?"

"No." I kneel beside my bed and crack open the small bushel of thorns. Inside sits Dayton's seashell necklace. Delicately, I take it in my hands and stand. "You'll need this for tomorrow. Your trident will be invaluable once I take control of the bow and we confront Kairyn." I drop the necklace into his palm without touching him. "Once you defeat the Bronze Knight with your newfound power, of course."

I move to turn, and he grips my wrist, tugging me back toward him. "You understand there's no other way. If I don't do this, I will be a wolf forever. All the fae of Summer in Castletree will be cursed forever. I *have* to do this."

"I know."

My heart clenches with a sorrow so profound, it feels as though the very earth beneath my feet mourns alongside me. Dayton stares down at me, his eyes a storm-swept sea, silently pleading with me to say more. The ache in my chest intensifies with every passing moment, a part of me desperate for him to leave. The other part wants to cling to him for every second we have left before . . .

Before . . .

Memories crash against my mind: the first moment we met, every time he made me laugh, the dreams that he could be mine. They feel like glass shells, shattering against the rocks, each piece bleeding my heart.

"This is how it has to be," I whisper, ripping my hand away. "You are bound to do right by your realm. My destiny led me to Summer, as well. To help my mother's people. My people. We are bound by duty to walk separate paths."

"Unless . . ." Dayton says, and his voice is hoarse, cracked.

Unless. A stupid star shower of hope fills my heart at the word. Tears blur my vision as I look up at him.

As if my gaze was the only invitation he needed, he crosses to me and takes my face roughly in his hands. "Tell me not to do it."

"What?"

We stagger across the room until he slams me against the stone wall. His face lowers closer, a tangle of blond hair brushing my cheek. "Tell me not to and I won't. Help me, Rosie, I'm barely holding on. Tell me now, and I swear to the gods, I'll never look at her again."

My heart blazes. *Tell him not to do it. Keep him. Stop him from doing this terrible thing.*

"I know it's hard, Blossom." His lips brush my cheek, and I close my eyes. "You're good. You're so good and perfect. But you can be selfish. You can do the wrong thing."

"Day—"

"No, no." His lips are by my ear, salty tears dripping onto my cheek. "Just think about it, Rosie. Think about what I'm going to have to do before you answer."

"Don't ask me to do that—" I snarl and flash my eyes open to see him a breath away from me. His hands grip my jaw hard.

"I have been with no woman since you, Rosalina, and I have no care to do so ever again," Dayton says. "You know my heart. You've seen it. It belongs to you. It belongs to you and Fare. So, tell me not to do this."

"Day …"

"Every swing of my sword is for you. Every word I utter, every action I take, every beat of my damned heart." His fingers tremble on my face. "Rosalina, I love you."

The earth seems to go out from under me, and I gasp in quick, short breaths. He *loves* me. He loves me.

"My love for you is deeper than all the depths of the sea." His forehead dips to mine. "I will do anything you ask. Please tell me not to do this."

The stones below my feet should be covered in blood with how his words pierce my heart. I break away from his touch. "I can't."

"Why?" Hurt and anger tremor in his voice. "Don't you feel *this*? Don't you love me?"

It's that question that destroys every piece of hope in my heart. "It's because I love you that I can't ask you to do this."

Tears fall down Dayton's cheeks, and he straightens. He leaves my room, closing the door behind him. But he opens it a moment later and he's holding his seashell necklace in one hand and the golden token of the Queen in the other.

"Farron made this necklace for me," he says, voice hitched. "It's the most precious thing I own."

"I can't take that."

But he's already stepping toward me, tying the shells around my neck. "Please. I want you to have some part of me forever."

"Until tomorrow, Day."

"Until tomorrow."

This time when he leaves, the door stays shut.

75

FARRON

The party unfurls before me like a silken veil. A part of me hates how beautiful it is. The prismatic courtyard of Cryptgarden is draped in pastel fabric. Sculpted crystal trees and flowers cast a glow over the guests. It's oddly reminiscent of Caspian's birthday party, and a part of me aches for the company of Ezryn and Keldarion, but most of all, for Day and Rosie.

Caspian again sits on a throne of briars, a black fox mask covering the upper half of his face. My own mask is an elk, brushed with burnished gold, long antlers jutting from the top. It covers my nose and everything above. I expected to feel uncomfortable dressed in Caspian's tight clothes, but there's a part of me that finds it a tad . . . thrilling. Tonight, I'm not the Prince of Autumn, but just another debauched citizen of the Below.

Hand trailing on the cool stair handle, I head down into the throng. The air is rich with the intoxicating blend of musk and sweet incense. A kaleidoscope pattern shines over the dancers, cast by the crystals, making them look like dreams—or nightmares—brought to life. Everyone is wearing a mask, but for some, that's all they're wearing. The outfits range from elegant gowns to nothing at all.

Fae grace the dance floor with a hypnotic rhythm, their movements akin to poetry in motion, as if ensorcelled by the enchantment of the night.

It's the drink, I think, having made sure to not have any myself. *It's working. They're all mad here.*

"Dance with me," a woman with a wolf's mask says. Her attire of silk and lace hugs her curves, leaving little to the imagination.

"I'm all right," I say, sidestepping away. I know we have to stay at this party long enough for Caspian to be seen, but it doesn't mean I have to dance with this stranger.

But she stalks me through the party, like a hunter after prey. Then she snags my arm. "Caught you," she laughs. Her lips, painted a deep crimson, curl into a playful smile.

"Sorry, Caterina," a smooth voice says. "His next dance is with me."

I'm enveloped in the scent of lavender as someone steps between us.

"Oh, Prince Caspian, of course," the woman in the wolf mask says before slinking back into the crowd.

"Try to act like you're enjoying this," Caspian says dryly, pulling me into a dance. "You are the one I'm going to disappear with later."

My words are all caught in my throat, and I can barely keep up with the footwork of the dance. How is he so good at this?

Caspian exudes majesty, wearing the finest midnight velvet. The fitted doublet hugs tight to his slim waist, its silver stitching reminiscent of the stars. A belt of woven gemstones adorns his waist, catching the light and casting prisms of color that dance across his figure. His cloak is a twilight-hued masterpiece of silk. As he moves, it billows behind him like moving shadows. Embroidered along the hem are stars and crescent moons, their celestial beauty mirroring his own.

As I watch him, I can't help but be swept away by the sheer enchantment of it all. He's like a character from a fairytale come to life, a prince of darkness with a charm and allure that are impossible to resist.

"I see you decided on a new cloak," I finally say.

He laughs. "Had to have something special for tonight."

Together, we move as one, our bodies swaying to the hypnotic rhythm of the music. The other partygoers track us with their eyes. Even with his mask, Caspian is impossible to ignore. Everyone here wants a piece of their prince.

"Well, I like it," I say.

I catch a flash of his lavender gaze from beneath the black fox mask. He pulls me closer so we're chest to chest, and I can feel the warmth of his breath on my cheek.

A sudden chill sweeps over the courtyard. The music stops abruptly.

Caspian must notice this a moment before me because thin briars wrap around my feet and shoot me across the dance floor, bumping me into people before I crash against a table laden with food and drink.

Gasping, I push myself up and stand just in time to see Sira enter the party. The crowd parts before her like grass bending to the wind. She wears a black dress with a silken spiderweb cloak.

Caspian regards her with a look of disinterest, leaning on some random half-dressed fae man. "Welcome, Mother."

"What is this?" Her voice is knife-sharp.

He gives a mocking smile, the kind of smile one might give if drunk. "Why, I do believe it's what some call a party."

"A party," Sira gleams and looks to the crowd. "Your prince makes merry while our enemies plot above?"

Caspian gives a mocking laugh. "Mother, life can be so boring if it's all work, work, work."

Why is he baiting her like this? It's like he wants to infuriate her. I push through the crowd to get closer.

"And *you*." Sira turns to the man Caspian leans against. "How are you enjoying this party, knowing it keeps your prince from thwarting those who would keep us down here in the dark forever?"

"Uh," the fae man stammers.

"As I thought," Sira says.

Shadows fall off her like water rolling off a rock. They gather on the ground before lashing up and devouring the man. Ash flutters away in a slight breeze.

Terror ripples through the crowd, but they don't scream. They don't even move. It's the kind of terror that freezes you to your core.

"There shall be no merrymaking, no parties, and no gallivanting until the Golden Rose is in our possession," Sira says. The sound of clanging metal rings behind her as black armored fae and goblins march to her side. "Return to your dwellings or reap the consequences."

Breath heavy in my throat, I back away into the crowd.

"And you," Sira says to her son, "follow me."

THE SOLDIERS BEGIN to direct the partygoers away from Caspian's palace and down the swirling steps to the city below.

This is bad. This is so, so bad. The party was supposed to be a distraction. What are we going to do now?

I dodge out of the way of the soldiers and walk deeper into the halls of Cryptgarden, trailing after Caspian and his mother. They're heading in the direction of his private chamber. Quickly, I double back, taking a shorter route Cas had showed me earlier in case of an emergency, and enter his room before they arrive. I'm sure he won't like me following him, but I can't let the soldiers direct me down to the city. I'd never get back in time to get to the pool.

I creep inside and tuck myself into Caspian's wardrobe, leaving just enough of a crack so I can peek out. The door opens and Sira and Caspian march in.

"It was just a little fun," Caspian says, running his hands through his hair.

Sira snatches the fox mask off his face and throws it to the ground. "Your sister is working tirelessly while you do nothing."

"I'm not the one who lost the Golden Rose," Caspian snaps, turning away.

Sira grabs his face with her hand. "But you can find her."

"I don't know where she is."

She pushes him away. "I find that hard to believe. Perhaps you have forgotten what's at stake. Perhaps you need the proper motivation. Vespera, come to me!"

A chill runs through my veins. I've heard whispers of that name before. One of Sira's main weapons in the War of Thorns.

Vespera, the Abyssal Sorceress.

The door begins to creep open.

"Mother," Caspian says quickly, only a tinge of panic audible. "If I could find the Golden Rose, I would but—"

"Wait," Sira says and the door halts.

"I do so hate to do this to you, my darling boy. I hate to see you look so frightened," Sira coos. "I suppose I did already remove one of your party guests. I know how you hate to see your people upset."

"I can begin my search tonight. I'll leave immediately."

"Very well." Sira lets out a long breath.

Relief courses through me.

The Queen of the Below turns to go but pauses near the door. "Though it is a shame to call Vespera up from deep Stygian Hollows for nothing."

"A little trip won't hurt her," Caspian sneers.

"Now that I think of it. . ." Sira gives a smile with no warmth behind it, "the Golden Rose was lost in Summer, which is your sister's domain. Perhaps Vespera can have a little fun with her as proper punishment?"

"No," Caspian says, and the word is so forceful that even Sira takes a step back. "I'll take it for her."

His mother whirls. "Oh, Caspian, darling. You wouldn't want to do that. You see, Vespera has brought the *hood*. I know how you hate the hood."

I can almost feel Caspian's fear as if it's my own, waves of it rippling through me so intensely, nausea overwhelms me. But all he says with that same cocky smile is, "Bring her in."

"Very well." Sira opens the door.

The Abyssal Sorceress glides in. Her skin an unnatural pale blue. Her dark hair floats like snakes. I've never seen her this close, only from a distance on the battlefield. It's her teeth that are truly the most horrific: rows of razor-sharp fangs and pale blue gums that ooze blood.

As she extends her hand, holding a tattered black hood, my heart quickens. Every fiber of my being screams at me to flee. But even if I could get away unseen, I know I can't leave Cas—not that he even knows I'm here.

"So, you haven't taken my advice and got those teeth checked out?" Caspian says, biting a nail. "I told you; the raw fish of the Hollows are no good for dental hygiene."

"Kneel," Vespera says, voice laced with venom. Blue blood splashes from between her lips, a few drops landing on Caspian's cheek.

He wipes it off, then obeys.

Vespera lifts the hood, her fingers long and bony. She draws it open and descends it over Caspian's head. At first, nothing happens.

Then I notice Caspian's chest, heaving in and out as his breath increases. He starts to scream, a chorus of agonized moans. Caspian pitches forward, clawing at the ground.

What is that thing doing to him? Vespera's smile widens, and she rubs her fingertips together.

My breath rises in my throat, and I place my palm flat against the wardrobe to steady myself. I wish I could help him. I wish there was something I could do. But revealing myself to Sira now would only jeopardize our plan, put Kel and George in danger, and ruin all chances of saving Rosalina's mother.

I know all this, but it doesn't make it any easier to watch.

A bloodcurdling scream tears from Caspian. Shadows leak from his body, briars burst through the floors, and emerald fire sprouts on his fingertips.

Enough. It has to be enough. His limbs are shaking, his room near destroyed. Sira has to stop this. But there is nothing but void emotion on her striking face.

Caspian's broken cries pierce the air like shattering glass, and the green fire begins to grow, curling around his arms.

Sira's eyes widen for a fraction of a second before she holds up her hand. "Stop. That is enough."

Vespera makes a bird-like screech and shuffles over the thorns and shadows, tearing the hood from his head.

I expect Caspian's face to be marred in some way—burned, scarred, broken—but the only difference is the black makeup smeared down his cheeks.

Sira wipes his face with the long sleeve of her dress and smooths back his hair. "What is your mission?"

Caspian opens his mouth, closes it. Opens it again, and when he speaks, his voice is hoarse and broken. "To bring you the Golden Rose."

"That's right." Sira smiles and bends to kiss his forehead. "Do not disappoint me again."

Like twin shadows, Sira and Vespera leave the room. I stay rooted in my spot, unsure how to proceed from here. Fear still grips me.

"You don't have to keep hiding," Caspian says without moving. "She won't come back."

Slowly, I crawl out from the wardrobe, catching my reflection in the mirror. My own cheeks are streaked with black paint. I've been crying too. I raise my mask over the top of my head.

Kneeling in front of Caspian, I ask, "What did the hood do to you? Does it show you visions? Nightmares?"

He shakes his head, as if trying to clear the memory. "The Soulrender's Hood can show many things. But today, it showed me wishes."

I study him and watch the ghost of a smile crawl over his lips. "My mother's wish for my future. One in which I kill you all, slowly, one by one. Ending with *her*."

"I know you're not going to bring her Rosalina."

His hard gaze is a challenge in the worst way. "I'll endure worse if I don't."

"Probably. But you still won't."

"What makes you so sure, Autumn Prince?"

I grab his hands. "Because you're her mate."

76

ROSALINA

The mattress is soaked with my tears. I'm not sure why I haven't left yet, like I told Dayton I was going to. I lack the will to summon my thorns and make myself leave.

Maybe it's the thought of being at Castletree when all the staff of Summer suddenly feel their curses break—of being around that joy. Dayton said I wasn't selfish, but I am. The thought of being around their happiness makes me sick.

Or maybe I can't go to Castletree because it still feels like something is tethering me here, and if I leave, it will snap entirely.

Idiot. I sit up and put my head in my hands. There's nothing binding me to Dayton.

My stomach rumbles, and I realize I haven't eaten anything all afternoon. A pang goes through me as I think of warm tea and cakes on a platter, of Astrid and Marigold's company.

But I still can't make myself leave.

Heaving in a breath, I quickly don my siren disguise and walk to the dining hall. It's mostly empty besides a few legionnaires sitting on long benches. Barley cakes and a pot of oatmeal are offered. I grab a tray and a large glass of water.

A few people nod hello to me, but I sit by myself, slowly nibbling at the bland food, knowing it'll sink like a rock in my gut.

"Wafer of the Above? It'll bring grand fortune in the battles ahead." A soft voice filters through the dining hall. The back of my neck prickles as Wrenley comes into view, holding a tray of wafers. This must be how she's allowed to come down to the barracks.

Come down and see Dayton.

Her acolyte robes are pristine, and her hair looks perfectly curled, bobbing just past her ears. There's makeup on her face, accenting her sapphire eyes, and rouge lining her lips. She looks stunning.

I can't be here, can't talk to her before she goes to see Dayton. Quickly, I stand, discard my tray, and head out the opposite end of the kitchen and into a narrow hall. I take a random corner, not caring where I'm going, just needing to get away.

There's a clatter as I smack hard into someone. A tray smashes to the ground, star-shaped wafers falling down like rain.

"Oh, I'm sorry, I didn't see you there," I say, bending down to pick them up. *Shit, shit, shit.*

"It's okay, Madison," Wrenley says, straightening the tray. But then she stills, her blue eyes wide. "What are you wearing?"

My hand unconsciously goes to my neck, where the seashell necklace hangs. The necklace isn't just made of shells Fare picked up. One of them was a gift from Wrenley.

"Dayton said I should wear it during the match tomorrow for luck," I say.

"He gave his necklace to a siren he *just* met?" Her eyes are fixated on me.

We both stand, the wafers discarded on the floor.

"I'm his partner."

"Of course," she says, and a bright smile appears on her face. "It's just, it's very delicate. I could hold on to it for you until after the fight, to make sure it's safe."

I touch it protectively. She already gets Dayton. She can't have this too. "I'll be careful. You gave Day one of these shells, didn't you?" Dayton had explained it was a gift from her father, but Wrenley had told me the truth. She never knew her father. So, what's the real story behind the shell?

Or maybe there's no story at all.

My fingers move across until I find it, the golden nautilus shell.

"A very special one," she says.

I tilt my chin down. My heart begins to hammer.

It's important, Rosie.

Images flash through my mind: lines of gold through the forest, grass

405

staining my knees as I fall before a patch of flowers. The will-o'-wisp leading me. The light shining at Caspian's chest last night. The Friar's Lantern flower that Farron sent. Sent from the Nightingale's collection of potions.

I look from Wrenley's familiar sapphire-blue gaze then down to the nautilus shell. Squinting, I peer into the tiny hole at the top of the shell. It would be so easy to miss, but I know what I'm looking for. There, within the shell, is a faint blue glow.

"You're the Nightingale," I breathe.

She tilts her head, hair falling across her brow, and laughs. A laugh I've never heard from the acolyte. "Here I was thinking you were as dimwitted as your Summer Prince." A cruel smile plays across her lips. "Rosalina."

Prismatic thorns break through the ground and swallow me whole.

77

ROSALINA

"Your plan isn't going to work," I snarl as Wrenley—as *the Nightingale*—snaps steel manacles around my wrists. Her prismatic thorns erupted me upward into what must be her private room somewhere in the Serenus Dusk Chambers. Tall windows show a perfect view of the arena. Chains attached to the stone wall snake down across the floor, leading to the steel manacles that clasp my wrists. I stand, tugging on the shackles, pulling the chains taut, but it's no use.

Wrenley laughs. "Isn't this such an adorable coincidence? We both figured out each other's disguises at the same time. Too bad I'm just a tad swifter. The siren ears were a nice touch though. I figured you would be too precious for our chivalrous High Prince of Summer to drag into the arena. I should have known nothing stops the indomitable Rosalina O'Connell!" Her tone is mocking, condescending.

I've let my siren disguise drop, coiling every bit of my magic deep inside. With a sneer, I say, "I guess spending all that time with us didn't teach you anything about what it means to care for other people. To have a heart."

Wrenley's laughter dies. "It's a privilege to have a heart, Rosalina. Count yourself lucky for possessing one for as long as you did before I tear it out."

Even disguised in the white and gold acolyte robes, I can't unsee the frenzy in her eyes. We led a snake right into our nest and fed her with our secrets.

It all makes sense now. Wrenley posed as an acolyte who served Kairyn because it allowed him to keep the Nightingale close. I'd never seen the Below's assassin at the same time as the acolyte and there were all these little inconsistencies in her story. No wonder I could never shake the feeling that Wrenley hated me; even she wasn't that good an actress.

But it was those eyes that finally gave it away. That look of frantic intensity, completely set sail from any sense of peace.

"So, what was your plan?" I spit at her. "Kairyn and Perth Quellos not good enough company? Couldn't make friends in the Below so you had to masquerade as one of us?"

"See, that's the thing about you and all the other puppets playing house in Castletree. You're so eager to believe everyone wants to hold hands and sing songs together. The world doesn't work that way, Rosalina. Trust is why you're in chains and I'm not." She shakes my steel manacles.

"Fine. You wanted to trick us. Well, you succeeded. But why pretend to be mates with Dayton?"

As the words fall out of my mouth, a ridiculous feeling overcomes me.

I'm imprisoned by an assassin who's tortured me and threatened my life. Yet, I feel *relief*.

She's not Dayton's mate. It was a lie. He doesn't belong to anyone else. He could still be mine—

My joy fades to fear. If that's true, he could have unlocked his true power. Would have had a chance in the arena tomorrow.

"You're asking why I went to all the trouble of seducing Dayton?" Wrenley blinks her eyes.

"You didn't seduce him," I snarl. "You tricked him with a fake mate bond. It's different."

"One of the simplest concoctions I've ever whipped up." She taps the golden nautilus shell still around my neck. "The Friar's Lantern did it all for me, truly. It was so simple; it almost makes me sick to think how easily he fell for it!"

"You played on his desire to save his realm. That's not weakness."

She rolls her eyes. "Ugh, don't you ever tire of being so righteous? You're so similar, the two of you. Honestly, the hardest part of the last few months was keeping that doe-eyed look around him when he was acting like such a heroic fool."

"Was this all because you hate me?" I whisper. "You wanted to take him away just to hurt me?"

"Everything's not about you, Rosalina." She says my name like it burns her mouth. "This is about something bigger, about the realms. They'll soon all belong to us, and your princes will be nothing but memories. Your precious Spring Prince was the easiest target. Kairyn was his only heir. Would have been easier to kill Ezryn outright, but so it goes, the ending was the same."

"Don't talk about Ezryn like that." I jerk forward, the steel manacles biting into my wrists.

Wrenley smiles and pats my head, despite the fact I'm taller than her. I step back against the wall to get away from her. "Simmer down," she says. "You're lucky Kairyn's soft. Now, Daytonales proves a different challenge. If we kill him outright, the Blessing will pass to his sister, which would just pose another problem. The only option is to have him pass the Blessing willingly. But who would he trust to receive such a precious gift?"

"His mate," I whisper. "Well, you're stupider than I thought. Dayton will never pass the Blessing to you, even if he believes you're his mate!"

She smiles. "He will if he thinks there's no other choice than to pass it to me or burden his beloved sister. See, there's this thing called 'subtlety,' dear Rosie. You don't seem to understand it, but trust me, I'm a master at it. These last three months I've reminded Dayton that passing the Blessing of Summer to his sister would not only be a horrible burden on her, but also her death sentence. I've told him how all his enemies will converge on her if she were to bear such a responsibility. Trust me, Dayton's too soft a man to let that happen to her."

"You're insane," I breathe.

"I'm efficient. The Summer Realm *will* be mine. Pathetic Perth Quellos may have failed his takeover of Winter and Autumn, but with Kairyn controlling Spring, myself controlling Summer, and Mother's new plans for Winter, it will be all too simple to make Autumn fall in line." She sticks out her bottom lip. "Though, I doubt you'll be around to see it."

Panic rises in my chest. The thought of Castletree's dark lines of rot fill my mind. If the princes lose control over two Blessings, what will become of our home? Of all the people who live in Castletree?

I look around for something, anything, to help me get out of here and warn Dayton. But there's only a bed with rumpled sheets, a vanity messy with makeup and hair accessories, and a dresser, though a few robes are scattered on the ground and not properly put away.

Then something catches my gaze tucked into the corner: the hovering golden orb with the rings around it. Dayton called it the Orb of Ancestors . . . It's what brought the warriors of light to life in the arena. The Nightingale has it constrained in a tangle of her prismatic thorns. Dark lines leech into the glowing surface. Is this how she corrupted the memory of Damocles and Decimus?

The door swings open and Kairyn's huge black frame takes up the whole doorway. His helm turns to me, chest heaving. "You did it," he breathes and looks to Wrenley. "You found her!"

He slams the door shut, and a joyous laugh bubbles up from Wrenley's throat. Kairyn crosses the distance between them in two steps and grabs Wrenley in his arms, swinging her around. The most genuine smile I've ever seen plays across her face. It's so big, the pink of her gums shows, and if she hadn't just told me I'm imminently going to die, I'd almost think it was cute.

"I'm so glad my presence pleases you both," I say dryly. "Now, if we could finish this interrogation so I could begin my escape, that would be great."

Kairyn drops Wrenley and stomps over to me. I can feel his grin behind the helm. "Do you know what these handcuffs are made of, Dandelion?"

I do. I recognize it from the Spring Realm. "Spring steel."

"Exactly. Try to use your briars to take you away and your arms will rip from their sockets before these chains break."

"Knowing her, she's stupid enough to try," Wrenley spits. She walks over to me and snatches my chin with one hand, while popping the cork off a small vial with her other. I try to thrash out of her grip, but she forces a thick, floral-tasting black liquid down my throat. "Say goodbye to your magic," she purrs.

"You can't keep me here!" I scream. "Dayton will realize I'm not there. He'll come for me!"

But they both ignore me, instead focused on the other. Kairyn smooths the hair back from her brow, his gloved hands so large compared to her delicate face.

"I can't believe you found her," he murmurs. "Everything's going to be okay."

She smiles up at him, then flicks her gaze to me and notices how intently I'm staring at them. Giving a tittering laugh, she pushes away from Kairyn and waltzes over to the vanity. "Of course I found her. It was only a matter of time." She puts a dab of rouge on her lips. "Now, for the next stage of our plan. Breaking the gladiator."

I don't care that I'm in chains, that there's two of them and only me. Primal instinct shoots through my chest. "I will kill you if you touch him."

Again, it's as if I'm nothing more than a nattering fly to these two. Kairyn rests a hand on Wrenley's shoulder. "I've got my knights at the ready. I'll have him brought to a cell and—"

"No!" Wrenley wheels around and glares at him. "I have the Summer Prince right where I want him. He's finally ready to trust his little mate." She looks at me with a self-satisfied smile. "How does it feel, Rosalina, to watch someone you love slip away? Now, do you understand what it feels like to be alone, to be left behind?"

The way she's speaking, it's like *this* has been her goal all along: to make me feel alone. Though I know it's not true. What she really wants is control over Summer. Yet still, there's a glint in her eyes that tells me she knows all too well the feeling she's describing.

"I'm not alone. Dayton isn't doing this for his mate. He's doing this for his realm," I say. "Even if Dayton sleeps with you, he'll never love you. Not how he loves Farron." I suck in a breath. "Not how he loves me."

Wrenley begins to roll her eyes, but Kairyn grabs her shoulders. "You're going through with it? You're going to bed him?"

"Yes," she snarls. "Now."

Kairyn staggers backward. "W-why would you do that? We have the Golden Rose. We can stop these mind games. We'll throw Daytonales in prison, use the Golden Rose as leverage. We can find a way to still get his Blessing—"

"We've come this far," she hisses. "This will work."

"Let us just kill him and be done with it!"

"What, so the Blessing passes to that whelp hiding out in the Ribs with your brother? No. We stick to the plan."

Ah, of course Wrenley would have told Kairyn about Ezryn's plan. I bet it's been driving him crazy, knowing where Ez is and not being able to go after him.

Kairyn paces back and forth, hands on his helm. "It's not going to work, Wrenley. If you sleep with him, he'll know you're not his mate."

"Yeah!" I say, then realize I'm agreeing with Kairyn and shut my mouth. Doesn't matter. Neither of them looks at me anyway. Distantly, I notice that Kairyn called her by the name she gave us. Is that her real name? Is there a piece of truth in all the lies she's told?

Wrenley begins aggressively brushing her short hair. "He's been waiting decades to find his mate and break the curse. Imagine what will happen to him when nothing changes? I'll convince him he's broken. He's too far gone to free himself of the curse. He'll be so devastated, he won't have the will to fight. In the arena, your Bronze Knight will beat him to within an inch of his life. Knowing death is upon him, he'll be greeted by me," she bats her eyelashes exaggeratedly, "his mate. I'll remind him that if he passes this burden to his sister, she'll be hunted down just as his brothers were. So he should pass it to me, an unassuming acolyte who will keep the Blessing safe until the Queen's eventual return."

"You'll never break Dayton," I say. "Not his body. Not his spirit."

She gives me a smirk. "Oh, I suspect he's already broken, and I think I have you to thank for that."

My legs weaken, and I nearly collapse to the floor. Dayton begged me to tell him not to go through with this. I let him walk straight into this trap.

Kairyn slams a hand against the wall. "There has to be another way!"

"Stop it, Kairyn," she snaps. "You said you were fine with this. You said you understood what's at stake."

"Of course I said that," he growls. "But now that the time has come, I cannot bring myself to let this happen."

"Well, you don't have a say."

"Give me more time." The distance between them vanishes as he sweeps her into his arms. "I will find another way to deliver you Summer's Blessing, I promise. Do not do this."

She shoves off him. "Just as you said you would deliver the Golden Rose? As always, the only person I can count on is myself."

"You wanted the monastery; I gave you the monastery! You wanted the Spring Realm; I gave you Spring!" Kairyn's voice hitches. "Yet, you still do not trust me," he adds.

Wrenley barks a laugh. "Those weren't for *me*. Those were for you. Do you remember how you were when I first found you? Miserable. Banished. You would never be content until you proved to your damned brother that you are the deserving ruler of Spring." Her steps echo through the chamber as she paces before him. "I made you into what you are. I took you to the Fates to see your destiny. I showed you the truth of Ezryn's curse. I turned you from a monastery boy into an Emperor!"

My heart thunders with the passion of her words. They've completely forgotten my presence now, so wrapped up in themselves. I test the steel again, knowing it's futile to try and break it. And Kairyn's right. Even if I could use my magic, I'd have to take the whole wall with me if I want to use my thorns.

Kairyn falls to his knees before Wrenley, clawing at her robes. "I have given you everything. All that I am. There's no part of my soul that hasn't been painted by you. This is the only thing I ask in return. Do not do this. Do not give yourself to *him*. You don't love him!"

Wrenley grabs Kairyn's wrists and flings them off her. "Love is poison."

Kairyn collapses to the ground, cape pooling around him. "I have nothing left. Would you have me rip out my heart and throw it on the ground before you? I will do it. I will do anything you ask."

She gives that sad, joyless laugh once again. "Oh, you've given me everything, have you, Kai? I told you to kill Ezryn and you left him alive to ravage the Summer sands. Those are destined to be *my* lands he's hunting! But is this how you play it in your mind, Sweetling? Everything all for darling Birdy girl?" Her blue eyes shimmer and her lip curls in disgust. "I fight for your attention with a godsdamned *ghost*. Someone who never existed! A brother who's scorned you since the first! You couldn't win his love, so you chose his hatred instead. Well, good luck trying that with me." Her whole body trembles and she turns away from him, stalking to the edge of the room. "I can't love you, but I won't hate you. So, what are you going to do about it?"

Kairyn stands, appearing as a looming shadow. I hold my breath, wondering if they're going to try to kill each other.

Then he moves. He rips off his helmet. It falls to the floor with a thud. Long black hair flows behind him as he rushes to Wrenley. In a single movement, he sweeps her into his arms and kisses her. Kisses her with the passion of a man undone.

Her eyes widen, shock registering on her face. Then she closes her eyes and melts against him, kissing him in return with the same passion.

Kairyn's helm lies on the floor, as discarded as I am. I narrow my eyes, hardly able to reconcile the usurper Prince of Spring with the . . . the *boy* in front of me. His hair reaches his shoulders, wavy and dark. He has the same tawny skin as Ezryn, and his brown eyes, too. I'm struck by how young he appears. Younger than me, even.

I suck in a breath. It *hurts* to see how alike he and Ezryn are. How young and handsome he is. I can picture the two of them beside each other, laughing.

Wrenley pulls away from him, her face shifting from bliss to horror. "What were you thinking? Your creed!"

He grabs her hands and brings them to his lips. "I don't care. My honor was forsaken long ago. You are my creed now, the temple that I worship. I have nothing else to offer you, to make you stay with me, but this." He places her palm on his cheek. "Please take it."

My heart catches. This . . . this is the most vulnerable a member of the Spring royal family could possibly be, to offer their face to someone who is not of their blood or fated mate. Kairyn must be truly desperate to forsake everything he knows for *her*.

Wrenley's chest heaves. Slowly, she takes a few shaky steps away from him. "I-I have to do this. I need the Blessing."

Kairyn falls to his knees. "It won't help you." He touches his chest. "It won't fix anything, Wren. It will only burn. Like there's a dagger digging deeper and deeper at every moment. If only Ezryn—"

"Ezryn!" she shrieks. "I'm not weak like you, Kairyn. You had your chance to kill him. Now, I have my chance to get Summer's Blessing. I'm not going to squander it."

Kairyn's stare turns inward. Those beautiful dark eyes glaze over. "There's nothing I can say to stop you, is there." He doesn't ask it but says it. A statement he knows in his heart.

"No."

Kairyn stands, movements stiff, jerky. He turns toward the door. "So be it. I will be taking my leave of Hadria presently."

"What?" She raises a brow. "Where are you going?"

He picks up the helm and puts it on, hiding the boy. "You want me to kill my brother? Fine. I'll kill my brother. I'll take my men to the Ribs and destroy him once and for all."

The words cut through me like arrows. No, no, no. I thought Kairyn had a chance of stopping Wrenley from hurting Dayton, not taking both him and Ezryn down! I thrash against the steel.

"You can't go to the Ribs," Wrenley breathes. "I need you here."

"Apparently not."

"I want you here."

"You don't know what you want," he growls.

I jerk forward, thrashing against the chains, but only manage to fall hard to the floor. "Leave Ezryn alone! You've taken enough from him!"

Kairyn tilts his head to me as if he's only just now remembered that I exist. For a moment, I think he's going to say something, but then he just opens the door and leaves, closing it softly behind him.

Silence echoes in his wake.

Wrenley stands in the middle of the room, shoulders shaking. She clenches her jaw so tight, it seems like her teeth may crack. Then with a scream, she grabs the hairbrush off her vanity and throws it against the mirror. Spiderwebs erupt across the surface, causing her reflection to turn into a hideous visage.

She runs to her bed, throws her head in the pillows and *screams*, a sorrowful keen. Tears spring to my own eyes at the sound. When she lifts her head, the kohl around her eyes is smudged, but the intensity in her gaze is back.

My heart thuds. This is my last chance to stop her. To have her stop Kairyn. As she walks past me, I reach out and grab her wrist. "I can see it on your face. You love him." It wasn't Dayton she had loved when we drank the truth wine. It was Kairyn. "Why risk that by doing this?"

She looks down at me. "Because I hate you more."

For a woman adept at disguises, this is the least convincing thing she's ever said.

78

DAYTON

I want a drink.

I really fucking want a drink. But to do this drunk wouldn't be fair to Wrenley or to me. I'm doing this to be better. To do right by my realm. To become the High Prince needed to save Summer.

Here stands the fool, who escapes within the flesh for fear of his fate. Who languishes his time and talent. Here stands a beast who will let his realm go to rot as long as his mind is muddled enough not to comprehend.

"Is this what you fucking wanted from me?" I snarl, thinking of the Enchantress. The Queen. "Did you want me to break your daughter's heart? Did you want to break *me*?"

Perhaps that is what she wanted. To reduce me to ash, to be remade.

Because by the damned gods, I know there won't be anything left of me after this.

I pace back and forth in my room before placing my hand on the wall that Rosie is behind.

Except she's not there. She's returned to Castletree.

Gritting my teeth, I slam my fist against the wall, causing a spiderweb of cracks. Rosalina didn't tell me not to go through with this. She didn't tell me no.

A soft knock sounds on my door. Nausea roils through me. "Come in."

Wrenley enters, wearing her white acolyte robes. Her gaze flits wildly back and forth. Her hair and clothes look rumpled, and her breathing is quick.

"Was there trouble getting away from Kairyn?" I ask.

Her gaze darts to me, wild and untethered. "Kairyn. What about him?"

"Is he going to notice you're missing?"

She stalks past me and grabs the wine I've been ignoring. "What do I care about that arrogant asshole? He thinks he can control my entire life, like he *knows* my entire life. He doesn't know a thing about me. Not really."

Something's upset her. Slowly, I hover a hand above her back before stepping away. "It's all right, Wren. We can figure out a safe space for you to stay."

"Oh yes, you would say that, noble prince." She falls to the bed in a flurry, wine goblet in hand.

Running my hand through my hair, I try to soften my expression, my words. "Tell me something about yourself. Something you've never told anyone."

Wrenley stills, an animal in a hunter's trap. She closes her eyes and breathes in a long breath. Then she opens her eyes and studies me, looking a lot more like the girl I'm used to. "I never knew I had magic, like *real* magic, until you showed me at the water fountain in Florendel. Now, I can feel it *everywhere.*"

"The world is full of magic." I sit down next to her and take her small hand in my own. "Anything else?"

"I always dreamed of living in the Summer Realm," she says softy. "Growing up, it felt like a place where no one could ever trap you. Like the sea could carry you far, far away from your problems."

"I know what you mean." But right now, trapped in these clay walls, the sea feels very far away.

"Now you tell me something," she says.

"Me? I don't have any secrets." I smirk. None that I think she would understand. "I once borrowed Kel's jacket and ripped it on one of the castle's thorns."

"Prickly little things," she says and downs the wine in the goblet. "I have one more. I've never . . . never done *this* with anyone before."

I swallow. "We don't have to—"

"No." She turns to me, and in a flash, all her shyness seems to have disappeared. She tosses the empty goblet to the floor. "You're my mate.

I've been dreaming of this moment my entire life. We belong together. Do you feel the same way about me?"

"O-of course I do," I say. The words taste like ash in my mouth.

Before I can think any more, her lips are covering mine.

"I'm sure we can figure this out," she murmurs, tugging at the laces of my shirt.

Dozens of responses filter through my mind, from the humorous to the downright raunchy, but all I can gasp out is, "If this is what you want."

"Of course it is. Who else would I want? You're my mate."

I'm not sure if I'm imagining it, but it almost seems like she's trying to convince herself as much as me. I kiss her again, this time running my lips from her jaw to her ear. I glide one hand through her hair, gripping her waist with the other.

"You're beautiful," she says, pulling away from me to look at my face. "Everyone in the palace goes on and on about it. Strong and handsome and tall. Though not as tall as Kairyn. He's—"

"A whiny giant, I know. Can we avoid talking about *him* right now?"

"Of course." She flushes and touches my hair. "Such a bright golden color."

"You're beautiful too, you know," I tell her. It might be the first truth I've said today. Her face, such a similar shape to Rosie's, that if I squint, I could almost pretend—

But I can't do that. It's not fair to her, and not fair to me.

Or Rosalina.

I roll Wrenley to her back, wondering how much longer we can delay this. I've done this with so many fae, so many times. Why can't I push my feelings away like I did with Fare for so many years?

Rosie brought those feelings to light, made me feel what it was like to love both of them. Anger courses through me. She shouldn't have done that. She had no right. Rosalina knew she had a mate, and yet she tried to get me to love her too.

And stupidly, she succeeded at it.

It feels like I'm going through the motions on where to place my hands, my mouth. Will this be enough to break the curse?

Wrenley moves to undo the laces of her robes, fingers trembling.

"Let me," I say, covering my hand with hers. "I have gotten you out of those robes before."

"When you rescued me." Wrenley gives me a half-lidded gaze. "You really are a good person, Daytonales."

"Haven't been told that too many times in my life."

She shakes her head. "It's going to be your downfall."

"Well," I say, removing her robes, revealing the silk chemise below. "You're about to learn just how *good* I can be."

Her breath hitches, and I kiss her again, trying to summon the time I rescued her to the forefront of my mind, picturing the shell she gave me, the light that bound us together in the field. Trying to feel anything.

I break away, gasping. I have to do this. I have to kiss her and . . .

The air feels suffocating, thick with the scent of perfume and dust. I swallow hard, trying to suppress the rising tide of panic. Anguish, shame, and a bitter sense of betrayal swirl together in a tumultuous whirlpool, threatening to drag me under.

Rosie's words echo in my mind: *I cannot keep away from you any more than the tides can resist the pull of the moon.*

I force myself to take a deep breath, willing my trembling limbs to obey as I run a hand over her collarbone.

Farron's voice invades my soul. *When we make love, it's different than anything I've experienced before. It's magic. It's enchanted. It's golden.*

I shake my head, ridding myself of auburn hair and the scent of crisp leaves and apples. The feel of his body entangled with mine. *Get out of my mind, Fare.*

I have no choice in this. Wrenley's hand touches my chest, no doubt feeling the hammer of my heartbeat. My body is not my own; it is merely a pawn in a cruel game of gaining power.

My heart must be locked away. If this is what it takes to be High Prince, then so be it. I lean down to Wrenley, steeling myself. Once this is done, a part of me will be lost forever.

The part that belonged to them.

"Ready, Wren?" I whisper.

She nods, hands gripping the ends of my shirt and pulling it over my head, causing my hair to fall wildly around my face. I slide my hand along her body to the hem of her dress and begin to drag it up.

Leaning down to capture her lips, it feels like cracks are forming all over my body.

And I . . .

"I can't do this," we both say at the same moment.

Her hands push hard against my chest.

Immediately, I stand, backing across the room. She sits up, drawing the blanket around her. "Wait, you can't do this?" she gasps.

"Wrenley, you said—"

She shakes her head, and the sad, desperate girl changes into one of anger. "Because you're in love with Rosalina, is that it? How can I be with you when you won't let her go?"

I throw my head back, hands in my hair. "I was trying."

She stands in a flurry, throwing on her robes. "You need to forget her, Dayton. She already has mates, and they're not you."

"I know."

Wrenley opens the door but pauses. "I really wanted to help you, Dayton."

The door slams shut, and I'm left alone.

Rosie is gone.

What if she doesn't return by tomorrow? What's even the point of fighting without my curse broken? I won't be able to win. I won't be able to protect her. We'll never get the bow.

The Bronze Knight is going to kill me.

I should run.

But instead, I stand and grab the jug of wine. Maybe I'll get drunk instead. What else would my realm expect of the drunken Prince of Summer?

79

CASPIAN

So, Farron knows Rosalina is my mate. It was always going to be impossible to hide it from him forever. I stand, trying to conceal the stiffness of my movements.

"Does Rosalina know?"

"No," I snap, whirling. "And you won't tell her."

Farron crosses to me, reaching for my arm, which I jerk away. "She deserves to know, Cas. I think a part of her already does. *I* felt you, I think. Your pain . . . And you've heard my thoughts, haven't you?"

"Mate of my mate. Yes, it's all very complicated." I open my wardrobe and pull out two plain black cloaks. "Put this on. It doesn't matter. If the Queen gives me what I want, there won't be a bond to worry about."

Farron slowly clasps the cloak around his shoulder, then puts his golden elk mask back on. "Caspian, for what it's worth . . . I'm not worried. Not anymore."

I still, concentrating on the feeling of the fabric in my hands so I don't collapse. "You would be if you'd seen what I did under that hood."

The Autumn Prince's earnest face is scrunched up in determination. "That won't happen. Rosalina won't allow it. I won't allow it."

He's so stupid.

"Besides, I'm not so sure turning human will break your mate bond," Farron says. "It's something I've been wondering about lately. The way

George talked about Aurelia . . . they must be mates and George is most certainly human."

Hope and fear mingle in my stomach. Could I become human and keep Rosalina? A short life with her would be worth a thousand years of living the future my mother has planned. A future of servitude to the Green Flame. A future of power.

A future without Rosalina is no future at all.

I throw my cloak over my shoulders. "We need to get going. We're already behind."

"What's the new plan? The party is over."

"My mother will assume I've already left for Summer. It's the perfect alibi. We just have to remain unseen."

We creep outside, following the halls until we get to the upper ring of the courtyard. Most of the party guests have left, though there are a dozen or so lingerers and a few soldiers attempting to round them up. More than half are engaged in sexual acts, too hopped up on the spiked wine to be afraid. Birdy's potion does its job again.

"Still a little chaos going on," Farron murmurs.

"This way." I grab his arm and lead him across the courtyard, head down, avoiding the notice of the guards with more pressing issues. My palace is perched on top of one of the tallest mountains in the Below. My city of Cryptgarden lies beneath it. Being the ever-generous ruler that I am, there are stairs carved into the mountain leading to my not-so-humble abode.

Farron and I take that spiraling path now. Halfway down the mountain, a track leads off to a lookout point lined with torches. I pull us in that direction.

"The pool is *in* the mountain that your castle is built on top of?" Farron hisses.

"Perhaps Mother thought it would help my magic," I say back. "All I know is its presence is quite annoying when you're trying to sleep. There's a secret notch in the rock wall. Only Mother and I know of it. She can't know I'm part of destroying the crystals."

"I know," Farron says. "Remember, she thinks you're in Summer."

"I know," I snap back, heart racing.

"Hey! What are you two doing here?" a stern voice calls. "Sira told everyone to leave these premises and go back to the main city!"

I freeze, the voice of a guard carrying behind us.

"Get us out of here. Use your thorns," Farron says.

"I can't. She'll see my thorns and know I was here." My mind races. There has to be something we can do. "He can't see me. He'll report my presence to her, and she'll do horrible things to me. Kel will fail and—"

The guard's footsteps get closer. The breath rages in my throat so fast I can barely breathe. How did I not realize someone was behind us? I was too distracted. I'm going to let them all down again. Green pulses on the edge of my vision.

Farron slams me against the wall, and all I catch is the glint of his golden elk mask before his lips are over mine. He's only an inch taller than me—I've measured—but there's a strength in his grip that I've never felt before. The power of a High Prince. His lips part as I'm engulfed in a wave of heat that ignites every nerve in my body, searing with the intensity of a thousand suns.

The guard's footsteps draw near, and the man grumbles. I suddenly realize what Farron's doing.

Something I really should have thought of. *Clever boy.* So, I weave my hands in his hair and kiss him back *hard*. With each brush of his lips, his tongue slips between my teeth, consuming me with a passion as wild and untamed as the Autumn winds.

"All right, break it up," the guard yells.

Farron licks from my lips to my ear and whispers, "Decent kiss, Cas, now be a good boy and keep playing along."

He spins us so fast my head whirls. His back is to the wall and my head is tucked into the crook of his neck.

"Oh, sorry, sir," he says in a slurred, arrogant tone, one far deeper than his own. One similar to a certain Summer Prince. "Looks like we got distracted."

"I've had enough of everyone's distractions tonight. Get out of here."

"Of course." He straightens, still keeping my head tucked in the crook of his neck.

I can only keep moving one foot in front of the other, waiting for the guard to call out my name, waiting for him to recognize me, but nothing comes. We descend the stairs, only stopping once we round the corner.

I fight for breath, then glare at him, slapping his chest. "Decent?"

He laughs, pulling up the mask and raising a brow, unable to stop the blush forming on his cheeks. "Rosie told me to kiss you. I couldn't let her down."

"Rosalina is a meddler and causes more trouble than she knows what to do with."

"Tell me something I don't know." He sighs then runs up a few steps to peer around the bend. "The guard's gone back up. I think if we hurry, we can get inside the mountain before he comes back."

My stomach knots, but I allow Farron to pull me back up the stairs to the lookout point. I press my palm against the hidden notch in the stone wall, feeling my magic bleed into the rock. It opens a crack. Green light washes over us both, and I turn to Farron. "Ready to piss off a cosmic god?"

His smile is dazzling. "As I'll ever be."

80

ROSALINA

I spent an uncomfortable, sleepless night trapped in Wrenley's room. I can tell by the position of the sun it's late morning, and the roar of the crowd is unlike anything I've heard before. It's like the trickle of rain working its way into a thunder. The High Prince of Summer must be stepping onto the sands. Desperately, I stretch my chains to look through Wrenley's window.

The arena is still full of broken columns, though most of Kairyn's plants have dried up in the heat.

Immediately, I know something is wrong. Dayton is stumbling. Oh my god, is he drunk?

"He thinks you've abandoned him," Wrenley purrs. She sits at her vanity, kicking her feet, an annoyingly smug expression on her face.

I wish I could feel some relief in the fact that they didn't sleep together. She'd come in late, ranting that her plan was still flawless, but I could see through the cracks. They both couldn't go through with it.

Wrenley hardly seems bothered by it all. It never mattered to her how to break Dayton, only that he's broken.

"Why would he think I abandoned him?" I snarl.

She cocks her head, the light from the Orb of Ancestors in the corner of the room shining in her hair. "Well, what else is he supposed to think when he woke up and you hadn't returned? It's not like he could even escape without your little thorns. His only choice is to face his destiny upon the sands."

"I would never leave him!" I shout, chains rattling as I surge toward her.

"I really couldn't have planned this better myself." She prances to the railing. "Now, we just have to wait for the Bronze Knight to do his job. It shouldn't take long."

I pull as hard as I can on the chains, getting as close as possible to the window. "Dayton!" I scream, but my voice is lost to the roar of the crowd. *Look here. See me.*

I'm just another face. Uncharacteristically, Dayton doesn't even look to the crowd, doesn't hold up his sword to their cheer. He just stares across the arena and shrugs his shoulders. "Let's get this over with."

The Bronze Knight, in his gleaming armor, strides forward, wielding the Lance of Valor. I feel a knot tighten in my chest. He lunges at Dayton and drives the lance down with deadly precision. The clash of steel rings out across the arena as Dayton just barely blocks him.

You idiot, I think. We weren't sure he could take the Bronze Knight without breaking his curse, and now he's trying it inebriated. I wish I was down there so I could smack him.

Below us, the Emperor's Box is empty, save for the Bow of Radiance gleaming on its pedestal. Kairyn hasn't returned. He must have traveled to the Ribs to hunt my mate.

I turn my attention back to the match. Dayton fights with reckless abandon, dual swords flashing in the sunlight, but his movements lack their usual finesse. Each blow he strikes is wild, uncontrolled, and I can see the pain etched into his features as he struggles to keep his footing.

"Come on, Day," I urge.

Wrenley gives me a sidelong glance, as if my pain and fear are a mystery to her. The crowd roars with delight, but they don't see it yet, how Dayton falters.

Wrenley chuckles. "I'm surprised he didn't try to run. He must know he can't win."

Dayton's cry of agony ripples through the arena as the Bronze Knight slices a red line across his back before kicking him face first to the sand. The Bronze Knight drives the lance down for another deadly blow, and Dayton rolls out of the way just in time, the lance still cutting his arm.

I can't tear my eyes away. Every strike that lands, every bruise that blooms on his skin, feels like a dagger to my heart. I want to scream, to beg for mercy, but I'm powerless to intervene.

"No!" Tears pour from my eyes, and I'm shaking. I'm the goddamn daughter of the Queen—there has to be something I can do. But the Nightingale's potion still runs through my veins, rendering my magic useless. Besides, in these chains I can't use my briars to spirit me away.

A gasp sounds from the crowd as the Bronze Knight lands a devastating blow, sending Dayton crashing to the ground. My breath catches in my throat as I watch him crumple, his swords slipping from his grasp, his golden hair stained with blood.

"I think that's my cue." Wrenley draws the white acolyte hood over her head. "I'll run to the sands and beg for the Blessing. With his dying breath, he'll grant it to me."

Rage and anger war within me. "He'll never give it to you."

"Oh, Rosalina, the perfect princess raised with love away from this deadly world." Her sapphire gaze narrows. "You have no idea what it is to be truly broken. You have no idea what one will do when they're truly desperate."

She leaves and I'm left alone.

"Dayton," I sob.

He lies in the middle of the sands, a drop of gold drowning in a pool of blood.

There has to be something I can do. I *need* my magic. More than that, I need to think clearly.

How can I concentrate when so much fear and sorrow tear through me? My heart is a thundering gallop, my breath ragged. I need to calm myself, but my own mind feels out of control. I slam my eyes shut, tears streaming down my cheeks.

Anastasia Steele from *Fifty Shades of Grey*. The name pops into my thoughts, and I catch a deep breath. Bilbo Baggins from *The Hobbit*. Claire Fraser from *Outlander*.

I may not have magic, but my stories are magic. They sheltered me from loneliness when I lived in Orca Cove, and they gave me strength when I was captured by Kairyn. Now, with each name I say in my head, I steady my breath.

When I reach Z and open my eyes, my mind feels clearer.

I need to save Dayton. To do that, I need my magic. To get my magic, I need to cure myself of the Nightingale's potion.

Memories wash over me of when Wrenley imprisoned me in the

monastery. She had so proudly bragged of her potions. They were all made of flowers.

The Queen's greatest strength was change. She transformed a tree into a castle and barren empty land into enchanted realms. Because she created it, she was connected to all of it. Justus had told me that. My mother made the Enchanted Vale; there is a part of it within me. The sirens, the fae, the animals, and the plants. Even the flower used to make this poison.

I turn my mind's eye inward. My body feels dark, where usually it beams with light. There's a shadow stifling my radiance. I know this shadow well; I spent three months under its hold below the sea.

I delve deeper into the recesses of my mind, picturing myself as a warrior of light, like one of the ancestors who fought in the arena. Wielding a gleaming blade and shield, I imagine myself cutting through the shadow, loosening its hold on my magic.

With each calm breath and steady beat of my heart, I feel for the flower's grip on me and purge it, metabolizing the poison as if it were part of me all along. In a way it is, as all living things in the Vale are.

Slowly, the light within me begins to beam again. My heart beats faster, not with fear, but with strength. With a final sweep of my mind's inner warrior, I neutralize the last remnants of the poison. My magic sparks into light, shining with the radiance of the sun.

I blink open my eyes, gasping. Carefully, I flick a white flame onto my fingers. *Back in business.* But now that I have my magic, what can I do to help Dayton while I'm trapped?

My gaze flits around the room until it lands on the Orb of Ancestors.

An artefact of the Above. One that holds all the memories of those who fought in the arena.

Summoning a golden briar, I weave it across the ground and wrap it around the orb. Carefully, my briar snakes back to me with the treasure.

Maybe there's nothing I can do, but there's something *they* can do.

All the warriors of Summer.

81

DAYTON

There's something sobering about losing half your weight in blood.

Sobering and fucking sticky.

Here lies the fool, coughing on his own blood. Who let his realm fall to a tyrant because his mind was too muddled to save it.

The blurred image of the Bronze Knight swims before me. Damn, I knew I'd lose to this bastard, but I thought at least I'd put on a show.

Have to hand it to the crowd, though. I guess in their own way, they're rooting for me. There's none of the applause that would normally arise when a kill is about to be made.

Horror cuts through me at the thought of what my death will mean for Delphia. Of the pain and burden she will feel in only moments—

"Wait!" A clear voice rings out across the arena, and I see the blurry shape of a girl in white running across the sand. "Wait, please!"

Wrenley. I can't even form words as she throws her slight body over mine.

"He's my *mate!*" Tears stream down her face as she looks up at the Bronze Knight. "Let me say goodbye!"

"Be quick," the Bronze Knight rumbles, "before I end the Summer Prince for good."

"Dayton." Wrenley takes my head in her hands.

"H-how did you . . ."

"I snuck past the guards. I couldn't watch this."

"Did . . ." I cough, blood splattering on my chest.

"Did what, Dayton?"

"Did Rosie come back?"

Wrenley's face turns to pity.

Just from her expression, I know the answer to my own question. "She didn't return, then."

"Dayton—"

We don't have much time; *I* don't have much time. "Wrenley, you need to get out of here. You need to find my sister and tell her she can't return to—"

"Kairyn has left the city," she whispers. "He's hunting Ezryn. What do you think he'll do when he feels her Blessing?"

Panic swells in my breast. I should have tried to escape the arena. Should have run like a coward to protect her. "Wren, I can't win this."

She drops her forehead to mine. "What if there was another way?"

"What way?" My breath rattles.

She strokes my hair, such a tender gesture. "Give your Blessing to me."

"What? I couldn't ask that of you."

"You're not asking me. Dayton, I would do this thing for you. I may not have been able to give you your true power—"

"That wasn't your fault," I rasp. "It was—"

"You're my mate." Wrenley places her hand over my slowing heart. "I want to protect you, and if I can't save you, let me save someone you love."

"Kairyn would come for you."

"I can escape before he returns," she says hastily.

My head falls to the sands, which are red now. My Blessing flickers inside me. A burden I never wanted.

Since the first moment I felt it blaze inside me, it has been nothing but tragedy. I imagine Delphia in the desert, feeling that weight transfer to her. She's already had to bear too much responsibility for the last twenty-five years.

Wrenley's no fool. There's a quiet sort of bravery about her. This choice will save Delphia, but not the Summer Realm.

Summer is as lost as me.

Gritting my teeth, I force myself up and look into my mate's eyes. "Wrenley . . ."

"I'm ready, Dayton."

82

KELDARION

"You need to tell me which way, George. Which way?"

George's eyes seek mine, but he can't focus. He looks past me, body twitching on the purple stone of the labyrinth. "Best to take the train. Slower, but better view. Best to take the train, yes, best to take the train. Though, we could travel coach—"

George's condition has worsened rapidly, each mile we travel eroding more of his strength and cognition. Thankfully, we haven't run into any more visitors or traps.

"Focus, George." I shake his shoulders. I've let him sleep as much as I could, but we're out of time. If he falls unconscious again, I'll have no way to find Anya. His connection to her is our only compass. My sole choice would be to abandon the mission and use the seed Caspian gave us to escape. But I'm not leaving here without the Queen.

His eyes find mine, and he blinks. "Kel."

"Yes." I breathe a sigh of relief and lift his head slightly. "Which way, George? Feel inside. Where is Anya?"

A grimace crosses his features. "I can't go on, boy. Everything hurts. I can't think straight. Everything inside of me is rotten."

I still my hands, which threaten to shake. "Don't say that, George. Everything's not rotten." I place my hand on his chest. "You feel that? Right by your heart? That's your connection to Anya. That can *never* be destroyed. She's so close now, George."

Tears stream down his cheeks. "It's all so far away. I'm so far away. I'm lost inside my mind—"

I grab his hand and squeeze it. "I'm right here. I'm going to keep you tethered to me, okay, George? Keep listening to my voice. Anya's waiting for you. Rose's mother. She wants to see you and Rosalina."

"I can't remember anything," George cries out. "It's all messed up."

"No, no, you remember. Like . . . like when you floated down the river on the wooden boat with Anya. You visited the big stone triangles. Remember that?"

His lip quivers. "The Pyramids. We went there a few weeks after we met. Then we sailed down the Nile . . ."

"Yes, yes!" I urge and pat his chest again. "And the two of you trekked through a great jungle and startled a huge spotted cat." The memories of his life, gifted to me by Clio, flood my mind, as real as if they were my own.

"I was working a dig in the Amazon. Thought that jaguar would be the end of us."

"Do you feel her?" I ask.

He closes his eyes and nods. "I think so."

"And the wooden house in the woods? Do you remember that?"

"Our cottage in Orca Cove. I took her to the place I was born, and she said she wanted to raise our daughter there."

I bring his hands to my lips. "You did. You raised the most amazing, wonderful woman in the world. You've got to tell Anya that. You've got to tell her how good her daughter is. How brilliant and funny and beautiful. Can you do it, George?"

George grits his teeth and attempts to stand. But he has no strength anymore. He can't raise himself up. "I c-can't . . ."

"Yes, you can," I growl then lace my arms underneath him. With a mighty thrust, I heave George over my shoulders and stagger to my feet. He's no small man, but I promised I'd carry him if I had to. I'm keeping that promise.

"Show me the way," I breathe.

There's a beat of silence, and I'm afraid he's lost consciousness. Then: "Left," George says assuredly.

So left we go.

"Follow along this wall then take a right."

"Straight past the turns to the end of the chamber. Take the leftmost passage."

"Keep on this path."

I follow each of his instructions, occasionally giving him a shake or pinching his leg. "Stay with me, George."

My shoulders ache from George's weight, but I keep myself in fae form. I don't want my beast to startle George when he's drifting in and out of the present and the past.

Slowly, the maze begins to change. The purple stone shifts to a dark jade. Brilliant scars of emerald light cut beneath the earth, reminding me of the walls of the Chasm.

"There are no more turns," George breathes. "Just keep going."

The sharp turns have given way to a circular pathway. I realize we're walking around a spiral. We're almost at the end.

A high-pitched cackle rattles the air. I steady myself and reposition George over my shoulders.

I knew there would be one more visit.

Ahead, the walls shift into brilliant emerald spires that connect with a jeweled archway. A small figure sits atop the keystone, swinging her legs through the air.

"One more Fate to speak with, George, then we're there," I murmur to him.

George doesn't respond.

The figure leaps off the keystone, hanging onto it with only her hands, then swings her body in a giant arc, somersaulting down to the ground.

"We've seen your sisters already, Melinora. We need no more gifts," I call as she runs forward.

She's short and slight, moving clumsily as if there are no bones within her. Perhaps that is true. Her skin appears made of straw, like a little doll woven by a fireplace. Two braids of multicolored yarn form her hair. Her eyes are big black buttons, and stitches hold her mouth in a permanent smile.

Melinora, the Mistress of Threads. My muscles stiffen at her approach. While her sisters unsettled me, there's something far darker about this Fate. She doesn't just see the past or the future; she sees the threads of life and cuts them when they fray.

Her joyous cackling echoes in the spiraling passageway. As she approaches, she dances in a circle around us, her limbs moving fluidly, bending in angles no fae could manage. "You're here! You're here! Never thought you'd get this far, no, I didn't! Not that I know. What does Melly know? Nothing, nothing. Philly sees it all, Clio reads your past. I only hold your lives hanging in the balance!"

I try to step away from her, but she moves too quickly, caging us in. George gives a shuddering breath.

Melinora stops moving. Her limbs slacken. Though it seems impossible, her grin widens. "Two," she says. "Two strings. The first." She holds up her hand, revealing a dangling thread. It's pale white but imbued with an ethereal blue glow. She strokes it across her straw face, and a shiver courses through me, like my bones are being licked clean.

"This one is so strong. Yes, so strong. Won't be cut for a very long time. For a very, very, very, very, very, very, *very* long time."

"Put that away," I growl.

She holds it up before her face, button eyes popping out for a closer look. A flappy cloth tongue licks across her sewn-on lips. "I watch it for fraying. Melly protects it."

"Put my thread away, Melinora. You don't need it right now," I say sternly.

She makes a sound that's half-hiss, half-pout, then tucks it into the pocket of her colorful dress. Her button eyes look to George.

"Now, this one," she says, "is a special one."

The thread she holds up is not like a string at all, but the branch of a willow tree. It looks . . . familiar.

I step closer. The top of it resembles a frosted branch in the dead of winter, the bark icy white. It melds to rich, dark brown with a sprig of cherry blossoms, followed by a lighter ash brown with a brilliant green palm sprig. The branch is capped by orange bark, a single maple leaf hanging on. Lines of black run up and down the branch and through the leaves, as if a sickness has taken root.

This branch . . . It reminds me of Castletree.

"This is a special one," Melinora repeats. "I've been ready to snip it for a long time. I watch it every day. Should have been snipped ages ago. Not right for it to go on this long. Not right for his kind."

Beads of sweat form on my brow despite the cool chamber. I grip George's wrist and leg tighter. Melinora's button eyes focus on him as she swings the branch back and forth. "Not right. Not right! Look at him! It needs to be snipped!"

George's thread is so different than mine. He shouldn't even have one in the first place; a human's life has no place being held by a fae.

"It needs to be cut!" Melinora shrieks. The stitches of her mouth rip open, and her jaw unhinges, chunks of red fluff falling out. "Cut! Cut! Cut!"

She whips up her other arm, revealing a pair of scissors sewn into the wrist.

"No!" I cry and lunge forward, nearly dropping George. But it's too late. The blades of the scissors snip around George's thread.

The branch doesn't cut. Melinora throws her head back and howls with laughter. She snips wildly at the branch, but nothing happens. "Can't cut it! Can't cut it!"

My heart hammers in my chest. I shove past the Fate, sprinting now through the maze. George's heaving chest rattles against me. I hardly feel his weight, my only thought to get us away from her.

When my lungs can barely take in air and my legs scream, I collapse against the wall, letting George slide to the ground. Every part of me shaking, I clamber over the old man and lift his back up until he's pressed to my chest.

The thread of his life looked like a piece of Castletree. He had been so sick in the Autumn Realm, but had awoken suddenly, renewed and filled with vigor.

Right after we had given our strength to Castletree.

"You're . . . you're connected to it, aren't you?" I whisper. *Aurelia, you are filled with tricks.*

For the love of her life, she would do anything. Just as I will, for the love of mine.

"Rosalina," I whisper, knowing she's too far away to hear me. "I'm going to save them. I promise you."

George's heart is weak, now. I don't know how to heal like Ezryn or how Farron transferred Dayton's life force back into Rosalina. But I've spent years giving my energy to Castletree.

Rosalina is my home, and by wandering into my castle uninvited, this man brought her into my life. In that way, he is a piece of my home.

"Anya's waiting for you," I whisper. "Let us finish this."

Energy flows through my body like a wind through barren trees. I think of Castletree, of uniting my magic with my brothers' as we poured it back into the home that shielded us. Magic ripples out of my body and into him.

George gasps, and I lean him away from me. He blinks, his blue eyes clear. "Keldarion?"

A delighted cackle sounds, and I look up to see Melinora holding up

George's thread. It shimmers with blue light, the black rot gone. "Such a strange little life!" Her button eyes turn to us. "Go on, go on, almost there now! Almost at the Golden Thread!"

George and I smile at each other. I help him to his feet, and he rubs his chest. "Anya."

Then he takes off, sprinting as if he were a young man. I sigh, muscles sore from carrying him for hours, and follow suit. Round and round we run, the green spiral pathway getting tighter and tighter. Anticipation bubbles within me. With each breath, I feel the pulsing energy in the air, propelling me forward. I can't even keep up with George.

We round another bend and . . .

The passageway opens up. An open-air chamber stands before us, punctured by four huge green crystals that emit a glow across the stone. Glowing, translucent green walls stand between all of the crystals, forming a box of phantasmal energy.

The world is silent. Neither George nor I breathe. Even my heart seems to slow.

There's only one thing to do.

I fall to my knees in a bow.

Because trapped within the cage is Aurelia, Queen of the Enchanted Vale.

83

DAYTON

My mate, Wrenley hovers above me, waiting for me to pass my Blessing.

I must do it to protect Delphie.

I reach out my arm to touch Wrenley when something catches the light. Something bright, hovering just beside the sun.

The light burning my eyes isn't the sun at all. It's the Orb of Ancestors. What, does Kairyn not think this knight will be enough to end me? He has to bring out some of the ancients to finish me off as well?

The orb sparks, jagged lines of light shooting out at all angles.

"Dayton," Wrenley says, her face flashing. "We have to do this now. The Bronze Knight won't wait."

"Hold on . . ." I rasp because there's another voice trying to break through.

I stare at the orb as it circles and spins. No warriors of light emerge, but there is something else emanating from it.

Energy, magic, light—

Never in a million years did I think I'd see little Daytonales on his back in the arena.

That voice, I know that voice. It's Damocles.

Don't fear, he's just lying in wait to surprise his enemy, Decimus says.

Wrenley and the Bronze Knight don't react. They can't hear my brothers. I must be closer to the afterlife than I thought.

This can't be the kid who bested me.

I recognize that voice too. Lucretia the Swift, a fierce gladiator from the past with unmatched speed and agility. I beat her spirit when I was still but a child, becoming the youngest champion to prevail against a warrior of light.

"Dayton!" Wrenley shakes my shoulders frantically. "Don't die before you pass your Blessing."

There's so much blood around me now. Blood like the ancestors shed. For thousands of years, the blood of the gladiators of Summer has soaked into the sand. They've given their bodies and spirits to this sacred space. In return, the crowd offers their excitement, their energy. It's symbiotic in a way, like a High Ruler's relationship with Castletree.

You always saw this place differently than your brothers. A voice I would know anywhere drifts into my mind. My mother. Sabine. *You saw the magic that was created here. The magic you created here.*

My eyes widen at the light, so bright it threatens to blind me.

More and more voices pour into my mind, warriors ancient and powerful. Words of courage, bravery, and honor. I feel the demand in all of it. *Fight!*

Little brother, is this how you want your story to end? Crushed on the sand by a man hidden by metal? Damocles says, and for a moment, I can almost see an echo of his face in the shimmering orb.

Wouldn't make a very striking mural, Decimus quips. It's like they're beside me, how they used to be. This isn't the version of them Kairyn brought to the arena before. This is a true memory of how they were.

The Blessing of Summer burns within you. Show the world you are worthy of it, Damocles says. *Our deeds break across the waves of time, creating a legacy that can never be forgotten. Stand and fight.*

I'm too broken to fight. Everything from my chest to my arms aches with fatigue.

Then mend your cracks with light. That voice . . . it sounds like her. Rosalina. *Rise, Dayton. Rise like the sun breaking over the horizon.*

Mend? I'm no healer, not like Ez, not like Fare. I clutch my arm, feeling the metal bargain band. *Through every storm and every season. . .*

Distantly, I hear Wrenley screaming. Shadows move, the Bronze Knight is getting closer.

I don't know how to heal. But I know what it felt like when Fare drew strength from me, taking my energy to fill his own well. I've watched Ezryn countless times, drawing life from plants.

My body may be broken, but there is life in the very stones of the colosseum, in the crackling air, in the blood-soaked sand. I have given myself countless times to this place. Now, I need to take a little back.

My hands fall to my sides, and I dig my fingers into the sand. Drawing the magic up through me, my well of power fills, and it swirls like a stream of light, knitting together wounds, repairing torn muscles, allowing oxygen to flow through my blood.

Gasping, I open my eyes. Wrenley is still above me. Slowly, I push myself to my feet. "Get somewhere safe. I've got a fight to win."

Confusion flashes in her features. "What? How are you standing?"

"You didn't think I'd lose my streak over a little wound, did you?"

"You can't possibly win!" Wrenley screams. "You don't have your full power! You haven't broken your curse."

Gently, I touch her shoulder. "And I never will. I'm sorry, Wrenley, I can't be your mate."

Her blue eyes blaze. "You can't just choose that!"

"Actually, I can," I say.

The Bronze Knight, seeing me on my feet, storms toward us, lance raised.

"He's going to fucking kill you anyway," Wrenley growls.

"I think this might help." From my pocket, I pull out the token of the Queen. There's no point in hiding it now.

As soon as it hits my neck, I feel a surge of energy within me. In my outstretched palm appears my trident, glowing a brilliant teal. I block the Bronze Knight's lance.

Power explodes between us as the two weapons collide. Digging my sandals into the sand, I slide back a few paces. There's an eruption in the stands, a crazed energy. It fuels me. Using all my strength, I push back against the Bronze Knight, hard enough that he stumbles.

Running a few paces away from him, I jump over a few broken columns and look upon the crowd. Below me, the Bronze Knight tries to scramble up, but he's too heavy, stone breaking beneath him.

"Citizens of Summer!" I yell to the crowd, beckoning the echosphere closer. "It's your High Prince, Dayton." There is a thunderous applause. "I can't help but notice the so-called Emperor has left. So perhaps it's time we took back the realm for ourselves!"

The ground shakes beneath me as the Bronze Knight crumbles the pillar. I fall hard, landing on my back. I bring the trident up to block before rolling away and leaping up. Distantly, I notice Wrenley standing off on the sidelines.

I have to set her free too.

"I have a confession to make to you, Summer," I say, parrying with the Bronze Knight as he charges. "Perhaps you've heard the rumors. The princes of Castletree are cursed."

A shocked murmur rumbles through the crowd, but I barely pay attention to it. They might not be in the stands to hear me, but I need to give the words to the wind. I need to speak my truth.

"It is true. I am. My own power has been shackled to the point that this idiot is giving me a good show." I smirk, feeding on the laughter from the crowd. "But I've realized that breaking the curse would come at too high a cost."

I dodge away from the knight and clamber up on a crumbled archway, buying me a few moments of reprieve. But a few moments are all I need. "It would mean forgoing the love of Farron, High Prince of Autumn, and Rosalina O'Connell, the Golden Rose, both of which hold my heart undisputedly."

The Bronze Knight drives the Lance of Valor into the archway. Spiderwebs crack beneath my feet. "I know now, all the magic in the world wouldn't give me strength without them. So instead of wallowing in that fact, I see it a different way. Maybe this curse isn't a curse at all. Maybe it's the gift Summer needs."

With that, I toss off my clothes, and shift into the golden wolf.

There is a shocked sound in the stands, followed by a glorious cheer.

The archway crumbles beneath my weight, and I leap from it, shoving the Bronze Knight to the ground. He drives the lance up at my belly, but I knock it away, pinning his hand down. Then, with a swipe of my other paw, I break the chain around his neck, and the maple leaf falls to the ground.

The Bronze Knight screams, his hand still around the Lance of Valor, grip pinned beneath my paw. He can't let go, and without the token, he can't wield the weapon without pain.

It's all right. I plan to put him out of his misery. I open my massive jaws and relieve the Bronze Knight of his head.

Blood coats my maw, and I shift back into my fae form. The trident re-forms in my hand and I don my breeches.

The crowd's roar is deafening, but I'm not done yet. I bend, picking up Autumn's token, and place it around my neck. I know this feeling, that of crisp nights and foggy mornings, of freckle-splattered cheeks and copper hair gleaming in the sun.

With the Trident of Honor in one hand and the Lance of Valor in the other, I look to the crowd. "I think that the Below has had a hold on the Summer Realm for too long. Let's take back what's ours."

I spin, pointing both the lance and trident. In a whirl of water and golden leaves, magic strikes the gates leading to the barracks. They collapse, and from behind them, Tilla and the other gladiators race out.

The crowd's roar has changed to a war cry as the people begin to fight back against those who would claim this land as theirs.

The fight for Summer has begun.

84

ROSALINA

He . . . did it. Dayton survived! He won against the Bronze Knight. Pride swells within me, mixing with a different emotion.

He chose me and Farron. Oh, how I wish the Autumn Prince could have heard those words. Dayton would rather remain cursed forever than give us up.

But if I get my way, he won't have to.

I need to get out of this Spring steel. Curse Ezryn's realm for making such sturdy things!

A screech sounds from the window ledge, and I turn to see a golden eagle perched there.

Justus, the first High Prince of Summer, had come just when I needed him. After pulling the Orb of Ancestors toward me, it had been surprisingly intuitive to connect with it. It had the same energy as Castletree. All I had to do was *ask* for help from the ancient fae. Their memories were eager to pass on words of wisdom to the High Prince.

And Justus had been the perfect help to carry the orb to the center of the arena.

"Thank you for helping me with the orb. Any ideas on what to do with these?" I shake my manacles. "See a key lying around?"

The bird quirks his head. "The Queen rarely found herself in binds she could not escape. There was nothing in the Vale that was not part of her."

I blow a strand of hair out of my face. "I think my water, wind, fire, and earth go a little beyond steel."

"Is steel not of the earth?" Justus says, flapping his wings. "Now, if you'll excuse me, I've got a rebellion to aid."

"Hey, wait!" I call, chains jingling, but the old mentor has already leaped off the building. "Stupid bird. Steel isn't earth."

Reforge it. Ezryn's words drift into my mind. I know he's far away, but for a moment, I let the presence of him and the Spring Realm sink into my skin. Our time together in Florendel. My visit to Draconhold Forge. *Reforge it.*

Walking through the smoky hall, seeing the red-hot steel in a forge. Red hot and malleable.

Could I change this steel back to that state? Not the manacles on my wrist, surely, or I'll burn my arms off. I follow my gaze to where the chains are bolted to the wall and crawl closer. I hover my hand above them.

My eyes flutter closed, thinking of the change this metal went through to be forged into such a state. *Reverse.* I think of fire, of heat, of the sun, and daylight. Warmth blooms against my palm, and I open my eyes to see the steel bubbling down the wall in thick red-hot globs.

"Yes!" I shriek and carefully tug my chains away. I'm free! Now, to find the key.

Where would Wrenley have hidden it? I spend a few minutes searching the room before my gaze turns to her vanity. Quickly, I rifle through her makeup before my hand grasps a large silver key.

Within a minute, I've freed myself of my shackles and am darting through the Serenus Dusk Chambers. There's something I'll need if I'm to win my own fight in the colosseum.

After I secure my precious cargo, I burst into the arena. The sunlight is blinding, and the whole Sun Colosseum is in an uproar. Tilla and the other trapped gladiators wage a battle against soldiers of the Green Rule. The stands are just as chaotic as the arena. The Summer fae are rallying.

Carefully, I search the arena. Something gleams across the way, shining in the Emperor's Box. The Bow of Radiance.

A familiar voice breaks through all else. Dayton. He stands on a pile of rubble, looking like a true god of the arena. Golden hair flowing, the Lance of Valor in one hand and his Trident of Honor in the other. His voice carries across the expanse, giving commands.

But stalking closer, ignored by the crowd, is an acolyte dressed in white.

Wrenley.

He doesn't know she's the Nightingale.

There's a detached expression on her face. What must she be thinking, as her plans crumble around her like stone? Dayton didn't give her his Blessing. Kairyn left her.

I need to get to him before she does. The bow will have to wait. No one else can wield it, anyway.

"Dayton, look out!" I scream across the arena, but there are so many voices, he doesn't hear me. I push past fighters. Green Rule soldiers try to quell the crowds as goblins attack with pikes.

Wrenley stalks closer, and I see the briefest glimpse of thorns stirring beneath the sands.

"Dayton!" I scream again, and then he turns, golden hair blowing.

"Rosie!" His face breaks out in the most glorious smile, and he steps down from the rubble.

Wrenley grabs his arm. Her expression changes to the doe-eyes I know are all fake. "Dayton, wait, as your mate—"

But I see beyond her words, to her hand, reaching for the two tokens around his neck. There's no way I'll be able to reach him in time. Not on my feet.

"Stop!" I shout, and they both turn to me. I rip the nautilus shell off my necklace and throw it to the ground. "She's *not* your mate!"

With my heel, I smash the shell. Florescent blue goo and petals spill over the sand. But it's not enough, not yet. Carefully, I brush aside my hair, where a small will-o'-wisp bobs. The one I asked to follow me from the Serenus Dusk Chambers.

"I need your help now," I whisper.

The little wisp flutters and lands upon my chest where it melds against my heart. Almost immediately, a golden line shoots from my chest to the smashed shell.

"A trick," Dayton growls, snatching Wrenley's wrist as she lurches for the tokens.

She cries out and tries to wiggle free, but he's too strong.

As I look down, something strange blossoms around my heart. The light no longer appears like a black tangle, as it did back in the Ember-wood Forest all those many months ago. The golden light glows bright as more lines—more mate bonds—burst forth. One brilliant bright light shoots to the ground, which must be to Farron and Kel in the Below, and another streams far into the horizon to Ezryn. But one line is brighter than all of them. One that blooms right before me.

Here in the arena.

Even if I didn't see it, I would feel it, this new light blooming in my chest, warmth flooding my body like the rising of the sun.

Tears flood my eyes as I look across at Dayton, to the light bursting on his chest, not to some necklace, but to his heart.

His teal gaze widens, and a look of pure, unfettered joy crosses his face. He shoves Wrenley away, where she falls to the ground in a cloud of dust and sand. The Summer Prince leaps down, the trident and the lance shimmering back into his tokens. He crosses to me in two steps, taking my face in his hands.

The light blooms between us like a newborn sun.

He tilts his head, giving me a curved smile. "Told you all along we were mates."

A half-bubbling sob bursts out of me. "You're such an idiot—" I start before my mate cuts me off with a kiss.

85

DAYTON

Rosie crashes against me like a wave upon the shore, and I can't pull her close enough. My mouth opens against her lips, drinking in the taste of her, this wonderful, glorious feeling bursting through me.

A laugh erupts from my chest as I kiss my way along her jaw to her ear. "So, if getting shot by half a dozen arrows and having amazing sex wasn't enough to unlock our bond, then what in the seven realms did it now?"

"I think," Rosalina trails a hand down my chest, "I've been in love with you for a long time, but you couldn't believe it. Just like you couldn't believe you were worthy of your Blessing."

"Nah, that idea sounds like it's all my fault," I whisper without meaning the words.

Rosie stiffens, then she whips out a hand, a golden briar erupting from the ground to smack away a prismatic thorn.

No! The Nightingale is here? But as the thorns fall away, all I can see is Wrenley staring at us. Her hair is disheveled, her face wild. Those bright sapphire eyes—

"I almost fucked the Nightingale!" I choke out.

"Yes, you idiot!" Rosie snarls at me.

"I distinctly remember you *not* stopping me from almost fucking the bloody Nightingale."

"Okay, we can argue about who's the bigger idiot later, but can we please go get my bow?"

"Pretty sure it'll still end up being me." I give a lopsided grin. "And yes, whatever you say, Blossom. If you asked for the stars, I'd pluck them from the sky."

I turn, and Wrenley—the Nightingale—is still staring at us. "The bow," she mouths. Then she turns, sprinting across the arena.

"She's going for the bow?" I choke out.

"We have to stop her!" Rosie yells, and we both take off in pursuit.

"Pretty sure the bow will stop her for us if she touches it!" I yell.

Something pained flits in Rosie's gaze, and she sprints faster. I summon the lance and trident from my necklaces, using the weapons to knock back our enemies as we run.

Voices rise up around us, excitement in the air as people notice Rosalina's golden briars. But Rosie seems wholly focused on catching the Nightingale. The bow gleams above us in the Emperor's Box. How are we going to—

A huge prismatic briar explodes from the ground and wraps around the Nightingale's waist, shooting her into the air. Rosie skids to a stop.

"Don't try it!" I shout.

But of course, she never listens to me. A golden briar bursts from the ground and propels Rosie higher and higher, right after the Nightingale. Who leaps from the air and into the Emperor's Box.

"Don't touch it!" Rosalina screams. "It'll burn you—"

There's a huge flash of light. Fuck, I have to get to her. I summon a rush of magic of my own. Wind bursts beneath my feet, carrying me high into the air.

I land in a crash on the Emperor's Box. Rosalina's arms are over me, helping me to my feet. I turn, expecting to see a charred acolyte and the bow . . . but there's no sign of either. Only a patch of prismatic briars.

"What happened?" I ask.

"I don't know," Rosalina whispers. "Maybe she carried it away with her thorns. I don't see how she could have gotten the token."

"We'll get it," I whisper and pull her against my chest. "You're safe. That's all that matters."

"What now?"

"Now, we secure the Sun Colosseum. Tomorrow, we retake the realm." I look out at the arena, then to her. "But tonight? Tonight, we seal our bond."

86

KELDARION

George lets out a heart's cry.

I stagger up, barely able to see clearly through my blurred vision.

Did I believe we'd truly find her? I was willing to take George into the unknown, willing to risk my own life, but that was because I knew he would never stop until we'd searched every corner of the Vale. Had I actually thought we'd find Aurelia here?

Not Aurelia, not to George.

This is his Anya.

He nearly falls over his own feet as he runs toward the glowing green cage. "Anya," he sobs.

She appears just as any other fae woman, her back against the glowing wall. Her features haven't changed much from George's memory, but she's more beleaguered. I wonder if in the sunlight, her hair would still have the slight hint of red as it did when she sailed down the river near the stone triangles.

Though Anya appeared as a human to George, she now looks fae. But I know better. The Queen is the closest thing to godhood the Vale has ever seen. She created our homes, our way of life. She saved the last pieces of the Gardens of Ithilias.

She bore the Golden Rose.

I want to fall back to my knees before her, to prick my hands and make vows in blood. I want to beg for her forgiveness and to tell her I understand now why she cursed me.

I never once believed in any of the centuries of my life that I would have this opportunity. But George has been waiting every second of his.

Keldarion, the cursed High Prince, can wait and so too can Kel, Rosalina's mate. My thoughts immediately turn to patrol, to guarding the single way in and out and observing for traps.

For this moment, I am here for George.

He stumbles forward, jaw trembling as if he's forgotten any word except her name. "Anya . . . my Anya."

The Queen slowly raises her head from her chest. Her shoulders are hunched forward, dirty feet splayed before her. She wears a white dress that seems clean enough, but dark circles rim her eyes.

"Anya!" George's voice cracks, tears streaming down his cheeks.

Anya blinks at him. Her eyes seem faded, faraway. A soft smile graces her chapped lips. "Hello, darling."

Her name claws out of his throat again, and George collapses to the ground before the translucent wall. He pounds on it with his fist, tries to tear it down. But we're too early. Farron and Caspian haven't destroyed the crystals yet.

Thank the seven realms, I think. If we had been too late, Sira would have imprisoned her some other way.

Anya's face hardens as she looks at George. She blinks once. Twice. Then looks around, as if expecting to see someone else.

Who? Sira? Does she assume this is all a trick?

"Anya?" George says quietly.

"Get it away from me," Anya snarls, voice harsh. "What is this?"

"It's me, Annie. I've come for you," George says.

"No, no, no." Anya covers her ears and collapses in on herself. "Get it away from me!"

I take in a shaky breath. She's been here for twenty-five years. Who knows what sort of things Sira's done to her in that time?

"Show her who you are, George," I call to him.

George's eyes widen. Despite the wrinkles on his face and his graying hair, there's a boyish fear about him now. "How?"

I tap my heart. "You know how."

George looks down, hands scratching at the wall. At first, I think he's going to stay there forever, the two of them so close, and yet so far away.

Then his voice rings out, low and quivering: "I will love you across the ages."

Anya looks up.

"I will love you in the desert, under a blazing sun, or in the deepest depths of the jungle. I will love you when the rain pours down and we're covered in mud, or when the night is so dark, the only light beams from your heart. No time nor distance nor magic can break my love for you."

A beat of silence echoes in the chamber before a guttural sob tears from her lips. "George!" She crawls forward, pressing her hand to his through the wall.

They stare at each other, their hands seeming to connect despite the barrier. Shock and love play across their features. My own heart swells, and I can't help but walk closer. If only Rosalina could witness this.

I imprint the image in my mind, taking note of every detail: the tremble of George's hands pressed to Anya's, the burst of color returning to her ashen face. The weight of their love rushes against me, and I understand now why it is so easy for Rosalina to love.

"What are you doing here?" Anya breathes.

A smile breaks across George's face. "We're here to rescue you."

Anya's body stills. She scrambles away from George. "No. No, no, you can't rescue me."

I take one last look at the entrance of the chamber then walk up behind George. For the first time, Anya seems to register me. "You?" she whispers.

I kneel down and bow my head. "My Queen."

She points at George. "Get him out of here. Now."

"We have a plan. My name is Keldarion, son of Erivor and—"

"And Runa, yes, yes. I know who you are, High Prince." A look of horror crosses her face. "Your curse is not broken."

"Well, you can fix that when we get you out," I grunt.

"Oh, no, no, no." Anya tugs at her hair. Her wild gaze falls to me. "Why are you trying to save me after what I did to you?"

"Because I am madly in love with your daughter, and she needs her mother."

A look of utter anguish cuts across her face.

"We have a plan," George assures. "Don't worry. You'll see her soon."

I try to keep my voice as steady as possible. "Farron, the High Prince of Autumn, and Caspian, the Prince of the Below, are working together to break your bonds—"

She lurches forward, hands reaching for me. They smack against the barrier. "Cas has decided to turn against Sira?"

Cas? "For today."

She blinks her eyes and smiles, giving a small laugh that reminds me of Rosalina. "I can't believe it."

"Your daughter can make the impossible happen," I say. "And that's what we're going to do. We're getting you out of here, my Queen."

George seems unable to say anything more. He just stares at her with stars in his eyes, a look of complete contentment on his face.

A single tear runs down Anya's cheek. "Oh, my George." Then she turns to me. "You are my daughter's mate. You know this."

"Yes," I breathe.

"Then, you will do anything for her. Is that correct?"

"Of course," I growl.

She stands, exuding all the grace and majesty of her title despite her prison garb. "Then you will take my husband and leave this place at once."

"No, Anya!" George stands. "This cage will be destroyed any minute. We'll escape together—"

"No, we will not," she says harshly. Then she sighs, and her whole body softens. "I can't leave here. If I do . . . Rosalina will take my place."

87

EZRYN

S and pelts my face, whipped by the wind so hard it slices my skin. My eyes are blurry with grit, and my mouth tastes of dust. Each step forward is a fight, but I keep moving.

It came upon us suddenly as we were traversing our way back across the Ribs toward Hadria. First, it was the wind, tearing at our clothes and making it nearly impossible to open our eyes. Then a red haze thick as clouds wafted over the horizon. Now, I can barely see a foot ahead of me.

"Ezryn! We can't keep going!" Delphia calls from behind me.

"Don't stop," I say back.

There's no other option. One foot in front of the other. If we stop, we die. If we go back, we die. There is only deeper into the storm.

There's a malice to this wind, something beyond the natural world. I wrap my cloak tighter around my face, but I can still feel it with each bite of sand. Like a malevolent voice stirs the wind to a riot.

"We have to take shelter," Nori says. "It's the only way to survive a sandstorm."

"There is no shelter," I growl. There's nothing out here: just the dunes and the wind and the damned sand. I *hate* sand. We can't go back to the Huntresses. Even if they would take us, I've lost sense of north or south. We can only keep moving.

Keep moving toward what? a voice asks in my head. *To Hadria, without the aid you promised? To Rosalina, with only your failures?*

This is all my fault. Of course I'm not a worthy representative of the Queen. I had fooled myself into thinking I could escape the Prince of Blood, but his legacy follows me everywhere. Now, I've shadowed Delphia with it.

If Dayton had chosen any other protector for his sister, would the Huntresses have given their support? I stagger forward a few steps. One of the girls calls my name but it's distant. "Keep moving," I rasp. Even though the only reason to do so is because I don't know what will happen to us if we stop.

"Ezryn, look ahead," Delphia snaps.

I squint, shielding my eyes from the stinging grains of sand. There's a dark shape within the swirling dust. A person, staggering toward us.

"Help," a man's voice cries. "Help me, I'm lost."

"Someone needs our help," Delphia says, catching up to me. "Hey! We're over here! Follow our voices!"

I stop, the wind threatening to bowl me over. "Shush."

She doesn't. "We'll help you!"

The man stumbles closer. His movements are heavy and clunky, weighed down by armor.

Golden armor.

A member of the Queen's Army.

Every muscle in my body tenses. The only members of the Queen's Army in Summer are those who left the monastery to follow Kairyn. Like the soldiers he left in Queen's Reach who nearly killed Rosalina. Like the troops sent around the Summer Realm to harass and intimidate the people.

These traitors are one of the reasons Kairyn's been able to cause the harm he has.

My chest heaves. All the rage and grief and frustration of failing our mission floods through me. I can't help Rosalina and Dayton in Hadria. I can't sway the Huntresses to fight for us. But I can still protect the girls. I won't let this renegade hurt them.

The frenzy surges up my blood. I no longer feel the sting of the sand or the bite of the wind. All I feel is hatred for this man and what his order has done. Murderers, invaders, traitors—

I cut through the storm and throw the man to the ground.

He gives a yelp that's cut off by the sound of my fist against his cheek.

"Stop, please!" he cries. I slug him and his nose sprays with blood. "Help!" The man starts to cry.

He needs to pay for what he's done, like Kairyn needs to pay. If the only thing I'm capable of is enacting justice, then so be it. I raise my fist again—

Something holds back my arm. Delphia wraps her arms around my bicep and stares at me unblinking. The wind whips her hair above her head like a crown. I grit my teeth and yank my arm free. When I turn back to the man, Eleanor covers his face with her body. There's a fire in her gaze.

"Ezryn," Delphia says lowly, "how will this help us?"

I take in a heavy breath, the dust coating my throat.

I want to kill him. I want to kill him because I'm so fucking angry, and I'm terrified he'll hurt you. The only thing I can do to help anyone is kill those who could wrong them.

None of that answers her question.

I stagger backward, collapsing in the sand. What . . . what was I about to do?

I hold my bloody hands up in front of my face. Was I right? Is this all that I am, all that I will ever be? What would Rosalina think of me? She looked into the eyes of a beast and found goodness. I looked at a set of armor and saw evil.

Delphia kneels beside me and takes my hand in hers, wiping the blood off with her sleeve. "You don't have to be afraid," she says. "Nori and I will look out for you."

She offers me forgiveness without a second thought. A childish, foolish decision—

Or am I the child? Too wrapped up in my own twisted sense of justice. Who am I to pass judgment on others when I have strayed so far from my own path?

The wind is too strong; I can't lie here anymore but I can't move either. The storm within me is painting my blood black.

"I don't mean you harm, sir, or you, madams," the man says, sitting up and adjusting his jaw. "I need shelter. This storm's going to eat us alive!"

"Look over there," Nori says. "The winds bending around those dunes. There could be a depression beyond it. We can shelter there."

"Come on, Ezryn." Delphia puts her arm under my back and hauls me to a seated position. "Follow us."

I let the child pull me to my feet, then follow her, fighting through the wind to get behind the dune. Nori was right; the storm has caused a trench to form. We duck down within it.

The lack of wind rushing through my ears is nearly eerie. I shake my head, sand running off my hair.

The soldier collapses to the floor a little distance from us and wipes the blood from his nose. "Didn't think I'd see another soul out here."

"We didn't either," Delphia says.

"I'm Mozi." He's young for a member of the Queen's Army; many of the soldiers lived during Aurelia's reign, but this fellow looks younger than me. Signing up for a life of servitude to a monarch who hasn't been seen in centuries—no one wonder he was so quick to defect to Kairyn's side.

"I'm Del. That's Nori, and that's, uh, well, we just call him Old Man."

Mozi nods. "Wish we met under different circumstances. Maybe we can help each other get out of this."

"You're a defector of the Queen's Army," I rasp. "You betrayed your vows to serve a tyrant." I drag my head to the side to stare at him. "Why should we help you?"

The boy's eyes flash. "It wasn't like that. Lord Kairyn protected the people of the monastery. It was filled with corruption; we watched him purge it, help the acolytes. Help us. He said we'd been waiting too long for a Queen who would never come to help the realms. But he'd help it. All we had to do was follow him." Mozi drops his head. "But it wasn't like that at all. He sided with the very thing we were taught to fight against. He took over the minds of the people of Spring. I saw it happen. Then he banished Prince Ezryn."

"The prince deserved it," I say.

"No one deserves that," Mozi whispers. "I didn't want to follow the Green Rule anymore, but it was too late. Yesterday, my squad was chosen to accompany Lord Kairyn out here to the Ribs. He took a whole fleet of airships. Once we landed, I saw an opportunity to escape and thought I could outrun the storm and make it to Autumn for a fresh start—"

"Wait." I crawl across the trench toward the boy and snag his chest plate. He gives a peep. "Kairyn is here?"

The boy gulps. "He's looking for his brother, Prince Ezryn, and the Princess of Summer, too. He wants them dead." Mozi looks into my eyes then to Delphie. "You're . . . you're them, aren't you? You're the ones he's looking for?"

I drop the boy and shuffle away, collapsing back against the side of the trench. I say nothing.

"How does he know we're here?" Delphia's eyes widen, and she grabs my arm. "Ezryn, what are we going to do?"

"How many soldiers does he have?" I ask.

"One hundred, Prince Ezryn. Five airships."

"I am no prince," I growl. *One hundred soldiers to catch me—*

Mozi crawls closer, eyes frantic now. "This storm's his doing, you know. He's trying to funnel you toward Solonius's Spine."

Solonius's Spine: the bridge at the end of the world. A passage between the Ribs and greater Summer. It had been too far away from the coast for us to take into the red clay sands, but it would be the closest route back to Hadria.

"We'll have to figure something out quick," Nori says in her monotone voice. "This trench is getting filled with sand by the second."

"I know how to get back to the bridge. You'll be safe from the storm, but his army is lying in wait, sir," Mozi says. "There's no way over the canyon but that crossing."

"No way over unless we take him down," Delphia says.

"He's got an army of one hundred soldiers," Nori says. "The odds are terrible."

Delphia shakes my shoulder. "Ez, what do we do? Fight or run?"

To run would be to lose ourselves in the sandstorm. If we make it out, we'll be even farther from Hadria. Rosalina and Dayton are counting on us.

But to fight . . .

I can't win against Kairyn. I know this. As much as every part of me screams to demand back my Blessing and to make him pay for what he's done, I can't lose myself in that storm again.

I keep expecting the world to change to one where the Prince of Blood isn't needed. But it's not the world shackling me to my vengeance. It's been me all along.

My strength doesn't come from my sword. It comes from my will to protect those I love. I don't need to kill to do that.

I don't need you anymore, I whisper in my mind to that dark shadow, the one I call the Prince of Blood. Maybe one day, I'll be able to say it to the beast.

I look at Delphia and Nori, staring up at me expectantly.

They need me to guide them.

I suck in a deep breath. "We're not going to fight."

Delphia starts to protest, but I interrupt her.

"And we're not going to run."

I look up at the swirling sands above our trench, the wind that screams and rages and roars. I know that feeling all too well. I picture Delphia, kneeling beside me and wiping my hands clean of blood. I can do the same for Kairyn. "We're going to talk."

88

KELDARION

"What do you mean, Rosalina will take your place?" George cries.

The Queen of the Vale kneels before us, head down.

I slam my hand against the glowing green barrier that cages her within. "So, you truly did make a bargain, didn't you?"

She sighs and holds up her hand. There's a single black band around the ring finger of her right hand. It has no design, no etching. Metal plain as prison bars.

The circular manifestation of a bargain.

I tear away from her cage with a growl. "What could ever possess you to involve your daughter in a bargain?"

"I didn't mean to!" she cries. Her eyes dart to the entrance. "I'll tell you quickly, but then you must leave. Promise?"

"No, I don't promise!" George says. "I've been searching for you for nearly half my life. I won't leave your side again."

"Oh, sweet George, it hasn't been nearly half your life. Not even close."

I storm back to the barrier. There's no way we can just leave, not when we have no answers and no direction. How could the Queen of the Vale have made a bargain without understanding the consequences? She's the bloody *Queen*. She created the realms, Castletree . . .

All this time, I thought with certainty that I was cursed because it was what I deserved. Now as I stare at Aurelia—at Anya—I wonder if she's as fallible as the rest of us.

"You'll understand when I explain." Anya touches her hands to the barrier and George places his against hers. "I had ruled the Vale for generations and I was tired of it all. Tired of war and noble squabbling and having to know the proper answer for everything. I was exhausted. I couldn't do it anymore! And I didn't need to be there. I left my four most trusted confidants in charge of the realms, assured that they would pass their power down to the worthy. Then I left."

"So, it's always been true," I growl. "You abandoned the Vale."

"I didn't *abandon* the Vale. The fae I left in charge were better suited to rule than I ever was," she snaps. "I had done my part. Suffered through wars, pushed my magic to its limits, sacrificed my happiness for the good of the people. It was my turn to *live!* And I did. Oh, I lived. I watched Shakespeare's plays at the Globe Theatre in London, sipped tea with Anne Boleyn in the gardens of Hampton Court Palace, marveled at Leonardo da Vinci's inventions in Milan, and sailed on the HMS *Beagle* with Charles Darwin." Her eyes shimmer. "I got to witness the rise of civilizations without having the pressure of designing them myself! To experience the world as it came to me . . . that was magic."

"What of your people?" I ask.

"I left them in the best hands I could," she says, voice short. "It's not my fault their descendants passed the Blessings down to those who refused to live with conviction."

The words find their mark. She did think me unworthy.

"Maybe I would have been more ready for the Blessing if my father hadn't died in a war, one you left us to fight alone," I say darkly. My anger surprises even me. This is the creator of my home, my way of being. The magic she saved flows through my veins. Yet, all I can think is whatever bargain she made threatens Rosalina.

Though . . . I suppose that doesn't make us so different.

Anya glares at me, then softens. "Fine. You're right and you have every reason to hate me, Keldarion. But I would not change my past. Not for anything. Because it led me to you." Her gaze drifts to George.

"I thought you were a fool when we first met," she says.

"I know. You told me all the time."

"I didn't expect to fall in love with you, George. I'd lived over a thousand years without falling in love. But this was greater than any adventure I'd been on. I was no stranger to grief. I'd mourned countless visionaries who'd inspired me, many leaders I admired. But not so many friends. I knew better than to get attached to someone whose life would vanish in a breath of mine."

Her voice gains strength as she speaks. "My fae life was far behind me, but I still remembered magic. I could turn fae to animals or some mixture of the two, but I'd never been able to create faedom. So how was I to keep you with me forever? How was I to cheat death?"

George's fingers curl against the barrier, as if he could wrap her hand in his. "I would have been grateful to have one lifetime with you, Annie."

"I know you would, darling." She smiles and a tear trails down her cheek. "But you know me. You said it all the time. 'Nothing's ever enough for you, is it, Annie?' One lifetime with you would never do me. Never ever."

A pit opens in my stomach. There was only one fae in the Vale who ever rivaled the Queen's power. If there was something Aurelia was incapable of—

"So, I did the only thing I could think of. I went to the one person who I thought might have been able to master this power. My enemy, Sira."

I knock my head hard against the barrier. "Thank the seven realms Rosalina got your looks and not your rashness."

She glares at me. "Are you one to speak of poor bargains, Keldarion? If so, please come and join me within my bars. We could pass another twenty-five years with the discussion."

"Enough, you two." George glares at us both. "Anya, go on. I need to know."

"I asked Sira how to extend a human's life, but some things are impossible for even the two of us. However, she did have other arcane knowledge. She offered to teach me how to tie your life force to an object. In return, I would make a bargain with her."

George's face crumples in anguish. "Say this isn't all for me."

"I'm selfish, I know it, George. What can I say? Well, I asked her what this bargain was. We were friends before she stole the rose from the Gardens, did you know that? I'm sure you didn't. You don't remember any of my stories, do you, George?"

He clutches his hair. "I don't know what I remember. There's bits and pieces falling at me, but I can't line them up. It's like I'm standing in a meteor storm just waiting to get hit."

Anya gives a sympathetic smile. "I'm sorry. That's my fault, too. But I'll get to it."

"The bargain," I growl. "What bargain did you agree to?"

Her voice takes on a dark resonance. "The bargain was thus: if I were ever to love anyone more than George, that person would belong to Sira completely: mind, body, and soul."

George and I both swear at the same time.

"It was a fine bargain!" Anya exclaims. "I'd lived a thousand lives and never loved anyone except George. I never thought it would be possible!"

"Until you had a child," I say.

"Well, yes. That comes later. You're moving too fast. I made the deal and felt quite chuffed about it, thinking I'd gotten exactly what I wanted from Sira without any sorrow. Of course, now I had to decide what I was going to do with George's life force. What object would live as long as I did?"

George's life-thread springs into my mind, his illness getting worse every time the High Princes were away from Castletree . . . "You tied it to Castletree."

"It was quite clever, if I do say so myself." She crosses her arms and tilts her nose into the air.

I pound a fist against the barrier. "Except you cursed us princes and now Castletree is dying!"

She puts her hands on her hips and glowers at me. "You have a lot of expectations of me, Keldarion. I didn't *want* to be Queen, did you know that? I only wanted to help my people. After I saved the roses from the Gardens and made the new realms, everyone proclaimed me Queen, and I just had to deal with it. I'll have you know that it's one thing to be a hero and another thing to be a Queen. I didn't always get it right."

I take a step back. That's exactly what she is. A hero. She saved the Gardens of Ithilias and traveled around the realms, rescuing fae who needed help.

Her restlessness simmers beneath her skin even now, her spirit undamaged even after twenty-five years in prison.

So many of the fae in the Enchanted Vale look up to her, thinking her a goddess. The army at Queen's Reach pledged their life to her.

But she's only a fae who saved the world and had to live with the consequences.

She sighs and looks away from me. "So, I tied George's life to Castletree and returned to the human realm. We went on all sorts of adventures. Do you remember them?"

"Yes, I think so," he says. "But they're only now coming back to me."

"You knew everything back then. What I was. Why you never aged. But our greatest adventure began in Orca Cove." She looks down and splays her fingers across her belly. "I had made the realms, grown Castle-tree from a sprout. But this was the greatest life I ever created."

"Did you not think of your bargain? Did you not ever consider you would have a child?" I exclaim.

"Of course I did! Sira led me to believe our bargain only included romantic love."

"You've got to be explicit in the wording of bargains," I mutter.

She glowers at me. "Thank you for such a helpful observation. Obviously, having time to reflect on everything, one could say I was a tad . . . optimistic about my deal."

I begin to interject that "optimistic" is far too *optimistic* of a way to view her mistakes, but she waves her hand to silence me and continues speaking. "At that point, I knew my adventures in the human realm were coming to a close. A half-fae daughter should be raised among her people. So, when Rosalina was one year old, I journeyed back to Castletree for the first time since I'd tied George's life to it decades ago."

"And you found us," I say solemnly.

Her face turns into a snarl. "I discovered a coward, a layabout, a menace, and . . . and you! You who were the Protector of the Realms. You who had so much potential. You who broke poor Caspian's heart!"

I throw my head back and laugh. "Poor Caspian? Broke his heart? Has this cage rotted your mind?"

"Keldarion!" George snaps.

I get as close to her face as I possibly can. "When did you first meet Caspian?"

She gives a wicked grin. "Offer still stands. Come and join me in here, Keldarion. I've got hundreds of Caspian stories."

"Another thing to thank the seven realms for! That Rosalina didn't get your twisted sense of humor!"

"A shame," Anya says. "Would you like the rest of my story or are you ready to leave?"

"The story," I growl. "Continue."

"I could have possibly forgiven the fact you four were useless at keeping the realms stable, protecting your people, and upholding every-thing Castletree stood for, but you committed an even worse sin." Anger flashes in her gaze at the memory. "You were my daughter's mates. I can feel these things, you know. Many from the Above can feel the deep

462

magic, like mate bonds. For my daughter to be mated to such pathetic, pitiful, ineffective, futile, disappointing—"

"I *get it*," I growl. "We weren't good enough for your daughter. Finally, something we agree on."

Her lip trembles. "I know you judge me for my actions, Keldarion. You think you know the horrors of war. Of loss. I *lived* it all, every pain, every horror. When I finally felt like I had set things to right, I left the Vale in the hands of those I trusted most. For me to return years later to see all of that work, all of that sacrifice torn to shreds—" Her words cut off in a sharp breath, and she looks up to the sky. "I didn't intend to leave you in such a state for long. I thought you needed to *feel* the consequences of your actions. But of course, things didn't go as I planned. Just another drop in the bucket of mistakes the Queen of the Vale has made."

I pause, musing on the tone of her voice, her choice of words. She seems . . . jaded. Resentful of her role as Queen. Mostly, I sense a feeling I know all too well: shame.

I have no words of comfort for her, and no defense for myself, so I ask, "The staff—did you have to curse them, too?"

Anya avoids my gaze. "Have you seen your people die, Keldarion?"

"Yes," I breathe. "I have been to battle."

"What of your citizens? Have you heard a mother's scream over her babe's dead body? A child wailing for parents they'll never see again? Have you watched your home be destroyed, every rock, every root?" Her voice darkens, each word a harsh accusation.

"I saw Frostfang fall to the Below's forces," I breathe.

She sneers at me. "A home you soon liberated. I was there when the Above crumbled. When every part of my life I'd ever known was ripped away from me. Pray you never feel pain like that."

"What does this have to do with our staff?" I snarl.

"I wanted you to *fight* for your people, Keldarion. To stand up for something, for someone. I planned to help you all reach your true potential, to free the innocent of my curse shortly after, but I didn't know . . . I didn't know . . ."

"Didn't know what?" George urges.

"Didn't know Sira would be waiting for me in the human realm. I think she was quite content to leave me there among the humans. Probably never would have made good on her bargain until I showed my face at Castletree and cursed all you princes. It was the perfect opportunity to gain control over the Vale. One she couldn't turn down. So, she came to collect the one I loved more than George. She came to collect our daughter."

The idea of Sira taking Rosalina . . . raising her in this place . . . My hands turn to fists.

George's breath becomes shaky. "No, not our girl."

"Of course I wasn't going to let that happen," Anya asserts. She twirls the ring around her finger. "But I didn't have many options. I was trapped in the bargain."

"So, you offered yourself in Rosalina's stead," I say.

"Smart boy." She smirks up at me. "Sira was more than happy to agree."

"Oh, Annie." George falls to his knees. "Why didn't you tell me? We could have figured something out. We could have—"

"Sira graced me with an extra day of freedom so I could see my daughter's first birthday. I had just enough time to do a few last things to help our Rosie girl. I put an enchantment on her to conceal her faedom. I didn't turn her human but disguised her a little bit. Then I planted a rose-bush in the forest outside our home. In my heart, I knew my daughter would eventually discover the Vale, and I had to give her a way. I made sure it wouldn't bloom for two and a half decades so that she could have a normal childhood. I wanted you to have a normal life, too, George." Anya's eyes fill with tears and her lip quivers. "It was the hardest thing I ever did, but I suppressed your memories. Changed them, so all thoughts of magic disappeared. Our adventures from the past were rewritten in your mind to fit a normal lifespan. Though with Castletree so weak, you seem to have begun aging as a human again."

Both Anya and George are near tears now. "You see, I may be selfish, George, but you're stubborn," she continues. "I couldn't have you following me or doing something even stupider, like trying to rescue me!" She gestures wildly, and somehow, all three of us laugh.

"You underestimated your husband," I tell the Queen. "Even without those memories, he spent every day searching for you."

"You fool," she whispers but somehow it sounds like "I love you."

"Here you've been all this time," George whispers.

"Here I've been. Sira's using my magic to power her portals to other worlds. She loves to visit me and gloat about her plans," Anya spits.

"Anya." I place my hand on the barrier. She places hers up against mine. "The weaker you get, the sicker Castletree becomes. It's killing George."

For the first time, her expression falters. Her voice is barely a whisper. "I can't leave."

"I know," I say.

She closes her eyes and leans her head up against the wall. "Tell me of her. Tell me of my girl before you go."

George's voice hitches. Tears pour down his face, but I see he's trying so hard to stay strong. "She looks just like you, Annie. Got your eyes."

"And your bravery," I add. "We princes failed you. Failed our realms. But if anyone can make it right, it's Rosalina."

"I thought so." Anya quickly brushes her tears away. Then she straightens her shoulders and stares at me with eyes that have seen a thousand wonders. "You were not worthy of my daughter, Keldarion. But maybe that's starting to change."

89

DAYTON

"We've taken control of the Sun Colosseum," Tilla says.

I stand beside the Spring warrior. She managed to raid the armory and has a long silver spear strapped to her back. Though it's nothing compared to the weapons of the Spring Realm, watching her today, I know she's just as deadly with it.

We're on the uppermost ring of the Sun Colosseum. Below, the legionnaires that rebelled against the Green Rule organize troops, treat the wounded, and find places in the Serenus Dusk Chambers for the civilians to sleep. There are enough supplies and food to last us for a while. My gaze turns outward to Hadria. The dusky afternoon light casts thick red waves over the stone buildings.

As much as I wanted to be alone with Rosalina right away, we both knew there was work to be done to secure the colosseum. Now, my mate has retired to the Dusk Chambers while I do a final check-in with Tilla.

"We don't have enough soldiers to take on the rest of the city," Tilla says. "Kairyn's forces have secured the outer walls and streets surrounding the arena."

"Not to mention their airships," I grit out. "I'm sure they're waiting for their master to return. No doubt that's where the Nightingale's slunk off to."

Was that Kairyn and Wrenley's—the Nightingale's—plan all along? To trick me into giving up my Blessing, so the two of them could rule Spring and Summer? To think I came so close to giving in, so close to falling for it, ignoring my own instincts. I never felt a connection to her, but I made myself believe it because of some stupid glowing light.

"We'll give them a fight. The people are inspired by you and your mate," Tilla says.

"She's incredible," I agree. Even if we didn't get the bow, Rosalina's presence and magic will be invaluable in the coming battle. We'll figure out a way to retrieve the bow later.

"Do you think Kairyn can find Ezryn in the desert?" Tilla asks.

"I don't know," I say. "But Ezryn will do anything to protect Delphia and Eleanor. He won't stop until they reach their goal."

"I hope beyond hope that he succeeds in bringing aid," Tilla says, tilting her face to the sun. "To see the Huntresses, now that would be a sight to behold."

Tension twists in my gut. Delphia really is our only hope. We may have won the battle today, but the war for Summer is just beginning. We'll need an army to take back this city. Kairyn only imprisoned half our legionnaires in the colosseum. The others are being held in Soltide Keep. There's no way to get to them.

Well, there may be one more hope. One I haven't even told Tilla about. If Farron and Kel succeed. If they rescue the Queen, would she come to the aid of Summer?

"Nothing more we can do tonight," Tilla says. "I'll keep an eye on things out here."

"What are you saying, Til?"

"I'm saying, Daytonales," she raises a knowing brow, "go get your girl."

PART FIVE
SUMMER'S DAWN

90

ROSALINA

Blissfully warm water embraces me. The marble bath sinks deep into the ground, stretching across half of the room. It's more like a tiny pool than a bathtub. Flickering candlelight casts a soft glow over the royal quarters in the Serenus Dusk Chambers attached to the colosseum. This is one of the few rooms not being used to house the citizens of Summer.

Fragrant rose petals float on the surface of the water, their sweet aroma mingling with the scent of jasmine-infused oils. I lean back against the edge of the bath, my gaze drifting lazily toward the bed, framed by gauzy curtains that sway gently in the breeze. Through the arched window, I can see Hadria, shining under the setting sun. From this high up in the Dusk Chambers, I feel as though I could touch the pink and orange clouds.

There hasn't been much relief these last few weeks, but tonight I can breathe. I try again to push away all my worries. I know Kairyn and Wrenley will return, and my heart aches not knowing how Ezryn, Kel, Cas, and Farron are. But I must have faith that we'll be together again.

I reach for a glass of wine resting on a nearby table and take a sip, letting the warmth spread through me.

Closing my eyes, I allow myself to simply be, to bask in the tranquility. The door opens and closes softly, and I don't need to look to know who's there. My bond rises like a sunrise beside my heart. Doubt clouded that bond for so long, but not anymore.

I crack my eyes open as Dayton walks across the chamber. It's like I'm seeing him for the first time, stomach flipping and butterflies fluttering. *I knew you belonged to me.*

"We first met in a bath," he says.

"I know."

Dayton drops his leather armor to the floor. There's not enough time to drink in the glorious sight of his body before he walks into the water. Candlelight glints off his broad shoulders. "This isn't quite as spectacular as Castletree's hot springs," he says.

I wade closer to him until we're only inches apart. "We'll remake it. After Kel and my father rescue my mother, she can help. Your rose will be healed and—"

He cups my face with one of his hands. "We'll do it, Blossom."

Warmth swells in my chest as I look up at him.

"When we first met, I asked if you knew how to beg," he says.

"I remember," I say. A flush that has nothing to do with the hot water spreads across my cheeks. His gaze doesn't drop to my naked form but remains solely fixated on my eyes.

"Now, I must beg something of you," he says, placing his other hand on my face. "Your forgiveness."

"My forgiveness? How very serious of you."

"Let me be serious, then. Just this once," he says, voice low. "Because I've never been so serious about anything as I am you."

"All right," I say gently.

"Forgive me for ever doubting. You told me we were mates long ago. You said you felt it, but I brushed it aside. I couldn't believe that loving me wouldn't ruin you. I think for a long time, I saw love as a cage that trapped everyone in it."

I place my hand over his. "Now, what do you believe?"

His lips tremble, and a single tear runs down his cheek. "Love is an endless sea, and in its depths, I find your strength."

Rising on my toes, I kiss the salty tear off his cheek. "You have my strength, and my lo—"

"I love you," he says quickly.

"W-what?"

"I wanted to tell you first." He smirks. "It sounded like you were ramping up to do that so—"

A laugh bursts from my chest. "You already told me you loved me."

"We were fighting," he says with a grin. "It didn't count."

I laugh and wrap my arms around his broad shoulders. "Well, I love you too, Day. Through all the tears, the fights, and the laughs."

He dips his head, lips parting against mine in a gentle kiss. Almost tentative, even as every inch of his body presses against mine. His fingers tangle in my hair and desire courses through my veins.

"Rosie."

"Day."

"I'm so happy you're my mate," he says, pulling away slightly, seeming content to just gaze at me. "If I haven't made that obvious."

"I can't wait until we tell Farron."

Dayton lightly touches the token of Autumn around his neck. "He's going to be so happy."

I kiss the skin above the bargain band around Dayton's arm. *We'll see you soon, Fare.*

Dayton strokes the back of my hair, keeping me pressed close. "I want you, Rosie," he says. "I want to make love to you as your mate."

I tilt my chin up to him. "I want that too," I say, though I'm unable to hide the nervousness in my voice.

"There's something wrong," he says. "Tell me."

I can't help the anxious flutter of my heart. "When Ezryn and I made love, when his bond was about to break, the power overwhelmed him . . ."

"Don't worry, Blossom. I'm not afraid anymore. You are the most wondrous woman in all the Vale. I will strive forever to be worthy of you. That means becoming the best version of myself, of accepting all of who I am. Accepting Summer's Blessing." He lifts me up, carrying me out of the water. "I'm ready to be High Prince and I've never been more ready for my princess. I intend to greet the sunset as a man with you in my arms."

91

ROSALINA

We fall to the bed as one, legs and arms tangled. It's so soft, sheets made of silk, gliding over my skin, a contrast to Dayton's calloused fingertips. His lips are gentle as a breeze.

"Rosalina." My name is a long exhale.

I straddle his hips and look down at him, admiring his beauty. Brushing the curtain of golden waves behind his ear, I caress his strong jaw and full lips, which curve into a smile at my touch. He lifts his face to my shoulder, lightly kissing his way up the tender skin of my neck, over my pointed ears, ending with a gentle kiss to my closed eyelids.

"Rosalina," he breathes again.

"Dayton." I stroke his muscles, knowing the strength that's coiled beneath. But he touches me like I'm a delicate piece of porcelain.

I've been with Dayton before, wild and frenzied, desperate and yearning, but never like this. This slow exploration. Like every brush of his fingers is him worshiping what's *his*.

I sigh deeply and lie fully over the top of him, feeling the hardness of his cock pressing against the soft curve of my stomach. But there's no urgency. I think the Prince of Summer would be content to lie together with me until the end of time.

"I can't believe you're here," he mumbles against me, "but more so, that you're mine."

"I'm yours," I whisper back, tasting the salty sweetness of his skin as my lips brush his shoulder.

"This ass. Did I tell you I love this ass yet?" His hands glide down my back to cup me, fingers kneading the soft flesh.

"Hey, you have a nice ass too," I say, giggling and grabbing his rock-hard muscles.

"Oh, I know." He grins.

"Cocky."

"Speaking of cocks, aren't you going to tell me that's nice too?"

A sly smile spreads across my face, and I slide off his body to lie beside him. I drag my hand down his chest to wrap my fingers around his large shaft, moaning at the sheer girth of it.

"You feel so good," I whisper and begin to stroke him up and down.

He groans deeply, then growls, "Bet I would feel even better in your mouth."

My core tightens, and I inhale a breathy moan. My other hand moves to cup his balls, feeling their weight in my palm, massaging them. "Would you like my mouth around your cock, my darling mate?"

He arches back into the pillow, then slides a hand between my legs. "Seems like you like that idea too."

His large hand cups my pussy, and I instinctively grind against his palm, feeling the delicious friction flutter through me.

"You're right." I slowly run my teeth over his neck, dragging my tongue down the valley of his chest while his hand is still between my legs. His finger teases my clit, making me moan. When I'm a mere breath away from his cock, inhaling his musk, he tangles his hands in my hair and stops me.

"Day?"

"I have a better idea." He grabs my hips and repositions me so I'm lying over his chest, my mouth right before his cock, and my pussy is . . . my pussy is on his lips.

"Sorry, love," he says, his fingers kneading the soft flesh of my ass. "Couldn't wait to taste you."

He licks my slick entrance before driving his tongue inside.

My whole body shudders with the sensation, and I grasp his muscular thighs. "I think you overestimate my ability to *think* when you're there," I gasp, "let alone do anything else."

He laughs, breaking away for a moment, kissing my inner thigh. "I have complete faith in you, Blossom."

Then he dives back inside me. "Oh, fuck," I moan, feeling his hot tongue teasing my sensitive clit. My head spins with pleasure, but I manage to keep my focus on the task at hand.

I take him into my mouth, my tongue swirling around the tip, then suck him deep, going as far as I can. His cock twitches in my mouth, and I know he's close to losing it too. He groans against my pussy and grabs my ass harder, pushing me into his mouth. Pleasure explodes inside me as he continues to lick, suckle, and nibble me.

"You taste so good, Day," I whisper, taking a moment to breathe before lapping at his length again.

"I could eat you forever."

Feeling his cock between my lips and his mouth between my legs has me on edge already. "I might—"

"Come, Blossom," he growls. "Remember my rule. Never just once."

I smile against his length, continuing to pleasure him as my inner walls tighten. His tongue is merciless, licking and sucking every inch of my sensitive flesh. I cry out, muffled by his cock in my mouth, trembling as pleasure crests through me.

He doesn't stop growling encouragements as I suck him hard, hollowing my cheeks. The vibrations of his voice send shivers through me. My pleasure soaks his lips.

"That's it, Baby, come in my mouth," he says. "That's it, that's it."

My body sings with euphoria, but it only makes me want more of him. I force myself not to gag as I take him deeper, deeper.

His fingers dig into my hips as I swirl my tongue around the head of his cock. I increase my pace, desperate to feel him come undone. His muscles tense. I glance back to see his chiseled jaw clenched, lips glistening, golden hair disheveled across the pillow.

"Gods, the mere sight of you," he groans. "Rosie, swallow my cum. Swallow it, Baby."

All I can do is blink, and then I'm drowning in the salty sweetness of his release, his seed flooding my mouth. He growls long and low, and I take it all.

Finally, I break away gasping, mouth still dripping. Dayton pulls me up, sealing our lips together. He kisses me hard.

"You taste amazing," I pant.

"Likewise, Rosie."

He brushes the hair out of my eyes, a soft smile on his face. "Pull me beneath your waves," he murmurs.

I press my lips to his again. "I want to drown in you."

He kisses me deeply then, and a tremor of delicious heat washes over us both. We know what's coming next. But again, Dayton seems in no rush. Only the first rays of sunset have started to wash over the room, painting it in vibrant red and casting shadows of rich violet. Sunbeams illuminate dusty sparkles, and I inhale the thick warm scent of sea, sand, and sunshine.

"I love you so much," I whisper.

He rolls us until I'm on my back, and sunlight beams behind him, silhouetting the Summer Prince in rays of gold.

"I will never stop loving you," Dayton whispers against me. "Not until my last breath."

A sudden terrible fear fills me for a moment, but he silences it with a devastating kiss. "I will mate you now, Rosalina."

My legs spread as he positions his cock, hard again, at my entrance, and then shoves himself inside with a deep male groan. A tiny whimper escapes my lips as my body adjusts to his size. The full width of him fills me completely with each inch that he slides deeper, deeper, deeper.

"More," I tremble, fingers clawing at his back. "I want all of you inside of me."

"Baby, can you take it?" he asks, voice raspy, his own pleasure rocking him.

"Yes," I say, thrusting my hips up. He sinks to the hilt.

Dayton's eyelids flutter and the muscles in his throat bob as he throws his head back. "Oh, Rosie."

I feel it too, this utter completeness. At last, I'm fulfilling the urge that has clawed at me ever since the first moment I laid eyes on the Summer Prince.

Dayton takes in a shuddering breath and looks as if he's almost nervous. I clasp my hands on each side of his perfect face.

"Your curse will break. Our love is that strong."

"I know. I believe in us, more than I believe in anything else."

It's a wicked sort of agony, the slow drag of his cock rubbing against my sensitive inner walls.

Through that pleasure, something uncoils within me, growing warmer and warmer next to my heart.

"Do you feel it?" I press a palm against his chest.

"Yes." His eyes shudder closed. "Surprised I'm not entirely made of flame."

"But you are," I gasp. "You are warmth and sunshine. My light in the darkest places."

It consumes me then, consumes us both. His lips press hard against mine, hands roaming over my body.

"I love you. I love you," he says, the sound of our bodies moving together filling the room. "Say you're mine."

"I'm yours," I think I say but the world has turned golden and hazy as he takes me like the tide sweeps the shore.

"Say it louder."

Everything within me splinters. "I'm yours," I cry out. "I'm yours."

Dayton's hand digs into the covers, the other weaving into my hair.

I press my lips to his cheeks, tasting salty tears. The Summer Prince is crying.

My body aches for release. I'm unable to comprehend anything beyond it. I surrender to our fire.

"I'm lost in your storm," I gasp against him. "I never want out."

A primal growl resounds in his chest. "This is it, Blossom. I'm going to claim you."

He moves, hands working their way over my body, my breasts, rubbing my clit as his cock thrusts powerfully into me.

My pleasure crests like a delirious ember, a burning beside my heart that can't be captured. The sun washes the whole world in light. "Dayton!" I cry out, unable to hold back the tidal wave of emotions.

He explodes, crying out my name like a prayer, spilling his seed deep inside.

Dayton collapses over me. His heart beats in time with mine, our breath mingling as we gasp for air.

I hold him close. "I'm yours," I whisper.

"And I'm yours," he pants, "forever."

We lie in the bed, unwilling to be parted from each other's bodies. He stays sheathed within me. Every so often, he tilts his head, placing a kiss to my ear, my jaw.

I am content to hold him close, to feel comfort in the press of his chest against mine, to weave my fingers through the thick strands of his hair.

Then, a fading light flickers over the bed, a golden beam playing across the muscles of his back, and it shimmers like starlight.

"Dayton," I whisper softly. "It's happening."

He lifts his head and gives a rueful smirk. "Is that what that tingly magical feeling inside of me is?"

I hold his gaze. This is how it's always been between Dayton and me, ever since our first meeting in the hot springs. Magical, tingly, explosive. For so long, we fought the threads of fate that bind us together. Our love has proven invincible. Nothing, not war nor lies nor our own fears or doubts can destroy it. This love has lived in me and given me strength, even when I didn't know what it was. "Yes, Dayton. Our love is magic."

"Stars, I know," he says and pulls me up until we're both sitting. Then, he kisses me.

I feel the powerful magic sparking off his lips, the change beginning within him. He breaks away with a smile on his face, bold and unafraid.

He leaves me, moving to stand at the edge of the bed, lean and powerful body rippling with golden light. He cries out, a burst of color appearing behind him, the silhouette of a wolf. The wolf howls once, then breaks apart into iridescent motes of daylight.

Dayton stands, shoulders broad, hair long, and face fiercer than I've ever seen it. Something tremors deep within me, something primal reacting to the power radiating off of him. The power of the unbridled High Prince of Summer.

His very skin seems to glow gold as he walks toward me and cups my face.

"Your curse is broken," I whisper.

"Because of you."

He gathers me into his arms and carries me onto the balcony, where the first stars are beginning to glimmer in the sky.

Dayton dips his head to my neck, inhaling. "My first act with no curse will be to take my mate under the stars."

"Dayton," I whisper dreamily, the full euphoria of it swelling inside me.

"I've never felt power like this before," he says. "And trust me, you haven't either."

Then he sheaths himself inside me. I tilt my head back, crying out to the stars above.

92

DAYTON

My mate in my arms, my cock deep inside her, the stars above me. How could a man want anything more? And how glorious it is to be a man beneath these stars and not at the whim of the moon.

Rosalina cries out, face in the crook of my neck, legs wrapped around my hips. I hold on to her ass, gripping tight to the soft flesh, as I move her up and down my length.

I took her slowly before. I wanted to feel every moment of us coming together. Now that our bond has awoken, something animalistic has taken over. A primal instinct to claim my mate. She's near feral right now, biting me, clawing at my back, shoving her wet pussy down hard on my cock.

It's so messy. I filled her to the brim with cum, and now I'm fucking it deep into her. I plan to fill her more, lots more, before this night is over.

"Dayton," Rosalina moans. My name on her lips is enough to have me completely lose all sense.

I clutch her tighter and walk us to the balcony railing, sitting her down on it. I slow my movements, and we both gaze down, watching our joining. My cock is covered in her slick arousal, veins throbbing with need. Using my thumb, I rub slow circles on her clit, intensifying her pleasure.

Rosalina's face scrunches, and she throws her head back, long brown curls catching in the wind. There's nothing behind her except open air, but I know she trusts me never to let her fall.

"You feel so good, Baby," I say, inching so slowly inside her. "The way you clench around my cock . . . not even the gods have known such pleasure."

Her laugh twinkles like the light of the stars, and she reaches forward to brush her fingers over my balls. A tingling sensation shudders through me, and a deep groan rumbles from my chest. I slam all the way into her.

"Oh," she gasps. "You liked that?"

"Mmm, I love anything you do to me," I murmur, bringing my mouth to her neck and sucking at the sensitive skin.

She cups my balls then with her hands, palming them and lightly scratching with her fingernails.

My groan deepens, and I thrust harder, my muscles tensing. I lean her further over the edge to gain better access to her chest and lower my mouth to her breasts. So fucking full and beautiful. I lap messily at them, my vision flashing with white as she squeezes tight.

Rosie's legs tighten around my hips as our movements become synchronized. I purse my lips around one of her bouncing breasts and suck deeply before taking a nipple between my teeth. I tug on it then let her breast fall free.

"Oh, Day, yes. I can't hold on much longer."

"Don't try, Baby, come around my cock. I'm not stopping."

"Day!"

She moans deep at my words, and I feel her inner muscles constrict. I capture her lips and slam deep into her. "Fucking yes, take my cock."

Her body trembles with the aftershocks of her orgasm, and I move to suck her other breast into my mouth. It's got to be fair. She clutches my face, breath heavy. "Don't stop," she gasps. "Don't ever stop."

"I don't intend to."

I lift her up and slide her off my cock, at which she gives a little whimper of protest. "Don't worry, Blossom, you'll be full again. Put your hands on the railing."

She turns around, back to me, glorious ass out. I brace my hands on her hips and sink back into her warmth, fucking her from behind. Rosie's fingers dig into the railing and her breath grows labored. She moans my name over and over, the sound drifting up to the stars.

I knot her long hair with my hands and force her head up, beautiful neck on full display. "What do you see before you?"

She makes small sounds of pleasure before finding her words. "The stars. Hadria. The sea."

I don't slow, fucking her harder as if to prove my point, using her hair like a bridle. "The Summer Realm. My realm. You know what?"

"What, High Prince?"

I lean over her, kissing her spine before drawing my lips up to her pointed ear. "Now, it's all yours. Because I'm yours. Everything I have, everything I am."

"Day," she breathes out in surrender, tilting her face so I can capture her lips in a slow kiss. "It's ours. Together. Always."

"Look upon our realm while being fucked like royalty." I straighten, repositioning one hand on her hip, the other reaching down to tug on her swaying breasts.

Her body trembles with another wave of pleasure, and I can feel her wetness coating my cock. "You're so freaking good at this," she breathes, her voice shaky with desire.

"I've dreamed of this for so long, Rosie. You have no idea how much I craved to be inside you. Think you can tear me away? No fucking way." I thrust deeper with each word before moving to a rapid pace, our bodies connecting with a slick, wet sound.

She looks so beautiful painted by the light of the stars and moon, an almost ethereal glow emitting from her body . . . and from mine. Is this our mate bond?

I move to massage her clit. Rosalina gives a broken moan, and I can sense she's close again. Her walls clench tighter, driving me closer and closer to the edge. This time, I'll finish with her.

My heart pounds in sync with her breath, the only other sound the distant crashing sea.

Rosalina arches her back, fingers digging into the railing for support. "Dayton, god, you're so deep."

I pause, my cock still buried within her tight, wet sheath. I turn her face, pulling her in for a searing kiss. "We're going to come together, Baby. Can you hold on a bit longer?"

She nods and bucks her hips under me, matching my rhythm, our bodies moving in perfect harmony. I watch her reflection in the glistening marble railing: her face contorted in pleasure, her features soft and ethereal as she gazes up at the night sky. For an instant, I find myself hypnotized by her beauty.

Then, I feel it. An unrelenting tension growing with each stroke. No more holding back.

"Rosie," I groan, my voice low with need. I slow my pace, drawing out the pleasure, my fingers still rubbing her clit, and I watch as she begins to succumb, her breaths ragged and shallow.

"Yes, Day," she pants, her eyes closed tight. "So close."

"Then come for me, love," I murmur. "Come, my beautiful mate."

Rosie's breath hitches as the waves of pleasure crash over her, her body convulsing. Quickly, I straighten her and draw her up against my chest. She turns her face toward me so I can see as her eyes roll back in her head, lost in the euphoria of her climax.

I cannot hold back any longer. "Rosie," I groan, my voice hoarse with need.

Her eyes flash open, meeting mine. So beautiful. I slam into her one final time, my cock jerking and twitching, and release deep within her. Rosie's fingers dig into my arms as she lets out a guttural cry, her body still convulsing in a fierce orgasm. The stars from the night sky seem to descend into my vision, the whole world lit up in sparkling lights.

Rosalina collapses in my arms, panting heavily as our bodies stay locked together.

The sound of the ocean crashing against the shore blends with our heavy breathing. I slide my hands over her slick skin, rubbing her still shaking thighs, her hips, her ass, drunk on the sight of her.

"I love you, Day."

"I love you." I lean down, pressing a tender kiss to the back of her neck, my heart swelling with the truth of it.

GROWING UP, I used to sneak my way down to the docks. Not the main docks of Hadria, but farther. I'd take my horse, Felix, and ride out of the city, over the hills, and to the smugglers' bay. It wasn't because I wanted to rebel against my parents, but because I loved to marvel at the stunning flags, the brilliant ships, and because the pirates had the best stories.

Maybe they knew I was a prince and humored me, or maybe I won them over with my jokes—which were hilarious even then. But I'd spend hours down there while they unloaded goods and sat around playing cards, and I soaked up their tales. They spoke of all their adventures, sailing over waves a hundred feet high, of smoky cannon fire, of siren songs. But there was one thing all these stories had in common, one thing these pirates searched for above all else.

Treasure.

"I'm going to find the biggest treasure in all the world," I'd proclaimed to Felix, riding back against a red-stained sky.

Now, many, many years later, I know I have the greatest treasure of all, wrapped in my arms.

Rosalina stirs, curling deeper into my chest. Silky moonlight illuminates her pale skin, and her dark hair falls in thick waves over the pillow. A thin sheet drapes over us, shielding against the nip of the sea breeze. She wears a fine nightdress of light cotton. Gently, I stroke my finger down the curve of her face.

"I will always love and protect you," I vow to my mate.

My mate. The feeling doesn't get old. Anticipation curls in my gut at the thought of telling the other princes. Kel and Ez might give me a hard time for taking so long to realize it, but I know they'll be as thrilled as I am to share a mate. I may have lost my own brothers, but I found brotherhood just as deep in the two of them.

My fingers drift to the maple leaf necklace. I'm most excited to tell Fare. Did he feel it already? Or is he too deep in the Below? Is this why it's always felt so magical between us because we had a mate destined to bind us together?

Something unsettling tingles at the back of my mind . . . the passion with which Caspian and Kel came together, how Farron had screamed at Rosalina that Caspian wasn't her mate . . .

Rosalina is the Queen's daughter, and mates with each of the High Princes. Surely, she is not destined to be with someone of the Below, as well.

I clutch her a little tighter. It doesn't matter. I will love and protect her through anything.

Warmth burns in my chest, and magic still tingles on my skin. My curse has ended. Gazing through the windows to the night sky fills me with hope.

I may not be a perfect man, but I understand now why I can't run from my problems or hide my troubles with drink and fake smiles. There are people worth fighting for, and I know I'd give my life to keep them safe.

The Enchantress's glowing image drifts into my mind. *I guess you decided I'm finally worthy of my mate, huh?* A laugh ripples up my chest. The funny thing is, I don't even care what the Enchantress thinks. *I decided I'm worthy of Rosalina, and that's what really matters.*

I'll spend the rest of my life proving it, I think, looking down at her.

Gently, I untangle from my mate and cross to the open balcony. The stars glitter in the sky, but Hadria gleams with its own sort of light. Candlelight flickering in the brick houses, moonlight making the sands shine white. In the distance, Soltide Keep gleams on a cliff above the sea, the illusion of Castletree behind it. That is where I belong.

The people of the Summer Realm have always been blessed with fierce leaders. Justus, my mother, Damocles, among the many other heroes of old. It is my turn to uphold their legacy. The thought used to make me want to disappear into the bottom of a wine bottle. Now, pride swells in my chest. Nothing will stop me from protecting what they worked for. I've fallen down and gotten up enough times now to know I can be the leader Hadria needs.

I deserve to see these stars as a man. I deserve to claim the title of High Prince of Summer.

I clasp my hands on the stone railing, feeling the tug of the wind through my hair.

"I will reclaim Hadria," I vow. "Sabine, Cenarius, Ovidius, Damocles, Decimus, and Delphia, I will make you proud. I promise to be a High Prince worthy of the Summer Realm."

93

ROSALINA

My dreams are sweet. There is no true image, no sounds, just an ethereal sense of contentment. A pastel haze encompasses my vision. My body is warm, safe. There's a sense of *rightness* in my chest. I want to stay here forever.

Time passes slowly as I float through my consciousness. Distantly, I notice I seem to be drifting somewhere. Down. Down. Down. The light turns to darkness, then to a spark of emerald green. But I'm not afraid. No, this also feels right. Like I'm getting close to—

"Keldarion," I whisper. The haze begins to form a silhouette. I would know the broadness of his shoulders, the shift in his stance, even in my dreams. "Kel!"

He turns to me, and a soft smile appears on his face as his features come more into focus. I float forward, my body not truly corporal yet.

"I've been looking for you," he murmurs. "I didn't think I'd be able to reach you in the labyrinth. But . . . it seems there's some strong magic here helping my own."

This isn't a dream anymore. This is the strength of our mate bond, connecting us from between the realms, the same way it did when he was in Winter, and I was in Spring. He's found me even when he's so far below the surface. My heart screams for him. My mate, my first mate.

I fly over to him, wrapping my arms around his neck. He grabs my waist and spins me. I laugh, giddy from the feel of him.

"Kiss me, Rose," he murmurs, and I do. Our lips touch, soft at first, savoring each other. I've missed the press of his mouth on mine, the steadiness in which he grips me, like he'll never let me go. Then, he changes, kissing me with the untamed wildness within him. A wildness I would traverse forever if I could.

I press my body tight to his, and he matches my intensity, fingers near bruising.

"Say we won't be apart much longer," I gasp between kisses.

"Not much longer. Soon, you'll be back in my arms for real, and I won't ever let you go."

My skin tingles. Right now, I'm able to touch him, but my hold on this place feels tenuous. "I'm so grateful to see you just for a moment. There's so much to tell you." I look around. Everything besides Kel is dark and hazy with that green glow. "Where is Papa? Is he all right?"

"Yes. We'll be making our way back home soon," he says.

"My mother?"

The gentlest of smiles appears on Kel's face. "That's why I was hoping I could bring you here. I wanted you to see her."

Kel takes my hand and leads me through the haze. Structures begin to form: giant crystals that gleam with a malevolence I can feel even across the realms. Between the crystals lies a cage with translucent green walls.

"They won't be able to see you," Kel whispers. "But I wanted you to see them."

My heart beats strong and steady in my chest as I step forward. The mist shifts, revealing two more figures: one out of the cage and one within.

Papa's sitting on the outside, leaning his head and palm against the transparent wall. Tears streak down his face as he stares at the figure inside.

A woman leans against him, her hand up to his. The barrier separates them from truly touching.

I know her. I know her from the photograph of us in front of the willow tree. I know her from stories Papa told and legends from the realms.

But more than that, I know her within. Her blood sings in my veins, sharing a thousand tales from a thousand years. I know her in a way that is so ingrained and visceral, it feels like I know her better than anyone else.

Her love was with us all this time. It was what brought me to the Vale.

It's what gave me the strength to pick up the Bow of Radiance. She is everything around us. She is everything within me.

My mother.

If I was more than a flit of mist, my legs would have given out. Instead, I drift over to my parents.

They stare at each other with a love that transcends all the ages of the world. Papa murmurs softly to her, and she laughs. Memories, I realize. They're reminiscing over memories.

"What's going on?" I murmur to Kel. "You're waiting until Caspian and Farron destroy the prison?"

Kel holds my gaze. I know that look. A look that says, "you're about to fall apart, but I'll hold you together." "Rose, it's not as simple as we thought."

"We didn't think it was simple, but we knew we would do it," I say, voice taking on a frantic note. "You have to get her out, Kel. No matter what, you have to get her out."

Kel reaches for me, hand shivering through my shoulder. My body's beginning to fade into incorporeality. "I wanted you to see your parents together."

No, no, no. Why is his voice so soft? Why couldn't I just see them together when she's freed? What is Kel saying?

"Rosalina."

I stiffen. The voice doesn't belong to Kel.

The woman in the cage is looking at me. She's very beautiful, but . . . tired. So tired.

I fall to the ground beside my father. He doesn't notice me. The haze starts to creep in, his figure obscured. The prison walls shift away, until only the woman sits before me. I know I'm visible only to her in this moment. "Mom?"

Her eyes crinkle, gorgeous lines like gold filament through cracked pottery appearing in the corners. "My brave girl. What a life you've lived!"

"You're coming home with us, Mom," I whisper. "I want to meet you for real."

"Oh, we've met before," she says. "We've met in the songs of Spring and in the tides of Summer. We've met with each harvest of Autumn, and through the storms of Winter. You'll find me there, dear one, whenever you need me."

"No." My voice hitches. "You have to come home."

"I'm there every time I close my eyes." A pained expression crosses her face. "You don't have long here. Rosalina, I . . ."

"What is it?" I try to grab her hand, but I don't have arms anymore. I'm fading away.

"I'm so sorry for everything. I have no right to ask you for anything—"

"Ask," I breathe.

She shifts forward, eyes wild with desperation. "You must protect Castletree. It is the heart of the Vale. My heart. Whatever happens, do not let it fall. Do you understand?"

"Yes, Mom." The words barely make it out.

"One more thing."

I need to hear what it is, but pieces of my essence are being torn away. I fight to stay here with her, with Kel and Papa.

My mother reaches out, and I feel her hand in mine like a tether. "You have a sister. I couldn't protect her. I wish I had a chance to get to know her. She doesn't deserve the life she's been given. Please, do what I could not. Save her. All I want is for her to have peace."

The shards of me shatter, erupting away. The mist bursts back in, forming shapes and figures once again: first the huge crystals, then the prison, then Papa, and Kel.

I am nothing but splinters of a person. Kel looks up at me as I drift away. *See you soon, darling,* he says in my mind.

See you soon, I say back.

Before there's nothing left, I fight for one last moment. "Papa," I whisper.

My father looks up at me, his blue-fire gaze holding onto mine.

Then I'm ripped away.

I wake up in my bed in Summer, gasping and gripping the sheets.

"Rosie?" Dayton's voice. He's standing on the balcony, dawn basking him in light as if the sun woke up just to grace his skin.

I can't catch my breath. My heart rams against my ribs.

"Rosie, what happened?" Dayton rushes over to the bed and puts his arms around me.

"I saw her . . . I saw my mother," I gasp.

But it's not her image I can't chase from my mind.

It's Papa's. His crystal-blue gaze.

I've seen that gaze before. Seen it angry, conniving, resentful. Seen it tired, desperate, sad. Seen it in tears because she was left with nothing.

While I grew up with my father.

"Dayton," I whisper. "Wrenley is my sister."

He leans back against the bedframe, eyes faraway. "The Nightingale. It can't be."

"I think she needs our help, Day."

He chokes out a laugh. "Only Rosalina O'Connell would want to help the assassin who tried to murder her! Not to mention seduce me."

"Come on." I poke his chest. "We've done weirder things."

He pulls me tight to him and kisses the top of my head. "As long as I get to do them with you."

I hold on to this moment. I will see Kel again, and my father. I don't know what's happening down Below, but I will not let my mother stay imprisoned.

And my sister . . .

What would our life have been like if we had the opportunity to grow up together? How alone she must have been all these years, raised by Sira in the dark. At least she had Caspian. He cares for her. Loves her, even.

Caspian's had the chance to know her in a way I never have. Despite working for Sira, I know Caspian's kind and funny and clever. If he loves Wrenley like a sister, there must be more to her than I know.

My mother believes she deserves peace. If I can give her that, I will. Even if she hates me. Even if she wants to kill me.

"We'll figure it out," I tell Dayton. "We always do."

94

EZRYN

I take cover behind the colossal sandstone pillars flanking Solonius's Spine, the bridge marking the boundary between the Ribs and the rest of Summer.

True to his word, the defector from Kairyn's army, Mozi, led us back to where he'd come from. The closer we got to Kairyn's camp, the less the storm raged. We emerged out of the swirling sands beaten, gritty, and weak, but alive.

The girls lean against a pillar, sharing a waterskin. We don't have many left. I tucked my last skins into their bags for them to find later. They'll need them, and I most likely won't.

Pillars guard the canyon before us, their surfaces etched with stories from epochs so old, only the Queen would remember them. A sense of awe strikes me as I run my hand over one of the carvings.

Before us stretches the bridge, a massive structure carved from the very bones of the desert itself. The weathered stone bears the weight of centuries; even the historians of Summer don't know who built it or why. Perhaps at one point in Summer's history, there was something in the Ribs worth traveling here for. Now the only greenery is bits of shrub growing between cracks in the stone.

The sun rises on the horizon, casting warm, golden light over the bridge.

A lone figure stands in the middle, dressed all in black, his cape snapping in the wind.

Kairyn's body is completely still, save for his arms, which jerk from left to right, up and down. *He's coaxing the winds*, I realize. I never mastered the art of the Spring storm; the only time I ever seemed to utilize such magic was when I was overpowered by it.

I don't know if I would say Kairyn has mastered it either; I felt the rage in his storm, the wildness with which his magic rioted the winds. How long has he been standing here?

At least he doesn't know I've arrived yet.

Across the canyon, on the other side of the bridge, is Kairyn's camp. Tents are set up and members of his army are stationed in neat rows. Five airships are docked at the back of the camp.

I intake a breath. All of this, to find me. If nothing else, I hope removing my brother and these troops from Hadria has given Rosie and Dayton an opening to win the games.

"Let me face him with you," Delphia says, stealing my focus from Kairyn. "You can't win by yourself."

Nori takes a glug of water. "His hammer is bigger than you are. If you look at the odds . . . They're not good."

I kneel down before the girls and take one of each of their hands. "This is my place. I could have walked a thousand paths, but they would all end here. I'm so glad I got to walk this path with both of you."

Delphia's bottom lip quivers. "We can help you—"

I smile. "You have."

All my life there's been a storm raging in my chest: the grief, the anger, the sadness, the shame. It's plagued every decision I've made my entire life. I thought I kept it at bay with blood, but instead, I fed it. Rosie tried to show me, but I was too afraid to listen.

Traveling with Delphia and Nori has showed me how much that storm devours those I care about. They've shown me that in its quiet eye, there is peace.

I take a deep breath to quell the gale in my mind.

There are a thousand reasons to run out on that bridge and attempt to kill my brother. A thousand reasons to flee into the desert.

But there are two good reasons to stand my ground.

I will give my life to protect the Princesses of Summer and Autumn. To give them time to escape. I am long past thoughts of redemption or justice; all I know is I don't want to be the slayer anymore. I will protect them, and in doing so, protect Rosalina the way I vowed I would.

I bring Delphie and Nori's hands to my lips and kiss their knuckles: a knight pledging allegiance to a princess. Then I stand and walk over to the next pillar, where Mozi hovers nervously. He keeps peering out at Kairyn and the rest of the army.

"Mozi." I put my hand on his shoulder. "I have been given more than my share of second chances. So, this one I extend to you. I will keep Kairyn occupied for as long as I possibly can. It will disrupt the magic he's using to create the sandstorm. You must take the princesses as far north as possible. Do not stop for anything."

"North?" Mozi gasps. "Back into the Ribs?"

I look up at the sky. "The Huntresses of Aura are always watching us. When you are clear of this place, call out for them. They will find you. Do not ask, but demand, that if they will not aid Hadria, then they must save a child of their blood. Tell them to fly the girls over the Briar to Copper-shire. They will be safe there."

Mozi nods, face twisted with emotion. Then he falls to one knee and places a hand over his breast. "I'll do anything you ask, Your Eminence. In my heart, you are the true High Prince of Spring."

A wave of sadness crests over me. Banished, I am no longer a Prince of Spring, but nor will I be the Prince of Blood. Not anymore. "You must make contact with the Huntresses before the storm begins again. And if it does . . . I have fallen."

"No, Ezryn!"

I turn around to see the girls. They rush forward and wrap their arms around my waist. I stagger, arms hovering awkwardly, before I embrace them back.

"You two are so strong and smart and brave. I've learned a great deal from traveling with you," I say softly.

"I don't want you to go," Delphia says.

"You will see your brothers again, I promise, and one day, you'll sit upon your thrones in the great halls of your keeps and remember how you braved the Ribs."

"But we failed," Nori says.

"You *lived*," I tell them. "As long as you live, the realms will have hope."

A sob chokes out of Delphia. "Don't die, okay, Ezryn?"

I look up at the sky. "I'm going to do my best." Then I nod to Mozi. He nudges the girls, and they pull away from me.

"Girls?"

"Yes?" Delphie turns back.

"If the storm begins again . . . Well, whenever you should see the Golden Rose, tell her . . . tell her not to be angry with me, all right? And tell her, thank you. For knowing me as I now know myself."

Delphia nods, then looks toward Kairyn. "Hey, Ez?"

"Hmm?"

"Don't be afraid to make a big move," she says and flashes me Dayton's signature grin.

"But do it logically," Nori adds.

I nod and offer them a genuine smile. They turn and follow Mozi into the desert. I watch until the three figures become silhouettes.

Now, there's nothing else left to do. I go and face my brother.

KAIRYN DOESN'T NOTICE me as I take my first steps onto the bridge; his helm is tilted skyward, and I know he's focusing everything on the sandstorm.

Against my better judgment, I cast a look over the side of the bridge. The canyon plummets down thousands of feet, so far that the bottom is hidden by darkness. I wonder if it goes all the way to the Below.

I know the moment Kairyn sees me because the world goes silent. The wind dies instantly. The sand stills. The desert doesn't even dare to breathe.

The morning light bathes Kairyn in a fiery halo. He stands rigid, his long shadow stretching before him. The token of the Queen hangs on a chain around his neck.

"Here we are, brother. Together at the end of the world." His voice booms over the expanse.

I say nothing.

"You know it has to be like this, don't you, brother? Alone in the darkness, you'd feel me, wouldn't you, as I feel you? A constant reminder that while one of us lives, the other must suffer." His words descend into a raspy growl. He touches the wooden token that hangs over his chest plate. A light flashes, materializing into a war hammer, one of the Queen's weapons: the Hammer of Hope.

496

"Even after I made you pay for your crimes, after I banished you, destroyed you in battle, you still continue to vex me!" Kairyn hauls the hammer over his shoulder, then brings it down, smashing a huge chunk of sandstone out of the railing. "You haunt my soldiers through the desert, disrupt my affairs, and steal the nobles I mean to make prisoner! Ever since we were children, I could never do anything well enough for you, could I? You always had to challenge me!" With another roar, he smashes the other side of the bridge.

I stay still, silent.

Kairyn stalks closer, light glinting off his hammer as he brings it down once again on the stone in front of him. "Is this what you wanted me to turn into, brother? Is this what you wanted to make me?"

My chest is heavy with grief at his words. "It's not too late, Kairyn. I'm not here to fight with you. I'm here to offer you a second chance. You don't have to side with Sira. We can fix this. Together."

A half-laugh, half-cry tears out of him. "How dare you speak to me of such notions? You failed me, just as you failed Mother. As you failed Father!"

I take in a deep breath. Feel the steadiness of my feet on the stone, the warmth of the sun on my skin. "I know I have, Kai. I am so sorry."

Kairyn staggers back, hammer crunching against the stone as it drags. "Stop. It's too late. I have nothing but what they give me."

"That's not true. You are a son of Spring, not of the Below. You have our people, our home. You have the beauty of the Vale and . . ." Unconsciously, I reach up and touch the ragged points of my ears. The storm that once swelled in my breast stays quiet. "And you have your brother's love."

Kairyn shakes his head back and forth. "There is no path to peace while both of us live. You couldn't kill me, yet you won't die!"

I close my eyes. So, this is how it will be. I only hope I can give Delphia and Nori enough time.

"Draw your blade," Kairyn says. "Draw it and let us see this through."

"I won't fight you."

"Then this will be the end of you, brother," Kairyn says sadly. "I will mourn you."

My brother attacks.

Kairyn charges at me, swinging his hammer with wild abandon. I dance away from his strikes. I do not draw my blade. I don't give in to the storm, nor do I fight it. With each frantic swing of my brother's hammer, I flow as the river flows, drift as the breeze drifts. I am the wings of the birds and the leap of the deer.

Kairyn roars, his grip too tight around the hammer. Each missed swing slams against the ancient stone, creating divots and cracks.

"Draw your blade!" Kairyn screams. "Fight me!"

I roll under another one of his rage-fueled swings. My mother's sword remains sheathed in its scabbard. I will not draw steel against Kairyn again.

"You're a coward." Great clouds of dust erupt from each of his heavy steps. "Why do you run but not flee? Take up steel, as a son of Spring should!"

But I am more than a son of Spring. I flick along the edges of the bridge, fast as one of Farron's flames. I dance backward to avoid a swing, my footwork honed from darting away from twin blades wielded by Dayton. I dash toward Kairyn, billowing past him and out of striking distance, as Kel always erupted upon a battlefield.

When Kairyn turns to face me, shoulders shaking with rage, fists clenched so tight around his hammer that the hilt seems close to snapping, I stand and face him as the Golden Rose stands and faces all the hurt of the world.

"What is this? A game?" Kairyn roars. "Either you or I die on this bridge. There is no other path for us!"

"Then I shall forge one," I say.

"Impossible!" Kairyn thrusts out his hand, and the hammer shimmers, disappearing into a ball of light that twinkles back into his necklace. With a roar, he lifts his hands to the sky. The desert grass that grows in the cracks of the bridge bursts forward, morphing into massive vines. They thump down on the bridge between us. The weight of one causes a chunk of bridge to fall away near my feet. I look down at the canyon yawning below.

"Free me of this torment and DIE!" The vines whip up like great cobras, snapping toward me. I keep my breath steady and my movements fluid, slipping through their grasp like water through a sieve. Every moment I spend here with Kairyn is another moment Delphia and Eleanor have to escape. That thought above all else keeps me centered here in this moment.

I do not need to kill my brother to protect them.

Peace fills me with the thought, even as the vines grasp for my limbs, desperately trying to entangle me. Kairyn screams as he whips his arms around, each movement making the vines more chaotic, more tangled.

Cracks spiderweb across the bridge's surface, and part of the railing crumbles away as a vine crashes into it. My feet barely touch the ground as I leap from the railing to the top of the vine to the railing on the other side.

Kairyn unleashes a roar of primal fury. With each passing second, his attacks grow more frenzied, more desperate. He hasn't hit me once, but once is all it would take to send me tumbling over the side and into the pit below. My heart beats strong and steady in my chest, but I don't know how much longer I can avoid him.

His movements are frantic, erratic. He'll do anything to get me in his grasp. But I know how these plants move. This was once my power; it lived inside of me for years.

I will not be caught in its turmoil again.

I dash behind Kairyn and take a single moment to catch my breath.

Don't be afraid to make a big move. But do it logically.

Jumping away just as a vine smashes down where I was, I sprint toward my brother. The bridge crumbles below my feet, stones falling away and revealing the abyss below.

Kairyn balks as I run straight toward him, but I slide to his left just before I reach him. His vine whips around to grab me. I dart up and circle him, the vine following me.

"Get out!" Kairyn screams. "Leave me alone!"

The vine tails right behind me as I roll to Kairyn's other side, then I'm up, jumping on the rail and propelling myself over my brother's head.

"Stop it! Stop running!" Kairyn screams.

"I'm not running," I say. "And I'm not fighting."

With a huge leap, I jump over Kairyn's head once more, then pull to a stop before him.

Kairyn gives a maniacal laugh. "So, that's it? You're giving up? You admit it finally. I am the strongest! I deserved Spring's Blessing all this time!"

The breath is ragged in my throat, my muscles ache. I hold steady.

"Then this is it," he laughs. "I'm not afraid. I'll be free. I'll be free when you're dead!"

But nothing happens. No vine comes to strike me down, no hammer emerges. My brother jerks his arms, but they don't move. His vines are twisted so tightly around him, his arms are pinned to his sides, his feet locked together.

Only his head can move. "What have you done? What have you done to me?"

"You have done this to yourself," I say.

"No," his voice cracks, almost boyish. "No. No, this isn't it. I have to kill you!"

"I'm sorry, brother. I cannot die today. Not while there are still those who need my protection."

"Ezryn!" he screams, my name echoing through the canyon. "Ezryn!"

I look down at my brother, thrashing helplessly in the cage of his own creation. Now, I draw my mother's blade and hold it to his neck.

"Do it," he growls. "Kill me. Take this misery from me. Rid me of it!"

My hand is steady as the steel fits perfectly beneath his helm. One push and I could cut clean through his neck.

I stare into the dark abyss of metal. The downturned feather brow melds away in my mind's eye. I can picture my little brother as he once was, can picture the man he could have been.

Could still be.

I made a vow to Rosalina. I promised I would return to her.

If I kill my brother and slay the last of my kin, I don't know what man would come back to her.

"Do it," my brother breathes. "Free me."

I move the blade slightly, just enough to slice through the chain around his neck. The token of Spring falls and I catch it midair. Without the Blessing, it is little more than a trinket to me, but at least this will keep the Hammer of Hope out of his hands. I tuck it safely into my pocket.

"You have the token and the hammer. Kill me and be done with this torment," Kairyn growls.

"I can't free you of your torment," I say softly. "Only you can do that."

With a cry, I bring my blade down. The tip of my sword digs into the cracks of the bridge. The stone beneath Kairyn gives way, crumbling into the abyss below. Kairyn falls, suspended in midair by his vines.

"Ezryn!" he screams. "You should have killed me! Ezryn! I *hate* you!"

I collapse to my knees as his cries echo through the canyon, suspended in the remnants of his own destruction.

A part of me wishes I could lie down here, in the remnants of mine.

But there are still those who would hunt Delphia and Eleanor.

I pick up the hilt of my mother's sword and walk into the sun toward my brother's army.

95

FARRON

I have been afraid many times in my life. So afraid, it felt as if the sun would never shine again through such darkness. Like when I hid in the alder tree as the goblins ravaged my home. Or when I looked into the eyes of the Enchantress and saw the worst parts of myself looking back at me. Or when I held my mother's dead body and realized that every challenge I would ever face, I would face without her guidance.

But standing before the pool is a different kind of fear entirely.

Green light flickers across my body from the giant diamond-shaped crystals that adorn the room. It's as if just being in their glow saps my body of will; I am small beneath their radiance. Their light seems to cut through my skin, leaving me a bare skeleton, my every weak thought, ripped apart and put on display.

In the middle of the stone chamber lies the reservoir: a large pool of ink-black water. Emerald stalagmites jut up from the ground, while deadly sharp stalactites jut down from the ceiling. Brilliant green energy flows from each crystal, surging through the ground toward the reservoir. When the lines of energy reach the pool, they drip into the water like liquid light, making the water appear oily and luminescent.

There's something lingering in the darkness. Something lying in wait.

Farron, Autumn-blood. Come—

"Have you finished?" Caspian's voice tears me from my thoughts.

I shake my head. "Yes. Everything is in place."

At the base of each of the huge crystals, I have planted mycelium from Nori's mushrooms. They'll need a spell to grow into the cracks in the stone and form a connection with each other. A connection powerful enough to siphon the energy from this place.

My spell will need to do more than bring them back to life though. I need to change their power. Instead of sucking the vitality from animals or plants, I need these mushrooms to suck magic.

"All right then!" Caspian claps his hands, the sound echoing through the chamber. "What are we waiting for? Bring this place crashing down."

My heart thunders in my chest. Have Kel and George found their way to the prison? *Are they even alive?*

I can show you, Farron, Autumn-blood.

I give my head another shake. We can't linger here. I have to do this now. "I need to say the spell."

"So, say it." Green light flickers off Caspian's features, making his handsome face sharp with shadows. His chest heaves with shallow breaths, and he can't stay still, pacing around the chamber as if he's a beast caught in a trap. *He refuses to look at the pool.*

When I don't reply, Caspian squints his eyes shut. "*Say it,* Farron."

Say the word, Farron, Autumn-blood. Let me help you.

My palms are sweaty, and I wipe them on my pants before kneeling down to the earth and placing my hands on the stone floor. I shouldn't be here. Every nerve in my body knows this place is wrong. But there's no choice.

I've rewritten the spell a thousand times in my head before landing on the words that felt ancient, connected to the oldest magic of the Vale. I am High Prince of Autumn. My mate bond has awakened and thrives in my heart. My curse is broken. If anyone can create a spell, it is I.

Besides, Caspian helped me with it. He knows this place better than anyone.

"Ancient whispers and shadows deep, hear our plea, let magic seep. Draw forth its essence, let it flow, where mystic forces ebb and grow." My voice is soft, coaxing the words to fulfill their duty.

"Louder," Caspian growls. "This has to work."

I clear my throat and speak with more strength: "Grown in the moon's ashes, a hidden vale, where enchantment thrives and spirits trail. Embrace the power, let it swell, in realms unseen, where the fae may dwell."

My words spark in the air, but there's no magic catching, no blaze of the spell finding its mark. My throat feels too dry.

I look up at the pool. Its presence is too great. There's too much sorrow . . .

Utter despair washes over me. How did we expect Kel to make it through the labyrinth? He'll be lying dead with George beside him, the Queen left to rot in her cage forever. Stars know where Ezryn is. Probably dead too, body already white bones now. An image flashes in my mind. Dayton on his back, blood draining into the sands of the arena, body ravaged by sword and arrow.

"Say the words, Farron," Caspian growls. "Keep going."

But why? I can see her, screaming my name. I can't protect her. Can't protect my mate. Shadows erupt from the ground, wrapping around Rosalina's arms, legs, body. Her eyes are wild as she searches for me.

There is no point for me to exist. No point left when everything we're doing will lead to—

"Say. The. Words." Caspian's in front of me, his purple gaze searing. Roughly, he grabs my shirt and puts his palm flat against my heart. "Whatever strength you have left in here, find it. Do not let him in, Farron. Guard your heart with everything you have. And say the damned words."

Stone against my palms. Green light over my skin. Caspian's hand on my heart. His touch tethers me back to this place.

"Slumber, oh magic, in silent rest. Your essence fades, yet still, it's blessed. Return to the depths, let the living see, and in your tranquil sleep, be free," I utter. My words need more power, more magic. *Find the strength within my heart.*

I turn my gaze inward, to that place I cannot see, but only feel. There's something within me, something precious and undiscovered . . .

A spark.

I gasp, then follow it further within myself. Tendrils of golden light. The bright crack of sun over the horizon, and the sparkle of a sea of stars both above and below. Something important has occurred.

Something worth fighting for.

"For magic knows no bounds, but journeys anew. A cycle unbound forever true," I say, a new cadence to my voice. My words echo over one another. Caspian gives a shaky smile, then clutches harder against my chest.

My fingers grip into the stone. "Your reign in this world now wanes. A peaceful sap as nature gains."

Silence haunts the chamber. Caspian and I look at each other, blinking. I stand, pulling him with me.

"Is it working?" he breathes.

The mushrooms stir, then straighten, their black domes growing in size. Dark tendrils of mycelium snake under the earth, crisscrossing the emerald rivers that flow into the pool.

The ground begins to shake, and I clutch Caspian closer to steady myself. Rocks fall from the ceiling, and the crystals tremble. Their glowing light flickers. I hold my breath.

With a deafening roar, the crystals shatter into a myriad of sparkling shards. They scatter across the floor, falling like poison rain. We duck down, sheltering our heads from the blows. A cacophony of screams fills the chamber, the sound of a woman crying over and over again.

The chamber falls into complete darkness.

"W-we did it," Caspian whispers. "We did it!"

But I can't respond. I can only stare into the darkness.

There's something coming out of the pool.

Someone.

"Welcome, Farron, Autumn-blood," the entity says, a choir of whispers and screams forged into one voice. "I have been looking forward to meeting you."

96

CASPIAN

I was born in the shadows. I am no stranger to the darkness.

But here, the shadows look back.

I will not break, I whisper in my mind. *I will not shatter. I will not—*

You will break. You will shatter. Then you will rise.

Even my thoughts are not safe. His voice courses through me, his whispers coming from within my mind. Though as much as I have longed to escape it, I know the truth.

He made me.

He *is* me.

I need something to break this paralyzing hold. I bite the inside of my cheek hard, drawing blood. The pain brings me back to myself. I stagger through the darkness, away from the pool.

Farron's spell worked; his mushrooms destroyed the magic within the crystals. I can only pray to the gods I don't believe in that the chain reaction we theorized worked, and that all the crystals connected to this magic have shattered as well.

But there's still magic in the pool. Enough Queen's essence within the reservoir to hold this connection to the worlds beyond. To where he lies in wait.

I must not give him what he seeks.

Finding my footing, I stand and stare into the darkness. "Hello, Father."

So jealous was Sira of Aurelia's ability to create life, she sought out powers from beyond our world. The Baron of the Green Flame answered. I don't know what one would call him. A god, a prophet, a phantom, a demon. He wears a cloak of ashes from the worlds he's ended. And if my mother succeeds, he'll be able to step through this gateway into our world and claim another.

Without the crystals, the chamber is pitch-black, except for a phantasmal glow radiating from the reservoir. My father floats atop the water. When I've been brought to him before, he appeared as a fae made giant, his hand twice the size of mine, his eyes like milky portals. I know there is another form, as well. One I have seen in my dreams: a calamity of green flame with the maws of a monstrous beast and gaping holes for eyes.

He takes the form of a fae of normal proportions now. His skin is bone white, waist-length hair, the pallid sheen of lichen adorning forgotten tombstones. His ears, longer than those of the fae of the Vale, taper to sharp points. Emerald-green clothing adorns his body, the draping and patterns unknown to me. A creature from a world away.

Ropes of green fire stretch out from his wrists and ankles. All the magic Sira siphoned from Aurelia has given this pool enough power to gift the Baron some corporality here, yet it's not strong enough to step through.

But that doesn't mean he can't still break me.

"I knew you would come back to me, son. The water speaks to me. I feel it in each ripple. I hear it in the tremor of your heart. You seek a gift. I will bestow one." His voice sounds like a thousand men speaking all around me, screams and cries lacing behind the authority in his words.

My knees buckle at the sound, but I hold myself upright. Gritting my teeth, I stare into his empty gaze. "I seek nothing from you."

"You seek everything."

His voice assaults me like a wind, and I scream, my own sound lost in the torrent. I dig my fingernails into my palms, feeling that bite of pain again to keep me here, keep me grounded.

"You have shattered my crystals, son. Did you think that would stop me?"

"I thought it might shut you up," I grit out.

"Every time you come before me and refuse to step into the pool, you break your mother's heart."

"Ah, so you don't know everything," I say, trying to affect an air of confidence. "My mother doesn't have a heart."

The Baron sighs, his breath creating a wind that blows back my hair. "Come, Caspian, my son. It is time. I will gift you everything. Every wish that has ever lain within your heart can come true. All you must do is join me in the pool. Step into the water. Accept your fate."

"No." This is what my mother has always wanted. The reason why my faedom has been a death sentence not only for me, but for all of the Vale. I know what happens when I step into that pool.

"I have seen it in the water," the Baron says. "It is your destiny."

"Fuck destiny." I turn away from him. I need to find Farron and get out of here. We've destroyed the crystals. It's up to Kel now.

Shoots of green flame erupt around me, caging me in on all sides. I stagger, searching for a way past.

"Caspian," the Baron says in a near sing-song voice, "you have come to me for a reason."

"Yes. To stop you." I turn in a circle, looking for a way through the flames. The only path leads back to him. Back to the pool.

"I can free you of her."

I snap my head to the Baron. "Free me from whom?"

"Your mother." His skull-white lips curl into a smile. "She haunts you. You feel the whip of her lash each time she looks at you. Though, there's someone else, isn't there, son? A girl."

"Silence," I growl.

"Sister," he hisses. "You worry for the one you've chosen as sister. Your mother will kill her, won't she? One day? You know this to be true. But you need not fear, son. Come. I shall show you all the paths of your life in which you can destroy your mother forever."

I take a shaky step toward him. "My mother brought you to this realm. She bore your child. Everything she does, she does for you, and you would have me destroy her?"

My father's milky gaze drifts over me. "I would have you, son. There are a great many wonders in this universe. Worlds upon worlds upon worlds. My own heart beats for another realm. But this one . . . oh, this one is so beautiful, isn't it? How sweet it will be to walk in its ashes. You must do this for me, son."

"No," I whisper.

He takes a step across the pool toward the edge. "Long have I searched for a vessel strong enough to bear my power. Sira was a mighty vessel for my heir, but you are the treasure. I will gift you power enough to make the very cosmos bend to your will. I will gift you this world, son. Take it for me. Sink your teeth into its skin. You will find one is not enough." He reaches out his hands. "There's so many of them, dangling across the universe like ripe fruit. One by one, I shall have them all."

I fall to my knees at the edge of the pool, my very skin feeling as if it wants to rip off and belong to him. "I do not wish for this power."

The Baron steps forward and bends down before me. His ghostly hand strokes my head then my cheek. His words are almost tender. "You do not get to choose. This path has been chosen for you. I have seen it and so shall you."

Fingers like claws dig into the back of my skull and drive my head down over the water. I scream and thrash against his pull, but I can't tear away.

The void looks at me, and I have to look back.

The pool erupts into images, each ripple a different path of the future and, in each one, I see the same: destruction. Horror. Power within power, unlike anything I've ever felt.

My eyes follow a particular ripple, larger and brighter than the rest. A ripple etched into the fabric of fate. I stand straight below the cosmos, a huge, white moon and glowing stars above me, dark clouds at my feet, and below, I see the Enchanted Vale. It looks like a battle map, one where I can move the pieces at will however I like.

The clouds part to reveal Castletree. It's different now, with bark of darkest black. Thorns wind around every branch, creating a keep of briars. My mother's body lies limp as a ragdoll, impaled by a thorn at the very peak of the tree. A proud display.

Something akin to joy flickers in my chest, but it's not joy exactly. It is too muted to be true happiness. It's more . . . satisfaction.

Someone walks out onto the balcony of Castletree, holding a bow of brilliant white light. My sister, Wrenley. Little Birdy, so beautiful—

Her eyes glow with a phantasmal green light. She smiles up at me in the clouds, then raises her bow in salute. Down below, standing at the base of Castletree, a massive army of skeletons writhing in green flame rattle their bones in cheer.

"You were born for this purpose," a voice says. A voice I love.

I turn to see Rosalina standing in the clouds beside me, looking down at the Vale. She's dressed in a gown of black, the fabric like thorns crawling up her body. A twisted crown of briars adorns her hair. There's an otherworldly beauty to her, one that catches in my throat.

"Princess," I whisper and reach for her.

She looks up, staring at me with eyes green as emeralds. "Why else are you here, Caspian? You were created to wield the Green Flame. This is your destiny, and I am your mate." A smile curves up her lips. "This is *our* destiny."

I take a step back. "No. I don't want this for you."

She looks back down at the Vale. "Your mother is dead. The High Princes have fallen. The Vale is ours, Caspian, and we shall rule it as we like. Everything you've ever dreamed of is within our grasp."

"Stop it, Rose. This isn't you," I whisper.

"All your life, you've wanted to rule under the sun. The Green Flame will cure you, Caspian. You'll have a real home. The whole Vale." Her voice grows in intensity, becoming excited, frantic even. "See these fae? They hated you. I will end them for you, my love. You'll finally have the respect you deserve. A place to belong."

I stagger backward, feet slipping on the edge. One more step, and I'll tumble from these clouds and fall to the Vale below.

Rosalina steps in front of me and holds out her hand. "You don't need to wait any longer, Caspian. I will be yours forever. Come with me. Our mate bond was written in the stars, as is your eternal dominion over this world."

I search her face, looking for any remnant of the Rosalina I know. The woman who gave up her freedom for her father. The woman who never let love leave her heart, even in the face of such abuse. The woman who believed there could be goodness in a villain.

"This isn't what you want, Flower," I whisper. "This isn't what I want."

Her lip curls into a sneer. "It doesn't matter what you want. You were born for this, and only this. You *are* the Green Flame!"

"No!" I scream and grab her shoulders. We tumble backward together, falling from the dark clouds. Wind rushes past us both, drops of water pelting my face—

I push myself up from the stone, reach around and snatch my father's wrist, tearing it from the back of my skull. My face is a breath away from the pool. I stagger backward from it, throwing the Baron away from me. He hisses.

"I am not your weapon," I say.

"You cannot escape your birthright," he snarls.

I find purchase on the stone floor and push myself to my feet. With all the hatred I can muster, I look up at him through my lashes and say,

"Something to learn about me, Father, is I love a little chaos. If I have to disrupt fate's plan, I'll do so gladly. After all," I purr, "what else are villains for?"

My father roars, a sound like the felling of a great tree, and floats back to the middle of the pool. "Fine. Pretend you can fight destiny. You'll come crawling to me before the end, Caspian, ember of the Green Flame. In the meantime, I'll set my sights elsewhere." He turns and looks toward the other side of the pool.

I follow his gaze. My stomach drops. "No."

Farron, eyes glowing green, steps toward the water.

97

EZRYN

I walk to the far side of the bridge. My brother's screams of anger have quieted. Now, there is only his army to deal with.

Though they call themselves the Green Rule, my brother's soldiers still wear the golden armor of the Queen's Army. They form ranks as I approach, drawing their spears before them. My blade is heavy in my hand. One hundred soldiers. One hundred lives. Did I take that many in Queen's Reach? What about during my journey across Summer, in pursuit of Rosalina?

This time, my thoughts are not clouded. I focus only on my one reason to wield my blade: Protect Delphia and Eleanor.

I'm nearly across the bridge when I feel a presence on either side of me. I look down.

Delphia struts to my right, swinging her twin blades. Nori shuffles on my left, holding two glowing pumpkins in each hand.

I stop and blink, not believing my eyes. "What are you two doing here?"

"I tried to stop them!" Mozi cries. He runs up beside us, breathless.

"When will you learn, we don't ever listen to what you have to say?" Delphia grins up at me.

"We waited until the masked man was dealt with," Nori says mildly. "You should be impressed with our patience."

I take a deep, steadying breath. It's too late to send them back. We step off the bridge onto the packed sand. The soldiers at the front of the ranks stare at all four of us. One steps forward.

"What have we got here?" He leans on his spear. "The Prince of Blood, the runaway princess, a defector, and a little girl."

"I'm older than Delphie," Nori mumbles under her breath, "and a princess too."

"What's your plan, Prince of Blood?" The soldier holds his arms out. "You going to slay all of us? I don't think so. Let me tell you how this is going to work. I'm going to cut all your throats, then free our Emperor."

A second member of the army shifts his stance, then says lowly, "They're little girls, sir. Emperor Kairyn gave orders to take them alive."

"I don't care," the first one snarls. "He'll want them dead after the defeat he just suffered. I'll take the glory for killing them myself!"

"Now, can we fight them?" Delphie growls, giving one of her blades a twirl.

"Not yet," I murmur. How easy it would be to walk over and take this man's head with a single swing. One hundred soldiers. I could do it—I could kill every single one of them if it meant keeping the girls safe. I could paint the sand with blood until it matched the red clay of the Ribs.

But I turn and look at Mozi. He steps forward, spear held protectively in front of us. "If you want them, you'll have to go through me."

The soldier laughs. "It will be my pleasure."

There may be one more Mozi in those ranks of soldiers. One more person who needs someone to look at them with forgiveness. One more person who needs a second chance.

Rosalina has given me that chance. Delphia and Eleanor have too.

And though I wouldn't admit it to myself, Keldarion had given me that chance, as well, to be his brother again, and I refused it.

I walk forward and sheathe my blade. The *ting* of Spring steel rings through the canyon. The soldier looks at me, confused, but I stare past him, holding the gazes of the men and women who once vowed their lives to Queen Aurelia.

"My name is Ezryn. I speak to you today not as a prince but as a man who has journeyed through the darkest of nights, who has been burdened with grief and despair." My voice booms out across the desert. "I know you all have walked this path, as well. You were once warriors of light. I beg you to find that spark once again."

The ranks are silent, not even the clink of spears or the shuffle of armor. "Even in this time of hopelessness, when you think yourselves abandoned and alone, hear me when I say, this is not true. There is hope if only we have the courage to find it. Queen Aurelia may never return, but that does not mean we give in to her enemies. You once swore vows to her because you believed in what she stood for. Unity. Balance, and, above all, love for our people, our realms, and ourselves. We must not let her memory fade into oblivion."

The sun burns my eyes, but I do not look away. I think of Rosalina, of how, no matter where she goes, her light shines on those around her. She is my hope. May she be theirs, as well. With all the conviction I bear in my heart, I continue: "Her daughter, the rightful heir to Castletree, needs you. She is our glimmer of hope. Though the storm may rage around us and within us, we can stand together and endure any tempest. I lost myself to the darkness, and the Golden Rose offered her forgiveness, as she will forgive you. Seek the sun as you once did and find your redemption." My voice radiates out, strong and sure. "I ask you now, warriors of light, who among you will remember the vow you once made? Who will stand with the Queen? Who will return to the light?"

Silence yawns back at me from across the ranks. My heart beats painfully against my chest.

"Aye," a voice calls from the back. A soldier breaks formation and walks forward, her spear pointed down. "I will stand with the new Queen."

She strides past her comrades and stands beside us. I nod at her, and she takes position behind Mozi.

The first soldier who threatened us tilts his head back and laughs. "More flesh for the vultures!"

Then another voice calls out, "I'll stand with the Queen." A different soldier breaks formation and comes to our side.

"Aye, me too!"

"Aye!"

"I remember my vow."

"As do I!"

I fight the astonished smile on my face as soldier after soldier leaves their lines to join us. Delphia gives a wicked grin and winks up at me. More and more tear away from the army until we are flanked on either side by soldiers.

I look around; the renewed Queen's Army has formed ranks around us. Now, only twenty of the Green Rule stand before us, faces a mask of shocked anger.

The first soldier spits onto the ground. "The Green Rule has been promised dominion over the Vale. We will not be cowed by weaklings who would pursue a false ideal of salvation!"

"The Green Rule may promise you dominion over the Vale, but it will be the dominion of a wasteland," I say. "They will take everything that is good and beautiful and turn it to ash. We are offering you a second chance. I urge you to take it."

He grits his teeth. "I'm going to fucking kill each and every one of you!"

Delphia nudges my arm. "*Now* can we fight?"

"I've got this," Nori says and steps forward. Just as I reach to pull her away, she draws back her arm and chucks her pumpkins, one after another. They fall among the remaining members of the Green Rule, murky, brownish-green sludge exploding over them.

"What is that?" Delphia asks.

"A substance I created from something I found in the harpy nest." A thin smile spreads across Nori's face. "Let's just say they're going to be very popular with the harpies."

I give the soldier a sympathetic shrug. "I'd run as far away from here as fast as you can, if I were you."

The soldier looks at his body, covered in the brownish-green muck, then turns to his comrades. "Retreat!" The Green Rule takes off, sprinting away from the bridge.

I ruffle Nori's hair, then look around, staring at the ranks. Eighty soldiers, sworn in renewal to the Queen. One hundred and one warriors I didn't have to kill.

I can't see my brother, dangling below the bridge, but one way or another, he'll get out of there. This isn't the end. He still has my Blessing, and I will have to face him again. But I can do it without losing who I am. Without losing the man Rosalina fell in love with.

I raise my mother's blade into the air. "For the Queen!"

"For the Queen!" my new soldiers echo. The sound of their spears rattles through the desert.

I turn to lead them back to Hadria when something drifts from the sky. I lean down and pick it up, holding it to the light.

It's a large white feather.

98

FARRON

Coppershire is beautiful at dusk. I walk through the grand living quarters of Keep Oakheart. Has it ever looked so lovely, drenched in dying sunlight? A warmth fills my chest, an almost drunken sense of peace.

My father sits on the couch, laughing with the twins. They wave to me as I walk past. Nori lounges in a chair nearby, legs stretched over the armrest as she flips through a book. She glances up at me as I pass and graces me with one of her rare smiles.

My family. My beautiful family that has stood by me throughout fire and ash.

The glass doors to the balcony are open, letting in the warm Autumn breeze. It smells of a rich harvest, my realm bountiful and prosperous. Kel and Ezryn lean on the wall beside the open doors, deep in conversation. Kel looks resplendent in the brilliant blue robes of Winter, his brow adorned with a sapphire circlet. Ezryn wears armor of starlight silver, his helm shining in the fading light. Both of them nod their heads toward me. My chest thrums with the strength of our brotherhood.

Two figures walk in from the balcony, their laughter a joyous sound. Dayton has his arm around Rosalina's shoulders, and she places a hand on his chest. When they see me, their eyes crinkle and smiles break across their faces. My heart swells. They are both so beautiful, backlit by the sun.

Rosalina strokes a hand along my arm as I walk past her onto the balcony. I stride to the railing and look out at the city. My citizens are busy in the streets, pulling carts of Autumn's bounty and selling hand-crafted wares. Each one of them is under my protection. They are my responsibility to keep safe.

"Is this not everything you've ever wanted?" a familiar voice asks.

I turn to see my mother standing beside me. Princess Niamh looks as elegant as ever, dressed in shining bronze armor with a golden thread woven through her braid. "Mother."

She takes my hand and kisses it, her smile so warm. "Your family safe. Your friends happy. Your realm thriving. You, surrounded by those you love. Is this what you want?"

"Of course it is." I run a hand along her cheek. "How are you here?"

"I came to show you the threads of destiny, clove." She puts a hand on my back and guides me to look into the living quarters. Everyone I love is in there.

"What would you do to protect those you love?" my mother breathes.

"Anything."

She stares at me. "What would you give?"

"Everything."

She smiles, then lurches backward. Her skin starts to turn ashen, crumbling away like dust to reveal bone beneath. Dark circles turn her eyes to pits. She looks down at a hole in her armor, revealing a wound in her stomach, a gaping thing that drips blood all over the ground. "Will you stop what happened to me from happening to them?"

"Mother!" I cry, then turn to look into the living quarters.

They're gone . . . replaced with a shadowy, ashen mockery of what had been my home. "Rosie!" I scream, running inside. "Father!"

It looks as if a fire has ripped through the keep, turning the furniture to piles of dust. The couch where my father sat with Billy and Dom . . . Now, there are three smiling skeletons. I fall to my knees, throwing up a plume of ash, and crawl over to them. "No! No, not my brothers!"

On the couch where Nori lounged, a skeleton has its legs up on the armrest, the burned pages of a book catching in its ribs. A guttural cry escapes me, and I spin.

Two skeletons lean against the wall near the balcony, one in tattered robes that may have once been blue, the other in charred armor. The bottom of the helm is seared off, revealing a jaw hanging on only by one hinge.

My heart feels like it will rip out of my chest. "Rosie. Day."

There, by the doorway to the balcony, are two skeletons clutched in an embrace, their mouths agape in a forever scream.

Numbness takes over my body. I waver on my knees, feeling as if I may black out. Hoping against all hope I will.

My mother's voice cuts through the shock: "I can give you the power to save them. To keep them with you forever."

Slowly, I look up. But it's not my mother standing above me. It's a man. He looks almost-fae, but his ears are too long, a sense of strangeness to his features. Long, pale white hair falls to his hips, but he has a kind smile. My mother's smile, I think distantly.

"Who are you?" I ask, voice weak.

"A friend," the man says. "I want to help you."

"How can I trust you?"

He kneels down and takes my head in his hands. His touch is the only thing keeping me upright, my whole body dizzy and numb.

"What would you do to save them?" he asks.

"Anything."

"What would you give?"

I meet his milky-white gaze and intake a sharp breath. My heart pounds a strong rhythm within my ribs. "Everything."

He stands. There's something cunning in his gaze, a knowing I can't help but admire. "Then trust in that."

He steps back, and I reach for him. "Wait—"

A smile crosses his clever mouth. He keeps walking backward. "Anything! Everything! That's it, Farron, Autumn-blood!"

My vision blurs with each of his steps, the ashen remains of Keep Oakheart drifting away to pure darkness. Suddenly, the only thing that remains is a pool glowing with green light as if lit from the depths itself and . . . and him.

The man floats above the water, arms outstretched to me. "Step into the pool, Farron, Autumn-blood. I shall give you the power you seek."

I blink. The water is so close, I can feel its pull like the moon to the tides. "And what will I give in return?"

The man smiles. "Anything. Everything."

Shakily, I get to my feet and stare into the deepness of the pool. The power to save them . . .

My mother didn't need to die. I don't need to live in fear every day that someone will take Dayton or Rosalina from me. I could keep them safe forever . . .

"Farron!" Someone screams my name.

The man above the water looks past me, face turning into a sneer. "Come into the water now, Farron, Autumn-blood."

"Farron," the other voice says again. "Listen to me. You are not alone."

"The water knows," the floating man says.

I tilt forward, peering into its depths. He's right. The water does know. Within are the answers I seek.

Fate decided by one step: either back to the voice, or forward into the pool.

"Farron, I'm right here with you," the voice says. "You can fight this."

He's right. I must fight this. Must fight death.

I know the step I must take to decide my fate.

99

KELDARION

I sit with my arms draped over my knees, head hanging low. How long has it been since we arrived in this chamber? Hours? Minutes? I guard the entrance, though there's been no sound or sign of anyone else. Why should they have patrols? No one could make it to the heart of the labyrinth.

No one without a tie connecting them to the Queen.

George and Anya whisper to each other, savoring what little time they have remaining. Was it a cruel thing to call Rosalina here, knowing we cannot take Anya home with us? Perhaps. But if this is her last chance to see her mother, I know she would want it.

Pain grips my heart. I've been away from my mate too long. Never again, I vow to myself. Once I have her back in my arms, I won't let her go.

And that means I must return to the surface. I touch the small seed Caspian gave us that will create a temporary portal back to Castletree. Hating myself for having to do so, I stand and walk over to George. "This prison could break any minute. If Anya won't come back with us, we shouldn't be here when it happens. It will only put us at risk."

"He's right. You should go now," Anya says.

George looks between the two of us. "N-no, not yet. There's still time..."

She smiles at her husband. "The sight of you has given my heart hope it has not had in years." She flicks her gaze up at me. "Both of you."

I bow low. "I will find a way to break our bargains. I swear it."

"We can't just leave," George exclaims. "There's still time—"

A sharp, piercing sound shatters through the chamber. There's the high-pitched clang of metal meeting metal, followed by an explosive pop that sends me barreling forward, knocking George to the ground and covering his body with mine.

The giant green crystals explode. Shards scatter through the air. A shockwave tremors through the ground.

Pieces of crystal skitter over my body, some embedding in my skin like needles. Then a haunting silence fills the chamber, the only sound the soft tinkle of the final pieces of crystal falling to the ground. I blink rapidly. The chamber is so dark, the green glow gone.

The only light comes from . . .

The Queen.

She stands in the middle of the room, radiating like she was born a part of the night sky.

They did it. Caspian and Farron fucking did it.

"Annie?" George struggles to his feet, pushing me off him. He blinks at his wife. "Annie!"

"George."

He runs to her, engulfing her in his arms. She curls into him. It's a strange thing; the Queen always seemed like an immense, otherworldly entity in my mind, but she appears small in George's embrace.

He kisses her, a man kept in darkness who has finally found the light. Their love emanates all around. Sparks fly from Anya, a tiny star shower illuminating even the darkest pit of the Below.

Every nerve in my body is alight. An ice dagger appears in both my hands. "George, I'm so sorry. We have to go now, or it will be too late."

George pulls away from Anya, frantically pushing her hair back from her face. "I can't. I won't. If you're not coming with us, then I'm not going either. I'll stay with you." He turns to me. "Kel, you're a good man. I trust you and after our time together, I love you as a son. Take care of our daughter. Tell her I love her—"

Anya smacks George on the side of his head. "Don't be a fool! You're not staying here. Go. Sira will have felt this destruction across every corner of the Below, and I'll be the first thing she secures. Leave now, while you still have the chance!"

"There is nothing that can tear me away from your side again," he says.

I hop from foot to foot, swinging my daggers in my hands. "George, come on."

"You're going," Anya snarls.

"I'm not!"

I feel it before I see it. A creeping, slithering sensation at my back. I whip around and swing my ice dagger. A ghastly cry erupts out as it connects; the shine of my dagger illuminates a twisting creature, a shadowy wraith with hollow eyes and a gaping mouth.

"We're not alone!" I call. That didn't take long. Sira's already sent her servants.

"Run, George!" Anya pushes on his chest.

Another shiver trembles at my left side, and I spin, dagger flying. Another wraith cries out, crumbling beneath my blade. How many are there? I can barely see. This whole place could be crawling with them.

He grabs her tight to him, pinning her arms to her sides. "I'm staying with you. Nothing can change my mind."

"We have another daughter!" Anya screams.

George lets her go. Staggers back. Quickly, I run and skid along the floor, dragging my daggers through a wraith hovering at George's back. My mind can only concentrate on detecting the shivers and the slight bits of movements in Anya's light, indicating a wraith. But did she say . . . another daughter?

Rosalina has a sister?

"What . . . what do you mean?" George whispers

Anya's chest heaves. She looks down at her arms, glowing with light, then shoves her hand to the left. A huge beam of light illuminates the quadrant. Three shadowy wraiths screech and wither. But more erupt up from the ground, taking their place. "I was pregnant," she growls, "when Sira took me to the Below. I didn't know! I didn't know, George!"

Another cluster of wraiths spin into being. My daggers cut one, two, three, but a fourth emerges at my side. I don't have time to cut it down before it wraps two shadowy tendrils around my body. I gasp, everything in me goes ice cold. A sense of hopelessness washes over me, every happy memory drained from my mind.

Anya cries out and a javelin of light shoots forward, stabbing through the monster. I collapse to the ground, freed, clutching my chest. She turns back to George. "I had to birth the baby in this prison. And then . . . and then Sira invoked the bargain again."

I try to make sense of it as I stagger back up to my feet, daggers at the ready. She once again loved someone more than George: a mother's love for her second child.

"She took the baby," Anya breathes. "I had nothing left to trade. Our second daughter belongs to her now."

George stumbles back again, eyes unblinking.

"I couldn't tell you before," she whispers. "I couldn't break your heart again."

Instinctual terror cuts through me as I look around. It doesn't matter how many of these wraiths I destroy. More and more sprout from the ground, an endless wave of horror. "George, it's now or never."

"This is my fate, love," Anya breathes. "But you can still save her. Find a way to save our daughter. I named her for the birds we used to love. Wrenley. Isn't that beautiful?"

George closes his eyes, a look of pure agony on his face. He collapses to his knees. "I can't—"

"You will. The longer you stay in the Vale, the more your memories will return. Treasure them, George." The Queen of the Vale kisses her mortal husband and steps back. She closes her eyes and raises her hands slowly into the air. Huge, golden briars erupt from the ground. They wrap around George's waist, then tangle up my legs and chest.

The Queen looks at me, and her eyes flash with power. "Keldarion, you are the Protector of the Realms. Our people are in your hands now. Help Rosalina lead. Together, do better than I did."

Then she turns to George. Her face softens, looking . . . human. "Goodbye, love. Protect our daughters."

The last thing I see are the wraiths leaping upon her, swallowing her up in their darkness, before her briars whip us into the earth and up toward the surface.

100

ROSALINA

I am wrapped in Dayton's arms, savoring the softness of the bed and the morning light drifting through the curtains, when a violent rumble shakes our room.

The whole palace trembles: a vase tumbles off the vanity and a painting falls to the ground. Dayton braces his body over mine.

"An earthquake?" I cry.

He stands, pulling me with him. I nearly fall over, my feet unable to find purchase amid the shaking. He guides me to the balcony.

"Rosie," he whispers. "Look."

Dark clouds rumble across the horizon.

No. Not clouds.

Shadows.

Like a storm rolling in from the sea, mass shadows cover the sky and drench the ground in darkness. Sitting atop the calamity of darkness is a figure, hands held high.

My throat tightens and a cold sweat breaks across my brow despite the heat. I know those eyes even from such a distance.

Sira, Queen of the Below, has come to the surface.

"It can't be," Dayton says. "Sira has never dared an outright attack."

"Maybe she just wants to talk," I murmur.

But we both know what this means. If Sira has come to the surface, it's because she's angry.

Very angry.

We did this, I realize. Whatever Caspian, Kel, Farron, and Papa did Below has enraged her.

If she chooses to attack, the blood of Hadria's citizens is on our hands.

A blustering wind blows back my hair, and I curl against Dayton's chest. He holds me tight, his mouth a firm line, eyes filled with rage as he glares into the clouds.

The shadows roll straight over the heart of Hadria, then stop. They undulate like thousands of snakes one over another. Sira looks to the colosseum. Looks to us.

"Citizens of the esteemed city of Hadria," she cries, her voice amplified to sound like the crack of thunder. "I am Sira, Queen of the Below and protector of the savants who long have rejected the tyranny of your nobility. An act of aggression has been waged upon the Below, and I must return it in kind. Hadria has been claimed by an Emperor of my choosing; the violent attacks against Cryptgarden and the soldiers of Hadria prove that a heavier hand is needed to restore order."

Screams erupt from the streets around the colosseum. A shiver courses up my spine as I take in her words.

"She says it like we've been oppressing her, and not as if her minions took over Spring and Summer," Dayton snarls. "Fuck this. I need to get to her and—"

"Wait." I grab his arm. "You challenge her right now and you're dead. You may have broken your curse, but she's been amassing her power for decades. Our priority must be the people of Hadria."

Dayton nods, but I can feel the tension in his chest, the rage building within it.

Or maybe that's my own rage. I stare up at her. This so-called *Queen* stole my mother and tore my family apart. Now, she's threatening the home of my mate.

I may not have shadow magic, but I do have something she doesn't.

The blood of a Queen.

Sira's voice echoes out again, each word a rumble of thunder: "In repentance for the wrong that has been committed against me, I hereby claim Hadria as my own. Citizens, you and your families will be safe," her shadows ripple, "as long as you swear fealty to the Below, and me as your Queen. Those who choose to maintain their misguided loyalty to Aurelia's dog, who you refer to as the High Prince of Summer, will suffer the same fate as the noble family of Summer." Lightning flashes behind her. "Complete and utter annihilation."

"You fucking tyrant!" Dayton screams. "Get out of my fucking city!"

She can't hear him. But she might be able to hear me.

I whisper to the wind, willing it to drift up to her. A promise. A vow. A covenant that I will see through to the end. *We will not kneel in the shadows. We will rule again from a throne among the stars.*

Sira snaps her head, eyes searching. I pull Dayton from the balcony and back inside, keeping an eye on the floating Queen through the window.

"If you will not kneel," she snarls, "then you will die."

Sira yanks upon her shadows as if they were a steed, and they turn, starting to roll back away from the city. "I will return at dawn to accept your fealty."

I take in a deep breath, knees buckling. She's leaving. We have time to figure this out, time to—

A darkness falls over the colosseum. Dayton and I look up through the window, Sira's shadow clouds are straight above us. I can't see her anymore, but her voice is louder than ever: "One last thing before I go. I cannot suffer the rebels who threaten the safety of those in Hadria to live. Let them be an example for those who think of rejecting my generosity." She sighs, and it's as if the city takes a breath. "Your precious colosseum and the lives of the rebels will be the balm that soothes my broken heart."

"What?" Dayton cries. "What does she—"

Before he can finish his words, a torrent of shadows descends from her cloud and flashes of emerald flame dot the arena.

A bloodcurdling scream erupts from the floor below us.

"Feast, my darlings," Sira's voice booms, "but only on the rebels in the colosseum. We wouldn't want to hurt one of my new loyal citizens."

With horror, I watch as her cloud carries her away from the city, but it's so much smaller now, one shadow after another pouring down into the arena. Skeletons, bodies imbued with emerald fire, manifest within the shadows, spreading across the sacred sands.

Another massive rumble shakes the building, and Dayton grabs me.

A sheet of blackness covers the window, its movements frantic, desperate. The glass cracks, and darkness seeps through the fractures. I scream and scramble away.

"We've got to get out of here," Dayton cries, quickly donning his dual blades and grabbing my hand.

He pulls me out of the room and into the hallway. Chunks of rock shatter on the ground, and pieces of the floor erupt up in plumes of dust and rock.

"The colosseum," I gasp. "They're destroying it."

101

ROSALINA

ayton's hand grips mine tightly, pulling me along as we navigate the labyrinthine corridors of the apartments attached to the colosseum. My heart pounds in my chest as the ground trembles beneath us. Dust and debris fill the air, choking my lungs as we push forward.

"Those fucking shadows are going to bring this whole place to the ground," Dayton snarls. "We've got to get out of here."

Screams of terror puncture the air. I chance a look out the window to see pillars falling into the arena. Gladiators we fought and lived among scatter across the sands. Skeletons cloaked in green flame attack from all sides, swarming the fighting ring and the stands. "We can't leave them."

"I won't risk you."

I touch his arm. "We're gladiators, Day. There's a fight on your sacred sands. We can't lose."

Dayton looks at me, his face etched with determination. Despite the chaos, there's a sense of calm in his eyes, a quiet strength that gives me hope despite everything else. He nods.

I don't wait another moment. With a cry, I reach down through the ancient stone. The cracks in the foundation made by the shadows help my briars find purchase. They shoot up, wrapping around me and Dayton, then propel us to the sands.

We move as one; Dayton swings his trident and I bring forth a torrent of dagger-sharp thorns. The maple leaf token glimmers on his neck. Within a minute of landing in the arena, we've brought down ten of the flaming skeletons.

But like the Green Flame goblins, these ones keep standing up.

"Nice of you to join the party," Tilla grunts, fighting over to us.

"We can't kill these things," Dayton says, blocking a skeleton's strike with his trident. "We've got to get the rebels out of here."

"How?" Tilla cries. "Even if we get past these skellies, those shadow freaks are blocking all the exits."

Breath comes ragged from my throat as I raise up a cluster of thorns to block the assault of three skeletons. I could use my briars to transport a few people out, but not everyone. At least, not quickly enough.

A death cry rings out as another gladiator falls, his body shriveling amid the flames. We have to do something *fast*.

My thoughts are cut off by the crackling scream of a giant skeleton as it lunges toward Dayton, jagged sword drawn over its head. Thorns coil around my arms like serpents ready to strike. With a roar of defiance, I launch myself into the giant skeleton's path, my briars lashing out with deadly precision.

My thorns instantly shrivel up as the skeleton's body flares with green flame. It turns its attention to me, and with a bone-rattling roar, strikes.

I'm yanked backward, just out of the blade's reach. Looking down, I see dark purple vines wrapped around my waist.

My breath catches in my throat as I look behind me.

Standing there, arms outstretched, a tumble of briars before him, is Caspian.

He gulps in air, eyes wild and dark. He looks . . . unsettled.

"Cas," I breathe. It's as if my limbs are not my own. I stumble toward him, the rest of the arena fading away.

"Can't keep yourself out of trouble, can you, Princess?" He smirks, a little of the normal Caspian coming back to him.

"You're one to talk." A fire radiates in my chest as someone steps out from behind Cas.

Tears spring to my eyes. "Farron!"

I rush to him, forgetting about the skeletons, the shadows, all of it. I throw my arms around his neck.

"Rosalina," he breathes, pulling me close. "You're all right."

"Not really," Caspian snarls, throwing up a huge wall of briars to block a surge of skeletons. "We're all kind of fucked right now."

I pull away from Farron to look up at him. Strands of messy auburn hair cast his eyes in dark shadows. "Are you okay?" I whisper. "What happened down there?"

Farron smiles at me, a smile that doesn't reach his eyes. "I've never been better, Rosie."

"Fare." Dayton's voice carries over the screams, clash of metal, and rattle of bones.

He walks with frenzied purpose, gaze unblinking, his trident blocking and slicing skeletons without him even having to look at them.

Dayton's trident disappears into his necklace. He snatches Farron in his arms and kisses him. Kisses him like a man possessed. My own bond leaps in my heart, and I join my briars with Caspian's to form a shield between us and the rest of the world, just to give them this moment together.

"Mmm." Caspian wiggles his shoulders and points to our briars interlaced together. "That tingles."

Dayton's hands tangle in Farron's hair, and Farron grips the side of Dayton's face, kissing him with equal passion.

"For stars' sake," Caspian snarls, erupting another huge wall of briars around us. "Are we fighting or kissing? You know I love the latter, but really, choose your moments, people!"

Finally, Farron pulls back and strokes the hair away from Dayton's eyes. "It's true. I thought I felt it, but it's really true." He looks at me. "You two are mates."

"Yes, I'm sure it's a whole glorious tale you can beguile us with later, but for now, can we get out of here?" Caspian taps his foot. "These briars aren't going to hold forever."

I ignore him and hold Farron's gaze. "It is true. We all belong together, just as you always believed."

Farron's mouth sets in a determined line. "I'll keep it that way. Forever."

Dayton calls the trident from his necklace in a shimmer of light. "We're not going anywhere, Caspian. I won't leave these people to be slaughtered."

Caspian's nose wrinkles. "Well, I really can't hang around. So, you're all going to have to—" He looks up, a laugh breaking free. "Never mind. Looks like you're sorted. Best of luck, then." He turns to Dayton. "I'll do what I can to aid you, but I've got to attract a little less attention. Only the gods know what trouble I've got myself into so far."

"Thank you, Caspian," Dayton says. "I mean it."

Caspian nods, then turns to Farron. In a quick motion, he snatches Farron's jaw and gives him a scathing look. "Watch yourself, Princeling. I know I will."

Farron shoves him away. "Yeah, nice traveling with you too, Cas."

Finally, Caspian turns to me. He bumps my shoulder and drops his lips to my ear. "Be careful, Princess." His eyes flick back toward Farron.

"What happened down there?" I whisper.

His mouth becomes a hard line. "Remember, even a warm hearth can leave you scorched."

I grab his wrist. "Are you really going to abandon us here?"

"Don't worry. You have friends in high places. Besides, I'll see you soon. I always do," he says with a smirk, as a thatch of briars erupts around him and sinks him down into the earth.

"Great! Of course, the traitor leaves right when we could use another blade," Dayton says, though his tone is only half-serious. "Think this will help, Fare?"

Dayton rips something off his neck and tosses it to Farron. The token of Autumn.

"Thanks, Day." Farron grins, throwing it over his head. In a flash of light, the Lance of Valor appears in his palm. Farron lunges forward, swinging the lance. A trail of orange flames and leaves sweeps behind it, taking out a whole row of skeletons. A moment later, the bones rattle as the skeletons rise again.

Farron furrows his brow. "It's not enough. Every time we kill one of these skeletons, they just get up and keep coming. We need to get all of the rebels out of here—"

Friends in high places. I look up. A shadow sprawls over me, but I am not afraid. A smile breaks across my face. "They found them. They found them!"

A legion of winged horses emerges across the horizon, their majestic forms silhouetted against the blazing sun. Each horse is adorned with shimmering armor, their powerful wings beating rhythmically.

Dayton's mouth falls open, then he laughs and hoots. He raises his trident in the air. "Summer called! The Huntresses answered!"

The horses dive, their armored riders reaching out with outstretched arms. One by one, they snatch the gladiators up from the grips of the skeletons, pulling them onto the backs of their horses.

A brilliant white horse sails toward us. The rider offers a gleaming smile, one I know so well because I admire it daily on the face of my mate. Delphia wears a brilliant golden helm adorned with wings. She clutches the reins with confidence, as if she were born to fly.

"Looks like you could use a ride, big brother!" she cries as her Pegasus flaps down toward us.

"Delphie, you brilliant little brat!" Dayton cries, practically jumping up and down. He runs over to her and nearly strangles her in a hug.

"Hurry, get on before one of these creepy things reaches us," she snaps.

"How do I land this thing?" another voice cries from above. A gray Pegasus flaps its massive wings, nearly knocking Farron and me over. Nori yanks on the reins with far less elegance than Delphie, eliciting an annoyed snort from her steed. When she's low enough to the ground, she levels us with a glare. "What are you waiting for? Let's go!"

Farron and I exchange a surprised look, then with a rush of excitement, I leap up behind his little sister. Farron jumps on behind me, the large creature just big enough for the three of us.

Our horses take flight into the sky, joining the rest of the legion in the air. Gladiators hold tight to stern-faced women, riding their steeds with effortless grace.

A golden eagle screeches as it flies in front of Delphia's horse. "Thanks for helping me find my brother, Justus," I hear her call over the wind.

I look down as the arena gets smaller beneath us. The green flames still flicker, each one a warning. Tomorrow, it won't just be the arena overrun. It will be all of Hadria.

"Amazing rescue," Dayton yells to his sister. "But what's the plan now?"

"The Huntresses weren't the only thing we found in the desert," she says back.

I follow her gaze ahead of the legion.

Drifting out of the clouds is a dark and terrible structure: the black sails of one of Kairyn's airships. Four others follow in its wake.

"Stop, Nori!" Farron cries. "That thing will blast us out of the sky!"

But something thrums to life in my chest, an urgent pull that sends shivers of electricity through my body. "No, Fare. That's exactly where we need to go."

More winged horses shoot out of the clouds, escorting the ships. As we get closer to the first one, I make out the figure at the helm.

His smile, such a rare sight, strikes me like an arrow to the heart.

Ezryn waves us forward, pointing at where our horses can land on the deck.

I look backward, toward the outskirts of the city where Sira's army lies in wait. A question tugs on my mind: is Wrenley down there? Did she run back to Sira's clutches? Or is she somewhere in the ruined colosseum?

I take a shaky breath. There are too many unknowns. But my princes are with me.

We may have a hope yet.

102

ROSALINA

The deck of the ship is a bustle of activity. Farron, Nori, and I dismount our Pegasus, and it takes off back into the sky, falling into formation with the other winged horses that flank the ship. Dayton's laugh booms over the shouts of the crew as he flings Delphia in a circle, squeezing her so tight all the breath shoots out of her in an exhale.

I scan all the faces aboard the ship before my gaze meets Ezryn's atop the bridge. My heart stutters. He came back, like he promised he would. Delphia and Nori are safe, and the Huntresses of Aura have come to our aid.

I never doubted you, I whisper across our bond.

The smallest flash of a smile flickers on his face. *Do you always have to be right?*

Yes, actually. At least when it comes to you four, I say in my mind, raising a brow.

His gaze narrows, and the small smile turns wolfish. *Get over here and let me kiss you.*

Eagerly, I dash across the deck, winding through the bustling crew. My heart hammers in my breast, every moment out of his arms feeling like an eternity.

Just as I'm about to reach the stairs leading up to the bridge, a voice calls my name: "Rosalina!"

I turn to see Delphia and Nori standing together.

"Girls." I walk over to them and pull them in for a group hug. "You did it! You survived the Ribs!"

They wiggle out of my grasp, and Delphia crosses her arms. "Wasn't like it was even hard," she says.

Nori picks at a fingernail. "Speak for yourself. I still have sand in my hair."

"I'm so proud of you both," I say.

"Yeah, well," Delphia shrugs before her eyes flick up to the bridge, "we had some help."

"Did you take good care of him?" I ask, following her gaze up to Ezryn. He's been intercepted by Dayton and Farron. Day seems to have begun an epic tale, to judge by the extensive hand gestures he's making, while Fare and Ez listen, enraptured. A flood of warmth rushes through my bond, and all three turn to look at me. My face heats under their combined intensity. More feelings rush through the bond: contentment, joy, relief. Dayton must be telling them about our mate bond.

"We took real good care of him," Delphia says. "He needed *a lot* of help."

"He'd probably still be wandering the desert if it wasn't for us," Nori says, words lacking any inflection.

I chuckle. "I don't doubt it. He's lucky to have had such capable travel companions."

Delphia shrugs. "It wouldn't be the worst thing to adventure with him again. He wasn't so bad."

"For an old man," Nori adds.

Laughing, I grab the girls in a hug again, then turn back to the bridge, anxious to get to Ezryn. As I start ascending the stairs, a hand grabs my wrist. I turn to look into a woman's harsh, weathered face. Based on the Pegasus feathers pinned in her hair, she must be one of the Huntresses of Aura.

"Rosalina O'Connell?"

"Yes?" I peep. Her hawk's gaze makes me nervous.

"I am Matron Valeria. Your mate, Ezryn, son of Isidora, says you are the Queen's daughter."

Forcing some command into my voice, I say, "This is true. I am daughter of Aurelia."

She looks me up and down, then nods. "Yes, I see this. Moreso, I *feel* this. Your mate was able to command the Queen's Army in your name."

My breath catches in my throat. Ezryn was able to sway the Queen's Army from his brother's side. "Ezryn is a remarkable leader."

"Of that, I was not certain." Valeria's gaze narrows. "When he first entered our domain, we tracked his movements across the desert. He seemed determined to serve only his own interests. So, when he came to us for aid, we sent him away. However, my heart urged me to keep watch over him and his young charges. I saw how he restored faith in the soldiers who found themselves adrift. To command an army is one thing, but to win their trust and loyalty is another. I knew then that the son of Isidora spoke honestly during his plea. To see the Queen's Army restored to their righteous purpose can only be a sign that the Queen has come again to bring balance to the Enchanted Vale. This is your path, Golden Rose, and the Huntresses will aid you and your mates in what ways we can."

I take her hand; it's rough and heavily calloused. "Thank you, Matron Valeria. It is an honor to fight beside you and your warriors."

The Huntress gives a stiff nod, then melds back into the crew. I let loose a breath and begin to make my way up the stairs again. I take one step before smacking into Ezryn's hard chest.

The moment I look up and meet his dark gaze, the bustle around us seems to quiet. Everyone else on this ship blurs away into ghosts. There's only me and him, the air between us sparking.

It was true what I said in my mind—I never doubted him. So why do I feel like my heart is going to explode out of my chest at the sight of him here?

I search his face, trying to pinpoint it. He's *different* somehow. On the outside, he's the same: ruggedly handsome face, intense gaze, clothing made for movement. But I feel something within him, something through the bond. Quiet. A tranquility, even. Like his inner self finally matches the stillness he embodies.

"Hi," I say.

"Hi," he responds.

The world rushes back in, the shouts of the crew, the flurry as people attend to the ship, the flapping wings of the Pegasus nearby. Delphie and Nori have found their big brothers, and the four of them stand in a circle, talking animatedly.

"It's really busy on the deck," I say quietly.

"Indeed it is," Ezryn says.

"Would be good for you and me to, you know . . . debrief."

"Absolutely, we should."

I bite my lip. "No real space up here."

Ezryn takes a step down until we're standing chest to chest. His dark eyes blaze. "There's a closet below deck."

"Perfect."

In a flash, Ezryn grabs my hand and tugs me across the deck and down into the galley. An excited giddiness fills my whole body as he pulls me faster. A few members of the Queen's Army Ezryn swayed to our side try to stop him to talk but he brushes them off.

"Get in. Quickly," he says, opening a door outside of the berth. It leads into a small broom closet, lit only by a flickering lamp. "Will this do?" he asks.

"Oh, it will do," I say at the exact same time as I push him against the wall, reach behind me for the handle to slam the door shut, then launch myself at him.

I kiss him hard, my mouth desperate for his. He matches my energy, wrapping me in his arms and pulling me tight against him. Stars, is he already hard? The realization sends a shot of electricity up my spine. "I missed you," I murmur in between kisses.

His hands cup either side of my face, and he pulls back to stare at me. The dim lamplight makes his eyes spark with a golden glow. "You were with me, Rose. Every decision I made, every action I took, I thought of you. You are my guiding compass."

My throat tightens, and I kiss him hard again to chase away my threatening tears. His mouth slows against mine, becoming gentle, exploratory. Like he's studying my lips with each tiny movement. The rough scratch of stubble is contradicted by the softness of his tongue.

"Thank you for coming back to me," I whisper.

His hand coasts across the point of my ear. "Thank you for leading me back."

Ezryn captures my mouth again, guiding me into the corner of the closet. His knee nudges my legs apart, then the hard muscle of his thigh presses against my aching center. I cry out, but he covers my mouth with his hand. "Shush, Petal. We don't want any unexpected visitors."

I nod, then narrow my gaze teasingly at him. I flick my tongue across the fingers covering my mouth, and he grits his teeth, barely holding back his own growl. I work my lips around the tip of one of his fingers, sucking it, licking its length, reminding him just what my mouth is capable of.

"How can you save my life and be the death of me all at once?" he says, voice low.

The closet is so small, his frame takes up most of the space. Despite my own height, I feel small, pushed into the corner, trapped by his leg between mine. Feverishly, I grab the edges of his tight shirt, pull it off, and chuck it to the floor. It lands with a wet slap, and we both look down to see it in a mop bucket. Whoops.

"That was an accident, I promise," I say, though I know I don't seem very sorry as my hands greedily run over the planes of his chest.

Ezryn lowers his brows. "Oh, you're going to pay for that."

My laugh is stolen by a moan as he drives his knee up against my throbbing pussy. The contact sends a blaze of need through me, and my fingernails sink into his shoulders. I'm still wearing my Summer sleeping dress, and he easily slips the bodice down, freeing my breasts. He pulls back, eyes locked onto my chest.

"Ez?"

"Sorry," he says, not even blinking. "I just need a moment to admire these."

I give a little laugh, then bring my hands to my breasts, fingers kneading the soft flesh.

"Stars, you *will* be the death of me," he practically growls. "Don't stop, beautiful."

I give him as best a show as I can in this cramped space, tugging on one nipple, then the other, lifting my breasts then letting them fall and bounce. Ezryn palms his hard cock through his pants, groaning with each move I make.

I lean forward and snag his bottom lip between my teeth, nipping lightly. "Now, *you're* the one being loud."

"Better give my mouth something to do then."

He shoves me back again, then sinks to his knees. He places his hands on either side of my hips, then stills in that cat-like way he does. I brush my fingers through his hair. The way he's looking up at me: it's both adoring and awed.

His fingers play down my stomach before pushing my dress up to my hips. "It is the greatest honor of my life to be on my knees to serve you."

Words escape me as he takes the waistband of my panties between his teeth. With a single swipe, he pulls them down. The cold air is replaced immediately with the warmth of his breath as he lays a kiss against my slit.

"Ez," I moan.

"Your only job is to be quiet and come on my tongue," he says, drawing one of my legs over his shoulder. "Do you understand, Petal?"

I nod frantically, then slam my head back against the wall as he draws a long, languishing line across my pussy.

I whimper, my legs trembling at the sheer pleasure of his mouth. He's always known exactly how to work my body, how to make me melt with a single touch, a single look. His tongue swirls around my clit, dipping inside of me and teasing every nerve ending I didn't know I had.

I bite my lip to stifle a moan as Ezryn's intensity grows, his fingers digging into the soft flesh of my thigh, his tongue flicking over my most sensitive spots, driving me wild with desire. I clench my fists on the wall for support, trying not to make a sound. He's relentless, and it's both agonizing and delicious.

"Ez," I whimper, my self-control crumbling. "I . . . I can't. . ."

He lifts his head just long enough to glare at me with those heated eyes before diving back in, this time zeroing in on my clit. His tongue is a wet, warm trail of exquisite torture, and I can feel myself teetering on the edge of release.

"Ezryn, I'm going to . . . oh gods, I'm . . ."

He doesn't relent; my words have only spurred him further. "Remember your orders, my Queen," he growls against my skin.

To stay quiet and to come on his tongue. I can definitely accomplish one of those things.

Ezryn hooks two fingers inside me at the same time as he captures my clit in his mouth. I let out a gasping moan as my orgasm crashes through me. Waves of pleasure cause my whole body to tremble, and his skillful tongue moves with each tremor. I sag against the wall, trying to muffle my cries by biting down on my fist. His fierce devouring of me turns into kisses on my thighs, my stomach, and then my breasts as he begins to stand, gently guiding my leg back to the ground.

"Good girl," he murmurs.

I can only give a dopey smile, my body still shivering with aftershocks, as he claims my mouth with a kiss. I taste myself on his lips.

"Now, I'm going to fuck you, my Queen," he says softly. "Fuck you and fill you and make you beg to scream my name."

Heady need roars up my body, and I claw at the back of his neck to bring him in for another searing kiss. My limbs still feel boneless from my orgasm, and I let him maneuver me as he pleases. My dress slips from my waist into a pool on the ground.

He turns me around, so my arms are up against the wall and my hips are flush against his cock.

I hear him fumble with his pants before they fall to the ground. Then, his steel-hard cock taps against my ass.

"Are you ready, Petal?"

I look over my shoulder, holding him with a narrowed gaze. "So ready, Daddy."

He laughs and shakes his head. "You've been spending too much time with Dayton."

"Maybe we can spend some time with Dayton together," I purr.

He makes a low sound in the back of his throat then plants a kiss at the top of my spine. "One thing at a time, my greedy girl." His words are affectionate, and a trill of joy rushes through me.

Because ever since I began living at Castletree, that's how I always felt. Greedy for wanting the princes for myself. But it wasn't selfishness at all. My heart knew we were bound together and that it was only a matter of our bonds weaving through the paths of fate.

Now, the thought of Ezryn and my newest mate sends my heart hammering. The command of Spring with the strength of Summer. . . I let loose a contented sigh and buck my hips back against Ezryn.

"Everyone's going to be wondering where we are, so I'm going to take you hard and I'm going to take you fast. Can you handle it?" he says, voice full of dark promise. I feel the head of his cock press against my pussy.

"I can handle it."

"Don't scream."

Ezryn thrusts inside of me. He must know me well, because just as a cry is about to leave my mouth, his hand covers my throat.

His pace is punishing, each stroke sending delirious heat through my body. I squeeze my eyes shut, biting my lip hard to keep from calling out his name.

"Stars, Rosalina, you're so good," he pants, dropping his hand from my throat. "Such a good girl."

My head buzzes. Maybe I'm crazy, but there's something about hiding away in this closet that's so exciting. I know Ezryn so well now—his history, his heart—but being taken like this almost makes it seem like we're brand new to one another. Two secret lovers stealing a moment wherever they can.

Each thrust drives further inside of me until I'm stuffed full. He pauses at the apex and swirls my hips against his. I moan out, the feeling of his cock grinding against my deepest point is complete ecstasy.

"If you keep doing that, I'm going to come," I pant.

He wraps his arms around my middle and pulls me even tighter against him. "How can I say no to that?"

Each movement he makes is intentional, every thrust and grind perfectly synced to send me over the edge. My legs begin to quake, and spots form in my peripheral vision.

"Ez, I'm going to . . . ah, Ez—"

"Beg me to let you say my name. Beg me to let you come."

"*Please,*" I cry out, my control a fraying thread. "Let me say your name as I come over your cock!"

He gives a satisfied growl then grabs my hips on either side, pace quickening. "Say my name, Baby Girl. Say my name and I'll bring you to oblivion."

"Ezryn!" I scream as his cock pulses inside of me. "Ezryn!"

He cries out himself. My climax sweeps over me like a tidal wave, and it takes him too; I feel his body explode within me, the thought only making my own release stronger. I ride out the tremors in his arms, sighing with each shiver.

Ezryn's warm breath caresses my neck as he straightens and unsheathes himself. He pulls me against his chest and kisses the top of my head. "Some debrief you give, Rose."

I snort a laugh and hug him around the middle. "You're one to talk."

That brand-new feeling lingers as we hold each other. Maybe I wasn't so crazy after all. Maybe there is something brand new about him. Maybe there's something brand new about me too.

IO3

EZRYN

Our bodies are slick with sweat, our heavy breathing the only sound. Rosalina leans against the wall of the closet. Her hair is tangled, face flushed. The exquisite look of a woman well fucked.

I try to back up to give her some room but end up shoving my foot in the mop bucket. I give it a kick, freeing myself with a *thunk*, and Rosalina bursts out laughing. My wet shirt sits beside it. A part of me thinks Rose did that on purpose so I'd have to stay shirtless.

I shush her with a kiss. "We'll get caught."

"If no one heard me screaming your name already, then I think we're safe." She runs a hand down my chest, her touch like a soothing balm.

My mate back in my arms, both of us reunited with Dayton and Farron . . . perhaps everything is not so hopeless after all.

Though, Rosalina and I should get back above deck. I'm sure Valeria and Mozi will have recruited Dayton into helping the rescued gladiators settle in with the rest of the fleet. Seeing Dayton again was like looking at the sun itself: a glowing, colossal entity with the confidence to bathe the world in light. *Mate of my mate.* Though he had quickly told me the story, I had felt the change as soon as I saw him. I always knew the brotherhood I shared with Dayton went beyond friendship—we are bound together in a fate from the stars.

"You kept your promise," Dayton had said to me when we first reunited, his eyes on Delphie. "You kept her safe. I knew you would."

"Actually," I'd managed to say, "she kept me safe."

And to see Farron again after all these months . . . I almost didn't recognize him. There wasn't time to hear about the journey he's been on since last I saw him in Spring, but I can tell it weighs on him. There was an emptiness to his expression . . . a voidness in his eyes I've never seen before. I'll have to speak with him when I can.

But all of that had to wait. I'd needed to take care of the most important business: claiming my mate. Although this closet is hardly worthy of Rosalina, it has served its purpose. The only private bedchamber on the airship is the captain's quarters, which I left free for the High Prince of Summer; this is his realm after all, and he deserves the command.

Rosalina doesn't seem to have minded our shabby quarters though. She's staring up at me like one might stare at the sun. Our mate bond seems to sing between us.

"We should probably get back up on deck," I murmur. "Dayton will want to hold a council soon."

Rosalina laces her fingers through my hair and pulls me down until my head rests in the crook of her neck. "Soon. Just one more moment here."

One more moment. I wish I could live in this broom closet with her forever, our own space without war, without meetings, without pain. I breathe in her scent, fingers trailing over her hips.

"This kind of reminds me of the first time you kissed me," she says. "I followed you into the closet and then you punched out a light. Do you remember?"

"How could I ever forget?" That world feels so far away. "I could break this light for you, if you want?"

She laughs, then runs her hands along the scruff growing over my chin. "No, I love to see your face. It is my right as your mate."

"Everyone has a right to it now," I murmur.

She pushes me back slightly so she can look me in the eye. "What happened out there in the desert, Ez? Did you see him? Your brother?"

"Yes." I look down, unable to hold her gaze. "We faced each other once again."

"And you live, even though he has Spring's Blessing . . ."

"He was blinded by rage. I used his anger against him." Memories of my brother's screams flood my mind.

"Is he still alive?"

The weight of the question hangs in the air before us. The words stick in my throat. Though I know why I chose the path I did, I don't know if anyone else will understand it. But I must try. "Yes. I could not kill him."

"Oh," she says.

I grab her hands and stare at her deeply. "Listen, Rosalina. I know how dangerous Kairyn is with that Blessing. I had the opportunity to end his life. But it was as if I could see my own life laid out before me. If I killed my brother, I would become like him. His rage, his sorrow, his pain . . . It would pass to me. I would not be the man you fell in love with."

A soft smile crosses her face, and she trails a hand over the curve of my tattered ears. "This is why I fell in love with you, Ezryn. Because of your gentle heart."

Gentle. A word I never thought would be used to describe me, a man cursed for his malice. "I have to hold on to the hope that there is still good in him," I whisper.

Rosalina rises to her tiptoes and presses her lips to mine, a whisper of a kiss. "I stand by you, Ezryn."

I grab my pants off the floor and rummage in the pocket. Then I hold out the Queen's token of Spring. "I took this from him. Without it, he won't be able to wield the Hammer of Hope nor travel to Castletree on a whim. Though he may be the High Ruler, he does not deserve to wield such power." I put it in her hand, closing her fingers around it. "You should look after it."

"It belongs to you," she whispers.

"No. It belongs to a deserving ruler of Spring. Until that person is found, you must safeguard this." I implore her with my gaze. "There may be an opportunity to grant this to someone who can save Spring. Please, Rosalina. Look after this. For my people."

She closes her eyes and nods. "I'll keep it safe, Ez." Then she wraps her arms around me. "I'll keep you safe."

I hold her as tight as I can, treasuring each inch of her skin on mine.

"One more moment here," I murmur.

"One more moment."

104

DAYTON

Somehow, the arguing voices are even louder than the whir of the airship. Never thought I'd be aboard one of these ugly things. I've caught a few of our crew looking nervously over the railings, but they had to pry me from the edge. I've stood on the bow of a ship with waves cresting the horizon, but there's something magical about sailing across billowing clouds.

It's a little more unsettling below deck, with the echoing metal floor and rattling pipes. I enter the meeting room. Even though I'm not late, it seems the arguing has already begun.

The scent of polished metal and oil fills my nostrils. The soft hum of machinery resonates through the floor, a reminder of the ship's power.

The Green Flame's power.

I guess if you can't beat them, use them however you can.

Justus, Valeria, Delphia, Nori, Ezryn, and Fare stand around a long table. Rosalina hovers a little way behind them, silently watching. I cross to her, placing a quick kiss to her temple, before stepping between my sister and Fare.

"Any of you geniuses figured out how to save Hadria yet?" I ask.

"Like I've explained," Nori says, "it's statistically impossible."

"Remember, Nori," Ezryn gives her a soft look, "that's what you said about finding the Huntresses."

She sighs, tucking her long hair behind a pointed ear. "Okay, then it's extremely unlikely."

"Nori's not wrong," Delphia says.

There's a thin layer of water over the table. Delphie stretches her hand over the surface. The water stirs, then rises and coalesces into a miniature model of Hadria. Delphie's eyes glow with focused intensity as she manipulates the water, shaping it to her will. Tiny ripples and waves form intricate details of the city's layout. It's a replica of the grand war table at Soltide Keep.

Nori stretches her hand out beside my sister. Tiny red flames dot up around the city, their light flickering in the water. Representations of Sira's army.

There are so many.

"This is just a guess, of course," Nori says. "We have no way to know where Sira will drop her army. Based on the numbers she let into the arena, this is a safe conclusion."

"Plus, we don't know when Kairyn will come slinking back," Delphie says.

"If my brother returns, I'll deal with him," Ezryn says. "Again."

"We also don't know where the Nightingale or the Bow of Radiance are," Rosalina adds.

"What about your new friend?" I ask, nudging Farron's shoulder. "Think Cas will be of any aid?"

Farron shakes his head. "I think he's trapped in a different way than we are."

Ezryn sneers. "Yes, he's trapped to reside over the city his mother conquered."

"Either way," Farron says slowly, "we can't expect his help in this."

"No word from Kel or my father?" Rosalina asks, stepping closer. "Your plan worked. Surely, my mother's cage must have broken. It would explain why Sira is so upset. But Kel still feels so far away."

Farron crosses to his mate—to *our* mate—and wraps an arm around her shoulder. "Kel can handle himself. We'll see him soon, I'm sure."

Rosalina nods and gazes at the water model of the city.

"So, what are you all saying?" I say, arms out. "We retreat? Leave every Summer citizen to Sira's cruel will? You heard her, if they don't submit, she'll *kill* them. Summer fae don't submit."

Ezryn gives a long sigh. "With the Huntresses, newly recruited

Queen's Army, your legionnaires, and your magic . . . it would have been enough to stop the forces Kairyn brought into the city."

"But not Sira's skeletons and shadows," I finish for him.

"Even if this is a hopeless cause, the Huntresses will see it through," Valeria says. "We have vowed to serve the Queen, and we will do so unto death."

Justus walks forward. "Even the Queen herself knew that sometimes a battle must be lost to win a war. Perhaps this is one of those times. I cannot see a way to save Hadria."

"We can't just admit defeat," Delphia yells.

Voices clash with one another as everyone begins talking at once, contradicting each other, arguing.

"Wait," Rosalina's voice rings out, silencing us all. She holds us with her gaze, eyes appearing more golden than brown. Rosie hovers her hand above Hadria, then points to the representation of the sea, where the water begins to bubble. "What if we didn't save Hadria? What if we destroyed it?"

DELPHIA SITS at the helm of the ship, face toward the clouds, dark curls blowing in the wind. On her lap rests a juvenile Pegasus.

"Who might this be?" I take a seat next to her.

"This is Drusilla," Delphie says. "We rescued her from a harpy's nest. She was supposed to stay back at the Ribs but looks like she followed us here."

"Sounds like a certain spirited princess I know." I tuck a curl behind her ear. "You did well. We never would have been able to bring all those people to safety if you hadn't found the Huntresses."

Delphie smiles and returns her gaze to the horizon. "You did well too, brother. You feel different."

"My curse is broken."

"I know but it's something deeper." She turns and taps my heart. "In here."

For once, I think I know what she means. "Once this is all over, you deserve all the time in the world to flit about and ignore duty. Twenty-five years, in fact, with interest."

Delphia laughs, weaving her fingers into the mane of the Pegasus.

"That might not be so bad. Bet I could get around the Vale quickly on one of these."

"Bet you could, Del," I say. "As long as you promise to come back and relay all the tales of your adventures to your poor, boring brother."

"I don't think your life will ever be boring, Day."

I knock her lightly on the chin. "Not if I can help it."

Delphia's gaze flits across the ship to where Farron and Nori are curled together under a tartan blanket, looking at the young princess's notebook. "Adventuring wouldn't be that much fun on my own, though."

"I happen to believe those Autumn royals aren't too bad for company."

Color darkens her cheeks, and she swipes a glare at me. "Nori knows a lot about plants. I would have eaten, like, twelve poisonous things already if she weren't around."

"Well, we wouldn't want that." I laugh, pulling her to my side.

She settles against me, and I reach around her to pet the Pegasus.

"You know," Delphia says after a while, "they'd say our plan tomorrow is crazy."

I don't need her to tell me who they are. Mother, our fathers, Damocles, and Decimus.

"They'd never approve of it," I agree.

"But I think," she whispers, "they'd be proud of us."

My gaze shifts over the edge of the ship, to Hadria far below, washed in the light of the setting sun. "I think so too, Del, and tomorrow, when we save our people, we will feel their blades beside us."

105

ROSALINA

I creak open the door to the captain's quarters to find Dayton. He stands by the bed, looking around the room. Though it's made of dark wood and metal forgings, the bedsheets black, with only the dim glow lamps to light the room, Dayton's presence feels warm as the sun itself.

He wears a tight black shirt and pants: the same attire as me. It's what the Queen's Army wear under their armor, and the only clean clothing we have aboard the ship. His hair is damp, and a trail of steam still drifts out of the private privy attached to this room. My own hair has just started to dry from the shower I took below deck. It's certainly not as luxurious as the privies in Spring or at Castletree, but anything is better than the gladiator bunks.

"Blossom." He smiles as I enter and click the door shut behind me. "Everything all right?"

I wrap my arms around him, leaning into his embrace. "Now it is."

We'd spoken until our lungs gave out in the meeting; there are no more words that need to be said, no other plans to be laid. Now, I just want to bask in his warmth. No matter what happens tomorrow, I want to have tonight.

"Hey, no being sad. We're on the edge of battle. In Summer, these kinds of evenings are a time of celebration."

"Trust me, every night with you is a celebration." I offer him a smile.

"Of course it is." Ever since he broke his curse, there's a spark of the old Dayton back, one I haven't seen in months. That charismatic poise I saw in the hot springs when we first met. But this time, it's tempered with something else: a strength and confidence that's brand new.

I run my hand down the skin visible between the deep V of his shirt. "Hey, Dayton, have you had a chance to talk with Farron since we came aboard?"

"A little, though I hope to rectify that soon."

"Do you think he's . . . okay?"

Dayton raises an eyebrow. "What do you mean?"

"I don't know." I chew on my bottom lip, trying to find the words. "It's hard to explain. It's just when I first saw him, I felt . . . something different."

"He's probably just worn out from spending so much time with Caspian. But the three of us are together again. Ez, too, and soon enough, you'll be back in the arms of that frosty bastard, Kel. It's going to be okay, Rosie. Everything's going to be okay."

I close my eyes, wanting beyond hope to believe him.

The door creaks open, and Farron pokes his head in. "Hey, I was looking for you two."

"Come on in." Dayton opens his arms.

Farron slinks in and closes the door behind him. He's wearing the same black undershirt and pants as Dayton and me. Maybe it's because I'm so used to seeing him always dressed in his finest, with fancy vests embroidered with golden thread or waistcoat made of the softest fabric, or with his gold reading glasses and a glittering cuff adorning one of his ears, but he looks different right now. The black doesn't suit him, and his hair falls straight in front of his eyes, casting shadows over his face.

He looks from me to Dayton. "Feels like the first chance I've had to breathe in days."

Neither of us respond. We stand there in the comfortable silence, just staring at one another.

Marveling that after so many trials and so much sadness, we're here. Together.

An invisible string of electricity seems to dart between Farron and Dayton as they hold one another's gaze. I'd known it from the first moment I saw them together in Dayton's room. They are in love. A love that goes beyond mate bonds or fate.

"I'm so sorry, Fare," Dayton breathes. "For everything these last few months. I never want to put you through pain and that's all I've done—"

"No, I'm sorry," Farron interrupts. "I should never have doubted what I've always known in my heart."

I step toward Farron and grab his hand, pulling him closer to Dayton and me. "Whatever happened in the past has only made us stronger. You, Farron, and you, Dayton, are my mates. Our love was written in the stars. The three of us were meant to be together."

A smile quirks at the corner of Farron's lip. "You're right. We are meant to stay together." Then he flings himself at Dayton, wraps his arms around his neck, and kisses him with everything he has, full and passionate and reckless. Dayton's eyes widen in surprise, before he wraps his arms around Farron's body and melts into him.

Farron breaks away with a fevered look, then roughly grabs me by the back of my neck. I fall against him, kissing him deeply. His hands trail down to grab my ass, and I moan into his mouth. Farron's touch is more assertive than I've felt before, and I'm completely at his mercy.

When Farron pulls away from me, Dayton places a hand on each of our cheeks. His blue eyes shine with desire. "This time will not be like our other times. It is a new beginning for us."

"Then make love to me, Prince of Summer. You as well, Prince of Autumn. Show me this love," I breathe.

I pull my black shirt over my head, freeing my breasts. Farron runs his tongue over his front teeth. Then I wiggle out of the tight pants, sliding them and my panties to the floor. The mere sight of their hungry eyes sets me on fire.

"It has been far too long since we shared our woman," Dayton says.

"Not just our woman, Day. Our *mate*," Farron corrects.

Four hands run over my body, stroking my hair, down my neck, along my collarbone. Dayton lifts one of my breasts, massaging the soft flesh, before holding it up to Farron like an offering. Farron leans his head down, greedily sucking on the nipple.

A whimper trembles out of me, and I arch into their touch.

"Let's see how wet you are for us," Dayton whispers in my ear. He slides his finger between my legs and moans. "Doesn't take much to excite our mate, does it, Farron?"

Farron licks up my nipple to the base of my neck, which he bites. A stinging pain shifts into arousal as he sucks the tender skin. "Her body is a temple, and we are devout worshipers."

"It's not fair," I whine. "The two of you are teaming up on me."

Dayton pulls his fingers out of my pussy and holds them up to the dim light, admiring the sheen. "Poor Blossom. Are we too cruel to her?"

Farron wraps his lips around Dayton's fingers and sucks deeply. My breath catches in my throat. Dayton lets out a purely male groan and palms his cock. It strains so much against the tight pants, I can practically see the veins bulging. After Farron has licked Dayton's fingers clean, he pulls back and says, "If this is cruel, I have no intention of being kind."

"Me neither." In a single movement, Dayton grabs my ass and hauls me up into the air.

I let out a giggling scream and wrap my legs around his waist. "What are you doing?"

"Making up for lost time," he murmurs in my ear before chucking me onto the bed. "Farron, get behind her. I don't want one inch of our mate not worshiped."

"My pleasure," Farron says and quickly yanks off his clothes. I lick my lips, staring at the smooth planes of his chest, the lean muscles that line his legs and at the steel-hard cock that looks all too delicious. He scrambles over to the top of the bed and sits with his back against the headboard. His legs lie out on either side of me.

I turn onto my belly, mouth lolling open unconsciously as I move for his cock.

"Not yet, Blossom." Dayton grabs my ankles and yanks me back before flipping me over. Farron links his arms under mine and pulls me up so I'm sitting between his legs. His hard cock presses into my back, filled with promises for later.

"Perfect," Farron purrs and begins massaging my breasts. He rolls one nipple between his thumb and forefinger, before pinching the other. His long fingers play across my skin like I'm an instrument he knows all the chords to.

"I couldn't agree more." Dayton stands at the end of the bed looking down at us.

"Give us a show, Day," I breathe.

He smiles that cocky, arrogant smile I love so much. I would kiss it straight off his face if Farron's hands didn't feel so fucking good.

Slowly, ever so slowly, Dayton pulls his shirt off, revealing each cord of muscle. His abdomen stretches with each breath. Then he digs his thumbs into the waistband of his pants and pulls them down. His enormous girth springs free of its confines. The tip is pearly with pre-cum, his desire evident.

Farron lets loose a sigh, his own cock straining against my back.

"Now," Dayton says, eyes shining with a feral glint, "I'm starving."

He dives straight between my legs. I cry out as the tip of his tongue traces the outside of my pussy.

"You can take it, Sweetheart," Farron says. "Does it feel good?"

"So good," I breathe, writhing in Farron's lap.

"Mmm," Dayton hums against my heat. "You taste divine. Like ambrosia."

Farron squeezes my breasts in time with Dayton's tongue-strokes. I squirm and tremble, trying to keep myself from falling apart between the two of them.

"I can't take much more," I pant.

Dayton retreats for a moment, licking his lips. "Good. I want your cum all over my tongue. Help me get her there, Fare."

Without a moment's delay, Dayton's mouth is back, sucking and licking. Farron places his lips to my ear, tugging at my earlobe as he kneads my breasts with even more fervor.

When Dayton sticks two fingers within me, I'm undone. "Day! Fare!" I cry out, body arching. This only seems to excite them more, and they both double down on my torment, Farron pinching both my nipples so hard, I scream, and Dayton sucking on my clit as his two fingers work me.

My orgasm erupts through me in waves of euphoria. Explosive, pulsating pleasure radiates throughout my body. Farron sits us up and reaches between my legs, spreading my pussy lips apart. "That's it, Dayton. Get every bit. Don't let a drop of our girl's sweetness go to waste."

I'm a quivering mess, collapsed against Farron's chest, but I know my mates aren't done with me yet. If they have their way, I'll be passed between them until I'm drained dry. But I'm starving, too.

Quickly, I jerk toward Dayton and away from Farron, then scramble up to all fours. I know my ass and swollen pussy will be right in Farron's face.

Dayton's now kneeling on the edge of the bed, heavy cock bobbing.

I don't give him a chance to protest; my lips wrap around his cock, swirling the tip and lapping up every bead of pre-cum. Dayton throws his head back, letting out a beastly roar.

"Is this what you want, Blossom? To choke on my cock?" he grunts, lacing his hands into my hair. In response, I just look up at him through my lashes. A plead and a promise.

"She knows what she's doing." I feel Farron kneel behind me, his cock slapping against my ass cheeks. Then the bulging head of his dick presses against the entrance of my pussy. "You know I can't resist you."

"Then let's give our woman what she's asking for," Dayton growls.

I cry out, the sound only a strangled whimper as Dayton thrusts his huge cock all the way to the back of my throat. At the same time, Farron plunges inside of me. They move in perfect unison, working my mouth and pussy with a forceful rhythm.

"Come here, Baby," I hear Dayton groan, then there are the sounds of kissing above me. I pull back slightly on Dayton's cock and arch my neck to look up.

Dayton has grabbed Farron by the back of the head and pulled him forward. They kiss, tongues battling. The sight of my mates together, taking pleasure in each other as they fuck me, is too much.

"I'm coming!" I try to scream around Dayton's cock.

"Fuck, I can feel it," Farron breathes, pulling back a little from Dayton.

"Don't stop," Dayton growls, his cock plunging harder and harder into my throat. Farron keeps his pace, my pussy clenching around him as my orgasm roils through me.

They both slow before pulling out at the same time. My knees buckle, and I wouldn't be surprised if my eyes were in the back of my head.

I look between them, voice shaky. "I want to watch you two now."

Dayton smiles then grabs Farron around the shoulders and pulls him to the bed so they're lying down. I laugh as he near-wrestles Farron in his arms until they're facing each other, looks of longing exchanged between them.

How long has it been since they've been together? I felt Farron's heartbreak as my own when we thought Dayton didn't belong to us.

Dayton kisses Farron slowly, deeply, and I feel tears welling in my eyes. I treasure their love just as much as I treasure my own with each of them. *How lucky we are,* I think, *to get to share in so many different kinds of love.*

Farron runs his hand over Dayton's chest, then up his face. Their bodies are so close together, it's hard to tell where one begins and the other ends. My eyes drift down to their cocks, rubbing together, both shining from being inside of me.

Unable to help myself, I lean forward and grab them both at the base of their cocks. They look up at me.

"Don't stop," I whisper.

Dayton goes back to kissing Farron with sensual slowness, and I take my time, stroking from base to tip, savoring the silky hardness of each of them.

I love you, I think. *Both of you. I want to love you forever and ever and ever. I want to have a thousand moments like this. A million. I never want us to be apart.* But I can't say any of it out loud, because my throat is tight. Blinking away the tears, I focus on how beautiful each of them is in their own way. Dayton, with his hair like sunshine, his body so strong and protective. Farron, eyes golden as the dawn, lean and elegant. They complete one another so beautifully, two pieces of my heart that have finally clicked perfectly into place.

"All right," Dayton breathes. "If you don't stop stroking me like that, I'm going to come all over my boy and, while I do love to do that, I think it's reserved for you today, Blossom."

"Come between us," Farron says, and grabs my arm, pulling me down to lie in the middle. He moves the hair away from my shoulder so he can kiss my neck, then gently guides me to lie on my side, facing Dayton. "Shall we fill you, Sweetheart?"

"Stuff you full?" Dayton asks, lying on his side before me. He palms my breasts and gives me a gentle kiss that turns into biting down on my bottom lip. I groan and press my ass back into Farron's cock.

"Yes, yes, both of you. I want both of you inside of me. At the same time."

I hear Farron spit onto his hand, then a slick finger rubs against my ass. "You've never had two cocks like this, Sweetheart. You tell us if it's too much, okay?"

"Okay."

He dips a finger inside of me, stretching me out, preparing me for his cock.

Dayton kisses me, and I feel his girth press against the entrance to my pussy. "Say that you love us."

"I love you," I breathe.

"Say that you want us."

"I want you." My words are a plea.

"She's ready, Day," Farron says.

Dayton's eyes flash. "Order us to fuck you, Blossom. To fuck you like the royalty you are."

My heart thrums in my chest with wild excitement. "Fuck me. Fuck me like the royalty I am!"

"Very good," he purrs and lifts my leg up onto his hip.

In a single breath, I'm suddenly stuffed full, one cock in my pussy, one in my ass. I cry out. There's a twinge of pain, but the pleasure overwhelms it.

"Oh, fuck," I moan. "Oh, fuck, that's so good."

The sensation is unlike anything I've ever felt before: fullness and stretching in every possible way. Dayton and Fare move together in perfect harmony, as if they've been waiting their whole lives to share me like this.

"We're going to take our time with you, Sweetheart," Farron whispers in my ear, his cock twitching inside of me. "Stretch you out nice and slow."

Dayton's hand comes up to my breast, squeezing my nipple between his fingers as he thrusts his hips against mine. "You feel so good," he groans. "So wet for us."

I can't find the words to respond, nor can I truly move. I'm captured between them, my body the vessel for their pleasure. My voice is a mixture of moans and cries.

"Can you feel my cock, Fare?" Dayton growls. "I can feel yours."

"Fuck yes," Farron breathes.

Dayton's pace quickens. "We're going to fill you so full of cum. You'll be dripping with both our seed. Do you like the thought of that, Blossom? Your legs are soaked."

"Yes, Day," I manage. Waves of pleasure course through me. At every crest, it feels like I'm falling, but one of them is always there to catch me.

Farron and Dayton's arms reach for each other over the top of me. Now, I don't know where they end, and I begin. I don't think I ever want to know.

My wave crests to its full height. Both of their cocks ram into me with fevered intensity, and my voice becomes a broken scream. I can't hold on any longer. I'm falling into oblivion.

Time seems to pause for one moment, and I become acutely aware of everything. The safety of being trapped within their arms. The smell of Dayton in front of me: that sea salt and musk that never leaves him even after he's bathed. The familiar rhythm of Farron's breath that has lulled me to sleep no matter where I am. The pleasurable ache inside of me as my body becomes a home for my mates.

"Come with me," I breathe, and I know instantly that they will.

Pleasure erupts within me, and both of them roar out my name. Everything outside of us ceases to exist. There is only the pleasure of this single, glorious moment.

Cum pours into my entrances, filling me to the brink of fullness. My eyes roll to the back of my head and stars explode across my vision.

My wave crests down. Both of my mates still remain inside of me, panting.

Then, Dayton laughs. "I fucking love you both."

"I love you both, too," Farron says.

I kiss Dayton, then twist my neck to find Farron's lips. "This love," I breathe, "is eternal."

106

FARRON

Dayton and Rosalina's laughter drifts over to me. I open the door from the attached privy to the bedchamber to see them still lying together, tangled in the sheets. I give a soft smile. They look so happy, their love finally blossomed in the way it was always meant to.

After our lovemaking, both of them washed up and immediately returned to bed, just happy to be in each other's arms. I excused myself to wash up, as well. They're waiting for me to return.

I click the door shut and take a staggering breath. Placing my hands on either side of the sink, I look into the mirror.

Who is it that's looking back at me?

It *looks* like me. Auburn hair. Thick brows. Same bone structure. But something's different. *I'm* different.

There's more to me than there ever has been before. The weakness is gone. The man looking back at me *feels* strong. Powerful.

Capable of doing what he must.

The corner of my lip curls up as the gold in my eyes flickers into flecks of green. Powerful energy washes over me, and pieces of me seem to drift away, nothing but motes of dust in a sunbeam. This energy . . . it's originating from *inside* of me.

The privy begins to dissolve, falling away like ash. I stumble away from the mirror. The ground falls out from beneath my feet, and suddenly I'm floating in a black sky. There are no stars, only huge chunks of rock whizzing past. I whirl in a circle, trying to place myself. A landmark catches my gaze.

A giant emerald throne floating in the air before me.

A man sits upon it, leaning an elbow against his knee. I know this man, this not-quite-fae. A familiar smile carves up his face—familiar because it's the same one on mine.

"Steady, Farron, Autumn-blood," he says, voice radiating from all around me. "There is much work ahead."

I blink and stumble backward. The sky disappears, the privy returning to me. I lose my footing and smack against the wall.

"Hey, you okay in there?" Dayton calls.

Breath comes ragged from my throat, but I steady myself and lean back over the sink.

Warmth floods my body, rushing down my arms and into my hands. Green flames erupt atop each of my palms.

"I'm fine," I call back. "In fact, I've never been better."

107

ROSALINA

Despite the warm air of Summer drifting in through the ship's window, despite being enveloped in Dayton and Farron's arms, despite it all, my dreams are cold.

Snow flurries melt on my heated cheeks, and a stiff wind tugs at my white nightdress. I stand and look around. I appear to be in a canyon, barricaded in on either side by tall, icy walls. My bare feet trudge through the snow. The flickering light of a fire cuts through the darkness.

My heart is drawn to it.

Keldarion's broad shape is hunched over the fire as he warms his hands above the flames. He glances my way as I approach, orange light tangling between the thick waves of his white hair.

"My Rose. You've come." He opens his cloak, and I quickly fall into his arms. He tugs me onto his lap, enveloping me in the warm fabric.

"Where's my father?" I whisper.

"He's resting." Keldarion gestures to the other side of the fire where a figure lies covered in blankets.

My voice cracks. "My mother?"

Keldarion is silent for a long moment. Finally, he sighs. "Rose, I'm so sorry. We couldn't get her out."

I close my eyes, each breath a painful rattle in my chest. "Oh," is all I manage to say.

"We failed, Rose. There is more keeping your mother in the Below than a cage. Something not so easily broken." Kel absentmindedly touches his bargain bracelet. "I'll explain everything when we are together again, I promise."

I nod, fighting back tears. *She's alive.* That's all I need to know. Seeing her, even for just one moment, has strengthened my resolve to free her. As much as I want to push Kel for all the details of her imprisonment, I know this dream will not keep me with him for long. If things go wrong tomorrow, I want this last moment with Kel.

"Thank you for trying," I say. "For keeping my father safe. I understand so much more than I did before. Through our connection, I even had the chance to speak with her."

"You did?" He pulls back to get a better view of my face. "What did she tell you?"

"I have a sister."

Kel nods. "Ah, she told you. She shared that with George, as well. Wrenley."

"Yes, Wrenley. But she's also the Nightingale," I say, desperation creeping into my voice. "My mother asked me to save her. After everything she's done to us, I would be crazy to try and help her, wouldn't I?"

"Wrenley and the Nightingale one in the same." Kel's eyes flash. "Dayton's mate?"

"Not Dayton's mate," I say.

Kel gives me a knowing look. A part of me suspects he's already felt the awakening of the bond between Dayton and me, but he'll wait for me to explain. "Do *you* want to save her, Rosalina?"

I look down at my hands, thinking. In the moments I've spent with Wrenley, there have always been cracks of light shining through her anger, small glimpses of someone who laughs and loves and grieves. There's a deep, overwhelming sadness within her.

When I was young, I fell through the ice and almost drowned.

A part of me thinks Wrenley has been drowning her entire life.

"Yes," I say to Kel. "I want to save her."

"Then trust your heart. A year ago, no one believed the princes of Castletree could be saved. Look what you've done for us, Rose."

I force a smile and touch his face. "Well, I'm still working on one of those princes of Castletree."

Keldarion weaves his fingers through my hair, gaze softening. "If only you could know all the ways you've already saved me. Your sister may not realize it yet, but she is so very lucky to have someone like you, Rose. You bring out the sunlight in a storm. Your love is magic."

"You saw something in Caspian that could be saved," I say softly. "Your love is magic, too."

Keldarion stiffens and his hand tightens in my hair. "Do not do yourself the disservice of equating us. When he wants to be, Caspian is untouchable, even by love. Be careful when it comes to him."

A flash of fear flickers in his eyes. Will he ever be able to trust the Prince of Thorns again? Though, perhaps Kel is the logical one. Here I am, trusting Caspian with my whole heart, even though a voice inside is screaming it could kill me.

I press away from Kel's chest and look around. It's hard to see anything beyond the flicker of flames on the icy cavern walls. "Where are we?"

"The Anelkrol Badlands. Your mother brought us here, though I can't ascertain as to why."

"She must have had a reason."

"I'm sure. She's different than how I expected the Queen to be. A bit . . . peculiar." He raises a brow. "Like a couple other O'Connells I know."

I laugh and fall against his chest.

"There's happiness radiating from you, Rose," Keldarion murmurs. "It's beautiful to see."

"It's Dayton. Our mate bond awoke. His curse is broken, Kel."

A smile breaks across Kel's face. "I suppose you won't appreciate me punching him in the nose anymore?"

Another laugh bubbles out of my chest. "Only when he deserves it."

"Well, it *is* Dayton, so I suppose I'll still have my chance. Even you being his mate won't stop him from acting like an idiot from time to time."

"I think we're both being idiots tomorrow," I whisper. "We fight for Hadria. So much relies on me. I don't know if I can do it."

Keldarion takes my face in his hands and pierces me with his gaze. "Do not let doubt cloud your courage. If it does, take every piece of mine."

"Kel . . ."

He kisses me deeply, then pulls back only a breath. "Inside you is power the realms have not seen in an age. Embrace your legacy. Let your heart guide you. This world was created by the same magic that flows through your veins. Do not doubt for a moment that you have the strength to shape it."

My hands grip his shirt. The winds of Winter begin to whip around me before turning to a warm breeze. "I'll see you soon, Kel. I promise."

"Wake now, Rose, to a glorious dawn. Shadows may be falling from the sky, but you are the sun. People pray for your light."

PART SIX
BENEATH THE WAVES

108

CASPIAN

My mother sits on her throne of shadows, suspended hundreds of feet in the air over the sands outside of Hadria. Beneath her, an army of thousands of skeletons marches back and forth, green inner fire flickering out of their eye sockets and from between their ribs. The walls around Hadria seem but a pathetic obstacle to such an army.

I lick my lips and force my heart to slow. As much as I'd love to believe this is the only path before me, I know there are others. I could denounce my loyalty to the Below, bring my alliance with the Golden Rose out into the daylight. I could run away, disappear into the human realm, and hide under a rock until the sickness takes me.

But instead, I'm doing what I've always done. One foot in the grave, the other ready to make a mad dash away. I made a promise long ago to protect both of Aurelia's daughters and if I'm to uphold that vow, then this is the only path forward.

My thorns arc me up through the air, my hold on them growing thinner and more tenuous as I ascend. Though this power originated in the Above, it doesn't seem to like being away from the earth. My mother doesn't say anything as I waver before her, suspended only by my thin thorns. Her long black hair billows in the wind as if it is one of her shadows. She sits stiff-backed, hands digging into the armrests.

I look around. What a strange sight this is: the bright blue sky of the

Summer Realm with this horrid splotch of dark shadow clouds. My mother's macabre throne floats over the sands like some sort of ghoul from a child's nightmare. If you ask me, the whole thing is completely tacky.

But of course, Sira would never ask me. My opinion has never been as valuable to her as my unquestioning loyalty.

My only hope is there's still a shred of it to keep me alive for the next few minutes.

"Mother." I bow my head before her. "Welcome to the Summer Realm."

She flicks her gaze toward me. On the outside, I'm perfectly still. On the inside, my pulse races. Can she tell how nervous I am? Does she know I was involved in the breaking of the crystals?

Did Father tell her or is this another one of our little secrets?

Her lip curls slightly. "I didn't expect to see you here. You always seem to be missing when I need you."

"Apologies," I breathe.

"Perhaps you can be of use. Sit." She waves a hand.

I nearly let loose a sigh of relief but keep my face a steady mask. I hate the feel of these shadows beneath my feet. It seems as if I should slip right through, but somehow my weight holds. Though, it's an always present reminder that anytime she wants, the Queen of the Below could whip them out from under me.

"You've brought the Baron's army to the gates of Hadria," I say mildly. "Birdy's plan wasn't working fast enough for you?"

I looked for my sister after leaving the parade of heroes, but she was nowhere to be found. With Dayton and Rosalina's mate bond forged, and her plan in shambles, I expect she's in no hurry to report to our mother.

A twinge of worry and unease passes through me. A desperate Birdy is a dangerous one. There's no telling what she's capable of in this state.

Sira doesn't respond for a long time, her gaze out on the horizon. There's something different about her face. Her black eyes are shiny . . .

She's about to cry, I realize. She's fighting not to.

My mother, the Queen of the Below, who I have never seen have another expression beyond what I call "intense constipation."

"She almost escaped, Cas," Sira breathes. "Where were you last night? I needed you. Everything broke down."

"I'm sorry, Mother. I was trying to find the Golden Rose."

She buries her face in her hands. "I am cursed with a flippant son! He leaves me defenseless against invaders!"

I gently place a hand on her arm. She peeks out from between her fingers at me. "I'm sorry, Mother."

Truly, I am. Even though every word from her mouth is a lie. I have never been flippant. She has never been defenseless, and I am no savior.

I see what mood she's in. One that strives to guilt and cajole. It still works on Birdy, but I was broken of my sympathy for her after the hundredth beating I received at her order.

In fact, these tears—however real they may be—make me sick. I need to leave, even if I choke on filth from my lungs. I can't sit here, batting my eyelashes anymore as she sits outside of a city filled with innocents.

But Birdy! What of Birdy girl?

"Those damned High Princes did something," Mother says. She grabs my hand with both of hers and wrings it tightly as if for support. "One of them got in, I think. Broke your father's crystals."

"Did Aurelia escape?" My voice is barely more than a whisper.

"No, of course not." Mother sits back on her throne. "She won't leave. I know it, too, but still the thought . . ." Those tears are back, glistening like oil down her face.

"She's still imprisoned?" Damn it, Kel! Everything Farron and I risked was for what? For nothing? She's still there. Rage and grief war up in my chest, and it takes everything I have to keep the gentle smile on my face.

"I'm going to do something drastic, Caspian. I don't want to. Draining her slowly is so much more effective in the long-term, but they've pushed me too far. I'll have to take all her magic. At once."

"She won't survive. You could lose everything if she dies too soon," I say, fighting my rising panic.

"I know. But there's always the Golden Rose." Mother waves a hand as if to displace the bothering thought. "Those pesky princes may have slowed us down, but we'll remake the crystals. We'll summon enough magic to turn the pool into a portal to bridge the gap between worlds. Your father will reunite with us, Caspian." She runs a hand along my cheek, a shaky smile on her face. "We'll be a family soon. Your father, me, you, and your sister. The four of us will see this world renewed from the ashes of the Green Flame."

"What a day it will be," I say.

Plans within plans within plans. My mother envisions a world ruled by the god she worships and the children she's broken. All while that god intends to use her as collateral.

Her grip becomes more urgent, fingers clawing down my face. Her expression breaks into a pained grimace. "When will you do it, son? When will you take up your father's mantle? His power flows through you. You have but to step into the pool—"

I grab her wrists and direct her hands away from my face, lest she scratches an eye. "I would not be so selfish as to take a drop of his power while the crystals need to be remade. Let us first work on refortifying. If the princes tried to break Aurelia out once, they will try again."

Sira gives her version of a laugh. "It doesn't matter. I could fling the doors wide open and invite them in. Aurelia won't leave."

Again, I steady every motion, every tic of my face. *Won't* leave. Not *can't*. *Won't*.

"How are you so certain?"

"Because she is a fool who loves her children," Sira says sadly, then looks to me. "The one thing we unfortunately have in common."

An ache I'd long abandoned re-emerges in my chest. Her love may be poisonous, but it does not mean I don't crave it all the same.

"The most tragic part of this whole ordeal is that I must retaliate," Sira says, peering down at the army below us. "I don't even know which damned prince it was who broke in, so I don't know what realm to obliterate. But figuring as your sister's been having such slow progress here, and I've heard word that Daytonales is stirring up trouble, why, it seemed like the perfect city to make an example of."

"Tragic because the people won't swear fealty to you?" I ask tentatively.

Mother rolls her eyes. "Tragic because I was saving this army to bring Frostfang to its knees. Never mind though. I'm sure they'll make quick work of the peasants here. Then we can march on Winter. We can take Autumn on the way!" She claps her hands. "Perhaps this isn't such a loss after all."

My composure begins to ebb out of me. "Or perhaps, there's another way. Give Wrenley some more time. She's close to getting the Blessing of Summer. If she takes the rule, then you will have the support of the people by law. Spring has stayed in line because they believe Kairyn to be the rightful ruler—"

"Silence!" Even the clouds ripple with the power and command in her voice. "You children are always making plans and schemes. I'm tired of it. You can have adoring subjects in another realm, Caspian. These fae, I would make an example of."

"What of Wrenley?" I ask.

"I'll figure out something to deal with that disappointment." She stares at me hard. "You're bothering me now. Not one subject has come to swear fealty to me, and it is almost dawn. Make yourself useful and go kill something."

I summon my thorns to lift me from my mother's clouds and give her a deep bow before departing. "My pleasure."

Then, I descend back to Hadria, panic rising in my chest.

For the first time in my life, I don't have a plan.

109

DAYTON

"Easy, girl, easy!" I say, patting the white mane of the winged horse. "Domitia, was it? You're a good girl, Dom. This way."

The giant wings of the horse beat as we descend to Rosalina. My mate stands knee-deep in ocean water, positioned in a small cove outside of the city. "Ready, love?" I ask.

Rosalina turns, dark hair blowing in the breeze. She wears a gleaming bronze breastplate over a long white tunic. A scarlet cloak billows behind her, a bow strung over her back. Stars, my mate looks beautiful dressed like one of the Huntresses of Aura.

"We're all ready," she says.

"Let's fly." I hold out my hand and hoist her up behind me. "Come on, Dom."

Domitia beats her powerful wings, and we rise high into the sky. I keep us hidden in cloud cover as we breach the city walls and hover above Hadria.

"Did you decide where we're doing this?" she asks.

"Somewhere high and close to the sea. No better place than Soltide Keep."

Dom swoops lower, leaving trails of wispy white clouds in her wake. The streets of Hadria are barren besides creatures of the Below stomping over the cobblestone. My citizens believe they must submit to the Queen of the Below or die. We're going to save them from that. All of them.

Dom circles over the spiral towers of Soltide Keep. The glittering white sandstone walls gleam with sea glass and shells, festooned by towers of pastel pink and teal. We land on the highest tower and slide off the Pegasus. The view is nothing short of resplendent.

The first hint of dawn brushes against the ocean's horizon. I look over my city, to the calm waters of the harbor, shielded by the rocky breakwater. For a moment, the world stands still, and I simply *feel*. It seeps into me: the gentle rustle of the breeze, the distant cry of seagulls, and the soft lullaby of waves kissing the shore.

Rosalina gently brushes my fingertips with her own. "Are you ready?"

The answer swells in my chest. "Yes."

Rolling my shoulders, I face the dawn. Navy shadows retreat, surrendering to the brilliance of the morning light, and the world awakens with a newfound vigor. The power of the Summer Realm flows into me. I'm going to need every ounce of it this morning.

I cannot fight this power. I must surrender to it. As magic flows freely between myself and Castletree, so does the Blessing flow between me and this land. Between me and the sea.

My eyes fly open, and my whole body tingles with electricity as I connect with the ocean. I grit my teeth, fighting to weave control through every wave, feeling my awareness spread over the surf. The ocean whispers to me, and I call back: *Help me free my people. Help me save my city. Let me wield your might as my own.*

"Dayton?" Rosalina says.

A smile breaks across my face. "Been a long time since us princes felt what our Blessings could really do."

Like a released breath, the ocean surrenders. I stretch my fingers out before me, feeling as if the world is in the palm of my hands. I flick my wrist and waves crash against a nearby shore.

"There you are," I grit out. Sweat drips down my brow. Power thrums within me, a tempest waiting to be unleashed. I feel the ebb and flow of the waves as they respond to my command. The air crackles with energy.

With agonizing effort, I draw the sea back . . .

Far on the horizon, a great wave rises from the depths of the ocean like a titan awakening from slumber, its towering crest garlanded with a frosty crown of foam.

"Oh my god," Rosalina whispers.

Digging my heels into the ground, my fingers flex as all my concentration pools into controlling this wave.

As it draws closer, its sheer magnitude becomes apparent, dwarfing everything in its path. The water surges forward with primal fury. The fury of the ocean. My fury. A deafening roar thunders.

Below, screams sound as people notice the tsunami on the horizon.

"It's so big, Day," Rosalina gasps. I turn and see a flicker of fear in her eyes.

But all I can do is let out a strained laugh. "That's the same thing you said last night."

"Day—"

"Hey, I make jokes when I'm nervous."

The thundering is immense now, roaring in my ears, my own rapid heartbeat drowning out everything else. I can taste the salt on my lips, feel the spray of the sea as it dances upon my skin. This is my domain, my birthright, and I shall not hesitate to wield it as I see fit.

With a primal roar that echoes across the skyline, I unleash the full might of my magic.

"Dayton!" Rosalina yells. "Release it! It's too close!"

"Not yet," I snarl.

The wave rises higher, a towering wall of water that roils closer and closer.

"Dayton!"

More screams sound, and I distantly hear my name being called. The people have noticed me up here.

"Dayton! It's too close!"

"Hope your fucking green skeletons know how to swim, Sira," I growl.

With a flick of my wrist, I command the great wave to halt its relentless advance just outside the breakwater, a singular barrier between destruction and salvation. It washes against the stones with a deafening roar. The impact sends a spray of mist cascading into the air.

For a heartbeat, the world holds its breath, teetering on the edge of calamity. Then, with a whispered command, I release the wave from my leash, allowing it to unfurl its fury upon Hadria.

The water surges forward like a ravenous beast, hungrily devouring everything in its path. Buildings tremble beneath the onslaught, their foundations shaken to the very core by the unyielding force of the tide. People flee in panic, and so do the monsters of the Green Flame.

Inside my body is on fire, my Blessing ablaze, magic pricking my fingertips. After being coiled for so long, it wanted to be used.

"Your plan is working." I guide the wave with a delicate precision, channeling its might into controlled torrents that cascade through the streets like rivers of liquid silver. Where once there was chaos, now there is order, as the water follows the path that I have laid out for it with unwavering obedience.

"The power of the sea," Rosalina whispers.

"I'd say we have about thirty minutes until the lower city floods, an hour till it makes it to the arena. By nightfall, the entire city of Hadria will be underwater." I turn to Rosalina and grip her face. "It's your turn, Blossom."

110

ROSALINA

The wave dissipates into a sea of churning currents as I stand with Dayton on Soltide Keep. The city lies before us, transformed by the power of the ocean into a landscape of surreal beauty and devastation. Transformed by my mate.

This is what the Blessing of Summer is capable of without being hindered by the curse. I can only imagine Dayton's power if Castletree was at full strength.

Panic rises in the city, but all I see is hope. A promise of renewal in the wake of destruction. My mate has unleashed the fury of the ocean upon Hadria. The city will not survive.

But its people will.

"I'm ready," I say.

Dayton grips my hand, and I feel the swell of his magic flow into me.

Change is a magic I inherited from the Queen. A power she used to save her people.

A magic I will use today.

As I close my eyes and immerse myself in the ethereal realm of magic, I feel the pulse of the Summer Realm echoing through my veins like a beam of sunlight. It calls to me, a whisper on the breeze, allowing me to weave enchantment to all those born from its embrace.

With a soft exhale, I extend my consciousness across the vast expanse of Hadria, reaching out to touch the hearts of its inhabitants. As when I cast my magic out in search of the sirens, there is a distinct difference to life born of the Vale and life touched by the Below. Even those who have sworn service to vile deeds are tainted by it.

But the citizens of Hadria each feel like a glowing star. I feel the warmth of their souls. Dayton's heart, the heart of the Summer Prince, guides me to them.

Fae of Hadria, today you must change to survive. I, the Golden Rose, will make it so.

I unleash the full extent of my power upon the people of the Summer Realm, infusing them with the essence of the sea and the song of the sirens. Their forms shimmer and shift, bathed in the iridescent glow.

There is a bone-deep knowing within me. When water touches their skin, they will feel the ancient call of the ocean stirring within them. With a single breath, they will be transformed, their fae shells melting away to reveal the radiant beauty of the sirens that lie dormant within.

Gasping, I open my eyes. Already the water has begun to flood the lower city.

"Is it working?" Dayton calls.

Then I see it, a woman running from a skeleton. The water rushes up to cover her. In a splash of light, her legs shift into a glorious tail. The skeleton, however, is swept away by the water, bones smashed in the wake.

"It's working!" I cry.

"And you succeeded in convincing our other friends to help?" Dayton asks.

"They are honoring my mother."

Like thousands of gems sparkling on the surface of the sea, sirens flood in through the harbor. I asked for their aid, to guide the people of Hadria to the safety of Aerantheis. To shelter and teach them the ways of the sea until we can rebuild their home.

Dayton turns to me, hair blowing across his face. "No, Rosalina. They are honoring you, the Golden Rose. Princess of the Enchanted Vale."

III

EZRYN

I dash through the narrow streets of Hadria, the sound of rushing water echoing off the stone walls. My boots are drenched from the rising tide, heart pounding as I work to get as many people to safety as I can.

Up ahead, a man huddles between two barrels, arms wrapped around two children. Each of them having sprouted the fin-like ears of a siren, their skin glinting with a metallic glow.

"Hurry!" I scream to them. "Get to the ocean! You'll be safe there."

Rosalina's magic has worked; the citizens of Hadria will be able to breathe underwater, to grow tails like the sirens who live in these seas. The sirens themselves wait at the ocean's edge, ushering the Hadrians out and bringing them to safety in their underwater city.

I place my hand on the man's shoulder, holding his fearful gaze steady. "The water is your friend. Be brave, now."

"What of the skeletons? Some have survived the flood," the man says, voice quivering.

I lift my mother's blade up to catch the light. "I'll deal with them."

The man nods, then takes his young children by the hand and sprints toward the south.

I look around, searching for any more citizens to urge forward or any skeletons to dismantle. A shadow passes overhead, and I look up to see a winged horse flying above, its rider shooting arrows down into the city, striking enemies from above.

My heart thunders. We may not claim victory this day, but neither will Sira. That in itself is a triumph. Though they will need to rebuild their city, the people of Hadria remain free. That is more than I can say for my own realm.

A rush of water sounds, and I run forward to see the canal has finally fully flooded. Water breaches the banks, spilling into the alleyways. Before I get swept away, I leap straight into the canal, landing on a barrel. The churning water makes the barrel spin, and I barely keep upright. Spotting a sturdier-looking wooden plank, I jump and land upon it. Briny water sprays up at me, blurring my vision. The plank starts to sink with my weight, and I jump again. Each leap is a gamble as I make my way down the canal, using pieces of debris as my stepping stones.

I land upon a broken door, barely keeping balance. A terracotta awning hangs from a stone wall overhead; above it is the upper quadrant of the city. A scream cuts over the rushing water. Propelling off the door, I grab hold of the awning and pull myself up. Tiles slide under my feet. Using brute force, I scramble up the stone wall and heave myself over onto dry pavement. It won't be long before this section of the city is flooded too.

The scream punctures the air again, and I run toward it. A young fae woman sprints down the alley in my direction, a skeleton only steps behind her. I charge forward, sword at the ready, taking the skull of the skeleton with a single swing. The green fire within the monster's chest wanes. I know it won't be long before it reanimates, but at least this will give the woman a chance to escape.

She looks to me, her wide eyes shining. "Th-thank you."

"Get to the sea! There will be people there waiting to help you."

Her eyes widen even more. "I saw it. When we go into the water, we're changing. What's happened to us?"

"You have been blessed by the Queen's magic," I say assuredly. "She has given you a great gift."

The woman looks up, a sense of awe on her face. "She has returned."

"Go! The water is safer than the land now. Tell everyone you see. Get to the water!"

The woman runs off, and I allow a moment to catch my breath. My own gaze drifts to the sky. Somewhere up there, Delphia and Nori are both on winged horseback, scouting for survivors. Rosalina and Dayton have completed the first part of their plan.

Dayton's power . . . It's incredible. He brought the entire ocean to his beck and call. The awe apparent on the woman's face from a moment ago—it is nothing if not warranted. Just as the Queen performed miracles an age ago, now so does her daughter.

I suck in another deep breath. I must do my part. I will clear this city and save as many as I can.

The marketplace is on this level of the city. There may be scared citizens hiding there. I take off at a run, cutting through a backstreet passage—

There's a figure at the end of the alley, turning in a circle as if he's lost or unsure what to do with himself. He's a fae, not a siren, and entirely too well-dressed for a battle.

Caspian.

My reaction surprises myself. Gone is the white-hot rage from the last time I saw him. Instead, it's as if my whole body has been plunged into freezing water. My muscles tense. My eyes narrow. Caspian . . . here. In the city.

Farron says they worked together to try and free the Queen. But I know better. So many people I love have been led astray by his charm and guile.

If he helped us once, it's only to lead us into a greater betrayal.

I understand now. This is fate. Everything between me and the Prince of Thorns has led to this moment. Everything I have learned from giving up my Blessing, from losing Florendel, and from traveling through the desert . . . it has led to this.

I feel the weight and strength of my blade. It is my duty to protect my family. To protect those I love.

And Caspian has always been a threat to that.

The son of Sira killed my father. He torments my mate. He destroyed the life of my best friend. Now, he helps his mother take over a city and slaughter innocents.

I will do what I must.

My feet have wings as I surge toward him.

Caspian turns and catches sight of me. His lavender eyes shimmer with mirth. "Ah, Ezryn! What a sight for sore eyes. Still gracing us with the helmet-less look, I see, and how fine it is! Now, it appears I've missed something important. Turning all of Hadria's citizens into sirens is certainly a bold move, but what else could I expect fro—"

I don't let him finish. The moment I reach him, I swing my sword down in a cleaving arc. He ducks out of the way with the agility of a cat.

He stumbles out of the alley to the open street. "Not exactly the greeting I was hoping for."

A growl sounds in my throat. "I told you that the next time I saw you, I would kill you. For all my evils, I do not break promises."

Caspian ducks under my next swing and smiles up at me with that smarmy grin. "I don't suppose you want to hear my side of things?"

I respond by slashing at him again.

He leans back so far, my blade skims over his chest. "I'll take that as a no."

I punctuate each word with a swing of my sword: "You. Killed. My. Father!"

Caspian lets loose a sigh, one of his thorns erupting out of the ground to whip him over my head and away from my attack. "I know, Ez, but trust me, it was the merciful choice. He'd been poisoned for months! Another moment and he'd have been one of Perth Quellos's monsters. Would it have been better if you'd killed him yourself?"

Rosalina told me the same thing. But she has yet to realize every word from the Prince of Thorns' forked tongue is twisted. "Liar."

Caspian lands and dusts off the shoulders of his coat. "I saved you from the fate of murdering both your parents."

The icy frost taming my rage begins to melt. An inhuman sound erupts from my throat, and I charge at him, sending Caspian skittering back and falling across the sandstone. Water splashes up around him, and only now do I realize this street is beginning to flood.

"It's the truth," Cas spits, touching a scrape along his cheek. "I did it, so you wouldn't have to."

My mind races. "And who poisoned him in the first place? One of your minions? The acolyte who pretended to serve him?"

If I didn't know better, I would say a look of remorse crosses his face. "I am genuinely sorry for your loss, and what my sister helped do to your people."

My shadow spills over Caspian. He still hasn't stood. Instead, he's crouched on all fours, water sloshing at his boots.

"I will kill you for everything you've done to me and those I love," I say and place the point of my sword at his neck.

Caspian rolls his eyes. "Really, Ezryn? Kairyn takes over two realms, banished and mutilated you, and you find forgiveness for him, but for me? Nothing?"

"I do not forgive Kairyn," I snarl. "I spared his life because he is my brother!" I whip my sword up in the air, preparing to strike.

Caspian gives a weak smile. "Weren't we also, Ez? Once upon a time?"

I freeze. No, no, it was never like that between us. I loved Kel, and because of that, I tolerated Caspian. But I always knew, in the depths of my heart, there was something wicked inside of him. "Never. I always knew you would betray Keldarion."

I swing my sword down. In a single movement, Caspian stands, drawing up a thick briar to block my attack. I growl and push harder, my blade slowly cutting through the wood.

"Kel betrayed me first," Caspian hisses. "He brought his army to Cryptgarden. He rampaged my city. His soldiers hurt people I cared about. I may have stabbed him in the back, but he drew the blade."

I push harder until Caspian's face is right in front of mine, only a breath away. In a moment, my sword will cleave through this briar and take his head from his shoulders. As he is to die, I tell him the truth. "It was never Kel. *I* ordered the attack on Cryptgarden."

Caspian blinks. "No. Keldarion said—"

"Keldarion *lied*," I growl. "I would have gladly admitted the truth, but Kel refused to let me say anything. He was worried you would kill me. But here we are, all the same. I knew you were plotting with Sira. I knew you'd strike Keldarion down at the first convenient moment. I had to strike first. If only Kel had told you the truth, we could have had this battle out in the open a long time ago."

My sword cracks through the briar, but Caspian leaps back. He bows his head, hair shading his eyes.

The air around us grows cold, and my shadow seeps out from in front of me to form a sword in Caspian's hand. A blade of pure darkness.

Caspian looks up at me, eyes glinting. "Then this has been a long time coming."

112

KELDARION

A shiver runs through my bones, and I wrap my coat tighter around myself. If I can feel it, I know it's cold. The sun blares down, heatless and intense, shining off the huge icy walls that pin us in on either side. Dark purple briars are frozen within the ice, terrifying visages of war.

Why did you send us here, Aurelia? Her briars could have taken us anywhere. She might have sent us back to Castletree. Or even somewhere in Frostfang. But no, the Queen of the Vale sent us to the coldest, most desolate place in all the Enchanted Vale. A place I once waged war. The Anelkrol Badlands.

Rosalina was able to find us here. Though I was only able to hold her for a few moments, her touch has given me the strength to continue, to find a way out of this barren wasteland. She will face her own battle today; the very least I can do is see her father to safety.

I know where in the Badlands we are because we're walking through a giant rift in the earth, the ground frozen beneath us, canyon walls made of ice so crystal clear I can see my reflection. Briars poke up here and there but are mostly frozen within the walls or under our feet. The canyon breaks off in different directions. Another damned labyrinth. I can't even use the seed Caspian gave us because the ground is so frozen, there's nowhere to plant it.

I hate this place. It's where Caspian and I did battle, just us two, when both our hearts were so ripped open, we needed the earth to reflect it.

George is far behind me, stumbling and shivering. His face is ghastly pale, eyes dull. I don't know if it's from Castletree's sickness or his own grief. I stop and wait for him to catch up.

"How are you holding up, George?"

No response.

"Would you prefer to ride on my back? I can shift."

Again, he wanders on like a lifeless corpse.

I jog back up beside him. "Once we're out of this canyon and onto the flatlands, I can navigate our way back to Voidseal Bridge. We'll rest there, then make the journey to Frostfang. It'll be a long road. How about a story? I think you only got halfway through your tale of the—what was it? The conservation of the ruins in Pompey? Pompeii? Yes, that was it."

George's chest heaves but he doesn't stop walking.

I sigh and follow behind him. "I'm sorry, George. I can only imagine how hard it was to leave Anya there. But there was no other choice."

George stops and turns to me. A spark finally appears in his eyes. "You," he growls. "You made me leave. I should be down there with her!"

I storm over to him. "You heard your wife. You have two daughters to look after now. Do you remember the prophecy given by the Fate? 'You are destined to find Rosalina shattered.' We can't let that happen. She needs us both."

George sneers and turns away. "It wasn't 'Rosalina shattered.' It was 'your rose shattered' and I'll do whatever it takes to protect my daughter. My . . . daughters."

Your rose shattered. What else could it mean? *Go back to the place where all was lost.*

My rose . . . all was lost.

I start to run.

I know this crack. It's where I sent a blast of air so powerful, it cut into the earth. Caspian's flames turned the ice brittle, and it collapsed a wall here. Yes, yes and then our magic met together creating a pit around this corner. It's still here, gaping down into the earth.

George yells my name, chasing after me, but I can't stop. I keep running, following the scars of our heartbreak across the landscape. I'd created a massive rift that turned into a fork. I take the right passage. Caspian had grown thorns so giant they formed a bridge over a crack in the ground. I run across them, feet slipping on the icy surface. George's voice follows behind me.

And here . . . here was where the calamity of our magic met. A crater forged within the canyon, the place where Caspian and I unleashed all the rage and grief and love from our time together.

The place where we destroyed the rose stolen from the Gardens of Ithilias.

My steps echo as I stumble out into the crater. Time has changed this place. The ice has turned to bluish-green crystal, infused with Caspian's magic. My reflection looks up at me as I cross the middle.

"Magnificent," George whispers, catching up to me.

"This is a place of destruction," I say. "Caspian and I spent years searching for the rose of Ithilias, only for it to be collateral damage in the battle. That rose could have changed the tide of war. Every monster Sira's ever created answers to its magic."

George's brow furrows. His pace increases and he walks out in front of me, then sinks to the ground, fingers feeling the furrows of crystal.

"I thought," I whisper, "maybe Aurelia sent me here for a reason. But it's probably because it was closest to the surface above the prison."

"Or maybe," George says, "it's because the prophecy is coming true."

He's staring straight down in the middle of the crater. I walk over, my heart the only sound I can hear.

There, beneath the blue-green crystal, are shattered pieces of a rose. Even now, I can see the shards still shine with a celestial light.

A fragment of the Above that could turn the tide of this war.

I turn to George. "You ever excavated an artefact out of ice?"

He smiles. "Oh, have I got a story for you."

113

DAYTON

Wind rushes past us as Rosalina and I scour the streets from the skies above Hadria. She clutches the reins of a winged horse, while I sit behind her, hands tight around her waist. Nearby, Farron rides a dark brown Pegasus, looking as if he's ridden one all his life. He's always had a way with animals. Probably why he's always had a way with me.

Our plan is . . . working. Below, sirens man the shoreline, guiding the newly turned fae down to refuge in Aerantheis. Most of Sira's army has been swept away, nothing but bones floundering in the sea. Even Sira herself has disappeared. Her shadow throne still hangs in the air, but it sits empty.

Meanwhile, the Huntresses scour the skies, looking for survivors to help or any rogue skeletons to destroy. I know Ezryn's taken to searching the city by foot to find anyone we can't see from above.

"Down here!" Farron shouts. "There's a family cowering on that rooftop. I'm going to go help them."

"You got it?" I call back.

"Yes, keep going. I'll catch up." Farron pulls on the reins and his horse folds its wings into a dive.

We keep flying. I look behind me at the shore, trying to find strength in all of the people of Hadria escaping. And yet . . . when I look down at what was once my home, it feels like my ribs are pulling apart. Down there was the theater my mother loved to drag me to. The stage is hidden by the blue-green sea, only the tip of its roof visible, and the street straight below us used to house the public baths. I imagine the entire room is underwater.

And just ahead of us is the arena. Has the water breached its walls yet? Are the sands once soaked with blood now cleansed by the sea?

"We should check the arena for anyone hiding there—" Rosalina begins before a gasp escapes her. She yanks hard on the reins, our winged horse jerking to the left just as a blinding bolt of light shoots past us.

"What the fuck was that?" I scream.

Rosalina doesn't have time to answer as she coaxes our Pegasus into a full-out dive, barely avoiding another golden beam of light. We balance out, our steed's wings spread wide. "It's her." Rosalina points to the arena.

I narrow my eyes. I can see the water pounding at the walls and closed doors of the stadium but some has seeped through. A figure stands in the middle of the arena, about knee-deep in water. She lowers a golden bow and glares up at us.

Ah. My sweet "mate." Wrenley.

"She finally got brave enough to try holding that damned thing," I growl. "You O'Connells and your Queen's blood."

"I have to talk to her," Rosalina says.

"Yeah, well, she doesn't really seem in the mood to talk." I grab Rosalina's shoulder. "Rosie, one strike from that bow could bring down a High Prince. If she hits you—"

Rosalina snaps the reins, the steed responding instantly, darting down into the arena. "I have to try to get through to her. She's my sister." Something dark and ruthless sounds in Rosalina's voice. "And that's my bow."

114

ROSALINA

As soon as we start descending into the arena, Wrenley stops shooting at us. Was she even trying to hit us before, or was it all just a challenge?

I see the wildness in her gaze, even from up here. It's different than the fierce look she has as the Nightingale. Dressed in soaking wet, torn acolyte robes, her hair a mess, her face visible without the mask, she appears even more frightening than in her armor. Her mouth twitches between a smile and a frown, and her pupils are needle points.

I pull on the reins when we're a few feet above the flooded ground. Dayton slips off, splashing in the water, and I follow suit. My feet sink into mud: the once sacred sand of the arena now turned to muck. Clicking my tongue like Delphia taught me to on the airship, I direct our steed to circle above us. There's nowhere for it to safely land here.

"The gilded flower has come at last to look upon the weed!" Wrenley throws her head back and laughs. "Well, this weed wields the ultimate ethereal power!" She draws back the string of light on the bow. A huge arc of radiance shoots out, smashing into the stands. The seats erupt in white flame.

"You need to put that down," I say calmly. "It could hurt you."

She cradles it, staring down adoringly. "That's what they always wanted me to believe. That I wasn't strong enough. Caspian. Kairyn. They didn't believe in me." Her blue gaze flicks up to mine. "But my blood is just as worthy as yours."

Dayton's sidestepped to her right. "We get it, Wrenley. You got your fancy bow. Good for you. But you've lost. Summer's Blessing will never belong to you!"

Wrenley's lip curls, and she gives Dayton a scathing look. "I had to endure months of your senseless rambling. Vex me further, and I'll shut your mouth for good."

Dayton responds with his thousand-watt smile. "Ah, come on, Wren. They weren't all bad times, were they?"

Don't provoke the unstable woman with a deadly weapon, I snap in my mind.

Instead, he tries to turn that smile on me. *Hey, this is fun! Your voice is just as sexy in my mind.*

Focus!

Dayton sighs, then draws his dual blades. "Enough's enough. Drop the bow, Wren."

"Never!" She smacks the bow down upon the water, sending up a spray.

"Listen to me." I chance a step forward. "You don't have to do this. I know how Sira treats people down Below. I know how she treats Caspian. If that's what you've experienced, I'm so sorry. We can work together—"

"You stupid, vain idiot!" she shrieks. Another blast of the bow shoots off into the stands. A rumble sounds: the breaking of wood and stone. "How easy the world has been for you, hasn't it, Princess? Coddled from birth like a kept dog! You know nothing of suffering!"

My heart thunders at her tight grip on the bow, but I dare another step closer to her. "Actually, my life hasn't always been easy. I've always known I was missing something. Missing part of my family." Steeling my heart, I close the final gap between us. She shivers at my proximity, every muscle in her body twitching as if she can't stay still. Her eyes waver like a stormy sea. "I was missing my sister."

Our eyes connect. I see Papa in her: in her tenacity, her stubbornness, in the horizon of her eyes, and I see our mother too, in the wave of her hair, the resilience of her spirit.

Her shriek splits the air between us. "Shut up! Shut up! Shut up!" Cradling the bow again, she sprints away from me before falling to her knees in the water.

"Wrenley!" I step toward her, but Dayton grabs my shoulder and holds me back.

My sister sits up, bow in her lap, and cries, "Summer is lost! Everything I worked for! Do you know what she'll do to me? I could have done it. I could have had it all." Her body stills, gaze flickering with inner fire. "Except you ruined it. *Again.*"

With a roar, she gets to her feet and draws back the bow. Blinding light after blinding light bombards the stands. Explosions of rock smash into the water. Dayton shields my body with his own.

"Are you insane?" he yells at her. "You hit the walls, and this place will be underwater in minutes! You hit a keystone, and we'll be trapped under rubble!"

Wrenley doesn't hear him. She shoots bolt after bolt, tears flinging from her eyes. "I have no sister! No brother! I have only myself!"

Water starts to flood faster into the arena, drenching me up to my waist. The breath comes ragged from my throat. I push away from Dayton and surge toward her.

She's facing away from me now, screeching and crying, fingers raw from shooting the bow. A chunk of the stands collapses inward, crumbling to the water. Still, she doesn't stop firing.

"Rosalina!" Dayton calls. "The foundation is falling apart. We have to go. Now!"

I can't go yet. Each step is an effort, but I don't stop. She doesn't even notice as I come up behind her. "You have me," I breathe. Then I wrap my arms around her waist and hug her to my body.

She stills. The bow lowers, dipping into the water.

"They left me," she whispers. "All of them. Kairyn chose his brother. Caspian chose you. It's so easy for them."

"I'm choosing you," I say into her shoulder. "I choose you, Wrenley. You're my sister by blood, but more than that, I want to know you."

"Why?" she breathes. "I . . . I hate you."

"I know. But trust me, you're not the first person I've had to win over."

She shakes slightly in my arms, and I wonder if it's the beginning of a laugh.

"Come with me," I say.

"I can't."

"You *can.* I know it's hard, but—"

Wrenley growls, then tears free of my grip. Her words are a pained shriek: "*I CAN'T!*"

I back up, afraid of the pure anger in her voice.

The colosseum groans around us.

"Rosalina, we have to go now!" Dayton calls, hand in a fist above his head: the signal for our steed to retrieve us. *We'll have to find another way to get the bow. She's damaged the integrity of the structure. This whole place is going to come down in a minute,* he says in my mind.

No, no, I was *so* close to getting through to her. I just need another moment, another piece of connection—

But it's as if she's descended back into that darkness, hands wringing around the glowing grip of the bow. "I need to kill you," she whispers. "It's the only way to fix this."

Rosalina! Dayton shouts in my mind at the same time as another voice echoes out across the arena: "Wrenley!"

I look behind me to see a dark silhouette peering out from the Emperor's Box above the arena. Kairyn's hand is outstretched, as if reaching for her.

Wrenley looks up at him, pain melting off her face. "Kai. You came back."

"Fucking great," Dayton groans. "Just what we need. Him."

But I don't think he even notices Dayton or me. His visor's gaze is entirely on Wrenley. Tendrils of seagrass spurt up from the water and wrap around his arms, carrying him down into the arena. The water has now drained in so deeply, it's up to his chest. He doesn't seem to care, wading toward her.

"I just got back to Hadria," he calls. "Are you all right? What's happened?"

Wrenley only manages a pathetic sob. "Kai!" She turns away from us and starts pushing through the water toward him, slinging the bow across her body.

"Now's our chance to escape!" Dayton calls. Our winged steed rushes down, and Dayton grabs its neck, hauling himself onto its back. I turn to move closer to them—

A thunderous roar shakes the arena as my feet go out from under me. I'm swept into the water, which is suddenly rushing. Kicking to the surface, I look in horror to see part of the arena has completely collapsed. The stands have fallen inward, and a yawning abyss has opened in the ground. Water and broken stone pour into the massive hole.

"Kairyn!" Wrenley screams, and I watch as his black armor drags him down under the water. All I see is his cape rising to the surface as he spills down into the hole.

My sister fights for purchase, but the current is too strong, the hole acting like a drain. With a panicked cry, she shoots an iridescent briar upward. It wraps around a pillar, but it's too weak from the explosion, crumbling under the force.

Her face breaks. "Mother! Help me!"

"Rosalina!" Dayton cries. His steed beats its powerful wings above me, and Dayton reaches down. I fling my arm up, and he snags me by the wrist.

"Mother!" Wrenley screams again.

Dark shadows materialize into the form of a woman: she has no features, only a shadowy, floating thing, but I recognize the Queen of the Below from feel alone. "Pity. You turned out to be such a disappointment, daughter," she says softly, but reaches her shadow hand down toward Wrenley, who surges closer to the hole.

Wrenley stretches her hand to grab her mother's . . . but the shadow snags the bow instead. It envelops the sacred weapon in darkness, smothering even its shine.

"Mother?" Wrenley cries.

"How many failures must I endure?" the shadow creature sighs. "We'll discuss this when you're home, daughter. If you make it home."

In a burst of darkness, the shadow figure and my bow disappear.

Wrenley lets out a wretched cry before careening down into the hole.

"I got you," Dayton says and begins to pull me up onto our horse.

I look up at him, my beautiful mate. How lucky I am to have had so much love in my life. Then, I look back toward the hole, filling faster and faster with more water.

"I'm sorry, Dayton," I say. "I have to save my sister."

I let go of his hand and fall.

115

ROSALINA

I plunge down the pit, roaring water swallowing me like the maw of an ancient beast. The world turns into a blur of white foam as I freefall. My stomach leaps into my throat. I don't have a moment to scream before I land in the water. Panic clenches my chest as water encapsulates me on all sides. There's nothing but darkness, no way to know up from down.

The deafening roar fades as I kick my legs furiously. There's a glimmer of light above me. My heart pounds in my ears until I break the surface, gasping in air.

This pit below the arena is vast and cavernous, the only light coming from the hole where the water surges through. Remnants of the arena bob around me: pillars, wooden benches from the stands, and even gladiator shields. Chunks of the stone structure still rise out of the water, forming islands.

I swim over to a raised pile of stone and pull myself up. Ancient faces peer back at me, and I realize this was once a mural. A flame sparks on my palm, illuminating the area around me. "Wrenley? Wrenley!"

I catch sight of her bobbing in the water. She's face up, but her eyes are closed, limbs spread around her. My flame whooshes out as I leap into the water and swim over to her. "Hold on." I wrap my arms under hers and use my feet to kick us back to the stone island. With a grunt, I haul her out of the water and lay her flat upon the rock.

Ear to her chest, I count her heartbeats. She's passed out, but her heart rate is steady and she's breathing. There's a gash over her eyebrow that drips blood down the curve of her jaw, but otherwise she seems okay.

I breathe a sigh of relief. "I'm going to keep you safe." She looks so innocent, her cheeks full, lashes long. In another universe, I would have gazed upon this face all my life. What would it have been like growing up with a sister? Would we have fought over the bathroom? Gone to movies together? Cried about boys? It all seems so . . . ordinary. "I would have liked some ordinary moments with you," I whisper.

I have to get her out of here. The water level is rising fast. I stand and look around. Going through the pit we came through won't work: the water's coming down too strong. Another glint of light catches my eye. Another part of the colosseum has collapsed, revealing a hole in the ceiling of this cavern. The brilliant Summer sky shines through the gap. That's my way out of here. Standing on my tiptoes, I catch a glimpse of a flat rooftop: part of the Serenus Dusk Chambers, I think. Looks stable enough. We'll be safe from the water there.

A wheeze echoes through the cavern. I spin in a circle, trying to locate the sound. Another gagging cough follows, and my gaze catches on a heap of piled stone about twenty feet away from us. A pillar has fallen on top of it and smashed in two. Lying beneath one of the pieces is . . .

Kairyn.

He makes another horrid sound. I turn away from him, concentrating on Wrenley.

"R-Rosalina." His voice echoes through the cavern.

I should pretend I never heard him, spirit Wrenley away and leave him here in the dark alone—

"Rosalina, please. I need to speak with you."

I squeeze my eyes shut and ball my hands into fists, cursing myself. Then, I look down at Wrenley. "I'll be right back."

I cross the distance between us in only moments, my body used to swimming now, and pull myself up on the rock platform. My breath catches in my throat as I look down at him. The giant pillar, still shimmering white, lies right over his chest. One of his arms is completely pinned, and the other is limp beside him.

His helm, that formidable owl's visage, is dented and scratched.

I kneel beside him. "You're hurt. Why would you want to see me?"

"My helm. Remove it. *Please.*"

A part of me begins to protest, but then I look at his body, completely broken beneath the pillar, and do as he asks. I remove it carefully, guiding the dented helm over his jaw and ears, before it comes fully free. I set it to the side.

Kairyn's dark eyes shine in the dim light, struggling to find my own. My throat tightens. He *is* just a boy, the same as I thought when I first saw his face without a helm. A man brand-new. I hate how much of Ezryn I see in him, not just in the features, but in the memories I envision of his life.

"Why did you want to speak with me?" I whisper.

He swallows. "Save her. Please. Please, don't let her die here in the dark."

He's talking about Wrenley, I realize.

"She hates the dark. Take her to the sunshine. Please, Rosalina. Don't leave her alone."

He doesn't know that's why I came here—to bring my sister back from the dark. I steady my breath. Maybe there's a chance here.

"Why should I save her?" I ask.

"Please! She's . . . your family."

"What do you know about family? You tried to kill your own brother."

"Yet, after everything I've done, he spared my life." Kairyn closes his eyes, and a tear squeezes out and drips down his face. "I wanted him to see me for who I truly was. In the end, he still hasn't. He would have murdered me if he had."

"Or maybe he sees something in you that you don't yet," I say quietly. I place a hand on his forehead.

He opens his eyes, blinks becoming slow and distant. "Will you do it, Golden Rose? Will you save her?"

"Yes." I wipe the tear off his cheek. "She will be safe."

He lets out a sigh and smiles. It's the first time I've ever seen it. It's different than Ezryn's, but beautiful in its own way, crooked and . . . soft. The one soft thing about him.

His movements are shaky as he reaches his one free hand to mine and lifts it onto his chest, over his heart. "Tell Ezryn . . . tell Ezryn I only ever wanted to make him proud."

He's dying. The thought comes to me all at once. I knew it in my heart, but now my mind has words for it. This boy is dying.

Spring will be without a High Ruler.

"Kairyn, what of your Blessing?"

His breath only wheezes now, his face drained of color. "I have no blood-heir. I must choose . . ."

A pit opens in my stomach. What will become of the Blessing? Of the people of Spring? Will Kairyn pass it to one of his minions who will rule with a tighter fist than he has? Or is the magic destined to vanish from the realms forever—

Kairyn offers me that smile again, and his eyes find mine. A warm glow trickles over my skin, the feeling of standing under a spring rain.

Where my hand touches his chest, a golden glow erupts forth.

Magic blooms within my heart. Whispers of Spring sparkle through my body. All at once, I am a cherry blossom unfurling under an azure sky, a blade of grass fighting for sunlight through the fresh earth. A sense of renewal sweeps through me, a caress that eases winter's icy grip and makes way for summer.

Every bud that blooms, every bird that sings, does so in a language older than words, and I know it all. Like a storm that makes way for new life, I feel the power of rejuvenation flow through me.

I am Kairyn. I am Ezryn. I am Isidora, and all the High Rulers of Spring that have come before.

I clutch my heart and gasp. "You . . . you gave me the Blessing of Spring."

Kairyn closes his eyes. "Find someone who will do better with the Blessing than I did."

I stagger to my feet and stumble a few feet away from him. I turn inward, as if speaking to this new magic. *I will keep you safe, I promise. Keep you safe until I find a heart worthy of wielding you.*

I leave Kairyn as his breathing slows to a near inaudible level and swim back to my sister. I have to get her to safety.

My magic feels strong and powerful, infused with Spring's Blessing. My vines find root within the rock and burst forth, glowing like shards of sunlight. Delicately, they cradle my sister and weave up through the cavern until they reach the flat roof beyond the small hole I saw earlier. I guide them to set her down safely.

Then, I place a hand on my vine, ready for it to pull me up. I look back over to the pillar, where Kairyn lies pinned.

I'd told Ezryn I fell in love with him because of his gentle heart. That gentle heart has carried him out of his malice. He found his way back to me by choosing mercy. My gaze drifts upward. My thick vines block

Wrenley from my view, but I know she's lying there. I have to believe there's good in her. Just as Ezryn has to believe there's good in Kairyn.

I don't think. I run, leaping over the water, my vines carrying me across the distance. Then, with a roar, I erupt another huge patch of briars. They wrap around the pillar, the strength of root and rock singing through my blood. The pillar lifts off of Kairyn, and my vines chuck it into the water.

I sink to my knees behind him and place my hands on either side of his head. Just through touch, I feel his body like a network of roots stretching out through the soil. His heartbeat is so weak . . .

I focus, channeling my newfound magic into him. A soft, golden glow emanates from my palms. My magic flows through that incorporeal root system I'd felt earlier, mending bones, restoring breath. With each passing moment, I sense the pain leaving his body.

His heartbeat strengthens and his breath regulates. His eyes do not open again, but I feel strength flow through him. I let go of his face, panting. Spring's Blessing is not just healing or renewal.

Like the first flower fighting against a frost, Spring is hope.

That is what I give to Ezryn. To Kairyn. And hopefully, to Wrenley.

Gently, I slide Kairyn's helmet over his face. I lace my arms under the unconscious former High Prince of Spring and pull him tight to my chest. Then my vines wrap around us and carry us into the light.

116

ROSALINA

My thorns whip Kairyn and me through the hole and out of the cavern. I blink against the bright sunlight, barely able to see as I guide us down to the flat rooftop. Waves crash against the sides, and the only visible monuments left of Hadria are towers.

The capital of the Summer Realm has sunk into the sea.

My feet hit the stone and the vines tremble away, leaving me to support the unconscious Kairyn. Gently, I lower him to the ground and look for Wrenley.

She's awake, standing, a hand pressed to her temple.

And she's not alone.

Sira stands beside her, shadows licking at her edges. The Bow of Radiance is suspended before Wrenley, held aloft by a pedestal of shadow.

I look from my sister to the Queen of the Below. What is she doing here? I thought she left when she got the bow!

She's come back for Wrenley.

That bow was my mother's. It belongs to *me*. A primal rage erupts through me, and white-hot flame explodes over my hands. Vines with spikes sharp as serpents' fangs crack out of the ground and bob beside me. "Give that to me."

Sira raises an eyebrow and crosses her arms, smirking at Wrenley. "Take the bow, darling."

I look at my sister. "Don't do it. You don't have to listen to her."

Wrenley blinks, expression disoriented.

"Take the bow," Sira snarls.

Wrenley reaches forward and clasps the grip.

I saved her life. Maybe it doesn't mean anything to her, but it means something to me. I *won't* give up on her. I take a tentative step forward. "Wrenley, come with me. You don't need her. I'll keep you safe."

Wrenley looks at Kairyn, lying unconscious beside me. "What did you do to him?"

"He's alive," I breathe.

A look of relief flashes on her face. Her iridescent vines lurch up from the ground, wrapping around Kairyn, fast as a snake's strike. Within a moment, he's sunk down beneath the earth.

Wrenley's grip tightens on the bow. Her whole body shakes, gaze faraway. "You don't understand. I told you and told you! Neither you nor Cas ever listen!"

"That's a good girl," Sira purrs. She pets Wrenley's head. "Now, Rosalina darling, you be a good girl too. There's no need to make your own sister shoot you, is there?"

Shadows start to lick across the ground toward me. I remember how they tangled up my arms, pinning me to the Tower of Nether Reach the last time Sira imprisoned me. I'll never be at her mercy again.

But if it comes down to a fight between me, Sira, and the Nightingale, I know one thing for certain.

Whoever has the Nightingale—and that bow—on their side wins.

I let my flame and thorns fall. "Wrenley, listen to me. So much has happened between the two of us. But I want to get to know you. The *real* you. This time, I am listening and I hear how scared you are."

Sira lets out a mocking laugh, and Wrenley just looks at me, resignation in her eyes.

"There's another way, Wrenley," I beg. "Sira would have let you die for that bow. But that's not how things work in our family. We look after each other, no matter what. We *are* family."

"No." Wrenley's eyes dart back and forth. "I've never been a part of your world. Never can be."

My voice breaks. "Our mother wants to meet you, Wrenley. *Our* mother. We can save her together."

Wrenley shuts her eyes and grits her teeth. A pained sound emits from her throat, before Sira steps forward. "Foolish words from a fool's daughter! Be silent or I'll rip your tongue from your mouth."

"Get away from her!" a booming voice shouts across the sky. There's the flap of wings, and I look behind me to see a Pegasus surging toward us, carrying Dayton.

He leaps off its back onto the stone rooftop, tucking into a roll. When he gets to his feet, a bright light flashes in his hand: the Trident of Honor.

His gaze is fiery, set on . . .

Set on Wrenley.

"I've had enough of this warmongering Summer Prince," Sira says. "I'll get just as much satisfaction from ripping Summer's Blessing out of your sister. Now, Wrenley, shoot him."

"She's not going to do what you say anymore," I call. "She doesn't need you, Sira."

A smile twitches at the corner of Sira's mouth. "You petulant child. All you surface folk worship your great Queen. If only you knew how selfish she was. Even the most sanctified are susceptible to the right bargain." Sira runs a hand through one of Wrenley's curls. "My darling daughter knows that she was collateral for her first mother. That's why you're so well-behaved most of the time, isn't it? You know I look after you. It's very rare I have to enact the power I gained through Aurelia's bargain. But I will do it. Won't I, daughter?"

Panic laces through my chest. Aurelia made a bargain with the Queen of the Below? No, it can't be true. "You're not her mother," I say.

"I *am*," Sira snarls. "Wrenley, *shoot him.*"

Wrenley's chest heaves. "Mother, please. Summer is already lost. There's no point in killing him."

I hold my breath. I see it in her gaze—there may yet be some lingering attachment to Dayton. To me. Wrenley won't do this. There is still good in her. I *know* it.

"I SAID SHOOT HIM!" Sira's voice explodes through the air with a thundering roar, a voice so terrible, it sounds as if she dredged up all the echoes of the dead to scream with her.

A glazed look crosses Wrenley's face. Her blue eyes seem to darken before shifting completely to black. Her body tenses, each muscle seeming to move of its own accord. Then she lifts the bow, draws the glowing string, and shoots.

Dayton staggers back, once, twice. The trident falls from his hand and clatters on the ground. He looks down, fingers tentatively prodding at the hole gaping through his stomach. Then, he looks to me.

"Rosie," he says, and then that's it.

He collapses to the ground.

Our mate bond goes slack.

117

CASPIAN

I am tired of fighting fate. Weighing every decision, calculating all the possible outcomes. Constantly leaping over obstacles for my own twisted idea of the greater good.

If Ezryn wants to fight me, fine. Fight me. Realms know I've been delaying this for centuries.

But if Ezryn wants to kill me . . . Well, that's not happening. Not today.

He's not the only one with people to protect.

The clang of his steel blade against my own, crafted of obsidian shadows, echoes through the marble pillars. We trade blows back and forth. Though I've trained in swordplay, I've never enjoyed it the way Keldarion does. But today, the fury inside of me finds solace in the brutality of steel seeking flesh.

I give ground, dancing back before jumping on the precipice that looks over the lower city below. The rising tide and flooded canal have turned it into nothing but rushing water, ready to swallow everything whole.

Ezryn leaps up to meet me, and again, I give ground, letting him be the aggressor. Every movement is a calculated risk. When I notice his foot too far over the edge, I strike, kicking him in the chest and backflipping onto the pavement with a cat-footed landing. Ezryn loses his balance, but the bastard recovers, mouth curved back in a snarl.

He lunges, blade slicing through the air with deadly precision. I parry, our swords a blur of silver and black. He fights with a grace that belies his strength. Even without a Blessing, he remains one of the best fighters in the realms. I'd almost be impressed if I wasn't so fucking furious.

I'm not even angry at Ezryn.

I'm angry at Kel.

All these years he's let me believe that he *betrayed* me. That he first broke the covenant of our love. Every action I've taken, from petty revenge, the hopelessness and despair I'd fallen into—

Oh, I'm going to fucking survive this fight. I'm going to fucking survive it just so I can get to Keldarion and tell him what a rotten, pigheaded, selfish, idiotic, icy bastard he is.

I press forward, the ache in my arms a welcome distraction. Below, the waters roar with triumph as the city falls.

"Does it make you feel powerful?" Ezryn yells, his words carrying over the clash of our blades. "To destroy the homes of the innocent? To unleash the undead upon the living?"

There's no bother trying to explain the truth of it. Besides, what defense do I hold?

I could have stopped this. Could have claimed the Green Flame.

But is one death better than another?

Instead, I draw from the decades-old grief I carry with me and hone it to anger. "Just as powerful as you must have felt ordering trained Winter soldiers upon the innocents of Cryptgarden."

"There are no innocents in Cryptgarden."

"Not anymore."

The pillars cast long shadows as we dance between them. How easy it would be to call upon all of my powers. I could propel myself upward with my thorns, wrap my shadows around his body, then eviscerate him with the Green Flame.

He'll never stop trying to kill me. One of us will have to die for the other to live.

Why shouldn't I do it?

Mercy. Empathy. Compassion. These have been my bane all these years. If only I'd never felt warmth from a woman in the desert. If only I'd never given a rose to a teetering child who taught herself to walk. If only I'd carved out my heart before my mate bond had a chance to find the most brilliant, brave woman. *Curse the O'Connell women! And curse the men who love them!*

Ezryn feints to my left, drawing my attention for a split second before pivoting and delivering a powerful blow to my wrist with his closed fist. My grip slackens, and the shadow blade spirals out of my hand, skittering across the ground.

"Every day that passes, I regret not killing you when you first stepped foot into Castletree." Ezryn kicks my chest, and I fall.

"You'll have to die with that regret," I say sadly. "I didn't want things to end like this, Ezryn. But I see there's no other way."

I'm done playing. This game, at least. One of us will have to die, and I have business to attend to. A sense of deep sadness fills my heart as my briars lift me up into the air. I steal the shadows from the pillars, drawing them to form spears at my side. I feel my eyes flash with internal flame. "I'm sorry, Ezryn. Just so you know . . . I cheated at one of our games. You've got one on me. I hope that brings you solace in the end."

Ezryn's eyes widen and he staggers backward as I draw my shadow spears up—

A guttural pain lances through my heart. I cry out, and fall forward out of my briars, landing hard on the stone. Ezryn makes a similar sound, collapsing to all fours. Both of us clutch our chests. There is no visible wound, yet it feels as if my soul is rendering apart. Tears flood my eyes, and I can't help but weep.

A sob wracks Ezryn's body, and I see tears are also pouring down his face. "Rosalina . . ."

He's dead! He's dead! He's dead! Rosalina's voice rips through my mind. Grief like I have never experienced floods through our bond and into my own self. I try to gain control over my emotions, but it's as if I'm being torn apart.

Something's terribly, horribly wrong. I have to get to her. Now.

I feel a presence over me and look up to see Ezryn. His face is streaked with tears, mouth a quivering line. "You feel it," he breathes.

"I feel it."

He closes his eyes and sighs deeply. In understanding. In resignation. "It is true, then. You are Rosalina's mate."

118

ROSALINA

"**N**O!" the word tears out of me. I fall to the ground, scrambling over to get to him. Stone rips open my knees and my palms as I cross the distance between me and Dayton.

He lies on his back, face up at the beaming sun. His eyes are open, but the familiar shine is gone. There's no light there anymore. The slightest hint of a smile seems trapped, imprisoned on his face even now.

"No, no, no, no." I touch his chest, his face, his arms. Then the wound. The bolt of light has cut straight through him, a gaping hole in his body at least a hand's width wide. "I-I can fix this. Hold on, Day."

But . . . what is there to fix? That *thing* in my heart that's called for him ever since we've met has vanished. A thread snapped straight through the middle. I place my hands on either side of his face like I did with Kairyn, feeling for the roots of his life. I have the most powerful healing magic in all the Vale. I *will* fix this.

But the roots have shriveled up. The soil of his life is barren. There's nothing to hold on to, not even a sliver . . .

If there was! If there was even one shard of him, I could do it. He's *mine*, my Day. I could unmake the world for him, if I had to.

No, I *would*.

I cradle his head in my lap. His vacant eyes terrify me, but so does looking away. I can't imagine not hearing his booming laugh, feeling basked in his love.

"Don't go," I sob, rocking back and forth. "I only just got you. Don't go."

There are voices around me, but I barely hear them. Who was with me? I don't care.

A wind picks up, tearing at my clothes and hair. I smooth his down. Then rain begins, pelting our skin. Dark clouds roll over the horizon, hiding the sun. No, no. Who's doing this? Dayton *loves* the sun. Thunder rumbles and then his skin is illuminated as a crack of lightning strikes the side of the building.

"Grab her and get us back to the Below before she takes us all down with her!"

Ah. I'm doing it.

It's as if a sick numbness spreads throughout my body, but my skin is alight with energy. How can there be so much power singing through my blood and not enough to save him?

Love. That's always what's powered me, driven every choice, every action. I love Dayton so much; it has to be enough to save him.

I brace my hands on his chest and *push* everything I am into everything he was. "Take it," I sob. "Take all of me. Take everything."

The storm rages more powerfully, chunks of rock shaking off the building with bursts of lightning, the rain growing so strong, I can barely see. "Everything I am, I give to him!"

But he's nothing but an empty shell. Our mate bond isn't just limp in my heart—it's gone completely.

No matter how much magic I have, even with Spring's Blessing and my mother's celestial blood coursing through my veins, there's nothing here to save.

My love is *worthless*.

A feeling cuts through the numbness.

Rage.

I peer through the rain and find the silhouettes of Sira and Wrenley. The Bow of Radiance glows bright enough to shine through even this storm.

My bow did this. My bow. *My bow!*

What good is my cursed love if it made me save the one who killed him? Killed he who is better than us all? He who loves and gives so much of himself?

No . . . He who *loved*. He who *gave*.

He's gone now.

Wrenley took him away. Because *I* saved her.

My compassion did this.

Gently, I place Dayton's head on the ground. Then I stand, body shaking. My voice echoes in every raindrop, every gale, every strike of lightning. "You have made a very poor choice, Queen of the Below."

I step through the storm until my eyes pierce Sira. "You will live to regret this."

Her only response is the slightest tremble of her lip. Then she turns to her daughter. "Now, Wrenley. Do it NOW!"

Wrenley is sitting on the ground, knees clutched to her chest, the bow tossed in front of her. She rocks back and forth before Sira's words cause her to straighten. Again, that voided darkness takes over her eyes.

Before I even have a chance to look back at my dead mate, iridescent vines leap over my body.

With my last moment of freedom before I'm pulled below the earth, I stare at the Queen of the Below, my gaze pure lightning, to remind her of my promise. *You will live to regret this.*

119

EZRYN

Dark clouds have rumbled over the horizon, shadowing all of Hadria in gloom. Rain pelts down, and I half-expect the familiar *ting* off my armor before remembering I'm not wearing any.

I can barely breathe through the pain. It's as if someone has reached through my ribs and seized my heart. My mate bond is taut with grief.

And . . . and so is his.

Caspian lies on the ground, nails digging into the stone. His face is contorted into a mask of anguish. *He feels it too.*

Mate of my mate.

I could slay him right now. It would be so easy; he's in no state to defend himself. But to kill him would be to kill a part of Rosalina's soul.

I will never hurt her again.

Right now, there's only one thing that matters.

I stalk over to Caspian and grab his forearm. He looks up at me, eyes shining. With a raspy growl, I say, "Can you take me to her?"

He nods, and his briars crack through the earth. Whatever has happened in our past, it will have to wait. The silent truce lays thick between us: Rosalina comes first.

My stomach churns as Caspian's vines whip us through the earth. We surge up, exploding onto a flat-topped roof looking over the churning sea that's swallowed Hadria.

I try to peer through the rain. "I don't see her."

"This is the last place I felt her magic," Caspian says.

There's no one here except . . . I spot it, a shadowed lump through the rain.

"Please, no." I sprint over, falling to my knees beside it.

My brother by bond, by choice, by friendship, lies dead. Dayton's body is stiff, eyes open and gazing into the void. A hole cuts through his stomach, so large and gaping it reveals the stone below.

A cry erupts from the darkest part of me. I grab his body and clutch him to my chest. My emotions meld with the ones pouring through the bond, our grief forming a tempest of its own.

I've brought him back from the brink of death before, but I'm too late now.

"How could you do this to me?" I ask him, tears merging with the rain, flooding down my face and into my mouth. "What am I to tell Delphie?"

Does she know already? Has Summer's Blessing passed to her? Oh realms, Delphie, poor Delphie.

"Farron?" I cry. "What am I to tell Farron?"

Because I know by the depths of grief rocking through my body that Rosalina already knows.

Rosalina.

I turn around, still clutching Dayton to my chest. "Where is she?" I roar.

Caspian's staring at us glassy-eyed. "Taken."

"Did you know?" I yell.

"No. Not until we arrived here, and I saw these." He kicks an iridescent briar lying limp upon the rooftop.

How could this happen? How could everything end like this? I lay my brother down and gently close his eyes. I press a kiss upon his brow. "I'll take care of them, Day. Del and Rose. I'll protect them in your name."

The sound of wings beating whooshes through the air. I look up to see a Pegasus descending to the rooftop. I squeeze my eyes shut, not sure how much more anguish my heart can bear. It's Farron. He'll see Dayton's body, know the love of his life is gone . . . I've already had to watch him lose his mother. If only I could take his pain.

Farron slips off the horse and walks over to us. He looks from Caspian to me. Then down at the body.

I stand on shaking legs and pull him into a hug. "I'm so sorry, Farron. I'm so, so sorry."

Farron doesn't say anything. He just starts to laugh.

I pull away and shake his shoulders. He barely reacts, still staring down at Dayton, damp auburn hair shadowing his face. "What's wrong with you?" I cry. "He's dead! Dayton is dead!"

"So he is." Farron looks up and his eyes glow a brilliant green. "And I'm going to bring him back."

120

FARRON

It's almost funny, thinking how I hesitated at the edge of the pool. I was so afraid of the unknown. But this time, my courage won out. I reached into the deep, dark place and I *took* what was offered.

Took what I deserve.

And look! Now, I need it. I told myself I would never be back in that place again. The field, with my mother cradled in my arms, a spear in her chest.

Ezryn is so upset, yelling at me, crying. The bond within my chest screams with grief. They don't understand. Not like I do.

Not like *he* does.

The Son stares at me, his purple eyes hard. Caspian. Shadow-blood. Flame-blood. "Do not do this thing, Farron," he says, voice dark and low. "Dayton would not want this."

Ah, The Son is always so cautious! So afraid. I was like that. Before the Baron helped me See.

I walk over to Dayton and kneel behind his head, brushing blond strands of hair away from his eyes. He is beautiful. "Look," I whisper. "Now, I'm the one protecting you."

Even more beautiful than my Summer-blood is what hovers above his chest. A tiny sun bursting with all the magic and power of the Summer Realm. Within this bright spark lies the ancestral memory of all the High Rulers of this realm. Summer's Blessing. It hovers by him, grieving in its own way. But very soon, it will try to make its way to the next in line. Yes, it will try.

And it will fail.

"We're not done here," I say to the Blessing. "You just wait a moment."

I hold my hand out to the magic, and it responds, leaping around my fingers joyously.

"Who are you talking to?" Ezryn asks gruffly. He and Caspian exchange a look.

Oh, they can't See it. Shadow-blood could if only he wasn't so afraid. He purposely weakens himself, keeping the sight locked away. He can't See. Not like I can. None of them can See the threads of life sparking brightly through their bodies. Or Dayton's threads, lying limp within him.

I can See all these things and more. Everything is clearer within the Green Flame.

Caspian grabs my shoulder. "Stop this madness, Farron. It is not the way of the world."

"Not the way of your world," I say matter-of-factly. "I make the world how I want it to be. It is what was promised."

A ragged breath tears out of his throat, and his eyes are bright with fear. "Dayton will never forgive you if you do this to him."

I look away from The Son and lay a kiss upon Dayton's brow. Peace fills my chest. "What use is forgiveness when I hold his life in my hands?"

Caspian grabs my shoulder and jerks me to look at him. "If you do this, you will not be the same." His voice lowers to a desperate hiss. "*He* will not be the same."

I put my hand on Caspian's and offer him a comforting smile. "That is how it should be. When one is incinerated by the Green Flame, they must be reborn anew."

Caspian staggers away from me, wide-eyed.

"What's going on?" Ezryn shouts. "Farron, what are you doing?"

I turn back to Dayton. "The ways of the world do not pertain to me. I follow no law, subscribe to no rule. I answer to one power alone, and it is not death." A green glow shines around my hands.

I have been in love with Daytonales for as long as the tides have rippled along Summer's shores, for as long as the harvests have grown in Autumn, for as long as the great icy caverns have stood in Winter and the rivers have cut through Spring. Because I was in love with Dayton before either of us ever existed; our love is eternal. It shone in the cosmos and plummeted to the earth in fragments of the stars.

I chose to become different—to become *more*—because I want to continue loving him through the ages. What a simple thing death is, and how easily it can occur. I have always been a logical man. I will not take chances with those I love.

His thread is gone. But from its frayed edges, I shall create a new one.

My magic seeps into his bones, his blood, his nerves, until I reach the filaments of his life's thread. A green flame lurks behind my own magic, bursting into those threads, remaking them from the ashes of what they once were. This is not creating a new life from the old, but rebuilding what was once there.

I find the strands of his strength, his goodness, his humor, and weave them with my flame as if I'm braiding a bracelet. His memories, beliefs, and preferences come next. It's all here, so easy for me to pick up and put back, right where it was. I'm particularly careful as I maneuver his mate bond. It's a strong power, quickly becoming taut as soon as I grace it with a bit of magic.

Last of all is the thing hovering above his chest. The thing that should have left a while ago, but stayed because it too was grieving. Because it too didn't believe that I am stronger than Death.

"It's time to go back," I tell Summer's Blessing, the little flitting sunburst over his heart. "It's okay. He's ready."

The bright light flutters back and forth, unsure.

"He's not dead," I tell it sternly. "At least, he won't be in a moment. Come now, I'm ready to finish."

Though it's nothing but light, it seems to look at me. It flits over his body, over the green thread shining in his chest. Almost as if it's *examining* him.

Then, it starts to back up.

"No," I say. "He's not dead! He's the rightful High Ruler of Summer! Get back inside of him!"

The Blessing slowly shakes back and forth.

"I have *remade* him," I growl. "*Get back!*"

The sunburst dashes away, but I'm quicker. Green flames erupt from my fingertips, caging the Blessing with my magic.

"What's happening?" Ezryn shouts and starts to lunge toward us.

Caspian grabs him around the chest. "Don't touch anything!"

I can't split my concentration; it requires everything in me to focus on the tendrils pulling, pulling, *pulling* the Blessing back into Dayton.

"He's not dead," I growl. "You belong to him."

The sunburst fights me, pulsing against the edges of my magic, desperate to get away. With a roar, an inferno of emerald flame explodes out of me, pouring over the sunburst. It goes limp within my fiery chains.

"Good," I breathe. Delicately, I direct it down upon Dayton's chest. The sunburst beams like a bright peridot before sinking beneath his skin.

With everything in place, I prepare to stitch the final thread within his life force. It was all so easy, this mending. But when you have the power to See, everything is easy.

"Come back to me," I breathe. "Come back."

And as the Green Flame promised, he does.

Dayton sucks in a breath then coughs. Ezryn shouts his name and collapses beside me, grabbing Dayton's hand.

I look behind me to smile at The Son. To show him the miracles his father can provide.

But Caspian has already started walking away.

Never mind. I turn back to Dayton, staring with pride at the mended skin, every rise of his chest. Each heartbeat is precious. Each heartbeat is what I was owed.

When Dayton's breath steadies, and he opens his eyes to look at me, they shine the most beautiful and ethereal green.

121

DAYTON

I open my eyes to darkness, feeling disoriented and sluggish. My limbs ache as if I've been sleeping for centuries. With a groan, I push myself up, feeling the soft bed beneath my hands. *Where am I?* Memories flicker in my mind like distant shadows—radiant light, searing pain, and then nothing . . .

Nothing until Farron's voice. A flash sparks across my vision, cutting like a blade. A light of emerald green. I grit my teeth.

"Dayton. Dayton." A hand touches my shoulder and I shudder. "He's awake."

I know that voice. "Del?"

As my vision adjusts to the dim light, I see my sister across from me, illuminated by glowing orbs on the wall. The air is thick with the scent of oil and rust.

I'm on an airship, lying on a cold bed.

Footsteps echo on metal, and more people crowd into the small room. Ez, Nori, and behind them, hovering by the door . . . Farron.

The way he's gazing at me, it's like I might not be real.

I wish I could reassure him otherwise, but I'm not exactly positive.

"What happened?" I rasp.

Delphie throws her arms around me, clambering onto the bed. Tears line her cheeks. "We thought we lost you, Day. The Nightingale shot you with the Bow of Radiance and Farron healed you."

Ezryn makes a sound in the back of his throat and shoots a strange look at Farron. Farron, who hasn't said a word, stays in the doorway.

"All that matters is that Dayton's back," Ezryn says. There's an odd pitch to his voice. One I've never heard before.

My thoughts are sluggish. *Back from where?*

"Hadria is lost, but so is Sira's army," Delphie says.

I strain, moving my stiff body to look out the round window. The airship hovers above the sea. Only the highest peaks of the Soltide Keep are visible above the waves.

"The people are safe," Delphia says. "The sirens spoke to me. They've given them shelter in Aerantheis."

"We'll rebuild it, Del," I say, touching her face. "I'll call the sea back and our people will return. Hadria will feel the sun's warmth once again."

"I know, brother." She curls into my embrace.

"The Huntresses have returned to their base," Ezryn says. There's an edge to his voice. "They await Summer's command for our next move. They've promised their aid to those who serve the Golden Rose."

"Our next move," I repeat, and then it hits me all at once. I scan the room once again, but the desperate ache in my chest is confirmation enough. "Rosalina?"

"Sira took her," Ezryn snarls.

More footsteps echo on the metal, and another figure strides in. Long black cape glistening, Caspian raises a brow at me, before turning to the group. "I have a way to get our mate to safety, but you aren't going to like it."

Our mate? *Our* mate? Rosalina is mated to a prince from each of the realms and the Below, while her own ancestry is that of the Above. The stars are cruel in their mischief.

Really, of *all* people . . . it had to be *Caspian*?

The Prince of Thorns crosses to the window, gaze faraway. "I'll tell you where you'll find her. Fair warning, it's going to be awfully cold. You might want to bundle up."

122

CASPIAN

Mother doesn't intend to lose her little Rose again. She's crafted a cell deep in the Below for the daughter of the Queen. Long rows of metal bars seal her away in a cavern made of crystals that shine blue, pink, and purple.

Sira hasn't infected these ones with the Baron's magic yet, though I'm sure it's only a matter of time. Regardless, they do a good enough job of leeching magic. I barely feel a whisper of my shadows this deep, never mind trying to summon a thorn here.

My heart races. I don't have much time. When Sira next visits the Baron, will he reveal what Farron and I have done? Does she already suspect?

Rosalina sits with her head in her hands, long brown hair spread before her. She wears only a short white shift, feet bare.

Hands in my pockets, I stand before the entrance to her cage. "Hello, Princess."

Rosalina lifts her head, and her gaze softens as she looks at me. She scrambles to the bars and wraps her hands around them. "Cas, you came. Tell me, please. I feel Dayton again. How is it possible? Am I going mad?"

Nausea roils in my stomach. "Farron saved him."

Though saved isn't the word I would use for *that*.

Relief paints Rosalina's face, and she rests her head against the bars. "Oh, thank god."

"Anyway," I say, placing my stolen key in the lock of her cell, "I'm here to rescue you."

Rosalina steps back as I enter. She raises a curved brow. "Forgive me, Cas, but wouldn't a rescue attempt have us leaving this cell?"

I close the door behind me. "Sira has a thousand guards stationed between here and where we'd first start to feel a semblance of magic."

"Then how are we going to escape?" Rosalina says, breath wispy.

Lightly, I touch the frosted thorn bracelet at my wrist. "They say a bargain is one of the most powerful forms of magic in the world, and the stronger the love, the stronger the bargain. Rosalina, I did love Kel. I loved him like the night sky must love the moon, to have been denied forever the promise of sunlight, yet still get to gaze on something so bright. Even now, every part of me aches for him, even though our love has always been a constellation of unattainable dreams. I love him because of it and despite it."

Her lips part, and she takes a step toward me, lightly touching the bargain bracelet. "You believe that love is strong enough to reach even down here? Strong enough to send me to Winter?"

"Yes." I drop my forehead to hers. "We can do it however you like. I don't think we'd even have to take off our clothes and—"

She grips my face, hands cold and soft. Then she places her lips to mine. I inhale her scent, taking her in my arms.

"Tell me, Caspian," she whispers.

"Tell you what?"

Her smile spreads against my cheek. "What we both already know."

My heart thunders in my chest, and a ringing sounds in my ear. "Rosalina."

"I am tired of your secrets." She pulls back, hair a dark frame around her face. "If we are to do this, I will have all of you. I will have all of my mate."

123

ROSALINA

There are a million questions I have for the Prince of Thorns. What truly happened down Below with Farron? Does he know his adopted sister is my blood one?

But that can wait. Right now, there's only his eyes, swirling like a galaxy, long dark lashes lowering. "How did you know?" he asks.

"I think my heart knew for a long time," I say, unable to stop my smile. To finally say the words my heart has been telling me all these months.

Caspian is my mate.

"You shouldn't be smiling like that for me," he says softly, hand cupping the side of my face. "I've already got enough of an ego."

I throw my arms around his shoulders, kissing him deeply. "Why did you take so long to tell me?"

He hesitates. "I didn't know I ever would. Rosalina, I may not have bars around me, but I'm a prisoner of the Below as much as you are. I just happen to have a unique way to free you."

"Won't they realize you helped me escape?"

"You know me, Flower. I always have a plan." He kisses me before I can catch his expression. "Are you sure you want this? We don't need to make it intimate."

I work on the clasp of his cloak. "If I'm to have you, Cas, I'll have you properly."

My gaze catches on something shimmering below his shirt. My moonstone necklace. "You kept it safe."

"Of course I did." He moves to remove it. "I suppose I should give it back to you now."

"Keep it," I breathe. "If we can't stay together, then at least a part of me can be with you."

A galaxy of emotions shimmers in his eyes, and his shoulders relax as if in surrender. "Very well, Princess. I shall not forget such a gift." He sweeps off the cloak and spreads it on the ground before gathering me in his arms and lowering us to the velvety surface. "We have to be quick."

Wild anticipation floods through me, fear and nerves and longing.

Caspian is my mate. Warmth blooms bright inside me, a feeling like morning mist running through my veins. It's always been simmering there, but finally, *finally*, he had the courage to tell me, and I had the courage to believe it.

And with Dayton's bond returned to full strength within my chest, I finally feel complete.

"You're so beautiful," Caspian murmurs, smoke-filled shadows in his voice. He kisses my neck.

"So are you," I whisper as he slides the strap of my white tunic off my shoulder and places his mouth on my bare skin. "I thought so the first moment I met you, when you saved me in the Briar."

He blinks, the iridescent lights of the crystals casting a rainbow across his face. "I hadn't felt anything in so long," he rasps. "It felt like my heart was caged in shadows, but something burst forth when you crawled through the rosebush. I followed that feeling straight to you."

Something clenches in my heart. All this time, he's been watching over me. Not just me, but Castletree, and in his own way, the Enchanted Vale. "You could have kept me then, but you brought me to Kel."

Caspian rolls the dress off my shoulders, and I lift my hips to wiggle out of it until I'm completely bare. His hand, the long delicate fingers, hover above me, almost like he's afraid to touch me. "I knew that's where you'd be safest," he says. "Now, back to his safety you must return."

His kiss crashes over me, and my skin rubs against the delicate fabric of his clothes. I unlace his shirt and slip him out of it, revealing his bare chest.

"Come with me." I press my lips to his collarbone. "Kel and I will protect you in Winter."

Sadness flickers across his features like the twinkle of starlight before he lowers his head to my neck. "The bargain will only send you. I belong here."

"No," I say, but my words cut off in a desperate cry as his mouth works my breast. Desire curls deep inside of me, like a caged animal thrashing to break free. "You belong with me."

"I wish it were so, Flower."

Desperately, I unbuckle his belt, and he kicks, breaking free of his pants entirely. He rises above me, dark hair falling over his eyes. "Of every wicked thing I've done in my life, this might just top them all."

"Wicked?" I gasp.

He smiles, and it's so soft and dazzling, a part of me melts inside. Caspian runs a rough hand along my body, gripping my thigh.

"This will save you, and the cost is only my greatest desire," he whispers. "Tell me, Princess, is that not wicked?"

I draw him toward me, capturing his lips. "Then let us descend into the shadows together."

He enters me then, slowly, swallowing me with his desperate kisses. His hands slide beneath my hips, raising them as he plunges deeper and deeper.

I've waited for this moment for so long. He's always been under my skin, but now, I finally have him inside of me. Stars crest at the edges of my vision, and Caspian weaves his hands in my hair.

"Rosalina, I would betray every god in every universe just to feel like this with you." His voice lowers to a growl as he slides to the hilt, and the sensation is otherworldly.

We find a rhythm, and my fingers dig into his back, feeling every rippled scar. Pleasure streaks hot down my spine like the strike of lightning, and I arch my back, meeting his thrusts.

"Caspian," I moan, head thrown back, eyes squeezed shut as I cling to him for support.

He kisses me sweetly at first but with an intensity that grows. His motions becoming more desperate. I wrap my legs around his waist, binding us closer still. There is no going back now. This has sealed our fates.

Magic prickles in the air, and my heart wars with itself, desperate to climb this peak with him, but knowing that the moment it's over . . .

"I have dreamed of this, Princess," he whispers against my neck as he kisses a path to my collarbone. "In the deepest dark of the Below, when I thought I would never see light again, all I could think of was you."

His words inflame me further, and I kiss him deeply. His breathing becomes more ragged, and a coil of desire tightens inside me.

"Caspian," I moan, my voice a mix of pleasure and need. "I have dreamed of you too."

Our movements become wild, eyes locked, hearts beating in sync. Magic swirls around us like a tempest. It crackles in the air, electric and alive, flooding our every touch, our every breath. A soft glow emits from my chest, and then his.

Like the crystals in this cavern, we are glowing.

Caspian gasps, "What is this?"

I lean up to kiss him deeply. "It's our mate bond," I whisper against his lips. "We're completing it."

Caspian's breath hitches and I can see the emotion painting his face. The happiness, the guilt, the fear. It's all there in his lavender eyes.

"Don't be afraid, Cas. This is right."

Caspian doesn't have a curse to break, but it's like he's shattering all the same, washing away the layers as light blooms across his skin. Long dark hair falls across his shining eyes.

"Call me your mate," I say.

He lets out a guttural cry, lifting my hips as he drives his cock deeper, then collapsing his weight on top of me. He grabs a fistful of my hair, and his lips move to my ear as he whispers desperately, "You are my mate, Rosalina. I do not know how you are bound to me, by the stars or by fate. But I know you belong to me, and I to you. Mate. My mate."

I tilt my head toward him, heart bursting with joy. "Caspian, I'll never doubt you again. I'll never doubt my heart again. It's been calling to you for so long."

"Every piece of you is mine," Caspian growls, his voice ragged with want. He bites at my neck, before lapping at the bruised skin.

Caspian thrusts like he's been waiting for this for a thousand years, stretching me to the brink of pain. A strange warmth bubbles inside me, as if the deepest parts of my soul are merging with his.

His fingers dig into my hips, pulling us closer. His lips find my nipple, teeth grazing the sensitive skin as he sucks fiercely. I arch my back, hissing in pleasure, feeling the connection between us deepen with every stroke, every kiss.

"Touch every part of me, mate," I gasp, my voice hoarse with desire.

The cavern seems to pulse in time with our rhythm, the stalactites above glowing softly as we move. Our bodies slide against one another, our skin slick with sweat.

He thrusts deeper, hitting a place inside that sends shockwaves of pleasure coursing through me. My core pulses around his cock. I dig my nails into his shoulders and rock my hips. *More, more, more.*

Anything, darling, his voice caresses my mind. *I would give you this world if you asked.*

His words drive me into a frenzy, and he reaches down between us, finding my clit. I cry out, and my spine arches off the cold, damp ground as the pleasure envelops me. My heart swells with love and lust. I grip his shoulders tighter, my nails digging in. Raw hunger emanates from his gaze as our eyes lock.

"I wish I had time to push you to your limits, Princess," he rasps, "to test just what they are."

His thrusts become more feral, and our bodies dance in a primal cadence. The cavern hums in harmony, the walls blurring in my starlit vision. Caspian's eyes are ablaze with desire, mirroring my own, as he thrusts deeper and harder, his hips grinding against me in a rhythm that sends tremors through the cavern walls. The stalactites above shudder, their crystalline forms resonating with our passion.

Stars, I wouldn't be surprised if we take down all of the Below.

His lips leave a trail of fire on my skin. With each thrust, I'm transported closer toward oblivion.

"It's almost time, Rose," he whispers.

"No," I say, tears pricking my eyes. "Not yet. Don't send me away yet."

His movements slow and tender, he leans down and kisses my eyelids. "Not yet, then."

I stare up at the canopy of crystals above us, and for a moment, I forget everything. The bargain, the Vale, my magic. All that matters is this feeling.

The world narrows, reduced to just the two of us as we move together in desperate tandem. The magic sparking between us grows brighter.

"Rosalina, Rosalina," Caspian mutters, a sort of delirium overtaking his voice. "You are a rose that blooms in the shadows, a star on the darkest night."

I clutch him. "Cas, I'm so glad you saved me."

"I love you, Rosalina," he whispers against my lips.

The words, so unexpected, send me over the edge. *I love you too.* I cling to him as wave after wave of pleasure washes over me. His arms tighten around me, and he cries out, his body tensing.

I arch my back, body writhing to crest with his even as tears spring to my eyes. The magic intensifies, swirling around us.

With a great sigh, he collapses on top of me, kissing my cheek, my nose, my temples.

"How long does it take?" I gasp. "How long does it take?"

There's a strange smile on his face as he looks at me. "Sometimes instantly, sometimes a few moments."

"If it works," I say.

His lavender gaze flicks to the thorn bracelet. "It'll work."

He sits up, loosely pulling on his pants and throwing on his shirt. I wrap his cloak around my shoulders, unable to take my eyes off the Prince of Thorns.

The ground rattles beneath us, tiny pebbles vibrating and then the first hint of a thorn breaks through.

"See?" Caspian raises a cocky brow.

"Okay, yes," I whisper. "You love Kel very much."

He leans toward me. "Give the icy bastard a kiss from me." Then his lips press over mine, even as I feel the purple thorns wrap around my body to claim me.

Something splashes into my mouth, a metallic sort of taste. Caspian coughs, and I pull back. Blood sputters from his mouth and splashes over my chest.

He looks down at his body, where a prismatic thorn impales his ribs.

"Very good," a dark voice slithers.

Sira.

The Queen of the Below stands behind us, the Nightingale beside her. My sister's eyes are a void black, the same as when Sira told her to shoot Dayton. Behind them, dozens of soldiers stand and wait.

"I knew your brother was up to something distasteful," Sira says.

"Caspian!" I scream. Rage billows inside me so hot, I feel it can burn through the crystals' barrier. How could she do this to her own *son*?

Caspian clutches his chest as blood pumps out between his fingers. But he just smiles. "You're too late."

Too late . . . too late.

"No!" I scream, but the magic of his bargain is already consuming me. Thorns swallow my body, dragging me under. "Caspian!"

He doesn't turn back to me as the guards drag him away, and I'm wrapped in thorns and shadows. My mind fills with mist. Keldarion. Keldarion, I'm going to Kel. I belong to Kel.

The last thought I have before my mind is entirely consumed with Kel is that I never told Caspian I loved him back.

124

KELDARION

Outside of Keep Wolfhelm, snow swirls in furious eddies, whipped by a fierce storm. George and I made it back to Frostfang just in time and we have retrieved a treasure long thought lost. That man really can excavate anything. The shards of the shattered rose are now delicately wrapped in cloth, hidden in my chambers. Though whether the rose still holds any power remains to be seen.

When our destination was in sight, George collapsed, falling into that broken sleep. I carried him the rest of the way. Now, he slumbers in the medical ward.

Castletree is weak, which means the other princes have not returned. I have heard no report on Summer. Where is my Rose? Feelings of turmoil and confusion flicker through the bond.

I know what I must do. Castletree, my home, lies dormant, its magic dwindling in my absence. I must return to restore its strength, to ensure George does not slip away forever. Then, I must find my own path to Summer, to Rosalina.

Yet, amid my concerns, there is a nagging absence. Caspian has not reached out to me as I expected. He and Farron broke the crystals. Why would he not come to me to gloat? Ice floods my veins at the thought of him, of the vision the Fates showed me: Rosalina, his dark princess . . . I will never let that come to pass.

As if in response to my thoughts, tendrils of purple briars erupt from the floor, coiling and twisting in an ominous display of power. A growl emits from my throat, and I turn to him, snarling, "I expected you sooner."

But there's no answer. Instead, I see the flash of skin through the briars. An unexpected wave of jealousy and anger flickers through me—another one of his twisted *presents*? He hasn't used our bargain so frivolously in months, since his birthday party in Cryptgarden. A part of me thought he'd given it up. To use it now, after the night we spent together, after he allied with us, and without so much as a word—

Warmth and longing bloom in my chest, and suddenly where I was once half, I am now whole. The briars fall away, revealing a figure partially covered by a dark cloak. The rest of their body is bare, smelling of blood, sex, and lavender.

Rosalina tilts her head, a spill of curls falling over her shoulder. She blinks her large brown eyes, but there's a milkiness to them.

"Keldarion," she purrs, "I belong to you."

125

WRENLEY

Fuck the twisting halls and the traps and fuck the Fates most of all and their weapons of words. They can spout their snarky prophecies at me all they want.

I write my own future.

The labyrinth is a misty haze behind me. Pressure rings in my ears. I've never been this deep in the Below before.

The prison comes into view. It's dark. Only small glowing orbs illuminate the figure sitting behind a transparent wall.

She's smaller than I expected.

I don't let my feet slow. If I do, I'll stop right here and never start again.

It seems Sira hasn't been able to regrow her crystals yet. But it's only a matter of time. *Cas, what were you thinking?*

The figure stands as I approach. She's about my height, and I hate that it's like looking into some sort of cursed mirror. Her brows lower as she takes me in, then her eyes widen, moisture pearling at the corners.

"Don't cry," I snarl. "I am here for one thing."

The former Queen's face hardens. She straightens, taking me in like I'm just another guard. "Very well. Tell me what you want, Wrenley."

She cannot stop the tremor in her voice as she says my name. It was the one thing Sira allowed me to keep from her.

I take in a shaky breath, desperate not to let my fear show. Not to her.

Not to this woman who bargained me away to Sira as if I were nothing more than a sack of flour. What did she even get for trading my life, my agency? I hope it was fucking worth it.

"I can summon briars, and more recently, water," I bite out. "But you could control all the elements. All the powers of the Enchanted Vale."

"Yes," she says simply.

I flick my gaze up at her. "I need you to teach me how to summon fire. I've tried everything. I've stolen mages from Autumn but they were useless. Read scripts and texts. Useless. I can't so much as create an ember, no less control it. But I know that power is inside me. I can *feel* it."

Aurelia tilts her head, studying me. "It is. I have no doubt. May I ask why you so urgently need this?"

I hiss and begin to pace before the cage as if I am the one trapped inside. "Your daughter has poisoned Caspian with her ideas. Sira suspects him of betrayal, of his unwillingness to accept his destiny. He has gotten . . . sloppy."

"I think the word you're looking for, darling, is brave."

"What would you know of it?" I slam my hands against the transparent wall. "What would you know of bravery? You fled from duty! You bargained away your own child!"

She doesn't so much as flinch. "This is not a fate I ever wanted for you."

Angry tears cascade down my face, and I turn away from her. "Then you shouldn't have made a deal with Sira."

"No."

I whirl around. "She has Caspian imprisoned above Cryptgarden, bound in a cage of fire. A mockery and a warning to all in the Below. She intends to keep him there until she can fix the damage and continue siphoning your magic. Every day, he screams in agony. I cannot take the cries anymore."

"So, you would learn fire to free him of this cage. To take him where? He cannot survive anywhere but the Below."

"Away from here," I say. "Better death than the fate that awaits him."

"What will she do to you if you are caught?"

"I'm sure I will be punished," I say. "But she will not kill me. Who would throw away a weapon they can control absolutely?"

There have only been a handful of times Sira has enacted such control over me.

But I remember everything from every one of those moments. The look on Dayton's face as I fired the arrow. The guttural sound Caspian made as my thorn pierced his back.

I remember it all.

I belong to Sira.

Because of *her*.

There's no escape from this life for me. Not when Sira can take control of me whenever she likes. But Caspian . . .

There may be a future for him. Even if it means he has to abandon me too.

"If it is what you desire, Wrenley," the Queen says, "then I will teach you how to unlock the depths of your magic."

"We don't have much time," I say, looking at the shattered crystals. "When Sira regains control, she doesn't intend to bleed you slowly like before. She will take your magic all at once. And with your death, she will bring the Green Flame to the Enchanted Vale."

The Queen smooths down the wrinkles in her dress. "Quite the predicament."

"Aren't you afraid?" I breathe.

She flashes me a strangely casual smile. "Oh, every day."

I shake my head. "Fine. What do you want in return for training me?"

"Nothing."

"Everyone wants something," I growl.

Her eyes soften. "I will never ask you for anything, Wrenley. I promise you that."

My mind rushes with frustrated confusion. "That's not how things work! I will not have charity from *you* of all people."

The Queen looks down, then flicks her gaze back up to mine, eyes shining. "Well, then, if I must ask for something, perhaps you could pass on a message from me to Caspian after you rescue him."

"What message?" I say in a low voice.

"Tell him," she smiles, "Anya O'Connell has another gift for him. One he'll need if he's going to defeat his father."

Thank you so much for reading Broken by Daylight! We hope you enjoyed your fourth adventure in the Enchanted Vale.

Reviews help others find our book. They are vital to authors. If you could take a moment to leave a review on Amazon and Goodreads, it would mean the world to us!

You can leave a review on Amazon here:

You can leave a review on Goodreads here:

THE ENCHANTMENT CONTINUES IN...

Beasts of the Briar Book 5

ACKNOWLEDGMENTS

You're not still mad at us, are you?! Okay, okay, but don't worry—Rosie and the boys are tough, and they'll be back in Book 5 to cause more trouble!

All jokes aside, the first acknowledgment here goes out to you, dear reader. Thank you for traveling with Rosie across the realms, for hanging off the cliff with us, and for being a part of our story. It is a dream come true to bring Rosalina's adventure to life, and we're so grateful you're all along for the ride.

A huge thank you to our agent, Susan Velazquez Colmant, who not only believes in Rosie, but believes in us. We could not ask for a better champion for our stories, and we're so eternally appreciative to have found someone who gets our weird ideas and helps us grow them into actual book-shaped things. I think we say, "What would we do without Susan?!" at least fifty times a week.

A heartfelt thank you to Stevie Finegan, dream agent, who works tirelessly to create opportunities for us and advocate for our stories. We are so lucky to have such an amazing person in our corner!

Thank you to the whole team at JABberwocky, with a special shout-out to Valentina who has gone to bat for us more times than we can count, and to Christina who is a behind-the-scenes magic-maker. We are so privileged to work with you all!

A massive thank you to Ajebowale Roberts. Thank you for knowing Rosalina and the boys to their core, for helping us breathe life into our stories, and for making so much enchantment happen inside the book and out. We have THE BEST time working with you, and we know our readers can feel the magic you bring to the stories, too!

To the Magpie team. It is truly an honor and a privilege to work with you, and we're so grateful our Rosie is in such good hands. A special shout-out to Rhian because we think you have the hardest job in the world and we are so, so grateful for your incredible eye! Another special thank you to Francine for putting up with all of our strange vocab and her fabulous attention to detail. Thank you also to Libby and Tanuja.

To our beloved beta readers who manage to put up with our massive typo-ridden tomes and still keep coming back for more: you guys are incredible. We don't ever laugh harder than when going through your comments. Thank you for cheering us on, putting up with us, and being a part of the journey. Huge love to Anne, Beate, Camille, Carlie, Jamie, Katie, Kaylee, Khepri, Lindsay, Natasha, Olivia, Renee, Sarah, Tatjana, Taylor C., and Taylor G.

To our online BFFS Hailey, Lindsay, and Stacey—forever grateful to the bookish world for introducing us to you. Here's to an IRL hangout sometime soon!

To Hazy and Salome, thank you for gracing our book with your beautiful art! You bring the characters to life in such an incredible way.

To our community of Roses: for the memes, the gifs, the fan art, the song recommendations, the cosplay . . . All of it is a dream come true. This is all we have ever wanted, and you make it happen. In return, we swear to torture you with angsty books for as long as we can.

Lastly, to our family for their love, support, and enthusiasm. There are so many things that would not have been possible without the support of our parents. Thank you for taking over shipping, for learning TikTok, for catching typos, for reading . . . for everything! To Graeme, I hope we did Malekai justice. Thank you for sitting side by side with me as I wrote his description. There's a part of you in all of it! As this is a Summer book, I'll end with the famous words from Batiatus . . . you know the ones!

Grab a coat, dear reader—we'll meet you in Winter!

XO,

Elizabeth and Helen

About the Authors

Elizabeth Helen is the combined pen-name of sister writing duo, Elizabeth and Helen. Elizabeth and Helen write fantasy romance and love creating enchanting adventures for their characters. When they're not writing, you can find them snuggling their cats, exploring their rainforest home, or rolling the dice for a game of Dungeons & Dragons. You can connect with them on TikTok, Instagram, or Facebook.

Facebook Readers' Group

Join our Facebook Readers' Group to interact with like-minded bookish people, get behind-the-scenes info on the creation of our books, receive sneak peeks for Book 5, and chat all about the Enchanted Vale and the fae princes!

facebook.com/groups/elizabethhelen

AuthorEizabethHelen.com

- facebook.com/elizabethhelenauthor
- instagram.com/author.elizabeth.helen
- tiktok.com/@authorelizabethhelen
- amazon.com/author/elizabethhelen
- goodreads.com/elizabeth_helen

Also by Elizabeth Helen

Beasts of the Briar

Bonded by Thorns

Woven by Gold

Forged by Malice

Broken by Daylight

Novella

Prince of the Arena

BEHIND THE SCENES

JOIN OUR NEWSLETTER

Join our newsletter for an exclusive behind-the-scenes look into our writing process and sneak peeks of the Beasts of the Briar series!

ElizabethHelen.SubStack.com

PLAYLIST

Spoilers ahead!
Scan the code with the Spotify app.

Giza Port | Jerry Goldsmith *(Prologue)*
The Prophecy | Taylor Swift *(A prince in hiding)*
this is what winter feels like |JVKE *(Kel and Cas make a plan)*
King | Florence + The Machine *(Rosie makes her escape)*
Wild Uncharted Waters | Jonah Bauer-King *(Dayton sets sail to rescue Rosalina)*
Starry | Marble Pawns *("What if I'm not worthy?")*
Triton's Fury | Alan Menken *(Destruction of the Summer Wing)*
Love Me Like You Do | Ellie Goulding *(One heartbeat at a time)*
Chiquitita | ABBA *(Sleepover)*
What Was I Made For? | Billie Eilish *(Memories and ice cream)*
Which Witch | Florence + The Machine *(Caspian visits with the Nightingale)*
Glimpse of Us | Joji *(Dayton tries to make peace with his fate)*
For the First Time | Halle *(Wrenley discovering the magic of Castletree/George's arrival)*
the lakes | Taylor Swift *(Forgiveness by the pond)*
Never Let Me Go| Florence + The Machine *("Use me however you want. Just please, don't ask me to leave.")*
The Battle of Kerak | Harry Gregson-Williams *(Attack on Corsa Tuga)*
Too Sweet | Hozier *(Vow it. On your knees.)*
Vanessa's Trick | Alan Menken *(Dayton shuts the door in Rosie's face)*
The Storm | Alan Menken *(Overboard)*
Across The Desert | James Newton Howard *(Ezryn and his charges search for the Ribs)*
Waiting in the Wings | Eden Espinosa *(Birdy's inner feelings)*
Uncharted | Bear McCreary *(Marooned)*
Harpy Song | Borislav Slavov *(Into the nests)*
If Only | Auli'i Cravalho, Graham Phillips *(Nightfire caterpillars)*
Crush Culture | Conan Gray *(Cas dresses Farron up)*
One Last Hope | Danny DeVito *(Dayton trains with Justus)*
The Tulkun Return | Simon Franglen *(Swimming with the sirens)*
Indiana Jones Theme | John Williams *(George drags Kel on an adventure)*
Cena Libera | Joseph Loduca *(Dayton enters the games)*
Would That I | Hozier *(Campfire in the desert)*
I Can Do It With a Broken Heart | Taylor Swift *(Rosie performs in the arena)*
The Mad Queen | Rok Nardin *(Keldarion, George, and the Fates)*
Gannicus | Joseph Loduca *(Dayton faces his brothers)*
Ludus Envy | Joseph Loduca *(Serenus Dusk Chambers)*

PLAYLIST

Breath Of Life | Florence + The Machine *(A rendezvous with the winner of the auction)*
3200 Years Ago | James Horner *(The Huntresses of Aura)*
El Tango De Roxanne | Aaron Tveit *("Please tell me not to do this.")*
Ritual | Within Temptation *(Party in the Below)*
Poor Unfortunate Souls (Reprise) | Jodi Benson *(The Nightingale reveals her plan)*
Ben and Rey Love Theme | Samuel Kim *(Kairyn removes his helm for Wrenley)*
Colours Of You | Baby Queen *(Farron and Cas kiss)*
Marion's Theme | John Williams *(George finds his wife)*
Now We Are Free | Hans Zimmer *(Dayton wins in the arena)*
The Kiss | Alan Menken *("Told you all along we were mates.")*
Spice | Hans Zimmer *(Lost in a sandstorm)*
Farewell | Alan Menken *(The Summer Prince breaks his curse)*
You Fought Well | Hans Zimmer *(Confrontation on Solonius's Spine)*
Doubt Comes In | Reeve Carney *(A god's offer accepted)*
august | Taylor Swift *(Three lovers)*
Calypso | Hans Zimmer *(Destruction of Hadria)*
Bad Parents | Simon Franglen *(A long awaited showdown)*
Main Title: Prologue | Alan Menken *(The shattered rose)*
Organization XIII | Yoko Shimomura *(Kairyn passes his Blessing)*
Hector's Death | James Horner *(End of the High Prince of Summer)*
The Iron Throne | Ramin Djawadi *(Farron, Autumn-blood)*
Destiny on Culloden Moor | Bear McCreary *("I will have all of you.")*
Running Up That Hill - Epic Version | Samuel Kim *(The Nightingale and the Queen)*

Made in the USA
Columbia, SC
17 September 2024

42514247R00400